WATCHER IN THE DARK

Everyone in the office is gone; the hallways are dark and empty. As I lock the front door behind me, I know I am closing a door forever.

Outside, the sleeting rain is cold and the wind is ferocious. It threatens to knock me off my feet as I step into the parking lot. With my head lowered against the deafening wind, I move toward the single spot of light in a world of dark. On my way to the street lamp I notice a car idling in the corner of the lot—in the dark. Thinking it's Max, I wave and begin to move toward it. The car begins to move toward me with its lights off.

At the same time, a second car enters the lot from the other side. Its lights are on bright and it, too, is moving fast toward me. The lights blind me for a moment. I hear a screech of brakes as the first car suddenly cuts away, making tight skidding circles on the wet asphalt. My heart leaps and I turn to run. I slip. . . .

SIGNATURE MURDER

PAT FRIEDER

BANTAM BOOKS

NEW YORK TORONTO LONDON SYDNEY AUCKLAND

To Brian . . .

Signature Murder
A Bantam Crime Line Book / May 1998

CRIME LINE and the portrayal of a boxed "cl" are trademarks of
Bantam Books, a division of Bantam Doubleday Dell Publishing
Group, Inc.

ISBN 0-553-57612-7

Published simultaneously in the United States and Canada

Bantam Books are published by Bantam Books, a division of Bantam Doubleday Dell Publishing Group, Inc. Its trademark, consist-
ing of the words "Bantam Books" and the portrayal of a rooster, is
Registered in U.S. Patent and Trademark Office and in other countries. Marca Registrada. Bantam Books, 1540 Broadway, New York,
New York 10036.

PRINTED IN THE UNITED STATES OF AMERICA
WCD 10 9 8 7 6 5 4 3 2 1

RULES OF EVIDENCE

RULE 404 (B)

Evidence of other crimes, wrongs or acts is not admissible to prove the character of a person in order to show action in conformity therewith. It may, however, be admissible for other purposes such as proof of motive, opportunity, intent, preparation, plan, knowledge, identity or absence of mistake or accident.

McCormick on Evidence

Evidence that the accused has committed another similar crime may be admitted. But much more is demanded than the mere repeated commission of the same crime. Indeed, it must be established that another like crime by the accused is so nearly identical in method as to earmark it as the handiwork of the accused.

The device or method used must be so unusual and distinctive as to be like a signature.

NOVEMBER

ONE

—◦◦◦—

FIRST I SMELL THE VOMIT. THEN I SMELL THE BLOOD. THEN I see the hand. Gnarled and arthritic, her manicured hands had often drawn my attention even in life, when both were still attached to the crazy old woman's wrists.

The vomit must have come from the housekeeper, Juanita Jakes. It is spewed at my feet over Mexican crockery, spilled coffee, and the runny orange eye of Isadora Stanton's three-minute egg. I've been here in Isadora's bedroom on many other mornings. I've watched, with sympathy and mild alarm, Juanita's balancing act with the old woman's breakfast tray. This morning, right about where I'm standing, just inside the bedroom door, Juanita must have seen the bloody horror in the bed, dropped her tray, and thrown up onto it.

In the fraction of a second that my mind works this out, another deeper part delivers the message, "This is my fault." As soon as I see the mutilated corpse on the bed, I know. It is my fault. Again! And I know, as certainly as I've ever known anything in life, that I will not be able to bear the guilt of another murder.

Even though it's nearly nine and already a bright November morning outside, the thick adobe walls and narrow windows keep the small rooms inside in perpetual shade. So it takes me a moment to realize there is a third person in the room. Juanita Jakes is still here, slumped in a straight-backed chair, facing away from the corpse and into the corner like some classroom dunce. Juanita is about six months pregnant. She moves her thumb to twist the unusual band on her left ring finger. Her body rocks very slightly. I wonder how long she's been like this.

"What happened? Did you see?" I ask.

Juanita looks up at me in dull bewilderment. She doesn't answer.

"Where's Teddy?" I ask, and this time something registers. Juanita raises her ring hand to point back over her shoulder. I follow her aim directly back to the corpse.

Isadora's hair is god-awful. She has been dying it deepening shades of red over the past fifty or so years until now it is nearly maroon. Dots of rouge the size of quarters overlay the maze of wrinkles and add to the clown-hag effect. She is laid out like Christ with her arms spread straight on each side of her frail body. A circle of blood blooms at the end of one empty wrist. There is no quilt or bedspread. A single fresh sheet is laid lightly over her from the foot of the bed to her waist. And there, placed neatly in the center of her chest, on her pink quilted bed jacket, lies her severed hand, curled like a claw on a brilliant cushion of blood.

At the start of every emergency I can remember, I've been dead calm like this. Years ago aunts and neighbors commented to my mother on my unchildlike behavior. They meant it as a sort of cautionary nudge, I think, but my mother chose to receive it as a compliment. My calm veneer always wears off, however. Not gradually but in sudden sloughed chunks like cheap nail polish. But in the immediate emergency, I'm steady and efficient.

And so I call 911 and turn my attention to Juanita Jakes. Juanita is mildly retarded, with the telltale flattened face of Fetal Alcohol Syndrome. She's been in Isadora's employ for more than a decade. As a girl of fourteen, Juanita came to help in Isadora's house not out of Isadora's need, but because charity toward FAS victims was a legacy from someone Isadora had loved a lifetime ago.

As the years went on and Isadora became more irascible, a string of housekeepers quit in exasperation. Eventually Juanita became what she is now—Isadora's housekeeper, cook, nurse, ward, and whipping boy. She arrives here six mornings a week before breakfast and leaves after the dinner dishes are put away.

I kneel on the floor before her now and take Juanita's wrists in my hands to hold her attention. I can feel her body tremble.

"Juanita, look at me." I lift my palm to her cheek, keep it there till her rocking stills and I hold her eyes with my own. With her freed hand she hooks a hank of hair and sticks it into her mouth.

"Were you here? Did you see what happened?" I keep my voice soft and steady.

She shakes her head slowly, in wide arcs.

"No," she answers. "I came in the back way like always. I made breakfast. I didn't know she was . . ." Tears form in her eyes. "I didn't know he . . ."

"He what?" I urge. "Didn't know *he* what?"

Juanita is suddenly looking more stricken. She chews on her hair with such vigor that I think she may gnaw through it.

"*He* who? You didn't know *he* . . . what? Juanita, who are you talking about? Teddy?" I guess. "Do you mean Teddy?"

Teddy Bellasandro is Isadora's driver, handyman, confidant, and best living friend. For the last few years, Teddy's been the only relevant "he" in Isadora Stanton's life. He should be here now, puttering around and filling the air with his Fats Domino impression.

"Teddy," Juanita echoes my last word and begins rocking her body again hard and fast so that I give up trying to get information and wrap my arms as far around her awkward girth as I can reach. I pat her thick strong back until she stills, then I coax her up out of the chair.

But before I can get her all the way through the rabbit warren of irregular rooms and out the front door, away from the horror in Isadora's bedroom, the first two police cars arrive. One of the officers takes Juanita back into the house. I don't envy him. Getting coherent information out of her is going to take some doing.

Standing on the front portal in the crisp fall air, I tell the other officer what I know about Isadora Stanton, starting with how I happened to be the one to find her.

"I live just up there." I point to the street. "Up Acequia Madre where it crosses Canyon Road. I usually walk to work and often stop here to check on her or, sometimes, to bring documents for her signature," I explain.

"Documents?"

I hand the policeman my card, deeply embossed in the middle with the firm name, *FREDERICK & DANFORTH PC. ATTORNEYS AT LAW*, and my own, *Matty Donahue*, in smaller print beneath. By this time, two plainclothed officers have arrived. The one in knife-creased jeans and a tweed sport coat introduces himself as Detective Daniel Baca. He has taken my card from the uniform; now he hands it back to me.

"You were Miss Stanton's lawyer?" Baca asks.

I nod and look out at the remnants of Isadora's garden. A few autumn chrysanthemums catch the sun and dazzle briefly. Strictly speaking, I am not—*was not*—Isadora's lawyer. Her real lawyer was burly, pompous Norman Frederick, one of the two senior partners. But Isadora's eccentricities proved a bit much for Norman. Soon after I came to work for Frederick & Danforth, Norman asked me to help him with her.

"Nothing much," he assured me. "Just a little assistance in delicate matters which may arise from time to time." It is my judgment on one of those "delicate matters" which fills my mind now. A judgment which may have led directly to the bloody mutilation inside.

• • •

The evening magistrate session was crowded with scofflaws waiting for the clerk to call their dog-leash or traffic case. Isadora sat purse-lipped next to me, pouting and fingering the hem of her skirt. Earlier she had thoroughly smelled that hem. She had lifted it to her nose and sniffed loudly and wetly for several minutes, leaving a lap full of white nylon slip for the delinquents to snigger at.

"I want to go home. It stinks in here," she announced.

She was right about the stink. More than sixty people were squeezed into a courtroom designed for thirty. The lack of air-conditioning on that August night allowed body odors to thrive.

"Look," I whispered sternly, as to a fidgety twelve-year-old, "we can't go home yet. We have to wait for the judge. He'll probably just slap your wrist, tell you to get your license renewed, and let you go. But . . ."

That was four years ago and I was twenty-nine at the time. Isadora was over eighty and had long since stopped taking advice from youngsters like me. And something on my face had captured her attention.

"Ink," she said.

"What?"

She pulled out a nearly clean hanky, licked a corner, and scrubbed the dewy linen against the corner of my mouth until she was satisfied, then tucked the hanky under her belt. Just as she ominously hawked something up from her throat, her case was called. Without waiting to see if she would swallow or spit, I stood and pulled her by her bony elbow up to the preposterously high magistrate's bench.

Though I'd lived in Santa Fe as a child, I had only recently returned to the "City Different" to practice law. I knew none of the judges yet, but this one seemed to know me.

"Well, Ms. Donahue, you honor us with your presence."

Judge Felix Sandoval was hiked up in his chair and looking down over smeared glasses balanced on the tip of his nose.

His black robe was worn like a golfing jacket, unzipped to display a yellow-and-green plaid shirt. The judge was full of asshole bonhomie. I thought, at first, that his irritation with me was only because the night Magistrate Court is a people's court. Here, the judge either acts as a clerk passing out tiny judgments as the assembly line of miscreants passes before his bench, or he holds forth on one or another of the world's troubles, as the mood strikes him. This judge didn't expect and didn't want lawyers mucking about. Apparently, he didn't want *me* in particular.

"Your Honor, this is Miss Isadora Stanton," I began.

"Yes, Ms. Donahue, it says that right here on the file, but . . ." Sandoval continued with open sarcasm, ". . . the court thanks you for your assistance." Then, ignoring me altogether, the judge smiled kindly down at Isadora.

"Now, Miss Stanton, what have we here? The officer's report indicates you were driving in the parking lot of the De Vargas Mall Shopping Center at six o'clock A.M. without a driver's license. Is that true, ma'am?"

"No! It is not!" screeched Isadora at the uniformed bailiff, the only official person she could see from her vantage point under the lip of the high bench. "I showed the cop my license."

Judge Sandoval winced at the word "cop" and lost his kindly tone.

"Yes, indeed." The judge raised his voice to oratorical level, held the open file high above his shoulder, and pretended to read from it. "Yes, indeed. The officer reports you did display a driver's license, a license which expired on September ninth . . ." Here, he paused for effect and began again, "September ninth, nineteen hundred and . . ." another pause while he looked down at the rows of captives, "Nineteen hundred . . . and . . . fifty-three! Now, Miss Stanton, I'm sure your able attorney here has informed you that it is illegal to drive on an expired license."

I was hastily considering the dead-loser argument that since my client was driving on private property, the motor vehicle code didn't apply, when Isadora spat the wad she had apparently stowed in her craw straight up at the top of Judge Felix Sandoval's bench. The room hushed. We all hung there with it as the gob of spit slid slowly down the huge sun symbol carved into the judge's bench.

The bailiff was the first to regain movement. Barney Fife-like, he was on his feet and bending Isadora's skinny right arm up her back. At this point Isadora drew herself up to her full five feet seven inches and, with her free hand, raised her walking cane above her head and actually demanded in a full strong voice, "Unhand me this *instant!*"

Small titters erupted from the audience and began to swell. The gavel came down . . . once . . . twice . . . a third time.

When the ruckus subsided sufficiently, Judge Sandoval focused his attention on me.

"Ms. Donahue, I've heard of your grandstanding in Albuquerque and Denver. I don't know what you think you're doing slumming in Santa Fe's Magistrate Court, but I hold you directly . . ."

Isadora had been unhanded by the bailiff pursuant to her demand and, apparently finished with this scene, was sauntering away. I made a grab for her but missed.

". . . directly responsible for this," Sandoval droned on. But the heat was out of his voice and he was watching in some dismay as the cause of all the turmoil strolled nonchalantly toward the exit.

"Oh, Miss Stanton," the judge called. "We're still here." He motioned for her with a curved index finger. "Won't you join us?"

When Isadora had returned docilely to her spot, led by the scowling bailiff, Sandoval sighed deeply, raised his gavel, and said, "License suspended pending completion of traffic school. Fifty dollars. Pay the clerk."

I was only too glad to get out of there. I thanked the court like a humble supplicant but, as I turned to go, Isadora piped up.

"You *can't* suspend my license, remember? I don't *have* a valid license." She crossed her arms like a satisfied debater who's won her point. "Besides, I don't need traffic school. I know how to—"

Felix Sandoval held a finger to his lips to signal silence. He squinted down at her. Then he squinted down at me and said softly, "You may ask your client, Ms. Donahue, if she prefers jail to traffic school."

"Jail!" declared Isadora promptly, a schoolyard scrapper daring the older bully.

We were at an impasse. Sandoval was on the bench by appointment and, in three months, had to stand for his first election. The story of his having jailed an elderly woman for such a trifle would be like manna from heaven to his opponent. He opened his mouth but nothing came out.

"If Your Honor please," I ventured. "I have a suggestion."

All eyes turned to me. Sandoval didn't stop me so I went on.

"Perhaps a full-time driver might be arranged for Miss Stanton," I improvised. "She can afford it, and . . ." I turned toward Isadora's stirring and gave her a *don't start up* look, "—and everyone's dignity could be preserved," I finished.

Sandoval pondered this, nodded once sharply, then nodded again. Isadora, to my happy astonishment, kept her mouth shut. I continued, hopefully, "Your Honor might keep the matter under advisement for six months, no sentence, contingent upon Miss Stanton's getting a driver by Monday and keeping him during the advisement period. I could make the arrangements."

The judge smothered whatever curse he was contemplating and settled into resignation. "So ordered," he said over his shoulder, heading back to his chambers behind the bench. He was shaking his head.

I looked at Isadora, who still had her bony arms folded across her chest, the cane end in one fist so that the long shaft rested like a rifle over her shoulder. Her whole body said, *This better be good.*

I laughed in spite of myself. "Come on," I urged. "You might even enjoy this."

When I made the offer to Sandoval, a fledgling idea had begun to stir in my brain. A few weeks earlier I'd met a guy who seemed perfect for the job of driving Isadora, just one of those serendipitous things.

I'd met him when my car was in the shop. I'd failed to make the Santa Fe-to-Albuquerque shuttle on the first day of a series of depositions in Albuquerque. And there, by the shuttle stop, sitting in a beat-up but spotless old Chevy, was a pock-marked, potbellied, unlicensed cabbie waiting to pick up strays like me. He was about fifty and looked every day of it, but was chock-full of attitude. He drove me that day, and when the promised completion of the car repairs was delayed and the deposition schedule was extended, I continued to use him. The cabbie reduced his regular fare to shuttle prices in return for a couple of weeks of regular business. As he could pick up fares illegally in Albuquerque as well as he could in Santa Fe, he seemed content to do that, then drive me home each night.

I got to know the guy. He was a tough-looking Cajun. Interesting and funny in an offbeat way. He told colorful stories of growing up in Louisiana. His gravelly voice even sounded like Bourbon Street. I liked him, and I thought this crazy old lady might like him, too. So, carelessly forgetting for that sticky moment in court my then-recent vow never to stick my neck out again, I brought Teddy Bellasandro into the life of the rich, mean, half-senile, funny, smart, old lady who was murdered last night.

Detective Baca is leaning in, concentrating on my face. I don't know how long he's been waiting for my answer.

"Uh-huh, yes," I say belatedly, to his last question. "I was Miss Stanton's lawyer."

After a period of questioning during which Baca is coming in and out of focus for me, I hike my hip up on the portal railing and the detective takes a seat on one of the old porch rockers like he's got all day. But his eyes are restless and he continues to confer every few minutes with one or another of the other officers. There is increasing activity inside the walled yard. Yellow crime-scene tapes have gone up. A uniformed woman has led Juanita Jakes waddling out of Isadora's house past the maze of cars and driven away with her. Men carrying cameras and other equipment have disappeared into the shadowy interior. One moves across my line of vision toward the squad cars carrying a metal toolbox carefully, in both gloved hands, away from his body as if it were a heavy wet baby.

From here, on the edge of the porch, the sky is that clear cobalt blue that the artists come to Santa Fe for. I see that Isadora's limo is carelessly parked and, even more uncharacteristically, sports a thick layer of dust. The remaining leaves on the giant cottonwood in the center of the yard are so brightly golden against that sky that my eyes hurt, and I turn them back to Detective Baca.

"Truth is, I was more like her keeper," I admit. "My boss, Norman Frederick, is officially her lawyer, but I probably know as much about her as anybody."

I tell the detective about Isadora's life, about her schedule and about people who knew her. I tell him about her next of kin, Faye Stanton, a surgical nurse in Albuquerque. "The Horrible Niece," Isadora used to call her. I tell him about the three or four people who actually spent any time with the old lady including, casually, Teddy Bellasandro. It was a thin fabric, this old lady's life.

"That's about all I know," I conclude.

Baca has his notepad open but isn't looking at it; he's watching me. He might look out of place in some police departments, but not in Santa Fe. Here, in every generation, there are shockingly beautiful Hispanic boys who grow into somber bureaucrats. Even so, Baca's battened-down good looks slightly disconcert me. His head is cocked now and he sucks his eye tooth, studying me.

"Got any ideas about who might have done this?" he asks.

I know that I should tell him the whole truth about Teddy Bellasandro right now. Later will be too late to seem innocent.

Teddy's criminal record can easily be pulled. And if that happens, Teddy Bellasandro will become Baca's number-one suspect.

I'm a commercial lawyer. The world of contracts and leases can seem as far from criminal law as from astrophysics or stand-up comedy. So maybe I'm wrong. But I don't think the cops or the D.A. will pull a thirty-year-old criminal record to find out about the old crime unless there is something else to tie Teddy to Isadora's murder. Or, unless someone tells them. Someone like me. Baca seems like a nice, competent guy. A good citizen would tell him all she knows. A lawyer thinking about keeping her license would, too. Even though I'm not such a hot lawyer anymore, being one is nearly all I've got.

But I fail to tell the detective about Teddy's past. I don't believe the evidence lying in there on that pink quilted bed jacket. Despite the obvious similarities, Teddy can't have done this thing. He was more than her driver. As I hoped on that first day in Judge Sandoval's courtroom, Isadora and Teddy had become more than friends. By the time the court-ordered six months ended, there was no turning back. In the following years, the two of them became like mother and son. They were the cantankerous nucleus of a bizarre little family of outcasts, an odd family which drew me gradually into its orbit. We cared about each other when nobody else wanted anything to do with any of us. Teddy loved Isadora. He can't be guilty.

Even as I psychologically circle the wagons to protect Teddy Bellasandro, I know he isn't the only one I'm protecting. If Teddy is guilty of this mutilation murder, then I'm guilty, too. Because for months I've known Teddy's dark secret, a past so horrible that most people would think him depraved if they knew. But the term "most people" didn't include Isadora Stanton. Teddy had volunteered his history to her. And it had been she who told me about Teddy's criminal record.

As I answer Baca's questions, the memory of the day Isadora told me the story wants to take root in my brain. Against my will, I remember Isadora's defense of Teddy. She had accepted his explanation for nearly incomprehensible acts. She had concluded that, in her opinion, Teddy was more saint than sinner. And I remember now that, at the time, I didn't disagree. Most of all, I remember that I made no move to interfere with their life and that I told no one.

I look at Baca again and answer his question. "No idea," I say.

TWO

—◦◦◦—

W HEN I OPEN MY EYES ON THE MORNING AFTER THE MUR-
der, the first thing I see is branches. I live in an apple
tree. This apartment, midway up on lower Canyon Road, is an
indulgence. It is poorly built and a royal pain in the ass in the
winter. I rented it four years ago this May when I was still
climbing out of the pit of self-loathing and when the tree was in
full blossom.

A rickety narrow staircase links the downstairs living and
kitchen area to the loft. At the top of these stairs sit my bedroom and bathroom. Both are sheathed in windows and em-
braced in the arms of the biggest blooming apple tree in Santa
Fe. At that time, I was still spending much of my time in bed
and this womb among the blossoms suited me fine. Still does.

Over these last four years I've learned a few tricks for keeping the more gruesome aspects of reality at bay. I've found
simple denial pretty effective. *It didn't happen and if it did*

happen, it doesn't concern me and if it does concern me, I'll deal with it later.

But this morning, the old tricks aren't working so well. I wash my hands and my left thumb lingers in the soft inner hollow of my right wrist. I banish the image of Isadora's severed hand quickly but not quickly enough. My other line of defense is to sleep until *"it"* goes away. I've tried that already. By the time Detective Baca finished questioning me yesterday, my protective bubble was near to bursting. So, rather than go in to work, I walked back home in a stupor, climbed the loft stairs, got into bed with my clothes on, and waited for sleep to erase the board.

No such luck! Here I am, eighteen hours later, and the picture of death and the prodding of guilt are still vivid and painfully insistent. This is too much like the last time, just after Thanksgiving four years ago. I can't keep the similarities out of my mind. My own history may be even more reprehensible than Teddy Bellasandro's. However horribly wrong it went, Teddy's excuse was protecting a parent. Mine was the lawyer's curse, ego.

To dispel the memory, I lose myself in the view out of the loft window down to the familiar compound and the more familiar street. My first reliable memories of life and all of my memories of childhood are of this odd city and on this famous street. I was about three when my young mother brought me back to Santa Fe with her to live with her parents. We lived in the house where she'd grown up and where her mother's mother's mother had grown up, only three blocks from this window.

My great-grandmother was one-half Jicarilla Apache and one-half Spanish. But this gift of connection with the racial and cultural history of this place was largely ignored by my Irish ancestors. So, by the time I was old enough to ask, no one remembered any of her stories or personal history.

Just until she could "get things straight," my mother had predicted the length of our proposed stay in Santa Fe. We lived in that little house up the hill for just over ten contented years without anything getting noticeably straighter.

My mother and I went through separate but confluent phases. She worked as a waitress and wrote sad short stories. I learned to read and found her stories funny. She rethought and revised and sent them off to humor sections of magazines that never wrote back. She became a welder of iron sculpture on the patio and I held my ears at the racket she made. She sculpted a gawky child with hands over her ears. The sculpture was accepted on consignment and eventually sold for a modest sum. She became a paralegal and told me, based upon that experience, that I should aim at becoming a lawyer because it was a ridiculously easy way to make a buck.

Before I turned fourteen, my mother and I left this street, and this city, for the first episode in what was to be her marriage phase. I liked most of her progressively more eccentric husbands *du jour* and considered myself no worse for the experience. I even liked the beginning of her travel phase until it threatened to untether me and we agreed that, whereas her stone would keep rolling, I actually preferred moss. My mother camped in the U.S. until I was safely enrolled at the University of New Mexico. Now, though I rarely see her, I look forward more than one might imagine to the monthly notes from Nepal or Singapore.

Home for me, however, has always been Santa Fe. So, when the bottom fell out of my life, after I decided not to die, I came back here. The house we moved into when I was a child is only a seven-minute climb up Canyon Road from this spot. I can walk by it, and being able to do that matters to me.

I don't often see clients anymore, so I wear whatever I feel like to work and nobody at Frederick & Danforth reminds me about the dress code. This morning, the day after Isadora's death, I yank a fairly clean pair of jeans off the hook and pull on a baggy black sweater. I pour a cup of coffee and settle into the rocker with the four-day-old Sunday *Times*. I know that this morning's *New Mexican* will be outside in the compound's driveway. I know that the story of Isadora's murder will be the headline in that paper. At the office, Norman and Joe will have read it by now. Soon, I have to tell them about Teddy. There is no way around it. They have a stake in this, too.

What I choose to do instead is read the book review section of the *Times*. Then I check the refrigerator. One quart of milk with yesterday's expiration date, two leftover burritos, an elephant garlic, two chocolate doughnuts in a white bakery bag, a can of Slim-Fast, and half a six-pack of Dos Equis. I eat both doughnuts and drink the milk from the carton fast, without smelling it.

There is a huge white "dry erase" board on my kitchen wall. In the old days, the board hung in my Albuquerque office and was usually covered with skeleton outlines of the trial in progress: each witness's name in a different color, matching abbreviations for the bits of evidence hoped for from each, check marks where the bits were sufficient to prove one of the legal elements. These days, I use the board for my grocery list. I pick up the marker and write *"milk."*

At ten-thirty, I've made no move to go the office. I can't hide forever, of course, but I figure I can get by with it for a while longer. So I ignore the first few calls, listening to Norman Frederick's secretary, Gloria Bachicha, on the answering machine while I pour myself another cup of coffee.

"Norman needs to see you immediately," says the machine.

I put on a Pavarotti tape, which drowns the sound of Gloria's second and third calls. I decide on the flu and am ready to sound authentic when she calls again. But when I pick up, it isn't Norman's secretary. It is Norman's partner, Joe Danforth.

"What's up, Matthew?" Joe asks, without preamble.

I'm sentimental about being called Matthew. My mother used to do it. Joe knows this because *he* was the fresh new lawyer with whom she'd once worked as a paralegal. He figures the old name might make me compliant. Joe doesn't miss too many tricks.

"I thought I would come in this afternoon," I say.

"Uh-huh," he says, less than pleased. "Is this about Isadora Stanton? It's all over the papers."

"I found the body, Joe; it was bad."

"Jesus H. Christ! The story I read didn't mention that. Are you all right?"

"Yeah, sure. I will be. You know, it just brings up memories."

"Oh, God, Matty. I'm sorry. I'd nearly forgotten."

How could he have forgotten? It was Joe I called after I'd become such a pariah in the legal community that no one would give me a job. It was Joe who reached out a hand and hired me even before my license to practice was restored. Joe who had let me follow him to a safe harbor. He'd remembered my mother and the fun of his salad days and without hesitation he'd said, "Sure, the firm could use some quality behind-the-scenes help."

It's been a perfect job for me. At Frederick & Danforth, I earn enough money as a back-office grunt to make restitution payments to former clients, and I don't have to deal much with judges or other lawyers who know my reputation. Except for Norman and Joe, I don't have to deal with much of anybody.

"Matty," Joe says, "you can't let this pull you down again."

After another long pause he says, "You hear me? You can't let this pull you back into that hole. You've got to get yourself together. Wasn't there someone you were seeing a couple of years ago? A therapist or something?"

"I'll be okay. Really."

"Matty, I'm so sorry . . . Do they know anything yet? I mean, about who might have done it?"

"No, Not as far as I know."

"Look," Joe says, "you take the rest of the day off if you need to. I'll talk to Norman. He's going ballistic. Says you were to have a brief ready for him yesterday."

"It's in his box. You know, the one on the corner of his desk where he insists that I put his stuff but where he never looks."

Joe laughs, a hardy short punch of sound. "Right. Well, see you tomorrow morning then?" he says with only a little of the demand showing through.

"Yeah," I say softly.

"Early?"

"Right."

With the phone still in my hand, I stare at the clock. Twenty more hours before I have to face the new reality head-on. Twenty more hours of aggressive escape from the new horror and the old horror. I need more distraction than I can get from Pavarotti. I switch off the CD and pick up the remote for the television. CNN is featuring a Vietnamese girl born in poverty and orphaned by the war who played a cello solo at Carnegie Hall last night. I begin to cry, slowly and steadily.

In spite of the most singular lesson to the contrary, or because of it, I'm sappy about people who overcome the odds and make second chances pay off. I don't, myself, play cello or even know anyone who does. And from my own experience, I know that trying to construct second chances has repercussions. In direct proportion to the force with which the naive hopeful hits the ball against the wall, that ball will come smashing back to crack his skull and embed itself in the brain, where it will kill him or remain forever as a reminder of the brutal lunacy of real life.

The sudden smash to my brain wasn't even connected to one of the high-profile cases which had begun to come my way in Albuquerque. It began as a favor for the man I was to marry. It was out of my area of expertise but nothing I hesitated to do. I was in love with John Elich. Four years ago, our wedding was set for the week before Christmas. And, my fiancé needed legal help.

John was twelve years older than me, with a teenage son named Tommy who'd been diagnosed with adolescent onset schizophrenia. Father and son had been close before John's divorce. And Tommy had been healthy. Against all medical evidence, John blamed himself for Tommy's illness, which came inexplicably at age fifteen. All at once, Tommy began hearing voices and refusing to leave his room.

The miracle drugs now known to contain schizophrenia were already showing remarkable results. But Tommy disliked the drugs. They dampened his inner journeys. So, for a while, at least, he required close supervision.

But the hospitalizations were terrible. Each time, Tommy emerged worse than when he went in. John refused to accept the doctors' designation "danger to himself or others," which meant more permanent institutionalization. Tommy said he would take his medicine. Tommy said his life depended on getting out of the hospital. Despite the disagreement of Tommy's mother, John wanted to take care of Tommy. Like John, I wasn't daunted.

A lawyer had to represent Tommy at the commitment hearing. But that first hearing wasn't the end of it. John's ex-wife, with the concurrence of the state, appealed the hearing officer's decision. And I found myself challenging experts, first to a review panel, and finally to a district court judge. I assured the judge that the loving father could guarantee medication would be taken. A secure reliable environment, I told the court, would give this lost boy a chance to reenter life; perhaps, one day, to again function well. I pointedly, forcefully, cross-examined the state's two psychologists, who faltered, unable to support their own opinion that Tommy was dangerous. The judge shook his head at the befuddled shrinks and ordered the boy's release.

Tommy came home.

On the fifth of December, amid wedding plans and Christmas plans, Tommy fired five shots into his father's head. He put the last bullet into his own brain.

After John was buried, I didn't leave my apartment for six months. During the first of those dark cavernous months, I mostly lay in bed on seldom-changed sheets, curled fetally on my right side where I could see the wall. When pain seeped into my hip from being too long in that position, I shifted to the left. But the view from my left side was toward the door, to the outside; so, when I lay that way, I kept my eyes closed.

By spring my law practice was gone and I didn't care. I'd been disciplined in absentia by the state bar association. Because my relationship with Tommy's father had "predictably" clouded my judgment and was a classic case of conflict of interest, they suspended my license to practice law for six months. After that, my license was suspended for an additional two months for neglecting the rest of my clients. Three of those neglected clients lost substantial sums of money during my absence. They said *because* of my absence. I didn't argue. I was advised by wise counsel to get on with the business of living or get on with the business of dying.

I've done neither. I agreed to pay each of the three pissed-off clients an amount they claimed was fair, in monthly amounts over six years. And I decided that I wanted to eat. So I've climbed out of hell and into purgatory. Now I've joined that segment of humanity that is content to live a life of short reach and small achievement. I do not want power or recognition any more. I want only to control my slight slice of going to work, coming home, eating, reading, and sleeping. I'm content to rely on others to make important decisions. I want never to be in a position of trust again. And just this minute, I very much want to keep the reality of Isadora Stanton's murder and my possible responsibility for her death from pushing me back over the edge again.

As the Asian girl plays her cello, I weep at the thought of second chances and second failures and try to keep my guilt for this third death at bay.

THREE

***

DESPITE THE WASTEFUL EXPENSE, THE FIRM OF FREDERICK & Danforth is still located in the lavish Santasteven offices. The original adobe structure was built in the early 1700's, and even after two centuries of tinkering, the building retains much of its early Spanish character. The central *sala* with its blood-cured dirt floor is not off-limits to lawyers of the firm. But it is so fragile and dimly lit that, as a practical matter, the room serves only as a historical curiosity to impress clients. Most of the additions are sunny, modern, big rooms with wide windows opening onto small remaining slices of once-magnificent estate grounds. But three of the rooms in use are renovated eighteenth-century cells with lots of charm but not enough floor space for a full-sized desk. Two of these have become storage closets for dead files. The third is my office.

On my way, I pass what is known as Norman's command post. Gloria Bachicha holds up a finger to stop me.

"Where have you been? Mr. Frederick has been looking for you for two days. He says you're to wait here."

Despite the fact that Norman and I clash on a regular basis, he continues to work closely with me because I do good work. Before my fall from grace, I earned as much money as a young lawyer on her own as Norman does now as a mature lawyer surrounded by support. I know more than any associate he can work with but I don't have a career agenda of my own. That is why I can dress the way I want and why I don't have to follow office rules. That is why Norman puts up with me.

My suspensions were published in the *Bar Bulletin*, which reports all disciplinary matters and which is distributed weekly to every lawyer in the state. At the time, my situation was the subject of much discussion among friends and associates. But, for the most part, nobody much cares or remembers anymore. It's all old news. Every once in a while, someone will still catch a glimpse of me and suddenly avert their face to save me the embarrassment. The worst of it is that my record is permanently on file for any prospective employer to see. I can't get another decent job. And that is why I put up with Norman.

I sink docilely into a client chair and instantly begin my favorite pastime, watching other people's lives. Gloria is neatly placing items on her desk for Norman's review. Billings to the left, court pleadings waiting for his signature at the top center, pink message slips next to them. She surveys this clerical Zen garden taking shape on the desktop with satisfaction before seating herself at the keyboard.

Her nails are perfectly manicured paste-ons in a brilliant crimson. As her fingers stroke the keys, I renew my wonder at how she can type like the wind with those contraptions attached to her fingertips. My own stubby, unpainted nails lie flat in my lap and I look at them for a while. Looking at hands is becoming a deep preoccupation with me.

After a while, Gloria rises to walk past my chair. Her small feet are encased in navy pumps with a bright red fine-line stripe. The shoes, with two-inch heels, bring her up to about five feet four. I don't think Gloria actually dislikes me. She barely notices me except when I interfere with something

Norman wants. Her pantyhose are flawless, as is her wool suit, in a shade of red which perfectly matches both her fingernails and the stripe in her shoes. I'm wearing jeans and a Levi jacket, as usual.

The smell of Old Spice reaches us even before the distinctive clop-clop of heavy orthopedic shoes against the brick floor of the reception room. Norman's tribulations with sore feet have been long and deep. As he nears Gloria's area rug, she turns on a dime and thrusts both arms forward to take the proffered camel-hair overcoat and metal briefcase. Norman stands facing her desk, fans the pink slips, deals out three to Gloria, pockets the rest, then turns his attention to the pleadings. Gloria's work is usually letter-perfect and the pleadings are run-of-the-mill. So he is taking about one second per page to read and sign, read and sign. As he replaces the last one on the stack, Gloria places a cup of steaming coffee into his hand.

I watch all this with a familiar bemusement. Even in my better days, I never had this geishalike service from a secretary.

Gloria precedes Norman into his office carrying the load of files he is to work on today. He follows with his steaming coffee and new pencils, and I bring up the rear. Only when he is seated behind his desk and Gloria has shut the door behind her, does Norman acknowledge my presence. He's forgotten again that it was he who wanted to see me.

He opens the first file and is reading it while he says, "You wanted something? Can it wait? I've go a few calls to make."

I shrug, nod, and exit without his looking up. As I pass Gloria, I shrug again, give her my best vacuous smile, and head down the long corridor to my office.

I close the door behind me and squeeze past the clutter to my chair. Absently, I let my fingers fondle and tap the phone receiver, raising and lowering it back into its cradle. I'd like some help but, this time, there is no one to call. I consider Joe Danforth's advice to call the therapist who helped me after I moved to Santa Fe. I punch the number from memory, listen to the answering machine, wait for the beep, then hang up without speaking. I'm the only one I've ever heard of who was actually

fired by her shrink. At his gentle insistence, Max Cortino and I
have parted company.

The sudden ringing of the phone under my hand startles me.

"It's a Detective Baca for you on line one; but Norman is
on the intercom line," the receptionist warns.

I pick up line one.

"Good morning, Ms. Donahue," Detective Baca says, overly
polite. "How are you this morning?"

"Not so hot."

"Sorry to hear that. We have a complication."

"Shoot," I say.

"Teddy Bellasandro, Miss Stanton's driver, he was arrested
last night. Assault and battery. He wants a lawyer. He wants
you."

"Assault and battery?" What's Baca talking about? "I don't
understand."

"Well, we weren't able to locate him for a time. Then, last
night, he showed up at the scene. We were out of there by then
but the niece had hired a private security guy. Mr. Bellasandro
broke the guy's jaw. Now he says he didn't know about the murder; says he just went a little nuts, but—"

The intercom-line light goes out and the desk speaker
squawks: "Now! In my office!" Norman's click is loud and echoes
slightly.

I tell Baca I've got to go.

Before I can get off he says, "Ms. Donahue, what I originally wanted to talk to you about is, do you happen to know
why Miss Stanton might have been interested in fake Indian
jewelry?"

"No. Why?"

"Ah . . . It's probably nothing, but we found a copy of the
Native American News in the backseat of the victim's limousine.
She'd circled an article about some counterfeit pieces showing
up in the market."

"No. I think Isadora subscribed to that paper because they
ran articles about Fetal Alcohol Syndrome from time to time.
She was interested because of Juanita Jakes."

"Ah, that explains it." He pauses. "Anyway, this Bellasandro says he wants you as his lawyer. There may be some conflict, you being a witness . . . but, I guess that's up to you."

"What happens if I don't respond?" I ask.

"Well, Bellasandro's only charged with the assault thing now . . . and he's entitled to a public defender. If you don't agree to represent him, somebody will be appointed before the arraignment."

"Uh-huh," I say. "I'll get back to you, Detective."

As I reenter Norman Frederick's office, he's standing by his conference table in the long window alcove, arranging documents in his metal courier case. He doesn't glance up and I move to settle myself in one of twelve soft gray swivel chairs facing the table. During the best of times, I'm this man's least favorite associate. He puts up with me, but he likes his associates younger, more conventionally dressed, more eager to please, and able to pee standing up.

"We won't talk about your being two days late," he says as he snaps the courier case shut. Then he gives me a couple of seconds to explain anyway. I don't.

"I found the brief," Norman goes on, without a hint of apology for yesterday's conniption fit. "It was okay, but I need that infringement research before my two o'clock appointment. You knew that."

"I have it; it's on my desk."

"Ms. Donahue, I believe I have made my wishes in these matters well known to you. When you are to be absent from these premises you will please deliver any items for which I may be waiting to the in basket on the corner of my desk." His lips purse and he points a manicured finger across the room to the in basket that he hadn't looked in for yesterday's brief.

Norman and I regularly play top-dog-and-under-dog games. When he's particularly upset, Norman distances himself by calling me Ms. Donahue. I always call him Norman.

"Isadora Stanton is dead," I say. "I guess you knew that."

Norman is a large man, about six feet two and carrying some extra pounds. His iron gray hair is parted slightly left of center and combed diagonally back like a thirties movie star. He looks like Ben Bradlee, knows it, and sometimes tries to affect a Boston Brahman attitude.

"Who did it? Do they know yet?" he asks.

After a pause that lasts too long I answer, "They don't know."

Norman hasn't been a trial lawyer for the past twenty-five years without knowing a thing or two about how to listen. He's heard something in my voice and in my hesitation. And, as he might with a deposition witness, he makes the guess. "But you . . . you do know?" he asks.

With eyes cast downward I've been making little fingerprint smears on his shiny metal case. I don't look up for a while. Again the silence speaks for me.

"Her hand was cut off," I say.

"Yes, that was in the papers. Bizarre."

"There's something you need to know, Norman. You remember Teddy Bellasandro? Isadora's driver?"

"Uh-huh. Bad news, in my opinion. I told her so." Norman has momentarily distracted himself with sorting the documents before him. "What about him?" he asks without much interest.

"Teddy killed a man, his stepfather. A long time ago. Thirty years ago."

"My God!" He sits down abruptly across from me, his composure ruffled. "And he's a suspect in this thing?"

"Apparently not yet. He's in custody now for hitting a security guard, but that's all."

Norman rises to pace as he begins the inquisition. "Did you know he had this record when you hired him to drive for my client?"

He has never before called Isadora his client. "No, not then."

"When?"

"About a year ago," I answer, remembering that crossroad moment. "Isadora told me."

"Why didn't you inform me immediately? Surely you could see a potential problem here. A person of normal sensitivity might have been expected to think about protecting such a client, to say nothing of protecting the reputation of this firm."

"Isadora told me not to tell you."

I'm pretty sure that Norman's eyeballs actually get bigger at this point.

"Miss Stanton was in no position to tell you not to inform me," he instructs. His voice is rising. "That woman was my client! Information my *client* gives to my *associate* obviously extends to *me*! What the hell were you thinking?"

"Yeah . . . well . . ." I say, "she asked me not to tell you . . . you, specifically."

He sits down again for nearly two minutes with his eyes squeezed shut. He is getting his irritation under control to do a damage assessment. My eyes wander over the gray-and-sand decor of his office and come to rest on a monumental abstract of gray mesas echoed by an apricot sunset.

"Any reason, other than the man being a murderer, to think he may be a suspect?" Norman's voice drips with weary sarcasm.

This is it, of course. The question I've been trying to hide from for two days.

"I suppose so," I begin like a stuttering engine unwilling to turn over. "The old crime . . . the old murder . . . the stepfather. His name was Lamont, Eldon Lamont. . . . He wasn't the only victim. Teddy Bellesandro's mother was—" I search for a palatable description that is nonetheless accurate, "—injured, too," I finish.

"What the hell are you talking about?"

"Teddy's mother."

"What about her?"

"Thirty years ago Teddy Bellesandro cut his mother's hand off," I say.

There, it's out.

I wait.

Norman's eyes open and narrow, and he leans toward me. Weirdly, this is the closest I've ever been to Norman's face and it feels oddly intimate.

"It was an accident," I add. "But I suppose he will be a suspect."

Suddenly he slams his fist against the table. Though I would've wished not to give him the satisfaction, I jump.

"You *suppose*? You fucking well *know* he's going to be a suspect!" he shouts. "And a hell of a lot more than a suspect, too!"

And then, exactly like me, and just as quickly, he says, "This is your fault! You brought a killer into Isadora Stanton's home. And you left him with her—even *after* you knew how dangerous he was. If it turns out that lunatic mutilated *our* client, it will be your fault. Won't it?"

Norman and I agree absolutely for once.

"Yes, Norman. If he did it, I did it."

"Yes, well. I've suspected that you weren't keeping a proper professional distance from Miss Stanton. Did you even consider that we—that this firm—could be held liable for your negligence? Negligence, hell! For goddamned *wanton disregard* for a client's safety. You have never shown an ounce of loyalty to this firm. I don't know why Joe puts up with you. But this! This is unbelievable!"

He's been nearly screaming at me, but now, unexpectedly, he lowers his voice and delivers his penultimate thrust with quiet deliberation. "Ms. Donahue, you have no business being in a position of trust."

We hold each other's eyes as in a children's game.

"Jesus . . ." he holds the stare, ". . . what in God's name have you done?"

From the moment I found the body, I've been waiting for this accusation. It ties me to that other moment, the one in which I might have made a difference.

My heart quickens and heat shoots through my limbs. I know without trying that my voice won't work properly. This has happened before and it feels exactly the same. Like riding a bike or sex, your brain never forgets the body-blow of guilt. I have no business being in a position of trust.

Norman punches Joe Danforth's intercom button. The reputation of Frederick and Danforth is threatened and tough-guy Norman Frederick turns to the steady calm leadership of his partner, Joseph Danforth.

"Yeah, she's sitting right here," Norman says into the

receiver. "Yeah they've arrested this Bellasandro but apparently not for the murder. I don't know. . . . What's your schedule? No, I don't think this should wait. We've got to work out a coordinated response. Our name . . . Your friend, Matty, says she's known for a year," Norman says to the receiver as he glares at me incredulously. "A year! Isadora Stanton told her this shit a year ago!"

FOUR

———✧❦✧———

"I PAY *YOU*. DON'T YOU FORGET THAT, MISTER." ISADORA wagged her long bony finger at Teddy. They were seated across from each other at the card table, their marked racing forms forgotten in the heat of the argument.

It was about noon when I arrived that autumn Saturday. I'd crossed into the courtyard off Acequia Madre and knocked on the open doorjamb. A typical hullabaloo was raging inside and one of them, I don't remember which one, pointed me to the couch where I waited more or less patiently for Isadora to remember why she had called me here. The parrot, called Angel Bird by Isadora and Rover by Teddy, squawked at Teddy from his perch on Isadora's frail sloping shoulder.

"I never did such a low unsanitary thing!" Isadora shouted at Teddy. "How dare you say I did!"

Teddy rose then and went to retrieve something from the desk drawer. He'd been complaining because his new dentures didn't fit and he claimed it was Isadora's fault. He said he'd had to buy new ones to replace the ones she'd stolen. He said she'd been using his false teeth for the past two months.

"Don't you believe him, Matty," Isadora said. "He's just trying to provoke me."

And then to him, "You just better watch yourself, young Theodore, I'm warning you! Matty's here to change the codicil to my will," she lied with practiced ease. "And we'll have to think again about who might like that limousine out there when I pass, won't we, Matty? It's a fine car. I didn't buy that automobile for you, mister; I bought it for *me*. I can do whatever I want with it. That car deserves a civilized owner. Not some—prevaricator—some . . ."

Teddy held his open palm out to her. In it lay a pink and pearly crescent. "Look here." He pointed out a small spot. "See, I etched your initial on the molar. Now you won't get mixed up."

She looked at the dentures in his hand, carelessly at first. Then with reluctant interest. She ran her tongue around the teeth in her mouth. All of a sudden her watery blue eyes got wetter behind her thick spectacles.

"Where did you find these?" she asked in the smallest voice she could find, nudging the uppers around on his calloused palm with her fingernail.

"In the parrot cage."

"You did not!" she huffed. "I put them in the glass by my bed!" Then, very softly, "I *always* put my teeth in that glass by my bed."

Teddy bent down and kissed Isadora's furrowed brow. "No, Izzy, you put *my teeth* in your glass. You been usin' *my teeth* since that fuckin' bird took yours. And this is the third time, too."

Her hovering tears gently crested.

Teddy averted his own eyes. "Here, now. It's okay." He patted her hand awkwardly. "It's my own damn fault. I got no business even takin' my teeth out in a decent lady's house. Anyway, I didn't need 'em much. I chew—" he said, expanding his substantial belly to its limit, "—and I just get a bigger pot."

He patted the aforementioned pot and winked at her. "Hey, now, this way neither one of us'll get mixed up, okay?"

Her face fell but her eyes rose up to his.

"What's wrong with me?" she asked him, and the tears spilled over. It was hard to watch her. Teddy laid her dentures gently down on the table and busied himself with tidying up, shooing the shrieking green Prussian Guard from the back of Izzy's chair and cursing at it. He peeked at her from time to time and waited for the tears to come to a natural finish. But for a long while she didn't finish. For a time in the middle, the weeping became loud and hard and changed to long heartfelt wails . . . at life, it seemed.

Finally, Isadora was nearly done. "I hate it when I get mixed up like that," she sniveled. "I hate it! I hate it!"

She was about to lose it again. The bird was imitating her crying sounds; "Oooohh" wailed Rover; "Ooohh," wailed Isadora.

"Okay, goddamn it, that's enough, old lady." Teddy slapped a racing form against the table, still not looking at her. "We had our cry today, that's a-goddamned-nough."

"Don't curse at her," I scolded him.

Isadora wheeled around to me, stiffened, and narrowed her eyes. "You leave him alone!" she spat. "What do you know? Teddy knows how to treat me! He doesn't act like I'm made of glass. We understand each other. You leave him a-G-D-lone! I'm no softy. I'm not, you know! You tell her, Teddy."

"She's not, you know," Teddy said to me and smiled at her with genuine warmth. "A little eccentric maybe, but our Izzy's no softy."

"I'm an old woman. I'm entitled to be eccentric."

He chuckled. "You're entitled to be just as eccentric as you can think up to be, old woman. And anytime you run out of eccentric ideas, you just ask me. I got a few of my own." He drew little circles in the air above his temple with his index finger.

Isadora began to cackle. "Play me some music, Teddy Bear. Sing me a song."

He obediently lumbered off to find the battered violin she had once played in the local symphony.

Once he was out of the room, she sighed deeply.

"I ever tell you that I had an abortion once?" she asked in a dreamy soft voice.

I was genuinely shocked. "When? I mean, they didn't do legal abortions in . . . it must have been—"

"Nineteen-thirty. I know. Nobody had abortions in 1930. Well, not nobody. And I'd waited until it was nearly too late . . ."

Rover climbed parrot-toed up her spine, which she deliberately humped to give the bird better purchase.

"My son would be middle-aged now," she said absently as Rover aimed an unblinking golden eye at the ceiling and slid his hard yellow beak along the length of one maroon strand of her hair after another, methodically grooming the old husk.

". . . Even older than Teddy. Can you imagine?" Isadora asked in pure wonderment. "The doctor showed me what he called the 'debris.' It looked like a spilled teacup of coagulated blood. It had a tiny bird-sized bone in it."

I'd moved from the couch and was standing at the open front door staring out at Isadora's courtyard and at Acequia Madre beyond.

Every useless extraneous detail of that scene has been etching itself into my brain over the last two days. The source ditch which gave the street its colorful name was dry then. It had been full during the summer, a slim river of fresh irrigation water flowing under child-sized footbridges. The toy bridges had been built by this century's residents in order to reach their dooryards more demurely. By that autumn day when I stood listening to Isadora behind me, the flow had stopped and some rich gringos in chinos and French-country straw hats had joined the few remaining Mexican families in the old custom of clearing weeds and readying the Acequia for winter.

"Have you thought about maybe having him live here?" I asked, my back to Isadora as I watched the communal activity outside. "You need somebody. You almost fell again last month, and—"

"He smokes cigars in bed." Isadora cut me off, sounding quarrelsome. "Says he won't give it up."

"Oh."

I must still have had my back to her when she began her story. I'm almost sure her voice came from behind me.

"It's not just the smoking. Teddy says he murdered some fellow. His stepfather, Eldon Lamont. He went to prison for it."

My fault.

Isadora had said it lightly. She threw the line away, really.

". . . Murdered some fellow . . ."

I don't think I turned around then, not yet.

Again.

My fault.

I can only see it in slow motion now. It gets slower every time I replay it.

"He was just a kid," Isadora explained. "He can't even remember most of it. He blocked it out. He only knows from the lawyers, really. But, I'm here to tell you he deserved what he got—the stepfather, I mean. Matty, Teddy's stepfather beat his mother. He beat that poor woman in front of her own son. Teddy grew up on a little backwoods farm in Louisiana. He grew up seeing that almost every day. The poor boy. You ask me, that boy was a hero. . . ."

I remember turning back slowly to face her. She was explaining to the wall, to the parrot, to the cards on the table. She didn't look at me.

"Well," she went on, indignant on Teddy's behalf, "he finally got old enough to do something about it!

"He was eighteen. He walked in on them. His mother was on the floor, bleeding. Matty, imagine! Her nose was bleeding. Her cheek was gashed open. He was her son . . . seeing that. Teddy says he must have gone nuts. Who wouldn't? He told me they kept an ax on the porch for snakes. Teddy grabbed it and raised it up to warn him, you know. Oh, oh . . . Matty, I don't—" Isadora stopped then and she looked into the distance at the picture she was painting.

"But his mother somehow . . . she got in the way—tried to stop what she saw coming, don't you see. I guess she must have put her arm between them."

I was staring at Isadora by that time with my mouth open. It was her own version of Teddy's story, full of defenses and rationales.

"She got cut. Oh, my God, Matty, Teddy told me he

remembers bringing that ax down. He remembers her screaming at him to stop. But he can't remember the rest."

We could hear the violin being plucked and tuned somewhere in the rear of the house. The sound was coming closer.

Isadora hurried on. "Her hand was severed. Both of them
were dead. Teddy didn't mean to do it. I know he didn't. He
couldn't do a thing like that. But they called it a double murder
and they put him in prison for all of his youth. Even if he did
mean it, even if he was too hot-blooded then," she argued,
breathless, "he was just a child. A person can change."

That was the moment. Norman doesn't know it but that is
the moment he blames me for. The moment it became my
fault.

"Shh!" she told me harshly, although I hadn't said a word.
"Listen, he's coming, shh . . ." Isadora thrust her hair back and
warned me with her eyes.

I remember every detail of how she looked, prim and untidy and expectant; how the room looked, mellow and Mexican; the sound of music walking down the hall toward us; the
faint scent of burning leaves from outside. What I can't remember is what was in my head. Where were the alarms? What was I
thinking?

When I was still in therapy, Max Cortino asked me to think
about what I was trying to replace by attaching myself to this
family of outcasts. At just the moment that Isadora declared "a
person can change," the answer to Max's question should have
been screaming at me: a child with a history of violence, a parent figure who rejects the implications of that history, and me
who so yearns to be part of happy domesticity that she's willing
to disregard her misgivings about safety and abet the dream.

Then he was back, shuffle-walking and rolling his shoulders to the Big Easy beat as he plucked. Teddy seemed to have
sucked rhythm through his boyhood pores in the bayou; he
used the violin like a fiddle to saw deep Cajun Zydeco.

"*Your grandma and my grandma sittin' by the fi'ire,*"
he sang.

Teddy bobbed and weaved in front of Isadora and she
clapped her hands.

"My grandma told your grandma—'m a-gonna set your flag on fi'ire," he sang.

"Hey now," she joined in.

"Hey now," he repeated and bent low until his mouth was inches from hers.

"Jackamo fee nah ney!" They sang the last line together and he danced away.

Isadora began to giggle and Rover squawked.

"Come on, you two," Teddy urged, raring back. "Let's see you *move!*" He demonstrated a little jig.

Isadora clapped and beamed at the middle-aged man dancing before us. And Teddy beamed back. At that moment these two were as happy as people get. She leaned sideways toward me without taking her eyes off him.

"A person can change," she insisted. "If a person can't change, what's the point?"

Oddly, the memory of that moment calms me. By the time Joe enters Norman's office, my panic has receded. Joe ignores the decorator's soft matching chairs and pulls a carved chair to the head of the conference table. He assumes his customary private office pose, straddling his chair backward and resting his elbows over the top as he faces us.

Like Norman, Joe is taller than average, but he is thin with a graceful, limber body, unusual in this sedentary profession. And unlike Norman, Joe actually is from a prestigious Boston family. Without vanity, he wears drugstore half-lens reading glasses on a cord around his neck. His clothes are always exquisitely cut, but faintly old-fashioned, as though his tailor were still using a pattern from his days at Harvard.

These two men are so different from each other. But, at moments like this, I remember that they are partners, that they have an adult lifetime of shared hopes and dreads. Both are good lawyers and both are hard-boiled, deeply logical men. Norman summarizes quickly. They waste not a single word in sympathy for the victim. They need to assess the potential damage to their firm and to do that they need information from me.

And they need that information now, before all hell breaks loose.

Norman lets Joe ask the questions. Joe doesn't allude to the sympathy he expressed to me on the phone yesterday and, though his tone is much gentler than Norman's, he too wants information.

"Did you tell the police? Who's the officer in charge?" Joe asks.

"Baca. Detective Daniel Baca."

"Did you tell Baca that you had personally engaged Bellasandro as a driver for Miss Stanton?"

"No."

"That Stanton was a client of this firm?"

"I said I handled some minor matters for her but that Norman was her real lawyer."

"Swell!" from Norman.

Joe ignores the interruption. "That Bellasandro had committed the identical crime in Louisiana?"

"It wasn't identical."

"Norman just said you told him it was."

"Well, alike, yes . . . but not identical. There are important differences. Not least of which is that there is no other victim here. It wasn't like the crazy heat-of-passion thing in Louisiana." I'm reaching for details now. Details I should have been certain of a long time ago. "There was less blood than, I don't know, than there should have been. It looked . . . it looked *controlled,* Joe. Her hand was placed . . . carefully."

Joe's eyes linger on mine.

"Christ!" Norman erupts but before he can continue, Joe holds up a restraining hand. Joe's authority is often displayed in little gestures like this. With a hand or an index finger, sometimes with an eyebrow, Joe exercises control.

"Matty," he starts gently, "I see you may think you have an interest in establishing that Bellasandro didn't do this thing." He takes off his glasses with one finger and shakes his head. His gray eyes are sad but his smile is charming. Some people think Joe uses charm to get whatever he's after. I don't disagree but I think that, like any good lawyer, he uses pretty much whatever works. With some people it's charm. With others it's intimidation. With me, Joe usually tries Dutch uncle. Dutch uncle usually works.

"We would all like that to be true, Matty, but listen to me and hear me. Although coincidence is certainly possible, the smart money is always on a connection. Where the coincidence is two identical deaths; where a hand is removed from two female victims; and where the man who mutilated the first woman is the employee of the second, it borders on insanity to deny the obvious. You made a mistake in judgment with this guy, Matty. A bad mistake! The thing about mistakes, though— no matter how serious they seem at the time—is that you make amends if you can; you let them go if you can't. You move on."

Joe likes lessons and this is always the gist of his wisdom: You do what you must.

"In this case," he continues, "you move on. So please, for all of our sakes, don't make things worse than they already are by denying the mistake."

For a second, Joe smiles at me with genuine warmth and I smile back.

"Now, did you tell Baca about the Louisiana mutilation?"

"No."

"So, in summary, before this murder, you knew Bellasandro had murdered someone and mutilated his own mother. You said nothing. Now, after an identical mutilation of a woman—by the way, a woman the right age to be his mother—am I correct?"

I nod.

"—you are questioned by the police and again you say nothing. Is that about right?"

"Yes."

Joe looks at me for a long while, his tongue lodged thoughtfully in his cheek. "Well, I'm all for discretion, Matthew, but we may be nudging the appearance of complicity here. Not precisely the note we're striving for, eh?"

I smile a goofy smile but have nothing to suggest.

"Matty, perhaps you should leave us now. Norman and I will work this out and let you know our thinking. Meanwhile, this is a small town. So far, there is no hint of our firm's liability in this matter. There will be some mention in the press of our association, of course, but Norman will control that."

He looks at Norman, who nods. Joe leans over the chair back, and stretches his hand across the table to me. "Meanwhile, Matty, let's not do *anything* to worsen the situation, okay?" I take his hand. "And, needless to say," he adds, "under no circumstances should anyone here be in contact with Bellasandro."

"He wants me to be his lawyer," I say.

At this news, Norman throws himself into the back of his rolling chair so hard it hits the wall. "What?!"

Joe squeezes my hand and asks, "What did you tell him?"

"Nothing yet. I want to go over there . . . to the jail . . . explain face-to-face that I can't get involved."

Norman has choice words about my decision but Joe again stills him with a look. His voice under tight control, Joe tells me: "All right. See the guy if you have to, to get it over with smoothly, but—" he stares directly into my eyes, "—end this association, Matty. End it *quick!*"

FIVE

―――∞∞∞―――

ONCE INSIDE THE DOUBLE STEEL DOORS, THE GUARD SEATS me at a cafeteria table in an open recreation room ringed by cells. These are apparently unlocked, since twelve or thirteen orange-suited men are wandering around unimpeded by either of the two guards. The inmates play Ping-Pong and hunch over card games. Two lean against the far wall appraising me without much interest. Lawyers are permitted into these misdemeanor cell-pods and permission isn't withdrawn for women lawyers.

I watch Teddy approach in his own orange jumpsuit. His muscle has long since gone to fat. Purple eagles are hidden under the mats of hair on his arms. Isadora once told me that Teddy claimed he got the tattoos when he was still too young for body hair. His pockmarked face is the same, but the crooked grin is gone.

Teddy arranges himself on one of the little metal seats attached to the table, takes a cigarette out of his jumpsuit pocket, and begins to tap it on the table.

"What happened to your face, Counselor?" His voice is like pumice.

When I saw my face in the mirror this morning I was a little shocked myself. During the past few days, my skin has begun to take on a grayish pallor and puffy circles have grown around my eyes.

"Murder makes me peaked, I guess."

Teddy snorts and gets absorbed with tapping the cigarette.

"I kind of expected you at the arraignment. Did you get my message? They said they'd tell you I asked for you."

"I got your message. I can't be your lawyer, Teddy."

"Ah, well, I figured. It don't matter." His voice doesn't change. He is not surprised by my defection. "They give me some public defender. You probably couldn't of done nothin' anyway. I'm guilty as shit, you know."

A rush goes through me. God forgive me, more than anything else I feel relief. Now there is no need for me to do anything. He's guilty, I'm guilty. Now I can go home, go back to bed. Maybe this time I'll stay there forever.

"I mean, I popped the guy," Teddy continues. "Fucker's gonna testify that I popped him, right? I mean, there don't seem to be no daylight in this thing, huh? The P.D. says plead it. I would've done it then, but the guy seemed a little flat-footed; you know? Not a sharpie like you, Counselor, and I figure maybe you got some ideas the P.D. don't."

The switch is too fast and it takes me too long to get it. He's not saying he killed Isadora.

"You're talking about assaulting the security guard?" I ask.

He gets very still for a few seconds. He stops playing with the cigarette.

"What the hell you think I'm talkin' about, Matty? You think I'm talkin' about Izzy? You think I'm sayin' I'm guilty of killin' Izzy?"

He's on his feet now, but the guard motions him down and he sits again and leans over close. His eyes narrow.

"The fuck is going on here? Nobody said nothin' to me

about a murder charge. What the fuck is going on? I'm one of the few people on the face of the earth who actually *liked* the goddamned harpy. We was family.

"Goddamn it, Matty!" Pleading tempers his outburst. "Maybe the cops don't know how me 'n Izzy was. Maybe nobody in this whole fuckin' world don't know that. But you! You were part of us. You know."

Memory floods through me. It's true. They invited me into their lives. For three years, I've seen Isadora cackling at Teddy as she spread her winning gin hand; seen Izzy using all of Teddy's tasteless gifts to keep from hurting his feelings. I've listened to Teddy sing to her. Isadora once told me she thought Teddy sounded like Harry Belafonte. She used to record him so she could hear his voice at bedtime. She claimed his singing helped her fall asleep; made her feel safe.

And, even the times she got crazy wild and he had to hold her back, he never hurt her.

"Ease on down, Izzy," he would croon. Teddy and Isadora had found in each other fun and even tenderness where the rest of the world saw a couple of tough, bizarre oddballs. Oddballs who'd made me laugh and made me welcome when nobody else could or would.

As I recall these scenes, I feel a quick prickly pressure behind my own eyes, but I am utterly unprepared for Teddy's tears. They roll down his sagging, pitted face until he wipes them away savagely with the back of his hand. He raises the cigarette in the air, and the guard comes over like a reluctant servant and lights it. After a moment, Teddy begins again, slowly and deliberately.

"Matty, what the hell you talkin' about here? Nobody has said anything about chargin' me with murder. Why would they? I was with Charlie Lee fishing at Puye Cliffs for three days. My vacation. You can check with Charlie."

"You were fishing at Puye in the middle of winter?" I hear the incredulity in my own voice. Puye Cliffs is a piece of forest land belonging to the Santa Clara Indians. It's an area about forty miles northwest of Santa Fe, dotted with ponds and remnants of fourteenth-century Anasazi dwellings along sheer cliff faces. As far as I know, the whole area is closed by the tribe during the winter.

"Sure, Charlie's a Santa Clara. He can get back in there whenever he wants. It's best in winter. Nobody else around in the winter. Sleep in sleeping bags and fry fish for breakfast. Me and Charlie been doing it every winter for three years."

"There's a witness?" I ask, my voice rising sharply. "A witness who will tell the district attorney you were with him the whole time?" I'm still sounding cautious but my heart is beginning to soar. The man has an alibi. He didn't do it. This whole thing is going to go away. Teddy probably won't even be *charged* with the murder. Even the assault charge may result in probation. Heat of the moment. Understandable.

I realize I'm grinning like an idiot and, though I quit eight years ago, I could use a cigarette myself just now.

"Damned straight there's a witness. But what do I need with a witness, Counselor? You better tell me why you thought they'd charge me with her killin'. What do you know that I don't know?" The question stops my grin.

"What I know," I answer slowly, "you know, too. I know about Eldon Lamont . . . and about your mother. I know what you did to your mother."

He doesn't respond, just puffs on his cigarette and stares at the wall. Puffs a long time.

Finally I say, "Maybe somebody else knew about that, too?"

He looks at me. "Yeah?"

"Yeah. . . . If you didn't do this, somebody went to a lot of trouble to make it look like you did."

As the day goes on, the weight I've been feeling is getting lighter and lighter, and by late afternoon, I'm beginning to whistle little repetitive snatches of long-forgotten songs. But before I float away completely, there is one call I need to make. The law labels the kind of person who would make such a call an "officious intermeddler." She's the nosy busybody everybody loves to hate. Me, too. I hate her, too. And yet, I can't help myself. I have to get over the edge of doubt that still might trip me up. So I make the call. Information gives me the number at the pueblo and he picks up the receiver himself.

Charlie Lee is wary. Probably he has heard about the mutilation murder by now and he probably knows that his friend, Teddy, worked for the victim. When I ask my questions, Charlie wants to know who wants to know. And when I tell him I'm a lawyer, he wants to know if I'm Teddy's lawyer.

"No," I admit. "I'm not his lawyer. I'm just a friend. I think I am, anyway. I'm concerned that Teddy may be charged in Isadora Stanton's murder. If he is, he's going to say he was with you at Puye for three days. Please tell me, is that true?"

This headlong tumble is met with a long silence. Eventually he speaks.

"We were at Puye."

It takes several seconds for me to know that he isn't offering any more.

"The whole time? Day and night?"

"Whole time."

"Together? I mean, were you actually together the whole time? Whose car were you in? Who was driving? Could Teddy have driven anywhere without you?"

Another long pause then, "Yeah," and ". . . My pickup . . . Me," and ". . . No."

I know this reticence. Every Anglo who has ever wanted something an Indian didn't want to give him knows this reticence. And—at least this Anglo—is daunted by it. There is something in this ability to live with long spaces that awes me and draws from me a shallow flood of words to ease the deep arid silence.

"Mr. Lee, maybe there's no reason you should tell me anything. I guess I'm asking mostly for myself. You see, I introduced Teddy to Isadora Stanton. They are both my friends. It's important to me to know whether he was involved in her murder. Do you understand?"

Finally, "I picked Belly up that morning . . . the eleventh . . . We stopped for a couple of beers in Espanola . . . We stayed there 'til dark."

"Yes, then what?"

"Then, I drove up the canyon to Third Pond." Charlie's voice is deep and flat. He swallows the ending of every word. "We made camp on the far side of the dam. We went to sleep."

"And?"

"We fished Third Pond."

"For how long?"

"All next day. Then I drove him home."

The downbeat of the last word sounds like closure again. My heartbeat accelerates.

"Wait! Don't hang up, please. One more thing. It's important! The truck keys. Did you have them?"

"Yes."

"All the time?"

"All the time. In my pocket."

"Are you sure?"

"Lady," Lee starts. His exasperation is showing now. To Charlie Lee, we are all officious intermeddlers who've been intermeddling for more than two centuries.

"Nobody drives my truck, ma'am. I sleep with the keys in my wallet, my wallet in my pocket, my butt on my pocket. You got any more questions?"

"No. No, really. I thank you." More to seem businesslike than anything else, I ask if he would be willing to give that statement to the district attorney should it become necessary.

"Mr Lee? Are you there?"

"I'm here."

"Will you?"

"I guess, if I got no other choice, that's what I'll do."

This time he hangs up before I can thank him again.

The rest of the day goes like a breeze. Teddy will be released soon. I'm not sure why that hasn't happened already. I'll call the public defender's office tomorrow and see what's going on. Meanwhile, I've got work to do. Norman seems like a benign buffoon today. I almost enjoy spending the afternoon with him reviewing a videotaped deposition and noting our objections for a pretrial motion.

•   •   •

When finally I pull my Toyota into the shadows of the compound of old adobes, I feel tired but happy, ready for the first good sleep in days. I let myself in, drop coat and purse in my living room, and pull myself up the narrow staircase to the loft. By the time I reach the top stair, I've strewn clothes on every riser. I turn on the water in the tub and diddle my fingers in the stream waiting for it to heat. In the spring, when the weather is warm, I sometimes fill the tub, kneel from the water and stretch out the bathroom window into a sea of white apple blossoms.

But this is the high desert and by November the brilliant days are turning into bitter cold nights. So tonight the window, which reaches from ceiling to tub, is closed tight. I like to bathe in the dark and so, as the tub fills, I switch off the light to let my eyes adjust to the darkness. I raise the window blind to bring the winter-bare branches nearer without fear of being visible from outside, and I feel decadent as I slip naked into the steaming water.

As my eyes adjust, I sink my shoulders beneath the hot water, and look at my own body. It's very far from perfect, but it is strong and well proportioned and my legs are my vanity. John's great-aunt once told me that "at least" I had good legs. She said that in her day, a girl auditioning to become a Ziegfeld Follies showgirl was asked to take four silver dollars and place them between her bare legs at the thigh, knee, calf, and ankle. If all four coins could be held in place and Flo Ziegfeld could see daylight in the vertical spaces between the coins, the girl passed the first test.

Later, in the privacy of the bedroom John and I shared, I stood naked before the full-length mirror and balanced coins between my legs as John lounged on the bed watching me.

Now, I lie here alone in the water, in the dark, remembering that day; remembering his reflection as he approached from behind. Our eyes met in the mirror as he feathered his fingers across my bare shoulders and down my spine. I let my mind play back the heat of that and other nights. In the churning mixture of hunger and sorrow, I ache for John. It has been such a long time since that life—which sometimes even now seems like my real life—ended. The muscles in my vagina begin to involuntarily squeeze and release. Steam rising from me, I stand to emerge from the tub. I lean one hand against the window to keep my balance and accidentally smear the steam away. And that is when I see it.

Below, crouching near my entry porch, a figure creeps nearer to the door. Is the door locked? My God, I can't remember if the door is locked.

A half-moon sheds the only light on the shadowy shapes below. Kneeling precariously in the slippery tub, I press my face to the wet glass. When nothing moves for several seconds, I begin to relax. It wouldn't be surprising, so soon after seeing murder and mutilation, if my imagination were working overtime. I decide to count slowly to ten. If nothing moves, I'll step out of the tub and survey the ground below from the better vantage of the bedroom window.

"One . . . two . . ." My skin is all goose flesh as the damp heat rushes from my body. By the time I reach nine and nothing has stirred below, I'm more concerned with getting warm than with an imagined danger.

Suddenly it moves!

Only a couple of steps, toward my living room window. The figure is directly below me now, and I can make out a cone shape, like a ski cap. A man, or maybe a large woman, stands in the shadows for an instant, then places both hands on the window. The hands are gloved. A wide glint of metal flashes briefly at the wrist as the person leans forward, close up, peering in. The figure, dressed thickly against the winter night, presses against the glass looking into my home while I, naked and shivering, press against the glass above looking down at him.

The figure moves. It is only three steps from the window to my front door. I turn away quickly. I have one foot out of the tub, dripping on the floor, when a dog bark pierces the silence and becomes instantly ferocious. My ankle twists and I land on my face on the tiled floor.

I lie motionless in the dark trying to will away the pain, blood spurting from my nose. I concentrate on the barking, which is beginning to break up now. I'm comforted by the dog's waning enthusiasm. Maybe it means the prowler has backed off. I don't know what's happening down there, but calling the cops seems like a good bet.

I crawl through the sudsy mess on the floor and, still on my knees, nudge the door open and move into the bedroom searching the plank flooring for the phone cord. When I find it, I pull until the telephone is in my naked lap and I dial 911 for the second time this week. Hunkered low, I tug the quilt from the bed, wrap myself in it, and wait, shivering with cold and listening to the endless rings at my ear and for sounds from below. Finally a woman answers, "Nine one one."

After providing my address, I hang up, crawl into the closet, and search the floor for yesterday's discarded clothes. Today's are on the stairs and I'm not quite willing to venture down yet. I find an old pair of Levi's with my underwear still in the crotch. Sitting on the floor, I pull both over my hips in two quick butt-hops. I can't find a bra among the stuff on the floor so I pull on a T-shirt over cold bare nipples.

By the time the two uniformed officers, both women, arrive, there's no sign of the intruder. The officers take my statement politely. I tell them, of course, about Isadora Stanton's murder. They don't discount the possibility of a connection but are more inclined toward the overactive-imagination theory.

"Sometimes," says the tall redheaded one, "after a trauma like that, people see things for awhile."

"Look, if it were just the shadowy shape I saw at first, maybe I would agree; but I saw a person. Standing. Looking into my window."

She stares at me with studied patience.

I'm frankly surprised to get this kind of crap from women and, maybe because of what feels like a small betrayal by one of my own, I don't go further. I don't mention what even I think I may have imagined. I don't say that I may have recognized the prowler. Something about the way the person moved, the general shape. I don't know; something made me think of Rickie Hadid.

Rickie Hadid is the surprise boyfriend of Isadora's housekeeper, Juanita Jakes. Any boyfriend at all would have been a surprise. With Fetal Alcohol Syndrome, the sins of her alcoholic mother have been written on Juanita's face and mind. Juanita's heavy flat face has short eye-openings, and a short, upturned nose. Her I.Q. level approaches ninety, which is at the high end of the intelligence scale for victims of this syndrome. Juanita is a person who makes you wonder again about the great inequities of God's gifts.

And, Rickie Hadid is *not* just *any* boyfriend. Rickie is smart and darkly, romantically, gloriously handsome. He looks like the young Turk on the old cigarette ads before Joe Camel. Rickie Hadid is, in fact, from Jordan. He is in this country on a student visa which ran out over a year ago, long after he had left his studies at the University of New Mexico.

Hadid's questionable status and his natural penchant for slick schemes used to trouble Isadora greatly. Though others might express wonder, sly old Izzy had not a doubt as to why Juanita had suddenly come up a winner in the romance sweepstakes. She had tried to warn Juanita but, vague as the girl was about everything else, she was adamant about Rickie.

I'd come late to Isadora's fiesta party last September. The few guests were grouped near the front door subtly vying for the best position from which to bolt. Isadora was in a particularly mean-spirited mood as she called Juanita over to where I stood. "Come here, Jakes, come here," the old woman shrilled. "Show Matty your ring."

Juanita's pregnancy was already showing by then. She obediently shuffled over, then offered a limp left hand for my appraisal. She kept her head down and slightly averted, but I could see the small play of a smile at the corners of her mouth and her eyes darting again and again to her own finger. The ring was a wide silver band which had been shaved and polished leaving a delicately carved pattern of cornstalks standing in bas-relief all the way around. The pattern was broken from time to time for slanting lines of turquoise stones. I'd never seen anything quite like it.

"Now, what do you think of that, Matty?" Isadora demanded. "Her Rickie, not his real name you know, has asked this poor child carrying a child to be his bride. And he's given her this as an engagement ring. Go on, tell Juanita what you think, Matty."

Even before she knew about the pregnancy, Isadora had sourly predicted that Rickie Hadid would try to wed his way into citizenship. Now the appearance of the ring on Juanita's bloated finger, along with the girl's unusual mulishness, had set Isadora off in vicious paroxysms of sarcasm.

"Tell us, dear, how do you suppose the handsome Mr. Hadid happened to choose you?"

"He likes me," Juanita mumbled.

"You think so, do you? I'd lay a wager that if I were to offer these old bones, he would drop you like a hot potato and I myself would be Mrs. Mohamar, alias 'Rickie,' Hadid before nightfall."

The old woman accompanied her small joke by lifting her napkin to cover her lower face in a pantomime of Arab female shyness. Juanita giggled. But, before Isadora was through, Juanita's worried eyes sought to pierce the darkness of the hall-way just beyond the main room. I looked to where she was star-ing. I found there another set of eyes looking back at us.

At the time, the scene had made me sad but hadn't frightened me. Rickie Hadid has always seemed fairly harmless to me. Now, as I lie here awake in my bed hearing every creaking board in the loft and remembering the figure which had lurked below, Rickie Hadid doesn't seem quite so harmless.

SIX

—⁂—

THE GRAVE-SITE SERVICE IS SPARSELY ATTENDED. THE CHILL autumn morning is cloudless and bright. Everyone is wearing dark glasses. Most of those gathered stand around a short row of folding chairs. They are strangers to me. The only two people, other than me, who gave a damn about Isadora aren't in attendance. Teddy hasn't been released yet and Juanita hasn't been heard from since the day after Isadora died.

Seated in the middle of the row of chairs near Isadora's coffin is a tall, angular woman with kinked, frosted hair out to here. A thin slit of face is visible between her dark designer glasses and the high collar of her black coat.

The Horrible Niece, I suppose; the only living relative. In three years of close contact with Isadora, I've never laid eyes on the niece. Since Isadora referred to her only as the Horrible Niece or Nurse Rat-shit, I'd dimly imagined that Faye Stanton would look like a gargoyle. So I'm a little surprised to see that she's maybe attractive under her Darth Vader gear. Seated next to her, a woman similarly masked reaches her gloved hand into Faye Stanton's lap; she finds Faye's bare fingers and squeezes them.

An assistant pastor who never met Isadora speaks movingly of this mortal coil so quickly shed. A lone man leans against a cottonwood tree at the edge of the circle. Shit, I think, as I recognize Eamonn Migill, the local gadfly reporter. A gaggle of four church ladies bow their heads in unison and pray for a soul that had remained belligerently closed to them during their duty visits. A fifth is worrying over a hand-held tape player.

Among the few remaining mourners are the three of us from Frederick & Danforth. I've been told that in the firm's glory days, a phalanx of associates always came to client funerals. But, since the beginning of the nineties, all law firms, and especially the natural resource specialists of the Southwest, have felt the economic pinch. Frederick, Danforth & Rodriguez were doubly hard hit when Gil Rodriguez left, taking with him not only his name on the letterhead but the firm's biggest client. Now, there is no longer a phalanx of associates. Are Joe and Norman here in person today because of the firm's reduced circumstance, or is there perhaps an agenda? At Frederick & Danforth there is often an agenda.

The eulogy over, the church lady with the tape player motions with flapping hands for everyone to remain where they are. "The deceased has made a request," she chirps. "As some of you may know, a group of us visited Miss Stanton from time to time. Though she wasn't able to attend services, Miss Stanton was quite generous with donations . . ."

I know for a fact that Isadora paid the ladies so that they would go away. I wonder idly if they know it, too.

". . . and in return she asked only one thing of us. She asked that this music—" she twirls the cassette in front of her, "—be played in the event of her death. As you see, the tape has no label. It has been quite a little mystery to the ladies and myself."

She fiddles a second or two more and then a surprisingly melodic gravel voice emanates from her little black box.

"Do you believe this?" Norman whispers across me to Joe. "We're to have a goddamned musical program." Joe is amused and everyone else listens curiously to the a cappella selection.

Small conversation erupts when it is over. Joe guesses that the singer is Tom Waits, the whiskey-voiced rock singer who dabbles in Gospel. But it is not Waits. I would know that voice anywhere. It is the deep scat basso of Teddy Bellasandro singing "Amazing Grace" directly to Isadora Stanton like it could save her life.

The service ends with a brief benediction, and Eamonn Migill leaves his place by the tree and saunters over to us.

"Ah, the Presidents," he says, tipping an imaginary hat. Only a few people in town refer to us that way anymore. It's an oblique reference to the original firm name Frederick, Danforth & Rodriguez, shorthanded to its familiar presidential initials, F.D.R. Norman likes it when people call us the Presidents.

"Eamonn," he says heartily. "Good to see you. Here to get a little set piece for your story?"

Eamonn Migill is the owner and editor of *At Large in Santa Fe*. He is also its only reporter. *Large* is primarily a throwaway shopper. But, except for a few dead weeks a year, the paper carries a single news story, or editorial, or torrent of gossip, according to Eamonn's whim. His interest is eclectic, his background knowledge deep, his mind very good, and his gossip frequently nasty. So the pieces generate discussion around watercoolers and on the plaza, where *Large* is distributed free at noon once a week.

I haven't seen Eamonn lately, which means he's been drying out somewhere. When Eamonn is sober, he's busy. You see him everywhere around town, cornering legislators during the session and generally nosing about. When he's drinking, he's at the Dragon Room, an expensive watering hole, where he's seated at a table everyone regards as his own. When he's drinking, the stories that get written by Eamonn are the ones that sit down next to him.

"I am, indeed, sir," he tells Norman now. "I suppose you heard this Bellasandro character was charged with the murder this morning? I'd be happy to have the Presidents' slant on the whole story if you gentlemen have a moment to spare."

Migill's words deliver an almost physical blow. I'd thought Teddy was home free. The police must have pulled Teddy's record after all. Why would they do that? And what happened to Charlie Lee, Teddy's airtight alibi?

Norman is happy to oblige Migill's request. Putting his slant on this story is probably the agenda, now that I think of it. "Bizarre tragedy. Nothing to do with us. Bound to be resolved quickly." Something like that.

As the three move away to talk, Faye Stanton, the new heiress, joins them. I steal a moment with the church lady. She shrugs agreement at my odd request and I drop the cassette tape into my purse. Finally, Norman is left to deal with the press and Isadora's heir while Joe and I made our way back to his car.

As soon as I shut the door on the Lexus, everything becomes profoundly still. When the Mozart begins, it's like being in a private, acoustically perfect concert hall. Joe's cars are always top of the line. He drives fast and sure, like he does most things. Headed to the office, he smoothly corners the continuous curve of Paseo de Peralta.

"Are you going to be able to get beyond this thing?" He keeps his eyes on the road as he asks.

"The music. 'Amazing Grace.' That was Teddy."

"What?"

"That tape, it was Teddy Bellasandro singing. Isadora loved his voice."

Joe drums his fingers on the wheel. "And . . . so?"

"Nothing, really, I guess. It's just that it sounded loving to me. Joe, their relationship was loving. I spent a lot of time with them, you know. The music sounded like how they were."

He lets this lie and we're quiet for a while. As he pulls into the parking area behind our office, he switches the Mozart off. A light wind skitters the pages of a torn newspaper across the dirt lot. He reaches for the door handle, but I know we've got to discuss the issue Eamonn Migill's news has raised.

"Joe, wait. I want to talk."

He closes the door but keeps his grip on the handle. His body language says he isn't going to give this discussion much time.

"What's up?" he asks.

"You want me to keep out of this—out of the murder investigation. I understand why you want that and I wish I could, but—"

"But?"

"But I need to know what happened."

Joe's exasperation shows. "For God's sake, Matty, you will know what happened in due time. It's only been six days since the murder. The cops do a pretty fair job, you know, and so does the District Attorney's office. The guy's going to have his own lawyer. A public defender has probably already been appointed."

"I know you're right; I just worry, you know, that they might miss something."

"What? Something you're going to see? With all your criminal law training?" The sarcasm is delivered with a pinched smile.

"Uhmm," I say. What I leave unsaid is, *Yes, goddamn it; something I'm going to see.*

"Matty, you're smarter than that."

"I think they're going to hang him, Joe. I don't believe he did it. I can't just sit by and do nothing. I won't." I'm arguing now.

"What makes you so sure he didn't do it?"

"It's simple. Even if you don't think he cared about her. Say I'm wrong about that. Say he secretly hated her or wanted her money. Anyway, say he wanted to kill her. Would he mutilate her? It's like leaving a big sign saying 'Teddy Bellasandro was here.' Nobody in their right mind would incriminate themselves like that."

Joe leans his head back and stares at the sunroof. He sighs deeply. "Matty, I don't think this guy *is* in his right mind. I don't think anybody who could do a thing like this even once could be in his right mind. Can you imagine it, Matty: cutting someone's hand off? Jesus! Doing a thing like that would make you crazy even if you weren't crazy before. Norman is right about this pervert, Matty. Teddy Bellasandro is bad news. The very last thing you need is to get mired in this. You know, your mother told me she thought she'd lose you the last time."

I didn't know this. I didn't even know they'd spoken about me. I guess I shouldn't be surprised that I couldn't have gotten this job without intervention and more than the skim of explanation I'd supplied. But I'm a little surprised that my mother would have talked to Joe so openly about my private grief.

"It's been four years; I'm healed to death," I tell him brusquely.

"You are scarred over, Matty. That's a far cry from healed. Those scars can reopen. And this situation is exactly the thing to do it, to tear you apart. You owe it to yourself to take care of Matty Donahue, not some rum-dum crazy. Innocent or not."

I take a deep breath. Joe's right about the scars. They're there. Even now, nothing terrifies me so much as revisiting the horror and guilt of the night when the man I loved died by his son's hand. I nod, then nod again like a dope. Maybe he's right about everything. Maybe I do have to take care of me first. Then he adds what he thinks is the clincher.

"Frankly, Matty, you owe it to us too, to the firm. You're okay today thanks, in no small part, to your job. It's been a safe haven for you. You don't want to carry the anxiety of trial work anymore? Okay, we let you work behind the scenes with almost no emotional demands and damned little stress."

"I know, Joe, and you know I've appreciated it. Really, I have."

"I know you have, kid. And, truth be told, we've more than gotten our money's worth from you. You're tenacious and you puzzle things through until you get results. Nobody puts together a discovery package or writes a brief like you do. You're as good as I am at seeing all the angles, all the possible scenarios. You're a good lawyer. But I guess I've thought it was a mutually beneficial thing. No?" He cocks his head and one eyebrow.

A car pulls in beside us. Norman and the niece emerge and hurry into the office.

"Except for Norman," I reply to Joe.

Joe laughs out loud and slaps my knee lightly in conclusion.

"Except for Norman," he agrees. "Come on, Matthew, let's go back to work."

He opens his door to a generous gust of winter air. As far as he's concerned the matter is concluded, but I still don't move.

"Wait. There's more." I hear myself explaining that I may be the only friend Teddy has left. And I admit again that I need to know that Teddy didn't kill Isadora Stanton, because if he did, I did.

"Exactly why you've got to stay away from it," says Joe. "Your real motive in this is to absolve yourself, isn't it? If Bellasandro didn't do it, you didn't do it. It's a lousy way to proceed, Matthew. It's just one more mistake. You've got to stop making these mistakes, Matty. Let it go. Walk away."

There's no way to argue with this. He's right about my motivation as far as he goes. But there's more to my tie to Teddy than that. Teddy and I are alike; both of us caused death and shattered our own lives once before. Teddy is living proof that, no matter what, second chances can work. And I need to believe in second chances. I need to believe in them now, more than ever. Also, I happen to like him.

"I saw him," I tell Joe, "in jail."

"And?"

"I told him I couldn't help him."

"Good!"

"But . . ."

"But?"

". . . but that was before he was charged with the murder. I didn't think they'd charge him. He said there was a witness, an alibi." I explain about Charlie Lee and the trip to Puye Cliffs. I tell him that apparently the D.A. hasn't followed up on this or Teddy wouldn't have been charged. Joe's interested.

"Alibi witness? Really? A Santa Clara Indian?" Then he drags his hand down his long face and sighs. "Just what the hell is it exactly you think you're going to do? You don't know jackshit about criminal law."

"I don't know. Be on his side. Try to figure it out. I know how ridiculous that sounds. But—"

And suddenly, without warning, I realize I've made up my

mind. I tell him calmly, "But that's what I'm going to do! I'm going to try to figure this out, try to find Charlie Lee, call the P.D.; whatever it takes."

Joe gives it a beat, then lets out a very long groan. "Oh, shit! I guess one of the things I've admired about you is that you're a bulldog. Why should this surprise me? Just give me some time to think about it, okay? Now, come on, Miss Marple, let's go in."

When I get to my office, there is a pink slip on my desk. *Max Cortino called,* it says. Firm policy at Frederick & Danforth is that the receptionist indicates on message slips, as closely as is practical, the exact words of callers. These slips often become part of case files and, where the quotes help a client or the firm against a client, they are trotted out. The pink slip on my desk does not relate to a client matter. It says, *What would Matty say to a cup of coffee? My place after work?*

Speaking of old wounds! After eighteen months of silence, what on earth can Max want?

About an hour later, Joe pops his head in my door. "Tell you what. You do what you have to do, but let's keep this as tight as possible. If Norman finds out you're snooping around, or whatever the hell you're going to be doing, the shit will hit the fan."

I'm genuinely grateful, and Joe must see it, because he grins and gives me a little wink. Then, as an afterthought, he adds, "It's not exactly that I don't trust your judgment on this thing, Matthew, but I don't exactly trust your judgment on this thing. How about you keep me informed on what you're doing, what you find out, just like you were doing discovery on a case for me? Okay?"

"You got it," I promise. I'm unreasonably happy, like a kid with her mother's permission to unearth worms in the backyard.

SEVEN

———◆◆◆———

AFTER JOE SHUTS THE DOOR, I SETTLE MYSELF BACK DOWN into the only chair in my office and let it soak in that I'm embarking on something that has more juice than anything I've done in four years. I glance around the diminutive cell where I've spent most of my waking hours for most of these years, and even the walls look different today.

The office is packed like a Japanese cracker box. I use the waist-high beehive fireplace to store my files. My computer, monitor, and printer are squeezed into the two-foot-deep window well. A wide shelf encircles the room with pie-shaped fans at each corner. This shelf is my desk. From the rolling, rocking, tufted oxblood leather swiveling chair, passed down from the departed Gil Rodriguez and located in the dead center of the room, I can touch everything in this office. The chair is yet another of the wombs I've arranged in my life. I've been going from treetop bed to this throne-in-a-closet, keeping life at a respectable distance.

Today, however, for the first time, the office feels claustrophobic. Leaning back with my feet on the shelf, I stare up at the high ceiling for divine inspiration. I review what I know about the crime. Not much. As I try to imagine the face of the killer, so little is clear: Is he old or young? Is he even a he? Could a woman have done this macabre thing? Was the killer an invited friend or a stranger, a guilt-free psychopath or a tortured soul?

The only thing that must be fact is that Isadora's killer almost certainly had to know about Teddy's past. No one else, other than Teddy himself, would have cut the victim's hand off. That someone had to know the facts of the Louisiana crime. So that is my litmus test. Who knew?

I drag a yellow pad from the shelf onto my lap and start scratching a list. Right now, it doesn't matter if they are likely murderers, only whether they knew about Teddy's past. I write:

TEDDY

ISADORA

MATTY

That's all I know for sure. But, of course, the three people on the list know other people. Until now, I've told no one, but Teddy's net spreads wide: the Louisiana cops who arrested him, the lawyers who prosecuted him in Louisiana, and the one who defended him—all knew the details of his crime. I write them down. Inmates he served with? Parole officer? Current friends? He told Isadora—why not others?

I write UNKNOWN ACQUAINTANCES and shudder. The list could go on forever. And any of dozens of people might have harbored a grudge, could have had a motive to frame Teddy.

And what about Isadora herself? She'd told me about Teddy. Who else would she have told? Juanita Jakes? Could Juanita have comprehended, let alone duplicated the crime? I remember my own rule. It doesn't matter if they are *likely* suspects, only whether they *may* have known about Teddy's past. I add Juanita's name to my list. Then, after staring at the names awhile longer, I add another: Juanita's boyfriend, Rickie Hadid. I can think of no other possible suspects.

I figure it's time to get some real information. Now that forensics has had time to work their magic, what do the cops know? The newspapers have been long on lurid descriptions of the severed hand, but short on significant details. What was the time of death? What about blood and fiber evidence? The weapon? And what about the alibi witness? Where is Charlie Lee?

A public defender will have been assigned to the case by now. I telephone the P. D.'s office. The phone rings endlessly before a gum-popping, young, female voice answers.

"Public Defender's office, hold please." *Click.*

I punch the speaker-phone button and go back to my list, prepared to wait as long as it takes. The P.D.'s office is a notorious zoo, where an undertrained skeleton-staff supports a small group of lawyers, each of whom handles scores of cases simultaneously.

"Who you holding for?" chirps the voice between pops.

"I want whoever has been assigned to the Theodore Bellasandro case. I think—"

"Felony or misdemeanor?"

"Felony, but it was originally a mis—"

"Hold, please."

Click. Some public defenders are excellent lawyers; a few are among the best in the profession. These are the ones, often, with a mission. They believe, without reservation, that they are the thin line protecting America's constitutionally guaranteed rights from predator prosecutors.

As I wait, I picture one of these paragons defending Teddy and wonder for a second if maybe Joe's right. These guys are experts. What can I add?

"Hello?" the receptionist says. "The P.D. assigned to Bellasandro is Stone Allen."

This can't be right! I know Stone Allen. Nobody would let Stone Allen handle a felony.

"Ma'am," says the voice, "are you still there?"

"Are you sure?" I ask. Maybe he was assigned to the assault. Maybe someone else is taking over now that there is a murder charge. "Please. Check again."

Click.

I went to law school with Stone Allen. His persistence and determination so far outpaced his intelligence that he became a minor legend among members of the bar. He took the entrance LSAT eight times before inching his score into an acceptable range to get into law school. He struggled pitifully through law school, begging mentoring from better students, including me. Stone's nickname back then was "Rocks," as much a play on the quality of his brain as on his name.

After graduation, Rocks took the bar exam every semester for five years with special refresher courses between each try. When finally, some six years after graduation, he was admitted to the New Mexico bar, he went to work immediately for the Public Defender's office. Everyone assumed he would stay pretty much at the bottom of that barrel for the length of his career. He could handle misdemeanor cases. He could plead low-grade felonies. He would never be responsible for using his legal skills, such as they are, to protect a life. I hadn't thought about Stone Allen for years. Now, a picture of John Steinbeck's Lennie with the doomed puppy in his big, clumsy hands floats to mind. I cringe.

"Yo, yeah, that's it. S. Allen, assigned to Theodore, a.k.a. Teddy Bellasandro, Murder One. You wanna leave a message?" I leave my number.

The logical place to start is with who stood to gain what if Isadora died. I turn to the computer, use Norman's access code, and call up Isadora's will and the accounting of her assets updated last year. I was right. With the house, Isadora's estate is worth about two million, all of it left to her niece, Faye Stanton. There is no codicil leaving the limosine to Teddy. As it turns out, I guess it's a good thing the old woman left nothing to Teddy. At least the prosecutors won't have that motive to parade before the jury.

What's she like I wonder? The hated niece who gets all the marbles. There's one way to get an idea quickly. While sitting in Joe's Lexus, I saw her walk into this building with Norman. Maybe she's still here. What the hell. In for a dime . . . I gather up one of Norman's working files to justify my visit.

His "What—" is generically brusque. When he sees it's me he adds, "—do *you* want? I'm tied up."

"Right. Sorry to bother you, Norman. But you said you wanted to look at these today. It'll just take—"

"No, no. This isn't a good time. Just leave them there." He waggles his finger vaguely at "our" box on his desk and then points to the door as a direction to me. When I don't immediately take the hint, he rises to hurry me out. He becomes courteous, "Just leave them. Don't worry, Matty. I'll take care of them."

The tone is just uncharacteristic enough to make me pause. And I pause just long enough to allow time for what he's been nervous about to happen. Out of his private bathroom emerges Faye Stanton, still in dark glasses but without the disguising coat. Her face is all cheekbone and hollows and taut smooth skin. She notices me but seems not to. She must be around forty but she moves like a young woman—like a dancer. She begins more or less swirling around the gray-and-sand room, moving from painting to sculpture to window. Her companion from this morning's funeral is nowhere in sight.

"Norman, I had no idea," she exclaims. "This is perfectly wonderful. You can't have done this yourself. Your wife?" she asks with eyebrows raised and a bemused smile on her face.

Norman's return smile is more of a twitch. He says, "Ms. Faye Stanton, this is Ms. Donahue, the ah . . ."

Norman seems stuck. I can imagine what he may be trying to say. *The ah . . . , flunky? The ah . . . , nemesis? The ah . . . , fuck-up?*

"Of course." Faye rescues us both. "My aunt's friend. I'm very pleased to meet you. Matty, isn't it?"

Faye is tall, bony, and agile. As she envelops my shoulders in one long arm, I have the feeling I'm about to be enfolded in a wing and flown to an aerie on a faraway cliff. She looks down at my face but only one eye focuses. The other glistens brightly but stares blindly over the top of my head. No wonder Norman is being such a twit. This lady is very peculiar.

But there's more to Norman's nervousness than that. She's giving him some sort of signal. Her eye flits to me and she makes a couple of quick sharp nods to him. He's struggling with something.

"Ah . . . Ms. Donahue, since you're here anyway . . ." Faye nods at him again, clearly telling him to get on with it, ". . . it would seem that we may need your assistance."

Norman resignedly continues. "As you may know, Faye here," he beams agreeably at her, "ah . . . Ms. Stanton, is the only beneficiary under her aunt's will. She is naturally quite anxious to have the will probated as soon as possible."

"Uh-huh," I say.

"And, certainly, I . . . *we*, would like to accommodate her," Norman adds.

"Uh-huh," I say again, and note that Faye Stanton has moved to the window and is staring out as though lost in thought and not engaged in Norman's stammering discourse at all. But her rapidly tapping toe suggests otherwise.

"But there is, of course, the question of whether there are any . . . may be any . . . ah . . . subsequent wills."

"Oh?" I say.

Faye Stanton, still staring out at the November day, says, "Would you know anything about a new will, Matty? Did Aunt Isadora mention anything to you about changing her will?"

"No, nothing, really. I mean, she was always threatening to write a codicil for personal items. But she never actually did even that, as far as I know. She certainly never mentioned anything to me about rewriting her whole will."

The change in Stanton is palpable. She's on the move again, swooping around the room and collapsing behind Norman's desk, in his chair, a smug satisfied smile on her face.

"Well, then, there's nothing to worry about, hey, Norm?"

Even Norman's wife doesn't call him Norm. I would lay odds that even Norman's mother didn't call him Norman.

"Ah . . . good, fine." Norman clears his throat. "Of course, publication is still necessary," he explains to Faye. "Required by law, you see. Additionally, just because Ms. Donahue doesn't know anything about a new will doesn't mean there wasn't one. Your aunt stood right here in this office and told me she wanted to write a new will, so we must assume that perhaps—"

"What?" I am stunned. "Isadora told you that she wanted to change her will?"

"Yes . . . ah . . . yes, she did."

"But you didn't do it?"

"No. No. We discussed it. I . . . ah . . . I was, as you know, concerned about her competence. I told her so. I was particularly concerned, given her choice of new beneficiary."

"Who was?" I'm interrogating now.

"Matty, this is a scream." Faye is fiddling with Norman's desktop family photo. "Aunt Izzy wanted to give her money to her murderer. It'll come to almost two million dollars. Two million dollars to some whacko handyman."

I look from one to the other and at the end stare at Norman. This little piece of information was left out of our last discussion, deliberately, I'm quite sure.

"Yes," says Norman uncomfortably. "For a time a few months ago, Isadora Stanton considered changing her will to include Bellasandro. We never actually got to the details of exactly how much or—"

I'm still catching up. "You told a client you wouldn't change her will because you thought she was incompetent?"

"I most certainly did." Norman says this as though this is the most normal behavior in the world. "She was, of course, free to go elsewhere."

"Uh-huh . . ."

Not only is telling a client she is incompetent to change her will a far cry from normal procedure, but this newly divulged incident—this wish to change beneficiaries—reeks of significance to the murder. I can't help wondering if, against every rule in the book, Norman passed on this tidbit to his friend Faye *before* Isadora was murdered. No wonder Norman is so nervous.

". . . Uh-huh," I repeat. "What exactly is it you want from me?"

"Well, Ms. Stanton—Faye here—felt that, given your relationship . . . ah . . . that you—"

"Jesus, Norman," Faye interrupts and focuses briefly on me. "I figured that if she hadn't talked this over with you, Matty, she'd probably dropped the whole thing. According to Norm, you were some kind of friend, right? Anyway, I wanted to know if she told you she was going to ask some other lawyer, maybe even you?" She anchors her good eye on me in evaluation.

"No, no," I say to Faye. "I guess she might have. But she didn't."

Why didn't Isadora mention any of this to me? Her niece has made a good guess. I am the logical person to have been privy to Isadora's dilemma. Why didn't she tell me she was thinking of changing her will?

"Well, then, Norman . . ." Faye is gathering her things. "Go ahead and start the publication period, if that's what has to be done. Let's get this show on the road."

I follow Faye out and continue to follow her well past Norman's earshot.

"Excuse me, Ms. Stanton," I call.

"Faye, for heaven's sake; call me Faye. I hate formality." She winks one of her eyes. I'm fascinated partly because I think she may have winked with the glass eye.

"Yes. Well, Faye, I was wondering. You have the keys to Isadora's house, don't you?"

"So far that's all I have, a set of house keys and Angel Bird. You wouldn't want that lousy parrot, would you?"

"No. No. I'd just like to get into the house if that would be okay with you."

When she moves close, with an easy familiarity I don't share, she's unsettling. "Into Aunt Izzy's house? Matty dear, what is this? A little extracurricular work? I had the distinct impression that our Norman wasn't eager to have you involved in any of this. What do we think we're doing?"

"Looking. I just want to look around," I say mildly. I realize agreeing to my request may be a risk to Faye if she has something to hide. But if she is threatened, she's a good actress. She merely seems curious. Very curious.

"I want to try to understand what was going on in your aunt's life that may have gotten her killed."

"Oh, fabulous! A murder mystery. Is that it? Nancy Drew going to solve a murder? This is too, too precious. Absolutely,

I'll be your loyal Bess. You name the time. I'll have to drive up from Albuquerque but I'll meet you there with bells on and we'll sleuth around like a couple of bloodhounds. Not a word to Norm, I'll bet. Right?"

I nod and watch her back as she flings the doors into the gathering storm outside. By the time I leave the office a few minutes later to keep my mysterious appointment with Max, the first snow of the season has begun to fall in fat, wet, Christmas-card flakes.

EIGHT

———◦◦◦◦———

T HE FOYER IS AS I REMEMBER IT. I STEP ACROSS NAVAJO AND
Oriental rugs scattered helter-skelter on polished brick
floors. The naked spots reflect the glow from the piñon-wood
fire in the tiny beehive-shaped fireplace in the corner. I settle
myself on the hard antique Spanish bench. Across from me, a
nicho hollowed deeply into the thick adobe wall holds, not the
religious figure for which it was originally intended, but a delicate six-inch bronze. The figure is a male dancer in midleap. He
is glued to the earth with a dab of bronze at his toe.

For a Brooklyn boy, Max has a good eye. In this nine-by-
six-foot space, he has created pure Santa Fe. I glance at the
carved door that leads to his residence, where I have never been.
I always went through that other door into the consulting
room. There Max keeps a couch that actually looks like the one
Freud used. I used to wonder whether other patients actually
lay on it. I never did. Every Wednesday afternoon at five-thirty

for over a year, Max and I sat facing each other from two over-stuffed chairs.

The consulting room door opens; an acne-stricken boy of about sixteen emerges. Max's hand rests easily on the kid's shoulder and guides him toward the exit.

"Next Tuesday, then. I'll be anxious to hear how it goes." For Max, there is no one else in the room but this kid. This kid is his patient and he's with him one hundred percent. It's only after the boy has shrugged a good-bye and closed the outer door behind him that Max turns to me.

"It's been a long time, Matty."

"I was more than a little surprised at your call," I answer. "I thought I wasn't allowed to come here anymore." It's a childish shot, but Max acts like he doesn't notice the remark.

"Let's go in and sit down. I have some coffee."

I move a step toward the consulting room but Max sweeps his arm gently toward the other door. Like a child in school who's maybe got it wrong, I stop still.

"You haven't seen the house. I'd like to show it to you."

I'm five feet six inches tall, and Max is only an inch or so taller. When he holds the door for me and I sidestep across the threshold to his home, we are eye to eye and belly to belly.

When he abruptly ended our therapy sessions all those months ago, he was gently adamant. We had traveled a piece of road together, he said, and now it was appropriate that I walk awhile with someone else. He gave me three names. I felt betrayed, but for a long time I sought an explanation. Surely Max had good reasons for this. Psychologists can't just dump neurotic patients. There are dangers. There are professional ethics.

He told me that I could grow healthy faster if I were weaned from him. I tried the other therapists he'd recommended. But nothing happened, except that I noticed one picked his nose and another forgot my name until he snuck peeks at the appointment pad. I called and Max said he understood. He was sorry. He wished it were easier for me. But, no! Coming back wasn't a good idea. From that day, I have given up the questionable luxury of psychological counseling. I've tried to shut Max out of my mind. Unfortunately, his is the voice of comfort, support, and sanity I carry inside me.

Coming here today after more than a year is electric. I'm still angry and full of leftover questions. But, more than anything, I want to talk to someone I trust about Isadora, about finding her dead. I need to talk about the memory of Isadora's blood flowing from the empty end of her arm.

As I think of Isadora's severed arthritic hand, Max's strong hand extends a hot mug of coffee. I hunker over it, warming my own hands in the steam. We sit facing each other across a low coffee table heaped with magazines.

"Just why *did* you call, Max? I was stunned that you did." Then I remember that I had called first, let the phone ring, but hung up rather than leave a message so he could rebuff me again.

"And apprehensive?" he guesses. "You sound apprehensive."

"How should I sound? You made it pretty clear you don't want me here. For a year you don't return my calls. Now, out of the blue, you invite me to afternoon coffee, for Christ's sake. I'm here anyway because I'm more than apprehensive—I'm scared shitless."

Like a fair number of Santa Fe professionals, Max is from New York. Dark curly hair sprinkled with gray begins far back into a receded hairline. Wire-frame glasses are forever being nudged up with his thumb. He does this now and flashes a grin.

"You're scared shitless?" Shrinks always repeat what you say.

"Yeah."

"You want to talk to me about it?" This, too, is pure shrink talk.

"Uh-huh."

But I don't talk and the silence lengthens. Finally Max moves to the window. He begins to pick rusty leaves off the geraniums on the deep ledge.

"Maybe you want to talk about your anger with me first," he suggests, with his back to me.

For over a year I've needed this invitation, needed to vent my rage at him. Still, I don't answer. I look at his back, see the faint shape of muscle under the shirt and see, for the first time, a small bald spot at the crown of his head. I don't know what the hell I want from this man.

"You remember Isadora Stanton?" I finally ask.

"Yes. I remember your funny stories about her. And, of course, I've read the papers. There's been little else in the news for the past week. It's why I called. I . . . uh . . . had a hang-up on the machine. I have caller ID, you know . . . I thought you might need a friend."

I'm sheepish about being caught and stupidly pleased at this gesture of friendship, but very confused. Max was my shrink, not my friend.

"I saw her," I say. "I mean, I saw her dead! Her body was still . . . Her hand. Oh, God, Max, her hand was just lying there on her body with no connection to anything." For maybe the sixth time today, my eyes go to my own hands and sturdy wrists. "How do you cut through this?" I ask, holding my forearm up.

Max is silent. I know he thinks I'm going to talk now of my feelings about vulnerability, death, blood; and that's what I thought I was going to talk about, too. But what I'm really interested in suddenly is weapons.

"How? What does a person use to cut through a human wrist?"

Facing me now, Max shrugs broadly. "I'm the wrong guy to be asking. If you really want to pursue this, ask the police."

"I guess I'm already pursuing it, Max. I've begun something that seems insane. What I want is . . . I want someone to tell me I'm not crazy."

"You're not crazy," he says.

"No, I mean you're supposed to tell me that *after* you hear the crazy idea."

Max is quite serious now. Sitting again in the facing chair, he leans toward me across the coffee table and takes my hands. "You're not crazy," he says. "You're smart, you're funny, you're sensitive, you're nice and you are, most definitely, *not* crazy." He releases my hands and leans back. "Now, tell me your crazy idea."

After I explain that I'm ankle-deep in a murder investigation of my own making with no clear idea of its parameters, I tell Max about Teddy's history, about my own silence concerning it. Max understands immediately why I so much want to prove Teddy innocent. He says nothing while I talk. He returns to the geraniums and resumes his pruning. I know from past experience that he is processing this, trying to decide whether my instinct is psychologically healthy or destructive. Apparently, the answer is not obvious, for the flowers are decimated before he turns to address me again.

"Whoever committed this crime is a dangerous person, Matty. If it was Bellasandro . . ." He tapers off and starts again. "But if you're right and it wasn't Bellasandro, and if you succeed in uncovering this other person, your own life may be in danger."

He delivers this gravely but with some heat. I decide this probably isn't a good time to tell him about my night prowler.

Then, he stuns me with a very nonprofessional plea.

"Matty, please, I don't want you to do this."

"Max?"

He paces, then sits, then paces again. Finally, he sighs and sits.

"Okay," he says. "What do you have in mind?"

"Well, among other things, I'm going to see Teddy again. Then I'm going to get into Isadora's house to see what I can find."

"No," he says.

"No?"

He pushes his glasses all the way up his high forehead and settles them at the hairline like puppy ears. He sighs again. "Do you want me to come with you?"

I can't believe I've heard him. "Come with me? Of course I don't want you to come with me. What can you be thinking of?"

He smiles bleakly. "Even shrinks get crazy ideas sometimes."

After more pruning and more coffee, he tells me I should do what I think best. I'm a big girl with a big brain and I should trust myself. By the time he gets to the end of this little feel-good speech, he's on his feet and I guess the interview is over.

"Will you call me?" he asks as we walk out through his

small terraced garden toward my car. "After you meet with Bellasandro, you may want someone to talk to about it. And I'd like to know you're okay. Promise me."

I promise to call.

Then he adds, "Maybe we could get something to eat?"

"Something to eat? You want to eat with me?"

I drive away more perplexed than when I arrived. His last words to me were, "And please, Matty, be careful."

NINE

꩜

NO CARD GAME OR LOUNGERS IN THIS HIGH-SECURITY SEC-
tion of the jail. Only one guard, and Teddy and I sharing
a cubicle separated by a sheet of bullet-proof plastic across a
gray metal shelf in a deliberately cheerless meeting room. The
air on his side is thick with cigarette smoke and with Teddy's
gloom. He talks in spurts with long silent intervals as I try to
move the conversation.

"Grand Jury didn't take long," I say.

The D.A. took the murder case to the Grand Jury two days
after filing the complaint. It took them less than an hour to enter a True Bill.

"But, you know," I hurry on, "the Grand Jury is really the
D.A.'s show. It doesn't mean—"

"Matty, I been here before, remember?"

"I talked to your P.D., Stone Allen," I persist. "He can't locate Charlie Lee. The Public Defender's office filed the required
Alibi Defense papers naming Charlie Lee but Lee went missing

a few days after talking to me. Did Rocks, I mean Stone, talk to you about that?"

"Stone Allen is a fuckin' idiot. Also, he figures I'm guilty. Says his boss calls this a signature murder so I'm gonna be hung out to dry. Says I should plead to Murder One now to get life instead of the chair. Matty, how can that be right? What's this jerk talking about?"

What the jerk is talking about is the practical effect, at a future trial, of a rarely used exception to a rule of evidence for a "signature crime." Rule 404 (B) prevents evidence of other old crimes from being admitted into evidence at the trial of a person accused of a recent crime. Too prejudicial is the reason. Jurors are too likely to jump to unjustified conclusions.

One of the several exceptions to this rule is for a crime which is so identical to a previous crime as to be "like a signature." Here, it is thought by the courts, prejudice is outweighed by relevance. So, the idiot, Stone Allen, or his boss, may be right to predict a disastrous verdict. When a prosecutor can tell a jury, "Ladies and gentlemen, the defendant committed this exact crime before. He did it once. Now, he's done it again," a drowsy juror's eyes are guaranteed to spring open.

I try to explain to Teddy about the evidence rule but he isn't listening. He already knows. He knows he's going to be fucked.

I tell him that if the new crime is different enough from the old one, the exception won't apply. Evidence of the old crime won't come in at all. "And that isn't the best part. I don't know what else the D.A. has on you but, if you can show the difference and if the rest of the evidence is thin, the indictment could get tossed in a pretrial motion. No trial at all. Teddy, are you listening?"

His face is a mask and I try to talk to the person behind it, telling him that he must show the judge the differences, that his P.D. could be of more help if Teddy would describe the Louisiana mutilation in detail.

"Listen to me," I urge. "Isadora's murder—with the mutilation—was a single crime with a single victim. Maybe the point of it was *specifically* to mutilate. Do you think? Not like in

Louisiana; Isadora said your mother just got in the way there; that it was an accident. You had good reason—"

"I don't remember," he interrupts savagely. "I swear to God, Matty, I can't remember shit about it. I know I wouldn't of hurt my mother on purpose. When I was little she always protected me from that bastard. I wouldn't of been alive if it wasn't for her. Later, I protected her. When I was sixteen, I moved out, tried to get her to come with me. She should've done it, too. I never knew why she didn't. I just know I wouldn't hurt her. But I did, didn't I? I *did* hurt her. Now I say I didn't hurt Izzy. Who's gonna believe me? Nobody!"

"Me! I'm going to believe you. You and I are alike, Teddy. We both caused the death of the person we loved most in the world. And we've so blended the grief with guilt that we can't separate the two." He must be thinking now about what happened thirty years ago because his body squeezes in, shoulders hunching together, as he crawls even further inside himself. This gruff middle-aged ex-con is looking more and more like a child to me.

"But, Teddy, life gives second chances." Simultaneously I hear my own intensity and see Teddy's wary reaction to it.

"You got a couple things of your own to prove here, Counselor?"

"Yeah, yeah, I guess I do. But that doesn't change what I'm telling you or what you need to hear. I believe you. And other people can believe you too, but you've got to help them by showing them the difference between your mother's death and Isadora's. You must have talked to people about it before; you talked to Isadora . . ."

"Mostly I know what my lawyer told me. And in the pen there was a group but it was all fucked up and after about three times they stopped meetin'. That was early on and I ain't said nothin' since. Except to Izzy. I wanted to tell her about bein' in the pen, you know. I figured she had a right to know. And when I started, somethin' shook loose and I got real close. Then it just went away."

He clamps his teeth together, then shakes his head hard like a wet dog. "I don't want to do this, Matty. Please understand. I *just can't remember.*"

Before he sinks too far I say, "Hey, I'm meeting with your favorite lawyer, Stone Allen. I knew him in law school. I'm going to offer to help."

His eyes meet mine. "Yeah?" he asks.

"Yeah," I reply. "But only if you help, too. You don't have to do it now but you've got to try to remember the first murder. When you can, think about Lamont . . . and about your mother . . . just a little at a time, huh? Quit when you need to. Maybe something will come, huh?"

He nods.

"But right now, Teddy, there's something else you have to remember. Help me understand what was going on with Isadora before she was killed."

We start slowly. But after a while his words are coming freely. Excitement enters his voice as he relates memories of the last few weeks of Isadora's life.

"Something was definitely going on. Izzy kept throwin' papers from files all over the place and rantin' and ravin' about shysters. Said, 'Skeeter would come back from the dead.' "

" 'Skeeter would come back from the dead?' What is that supposed to mean?"

"She used to call some old biddy friend of hers 'Skeeter,' remember?"

"Vaguely. Anyway, raving about shysters sounds pretty reasonable to me. Sounds like business as usual with Isadora."

Teddy shakes his head stubbornly. "This time it was different. She was way over the top. She kept swinging that cane of hers around like a fuckin' baton. She even threatened to bash ol' Jakes in the head with it couple weeks ago."

"What?" Threatening Juanita sounds bad, even for Isadora. "Why would she do such a thing?"

"Hell, I don't know, Matty. Like I say, Izzy was going generally nuts her own self, but something was up with Juanita, too. Maybe it was just the baby comin'; I don't know. But since she got that ring, she an' Izzy was a sight to watch. Juanita played with the goddamned thing all the time. She'd polish it, then look at herself in the mirror and wiggle her fingers like she's some kid waitin' for Prince Charming."

"Rickie Hadid is her Prince Charming. And Juanita really is a kid—"

"Yeah, that's the problem. Jakes is almost thirty, but you know how she is. And Izzy says—I mean said—that even girls with brains in their heads get royally fucked by men every day; and Juanita, she's gonna get hurt for sure. Izzy tried about a hundred times to reason with her. Subtle as a tank. You know how Izzy was."

"I take it it didn't work," I say.

"Hell, Juanita would listen a minute, then she'd start fiddling with that engagement ring in that dreamy way she has. She'd look up and say, maybe she's gonna move to France or maybe Arabia. Izzy'd go nuts. One day Jakes takes the ring off while she's chopping vegetables. Goddamned if Isadora don't grab it and threaten to swallow it like she does. Woman swallowed the ace of spades once to keep me from hittin' blackjack, and she—"

I need to keep him on track. "Are you telling me that Isadora swallowed Juanita's engagement ring?"

"Naw, she put it in the drawer of her nightstand. Said Jakes wasn't going nowhere and the sooner that girl knew it the better. So Jakes sulks. For a while she wouldn't cook and she wasn't cleanin' much either. She'd leave at night, come back in the mornin', pout all day, then leave again. Place looked like a pigsty. Never saw Jakes like that. Said she wanted Izzy to say she's sorry. Now, there's a picture for you: Izzy apologizin' to Jakes." He snorts at the impossibility of it.

"Isadora took Juanita's ring?" I ask. I'm remembering the morning I discovered the body, remembering Juanita Jakes in the chair facing the corner, twisting that unusual ring around on her finger. "Did Isadora ever give the ring back?"

"Damned if I know. Had to guess, I'd say no way. Why?"

I explain briefly about Juanita having the ring back on her finger. Both of us think she is the most unlikely murderer we can imagine. "But you can't really consider Jakes alone," I tell Teddy. "She's joined at the hip to Hadid." I tell Teddy about the night the prowler was staring into my window. "He looked a lit-tle like Hadid. But I only saw a silhouette, really."

"Hey, listen," he says sternly, shaking his fat, calloused in-dex finger at me. "I think this is way too dangerous for you. Did you call the cops?"

"I did. They're following up and watching the house." I lie to him with an absolutely straight face. "I'm fine. And I'll tell you something else. I bet I know what all that shyster talk and paper-tossing was about. Isadora wanted to make a new will. She and Norman Frederick even argued about it."

Teddy's face is blank. He doesn't seem to know that Isadora was about to make him rich. And if he *had* known, no *sane* per-son would kill his benefactor *before* she bequeathed him two million dollars.

"Oh," he says. "Well, it ain't only the Jakes thing. Izzy was really off on some kind of toot. The morning my vacation starts, I'm dumpin' my gear in Charlie's truck. She's in the kitchen readin' her little newspaper. She's got a magnifying glass and she's bent way down so her head's about a inch from the paper. She'd been doing that for days with that same newspaper. She couldn't see for shit. All of a sudden like, she makes up her mind. She says, 'Let's go; I've got to go to Canoncito.' She's forgot all about I'm takin' three days off."

"Canoncito? Where is that?"

"Fuckin' nowhere is where Canoncito is. Village south of here, just west of Albuquerque. On the Rez. Navajo, I think. Nothin' there. Anyway, I got plans. First time I'm goin' fishin' since last year. I ain't givin' it up to drive her a hundred and fifty miles in the opposite direction."

"Do you know why she wanted to go?"

"I got no idea. I guess she would'a told me but she got pissed right away, started swearing at me, said she didn't need my help. That I was no damned use to her. I said 'screw this' and left. I never saw her after that."

"Why? You mean this happened *just* before she was killed?"

"Yeah. I'm all screwed up about time now. But it must'a been that morning or the day before. Somethin' like that."

"Teddy, this is important. Isadora having raving fits and

wanting to go to Indian villages on the day she dies. Did you tell Stone Allen about this?"

Teddy snorts again.

"Had that happened before?" I ask. "Had she gone there before? To Canoncito?"

"That old broad ain't been out of Santa Fe for two years. Far as I know, she's never been to Canoncito in her life."

We spend the next few minutes talking about the days to come. He's got no money for a private lawyer. I tell him I'll do what I can to goose Rocks.

Before I leave, Teddy calls me back. "Uh, about Jakes . . . You know, with Izzy gone and the baby comin', ain't no tellin' what's happenin' to her. You think you could maybe look in on Jakes?"

Great! Mother hen to a nest of wounded suspects.

TEN

———◦◦◦———

I'M DRESSED FOR WINTER AS I LEAVE THE COMPOUND AND start walking down Canyon Road toward town. But the sun is out again, brightening the few inches of the last snow. The chunky old adobe structures with their sculptured roofs look like frosted ginger cakes. November is one of the best months in Santa Fe. The summer tourist season is over and the skiers haven't arrived yet. The emptiness is especially rare and sweet here on my street.

Canyon Road is one of Santa Fe's oldest streets, a natural spoke radiating out from the center of town. The road begins beside a shallow creek bed which deepens as you move out and up toward the mountains. The movie stars' houses on Upper Canyon Road cling to the ridge of a true canyon.

Lower Canyon Road, where I live, is the traditional home of artists in Santa Fe. Small alleyways and crudely defined circle compounds line a street too narrow for two-way traffic. In the thirties and forties, around the time Isadora moved here, these compounds were occupied by artists living in communal close-ness and painting on every available surface, including the inte-rior walls of their homes. A few of those murals are still visible in the houses I pass. But most of the old interior walls have been whitewashed or torn down to make gallery space.

Today, lower Canyon Road is primarily a street of galleries and restaurants housed in the original turn-of-the-century flat-topped adobes. But in November only the locals are out on the street and Santa Fe feels just a little like the small Spanish town it once was.

By the time I reach the hub end of Canyon Road and cross Paseo de Peralta, my mind is focused on today's meeting with Stone Allen. On the phone, Rocks had seemed pleased to hear from me. "Great," he declared. "Can't wait to see you again, Matty. I'll pick your brain. It'll be like old times."

When I arrived at my office, he's already there, looking like Garth Brooks, standing before the fireplace in the reception area with one booted foot on the adobe *banco*. He's dressed like an ad for a dude ranch in new jeans, carved black cowboy boots, a pink western-cut shirt buttoned to the collar, and a turquoise bolo tie. His baby face hasn't changed in ten years.

While I'd set this meeting early enough to avoid Joe and Norman, one glance at Gloria Bachicha, Norman's own private snoop, tells me that meeting Rocks here was a mistake. Oh, well, Gloria surely won't recognize a public defender by sight and she probably doesn't even know about Norman's com-mand that I stay out of the Stanton investigation. She's proba-bly just sniffing the air on general principles.

Rocks is looking around the plush offices of Frederick & Danforth appreciatively, his lips pursed in a silent whistle. "Nice digs," he comments. He rubbernecks all the way back to my door effusing about how great it is to see me again; how he lost track of me a few years ago. "It's like you fell off the end of the earth. One day, Matty Donahue's name is in the paper every day. You couldn't turn around but what you had some big new case in Albuquerque." Finally, his eyes light on me and stay. "So what happened to the star of our class, anyway?"

Apparently Rocks doesn't follow disciplinary proceedings.

I watch his face fall as I usher him into my monk's cell. There's no place for him to sit unless he takes my chair. I cock my head at it and he lowers himself reluctantly, making a face like a guy about to sit in a cow paddy. These cramped quarters aren't what he expected from his old hero and new helpmate.

"I haven't been doing much of anything," I reply, scooting a few manila folders aside and hoisting myself up on my desk shelf. "I moved to Santa Fe over three years ago, just after you joined the Public Defender's office. I've settled down, I guess."

Rocks is wrinkling his nose at me expecting some explanation, like maybe I'm secretly a full partner and my spacious real office is being redecorated.

"Now, Stone, tell me about Teddy Bellasandro."

His interest in my fate is promptly forgotten in favor of interest in his own.

"Matty, it's my first murder case. Just luck I got it! I was assigned weeks ago when it was only an assault. But now my boss, Joleen Fische, says I can keep it. It's the highest-profile case in the office. Joleen says I'll do fine. Course, we'll plead it. Hey, I guess I shouldn't be talking to you about that. You know, about my strategy."

"Don't worry, Stone. Nothing you say leaves this office. I promise." Let's see. This would make how many conflicting promises I've made this week?

He's eager to believe me, so he does. "What do you think? Joleen says maybe there's an insanity defense here. But I'm thinking probably just plead to Murder Two if we can get it. D.A.'s already offered Murder One, without the death penalty. Joleen says I should tell him where to stick his offer, but it's my decision. What do you think, Matty?"

This is a very scary conversation. Four years in practice, and this guy is no more prepared to deal with a serious criminal case than Juanita Jakes would be.

"I think he's innocent!" I tell Stone Allen. "I think Teddy shouldn't even have been indicted. I think you should be finding that missing alibi witness and getting a polygraph set up for Teddy. But the *most* important thing you should be doing is getting the detailed report on the Louisiana crime! Then you've got to differentiate the two crimes. Make separate lists of all of the facts of each crime so that in a pretrial motion you can—"

"Hold on! Hey! Whoa! Man, oh, man. You're something else. I remember now, how you used to be. But you just hold on; this is my case. I shouldn't probably even be talking to you about this. You're not the star anymore, Matty." He's swiveling around and around in my chair starting a new sentence with each pass. "You don't even have criminal experience, do you? You don't understand how these things work. We plead out almost all our cases."

A horrible thought crosses my mind. "Stone, have you ever actually tried a felony case?"

". . . Sure . . . I have."

If I want to keep from souring this meeting completely I've got to swallow my disapproval. Any hope of making an ally out of this legal mule is going to require a hell of a lot more combing and currying.

"I know you're right, Stone. That's the system. You guys are so overworked, it's a wonder you can try any cases at all."

Stone looks stoned. "That's right," he says.

"It's a damned shame, though. How could you know if you've got the one-in-a-million innocent guy, a defense lawyer's reputation-maker, when you've got a hundred open files? Like with Teddy Bellasandro, I'll bet you haven't even had the luxury of a full interview, have you?"

"No. Well, you know, I talked to him at the arraignment, like always. I got his side."

"Stone, I envy you."

"Yeah?"

"Yeah. You've lucked into the case of a lifetime. Bellasandro *looks* guilty because of the similarity to the Louisiana crime, but there isn't any real evidence against him, is there? If you can show the differences between the two, you have a chance here of turning your first murder case into a verdict for acquittal. Maybe even a dismissal before trial." I sigh enviously.

"I don't see that, Matty. There's hardly anything in the Louisiana record. Apparently Bellasandro confessed and pled so fast that no case was really developed back there. The record is two paragraphs. But it's enough. Guy and his wife were hacked with an axe. The wife's hand was severed."

"That's all? Nothing in the record about Teddy protecting the woman, his mother?"

"Nuh-uh, that's it. But I read up on this stuff; that's all they need. We got a very unique mutilation here. It fits the signature crime definition. 'So much like the old crime,'" Stone pantomimes quotation marks, "'as to be like a signature.' And, Joleen says nobody ever wins signature crime cases."

"But, Stone, that's the point! We've got to keep it from becoming a signature crime case. If the judge can see that the two crimes are *not* similar, the case may never get to trial. We've got to get all of the details of the old crime and then make the motion to the judge before—"

"I can't see me . . . well . . . you know . . . Matty, I haven't really had that much experience with complicated evidentiary motions."

That's an understatement. "But I have," I say. Although I have no criminal experience, I've argued pretrial motions in hundreds of business and personal injury cases. "If it comes to that, I could help. Strictly in the background, of course."

He screws up his face and I can't tell if he's eager or skeptical or just has to fart.

"Look," I persist, "there is a real shot here. There can't be much other evidence against him. You could save a man's life." Not too subtly I add, "And nobody will ever call you Rocks again."

He appreciates the potential of actually getting respect from his peers but shakes his head.

"You're wrong, Matty; there *is* other evidence against him." He says this slowly as he tugs at the end of his nose. "It's not good." Then, he carefully straight-arms some of my clutter aside, lugs his briefcase onto my desk shelf, and thumbs the latches open. He gestures toward the case and departs for the men's room, leaving me with all of his files on the Bellasandro case.

He's gone a long time and I try not to think of who he may be chatting with out there. Carefully I go over the entire police report and medical examiner's report, which are public information. I sort through the rest of the District Attorney's file, including the internal memoranda which isn't public information.

Discovery rules provide that the D.A. must give the P.D. everything that the state intends to use at the trial and anything else that may be exculpatory. These days, after years of struggle on this subject, the D.A.'s office often makes extra copies of everything in their file for the P.D. routinely. The combination of these reports and memoranda answer many of my questions.

The medical examiner's report tells me that Isadora Stanton died between eight-thirty P.M. and ten-thirty A.M. on November eleventh. Her stomach contents included the remnants of a bean burrito, and a partially digested gum wrapper.

The probable cause of death was shock as a result of the amputation. But the M.E. has noted other damage to the victim: a blunt trauma at the base of the skull and two small puncture wounds on the wrist so close to the severing cut that the punctures were nearly missed. A long section on lividity and extent of bleeding concludes that both trauma and puncture wounds preceded death by between fifteen to sixty minutes.

My question to Max about what kind of weapon cuts through a human wrist is only partially answered. The weapon responsible for Isadora's mutilation is identified as "possibly" a cleaver or small hatchet sharpened to a fine edge. Each of the cleavers in the Stanton kitchen was tested for the presence of blood. No trace of human blood was found. Each was compared by size and shape to the wound and eliminated. No other likely instrument was found at the scene.

The relative lack of blood and the complete lack of cuts in the bedding or mattress are the subjects of a series of fax correspondences between the case officer, Daniel Baca, and the medical examiner. The gist of their conclusion is that the amputation probably required the presence of what the M.E. describes as a "resisting device" or anvil for the blow required to sever the wrist. Baca has speculated that there must have been a blood-catching medium such as a drop cloth, which was removed from the scene.

I remember the quilts Isadora used to keep on her bed,

yellow- and blue-flowered to match those on the wall. Specially made for her—several of them. And I force my mind back to the morning I found her. The sheet pulled up neatly to the edge of her pink bed jacket. Was one of those quilts there? I squeeze my eyes tight in an effort to pry the memory loose.

I switch back to Baca's report. Dozens of full fingerprints of Teddy and Juanita as well as those of Isadora were found. A few of mine were identified, too. And, although there were other partial prints, none were identified by the F.B.I.'s computer. I doubt seriously whether Faye Stanton has fingerprints on file with the feds. But Rickie Hadid might.

Unusual trace and fiber evidence included microscopic metal filings found among Isadora's sheets and a shred of #70 base weight blue paper found on the floor near the bed. No other specifically suspicious fibers on or around the corpse have been noted. Of course, Isadora and Teddy and Juanita, who'd been in the house together nearly every day for years, had left evidence from their bodies everywhere. A single drop of blood tentatively identified as the victim's and described only as "recent" was found on a metal toolbox in the pantry. The toolbox was identified as belonging to the suspect, Theodore, a.k.a. Teddy Bellasandro.

I'm feeling pretty vindicated. I assume that the lack of identifiable alien prints means Isadora's killer wore gloves or simply doesn't have prints on file. The lack of specific fiber evidence which can be directly connected to someone else isn't great, but it's probably no worse than neutral. Even the blood on the toolbox can be explained in many ways. There is no real evidence against Teddy here. My relief begins to turn to excitement. They really do have the wrong man! I'm right to be pushing the envelope of ethics with Rocks. But then I get to the witness statements.

Juanita Jakes has provided an astonishing statement. About two hours after the policewoman led her away, Juanita told the officer that when she left Isadora's house on the night of the murder, Teddy Bellasandro and Isadora Stanton were arguing loudly. The report quotes her verbatim: *"They were both yelling and yelling, I don't like it when they do that."* Juanita had not

been able to provide the exact time of the alleged argument.
She had not remembered the subject matter of the argument.
She could not state even approximately when it started. The of-
ficer noted that Ms. Jakes appeared to be mildly retarded and
was clearly distressed during questioning about this matter. But
Juanita had repeated the accusation three separate times.

By the time Rocks returns, my head is in my hands.

"See," he says, "this isn't as easy as you think."

I do see. Maybe she's mistaken, maybe she's lying, protecting someone else. But Juanita's description sounds right on.
And, since it puts Teddy at the scene raging at the victim shortly
before she was killed, there's much less hope for a quick easy
dismissal before trial.

But worse than that is the queasy feeling starting in my
stomach. If Juanita isn't mistaken or lying, then Teddy lied to
me about being out of town at Puye Cliffs. And Charlie Lee,
who is suddenly among the missing, lied to me, too. I swallow
hard and go on looking through the file with a somewhat less
righteous enthusiasm.

Since Stone isn't stopping me, I look through copies of the
D.A.'s internal office notes. Something new catches my attention. "There's a notation here," I tell Rocks, "that the D.A.'s office did a criminal records check on Bellasandro. They pulled
the same report on the Louisiana crime that you described.
More than three weeks *before* the murder. What's that about?"

"Huh? Let me see." Stone looks at the notation without en-
lightenment. "I dunno. Why? Is it important?"

I tell him about my litmus test. Whoever murdered Isadora
had to know about Teddy's past.

"Look at this." I point. "Here. Someone deliberately ran
a records check. Three weeks before Isadora Stanton's hand
was cut off, someone found out that Teddy Bellasandro had
once cut off his mother's hand. So that someone knew how to
copy Teddy's signature! You better believe it's important," I say
firmly. "Who did this? Who wanted this information?"

Stone isn't excited about my questions. This has the feel of
more work with little reward for him. He suddenly notices or
suddenly cares that I'm looking at a file he hadn't intended to

show me. He busies himself stuffing everything back into his case. I have to beg him to request the information from the D.A.'s office.

He scowls. "But this isn't about this murder case," he argues. "I don't think they'll give it to me."

"You're entitled to the discovery," I insist. "Besides, why would they care? The D.A. doesn't have anything to hide. Just ask who requested this information and why. If they don't voluntarily tell you, I think we—*you*—can get a court order. Come on, Stone, you're going to end up the hero of the hour. Trust me."

Stone Allen doesn't understand yet that I should never be in a position of trust. He remembers a sure-footed and often-right Matty Donahue. He sees a Matty Donahue who can maybe do him some good, and so when I insist, he promises. He'll try to find out who requested Bellesandro's criminal record, even though he can't see the use. But he won't do anything else. Rocks doesn't really believe in miracles.

ELEVEN

---◈◈◈---

Thanksgiving morning dawns crisp and clear. The recent snow came and went so softly that no wind scoured the trees, and now dots of autumn color shimmer again in the sun. A perfect day for turkey and trimmings, for family and friends. It's been a while since I had a Thanksgiving like that and I'm in some danger of getting maudlin about the loss.

My refrigerator holds the same three inches of salami and an inch less of Margarita mix. The only new items are a pound and a half of cheddar cheese, a couple of limes, some onions, and a bag of slightly wormy apples from my own tree. The backyard is a lumpy swamp of rotting fruit. The smell of hard cider brewing with the compost of fallen leaves nearly knocks me out when I open the door. The scent lingers in the kitchen as I wander around absently wiping countertops.

I move to the dry board on the wall with the idea of creating a real grocery list. This barren Thanksgiving is so pathetic I conjure a future of fresh milk and eggs and drawers full of crisp vegetables. But instead, I write the suspect list I had begun in my office.

This time, I leave the distant, unlikely candidates off. Teddy is almost certain that, except for Isadora and his aborted prison therapy group, he never talked to anyone about the Louisiana mutilation. I look at the board for a while and add a name, *Faye Stanton*. Maybe Faye could have known about what happened in Louisiana. Maybe hating her niece doesn't necessarily mean Isadora didn't talk to her. Maybe even about her driver's past. They were family, after all.

I rearrange the list of names on the far left of the board to form the left leg of a chart: Teddy Bellasandro, Juanita Jakes, Rickie Hadid, Faye Stanton. At the bottom I add another suspect, this one with no name. I write *Inquirer* for whoever made the D.A.'s request for Teddy's record three weeks before Isadora died. Along the top axis, I title three columns with the age-old questions—MOTIVE, OPPORTUNITY, MEANS. I add a fourth, KNOWLEDGE, by which I mean knowledge of Teddy's criminal past.

I review each name methodically and jot notes in the squares. I don't ignore Teddy. He certainly had knowledge of his old crime. If Juanita Jakes is telling the truth and Teddy was there that night, he had opportunity. As to motive, I open my mind to the possibility that maybe there is more to the proposed change in Isadora's will than I know. What if, despite appearances, Teddy did know that she intended to leave him a small fortune? What if she'd changed her mind and decided not to leave him the money after all? Juanita Jakes told the cops that they were "yelling and yelling."

What if Isadora got abusive and swung her cane at Teddy? Might he not have pushed her, hit her head on the bed? It could have happened that way. This may be the story a jury will hear. But some of this scenario could apply to anyone on the list. And none of this scenario explains the mutilation.

And what about Jakes and her lover? If Isadora told Juanita about Teddy, then Rickie Hadid surely knew about it, too. Teddy claimed Isadora had threatened Juanita with her cane. Both Juanita and Hadid were angry over Isadora's opposition to their intended marriage, even before Isadora took the engagement ring.

As I pace the distance between kitchen and living room, I'm deep in thought, trying to remember what I know about the Arab culture's view of stealing. Would Hadid consider Isadora's taking of his faincée's ring to be theft?

The sound of the telephone intrudes on my thoughts. It is Max. As promised, I left word on his answering machine after my visit with Teddy, and now he's returning my call.

"I didn't know if I'd find you home today."

Before I can be embarrassed at having no invitations to Thanksgiving dinner, he adds, "I'm glad I did. My own plans fell through at the last minute. Friend's wife is having a baby. Labor pains interrupted turkey stuffing."

For reasons I cannot explain, the domestic scene his words conjure calls forth tears, and suddenly I don't trust my voice.

"Do you have plans?" he asks, and into the void he moves on. "Because if you don't mind, maybe we can get together."

"Now?" I squeak.

"Matty, are you all right?"

He fails to hear my nod.

"Tell you what. I was supposed to bring wine to the dinner party. How about if I bring it to your house instead? Sound okay?"

In a little eddy of excitement and inexplicable sorrow I give him directions to the compound.

Max has poured me a glass of the German Auslese he brought and has guided me away from my distress at my pitiful refrigerator.

"I'm sorry. I don't have anything." I've said this twice now.

"Sit here," he says and indicates the kitchen stool. And, there, perched and drinking expensive wine, I watch him begin to create a feast from nothing at all. Decorating the outside of my door is a hanging *riestra* of red chiles. A hundred years ago most families in this part of the world hung these strings of chile to dry prior to making chile sauce. Today, only a few of the oldest Hispanic families still do this. The gringos, like me, hang them strictly for atmosphere. So I'm pretty knocked out when Max takes them down, unwinds the burlap string and removes a dozen or so.

"This looks pretty good," he comments as he hands me the single head of garlic from the fridge and tells me to peel and dice it. He begins to clean the chile pods slowly, one by one, careful to take out the fiery heart and its dried brown veins. He nods at my chart.

"This what you've been up to?"

"Yeah. Max, do you know anything about how the Arabs deal with theft? Is it true that they cut the hands off of thieves because it is the hand which committed the offense?"

Max closes his eyes for a second. "I was afraid this is how you'd be spending your time today," he says.

Getting pissed out loud at Max is becoming easier. "You got a problem with how I spend my time?" I spit at him.

"No, I don't have a problem. In fact, if you let me, I'd like to be a sounding board for you. But, how about *after* dinner? I thought you might need a nice dinner today." His eyes hold mine and my earlier tears edge back.

"You remember telling me about the Thanksgiving before John's death?" he asks. "You'd fixed a big turkey, the whole nine yards, on your own? How you sat at the table and looked across at John and Tommy and thought that your lives were going to turn out normal after all?"

As soon as he says it out loud, I know that this is what the weepiness this morning has been about. Thanksgiving was the last holiday I had with John. Less than two weeks later, he was dead. In therapy I had told Max about that day. And today, he has remembered. I had forgotten, but he has remembered.

Max tries to explain my tears away.

"Most people think the heat that stings your eyes comes from the seeds of the chile pepper," he says. "But it really comes from something called capsaicin in the veins near the stem." He places the pods into my blender and adds diced garlic. Next, he finds the salt, oregano, and coriander. "Just enough water to make the blender work," he says and turns the switch.

The noise makes talking impossible for a while. I'm mildly

chagrined as Max flicks dead bug husks out of the handful of flour he tosses into hot olive oil.

"Browned flour is the secret of good red chile sauce," he shouts over the whining of the blender.

He pours the chile puree onto the browned flour and stirs the concoction together, announcing, "This'll boil for at least ten minutes. You always boil red chile, but you never boil green chile. Green chile has been cooked when it was roasted to pop off the skin; recooking just kills the flavor of green."

"How do you know all this stuff?" I ask.

"Well, the first year I came out from New York and opened my practice in my house, you can imagine, I had a lot of spare time on my hands. My neighbor, Dolores Valdez, is eighty-something. One of the original residents of Santa Fe. Dolores took pity on the lonely Italian-Jew boy and brought me enchiladas and *rellenos*. One day I begged her to teach me. I've been learning ever since."

As the sweet smell of cooking chile begins to fill my kitchen, Max is busily sorting through half a bag of Masa Harina de Maiz he found in my cabinet. No telling how many years the corn flour has been under there. "No bugs in here," he announces cheerfully. In minutes he has me kneading damp *masa* into a ball of dough.

While Max dices and sautes onions, grates the block of cheese, and checks the bubbling red chile sauce, I'm lost in the sensual pleasure of kneading the dough and inhaling the aromas. The windows are steaming up and my hands are working on their own accord.

"Whoa, hold it!" Max gently grabs both my wrists. "It isn't delicate like pie dough, but I think you *can* knead this stuff too much."

Max's forehead is as sweaty as the windows and my hands are dry and soft from the flour. A small bead of sweat drops from his brow onto the back of my hand and creates a warm circle of skin in the flour dust.

"It may not be the dough that I need too much," I say.

Max winces at the pun. "You need to break off pieces of this dough and shape them into little mushroom caps about the size of golf balls, is what you need. I suppose a tortilla press is too much to ask for?"

I raise one eyebrow.

"No problem." He grins, then places a saucer inside each of two plastic baggies, puts one of the dough balls between the sheathed saucers and presses down hard and quick.

"*Voilà*," he says theatrically as he lifts the top saucer off. "A corn tortilla."

"Amazing," I applaud.

As he manufactures one after another, I toast the tortillas lightly in the skillet. Then we start the stacking: red sauce, tortilla, sprinkle of onion, sprinkle of cheese, more sauce, and repeat until we are four tortillas deep; then into the oven. I set the table as Max comes with hot plates in hot-padded hands. I pop the tops of two Dos Equis and hand one to Max. As if rehearsed, we both pick up lime wedges and run them around the rims of our glasses.

"To keep away the flies," Max laughs.

We each drop our wedge into our glass, cover it with beer, and touch the edges together across the table.

"Happy Thanksgiving," he says.

After dinner, he's as good as his word. We are stretched out at opposite ends of the couch, letting the wonderful food settle and drinking coffee.

He begins where I left off. "Matty, I think you're right that, at least in the past, it used to be common in Arab countries to cut the hand off a thief. But I think that was official public punishment, not private retribution. Then, not now, and on the other side of the world, not here. Dolores Valdez, my resident expert on all things New Mexican, says there have been groups of people from the Middle East around here for as long as she can remember. The climate and the terrain in New Mexico is like their homeland."

"I guess I never really thought about it."

"There are other similarities such as the Spanish-Moorish architecture, the use of adobe and tiles. And the repetitive geometric designs of Arabic art. They're not unlike—"

"—those of the southwestern Indians," I finish. "You know,

Isadora took Juanita's engagement ring a few weeks before she was murdered. At the time I thought it was just because she opposed the marriage. But it isn't a regular band or chip of diamond. It's an unusual Indian piece. And it turns out that Isadora had been reading about a new wrinkle in the Native American knock-off game involving Arab groups."

"Everybody and his brother tries to get into the knock-off business around here." Max sighs. "It's only illegal if they claim the stuff is handmade by the tribes. Besides, these days Arab bashing's becoming almost as popular as Jew bashing used to be. I'd take it with a grain of salt. Arabs are as likely to be honest as the rest of us."

"And as dishonest."

"That, too. You have any instinct about Hadid?"

"Well, I've always kind of liked Juanita, even now that she's implicating Teddy. And, the truth is, I used to think her boyfriend was a hoot. A gorgeous, illegal-alien hoot to be sure, but, really, more funny than sinister. But Isadora was right. All things being equal, Rickie was way too good a catch for Juanita."

"Stranger matches have happened."

I'm telling him about weird Faye Stanton and her training as a surgical nurse, wondering if maybe she's blasé about cutting through human flesh and bone, when the phone rings.

"Matty? Stone Allen here. Sorry to bother you on a holiday but since I didn't have anyplace to go, I came down to the office to work."

In my generous mood, I feel sorry for Rocks with no one to be with on Thanksgiving. I assure him he's not bothering me in the least and ask what's up.

"The answers to our latest discovery motion came in over the fax yesterday. One of them is the answer you asked for. And Matty, it's a dilly. Hold on to your hat."

"Consider my hat held onto. Who ordered Teddy's old record?"

"You won't believe it."

Rocks is really milking this.

"Unless the Pope ordered it, I promise, I'll believe it," I say.

"Frederick and Danforth."

I roll my eyes at Max because Rocks is taking so much time getting around to it. "Frederick and Danforth, what?"

"Frederick and Danforth, Matty. *Your* office requested the District Attorney to run Bellasandro's criminal record. It was ordered in September. The report came in and was delivered to your office, let's see . . . October . . . nineteenth."

I just blink. What the hell?

"Who? I mean in our office, can you tell who specifically made the request?"

"Sure, it's right here. The request was made by Norman Frederick. Weird. Private citizens don't usually have enough stroke to get a record pulled. Anyway, does this help our case?"

But I'm not listening anymore. I say good-bye, then, after I hang up, I stare at the wall for a while. Max watches me in silence as I get up and move to the chart. I move my finger slowly back and forth across one of the entries, the one that says *inquirer,* until the word is erased. Then I pick up the marker and write in the name of the new suspect in the brutal mutilation-murder of Isadora Stanton. I write the name of my boss: NORMAN FREDERICK.

"What the shit is this?" I say aloud.

DECEMBER

TWELVE

—⚬⚬⚬—

MONDAY, DECEMBER 2

On this Monday after Thanksgiving, I've decided to drive to work instead of walking the two miles. The long weekend has been spent chaotically: scrubbing the refrigerator vegetable bins, thinking about Max and fantasizing a little, worrying about Teddy's fate at the hands of pebble-brained Stone Allen, buying new sheets—a direct result of the fantasies—and brooding about Juanita Jakes. I've tried to find her, but her ex-roommate said Juanita moved out and got a place with Rickie Hadid weeks before Isadora's murder. The roommate had no idea where that place might be.

Mostly though, I've been thinking about Norman Frederick. I'm still shaking my head as I maneuver the narrow one-way around the plaza. How I have disliked that man! I've thought him arrogant and pompous, smug and even cruel. But I've never before imagined a criminal Norman Frederick. I'm trying to get my mind around it now.

I figure Norman somehow got the D.A. to run a check on

Teddy on a hunch. It must've been about Isadora wanting to change her will in Teddy's favor. But why? And, the real kicker, why not admit it? Teddy's record and Norman's argument with Isadora about her will have been wide-open subjects for days. But Norman had acted so shocked when I'd told him. I remember that first morning in his office, remember Norman's apparent disinterest in Teddy before I told him about the Louisiana killings.

"Yes," he'd said then, "it was in the papers. So?" And his apparent shock, the accusation: "This is your fault," he'd said to me about keeping Teddy's secret. Why behave that way if he already knew all about Teddy's past, unless he, himself, was keeping secrets? Unless he's hiding much more than prior knowledge of Teddy's record? I pull into the parking lot and see that everyone is here before me.

Joe's Lexus reminds me again about the sole condition he'd imposed on my investigation, to keep him informed. I've told Joe about the alibi witness and about my night prowler. I had every intention of telling him about the unknown "inquirer," too. But, how do I go in there and tell him that the inquirer turns out to be his own partner? If I do, he will shut this investigation down in a New York minute. If I don't tell him and he finds out, I'll be fired. If I get fired over what will surely be called insubordination or betrayal of trust, I'm finished in this profession.

My solution, once again, is to ignore the problem. I spend the morning answering mail and revising a Condominium Declaration for one of Joe's Hollywood clients. Santa Fe is becoming a permanent movie colony as California investment money keeps flowing into it. In the office, these clients are known as money on the hoof, and they belong exclusively to Joe. I wait until almost noon to take the huge stack of revisions to him in the hope that he's already left for lunch. He has.

My own lunch date is with Stone Allen at the Coyote Café. In jeans and parka, I'm a little scruffy for the Coyote. Trendy restaurants come and go here with the seasons. So, after ten years as an "in" place, the Coyote is practically an institution. Wait-persons are likely to be New-Agers with a couple of master's degrees. I take the low steps in the wide curve of stairs two at a time. Rocks is already at the top standing beside a man-sized statue of a coyote.

"Matty, here!" He motions me up. "I got us a table." I follow him to one of the waist-high half-moons of white adobe that encircle each booth. As we scoot in, Stone explains that his loose association with me has become known to his supervisor in the Public Defender's office. "Joleen was pretty pissed that you saw the D.A.'s file and that I called you, you know, about that thing with Norman Frederick."

"Uh-huh," I say. "Have you done anything about getting the details of the Louisiana case?"

"Look, Matty, I told you, Joleen is already really pissed. She says your role has to be clarified. Joleen says if you want any more information you've got to talk to her."

"Come on, Stone, I'm sure Joleen wouldn't object if you just shared information that's already in the public record. Any citizen is entitled to have that."

But Rocks isn't listening. His attention is fastened on a woman approaching our table, muscling through the crowd like a stevedore. Rocks says, "Uh, Matty, I think it's kinda out of my hands now."

Joleen is overweight, with prematurely gray hair frizzed n a tight cap of curls which looks like it's never seen a comb. She's wearing stiff new Wrangler jeans which interfere with her ability to bend herself into our booth.

"Joleen Fische," she says curtly to me without extending her hand. "I think we've got a problem, Ms. Donahue."

"Oh?"

"I gather from Stone here that you're trying to get access to confidential information in the Bellasandro case. Is that right?"

Into my silence she cracks each of the knuckles of one hand.

"And—you want to yank Stone around without my okay. You appear to want to control the Bellasandro case with no personal exposure and no real responsibility. How am I doing so far?" Her eyes bore into mine.

"Well, I . . . uh . . . see your point," I stammer. "It's just that your office, that is, Stone didn't seem to be pursuing leads, even the Louisiana record, and—"

"*Stone!*" Joleen orders sharply. "You get up and go tell that ponytailed Ph.D. in aroma therapy who's masquerading as our waiter to get me a cup of coffee. Give him your own order while you're at it. Hers, too. And take your time."

As Rocks rises in a subdued huff, Joleen continues. "Ms. Donahue, what Stone is pursuing and what the P.D.'s office is pursuing are not always precisely the same thing."

"Then you *are* developing evidence that the Stanton murder is different from the Louisiana killing? What've you found? Are you preparing a motion to exclude the Louisiana stuff?"

"First question, yes. We're looking into it. But, we have a very fucking short window of time. We've got three weeks before we have to put this thing to bed."

"*Three weeks!* What do you mean, three weeks? You won't go to trial for months."

"*I* won't be going to trial at all. I don't try cases any more. I supervise, I support, I turn my hand to predicaments and strategies, and I argue a motion now and then. No," Joleen sighs deeply and motions across the room. "Our lad over there is the attorney of record. And our time problem began when he took his first independent step in *State* v. *Bellasandro*. As you know, each side is entitled to disqualify an assigned judge in any case—but only one judge. I'm afraid he's used up our single judicial disqualification rather imprudently. He used it to get rid of a judge who once insulted him, told Stone he was 'dumb as a box of rocks.' So now we've got no choice who's going to sit on the bench in this case. It's been automatically reassigned to Eduardo Peña."

"So? That's great, isn't it?" I know Peña to be a superb judge. He's knowledgeable, thoughtful, and can be relied upon to follow the rules of evidence even if he doesn't like the result.

"Let's just say it would have been great," Joleen mutters. "It might still be great if we can pull off a miracle. But it may turn out to be a disaster."

"Oh, right! I forgot about Judge Peña's retirement. You can

see how many cases I try these days. So, Peña is set to go off the bench . . . when?"

"End of this year. Twenty-nine days from today. And we might as well subtract seven days for the Christmas break. Any case Peña has pending on the first day of the new year will go automatically to his successor, Ann Chestnut. You know anything about that lady?"

"She used to be a prosecutor, didn't she?"

"A mad-dog prosecutor. Chestnut'll eat Stone alive. But what's worse is her position on the rules of evidence. When Ann Chestnut ran for Peña's position, her campaign slogan was: *Exclude the exclusionary rules. Give juries the whole picture.* And she doesn't just mean the rules excluding evidence from illegal searches and so forth. She means *all* evidence. Her position is that keeping *any* evidence away from a jury is wrong. The evidence of another, similar, crime committed by Bellasandro will be red meat to her. Trust me, if Chestnut gets this case, she'll hold the platter while the goddamned D.A. serves up a bloody hand to the jury. Fuck the rules."

"She can't get away with that. She'll be reversed," I argue.

"Yeah, someday soon, in the right case she will be reversed. And when the times comes, I'm personally looking forward to holding Ms. Ann Chestnut's chestnuts to the white-hot fire of the CON-STI-TU-TION." Joleen enunciates the last word like the late Barbara Jordan.

"But *this* isn't that case," she continues glumly. "If these two crimes are even remotely similar, the appellate court will say she was within her discretion. They won't reverse. And when she lets that evidence in, when the D.A. tells the jury, 'He has done it again,' your friend hangs. So," she cracks her neck loudly, "there's really only one solution. Get the case to Peña first. Get him to make the evidentiary ruling before it becomes Chestnut's case."

"It's too fast. And what if he rules against you? And he may turn it over to Chestnut anyway if she's going to try it."

"Not if I frame it as a Motion to Dismiss, he won't. And if he rules against me, I'll fall on my sword right then and there.

Bellasandro will enter a plea of not guilty by reason of insanity, or guilty but insane, depending on what our shrink says. Either will at least buy him a safe bed. Maybe more. I'll have a deal with the D.A. in my pocket before I walk out of that courtroom." Joleen sounds unshakably certain.

"My God! It's way too fast. No matter what, Teddy can't plead that soon." My voice is a decibel or so higher than the general buzz around us and it brings momentary attention.

Joleen twists to reach the folded document sticking out of her back pocket. She slaps it on the table. "I've already filed the Motion to Dismiss," she says flatly. "The hearing on it is set for Monday, December twenty-third. Three weeks from today."

I slam my fist on the table. "Hold on! There are other questions that have to be answered!"

"Such as?" Joleen is unaffected by our audience but I lower my volume.

"Such as—who really killed Isadora? Without the Louisiana thing, Teddy isn't even the most likely suspect. The niece stood to lose her inheritance, the housekeeper had an Arab boyfriend who was pissed at Isadora—"

Joleen laughs out loud, bringing us more attention from the other diners. "Fanfuckin'tastic!" she chokes. "You got us an Arab diversion, someone everybody will hate even worse than our guy. This could be useful. Go on, go on, what else you got?"

"Norman," I hiss into her mockery. "I think someone should look into . . ."

"Oh, right! How could I forget? Stone tells me you think you've got your anal-retentive boss dead to rights. Frederick improperly requested a records check on Bellasandro. Possibly, I might add, at the victim's request. How many years you figure Mr. Straightarrow will get for a crime of that magnitude?"

"Goddamn it!" I explode. "The point is that he's the only one who had enough information to duplicate the crime. Don't you have any interest at all in looking at who might have actually murdered Isadora Stanton? You're Teddy's lawyer, for Christ's sake. I can't believe you don't care about finding out who really did it!"

I'm momentarily saved from making a scene by the arrival of lunch. Polenta topped with fresh red chile and goat cheese for Rocks and a spectacularly good shark-meat enchilada for me. It's not possible to order anything normal at the Coyote Café. Like the patrons here, the food is to be looked at and remarked upon. Without skipping a beat, Joleen dives into Rocks's polenta.

"Let's get something clear, Matty," she says around bites. "Who really *did* it isn't my problem. I don't have to figure out jack about who did it. Only who *didn't* do it. Or, more precisely, who can't be proven to have done it."

She shovels more food into her mouth as she talks. By the time Rocks returns to sit with us, she's doing some serious damage to his lunch. "I don't have the budget, I don't have the personnel, and, frankly, I don't have the interest," Joleen says. "It isn't the way cases are won or lost in the real world."

"Well, there happens to be an alibi witness somewhere. Is that real enough for you?"

"Okay, okay," she says, apparently enjoying the skirmish. "I didn't say there was nothing to do, just that I'm not the one who is going to do it. And my staff here," she tweaks Stone's cheek, "isn't going to do it either. And that, Ms. Donahue, is what brings me here to meet you today. Stone told me you used to be some kind of hot-shit lawyer. So I looked you up."

She suspends a forkful of mush halfway to her mouth and appraises me. When I don't try to explain away my record, she moves on.

"I should have expected something like that. Good lawyers don't usually hibernate in a cave. When they do, there's usually some dirty secret curled up in there with them." She picks her teeth with her fingernail and continues to take my measure. "I'm surprised you were hired by any decent private firm, much less Frederick and Danforth. What's the story there? And why in God's name would you risk the only good job you're going to get for Theodore Bellasandro? What is this guy to you, anyway?"

I'm tired of trying to answer this question. After a beat or two she goes on.

"Shit. I guess your motives are your business. Anyway, if you want to work on this case, here's the deal. Sometimes, the Public Defender's office puts outside lawyers on contract for a case or two. But with your record, the office would never approve a contract. I assume you couldn't clear it with Frederick and Danforth to take a contract with us, anyway."

I nod.

"But"—she shrugs—"if this is how you want to spend your time, we could use a little help. But you got to stop that puppetmaster crap with the lad. And you got to play by my rules." She doesn't wait for assent, just starts ticking off the limitations. "We've got zero budget for investigation. So even if I could hire you I couldn't pay you."

"That's okay."

"Yeah, I figured."

"You're not entitled to confidential information. What you know isn't protected by the privilege, so you just can't know some things."

"Okay."

"And, I may pull the plug on this little arrangement at any time."

"Okay."

"Okay." She sticks her beefy thumb up and in the same moment undercuts the gesture with a wink as though this might be a joke. "As of now you are an unofficial, unpaid, unrecognized servant of the great unwashed and falsely accused. If you actually turn up anything, let me know."

I recognize that I'm smiling and I try to quit. Joleen sees and snorts.

"Look," she tosses several crumpled bills on the table, "some of this crap of yours might be useful. I like the Arab as a wild card. You got you some smoke and you got you some mirrors there. Also, Bellasandro's alibi witness, Charlie Lee, is nowhere to be found. The cops won't talk to us at all about whether they've located him. D.A. loves to spring that shit on us at the last minute. You want to try shaking something loose from the boys in blue?"

She stands and motions Rocks up. "I don't know why you

want to do this," she tells me. "I predict it's going to end up costing you something, so if you decide to forget it, let me know. But if you are going to come up with anything that matters," she keeps her eyes on me, "you do it in three weeks, my dear. Otherwise the lad here tries his first felony case to the mad dog."

For a long time after they leave, I stare at the money she left, at blue china etched with red coyotes, and at globs of goat cheese recongealing on the white linen. I hear the tinkle of glass and girlish giggles somewhere in the room. I sense someone nearing. I look up to up to see the smiling face of Liza Danforth, Joe's wife.

My heart sinks.

"Liza! Hi."

"What in the world was *that* all about, Matty? I was beginning to think you might need to be rescued."

Butt tucked and encased in black suede, face-lifted and lovely, Liza ignores my reticence and greets me by kissing the air and squeezing my elbow.

"Whatever. Anyway, did Joe remember to give you the invitation to our Christmas party? You've got to be there, you know."

Every year, Liza's Christmas parties get more elaborate. Because she used to be Joe's office manager in another lifetime, she still feels free to order office associates to do her bidding. Joe, who adores her, does little to rein her in. Now it appears that she and I are headed in the same direction so, with no way to escape gracefully, I walk back toward the office with Liza. Once there, she hands stacks of invitations to the receptionist and asks her to be a dear.

As Norman joins Liza, I escape to my office wondering what she will have to say to him about the scene she witnessed at the Coyote. Once in my chair, I collapse and rub my temples, feeling the deep squeeze between a rock and a hard place.

There are two new message slips on my desk. One from somebody named Carla and one from Faye Stanton. *How about*

Friday noon? Faye's message says. *I'll play hooky and meet you at Aunt Izzy's.*

I return Carla's call first. Carla is the name of Juanita Jakes's ex-roommate. I'd given her twenty dollars to call me if she found out where Juanita Jakes is living. She has.

THIRTEEN

—⁓∾⁓—

TUESDAY, DECEMBER 3

JUANITA OPENS THE TRAILER DOOR AND FLINCHES WHEN SHE sees me. She's wearing a loose flower-print house dress, and a heavy pink sweater. She's changed subtly. Her face is fuller. Her hair has been rolled up and let down in unruly hanks of Shirley Temple curls. She has applied makeup to her features. Pink lipstick and cheek blush done with a heavy hand. The effect, ironically, is to make her seem even more naive than usual. She doesn't want to let me in, but a lifetime of learned good manners apparently wins out. So she steps back and edges the door open just wide enough for me to squeeze past her extended belly.

It's cold inside and I shiver involuntarily. There are gas space heaters built into the trailer walls, but they produce no heat. The tiny combination kitchen/living room is exceptionally tidy and has been prettified with coffee cups filled with dried flowers and winter weeds. Juanita doesn't invite me to sit, but I slip into a narrow bench seat beside the kitchen table.

Juanita stands and looks around the room as though searching for an escape hatch.

Eventually she says, "Would you like coffee? I could make coffee."

In hopes of warming both my body and Juanita's chill reticence, I accept and watch as she silently and efficiently goes about her task. She ladles water for the pot from a bucket sitting in the sink. The whole process takes a long time and she doesn't look back at me until she has set two cups of coffee in two plastic saucers on the table. I stare at her hand. At that odd ring still on her finger.

"Are your utilities turned off?" I ask.

"Not the electricity," she answers defensively. Like living without gas or water is no big deal if you have electricity.

"I've been trying to find you for weeks," I say. "Where did they take you that day? I mean the day . . ."

She knows immediately which day I mean. The last day we saw each other, the morning after the murder.

"They took me for questions. I did okay. They said I could go after I slept. I didn't have to stay."

Maybe this means they brought her to the police station to take her statement. But, more likely, seeing Juanita Jakes's emotional state on the morning after the murder, the cops drove her to St. Vincent's Hospital for evaluation. Maybe both. I wonder in which order they might have done these things. Given Juanita's finger-pointing at Teddy, this may not be an idle question.

"Teddy asked me to look in on you," I tell her. "To find out if you're okay."

"He did?" This seems to please her. "Tell him I'm okay. I've got the electric stove. I turn up the oven at night and open the little door. It's real warm."

"Juanita, whose trailer is this?"

"Mine; the trailer's mine. My father gave it to me." She says this very quickly and with practiced certainty.

"I thought your father was dead." I'm not on very solid ground here, just fishing.

She grabs a curl at her ear and begins to twist it. "Yes, uh-huh, yes, he's dead, but he left it for me."

"Did you know that Teddy is in jail?"

Juanita's eyes get wide and watery. "Why?"

"They think he killed Isadora."

"They do?" She says this with surprise so genuine it must be real. "Miss Isadora liked Teddy. Why did he kill her?"

"I don't think he did, Juanita. I think somebody else killed her. The police think Teddy killed her partly because of something you told them."

She looks confused, but then understanding and then something else crosses her features. She frowns deeply, as if working through a difficult problem. There is a small lint ball on the elbow of her pink sweater. Juanita picks at it with the tips of newly polished nails, delicately, so as not to disturb the weave.

"Juanita, did you tell the police that you heard Teddy and Isadora arguing the night she was killed? Did you tell the police that they were yelling at each other?"

"Yelling and yelling; getting really mad." Juanita speaks with some heat. "I was scared. I don't like it when people yell."

This, too, has the unfortunate ring of truth, but I press on. "Could you hear what they were saying?"

She shakes her head hastily and returns her attention to the lint ball.

"Juanita, are you absolutely sure it was Teddy doing the yelling? Could it have been somebody else? Are you sure it was the night of the murder that you remember? Did you see Teddy or did you just hear him?"

"Did I get Teddy in trouble?" Her head is bowed but she raises her eyes to mine. Her expression is unexpectedly crafty.

What I don't want to do here is put words into Juanita's mouth. So I utter the standard advice: "Just tell the truth," I say blandly.

Juanita's fingers have begun to work further down at the bottom of the ribbing, scratching the wool with her thumbnail; deliberately making balls now, rolling each one tighter and tighter between thumb and forefinger until it snaps from its moorings. A small pyramid of hard pink balls the size of pin-heads is in front of her on the table before she answers.

"Maybe," she mumbles. "Maybe it was a rapist."

I almost spit my coffee out in the spasm this suggestion starts in my throat.

"A rapist?" I ask with a straight face. "Why do you think it might have been a rapist?"

"There are a lot of rapists," she suggests. "I have to lock the trailer even in the daytime because there might be rapists. You never know."

"Who told you that?" I have a pretty fair guess at the answer.

"My father," she says slowly with a lilt at the end.

"Would that be the dead father?" I ask.

Juanita clamps her teeth tight at being caught in a lie. She uses her thumb to hide the pile of pink balls under the edge of her saucer.

"Where is Rickie?" I ask softly. It's the next logical question. She's begun to tremble slightly; her head shakes in repetitious arcs like a metronome.

"This is Rickie's trailer, isn't it, Juanita? Tell me the truth. Does Rickie rent this trailer? Are you living with Rickie?"

"Uh-huh. Rickie rented the trailer," she admits in a slow voice. "When we get married we'll have a house in Albuquerque. Or New York."

"Where is Rickie now, Juanita?"

She looks down and begins to unravel her sweater again.

"I don't know," she confesses. "Rickie went to Gallup with a man to get some money. He said he'd be back by now. Don't tell anybody, Matty. Rickie says people might blame him for Miss Isadora because he's from Arabia. Rickie says everyone blames people from Arabia for things even if they didn't do anything."

"I'm sure that's true," I say sympathetically, just as though I wasn't the person offering up Arab diversions to Joleen Fische.

Juanita drops her voice and says, "They said he has to come home to the family now. But Rickie doesn't want to go home, Matty. He says his son—" she points to the mound in her lap,

"—is going to be an American. We're going to stay no matter what they say. No matter how mad they are."

"Rickie's family? Why is his family mad at him?"

Juanita shrugs. "I don't know, Matty. Rickie was supposed to finish school. Then he started helping some people from his village over there." She points out the trailer window toward the desert. "They make pretty things."

"And Rickie's family is mad about that? About making pretty things?"

"They wrote a mean letter. They sent Agi back again. Agi won't let Rickie have any more money. Agi says Rickie's messing everything up."

Who's Agi? But I force myself to ask one question at a time. I don't want to confuse her. "Messing up what, Juanita?"

"I don't understand it." Tears form and hover but she bites them back. "He needs a lawyer, I think. They're going to make him go home. I told him to go see you, but I guess he didn't want to." She looks hopefully at me and says, "After Miss Isadora died, Agi got really mad."

"Who's Agi?" I ask.

"Agi is Rickie's cousin. Agi takes them all over the world to sell. Agi says Rickie isn't careful. That's why he has to go home."

"Was Rickie at Isadora's house that night, Juanita?"

She switches on the metronome again. "It was probably a rapist," she announces and turns her face so far away that her forehead touches the trailer wall.

"Juanita, do you have money to turn on the utilities?" No answer. "Do you know where Rickie is?" No answer. "Has the rent been paid?" Still no reply.

More gently, I say, "I may be able to help you. Call me if you need anything. You know my number . . . even if you just want to talk, okay?"

Reluctantly, she finally turns to me. She nods dully.

"Juanita, if Rickie saw something that night, it could really help Teddy. If Rickie needs help staying in the country, I know somebody. Mention that to Rickie, okay?"

She begins to shiver and rock herself. "Please go away now, Matty," she mutters.

•   •   •   •

As I drive the long stretch of Cerrillos Road back into the heart of Santa Fe, I am picturing Juanita Jakes on the witness stand. Obviously, her eyewitness testimony putting Teddy on the scene that night isn't worth spit. I can't be the one to press her along these lines. But even a mediocre lawyer could drive a truckload of reasonable doubt through Juanita's version. Of course, we're not talking about a mediocre lawyer. We're talking about Stone Allen.

FOURTEEN

—◆◇◆—

THURSDAY, DECEMBER 5

GLORIA BACHICHA AND I HAVE BEEN WORKING ALL MORN-ing in the computer room, I summarizing from hard copy, and she inputting the data in neat columns. It's a mindless task and we continue through lunch. Eating from each other's brown bags and sharing office gossip is the closest we're ever going to come to chumminess. Gloria probably knows at least one of the answers I need. Here she is, right in front of me, and Teddy doesn't have enough time for me to screw around. I've begun to worry about whether Teddy can even last the three weeks until the hearing.

I've called the jail nearly every day since my first visit to Teddy, distorting my role—well, deliberately lying to the jail personnel—calling myself Teddy's lawyer so they will send him to the phone. I called again this morning to try to cheer him up; I told him Juanita's statement implicating him was fragile.

"It'll evaporate," I assured him.

But, one more, Teddy wasn't listening. Every day on the phone he has sounded lower than the day before. Even good news isn't getting through. He doesn't seem to care about anything I say. I recall my own months of depression and think his isn't very surprising. He's lost the deepest connection to life he had. He may go to prison again, this time forever. I can't imagine how hard it must be for him.

"Teddy, really. This is good. The only other thing they have is the signature murder angle, and if that connection is weakened—"

"Hey, Matty, I gotta get off the phone now."

"What's going on, Teddy?"

"Listen, Matty, I gotta go. I can't talk about . . . I can't talk now."

I take a deep breath, smile at Gloria, and blunder ahead like a blind rhino in the underbrush.

"Who's Norman's contact in the D.A.'s office?" I ask.

"Pardon?"

"I need some information from the National Criminal Record files. I don't know how that stuff is kept." I scratch my temple in woolly-headed confusion. "I suppose there's a centralized computer file. I think Norman mentioned he knew someone in the D.A.'s office who could get that stuff."

"Freddy Martinez, usually," Gloria says, without looking away from her computer screen.

"Did he run a records check for Norman? Did you get something like that from Martinez in October?"

"I wouldn't know," Gloria says. "I was out for two weeks in October. Why do you ask?"

"It would have come across your desk, wouldn't it? A records check? Would you remember something like that?"

"If it came in the mail while I was here, of course I would," she answers, tapping keys as she talks. "But . . . Freddy could have delivered it in person if they were having lunch or something . . . or it could have come over by courier, theirs or ours."

"Would you have made the request for that kind of record yourself?" I persist. "By phone or in writing—"

"What exactly are you wondering about?" Her voice has taken on a cautious note and she turns to look directly at me.

"Nothing, really," I mumble, yawning and stretching. "I'll get the last batch of files. Be right back."

Sometimes I'm not bright. This becomes painfully obvious later that afternoon in Norman's office.

"I've got the paper transcripts of the videotaped Tri-Con deposition," I tell Norman. "I marked our objections and noted the legal basis for each one. Do you want me to handle the motion in court tomorrow, or will you?"

"Mmmm." He's absorbed in a file. "Leave it. I'll look it over and let you know by noon tomorrow."

I make no move to leave and eventually he looks up. "Is that all?"

I study him, wondering if he will lie to me again. "I would like to know if you asked the District Attorney's office to run Teddy Bellasandro's criminal record before Isadora was murdered."

His eyes narrow slightly. After a moment, he aligns the file with a pencil on his desk. "I did." He makes the word "did" sound like it has three syllables. "And how does this concern you, Ms. Donahue?"

"Why did you do that?" I say.

He chews the corner of his lip and drums his fingers on the desk. Then he nods sharply. "Okay. I don't care for the interrogation approach and I would appreciate it if you'd refrain from using that tone with me in the future. But as I brought up the subject of Miss Stanton's will with you, perhaps you are . . . entitled to some explanation."

The room darkens. We are probably in for another storm. Norman flips on the desk lamp. He studies me over a tent of fingers.

"I was, as I've told you, concerned about Miss Stanton's competence. I felt that her decision to change her will, to disinherit her niece in favor of some recent employee, was, at best, imprudent. It smacked of duress."

"Oh?"

"You haven't dealt much with inheritance issues, Ms Donahue. But I've often seen older clients influenced by daily caretakers to make changes in their will. I'm extremely uncomfortable with these situations. My own father . . . Well, that's another story. Suffice it to say I'm always deeply concerned at a sudden change, cutting out family in favor of new friends."

Norman sucks in breath and snorts it out as though he already deeply regrets having embarked upon this explanation to me.

But he continues. "Freddy Martinez and I cochair the Judicial Selection Committee of the Bar." Freddy Martinez is an Assistant District Attorney. "He and I lunch together often on committee business and happened to do so on the day after Miss Stanton raged around here like a madwoman. It was on my mind, so, not surprisingly, our talk got around to the problem of older people being so vulnerable to potential con artists. One thing led to another. I asked, and Freddy agreed, to run a check on Bellasandro."

I must admit, Norman's explanation doesn't sound unreasonable. Unusual, maybe, but it could have happened just that way.

"Satisfied?" he asks.

"Sure. And I'm sorry about my tone. Just one more thing . . ."

Outside, storm clouds move fast and low across the windows.

"Why didn't you say that you knew about the Louisiana record?" I ask. "I sat in this office and told you that Teddy had a criminal record; you acted like you were surprised to hear that."

"And so I was. I just told you that Freddy Martinez agreed to order the record search. I didn't say I got the result. I didn't get it. I assume he decided it was improper to provide the information to me, or that he never even got around to requesting it."

Gloria comes in, pointedly avoids looking at me, drops

a note on Norman's desk, and hovers, waiting for him to read it. He nods to her. When she leaves, he flashes the note briefly at me.

"Miss Bachicha tells me you were asking her questions about this subject, too."

"Yes, I—"

"You what? Here I've been civil enough to indulge your curiosity in a matter which, if I recall correctly, you promised to stay out of. Now I find out that you have been . . . What shall we call this sneaky behavior, Ms. Donahue?"

"Norman, I'm sorry if I've overstepped but I need to understand this. And I don't. Why would you—?"

"Okay! That's it! That is quite enough. I do not intend to have any further conversations with you on this subject and I hope not to have to repeat this again." He's standing now and leaning far across the desk. "You keep your nose out of this. You hear me? If you want to continue as a member of this law firm, stop acting like you are this creep's lawyer. I—won't—have—it!"

I'm thinking as I turn toward the door that, unless there is some break in this case soon, my days in this job are numbered in single digits. I still owe sixty thousand dollars in restitution to old clients. Fingers of cold squeeze my heart each time I think about how much I need this job.

As I reach for the knob, Norman surprises me by adding, "We were better off when you were still acting like a rabbit."

"What?"

He's still standing, red in the face and leaning across his big desk. "For four years you've been scared shitless of making a mistake, unwilling to act as lead counsel, always insisting that we recheck your work like you were some law student or paralegal. You've been a royal pain in the ass. Joe wanted to help you because he said you'd come out of it eventually. As far as I'm concerned, you're just one more of the legion of lawyers who prance around the courtroom until the first time the shit hits the fan and then deflate like a popped balloon. There isn't a lawyer in this world who doesn't lose sleep over the mistakes he's made and will make. The good ones work through it; they grapple with their inadequacies. The sheep run out to pasture."

It's funny, but sometimes friends can talk till they're blue in the face trying to get you to see yourself and nothing happens. Then, an enemy holds the mirror up for a second and the image you see pierces your soul.

FIFTEEN

---〰〰〰---

FRIDAY, DECEMBER 6

THE HOUSE ON ACEQUIA MADRE IS SILENT NOW. MORE THAN
on that first day when Isadora's corpse was still oozing
blood, I feel that she's gone. Now, there is nothing—no sound,
no disorder to show that someone moves through these rooms.
Drapes have been pulled nearly closed. Long blades of dusty
sunlight cut through the dimness.

What am I looking for here? I don't know. But something
was going on in Isadora's life in the weeks before she was murdered. Whatever it was must have left traces. Maybe, if I just
keep my eyes open and my mind receptive, I will see something
that others have missed.

The police have completed their investigation of the crime
scene; the yellow tapes are gone and the bedroom has been
cleaned. A fresh yellow sheet covers the mattress. Otherwise, the
room is as when I'd last seen it, the morning after its occupant's
murder. Painted flowers of light yellow and blue decorate
the wall around the doorway and closet. Isadora's elaborate

bedspreads, nowhere in evidence now, had echoed the painted blossoms. A band of punched tin frames the wavy mirror above a long hand-hewn table. The straw-seated ladder-back chair where Juanita sat that day is still pulled out into the room facing the corner, away from the bed.

The leather-bound photo album on the table is one of the things I came to look at today. I flip through its thick pages. Judging from the dress and cars, these black-and-white photos span the second quarter of the twentieth century. Only a few of the pictures have any inscription to tell me when or where they were taken.

Who were these robust, good-looking people: a gathering of men and women in fiesta clothes playfully struggling for a bottle of tequila, a man and woman kissing through the window of a vintage Ford? I study the image of a beautiful woman astride an Arabian horse, her long, dark hair and shirt beaten against her body by the wind, before it dawns on me I'm looking at young Isadora Stanton. In shades of gray, the photographs evoke a poignancy that Kodachrome will never attain.

I'm so absorbed that for a time I forget the presence of Faye Stanton, elsewhere in the bowels of the house, so she startles me when she enters. Dressed in a long flasher's trench coat, Faye closes the space between us greedily like a giant vulture and stands peering over my shoulder.

"God, she looked like me, didn't she? I never quite realized that before," Faye says.

She's right. Isadora at thirty could have been her niece's twin.

"What are you looking for?" she asks.

Faye is once more standing entirely too close for my comfort and flexing her bony shoulders as though readying herself for flight or attack. One gray eye is looking back at me; her breath smells of almond tea.

"How did you lose your eye?" I ask.

She cocks her head appraisingly, gives a startled laugh, and pivots away. Sweeping her open trench coat in a wide arc to reveal spangles beneath, she settles herself, butt, elbows, and one long leg on top of Isadora's bed, seemingly oblivious of the recent history beneath the sunshine-fresh sheet.

"Yeah, it was pretty much the last straw," she says flatly. "Before I lost the eye, there was always some tiny hope that I could turn out normal after all."

I'm reminded of Max quoting me about Thanksgivings past: *"I thought we might live a normal life after all."*

Is everyone terrified of being abnormal? Of being alien in a world where the rules seem so obvious to everyone else? Or is it only a few stragglers like this glamorous crone and me who are locked on the wrong side of the magic door?

Reading my mind, Faye says, "Guess normal isn't in the cards for some of us."

"How did you lose it?" I ask again.

"The emergency room, a few years ago. I was holding down some guy on crack while the orderly was cutting off his bloody shirt. Guy grabs the scissors and starts slashing. They told me later that when he plunged the blade in, my eye plopped out completely and dangled on my cheek. The guy starts laughing then and drops the scissors. He can't stop laughing. He dies on the table, dies laughing."

"My God!"

"Yeah."

The random meaningless horrors perpetrated on some of us by others of us hits me again. But Faye appears well recovered. And that's even more startling, when you think of it. How do we keep recovering? . . . Appearing to recover?

"Who's this?" I'm pointing to the woman who keeps showing up in the pictures arm-in-arm with young Isadora or in antic poses, doing the cancan, smirking at the camera.

Faye raises her brows a couple of times like Groucho Marx. "Think it runs in the family?" she asks suggestively.

I remember Faye's companion gently squeezing her hand at the funeral. I look back at the photos. In those days who ever questioned the close friendship of women?

"Faye, do you know anything about these people? I mean about Isadora's young life?"

Her nose wrinkles in thought. "My father was Aunt Isadora's younger brother, and except for those few terrible weeks I lived here, most of what I know about Aunt Izzy, I heard second-hand from Dad."

"You lived here? You mean lived here with Isadora? I never heard about that."

"No, you wouldn't have. That's when I became 'the Horrible Niece.' It was a few years ago. Aunt Izzy had broken her hip, and the regular housekeeper quit because the old lady was being more of a pill than usual. Of course, poor Juanita couldn't cope. I was sort of between phases myself. It seemed like a nice solution for both of us."

"But it wasn't?" I guess, knowing the answer.

"It was a disaster. Suffice it to say, that woman could bring out the devil in Saint Peter and I didn't start out all that saintly. I saw a side of myself I didn't even know I had. Every night, Aunt Izzy insisted on getting out of bed without help. She was so weak that she would fall and hurt herself again. It was a nightmare. I was at my wit's end, trying to keep her from breaking her own neck. First, I bought a Posey jacket. You know those crossed-arm things they use in nursing homes?"

I don't know but the image appalls me. "Like a straitjacket?"

"She burned it."

"Good for her," I say.

Faye gives a microscopic nod before going on. "So, I threatened to restrain her with handcuffs. I even bought a pair. God, the old bat was pissed. She grabbed the cuffs and refused to give them back. Every time I wanted to bathe her or take her someplace after that, she'd cuff herself to the bedpost. Here, I'll show you."

Faye stretches her entire length across the bed to reach the nightstand at the far side, slides open the drawer, and fishes in the contents.

"Huh? They're not here. This is where the old dear always kept them just in case she wanted to cause trouble." Faye slams the drawer and gets up, wiping her hands together. "Anyway, from then on, things just went from bad to worse. After I moved out, I used to call but she always told Juanita to tell 'Nurse Rat-shit' to go to hell."

I'd like to know more about this old quarrel. Faye is, after all, the one who profits most from Isadora's murder. But, because of what Teddy said, I've been looking for something specific in the album and I think I've found it. I'm riveted by the inscription on the back of the photograph in my hand: *Me & Skeeter Marlson 1943.* Teddy said that when Isadora was upset the day she died, she'd told him, "Skeeter would turn over in her grave."

I hand Faye the photo and point to the inscription. "I don't suppose your father would have known much about his sister's friends?"

"Not ordinarily." Faye reads and turns the picture over. "Aunt Izzy moved from the family home in South Carolina when she was young. But . . ." she studies the writing again, ". . . but, this name even I know." She taps her nail on the inscription. "There was a rich family in Ashton, just outside of Charlottesville, by the name of Marlson. The Marlsons practically ran Ashton. My father talked about them all the time. He said the Marlsons got rich bootlegging during Prohibition and afterwards got even richer as a legal distiller and bottler. My dad said that old man Marlson was mighty fond of his own product. His wife, too, the gossip went.

"My father disapproved and was jealous because Aunt Izzy went to a fancy girl's college—Radcliffe, I think it was. He was the boy and, you know, in those days if anybody was going to go to college—"

"What's that got to do with—"

"Hold on, I'm coming to that. The reason Aunt Izzy got that special attention and a chance at a swankier life was because of the Marlson daughter. Alice Marlson was Aunt Izzy's best friend. Alice and Izzy had been close since they were little girls. Mr. Marlson came personally to talk to my grandparents. The Marlsons wanted Alice to go to Radcliffe. But she refused to go without Isadora. Dad always thought maybe old man Marlson bribed Grandpa, paid Aunt Izzy's tuition and more."

"How do you know so much about it?"

"It was family legend. Because Isadora left home and

couldn't help in the store, Dad ended up doing it. He blamed Aunt Izzy and Alice Marlson, the airs they put on, for his own mediocre life. Stupid, but that's the way it was. Then to make matters worse, when Grandpa died, he left all his money to Aunt Izzy. Dad just got the store and all the debts that went with it."

"So, Alice is Skeeter Marlson?"

Faye looks down at the old photo, then shrugs. "Who knows?"

"Is this all there is? Are there any more pictures, anything?"

"Not in the house. I would have come across anything like that. I've been cleaning all day. Which reminds me, I could use some help with this place. Living in Albuquerque, I can't even keep it secure. Do you know anybody I could get to stay here and watch the place—maybe clean a little?"

My mind immediately turns to Juanita but on second thought, I keep my mouth shut. "How about the shed?" I ask instead. "Anything out there?"

"Maybe. There's a bunch of old junk out there. I was going to throw it out. If you're interested, I guess—"

I don't know what the hell Isadora was talking about, but this *Skeeter* had something to do with all the carrying on Isadora was doing. "I'm interested," I tell Faye.

I follow Faye through the pantry, where I steal a glance at the empty shelf where Teddy's toolbox belonged. In the kitchen, I pause at the calendar on the wall. It's still showing the month of November. There is almost nothing noted on it. No appointments with lawyers to change her will, nothing to indicate she planned a trip to Canoncito. The only entry is for November fourth, a week before her murder. In that square, Isadora has written: Celestine Abeyta C'de Baca and a phone number.

Everyone in town knows Celestine Abeyta C'de Baca, but a call to Celestine is definitely out of character for Isadora. These two women had zero in common. Isadora neither knew nor cared about the intricacies of Santa Fe society—called those who did care "dodoes" and "pencil-necked geeks." She'd paid no attention to art openings or the opera season. Celestine, on the other hand, knows everything about everybody and everything Santa Fe. She is art critic, historian, and pompous caretaker of "Santa Fe style." Isadora wouldn't have liked her. Yet Isadora had called her. Had, apparently, made an appointment to meet with her.

I tear out the calender page and stuff it into my pocket. Maybe I can make something of it later. I go out the back door and into the gardening shed. Alone in the unlocked unheated shack, I take in the shelves and boxes, the pots and sacks, the wall hooks holding garden tools and an assortment of keys. I finger the keys. The one labled "shed" looks like a house key. I slip out to try it in Isadora's back door. It fits. Another nice little question of conscience. What the hell. Next time I want access, Faye may not be so obliging. I dig my own key ring from my pocket and clip the house key to it.

Back in the shack I stare at more old junk and finally settle in to pore through stacks of old magazines and newspapers. Among them are about twenty old copies of the *Native American News*. I thumb through a couple and stop to read the passages Isadora has underlined in articles about Fetal Alcohol Syndrome. On the potting table are two wilted cardboard boxes crammed with papers. At first glance, this stuff looks irretrievable. Over the years, dampness has soaked into the boxes. The bottom third of each is a sodden mess, and the layer above that is dappled with mildew. However, some of the pages near the top may be salvageable, and I begin by spreading these apart. After an hour, I've sorted the contents along the plant potting table into two piles: barely decipherable and totally indecipherable. The decipherable letters are fragments of Isadora's life which I have never glimpsed and wouldn't have imagined. At the top of the first pile I've placed a letter postmarked a decade ago, and return-addressed to A. Marlson.

Unaccountably, my fingers tremble slightly in anticipation and I nearly tear the old tissue-thin airmail envelope with its red-and-blue striped border. Although the letter inside is in a slanted, irregular script, as though written by a child, the voice that emerges from the page is clear and literate.

Iz,

> *I'm dying. I don't mean the regular "I'm dying" like I've been dying for the last five years. I mean now. Doctor Tucker, who I'm using since Simon had the bad grace to die before his patient, tells me we're talking weeks now. I know it's true because the shaking has almost stopped. I'm finally too weak to shake and I'm so grateful to have a few weeks of life without shaking that I'm almost ready to accept that demented trickster they call God into my heart.*

The next lines are too smudged for me to make out. "Demented trickster?" I don't know anyone who talks that way in letters to friends. This writer was born into a world of privilege and the literary tradition of another generation.

I struggle to decipher the rest:

> *Since I don't figure to dance the weeks away and the shaking has quieted enough to allow me to write, I decided to take the opportunity to tell people what I really think of them. So, I'm writing letters. Can you imagine? In seventy years I've never told the whole unvarnished truth to anyone except, almost, to you. Between naps, I've been writing for two solid days. I'm even writing to dead people. Actually, I'm mostly writing to dead people. Iz, I told my poor dead mother that I forgave her for all the years of booze. An hour later I wrote another letter to her, asked her to forgive me. As you know, my financial accounts are all settled. The trust provisions are finalized. Now I'm settling personal matters.*
>
> *Isadora, I have had no special urge to make a letter for you because you already know everything in my heart. You have been my friend longer than I've even known any other living person and our friendship is as full of grief and laughter and trust as a relationship could ever be.*

I rest the letter on the plank potting table for a moment and pace to dispel the chill. I try to understand the recipient of this letter, the odd old coot with the maroon hair and the vile temper, as the young vibrant woman Isadora must once have been. You can tell a lot about a person by the friends they make; I find myself envying these two who managed to keep a special friendship alive for over five decades.

You know, of course, the letter goes on, *the letter I want to write is to Jeff. Not the now Jeff; but the Jeff who, I believe with all my heart, he will someday become.*

I'm sitting here right now holding a picture of Jeffy in my unshaking hand. He's about five, got his chin stuck out to here daring someone to take him on. Iz, he was so much like me when he was little. The genes just skipped right over his father and took root in that boy. I never loved anyone in my life so much as I've loved Jeffy. Not parent, husband, lover, nor child. I'm ashamed to admit that I was probably a little in love with myself, new and shiny and wrapped in a just-starting life with all the potential still intact.

Of course, that's not so anymore. The other picture of him is the one I'm enclosing.

I stop reading and glance at the color photo of a good-looking long-haired boy throwing the bird at the camera.

. . . It's the last picture I ever saw of Jeffy. It was taken last year when he was twenty. That teeth-over-the-lower-lip rabbity look is the first sound in "Fuck you," his favorite expression these days. It's what he said to me when I told him I wasn't giving him his promised inheritance when he turned twenty-one. He has his generation's version of our family curse. I told him he was a junkie and I wouldn't put my money into his arm or up his nose. That was more than a year ago and he didn't know how sick I was.

The only reason to put with the shaking and the pain and the medication has been to see my Jeffy whole again. I see him in my mind every day. More clearly, as I got closer to the end. I can close my eyes now and see other photographs yet to be taken: Jeff throwing his mortarboard in the

*air, Jeff looking into his bride's eyes, Jeff with his own child
straddled on his back.*

   *Izzy, those pictures or some other "good life" pictures of
my grandson will be real someday. That little boy, with all
his promise, is in there someplace. One day my Jeff will be
whole again. I would give everything to be alive and to
know him then. But Dr. Tucker says it is not to be.*

   *So, my friend, I want you to do a last thing for me. If I
can't see my grandson, then at least I can send a message
now to the future Jeffrey Marlson. I entrust the enclosed letter to you. It is to Jeff. Hold it and give it to him when he is
well. I want him to know that I have loved him all of his life
and do now, at the end of my own.*

                                              Always,
                                              Skeeter
   *P.S. As you know, the lawyers are keeping track of his
whereabouts for the estate. So, if you ever need to find him,
they can help.*

I jiggle the envelope but find no letter to Jeffy enclosed. I
toss the letter into my sack of flotsam and jetsam and shake my
head. This little excursion into unknown lives has not been a
good thing. "Skeeter" and her problems have no connection I
can see to Isadora's murder. The woman appears to have died
more than ten years ago. This has all been a waste of time, no
use to Teddy at all. And Skeeter Marlson's unrequited love for a
delinquent grandson is too close to my own nightmares of John
and his son for comfort. Twisted reminders seem to be everywhere lately.

   Damn it, I think for the umpteenth time. I really don't
know what I'm doing. Nobody should be depending on me for
anything. Least of all for his life.

SIXTEEN

~~~

SATURDAY, DECEMBER 7

"So, what's the catastrophe?"

Max asks this as he maneuvers backward up my narrow staircase to the loft. He's wearing gray sweats and his glasses keep falling forward over his nose, but he hasn't a free hand to push them back up. He's holding one end of a large cardboard box. I have the other. "What's the catastrophe?" is a game we used to play when we were patient and shrink rather than whatever we are becoming now.

"You mean about losing my job?" I ask, grunting under the weight. This is the third carton of case files we've toted up these stairs and we've got two big ones to go. This morning, I brazenly called to ask Max for strong-back help, which I probably could have done without.

"Okay," he says, using his foot to shove the box against the wall with the others. "Let's say I mean about losing your job."

"Well, for one thing, there's the matter of eating and paying my rent, to say nothing of the fifteen hundred I pay each month to former clients."

"You can get another job," Max advises. He's headed back downstairs for the rest of the load. I lean over the loft balcony railing and watch as he hoists the next box on his shoulder like a strapping, brawny boy and takes the steps two at a time.

"Showoff," I say.

He dumps the box with a loud and dusty thud, flexes his muscles like Popeye, and grins. I sigh and follow him down the stairs. These are, after all, my boxes and I ought to carry my share. We work in silence until the last carton is placed on the top of the cardboard pyramid against my bedroom wall.

"Maybe in your world, I could get another job," I tell Max. "But I abandoned clients and pissed off judges. Compassion for fallen brethren isn't the standard in my gang. I only got this job because my mother worked on Joe. Otherwise I'd still be in that apartment in Albuquerque watching gnats fly out of rotten fruit baskets with sympathy cards."

"Is it really such an insurmountable obstacle?" he asks. "I mean, explaining what happened to you to a prospective employer? You made a mistake in judgment once and you had a bad time because of it. I guarantee you, most of the people you'll be talking to have made mistakes, big ones. Four years is a long time to pay for a mistake. Maybe long enough?"

"My mistake got two people killed, Max. You think four years is long enough to pay for that?"

"Yeah, Matty, yeah, I do."

"Maybe, maybe it was. Until this. But now . . . now . . . I suppose the catastrophe is really Teddy being convicted of Isadora's murder. You understand that, don't you?"

"Help me to understand it, Matty."

"A person might be able to survive this once, Max. This massacre by accident, by good deed and poor judgment, this killing people by thinking I knew better than everybody else, by thinking I could fix anything . . . this . . . assassination by . . . hubris. But not twice. Not twice, Max. Not me, anyway."

Max says that it isn't fair, that nobody should have to be caught in a crisis of the soul like this twice in one lifetime. But then he wonders if maybe therapy—*not with him,* but he could give me some names—wouldn't be better than focusing so exclusively on proving Teddy's innocence.

"Understand what you've done and let it go," Max advises.

I tell him that I've seen his recommendation, the nose picker, and I think I'll pass.

"Besides," I argue, "this is the first thing I've been committed to in a long time. Teddy didn't kill Isadora. I need to prove that. For his sake . . . and for mine. Maybe when he's out. Maybe then, I can work on looking at my mistakes. Maybe even forgiving myself."

He peers at me and nods, and I'm pretty sure he understands until he says, "That's not the way it works, Matty."

I'm embarrassed to be shrink-rapped like this. To change the subject I kick the heap of boxes, painfully stubbing my toe.

"Look at all this shit!" I exclaim, sitting on the bed to massage my foot. "Just when I need it least, Joe and Norman are really piling it on."

"Yeah, I was wondering about all this. " Max indicates the pyramid. "What is it?"

He has always been good at letting me change the subject. "It's your hour," he used to say. Is it still my hour, I wonder?

"These two boxes are copies of depositions from expert witnesses. Not only depositions that we've taken, but all of the depositions these experts have given in every case they've testified in during their lifetimes. I've got to go over each of them with a fine-tooth comb for inconsistencies."

"Why?"

"So Joe can make these guys look bad on the witness stand. These so-called experts have testified so many times, in so many cases—not always on the same side philosophically. So, you can set them up in a deposition. They will remember what they told you in a recent deposition well enough to say the same thing at trial. But they can't remember what they said in the old cases. When they testify differently, you pull out their old depositions from other cases. 'But, Doctor, six years ago, didn't you say, under oath . . .' Unless they're absolutely consistent, Joe has holes for them to fall into. Joe and I spend hours before a trial working out alternative scenarios depending on which way a witness steps."

Max is looking extremely wary. He's probably testified as an expert himself.

"You guys always do this?" he asks.

"I used to think it was fun. Lawyers are a goddamned tricky bunch and I used to like the tricks, the maneuvers."

I lie back on the bed and fold my arms over my face. I hate the melodrama but whenever I get close to this subject, the tangle of grief and guilt defeats me. "Since Tommy killed John, it hasn't seemed like so much fun."

I feel him sit down on the edge of the bed.

"It's how I got Tommy out," I continue softly.

"What do you mean, it's how you got Tommy out? Out of the psychiatric care unit?"

"Yeah."

"What are you talking about?"

"Two shrinks testified that Tommy was a danger to himself or others. But, me, I'm a B.F.L. So, I spend a week going through the two shrinks' backgrounds their résumés, their previous testimony." I wave a hand in the direction of the boxes. "Especially their depositions in previous cases."

"B.F.L.?" Max asks.

"Big Fucking Lawyer. Naturally, there were inconsistencies. I enjoyed making the so-called experts look like idiots or liars. I really got off on it."

"You never mentioned this part in therapy," he says.

"I didn't want to offend you. These guys are your . . . You know . . . You're one of them."

"So you were what? Protecting me?"

I shift the elbow over my right eye and peer at him through the crook. "Not a good thing?"

"Sit up."

"What?"

"Sit up. I want to hold you and I don't think it's a good idea for me to do that in a horizontal position just now."

I raise myself on one elbow and cock my head at him. I don't know if—

The phone rings and both of us leap up like teenagers whose mother has just opened the bedroom door.

"Good morning, Ms. Donahue. Daniel Baca here. I'm sorry I couldn't return your calls earlier."

I've left messages for Detective Baca twice a day for the past week without getting an answer, so I spiced up the last one. It seems to have worked.

He continues, "This last message here says you have some new information in the Bellasandro case?"

"Well, yes. I do." It's such a small lie. "Also, I was wondering what progress had been made in trying to find the witness, Charlie Lee. I thought perhaps we could meet to talk."

"Uh-huh. Well, I'm afraid that won't really be convenient, ma'am. I'm about to go off shift and I have a meeting, ah, a civilian, ah, civic thing."

"But Detective, I spoke to Lee. I called your office, made a statement. Charlie Lee verified Teddy's story. Didn't you—?"

"Hold on, ma'am. We got your statement and an officer visited the Santa Clara Pueblo two weeks ago. Spoke to the guy's girlfriend. Lee had taken off before we got there; Hollywood, he told his family. Going to be a Native American movie star. Now, what have you—?"

"Hollywood? Is he an actor? I mean has he ever—"

"I'm sorry, ma'am. That's all I got." Baca's voice is firm and slightly bored. "Now, was there something you wanted to report?"

I'm not doing any good here. I raise my eyebrows at Max, and start, "Do you know anything about a guy named Rickie Hadid, an Arab, a friend of Juanita Jakes?"

"What should I know?" asks the cagy Baca.

"Well, for starters that he exists, that he hung around Isadora's house, that he's got trouble with the immigration service, that he was pissed at the victim . . ." I falter. I'm a good deal less than certain that Hadid has any connection to the case but I need to get Baca's attention.

"Uh-huh," he says, followed by a long silence.

"And," I add, "that he's disappeared. There's more. You remember the newspaper you found in Isadora's car, the circled article? It may have something to do with Hadid. I'd really like to talk to you. Maybe you could bring a copy of the article?"

I can hear a slow gush of air before he speaks. "Tell you what, Ms. Donahue, the civic thing, it's a low-rider meeting. I used to judge the cars. Now, I'm a kind of unofficial sponsor for one of the clubs. They're meeting about three o'clock at the Denny's on Cerrillos Road down a bit from the station. You know the place? Maybe, if you could meet me there in about fifteen minutes . . . ?"

I grab for a jacket even before I hang up the phone.

"Come on," I tell Max. "Go for a ride with me."

Detective Baca is already in the booth. A pretty young waitress is leaning partially across the table on one arm. She's a little disconcerted when I scoot in across from Baca all the way to the window and Max takes the outside. The waitress straightens, drags her pad out, and poises her pencil.

"Regular for you, Danny?" He nods and she turns to us. Her name plate reads *Annette*.

"You folks need menus?"

"Two coffees, black," says Max with a smile and without asking me.

Max and I are still in sweat clothes. Baca wears a sports coat and knife-creased jeans. His off-duty outfit differs from his on-duty outfit only in that the collar of his pastel shirt is unbuttoned one button and there is no tie. I introduce the two men. Baca has a pad out on the table and now he thumbs the cap off a Bic.

"Okay, what's this new information you have for me, Ms. Donahue?"

"Do you mind telling me more about the search for Charlie Lee first? Is this one trip to Santa Clara all you'll do to find him? I mean, Lee can establish that Teddy didn't do it."

He turns to me with resignation.

"Yes, ma'am, it is. Because your statement corroborated the subject's alibi claim, my men spent hours out at Santa Clara. We were lucky. The tribal elders told the members to cooperate, which isn't all that usual. When the elders do give the okay, we usually get the straight story. So my guys went house to house. And the story is, Ms. Donahue, that Charlie Lee is absolutely, positively gone. No question about it. Lee's girlfriend, his brother—everybody—said Lee suddenly got an urge to go to Hollywood and just took off. They saw him pack. They saw him drive away. Nobody's heard from him since." He shrugs.

"Now if you ask me, that's not too surprising. A man like that, friend of a scum . . . you know, a friend of an undesirable like this defendant. Suddenly somebody's looking to him to bear witness, under oath, for that kind of friend—to say where they were together, when, and so forth. Lotta details to get tripped up on. In my experience, a man like that, he's not likely to want to be found. It's easier just to disappear. Become a movie star, something like that. It happens all the time."

Baca laughs gently and takes a swig of his coffee. "Now, that's all I have to say about the so-called witness. Or about anything else. I ask you again: What is your new information?"

"And what about Faye Stanton?"

Irritation swiftly replaces amusement. He'd leave if Annette weren't back with a big oval plate of eggs over easy, sausage, and hash-browns. I watch in fascination as he begins to put the heavy food away. No matter what's going on I always stop to notice when thin people eat like this.

"Have you considered Faye Stanton?" I ask again. "Does she have an alibi for that night?"

"Look, Ms. Donahue—"

"Matty, please."

"Uh-huh," Baca says. "Please, Ms. Donahue, whatever you think you're doing, ma'am, it's not likely to help. I'll tell you this much, so maybe you can let it go: Yes, we checked out Miss Stanton. We know she inherits and that kind of money's motive enough if a lady's so inclined. So, we checked. She was at a medical conference in Los Alamos for two days and two nights. Witnesses out the wazoo. Now please, leave it alone!!"

"Surely not for the whole two days."

"What?"

"The medical conference. If they're like legal conferences,

it's pretty easy to sneak out without anybody noticing. Especially during the evening. And Los Alamos is only, what, thirty minutes from Santa Fe?"

Baca shakes his head wearily and begins to edge out of his seat again but is interrupted by three kids suddenly standing at the end of our booth. They look to me like gang kids, but Baca gives them a big grin and one of them gives him a complicated high five.

"How ya doin', Sherlock?" says the kid to Baca as his eyes take in the other two of us without noticeable attitude of any kind. "Be in the back," he says to Baca. "Set the tables up. Meetin' starts at three, bro." The boy taps an invisible watch at his wrist. Then he flicks his chin toward the window. "Check out Chuey's wheels, man."

We all look. The car is gleaming and about four inches off the ground, with oversized chrome wheels. It is painted scarlet. Yellow and blue flames streak down the side, and a quite artistic rendering of the Madonna in blue and white decorates the hood.

"Oooo, that's fine," Baca tells Chuey. "But, hey. I'm ready to go now. I'll help set up." He wipes his mouth and once more starts to rise with a little salute to me.

"Wow," says Max, who's been silent until now. "Is that a '68 Impala?"

"You like it?" says the kid, like a kid.

"Wow," says Max again, also like a kid. "Could I take a look? Do you mind?"

"Does he mind?" laughs Baca. "Chuey lives for the chance to initiate *novicios*."

Max, God bless him, is out of the door with the boys in a flash, more or less forcing Baca to continue talking to me.

I push the advantage. "Did you bring the copy of the article you found under Isadora's bed?"

"You two are quite a tag team." Baca shakes his head and then, to my relief, laughs and opens the leather folder on the seat beside him. The sheaf of pages he pulls out are a photocopy of the November issue of the *Native American News*.

"There, on the third page, where the circle is. That's the stuff on the fakes."

Baca turns to the window where the three kids and Max are beginning a slow inspection walk around the car like they're circling the Venus de Milo in the Louvre.

I turn to the paper. As usual, for this paper, there are several pieces about Fetal Alcohol Syndrome. The subject is of abiding concern to the tribes, because the incidence of Fetal Alcohol Syndrome among Native Americans is more than ten times that of the general population. Because of Juanita, Isadora had the paper delivered and regularly read these articles.

But these aren't the stories Isadora has marked in this issue. A stubby circle is drawn around two brief paragraphs about allegations that a group of Arabs have been operating locally, selling imitations of Native American jewelry. There is nothing in it by way of details and nothing I didn't already know. But, it makes sense that Isadora would have noted it. Given her attitude about Rickie Hadid and her attempts to interfere with Juanita's marriage to him, she would have loved thinking maybe Rickie, himself, was a real criminal.

"Can I keep this?"

Outside, Max is getting behind the wheel. Baca and I watch as the engine turns over. The car begins to vibrate slightly and whisper exhaust. Baca doesn't turn from the window as he says, "I made the copy for you. Now, Ms. Donahue, if you're finished with *your* investigation, maybe we could begin with *mine*. Do you actually have any useful information?"

"I honestly don't know, Detective. This," I point to the paper, "may tie to a man named Rickie Hadid." I explain everything I know about Rickie, including the night-prowler incident.

"That his real name—Rickie?"

I shrug. "Isadora used to call him 'Rickie—alias—Mohamar.' But I doubt if she really knew. She didn't like him using Juanita. In spite of her own sins, Isadora was very protective of Juanita."

Baca is writing in tight neat script on his pad. He wants to know the date and time of the reported prowler, and Hadid's address. I explain about the trailer in the Cactus Trailer Park and my talk with Juanita.

"What does he look like, this Hadid?" he asks.

I look up from his plate of grease and into his face. "It's a funny thing to say, but he looks like you."

"Handsome devil, huh?" supplies Annette who has materialized as she pours him a cup of coffee but ignores my empty cup.

Baca gives her a look like "get outta here," but friendly.

"No," I say. "She's right. The most noticeable thing about Rickie is how handsome he is. Dark curly hair, deep-set black eyes, olive skin, teeth a toothpaste model would kill for. He's fairly well educated, I think. Dropped out of UNM a year or so ago; been illegal since then because that invalidated his visa. And, I don't know—" I point to the article, "—if he's involved in any of this or not. But I'll bet it occurred to Isadora that he might have been."

I fill him in on the details of Hadid's anger at Isadora's "theft" of Juanita's engagement ring and the reappearance of that ring by the morning after Isadora died. I even speculate that it may have been Rickie that Juanita heard "yelling and yelling" the night of the murder.

Baca shakes his head. "Makes an interesting image. No wonder the old woman was concerned."

"Juanita wants to protect Rickie," I say. "She maybe only thought to supply Teddy's name to the officer because I put it in her head that morning. I said to her: 'Teddy? Where's Teddy?' Could be she was just repeating the last thing she heard. When I talked to her later at the trailer, she wasn't sure anymore. Told me maybe it was a rapist."

Baca sighs and flips his notebook shut. "Well, Ms. Donahue, I appreciate your coming forward."

Annette ambles back over. Baca puts a ten-dollar bill on the table; Annette looks at it like it's maybe a frog.

"What's this, Danny?" Then she looks at me and gets it.

"Thank you, sir," she says, and pockets the ten without presenting a tab.

The "boys," including Max, are making their way back to the table.

"Man, oh, man. That car is fantastic. Chuey tells me you used to drive one of those things," Max says to Baca.

"Yeah, I was a homeboy. You got a couple of choices in some neighborhoods. Cars was the best one."

Max drives my car to his house. On the way we talk about Detective Baca. I remark that he's not a typical cop.

"I think there may not be typical cops or typical lawyers or typical anybodies," replies Max. "As soon as you get to know someone, he turns into yet another complex exception to the rule."

I intend to drop him off at his door, but when we get there, he asks me in and I say yes. He has another bottle of Auslese in the refrigerator. He asks me to get the glasses and a corkscrew. He'll light the piñon log already laid in the corner fireplace.

"Did you really like that car?" I ask. "Or were you just trying to give me more time with Baca?"

"It crossed my mind that you might need some help keeping him there but, yeah, I really did like the car. Beauty comes in all kinds of packages. Some of the low-rider cars are works of art. I've been a fan for a long time. A '68 Impala is a real prize."

"I guess I've got some things to learn about you. It's not fair. You already know all my secrets."

Max is silent and I settle in, putting my sock-feet up on his coffee table. We watch the flames.

"This wine is way too good," I say, after a while.

"You're right. There are some things you ought to know about me. Like why I terminated your therapy."

"You said we'd gone as far as we could. That I'd be better off with somebody else."

"Yeah, that's what I said."

"That wasn't the real reason? It wasn't the truth?"

"It was the truth. It was a real reason. But it wasn't the only reason. I had begun to . . ." Max rests his elbows on his knees and falls silent again.

I look at him. I know. I know about his forbidden feelings for me. I don't know when I first knew. I'm pretty sure I didn't guess when I was in therapy, but it's been hard to miss recently.

"What do they do," I ask him, "drum you out of the corps

for getting a crush on a client? Even if you do the honorable thing and terminate the therapy?"

He lifts his head and reaches his arm across the back of the couch and touches my neck. The touch is electric. It's been nearly half a decade since a man has touched me like this. I feel like Sleeping Beauty, awakening all at once. A very horny Sleeping Beauty. My breath comes quickly and I move into his arms.

"Would they? Drum you out of the corps?"

His lips are on my neck and his breathing, too, has become labored. "Maybe," he says.

SEVENTEEN

———❧———

SUNDAY, DECEMBER 8

THE COFFEE IS BITTER AND I'M ON MY THIRD CUP. IT'S ALmost midnight and I can't stand working on these damned depositions another minute. But I've got to go on. I know the reason Joe is pouring on work is to keep me from doing much of anything else. Specifically, to keep me from doing what I want to be doing.

It will be a week tomorrow since Joleen told me I had only three weeks to get information to help Teddy. For the last few days, as though they knew I was trying to steal time from work, either Joe or Norman has come up with some new task that had to be done ASAP. *Urgent* slips clipped to manila folders litter the desk in my office.

At least working at home in the middle of the night allows me to focus without interruption. Files and case notes are stacked all over the bed. I pull another off the nearest pile, arrange the blankets and the pillows behind my head and dive back in. By the time I look up again, it's nearly three in the morning. But I'm finished with their stuff for now. I still have a couple of hours for mine.

I yawn and stretch, put a sweater on over my nightgown, and head downstairs where I put on one more fresh pot. As it brews, I rearrange my work boards. I've bought a second dry-erase board and a bulletin board, as well as a rainbow of marking pens. A small area in the kitchen has been given over to organizing information about the murder. I have the three boards propped on three kitchen chairs arranged like a flying buttress around a fourth where I plunk myself down.

On the bulletin board to my left are pinned: a copy of the M.E. report that Joleen deigned to let me have, Baca's copy of the *Native American News* folded so the circled article is on the top, the two-paragraph police report from Louisiana, and a duplicate of Isadora's will from Norman's files. Finally, a single sheet of paper titled WHATEVER HAPPENED TO? upon which I've listed: *Charlie Lee, the D.A. Report.*

I sip the coffee and try to make sense of what I've gathered. The board in the center contains a list of everything I've learned so far about what Isadora did in the weeks before her death. I've been coming back to this particular board again and again. On it, I've written that Isadora:

> *Took Juanita's ring*
> *Read NA News about Indian Jewelry*
> *Made an appointment with Celestine Abeyta C'de Baca*
> *Wanted to go to Canoncito*
> *Said Skeeter would turn over in her grave*
> *Wanted to change her will*
> *Ranted about shysters (at least to Teddy)*
> *Ate a burrito*
> *Swallowed a gum wrapper*
> *Maybe got a drop of blood on Teddy's toolbox*
> *Argued with Teddy?*

I think that what Isadora, herself, did before she died may have everything to do with why she died. And why she died has everything to do with who killed her. Compared to what a regular human being does in the course of two weeks, the list before me is pretty paltry. And what I need, in order to make sense of things, may not even be on it yet. I begin to jot down the jobs the list suggests I should do today. The kitchen clock informs me that today begins in three hours.

I don't know if I've been asleep for hours or minutes when the phone rings. It takes several rings before I can pull my body up to answer it. My tongue is numb so I slosh cold coffee around in it while I answer Joleen's questions and bring her up to speed on my activities.

". . . okay, that's what Norman Frederick told you," she prompts impatiently. "Do you believe him—that he never got the report on Teddy at all?"

"I don't know." I yawn. "The assistant D.A. shouldn't have given a record like that to just anybody who asked. So that may turn out to be a dead end after all."

"Okel dokel, then," she says, giving the impression that this is pretty much how lame she expected my investigation to be that day at the Coyote Café when she so graciously consented to our one-way relationship. The one in which I get to be her unpaid assistant and she gets to give me no information and can pull the plug whenever she wants.

"And how goes the *jihad* angle?" she asks sarcastically.

"Hadid lives in a trailer with Juanita," I answer, "but he hasn't been there for a while. I'm going back out to the trailer park again today. After work," I add.

"Tick, tock."

"I know, I know, Joleen. Just two more weeks. But I have to go in to work this morning. And speaking of ticking clocks, what about you? Anything from Louisiana yet?"

"If I had any real information, you know I couldn't tell you. But, as it happens, there are only dead ends so far. There's no more to the paper record than you saw. I hoped we could reach somebody who actually worked that case. A bloody mutilation like that, it's the kind of thing a cop would remember, even if it's thirty years old. But the cop who worked it is dead. No one in the prosecutor's office is around anymore. I did locate an old guy who worked at the Louisiana State Prison years ago. He ran a therapy group that Teddy was in. He has some records of what went on in that group. But one, those notes are after-the-fact double hearsay. And two, he won't release them without a waiver from Teddy and Teddy's balking. I'll prod him a little but if Bellasandro doesn't want this therapist to divulge his notes, maybe there's a reason, huh?"

I don't have an answer to that. I'm quiet, listening to the silence. But . . . it isn't quite silence.

Maybe a click. Maybe insect scratching. In my ear.

"Joleen, did you hear that?"

"What are you talking about?"

The volume of her voice is suddenly lower—difficult to hear.

"Joleen, talk some more. Something is wrong with the telephone."

"Oookay . . . I'm talking. This is me talking . . . okay? What's this all about?"

"First there was a click then, all at once, your voice got lower—harder to hear."

"Can you open the receiver?"

My hands are shaking. I've never been bugged as far as I know. "It doesn't come off! It's all one piece."

"Get a screw driver," Joleen yells. "Pry off the ends."

I use the prong of a fork until the top of the receiver pops and I twist and pry until I can see the innards of the mouthpiece: A green computer chip, four thin, colored wires, and a black housing with no seams. No bug. I jam the cord plug back in place and speak into the dismantled handset. "There's nothing here."

Another click just before Joleen answers.

"Well, good," the volume of her voice is so noticeably and suddenly louder that the relief from finding no bug in the phone dies aborning.

"Is there another way they could be tapping this phone—without putting anything in the receiver?"

"Well . . . I suppose a line tap," she says doubtfully. "I defended a jealous husband once who used one of those. But I think they'd have to physically get pretty close for that—to make sure it was your line. You live in an apartment?

"Yeah."

"Then they'd have to be practically in your yard right now."

I drop the receiver and run to the door. It's now or never. If someone was listening just now, he knows I know he was listening. He won't be back.

I remember too late I don't have shoes on and that the gravel in the compound is sharp. I hear a car door slam and I run anyway. I make it around the corner too late to see anything but a car's rear fender, gray. And the last number of the New Mexico plate: nine.

EIGHTEEN

---∽∾∽---

MONDAY, DECEMBER 9

"WAIT, DON'T GO IN YET." JOE IS EASING THE DOOR TO his Lexus closed as he shouts across the parking lot, stopping me before I get to the office door.

He catches up. "You eat breakfast yet?"

I got off the phone with Joleen about thirty minutes ago. I've had two pots of coffee and maybe two hours' sleep.

"Just coffee," I answer.

He motioned toward the dirty alley with his head. "Walk with me. I'm on my way to pick up a Christmas present for Liza. Thought I'd stop at Pasqual's for a real breakfast. Come on. It'll give us a change to talk."

We walk together in silence. I know I should have spoken to him sooner. Surely by now Norman has given Joe an earful. As we pass by the side entrance to the New Mexico Supreme Court and round the corner to the gold-plated front doors, Joe regales me with stories of great arguments made in that building, which remind him of other courtroom war stories, his and others', some true, most myth.

"I ever tell you the one about Greyhound Means?"

Greyhound Means is a Texas lawyer of star dimension. Most of the stories about Means are apocryphal. I've surely heard this one but I'm really not ready to talk about Norman yet.

"What? Tell me?" I ask Joe.

"He's in front of the jury making his summation. He's defending a bad-ass motorcycle gang accused of, among other things, nailing a couple of tourists to a tree. Supposedly they wrapped these people's arms around a big cottonwood, then pounded a nail through the fleshy part of each hand. So, Greyhound is making his summation and he walks nonchalantly over to counsel table and, without breaking stride, picture this—without interrupting his speech, he lays his left hand on a length of two-by-four he's laid out there, and in midsentence his associate at the table picks up a nail and places it in that same fleshy part between the thumb and forefinger. Greyhound picks up a hammer and, wham! he bangs the nail home with one blow.

"Now, Greyhound, he goes on talking, without missing a beat. That board is nailed to his hand. He walks back to the jury and finishes his summation. He talks for maybe half an hour more, gesturing, swinging his arms around. Never mentions the board he's nailed to. At the very end he holds his hand up to show the jury as though he's just noticed the nail. He says, 'Huh, no blood.' He looks like he's thinking, then adds, 'No pain, either.' "

We're nearing the entrance to Pasqual's. As usual, there is a cluster of people outside the restaurant waiting for a table inside.

"See, Matty, there are almost no nerve endings in the flesh there. Means knows this, has surely tried it a couple of times, and—"

"Joe, don't you worry about the games?"

Joe looks at me like I just arrived from a not-so-near planet.

". . . and, as I was saying, the damn stunt worked! Ask me if he won the case, if his clients got the lesser count," he demands.

"I've heard the story before. I know they did. I'm just saying that in my old age I'm beginning to have some respect for reasonable rules in the courtroom."

"Means pushed the rules to the edge. It was a calculated risk. But a reasonable one to take. He gambled and he won. Neither he nor his client was punished for his behavior. What he did resulted in his client spending fifteen fewer years behind bars. Hold on for a minute, let me put my name on the waiting list."

It takes a minute or two for Joe to muscle through the crowd into the restaurant and then through it again back to the street. A couple of voices call to him and he stops to glad-hand.

"I left my name but it'll probably be thirty-five minutes before we can get a table," Joe tells me. "Come on, we'll walk over to Infeld's so I can get my Christmas stuff. Then we'll come back."

By the time we reach the corner of the plaza, Greyhound Means is forgotten and the heaviness of the unspoken is between us again. Finally, Joe says, "Norman says you accused him of some complicity in the Stanton murder."

"Did he? Is that really what he said?"

"Well, did you?"

"Did I? Accuse him? Maybe, in my heart. But I don't think I said so out loud."

"Well, surprising as it may be, Norman must have been listening to your heart, Matty. He says you accused him. That he kicked you out of his office. Norman had a lot to say about you and your little murder investigation. Now, the surprising thing is that I heard this from Norman, not from the lady who agreed to keep me apprised of *everything*." Joe is wearing sunglasses against the winter glare and he lowers his head to look over the rims at me.

"Okay, I'm sorry. Really, I am. I thought if I said anything to you in advance you'd stop me from talking to Norman."

"Um-hm, yes. I'd say that's exactly what would have happened. The very thing I had in mind when I asked you to keep me informed. I didn't exactly trust your judgment on this thing, remember? And it looks like I was right."

We reach Infeld's. I wait outside while he goes into the store. This is the heart of Santa Fe. Across the street is the La Fonda Hotel. It's been there for a century, looking more or less as it does right now: thick sloping pueblo-style walls and flat-terraced parapets at the various roof lines. The parapets now sport newfangled plastic *luminarios* which everywhere replace the candles in sand-filled paper bags that lined the streets and flat rooftops during my childhood Christmases.

In front of me is the plaza, the central square which, in this small city, is still a center for civic activity. Today, they're setting up a bandstand there for the Christmas carolers who will gather every night for the next few weeks.

When he comes out, Joe is carrying three small flat boxes neatly stacked and tied together with a green velvet ribbon. The trinkets in Infeld's start at about a thousand dollars.

"Liza wants to know if you'll be at the Christmas party— you didn't RSVP."

"Sure, fine," I say. "And look, about Norman. I don't think he *did* anything. I thought he knew about Teddy's background so that just made him a suspect in my mind. Apparently he didn't. But he got so pissed. That, by itself, made me wonder if he had something to hide."

Another five-minute stroll and we're back at Pasqual's. We squeeze in through a fresh batch of waiting customers. I move deftly between the closely packed tables to take the gunfighter's seat at a dime-sized table, my back to the wall. Joe orders *chorizo* and eggs and I ask for blackberry cobbler. I haven't eaten pie for breakfast since the old days, in the middle of trial anxiety.

"With heavy cream," I add at the last possible second.

Joe makes no comment about my dietary choice.

"So," he says, as the waiter walks away, "maybe we should start with what you would have told me if you had been telling me anything. What's been going on? Liza says she saw you lunching with the gargoyle from the P.D's office. What have you been up to?"

"Liza knew Joleen Fische was from the P.D.'s office?"

"The question is what do *you* know, Matty? What do you know now that you didn't know before? Anything?"

"Not too much, actually. Some dead ends, or at least paths that've narrowed. I talked to Baca about Charlie Lee."

"The police? You're talking to the police?"

"I called him. I wanted to know about Charlie Lee. What they'd found, you know."

"Bellasandro's so-called alibi witness?"

"Um-hmm."

"And?"

"He's vanished. All they know is that he's gone; maybe to L.A. They're not going to look anymore. I'm thinking I could drive out to Santa Clara, try to talk to his girlfriend myself. Something."

Joe shakes his head. "Doesn't sound like much on that front. What else?"

"Faye Stanton has an alibi. Tons of witnesses, according to Baca."

"Uh-huh. So far this private detecting thing sounds like a bust. Anything else?"

"Well, maybe. There's Rickie Hadid—"

"Who?"

"Hadid, Rickie. Juanita Jakes's boyfriend."

"Who?"

"Juanita Jakes. Isadora's housekeeper. Hadid is Juanita's boyfriend. I guess her fiancé, maybe even her husband by now. He's from the Middle East and in some kind of trouble with his family, and probably with the I.N.S., too. Rickie was furious with Isadora for taking Juanita's engagement ring. I think he might have been there the night she was killed, arguing with her. Somebody was, anyway. And the next morning, Juanita's ring is back on her finger. Either Hadid did something that night or he saw something that night. Either way, he's important. I told Detective Baca about him. He said he'd look into it."

Joe is listening attentively, but abruptly changes the subject. "This *chorizo* is fabulous. Want a bite?"

The *chorizo* does look good but I've got a mouthful of

cobbler and cream and I shake my head. I go on about Indian
jewelry and the history of Arabs in New Mexico but Joe seems
distracted, absorbed in his own thoughts. It's only when I say
I'm going back to Juanita's to look for Hadid that his attention
snaps back.

"No. No, you're not going to do that. We've reached the
end of this, Matty. What Norman actually said to me is, 'I want
her out of here.' Meaning *you*, Matty. I explained that this was
probably my fault, that I'd given you a tacit go-ahead. But I've
never seen him so furious, Matty. Norman's been my partner
for fourteen years. We've had some knock-down-drag-outs, but
nothing like this. I can't say I really blame him. It was a bad call
on my part, letting you do this, keeping your involvement from
him. And I'll tell you the truth, when I saw his fury at what he
called my betrayal, I didn't really have any comeback. He's
right. I told him so."

Joe pauses but now I, too, have no response.

"Norman's bottom line," he goes on, "is either your investigation ends immediately, or we give you notice today. He's
really pissed, Matty. I don't think this'll blow over. I told him I'd
talk to you. I am sorry, Matty. But it's up to me to see that it
stops. You're not going to interview Hadid. You're not going to
Santa Clara. You're going back to work, okay? You understand?"

"Yes," I say.

Joe pays and we trek back up the hill to the office. I break
the silence. "It's not only that Hadid may be involved or know
something about Isadora's murder. It's Juanita Jakes, too. She's
pregnant. I'm worried that she may need help."

All signs of Joe's friendship evaporate before my eyes.
"What the hell is it with you and this troupe of losers, Matty?
Even if it doesn't have to do with the murder, I don't think Nor-
man's going to appreciate the fine distinction. It's all got to stop.
And stop now."

Joe halts abruptly. He grips my shoulders and when he
speaks, anger simmers in his voice.

"In case I haven't made myself clear, Matty, this has come
to an end. Do not—I repeat—do not contact the pregnant girl
or her rag-head boyfriend! Do not voluntarily speak to the

police again! Do not go to Santa Clara. Have no further contact with Bellasandro. Have nothing more to do with this case. I intend to meet with Norman today and bring him up to date on your activities. I'll tell him that you've agreed to stop immediately. My partnership is not going to be further jeopardized by this foolishness. Are we clear, Matthew?"

"Please, Joe, you're hurting my shoulders. I hear you and I understand you. Please, let go."

He does, quickly, as if surprised at himself. "Good," he says. "Well, then, about those depositions . . ."

As I finally enter my own office this morning, the phone is ringing.

"I've been thinking about what you told me, you know," Teddy says without preamble. "About how Juanita lied about me and how maybe she's try'n to protect what's-his-name."

"Yeah," I say, cautiously listening for clicks or volume changes but hearing none. But I do notice his manner is lighter today, less despairing. I'm thinking this is a good sign; thinking he's finally taking an interest in helping himself. "What about it?"

"You say she's got no heat at her place? Living alone? Jakes can't get by that way, Matty. And maybe it's worse the Arab comes back." He pronounces Arab with a long "A." "You think she's in trouble? I mean, it ain't like her to lie. Maybe she's afraid of him. You know, Izzy wouldn't want no harm to come to Jakes. Her condition and all. I was thinkin' it wouldn't hurt you to go out there again just to see she's safe."

"This is what you called me about? Did you sign the waiver for Joleen—to let her get the Louisiana prison therapist's notes?"

"Joleen an' me's workin' things out our own selves. I'm just worried about Jakes, okay? So will you do it? Go out there? See does she need anything."

Now, as I drive out Cerrillos Road, toward the Cactus Trailer Park, it's too late to turn back. Physically, of course, I could whip a U-turn right now. But I've already called Juanita and said I'd come. She was glad. Seems Rickie's back. He wanted to talk to me, too, so he got on the phone. I try to tell myself I'm going out there just to check on Juanita's welfare. Just because Teddy is worried.

It's no wonder I'm not too good at sticking to the truth with other people. Here I am lying to myself again. The reason I'm not turning around is that I'm intrigued. On the phone, Hadid hooked me with the one bait he knew I couldn't resist.

So, here I am. Thirty minutes after implying a promise, I'm breaking my word and jeopardizing my career. Oh, well, what's the catastrophe?

NINETEEN

—◦◦◦—

"NO, NO, NO. IT IS A CATASTROPHE!" DECLARES RICKIE.
"It is a cruel deception, a conspiracy. Your government and my family conspire to strip me of my freedom. I am a man. I am no longer a child to be told where I may live and how I must behave. I have worked hard. My business dealings harm no one. They are not the concern of my family. Now, they conspire to bring me home. Just as I begin to see the return of a few dollars. No! Less than dollars; pennies, pennies!"

This diatribe has been going on for nearly twenty minutes and now, in its third repetition, it has begun to make my eyes cross. The trailer is quite warm now, thanks to an illegal butane tank hookup. We sit in lamplight, curtains drawn to shut out the afternoon sun. At every snap of Rickie's fingers, Juanita has served us a variety of very tasty, though unrecognizable, morsels on a large tin tray which now sits in the center of the table between Rickie and me. We use our fingers, even for the gooey stuff. The orange gingery things are really good. I've eaten them all and am stuck now with the small purple bean balls.

". . . but they must come to know that I am not without friends. I have protective armor. Once you have set up a second meeting with the I.N.S., you can easily show my marriage is valid. I am entitled to the fruits of my labor. You will explain to them that—"

"Wait!" I hold up my hand like a stop sign. Rickie deliberately misunderstands. He snaps his fingers at Juanita, who produces more orange ginger food from nowhere.

"No—well, okay . . . yes. . . . Thank you, Juanita," I look into her face as she leans close. She's radiant. "Look, you say you're married now—I believe you, but I'm not an immigration specialist, Rickie. I've given you the name—"

"No, I'm telling you definitely, no! You shall make us desolate—"

"Stop, please have mercy." I try to shake my head clear. "Rickie, you and I both know that I came all the way out here because you suggested on the phone that you knew something about Miss Stanton's murder and mutilation. Do you or don't you?"

"Of course, of course! I am a person bound by the honor of my word. We have a reciprocal understanding I am sure now. You Americans have an expression which you certainly understand. It has to do with massaging your backs."

"Scratching."

"Yes, yes, scratching. Now I shall scratch you. I can tell you in confidence. . . . This is your rule, is it not? I speak to my lawyer in confidence?"

Nice ethical question—heavily tinged with conflict of interest. The very kind of thing which cost me my license once before. It causes me to grind my teeth now.

"I'm not your lawyer. The confidentiality rule only applies if I am your lawyer and you are my client. And you must know that my loyalty in the Stanton case is to Teddy Bellasandro."

"You are his lawyer?"

"Nooo, not exactly."

"So you can be my lawyer, then?"

"Look," I sigh, "What I can do and will do as a private citizen is to voluntarily keep your confidence—under certain conditions."

"Ah, good, we will deal."

"I'd like your permission to tell Teddy and his lawyer anything that will help his case. And, if he needs you to say what you know to others, I'll urge you to do it. But I will not voluntarily repeat what you say to me to the police or other authority during your lifetime. How does that sound?"

"But, you could be my lawyer at the I.N.S.?"

"Perhaps I could, but—"

"Good. Good. You want to know what I have to say. And you will be my lawyer at the I.N.S. to hear it."

"No, Mr. Hadid. That is not—"

"Fine, fine. Our trust is of the highest order. My family will come to know who they are dealing with. I am happy to help my friend. What do you wish to know?"

"Here's what I think happened that night, Rickie. I think you were there. At Isadora's house. That you probably went there to get the ring Isadora had taken from Juanita. She obviously has it back."

Juanita is gazing at the ring as I speak. Rickie nods.

"I think you argued with Isadora. Maybe fought with her, right?"

"Who has suggested such a thing?"

"Without meaning to, Juanita—"

His eyes flash immediately toward her. "What is this you have said? As Allah is my witness, I shall—"

"Hey, knock it off," I interrupt. "She didn't tell me it was you who was arguing with Isadora. I guessed that part."

"No. No. Juanita knows nothing at all. She is too timid. An American woman, but like a mouse. But, yes, if this is what you want to talk about, fine. I will tell you that because of my wife's cowardice, I was forced to act myself. I insisted that the old woman return to me the fruit of her thievery. I have done nothing wrong, of course. She was a wicked old woman. A most wicked old woman. She . . . yes, we argued. She would not give me the ring, though it was my absolute right to demand its return. Juanita told me she was hiding it in the drawer next to her bed. She was a stubborn old hag; she raised her cane to me. I did not raise my hand to her."

"But you did take the ring?"

He grows cautious. "Such a thing could be interpreted as theft by your ridiculous law. Could it not?"

"Perhaps, technically. But nobody's interested in prosecuting."

"Very well. The drama you see in your mind is close to what happened. The crone and I had more words. I opened the drawer. It was full of old-woman junk. There were medicines and eyeglasses, even, as Allah is my witness, handcuffs. Beneath this lot was my ring. I reclaimed it."

"And then?"

"I left, of course. I did not harm the harridan. I am not a violent man."

"Let me ask you this," I say. "Did you see anything important while you were there? Anything or anyone?"

"Yes. I know this is the thing you want to know, the thing that will help your friend. Yes, my answer is emphatically yes! I am able to tell you that I have seen something of great significance. I am anxious to tell my friend. My dear wife has urged that I tell you. I am most happy to be of some small help in this matter."

"What? What did you see?" I'm drowning in his verbiage.

"First, we must speak of this ridiculous deportation trivia."

"Um-hmm. Why, exactly? Isn't the other lawyer I suggested okay with you? Carl Atwater is an immigration specialist. He could do much more . . ."

Hadid averts his eyes. "It is a matter of great humiliation. I am unable, temporarily, just for this moment, to pay this lawyer's fees."

"And you expected me to do it for free?"

"No, of course not. Today I am giving you a great gift. It is worth much to your friend and to Juanita's friend, Teddy Bellasandro, is this not so?"

I don't speak for a minute or so, and Hadid misunderstands my silence. As though suddenly in the grip of an inspired vision, he jumps up, retrieves something from what sounds like

Fibber Magee's closet, and returns holding a fantastic-looking silver concho belt.

The New Mexico tribes usually create fairly simple designs of silver ovals affixed to a plain strip of leather. Sometimes the individual conchos may be embedded with a single turquoise stone in the center. But on the belt Hadid holds out to me, the conchos are intricately festooned with turquoise, coral, and lapis. What makes this piece even more astonishing, not to say unbelievable, is the frayed tag tied to the belt with aged string and bearing a number.

"Old pawn," as they call Indian jewelry that was pawned at trading posts from the turn of the century through the sixties, has become most valuable as collectors' items. This piece, if genuine, is worth maybe forty thousand dollars. Though the tag is authentic-looking and the belt itself apparently aged, it is far too elaborate for local old Indian pawn. So if this guy is so poor he can't keep the gas on, what's he doing with forty grand worth of jewelry?

His foolish grin disappears as Rickie hears something at the trailer door. The stranger who enters is about Rickie's size. The two men look similar except the newcomer is not grinning. The moment he sees the belt he is seething. He rips the belt from Rickie's hands and replaces it with great clatter into the closet, while speaking rapidly and furiously in a mixture of English and what I suspect is Arabic. Rickie responds in the same vein until the man grabs his shirt and yanks him toward the back of the trailer. I hear the stranger hiss, "You are a reckless little boy. But you will not destroy what our family has built."

"Rickie's family?" I ask Juanita.

Juanita lowers her voice to a whisper and leans close. "His cousin. Agi gets so mad when Rickie gives jewelry to people."

"Does that happen often?"

"Not any more."

"Juanita, quick! Before they come back. Isadora was reading a newspaper article about some people who are making pretend Indian jewelry. Did she ask you about that?" I'm whispering, too.

"Miss Isadora said I shouldn't marry Rickie. But he's my baby's daddy. I love Rickie. I—"

Agi reenters the room and snaps his ornamented fingers at Juanita, then flips on the television. He sits to watch MTV with the sound off as Juanita obediently hoists her heavy body up and produces a freshly piled tray for him. Rickie emerges from the back and flashes a pleasant smile at one and all. Only the slight tremor at its corners betrays any anxiety.

"Forgive me," he says to me. "I wished only to show my great gratitude, but . . ." He shrugs at Agi. "But, you see how it is. Temporarily, I am not free. Although I would wish to reward you handsomely, I must rely on your generous friendship. As I was telling you most honestly, as a man of honor, I have seen something which is of value to you. I will tell you now what I have seen, and you will return this very great favor as you see fit, yes?"

I nod to signal my abject defeat.

"Good. Good. It is agreed. Yes. On that fateful evening, after I left Miss Stanton's home, I did a foolish thing. I waited in the bushes across the street for nearly an hour. I wanted to see if the old woman would summon the police. I needed to know this, you understand. She did not. Or, at least in that hour, none came.

"But someone else did come. A stranger walked with purpose to the gate and looked about in all directions. I stayed only until the door had opened and shut again.

"The next day, when I saw on television that the old woman was dead, of course I knew that what I had observed was important. But you understand how impossible my situation was, do you not? Also I have other considerations which . . ." he steals a glance at Agi. ". . . which mandate that I keep a low profile."

"What did he look like?"

"Ah, the stranger. I did not say that the stranger was a he, did I? No, and that is precisely correct. It was quite dark; there was no moon. I could not see the person's face, could not even swear that it was a man. Few women are so tall, but all things are possible." He shrugs.

"Is that it?" I ask. "That's all you saw: a tall, faceless person of unknown sex entering Isadora's house? Incidently, how did he or she get in?"

"I do not know. I myself opened the door with Juanita's key. When I departed, I am humiliated to tell you that in my rush, I may have left the door unlocked, perhaps even open. The crone was in bed. But why do you ask 'is that all?'? Is this not important? Your Teddy is not a tall man. He is exonerated by my word. Is this not so?"

"It's nothing," I say. "Nothing at all. Even if you were willing to say all this under oath, it exonerates no one. Not even you. Probably—especially—not you."

At this, Agi stands. He says to Rickie, "You see. This is not going to help you. Now you have only brought more unwanted attention to yourself." Unexpectedly, Agi's accent is closer to European than Middle Eastern. He turns to me. "My cousin has nothing further to say to you, madam."

Rickie attempts to ignore this interruption. He says to me, "Does this mean you will not represent us?" He grabs Juanita around the waist and pulls her to his lap. She does her wifely part by looking doe-eyed at me.

Agi suddenly pulls Rickie to his feet, nearly dumping Juanita to the floor in the process. To me he says firmly, "We shall all be leaving your country very soon. Mohammed and his wife shall not be seeing you again."

Rickie moves deftly between Agi and me. He holds out his hand to me with elaborate courtesy. "I will see you out." I send a terrified glance to Juanita but she seems unperturbed. I rise and Rickie follows me out saying nothing until we are a respectable distance from the trailer.

"Have no fear," he says. "No matter what my cousin or my father or my father's father wants, Juanita is not going anywhere. Nor am I. But, to my great embarrassment, we do need your help. My family has alerted the immigration authorities and they are being most unpleasant. I need a lawyer."

I shake my head. "Look, I'll call the immigration lawyer for you and see if he'll reduce his fee. I'll pay the retainer for you; it's probably about five hundred dollars." I say this like a person with a secure economic future. "You can repay me when—" I nod toward the trailer "—when your ship comes in. You've probably got a good case. Assuming the marriage is valid."

A huge smile lights Rickie's handsome face. "This is most generous. Yes, this will work. You will explain everything to Mr. Carl. You will set up a meeting; you will pay the fee. Yes, yes, a thousand thanks. You will be prosperous and blessed, Allah willing."

I feel like I've been run over by a camel caravan as I open my car door.

Rickie adds an afterthought. "Perhaps this will help. The person. The tall person that night, he carried a silver box."

"A what?"

"Yes, this is true; a silver box, large, almost like a suitcase."

"Like what, this big?" I place my hands about a foot apart and he spreads them slightly and pantomimes the rest of the shape.

"Like a briefcase? A silver briefcase? Could this have been steel or aluminum?" I ask, excited, remembering. "Like an attaché or courier case?"

"Is this good? Is it helpful?"

"Perhaps. I think so." This information scares me stiff. I know someone who has such a case. "Or was it more like a metal toolbox?"

"Of course," says Rickie. "It is exactly as you say. A metal courier case."

"And you wouldn't be agreeing to whatever I wanted to hear, would you?"

Rickie looks sensuously aggrieved. I sigh.

"Okay, then. Will you say that to the police?"

"Ah, that is a problem, as I have said. Perhaps, if I were already a citizen, there would be less danger to myself and my wife. We shall see."

"All right, you win for now. But tell me something else. I had a prowler a few weeks ago. Juanita said you were thinking about getting in touch with me. Was it you?"

Rickie glances back at the trailer. Agi has come to stand in the door to watch us. Rickie's eyes dart away from the dominating cousin. Then he says to me, "My cousin, alas, is a creature of intrigue. He is a protective man and a suspicious man. He endeavors to remain invisible while he spies on every one else. He is not at all like me."

"What are you saying?"

"Do I still have your personal word—to keep what I say to you private, even about my cousin?"

"No. No, Agi is not part of the deal."

"Then we shall say nothing further for the time being."

We've reached an impasse. On an impulse, I suggest, "I'm worried about Juanita. Perhaps she could stay with me for a while."

"May Allah increase your well-being," he says, literally slamming the door on my suggestion.

As I back out, Rickie is at the trailer waving and flashing those perfect white teeth.

TWENTY

"SO WHAT YOU'RE SAYING IS YOU'VE SOLVED THE CASE WITH ten days to spare, the bad guy's some Arab criminal named Agi something, who nobody gives a shit about. And Bellasandro's going to be set free thanks to your keen investigative skills. Well, I'm glad it all worked out so well, Matty. When are you going to call a gathering of suspects in the library for confessions?"

"Look, Joleen, I told you I'm sorry I didn't call you first. But all I did was call Detective Baca and tell him about the cousin."

"Matty, you are not a free frigging agent. You are *supposed* to be helping the *Public Defender's* office. So let me say this slowly. When we have information, we give it to Joleen. And JOLEEN decides how and if to dole it out to the police."

"Fine," I say, so weary of other people's egos and agendas I could cry. "I just thought Baca might be able to get a line on Agi. Rickie as a killer doesn't make any sense to me. Would he be fighting to stay in this country if he were worried about hiding a murder? But his cousin may be a different matter. I saw him. He's one scary guy. I just thought he was worth looking into—and that the police had the ability to do that. Anyway. I'm telling you everything now . . . if you want to hear."

To her credit, Joleen swallows her snit-fit and says, "Okay, okay, run this by me again."

"All right, look at this from Isadora's point of view. First, Juanita Jakes turns up with a fantastic engagement ring given to her by an unemployed Jordanian. Then Isadora reads in the paper that Arabs have been working in New Mexico duplicating Native jewelry. What does she do?"

"I give up."

"She makes an appointment with Celestine Abeyta C'de Baca is what she does. And she did. I saw it on her calendar."

"Who the fuck is Celestine Abeyta C'de Baca?"

"I take it you don't read the arts columns."

"Are you kidding me?"

"Well if you did, you'd know that Celestine Abeyta C'de Baca is who you would call if you had, say, an unusual Indian ring you wanted to know about. She knows more about Indian arts and crafts than God."

"So, what did she say, the C'de Baca woman?"

"Nothing. I've called but she's out of town. She'll be back for the party season, though, probably be at the Danforths' Christmas party on Friday. But, you have to admit, it all seems to fit together. Damn it, Joleen, I think Teddy really is going to be set free."

"You sound insufferably pleased with yourself. You won't be offended, will you, if I keep preparing for the hearing on the twenty-third? Just in case some actual lawyering might still be necessary."

When I laugh she adds, "But let's say you're right. Let's say there's a bad guy out there and you're onto him. And let's even suppose he *is* looking in your windows and tapping your phones. You better get yourself some locks on your doors and windows."

"As we speak," I say, looking over at Max, who is chiseling

out a square in the frame of my front door to fit the new dead bolt.

I hang up and slip an old Patsy Cline disk on the CD player. I warm a can of Texas chili and Max and I sit together quietly, by the fire, as we eat. He hums a snatch of "Please Release Me" and brushes the back of my hand. Since Saturday at his place, he hasn't touched me. I grab his hand before he can pull back. I nod at the new lock. "Thank you. It makes me feel safer."

Max gives my hand a brief squeeze, then shakes it off, ostensibly to clean away the handyman clutter. He slept on my couch last night because he's worried about prowlers but he won't touch me. He won't talk about his doctor-patient dilemma with me and he won't touch me. I figure he'll let me know how it comes out. When the chili is gone and the CD is done, Max drives me into work.

I feel uncomfortable in the office. I wish I could tell Joe what I've put together. I don't like lying to him.

When I open my office door I smell a familiar odor. A couple of sniffs at the air confirm that it's Old Spice. Surprising. Norman doesn't usually come this far into the aged part of the building. He prefers the buzz-and-yell method of getting my attention. And despite the *urgent* notes he's attached to the files he's left on my desk, there is nothing remotely pressing about any of them.

I settle in for the long haul, dispatching the litter and dross stacked on my desk as rapidly as possible. Around three, I stop to make some calls. One is to the city jail. I set up a special session with Teddy for tomorrow outside of regular visiting hours. Once again, I have to tell them I'm a lawyer working on his case to get this treatment. Lies are beginning to spring more naturally from my lips daily. A little like the old days. Not altogether a good sign. Not altogether a bad one, I decide.

I fiddle around, putting Max's number on my speed dial, and give it a try. His answering machine is repeatedly cordial. "*. . . but I want to return your call,*" it tells me in his voice.

"Please leave a message of any length . . ." I ponder what messages of any length might be on a shrink's answering machine. I tell Max's machine that he doesn't have to pick me up; that I'll walk home. But not yet.

It's the tenth of December, the deadline for getting November's time sheets in to bookkeeping. So I head to the mail room at the far end of the building with mine. The large open space is lined with work stations. Several women are working at the long tables in the center of the room. Paralegals direct temps who are sorting and collating documents. The only two men in the room, the bookkeeper and the office courier, are playing a game of hearts. They give me the high sign.

"Wayne, I'm going to dump these time sheets on your desk," I say to the bookkeeper.

"Matty, tell George here why Saint Peter thought lawyers lived longer than any—"

"Yeah, yeah," I interrupt, "according to their time sheets they were two hundred years old."

George, the courier, and I both groan at the same time. "Want to take a hand?" George asks, folding his cards. "It's time I got out of here. I've got almost twenty deliveries and as many pickups before five."

George is a skinny old hippie who's been with Frederick & Danforth for nearly thirteen years. He knows more about the Byzantine belly of the court system and its complex flow of paper than most lawyers and even many secretaries and he considers himself smarter than all of us. He is sorting items and tossing a few into a metal courier case. A metal case like Norman's.

My attention is riveted. "George where did you get this?"

"Same place as you got your fancy desk chair. Gil Rodriguez gave lots of his stuff away when he left. He said I was a courier and I needed a real courier case. He didn't want it anymore because of the initials, you know."

"Initials?"

George holds down the handle and points to a spot beneath where three letters, "F.D.R.," are etched directly into the metal. "F.D.R.": Frederick, Danforth & Rodriguez. A firm which no longer exists. Gil wouldn't have wanted such an identification after he left the firm.

"It looks exactly like Norman's. Does Norman's have the 'F.D.R.' initials on it, too?"

"Guess so. Why?"

"No reason. They're so small," I say, running my fingers over the etched letters. "I never noticed them before."

George quickly sorts the items to be delivered and checks them against his log. As I watch, a question begins to surface.

I don't ask it right away. It crosses my mind that I'd be better off not knowing the answer. But I can't resist. "You keep a log of all or your pickups and deliveries?"

"Yep."

"For how long?"

"Seven, eight years. Office policy. Why?"

I've become constitutionally incapable of leaving well enough alone. "Would you have a log from October? I was just wondering if you'd picked up something from the District Attorney's office and delivered it to our office? Would you be able to check that?"

"Let's take a look."

George turns several sheets on the clipboard before he finds it. When he does he points, and turns the log so I can see the entry.

"Sure enough," he says.

Just that easy and just that quick, I'm back to square one.

Why would Norman lie? Of course, there could be some other explanation. It could be just a coincidence that Norman asked the D.A. for Teddy's criminal record in September and the D.A. sent a package to our office in October.

My mind wants to pace, so my feet cooperate. I circle the mail room twice, my time sheets still in my hand, before I return to the table to tell more lies.

"Wayne," I say to the bookkeeper as he steps into his own double cubicle, "I've got a problem. I've lost my time sheets for the eleventh and twelfth of November and I've got to recreate them."

"Little creative recordkeeping, huh?"

"Look, Wayne," I persist, "I could probably figure accurately how I sent my time if I could compare Norman's records for those days. I was working with him. Could you check?"

"Sure. Norman's time sheets are always in ahead of time." Wayne runs his finger down some sort of ledger sheet, then rolls his chair over to a black filing cabinet and brings out a couple of folders.

"Here we go. But you must be remembering wrong, Matty, because Norman was out of town both days. Let's see. Yeah, he was at a medical-legal seminar. Gave the keynote address at a dinner on the evening of the eleventh, didn't return until the thirteenth. You in on that?" asked Wayne.

"Nooo. No. I wasn't. I guess I'm misremembering. Well, you're right, a little creativity with the time sheets *is* in order. I'll get them back to you this afternoon. By the way, where was the medical-legal conference?"

"Hold on a sec. Okay. L.A."

"California? Norman was in California?"

"No, Matty. L.A. is how Normal designates Los Alamos."

"You don't say?"

Detective Baca told me that Faye Stanton's alibi for the murder was a conference in Los Alamos. Coincidences abound! I wonder what Joe, who doesn't believe in coincidences, would make of these.

"Wayne, did Norman include the printed agenda with his receipts?"

"Uh, hold on, yeah, sure did—receipts attached to the brochure like he always does. I wish everybody would organize their receipts like Norman does. You could take a lesson."

"I could, indeed. Could you look on the brochure? What time was his speech, does it say?" I ask.

"Says here, '*Keynote—Norman Frederick—5:30 P.M., Dinner— 6:00 P.M., Conclusion Opening Session —7:30 P.M.*'"

Plenty of time after 7:30 to get to Santa Fe by the time a monster severed Isadora's hand from her body.

•   •   •

I've been sitting for too long staring at the neat stack of make-work memos on my desk. Long enough to consider the implications of today's events, to let them swirl like the sleet and hail outside my window. My reluctance to take this finished work down the hall to Norman has become a palpable dread.

Until I saw George's log, I'd actually bought Norman's story that he'd never seen a copy of Teddy's criminal record. Now I let myself picture Norman and Faye plotting a murder together in a hotel room in Los Alamos. My mind reels at the thought of those two doing anything else in a hotel room in Los Alamos.

Still, even with all that, never far from the pit of my stomach is the queasy dread of being wrong again. If I'm right now, I was wrong this morning about Agi Hadid. But it can't be helped. Rather than sit here paralyzed, I scoop up the files and the memos and head down the hall.

Norman isn't in his office. But I know he hasn't left for the day because his metal briefcase is still on his desk. That damned ubiquitous briefcase that he carries everywhere. I touch its cold side, twirl the combination with my thumb, and test the latch. I lift the handle, glide my thumb across the metal beneath until I feel the lettering. An "F," a "D," and an "R."

"Son of a bitch," I say aloud. But what I have my hand on is, indeed, a silver box.

I bolt from Norman's office and race to my own. I punch the speed dial for Max, and this time I tell his machine to pick me up after all. And I wait—and think.

There is only one way to make anyone take Norman seriously as a murder suspect and that is to find his motive. Isadora's money can't be enough. He's richer than she was. He's in love with his upright position in the community. But hell, maybe Faye has introduced him to some new positions, taken the waif to Babylon. And Isadora's money seemed to interest Faye very much.

I turn to my computer and call up Isadora's files. I spend some time going through her real estate and stock holdings looking for hanky-panky but finding none. I surely would have noticed it earlier if Norman had been messing around with

Isadora's assets while she was alive. Still, there seem to be a few things about both Norman and Isadora that I missed.

Finally, I turn to Isadora's probate file. Nothing odd here, either. Of course, the computer doesn't show the letters or documents which weren't generated by this office. Those are in the hard-copy files only, under Gloria Bachicha's control. But the computer file gives me a pretty good idea of what's happened so far. The will has been filed for probate. Notifications have gone out. Forms which will be sent later in the process have already been generated in final form. All is as it should be. And then, I come upon this letter:

> *Gus Fullerton, Esq.*
> *510 Central Ave., SW*
> *Albuquerque, NM, 87102*
>
> Re: <u>*Isadora Marie Stanton, Will, Your file #351*</u>
> *Dear Mr. Fullerton:*
> *I am in receipt of your recent correspondence regarding the Last Will and Testament of Isadora Marie Stanton. Thank you for responding to the Bar Bulletin Publication. I have reviewed the instrument prepared by you on the eleventh of November, this year. By date, it would appear to supersede the Will prepared for Miss Stanton in this office.*
> *I must tell you that Miss Faye Elizabeth Stanton, the sole heir under the original Will, has been notified by this office that her aunt appears to have executed a subsequent Will. Upon being informed that the document in your possession divides the residual estate into four equal shares and that only one of these shares goes to her, Miss Faye Stanton has expressed an interest in contesting the Will drafted by you. Among the grounds she may assert is the recent incarceration of one of the putative heirs. I believe you will find the enclosed news clippings detailing the charges against Theodore Bellasandro of interest. Further, as you recognize, the Will prepared by you contain several irregularities which may render it null and void.*
> *I enclose a copy of the original Last Will and Testament*

as well as a Memorandum of Law on the subject of multiple wills which you may find pertinent.

Finally, regarding your other inquiry, I have no information as to the whereabouts of either Juanita Marguerite Jakes or Jeffrey Thomas Marlson.

Sincerely
Norman J. Frederick, Esq.

Apparently, Isadora has left some money to Jeffrey Marlson, the grandson of her old friend, Skeeter. There is nothing further on the hard drive. I hurry to copy the address and phone number of the Albuquerque lawyer on notepaper and stuff it in my purse.

When I look up, I'm surprised to see how dark it has grown outside. Santa Fe's ever-changing winter weather is growing worse, and I punch Max's number again. This time he answers. I close everything down and head for the parking lot to wait for him.

Everyone is gone; the hallways are dark and empty. As I lock the front door behind me I know I am closing a door forever.

Outside, the sleeting rain is cold and the wind is ferocious. It threatens to knock me off my feet as I step into the parking lot. With my head lowered against the deafening wind, I move toward the single spot of light in a world of dark. On my way to the street lamp I notice a car idling in the corner of the lot—in the dark. Thinking it's Max, I wave and begin to move toward it. The car begins to move toward me with its lights off.

At the same time, a second car enters the lot from the other side. Its lights are on bright and it, too, is moving fast toward me. The lights blind me for a moment. I hear a screech of brakes as the first car suddenly cuts away, making tight skidding circles on the wet asphalt. My heart leaps and I turn to run. I slip. I regain my balance. I don't know who is friend and who is foe. Snow is clinging to my face, freezing me and obscuring my vision. Both cars are moving. One car reaches me as the other pulls out of its skid, and as it speeds off, passing under the streetlight, I think that it is gray.

The second car slides to a stop before me. Max throws the passenger door open and I run to it. He grabs my arms with both hands and pulls me to him so hard I can't breathe.

"Are you all right, Matty? Who was that? Are you all right? I thought he was going to hit you."

Through chattering teeth, I explain about silver boxes and the Los Alamos "coincidence."

Max is shaking himself as he backs out into the falling snow and heads up the hill. Although his car's heater is on full blast, I cannot stop my body from shivering. My story of this night comes out in little bursts.

"He did it," I stutter. "I think Norman killed her. It makes no sense, I know. Oh, God, Max, I'm so cold. I've never been so cold in my life. I can't stop shaking."

At my apartment, Max takes charge. He is all efficiency. The hot shower is started. My bed in the loft is stripped and re-made with fresh sheets. The heat is turned on high and a fire is set in the kiva below. When I emerge from the shower, I think that I'm ready for sleep and I think that I'm warm.

But, when Max touches my bare shoulder above the towel, the heat of his touch sears me. It is as though I have never felt heat until this instant, never been warm until now.

TWENTY-ONE

T HE FIRST TIME IS FAST AND GREEDY. BOTH OF US ARE AG-
gressive. I take quick hard breaths when I can tear my lips
from his flesh. It's over almost at once for him and he's a little
embarrassed.

"It's been a long time for me, too, I guess," he says.

He gets up then and I hear him downstairs fussing in the
kitchen. He comes back with tea and brandy and we talk some
more about the day, about my discoveries and my decisions.

"He did it!" I repeat. "I couldn't believe it but the son of a
bitch killed her. He must have, don't—"

"Shh, be quiet," he says. And I am.

We lie in the glow of firelight from below and I see in profile the edge of his nose and the curl of lip. I feel his hand begin
to move again.

The second time is slower and I come to know that he is,
after all, practiced and artful and I wonder a little about that. At
the top of the excruciating rise, up past tonight's fear and up

through the past years of dormancy, up past death and my own half-death, I reach a higher peak than I've ever felt before. Death has left the room and taken terror along.

Afterward, he rests his weight on me and strokes my hair. I haven't felt this spent-man heaviness pressing me into a mattress for four years and I squirm a bit. When he rolls away, we sleep and I do not wake again for over ten hours.

"So, this Joleen. She's a tough cookie, but sharp; you know, not like numb nuts. What do you call him? Rocks?"

Teddy's different today. The flashes of anger of our first session and the deep gloom of the last have been replaced by an eerie kind of calm. We could be neighbors chatting over the mailbox instead of through bullet-proof plastic. I haven't told him my news yet.

"She's all business," Teddy explains. "I kinda like her. She tells me we're gonna make decisions and we're gonna make 'em fast. Do I want a polygraph, yes or no? She told me which plea options she thinks I should consider and they sound a hell of a lot better comin' from her than from that box of Rocks. She even makes the insanity defense seem not too bad."

"Has Joleen talked to you about getting your record from the prison shrink in Baton Rouge?" I ask.

"Way she explained it, we may not be usin' that."

"What?"

"She says I should tell you to call her about that. She says she ain't too keen on me tryin' to explain it to you."

"I can imagine."

"Yeah, she says maybe my talkin' to you ain't such a hot idea at all anymore. She says my so-called friends are killin' me. Says, 'if these are your friends . . .'—well, you know. Her point—" Teddy holds up three fingers. "—first is, Charlie Lee flew the coop and ain't to be found to testify for me. Two, Jakes practically told the cops I did it. And you . . ." With the remaining finger he scratches the tip of his nose. ". . . You, she says, she'll talk to soon, but I'm supposed to tell you, butt out!"

A cold spot abruptly swells in my chest and then dissipates

slowly like the pain from a quick punch. I ask: "Is that what you want, for me to butt out?"

"Hell, no!"

The exclamation startles the guard. He wags his head a couple of times at Teddy, who ignores him and continues.

"You're my friend, Matty. I know you been tryin' to help me. I know what that's like, tryin' to help and sometimes screwin' up. But Joleen thinks maybe—"

The "screwing up" reference hurts my feelings a little and I start to interrupt, but he's going on.

"Hey, I'm not pissed at anybody," he says, leaning his chair back on two legs and pulling a cigarette from behind his ear. "I'm not even pissed at Charlie. He don't want to get involved. So, that's the way Charlie is. What good does it do to wish it was some other way? And Jakes, well, hell—"

"Stop! Stop being such a saint, will you! That's part of what I came here to tell you. I saw Jaunita again like you asked me to do. She's with Rickie and there's no chance she's leaving Hadid voluntarily. Which means she's with the cousin, too. Did Joleen tell you about Agi, Hadid's cousin?"

"Yeah, and that you got the cops involved to find out about him without her say-so. Joleen says she's got to control this case and you're too much of a loose cannon, Matty. How'd she put it? Your judgment is 'suspect' and she ain't sure you're worth 'baby-sitting.' "

Pretty much all of the breath is knocked out of me with that one.

"Okay," I say. "If that's the way it is, okay. But Rickie Hadid was there the night Isadora was killed, I'm certain of it. And he saw something."

Teddy brings his chair down flat. "You're shittin' me! What else did he say? What did he see?"

"He says he saw a guy with a metal case going into the house. Well, what Hadid actually said was 'a man with a silver box.' Anyway, the thing is, guess who has a metal case with a steel handle?"

Teddy shakes his head. He is staring intently at me.

"Norman Frederick, my boss!"

"No shit! And the Arab'll tell the cops this? Did you talk to that cop, Baca?"

"There's a problem . . ." I explain about Hadid's terror of deportation and his small extortion of money and about my hope of solving his other legal problem. "When he feels safe," I tell Teddy, "I think he'll talk, unless he's got more to fear from police questioning than he admits. Like maybe he's lying through his teeth, which is a distinct possibility."

"In spite of which, you mailed this immigration lawyer a five-hundred-buck retainer? Did you tell Joleen about what he saw?"

"Teddy, I've already told Joleen everything about both Rickie and Agi that I know. Hadid agreed I could tell you and her but he won't talk to anyone else until the I.N.S. thing is cleared up. I think he might skip if he's pressured. But there isn't enough time to deal with the I.N.S. before your own hearing in twelve days. Joleen must really press the judge to exclude the Louisiana evidence. Are you helping her? Trying to remember?"

"Well, see, Matty . . . there's somethin' you need to understand. Reason I'm feelin' better today is I come to a decision. Which is, I ain't goin' to trial on this thing no matter what."

He's picking a loose piece of tobacco from the end of the cigarette. He gives the job a lot of concentrated attention.

"You're not going to trial?" I'm stunned. "What the hell does that mean? You mean even if Joleen loses the motion on the twenty-third?"

"It means I ain't goin' to trial. Period! No matter what it takes. Joleen explained to me that they'll try to show how Izzy's mutilation . . . how it's like that thing before." There is panic in his voice. "They'll go into details. All the details about Louisiana."

"Yes," I say. "Yes! But only if the judge lets that evidence into the trial. That's what the motion on the twenty-third is all about. If you can help Joleen show the judge how it was different, the whole Louisiana thing can be kept out. You said you'd try . . ." I hear the plea in my voice and can't stop it, ". . . a little at a time. Remember, you said—"

"I did try, Matty. It's no good!" He says with grim resolve, "I ain't gonna relive that thing again, no matter what. I shut it out of my head even before it happened. I couldn'ta lived all these years if I didn't. It's been tearin' me up since you made me promise to remember. Izzy's gone. Now, I start thinkin' about Louisiana, all that again. Couple nights ago I woke up screamin' in my cell."

"I didn't know," I say. "I'm sorry. But Teddy, I think you've got to do it. Your life depends on it."

Smoke curls before his eyes and he closes his lids, shutting me out. The guard clears his throat a little and Teddy comes back from wherever he's been.

"Nope. I don't," says Teddy. "Goin' to the joint don't mean all that much to me. I done it once and lived to tell about it. I know how to handle myself on the inside. I don't wanna do it again, but there's worse things."

My instinct is to start arguing, to talk him out of this self-defeat. I can help him. I can keep a trial from happening because I can find out the truth before it comes to that. He doesn't have to consider a plea. But can I promise that? Do I trust myself? This much?

"Dammit, Teddy, you've got to find a way to go on from here."

Teddy starts choking and the guard comes over, takes the cigarette, stubs it out and doesn't move away. Teddy scoots his chair back and starts to rise.

"Yeah. I done that. I found my own way to go on. Now leave me be."

"Wait! Teddy, please wait, just a minute, please."

He sits back down listlessly and the guard retreats.

"Please, at least until the hearing. It's only twelve more days. I don't promise to come up with something, but let me try a little more. Just a few more days."

He puts his fingertips to the smudged plastic between us. "Just so long as you understand, I ain't goin' to trial."

I nod. "I just need some information from you."

"Okay, shoot," Teddy says wearily.

I ask and jot down his answers and ask some more. When I

leave the visiting room, I stop in the lobby to organize my notes: TITO SENA—*wood yard guy—drove Isadora sometimes before she hired Teddy.* MARIA TAFOYA—*Charlie Lee's girlfriend. No address except Santa Clara Pueblo.* JEFF MARLSON—*dead.*

Teddy hadn't remebered much, but he did remember a time a couple of years ago when he'd found Isadora crying. She told him she just got notice from the lawyers that Skeeter's grandson had died.

"So, what am I to make of that, do you think?" I demand of Max as he snips loose threads from my bathrobe sleeve with his toenail clippers.

"Teddy says that some years ago, Isadora cried when Skeeter Marlson's young grandson died. But a month ago, according to Norman's letter to an Albuquerque lawyer, Isadora may have made that same grandson one of her beneficiaries under a new will written the afternoon before she died. It makes no sense, does it?"

"No sense." Max has been answering in monosyllables like this for several minutes. I've worn both of us down after nearly two hours of going over and over the territory. Now he holds up one of my sleeves and then the other for inspection. "Neat as a pin," he decides.

"Okay, let's drop Jeff Marlson," I yield. "What I want is your expert opinion on Teddy's change in attitude, which I just don't get. He'd rather go to prison for the rest of his life than remember what happened?"

Max is of the opinion that it is sometimes dangerous to open past wounds.

"I thought the heart of your profession was uncovering and dealing with the awful events locked up in our minds. That was the prescription for me and my ugly past, as I recall."

"First, you were in a controlled setting with a professional." He shruggs at his lack of humility. "Second, you were able to examine your past and your own responsibility without your personality disintegrating. Third, that was *your* past. Mr. Bellasandro's past is something else. What he did as a young man is grotesque. The mutilation he refuses to remember may be tied up in childhood abuse—abuse of himself and of his mother, at the hands of a father figure. Maybe with the complicity or the ambivalence of his mother."

"How can you possibly know that?" I demand.

"I can't, of course, but it squares with what you've told me. He didn't mutilate *only* his stepfather, you know. I'm speculating, but it's a pretty classic formula for the rage that apparently erupted from him."

Both of us are silent, imagining our own version of another person's hell.

"Even so," I persist, "do you really think it's healthier to go to jail for a crime he didn't commit that to face his old crime?"

"I didn't say that, Matty. I just mean that sometimes the patient is the best judge of what he can handle at a given time. It's something like having a tumor tightly contained in a hard chrysalis somewhere in your body. Maybe the chrysalis can be opened, allowing the diseased cells to flood the body. Maybe the immune system is strong enough to destroy the cancer. But maybe the host is weak and the stuff behind the walls of the chrysalis is strong and avaricious. There are no X rays or blood tests to measure the aggression of a tumor of the soul. If the patient tells you it will kill him to open up the chrysalis, it can be terribly dangerous to pry open the casing without a life support system in place. Dangerous to release the memories."

"And dangerous not to?"

"Yes, that too."

"What about me?"

"What about you?"

"Your analogy: how does it apply to me? Do you think I— *we*—opened my sack of killer cells during therapy? And if we did, did the patient live or die?"

Max's hands, which have been rubbing my shoulders, still. My immediate impression is that we have reverted without warning back to doctor and patient.

"What do *you* think?" he asks me.

I hesitate. "I think it's the wrong illness metaphor. My mistakes and failure and guilt, they're more like malaria. They laid me out; sapped my vitality. This disease never quite killed me; never quite let me live."

Max leans down to kiss my head very, very gently.

"Until now," I go on firmly. "I feel something like potency, validity again. God forbid, Max, I feel almost righteous."

"You're involved," he says. "Now that the gears have meshed, you're moving again. This is pretty heady stuff, Matty. It's also very tricky stuff. When this is over you may not be able to go back to cohabiting with your old demons."

I begin rubbing my temples and now Max's fingers cover my own until he is doing the massage, which spreads from my temples down to my face to my neck and shoulders. My arms circle his hips and I pull him to me. It is in that position that he tells me for the first time about Sarah.

Sarah Cortino is eight years old and lives with her mother Enid, a shrink, in New York City. Enid no longer uses the name Cortino. She resumed use of her maiden name when she and Max concluded what he describes as the world's most amicable divorce. Sarah, whom I never heard about until this second, turns out to be the center of Max's life. They spend at least three months a year together, he explains. In the summer, she comes to live with him in Santa Fe and one month a year, this month, he travels to New York where he stays with his daughter. Guess where?

By the time all of this comes out, we have left the kitchen, paced the living room, returned to the kitchen, washed dishes together and he has followed me upstairs to the bathroom in the loft. He now sits on the edge of the tub and watches me brush my teeth.

"There was no reason to tell you before, Matty. And what's happening to you and me has been happening so fast there's been no time."

At my raised brow he squirms a bit.

"Okay," he allows. "You're right. I should've told you sooner. But I was worried. I still am. Having another guy in your life with a child from a previous marriage isn't a scenario I would have wished for you. For that matter, having an ex-therapist who can't keep his hands off of you isn't exactly a prescription for mental health either."

"Is it my mental health you're worried about or yours?"

"Either. Both. Do you know there is actually a New Mexico law against what we did last night?"

I cock my head in disbelief.

He sighs. "Well, association rules and regulations anyway. A psychologist may not engage in sexual intimacies with a client or former client to whom he has rendered professional services within the previous twenty-four months."

"You been memorizing the Code of Professional Conduct?"

"I looked it up. Seemed relevant."

"So let me see . . . six months until making love isn't moral turpitude?" I sneer. "Last night was very, very premature ejaculation?"

He looks miserable, but I don't much care. Fuck other people's moral prescriptions. If he wants to feel guilty about something, he can feel guilty about neglecting to tell me about his little upcoming trip to stay with his wonderful ex-wife. God-damn him to hell anyway!

"When are you leaving? When are you coming back?" I'm all business now, brushing my hair and watching him in the mirror.

"I would have been leaving in three days. I usually stay in the city for four weeks. I clear my calendar every year for this. It's our time, Sarah's and mine. You understand? But I can't leave you like this." He motions to the new double locks on the doors and windows.

"Do not dare to presume that I'm going to let you martyr yourself to stay here and protect me," I snap. "So, you are leaving in three days and you will live . . ." I ask incredulously, ". . . you will live in your ex-wife's house . . . for a month?"

"Enid and I are friends. She's Sarah's mother. I care about her and I respect her, Matty. But the romance died long ago. There was never a moment in our marriage when I felt the kind of passion I felt with you last night."

We've worked our way through my nighttime ablutions. I'm washed and combed and dressed for bed. There is nothing more to do but to get into it. Certainly I had expected, when I came home to find him in my kitchen, that we would end up at this point together, as we had last night and as I'd begun to hope we would for nights to come. He looks wretched and I care a little more than I did a moment ago.

"Go home," I say. "Let's talk tomorrow."

After he leaves, I can't sleep. I hunt restlessly for something to read. As though drawn by a magnet I end up in the fortress of dry-erase boards amid my investigation notes. I unpin the *Native American News* and read the whole thing. I read about Native American art, and about Native American health issues. I peruse the story about Fetal Alcohol Syndrome:

"FAS children," the article says, *"have a considerable range of intellectual functioning, with IQ scores from 16 to 105. Many are of short stature, slight build, and have a small head."* Juanita is definitely not of slight build, I think. *"Such children are hungry for attention and, despite their many problems, have a great capacity for love."*

Above the article is a fuzzy picture of a group of grown-ups with FAS children. The caption reads: *"Care often involves foster or adoptive parenting."* Why did Isadora keep such articles? Because she was responsible for Juanita. She tried, in her own way, to do her best for the girl. Below the article is a list of helpful steps such parents can take. Isadora has underlined these.

The inexplicable detritus of Isadora's life is scattered at my feet and pinned and scrambled on the boards before my eyes.

TWENTY-TWO

FRIDAY, DECEMBER 13

I ALWAYS LIKE THE DRIVE TO JOE'S HOUSE. THE GRADUATING foothills leading to the Sangre de Cristo range begin just north of town and ascend in steps to snow-capped peaks. Once again the weather has made a radical turnabout and the evening is mild and lovely. I had to call Joe. I owed him that much. But he was out of the city and wouldn't be back until tonight's Christmas party.

Liza had insisted I come. "You can talk to Joe there. Don't be a goose. Of course you're coming."

Bishop's Lodge Road continues past the turnoffs to the ski basin on my right and the Governor's Mansion on my left, toward Bishop's Lodge, once a retreat for Willa Cather's Bishop Lamy, now another tourist hotel.

I started to beg off but Liza added, "If you're worried about Norman, he won't be here." I didn't even ask how she knew I would be worried about seeing Norman. But into my hesitation she laughed and explained, "Joe tells me everything, my dear."

A couple of miles into the piñon- and juniper-spotted knolls, I turn off onto an unnamed dirt road, down-shift, and climb until I reach the circle drive at the cap of the highest dot of land for miles.

Tonight, the parking tarmac around the Danforth house is jammed with Mercedeses, Jeeps, Cadillacs, and battered pickups, reflecting the deliberately egalitarian guest list which marks most Santa Fe events. I notice that about a quarter of them are gray. I find a place far down the dirt road and begin the climb back to the house on foot, marveling as I walk at the vision spread out below me. Joe is a lucky guy. From here, you can see all of Santa Fe's night lights, the thin crimson line of sunset in the distant western sky, and the face of the snow-clad peaks of the Sangre de Cristos, 180 degrees to the east. The lot alone must have cost a fortune. Why am I here?

Liza had sweetened the pot. "Celestine is back in town. She'll be here."

"How did you know I was interested in—?"

"I talked to her this morning. She's just back from Mexico City, you know. She told me she had umpteen messages from you."

And so I agreed to come.

As I approach, the brick walkway and lower third of the house are awash with crescents of soft light emanating from an in-ground system. Guests mill and cluster on the broad flagstone entryway, taking in the unseasonably warm December night. As I angle my way around and among them, I crane a little to get better views and pick up snippets of conversation. This I do for no better reason than to feed my party curiosity. I don't party well, but I always imagine that everyone else is having a great time.

I know from previous visits that the back part of the Danforth house hangs over an embankment and is two stories deep, with floor-to-ceiling windows on both levels. But the front is low-slung, giving the deceptive first impression that this lavish and complicated modern home is really an old New Mexican hacienda. The visual white lie is ubiquitous in Santa Fe, where many choose to disguise twenty-first-century convenience in eighteenth-century charm, and city ordinances even mandate architecture that harkens back to Spanish colonial days.

The flagstone gives way to brick as I pass under a portico roofed with sturdy log vigas and crisscrossed twig *latias*. The entrance doors are hand-carved antiques rescued by Liza Danforth herself from an abandoned church in Mexico. Tonight, these doors are flung wide, and laughter and live music spills out. Two guests or servants of indeterminate sex dressed in matching red velvet fringe, each holding a small bouquet of tulip glasses, hug me between them, press a glass into each of my hands, and move on to others arriving behind me. I glimpse Joe and Liza in a loose receiving line across the foyer and wave tentatively with one of the glasses of champagne. I skirt the knot of people and move beyond the foyer down into the immense sunken center of the house.

The fourteen-foot-high ceiling of this room is domed in glass like a planetarium. Just below the dome but well above the heads of noisy guests are sheets of painted canvas twisted into streamers. I know that these streamers are art but they look for all the world like decorations at a high school prom.

"Drinking for two, I see."

The voice from somewhere over my shoulder is Eamonn Migill's. I arrange a smile and turn to face him. The reporter is drinking from a blue bottle of mineral water.

"This crowd seems to get bigger every year, doesn't it?" I say.

"Indeed. The first real party of the season. Liza has become quite the significant hostess. And how not?" Eamonn points with his blue bottle around the room at each of the three bars, every one a unique little spectacle in decorator magic.

"The food alone can't be beat this side of the real White House, eh? The firm must be doing extremely well. Or is this, perhaps, Lady Liza's very own doing?" Eamonn continues with a half wink. "Rumor is that there is Old Boston family money there." Eamonn never stops digging for information. His method is to drop tidbits of his own, then to be so persistent that if you speak to him at all you end up telling him more than you wished you had. I sip champagne to avoid conversation and the instant it hits my tongue I recognize that this is the good stuff.

Eamonn sees my expression and nods knowingly. "And multiply that, say, fifty dollars a bottle, by a hundred and fifty or so very thirsty visitors."

I've thought about Joe's wealth before, of course. Maybe the old Frederick, Danforth & Rodriguez could have supported the lifestyle of Joe and Liza Danforth, with this house, another in Vail, expensive vacations, two children in good schools, and a third "finding himself" in Europe, more or less permanently. But these days law firm profits can't support this opulence. The money could be coming from Joe's investments; he's known to be shrewd and lucky. But I, too, have heard the gossip that Liza came from money and that she's the one who notches their lifestyle up from mere comfort to grandeur.

As Eamonn and I reach something of a conversational standoff, an even less welcome guest makes his way over to us. Judge Felix Sandoval reaches his hand out to me, then to Eamonn, and gives each of us a perfunctory little shake. My guess is Sandoval doesn't like Eamonn any more than he likes me, but the judge is not the only one in this political town who works to stay in touch with the press. In the years since Isadora and I stood before him to defend her traffic violation, Sandoval has risen a judicial notch and now sits on the bench of the State District Court.

"Quite a shindig," he says. He speaks with a slight slur.

"Good to see you, Your Honor," says Eamonn. "Yes, Matty here and I were just saying the Danforth parties are becoming quite famous. Carol Burnett and John Ehrlichman were guests at the last dinner party I attended here. The place is lousy with luminaries tonight."

"I'm surprised you're not out there rubbing elbows among them, Eamonn," I hear myself saying. "You kind of thing, I would think."

"Uh-huh, well, Ms. Donahue, I'm getting a little long in the tooth to be star-struck. Actually, at the moment, I'm more interested in the hot local story. What's the word these days on the Stanton murder?"

I smile, but look for a graceful exit. I don't want to have this discussion.

"Thought you might be able to add some insight," Migill persists. "What was the old lady really like? How did she get hooked up with this Bellasandro creep in the first place?"

Judge Sandoval has been listening with undisguised interest and now takes a deep swig of something that looks like glue out of an oversized tumbler.

"Well, that's an interesting story, isn't it, Ms. Donahue?" The judge has been drinking too much. He seems primed to titillate the press at my expense.

"Is it, now?" asks Eamonn, opening both arms wide to gather in the two of us, hapless bits of fodder. "Is it, indeed?"

I am rescued by the arrival of Liza, with Joe in tow. She is resplendent in black and silver tonight.

"Felix, I didn't see you come in." Liza does a little cheek-aiming lip-popping thing with Sandoval and then taps her knuckles against Eamonn's chest. "What is this old reprobate digging for now, Judge?"

Sandoval ho-hos silently like Dopey chucked under the chin by Snow White. Joe is nuzzling Liza's neck but she shrugs herself free and beckons to me with her forefinger. Obediently, I follow her through the crowd to a group of native Santa Feans bedecked in enough silver and turquoise to sink a ship or mount a war.

"Celestine, dear, look who I have here. This is Matty Donahue."

The group opens to make room for us. Though a tiny woman, Celestine Abeyta C'de Baca controls the center of the group. She is wearing a wine-colored velvet Navajo shirt over what used to be called a squaw skirt and used to sell in Penney's for less than ten dollars. In the age of political correctness this tiered and roughly pleated garment, once common in the villages, has been renamed a "straw" skirt and is now sold from Taos to New York for hundreds of dollars. But it isn't Celestine's clothes one notices. It is the jewelry that nearly engulfs her. An enormous and genuine concho belt circles her waist. Not one, but two, silver-and-turquoise squash-blossom necklaces cover her chest. Three bracelets on each arm and silver rings on nearly every finger. Her long steel-gray hair is piled high and held by an ornament resembling a tiara more than a silver comb.

Celestine says to me, "Why, Matty, how nice. I've been meaning to return your calls."

"I called to ask about Isadora Stanton," I say. "She made an appointment with you?"

"She certainly did. I'd only just returned when Liza told me the terrible news. Of course, I thought immediately about Isadora Stanton's visit. I even thought to call the police, but one gets so busy. And they already had their man, don't you know."

Celestine claims to trace her ancestry to the conquistadores. She lets everyone know she is entitled to deference, so she gets it. The others in the group stop to listen to us.

"What did Isadora want?" I ask. "Was it about an engagement ring. An Indian piece?"

"Aren't you the prescient one? But it wasn't an engagement ring and it wasn't an Indian piece."

"What then?"

"It appeared to be a Zuni nature ring made by Charles La Loma. His rings have become quite valuable. The last La Loma I remember being sold fetched over thirty thousand dollars at a private auction. One simply cannot compete any more. That piece was bought by a Japanese group."

"Japanese?"

"Matty, dear, these days the real market for the very old pieces is international. At the moment, it seems, the world is hungry for genuine tribal jewelry. We just have to ride it out. We can pick them up on the way down in five years."

"But you said this wasn't an Indian piece, the one Isadora brought to you?"

"No. The counterfeiter didn't know the artist's personal history. The initials 'CLL' were carved on the inside—customary for Zuni artists to sign their pieces with initials." She turns to the others. "But La Loma never used his own initials. He used a personal stamp—a tiny three-dimensional pyramid stamped into every piece," she explains. "I hadn't yet seen one of the new Middle Eastern counterfeits. But that was my guess."

"They're taking over," a woman in bright red interrupts.

"Thirty years ago, when all this started, it did no harm. Some of the tribal turquoise mines were playing out, so local artists had to look elsewhere. Iran, where they had been mining turquoise since the days of Persian princes, became the new source. But when the Shah was gone, friendly business with Iran ended."

Celestine gives the woman in red a cold look. She is the expert, after all. "So, Matty, other countries in the area, acting as middlemen, got into the act. Initially, they just supplied the stone. Then some Arab merchant families began to manufacture pieces for the foreign markets themselves."

Everyone in the group is contributing something now. "They called them 'Ancient Persian,' " says one.

"When the appetite for authentic pieces from our southwest tribes reached Europe, it was a natural transition. The merchant families were already in place from Zurich to Shanghai," says another.

Celestine frowns them into silence and continues the explanation herself. "To make them seem authentic, you see, they build a history here, from the old trading posts through discovery in family collections, to auctions or private sales here in New Mexico. That's partly why they keep an operation here. And the fact that this is where the design knowledge is. Left to their own devices, the Arabs stray from the authentic designs. Their ornamentation gets ever more elaborate."

"Bad for the reputation of the whole state," opines the woman in red.

Suddenly Liza draws me aside again. "Whoops," she says. "I'm really sorry, Matty. Honestly, I didn't expect him to come. You won't make a scene, will you?"

I follow her eyes. Norman is standing stiffly with his sturdy wife Barbara, among a group of other lawyers standing stiffly with their own sturdy spouses, near a minibar commandeered by them so as to avoid the glitteratti. Norman has always been more comfortable with his own kind. Or so I thought until I began to imagine a new picture: a picture of stuffy and righteous Norman Frederick in cahoots with—if not in bed with—a one-eyed, amoral bisexual trying to steal back her inheritance.

Liza and Celestine eventually separate and a new conflu-
ence of guests forms, leaving me in a little backwater eddy.

I stare at Norman for a long contemplative moment. My
second glass of champagne is gone and a third or fourth has appeared magically in my hand. I suck the courage out of it and
move across the room, as stately as the Titanic.

"Good evening, Norman . . . Barbara." I exchange nods
with the other two attorneys and tentative smiles with their
wives. Norman becomes even more rigid and tries to kill me
with his aura.

"I'm surprised to see you here, Ms. Donahue. Since you
haven't been at work I assumed perhaps you'd made other
arrangements."

"Well, Norman, I haven't been to work for three days because on Tuesday I made a couple of interesting discoveries.
Would you like to know what they were?"

"Ms. Donahue, it really isn't appropriate to be discussing
office business here. Perhaps next week." He grimaces an apology
for my lack of courtesy to the other lawyers.

"I discovered that a packet from the District Attorney's office had been delivered to you, after all."

"I don't know what you're talking about and frankly I don't
care." He turns to the others. "I must ask you to excuse—"

"And should I assume you don't know anything about
what happened in the office parking lot late Wednesday night,
either?"

Barbara Frederick tries nervously to salvage something
civil by explaining to the others how hard her husband works.
"Why, it's nothing for this man to work all night and into—"

"Which reminds me," I interrupt, nodding toward Barbara,
"you probably don't know anything about a hotel room in Los
Alamos either." Ah, to hell with it, I think, and face him directly.
"It's one thing, Norman, to help Faye Stanton. Another to risk
your license for her."

Talk of risking licenses tends to cause constricting spasms
in the throats of Esquires. And Barbara's face, which she is
slowly turning to Norman, is stricken.

"Faye Stanton?" Her voice starts flat and soft but gathers

energy fast. "What have you been doing with that creature?" she asks Norman. "What is she talking about?" Barbara sloshes her champagne in my direction.

The others have copped quick mutual glances and now they keep identical smile-masks on as they back away. Norman's attention is torn between the gathering storm at his right and me, sweet and calm, as the eye.

"Now, Babs," he begins, "Faye's a client—"

"You said never again! You said you were disgusted with her life-style. You promised. You—"

I leave them like that and make my way to the door. I don't know a lot more than when I came in, but I do know that I haven't been completely wrong. It gratifies me one jot, like a two-dollar player whose sure thing has just come in.

Max is asleep on my couch and my turning the key in the lock doesn't rouse him. I slip off the high heels that I wear once or twice a year, pour a glass of wine, and sit in the rocking chair across from him waiting for him to waken. I study his sleeping features and try to picture the next month, or forever, without him. There is a French proverb that goes, *Patirr c'est mourir un peu*—to part is to die a little. How much of me would die if I never saw this man again?

The partings in my life began with my father when I was three and continued with my mother's wanderings during my adolescence. Then John and Tommy and, of course, Isadora. Max's fingers loosely hold a stem of his eyeglasses and his face seems simpler without them, more vulnerable.

Over the last twenty-four hours, I've given the situation some thought and concluded that I'm glad he cares so much about his daughter. I don't give a rat's ass if he stays in his ex-wife's house. I want him back. But what I do care about, what I can't ignore, is his obviously deep dilemma about my status as former patient and current lover.

What do I do about that? If I let my neurosis surface, what does Max, my lover, do? Call in Max, my shrink? And what if I try to keep my fears and dreads under wrap? Not possible. Not real. Watching him sleep is restful, though, and pretty soon my own eyes begin to close.

When I open them again, he's gone. The letter he's left behind is quite wonderful and I feel the love coming through the words. But the bottom line is that he has some issues to work out. He has to do it himself. He'll call every week from New York, and if I need him he'll come back at a moment's notice.

TWENTY-THREE

---◦◦◦---

I WAKE UP IN MY COLD BED THIS MORNING, MY MIND CLING-ing to a dream of Isadora in *her* bed on the last night of her life. My plan this morning is to drive seventy miles south to pay a visit to the Albuquerque lawyer, Gus Fullerton. So I try to shake the dream fragment. But my mind has a mind of its own. I give in and consciously help get the picture of Isadora in better focus. I've visited her in the evenings so many times I could imitate her evening ritual. So I do.

I raise myself to a sitting position and fluff the pillows around my back as she did every night. She would have been wearing her bed jacket. For verisimilitude, I slip on a sweater and am grateful for the warmth. Isadora was murdered on a cold November night. She would have had the quilt pulled up over her skinny legs. The next morning, there was no quilt. What else is missing? I close my eyes, deliberately recreating Isadora's bedroom behind my lids. The tin-framed mirror above the long table, the chair pulled into the center of the room, the nightstand next to her bed where she kept—what had Rickie Hadid called the contents—"Old-woman junk?"

I mentally sort through his listing: the engagement ring, medicines, eyeglasses, and, "As Allah is my witness, handcuffs." If Hadid is to be believed, he saw handcuffs in the drawer within hours or even minutes of Isadora's murder. I remember Faye Stanton's explanation of how they got there, how Isadora used to cuff herself to things to keep people from budging her around against her will. I shake my head at the thought. Isadora's behavior frequently looked loony from the outside. But from the inside, I think she was often battling for something more precious than life. Once, Isadora deigned to explain her curmudgeon ways to Teddy and me. She said, "By the time a woman's ninety, she better be wily and she better be cussed. Soon as she's not, they'll start stealing her freedom away a tea-spoon at a time."

When Faye looked into the drawer weeks after the murder, the handcuffs were no longer there. Perhaps the police took them. I race downstairs and untack my copy of the police re-port from the dry board. There is no mention of handcuffs.

While I dress for the drive to Albuquerque, I try again to conjure the murder scene; I wonder if the Isadora who sat against fluffed pillows facing her killer was the loony Isadora or the wily, cussed Isadora.

Gus Fullerton's office is in a white clapboard Victorian on a narrow lot wedged between a burrito stand and a sleek modern office building. The irregular blent of high-rise and humble in this area of Albuquerque is the bite-print of a city eating its past.

There is no parking space next to the house so I park, as all of Fullerton's visitors must, in the paved lot of the modern building next door. A directory on that building identifies each of its twenty-three occupants as attorneys.

Crossing the parking lot to Fullerton's lowly dwelling I skip down a dozen or so notches in the professional pecking order. In Fullerton's window, a sign made with gold-rimmed stick-on letters identifies G. Fullerton as a solo practitioner. Like his yellow page ad, it says he keeps Saturday hours, takes Visa and MasterCard, and that no appointment is necessary.

The door is ajar so I push it a bit and call "Hello . . ." When no one answers, I move through the tiny reception area to an office in back. Computer stations and file cabinets surround a desk behind which a doughy pink man with a fringe of red hair sits. He looks up and smiles.

"I'm sorry," I say, "there was no one out there. . . . Do you have a minute?"

"Come in, come in. There's never anyone out there anymore. Secretaries are a waste of my clients' money. I can do everything on a computer a secretary could do, and I can do it twice as fast . . . And . . . I can always spare time for a new client. What can I do you for?"

"I, uh, I'm not a client."

Fullerton tugs at his ear. "Bill collector? Fortune teller? Lost waif?"

"Lawyer."

"Be darned. I was hoping for lost waif. For other lawyers, I can spare about five minutes."

"I'm with Frederick and Danforth . . . in Santa Fe."

"Shee—it." Fullerton grimaces like he just sucked on a lime. "Look, miss, I went over the crap Normal Frederick sent down and I've already agreed that the will I drafted for Isadora Stanton has a few problems—no addresses on the beneficiaries, no named executor. She was in such a hurry and she said she'd send me that information later. Well . . . you must know the rest. Personally, I don't think the problems are fatal, but I don't have a client to protect, and except for the old lady's killer, I still don't even know where any of the putative heirs are. Like I told your boss, I had to file the thing but he's got no big quarrel with me. So, what did he send you down here for?"

"Norman didn't send me. I'm here on my own. I do know where one of the heirs is, but I'm not here to cause you any trouble. I'd just like a little information about what happened the day before Miss Stanton died. How did she find you? What kind of mood was she in? Did she say why . . . ?"

As I'm talking, Gus Fullerton turns to the bank of file cabinets behind his desk, opens a couple of drawers, pulls a pint of Old Granddad out of one and a thin manila folder out of the other. He pours the whisky into his coffee cup and taps the file nervously.

"Look, I don't want grief over this."

Whether he wants grief or not, Fullerton's probably going to get some over this. But not from me. Not right now. I nod, and reluctantly he shows me the file and tells me what he knows about that day.

Isadora came in about two in the afternoon of November eleventh, he tells me, demanding that he write her up a new will "right now!" She'd already tried any number of the twenty-three gray suits next door, but she was apparently so disagreeable some annoyed soul had sent her over here to Gus.

"And I must admit"—he laughs—"that old lady was a pip. Here she comes dragging in this old guy, even older than she is. First, I figured he was the husband and they wanted a simple will drawn up. This is the kind of junk they send me from next door all the time. So I called up one of the pre-programmed form-wills on my computer. But, it turns out, the woman's got a couple *million* bucks and the old man's *not* the husband after all. His name is Tito Sena; he's her chauffeur or something and she just dragged him in here to witness her will. Some witness—read no English whatsoever. I suppose your boss told you that, too."

Fullerton floats a brief mea culpa for the too common sin among street lawyers of taking on work they don't have the expertise to do. His defense basically is that Isadora wouldn't go away unless he drafted a new will for her. She didn't tell him where she'd been earlier that day or why the new will was so urgent. She just banged her cane on his desk, declared tomorrow wasn't soon enough, and threw hundred-dollar bills at him. He figured what the hell, took the necessary information from her, and sent them to wait at the burrito stand while he filled in the blanks. Isadora was satisfied and on her way back to Santa Fe by four in the afternoon of the day she died.

Fullerton pours himself another healthy shot and repeats that he doesn't want any trouble. While he sips, I scan the provisions of the will Isadora had tried to make. There are a few specific bequests, after which the residue of her estate is to be divided equally among Theodore Bellasandro, Juanita Jakes, Faye Stanton, and Jeffrey Marlson. Among the specific bequests are three names I recognize well. They are the names on the checks I write once every month—my ex-clients who get payments from me in recompense for my past sins. So this is why Isadora didn't share her intention to change her will with me. She intended to pay off my debts. Jesus!

"Look . . ." says Fullerton, " . . . you take that copy if you want to. If you find the people she named there . . . well, I guess a judge can decide whether it's a valid will or not. If it turns out this thing is void, so be it. But I've been sued before and I'm telling you right now, I've got no malpractice insurance and I've got no assets."

I leave my car in the law firm's lot and walk in the other direction—toward the sleazier end of the street. Small law offices in stucco houses give way to bail-bondsmen and pawn shops.

Did Isadora use her handcuffs the night she died? Why? And who has them now?

The pawn shop I choose is a once-white cinder-block building covered with graffiti and heavy iron grillwork. The door has been reinforced with rusty metal plates and I have to shove hard to open it. Inside is a world of little light; crowded rows of military gear, luggage, boom boxes, cassettes; walls of weapons and guitars.

Near the service counter, two guys are drinking coffee out of Styrofoam cups and leaning their kitchenette chairs back against the wall. The one who looks like Charles Manson doesn't move. The other one sports a military buzz-cut and a baby blue T-shirt that fails to encase either his bulging biceps or his hard potbelly. This one rises, moves to the counter, and offers to help me.

"I, uh, I'd like to look at some handcuffs, if you have any."

The buzz-cut grins at Manson briefly but then begins to sort through items behind the counter. Manson says, "Show the lady the fur-lined cuffs," and "Hey, lady, what ya want is a pair of leg-irons to go with 'em. Give your man his money's worth . . ." I try to ignore his continuing commentary in this vein while the guy at the counter, who says he's an off-duty sheriff's deputy, demonstrates the cuffs.

"See," he says, swinging out a sawtoothed curve of shining chrome. He slaps it on my wrist and the jaw snaps home. The cuff feels heavy, firm, and cold. The chain is much shorter than I'd imagined, only two links. Buzz-cut explains that a long chain is dangerous, a felon can wrap it around a cop's neck. I pay thirty-two dollars for the handcuffs and I'm glad to be getting out of here. Manson has begun to sing "Anticipation."

But on my way out, I notice five or six metal cases hanging on the wall above the used-luggage bin. Did Norman sever Isadora's hand because he wanted to frame Teddy for the murder he was about to commit? Or was it because of the handcuffs? The handcuffs and his briefcase? I ask Buzz-cut to get the cases down. He lectures while I examine the handles and connecting rivets.

"Like this one here," he points to a cheap dented case, "you got no security whatsoever with this."

"But some of 'em's tight as a nun's pussy," contributes Manson, who has roused himself to follow us.

I choose the case which most resembles Norman's and try the short-linked handcuffs in two or three positions. I try opening the case with my free hand and I try opening the cuffs with the key while my other hand is still attached to the case.

"How would you get the handcuffs off?" I ask Buzz-cut. "I mean, if you didn't have a key?"

"You got heavy-duty bolt-cutters?"

"I don't know. Let's say I don't, how do I get them off?"

"You don't."

                    •   •   •

The drive back to Santa Fe is grimly satisfying. For weeks my mind has been stirring a muddy mix of obscure bits and pieces surrounding the murder. But now, as long afternoon shadows obscure the desert landscape, the image of the last moments of Isadora's life is finally starting to clear.

TWENTY-FOUR

———◦◦◦———

Monday, December 16

THEY SAY THAT BAD THINGS COME IN THREES.

Mine come in fours.

On my kitchen table lay the four things that came to me today.

An hour or so ago, I cut the story in *At Large* and laid it beside the three letters. I've read all four pieces of paper several times. And now I shuffle them around like the objects in a shell game, arranging and rearranging, wondering if there is any logical order in which to put them.

Each represents a different kind of termination: my job, my reputation, my new mission, my friendship. Like the dead ends of a maze. The first message of ending was expected. The second was damaging, and the third baffling and painful. But, curiously enough, it is the fourth which devastates me.

FREDERICK & DANFORTH P.C.
Attorneys at Law
227 South Don Conderras
Santa Fe, New Mexico 87502

Ms. Matty Donahue
940 Canyon Road
Santa Fe, New Mexico 87502

Re: Termination

Dear Ms. Donahue:

Your services on behalf of clients at the firm of Frederick & Danforth are no longer desired. Your employment is hereby terminated, effective immediately.

Pursuant to your employment contract, you are entitled to compensation through this date, plus two weeks' severance pay and a pro-rata share of the calculated bonus. A check for that amount is enclosed.

You may have anticipated that the firm would provide a favorable reference. Under the circumstances, we are not willing to do so.

The office courier, George Perea, will contact you shortly. Please turn over to Mr. Perea any files or other property of the firm you may have in your possession.

AT LARGE IN SANTA FE

MURDER AND MUTILATION—
ONE LAWYER'S JUDGMENT
BY: EAMONN MIGILL

AS THE TOP LAYER OF MYSTERY CLEARS FROM THE STANTON MURDER CASE, A SUBTERRANEAN WORLD OF INTRIGUE IS REVEALED

BELOW. THE INVESTIGATION OF THIS CITY'S MOST GRUESOME CRIME RENDERED UP AN EXPLANATION IN RECORD TIME. WE ALL KNOW NOW THAT THEODORE BELLASANDRO, ISADORA STANTON'S ALLEGED ASSAILANT, HAS A HISTORY STEEPED IN BLOOD AND MUTILATION. WHAT WE HAVEN'T KNOWN UNTIL NOW IS THAT THE CONNECTION WHICH BINDS VICTIM AND ACCUSED IS A LOCAL MEMBER OF THE BAR WITH A HISTORY OF HER OWN.

THIS REPORTER HAS LEARNED THAT MATTY DONAHUE, A LAWYER WITH THE FIRM OF FREDERICK & DANFORTH, PLAYED A PIVOTAL ROLE IN PLACING BELLASANDRO IN THE HOME OF HER CLIENT, ISADORA STANTON. MAGISTRATE COURT DOCUMENTS REVEAL THAT IN A THREE-YEAR-OLD CASE AGAINST THE DECEASED, IT WAS MS. DONAHUE WHO REQUESTED THAT THE COURT APPLY A UNIQUE SOLUTION TO A RELATIVELY MINOR DRIVING VIOLATION.

THE SOLUTION? INSTALL THEODORE BELLASANDRO IN THE EMPLOY OF ISADORA STANTON. ALTHOUGH BELLASANDRO'S PREVIOUS MURDER CONVICTION WAS THEN A MATTER OF PUBLIC RECORD IN LOUISIANA, THERE IS NO ASSERTION, AT THIS TIME, THAT DONAHUE KNEW HE WAS A MONSTROUS KILLER WHEN SHE REQUESTED THE COURT ORDER.

DISTRICT JUDGE FELIX SANDOVAL, WHO SAT ON THE MAGISTRATE BENCH AT THAT TIME, WOULD LIKE TO SEE THAT QUESTION INVESTIGATED. "THERE WERE IMPLIED ASSURANCES TO THE COURT BY A MEMBER OF THE BAR,"

HE TOLD THIS REPORTER. JUDGE SANDOVAL CALLED IT "A VERY SERIOUS MATTER."

THIS IS NOT MS. DONAHUE'S FIRST BRUSH WITH THE BAR. ONLY FOUR YEARS AGO, SHE WAS DISCIPLINED FOR VIOLATING RULES AGAINST CONFLICT OF INTEREST AND NEGLECTING CLIENTS. THE NEGLECT WAS APPARENTLY PRECIPITATED BY THE WIDELY REPORTED MURDER-SUICIDE OF A FATHER AND SON IN ALBUQUERQUE. WHAT WAS NOT WIDELY REPORTED AT THE TIME WAS THAT THE SON, WHO FIRED FIVE BULLETS INTO HIS FATHER'S BODY BEFORE TURNING THE GUN ON HIMSELF, WAS MS. DONAHUE'S CLIENT.

WHAT WAS LIKEWISE NOT REPORTED AT THAT TIME WAS THAT THE SAME MATTY DONAHUE ARGUED LONG AND HARD AND, UNFORTUNATELY FOR ALL CONCERNED, SUCCESSFULLY, THROUGH ADMINISTRATIVE APPEALS AND TO THE DISTRICT COURT, TO HAVE THE SON, THOMAS ELICH, RELEASED FROM THE JUVENILE PSYCHIATRIC CARE UNIT. IS IT COINCIDENCE WHEN A LAWYER TWICE USES THE COURTS TO PLACE KILLERS NOT ONLY IN OUR MIDST BUT IN THE VERY HOMES OF THEIR VICTIMS? PERHAPS IT IS COINCIDENCE; PERHAPS, POOR JUDGMENT. THIS REPORTER HOPES, WITH YOU, THAT IT IS NOTHING MORE.

OFFICE OF THE PUBLIC DEFENDER
STATE OF NEW MEXICO
FIRST JUDICIAL DISTRICT OFFICE

1201 N. Chavez Road
Santa Fe, New Mexico 87501

In Re: *Theodore Bellasandro*

Dear Ms. Donahue:

I regret that this letter has become necessary. I recognize that we have a mutual interest in mounting the best possible defense for Teddy Bellasandro. However, an issue has arisen which mitigates against your continued involvement in that defense.

Mr. Bellasandro now believes he would be better off without further contact from you. He has asked me to inform you that we believe his best course of action at this time is to enter into plea negotiations with the District Attorney's Office. He has authorized me to tell you that his polygraph results were ambiguous. I regard such a result as positive and believe it improves our negotiating position. If you wish any further information in this regard, I specifically ask that you contact me rather than Mr. Bellasandro.

In anticipation that you may not wish to take my word for this, I enclose a note from Mr. Bellasandro.

Yours,
Joleen Fische
Public Defender

The sheet of yellow foolscap folded behind the letter is from Teddy; it says:

Matty,

> *I'm sorry. I don't want to go to trial. I'm grateful for what you done.*

> *Teddy*

"What the hell is this?" I ask Joleen when she finally returns my calls.

She sighs deeply, then talks fast as if to get it over with. "I spoke to the prison therapist in Baton Rouge. He's some kind of minister or pastor. He knows nothing that can help me with the motion, but he had plenty to say about handling Bellasandro. I'm breaking more than a few rules to tell you this, and I sure as hell wasn't going to put it in a letter, but here's the situation.

"When this preacher urged Teddy to face his *sin,* as he put it, all hell broke loose. Jarring the memory of his mother's death and mutilation sent Bellasandro into a tailspin. He wrecked the room, knocked around a couple of other inmates, threw the good pastor, while seated in his chair, across the room, broke a guard's arm. Before he could be subdued, he tried to put his own head through a concrete wall."

"This is because he was forced to remember his mother's death?" I ask.

"That's right. Later, in isolation, he managed to cut his wrist on a snag in a drainpipe. He almost bled to death.

"But when he got off suicide watch, it was like nothing happened. He barely remembered the incident. And what's more, in his new condition, he remembered nothing at all about his mother's death. Zero. After that, the preacher left him alone and nobody else messed with him. So, I've talked to a local shrink. He says to leave Bellasandro alone. Don't push him.

"Then you go out there and push him some more, urging him to remember. Right after you left, he exploded. They sedated him. This is when it comes to light that you've been there to see him more than once, claiming to be his attorney. Our office was notified."

Joleen sighs. "All things considered, my decision is to cut you loose. I've notified the jail. Starting now, you have no access of any kind to Bellasandro."

"But we've still got seven days left before the hearing—"

"Make that *I've* still got seven days left before the hearing," Joleen interrupts crisply. "You've got no time left at all."

"I've got information."

"Fine, but I've got a real job to do here."

"WAIT! It's about Norman."

"Oh, fuck."

"Joleen. Surely you've considered that Charlie Lee's disappearance isn't accidental. And if somebody is getting rid of witnesses who know Teddy didn't do it, it strikes me that Rickie Hadid may be in danger, too."

"Give me a break, will you, Donahue. The last time I looked, you thought one of the Hadids was the murderer."

"But—"

"Look, if you have something, put it in writing. Mail it to Stone. If there's still any case left in seven days, it's Stone's."

TWENTY-FIVE

⸺◦◦◦⸺

WEDNESDAY, DECEMBER 18

T HIS IS A NEW KIND OF DEPRESSION. IT HAS TWO FACES. Yesterday, I spent the morning cleaning closets, salvaging clothes destined for the trash pile and mending them carefully with tiny stitches. I occupied my day with such mindless chores, keeping a heavy lid on the corrosive upheaval beneath. Familiar sentiments about the fundamental injustice and lunacy of life on this planet threaten to surface. To expel self-pity, I spritz years of accumulated dirt and grease from the tops of spice bottles and organize them in alphabetical order.

But when I closed my eyes and allowed sleep to deepen to the place below my control, my dream took on a nightmarish quality. Last night it began with a real-life memory of me in the courtroom many years ago. The jury has just come in with a verdict for my client, the largest monetary award in the history of the state. I wait until the members of the jury have exited through the door at the rear of their box before erupting in a power fist. The word "yes" swells in me and bursts forth louder than is permitted in the court room. In the real-life memory, John, who knows how much this victory means to me and who has taken the day off from work to be in court, comes from around the bar separating spectators from lawyers with a grin of pride and love. John raises his flat palm and slaps mine in the air in congratulation. When it touches my searing red-hot hand, his hand bursts into flame.

The burning continues down his body until he falls and begins to break up into embers like a spent log. Smoldering ash on the courtroom floor brings other spectators to look. I hold my hot hand out to them and they back away with wide eyes, mouthing like a Greek chorus the words, "No, No, No."

I've talked to Max, told him about Eamonn Migill's article and about the drier, less histrionic, follow-up story in today's *New Mexican*.

"But the *New Mexican* carried a picture of me with the story so now I'm not only a villain, but a recognizable villain."

I'd meant it to sound like a joke but, to my ears, it sounded like whining. I tried again. "I guess that was the catastrophe," I told Max.

"I'm coming home," he told me.

"No, you aren't. Not now." I spoke with all the certainty I could muster. "If we have any chance of being other than patient and therapist, you can't come to me right now. But you can . . . keep calling, from time to time . . . if you like."

"I like," Max said.

This morning, I scraped small wood slivers off of the stair risers and contemplated the practical implications of my new status as pariah. Where do I go from here? How long will the money last? I've written my monthly restitution checks to the three former clients and paid my rent. My bank balance is now $433.26. By this afternoon, it has become something of an obsession with me to figure out how long I can go before I must buy groceries again.

I've been working around the dry boards and bulletin boards I'd arranged in the kitchen, avoiding them but not yet dismantling them. In five days, the court will hear the motion to dismiss *State* v. *Bellesandro*, if there is anything left of the motion at that point. I tell myself that the court calendar is no longer my concern. Whatever is going to happen is going to happen without me. I can't help Teddy. I may even have actually endangered Juanita. Feeling worse than useless, I slump into the chair and stare blindly at the boards.

But the gloom of failure doesn't go as deep as it once did. I realize with a small jolt that I'm not as fragile as I was four years ago. And I'm entering the stream from a different place. Little by little a new thought begins to creep in: If I can't do anything for anyone else, how about doing something for me? Whether it helps Teddy or not; whether it hurts Juanita or not; whether I ever work as a lawyer again or not, I want to finish what I've begun. I want to understand what happened to Isadora. No one needs to approve or give me permission to do that. Like sunlight through a canopy of leaves, a sense of freedom begins to dapple the gloomy underbrush. I go back to work.

By the time Max calls again, I'm absorbed in the M.E.'s report. By unspoken agreement, Max doesn't express his worry about me nor any hint of commitment. I ask and he tells me a little about Sarah, promises to send pictures. In order not to ask for or offer anything we won't deliver, we begin to talk about what I have in front of me.

"Okay, so summarize," he instructs.

"Toolbox on the floor—metal shavings among the sheets—fragment of blue paper." I explain that the small shred of paper found among Isadora's sheets is a fairly heavy grade. "And it was blue."

"So, it was a scrap of heavy, blue paper. So?"

"It's like the backing paper that was used for wills and trusts twenty or so years ago."

"But no longer used?"

"The days of long, legal-sized documents and fancy blue backing have gone the way of sealing wax and quill pens."

"Okay, you've clearly made something of all this. Tell me."

"An argument over changing a very old will, perhaps? Teddy said she'd been ranting about lawyers. And she'd just returned from Albuquerque where she'd had a new will drawn cutting Faye's inheritance. I don't know how Norman found out and got here so quickly, but I can picture the old fart trying to bully her into rethinking her will yet again. Maybe Isadora cuffed herself to his briefcase because her new will was in it and—"

"You think he cut off her hand because she disinherited Faye?" he interrupts. He sounds incredulous.

"—and he must have gotten some kind of tool to try to remove the cuffs and—"

"Jesus, Matty, stop. It's too bizarre. . . . Do you worry that you may be skewing the evidence to point to Norman because you hate him so?"

A long moment passes before I answer.

"I do."

With that, we fall silent. I fiddle with the phone cord, not yet ready to break the connection.

"Matty . . ." he says and doesn't finish.

After more silence I tell him the lawyer in Albuquerque described on old man who came with Isadora and witnessed her will. "Tito Sena was his name."

"Ahh." He feigns interest. "Does that help?"

"There's a wood yard down the street. It's called the Sena Woodyard. An old guy runs it. . . . Teddy told me a Tito Sena used to drive for Isadora once in while before she hired him."

". . . Matty, I miss you."

Jesus, I want Max to come home.

"What do you want to do?" he asks.

Deliberately misunderstanding, I tell him what I want to do is talk to Tito Sena. "Isadora wasn't in Albuquerque until two that afternoon. Maybe Tito Sena can tell me how she spent the rest of the last day of her life."

Continuing with his own conversation Max says, "Matty, I'm so goddamned worried about you—"

"Well, stop it," I say.

• • •

The Sena wood yard is a relic of the past. The half-acre of stacked cordwood nestled between a three-star restaurant and a yuppie dance studio is probably worth enough for Tito Sena to retire his grandchildren, but his family has been selling firewood in this spot for generations.

Hunched and suspicious he surveys me with narrowed eyes until I tell him I was Isadora Stanton's friend and I want to talk to him about the day she died. Then he grins broadly, showing a row of perfect dentures too large for his crumpled mouth. It turns out he's been waiting for someone to come and ask about this. He's anxious to tell me about the trip to Canoncito with Isadora, the one Teddy wouldn't take.

Back at home in my kitchen, spice bottles, stair risers and even budgets are forgotten as I work at the board before me. Hour by hour, with fragments gathered from Teddy and Tito Sena and Gus Fullerton, I can almost account for Isadora's last day of life.

Early in the morning of November eleventh, she was demanding that Teddy take her to Canoncito. Less than an hour later, around nine A.M., she'd convinced or bullied Tito Sena into driving her instead.

The trip to the far west side of Albuquerque takes about an hour and a half; then, say, another half hour to reach Canoncito. I write in blue marker, "11:00 A.M."

Sena was little help about what she might have done while in Canoncito. He only knew where she told him to stop and where she went in. He slept in the car and waited until she tapped her cane on the windshield. He didn't remember how long he'd slept.

But Fullerton told me that Isadora reached his office about two o'clock that afternoon, meaning that, after subtracting the driving time back into Albuquerque, she must have spent an hour and a half in Canoncito. According to Fullerton, the computer-generated form will had been edited, signed, and

witnessed by four P.M. Meaning Isadora was back in Santa Fe by
five-fifteen that evening.

Sena recalled that Isadora reached new heights of indigna-
tion on the way back into Santa Fe. Complaining about all shysters everywhere gave way, he told me, to threatening to end the
career of one lawyer in particular.

"Lady was loco," he'd said, rolling his eyes.

At the end of the work day, the pair had made one more stop,
and this is the part of Tito Sena's story I find most enlightening.

At Isadora's direction, Sena pulled up at the law offices of
Frederick & Danforth just before five-thirty P.M. on the day she
died. She entered the building in a state but, according to Sena,
came out a little calmer less than half hour later.

She told Tito Sena that she had looked the devil in the eye
and spat! "She looked kind of satisfied-like, you know," Sena
had concluded.

By midnight, I've gone as far as I can sitting in my own
kitchen. If I'm to understand what was going on in Isadora's
head that last day, a trip to the Navajo village of Canoncito is in
order.

Very early the next morning, long before I rise to set out for
Canoncito, I get another call and, as Max is the only person
speaking to me these days, I answer with a casual and slightly
sexy, "Good-morning—"

"Matty, turn on your TV. *Now!*"

The voice is familiar. Someone I've talked to recently.
"Rocks . . . ?" I mumble. "Stone? Is that you?"

"Right. Turn on your TV, Matty! There's been an explosion. That guy . . . Hadid . . . his trailer!"

TWENTY-SIX

――◈◈◈――

THURSDAY, DECEMBER 19

I LEAP UP, TOSS THE PHONE INTO A HEAP OF QUILTS, CLICK ON the set, and punch the remote until I find what Stone Allen is talking about.

". . . The flames were so hot," purrs the blonde with the Channel Seven mike, "they buckled the metal skin of the trailers on both sides and melted plastic awnings more than fifty feet from the site of the explosion."

Behind her is bright gray sky. I can see part of a fire truck and people milling and gawking. Then the camera pans the small plot where Juanita and Rickie's trailer stood. Only charred debris and smouldering ash are visible. The scene suddenly changes to a shaky night-scape with flames shooting into the night sky. "A neighbor with a new camcorder shot this video just after dark," explains the reporter helpfully.

I'm throwing clothes on while I listen and try to glimpse Juanita or Rickie among the crowd on the screen.

"One body confirmed. No information will be available as to identity for some time," the reporter wraps up cheerfully.

I scoop the phone up with one hand and my keys with the other. "Stone, I'm going out there. Thanks for the call."

"Let me know," he says, "what you find out. By the way, I'm sorry. You know, how things turned out."

By the time I get to the Cactus Trailer Park, the scene is cordoned off. Most of the residents of the park stand behind the tape in sweats and bathrobes watching the activity, conferring idly and drinking coffee.

I see Baca headed my way and I wait for him. When we are face to face he shakes his head. "Well, I can't say I'm surprised to see you here. That was an interesting piece about you in *At Large*."

"The body. Who—?"

"Don't know yet." He answers tersely. "The fire incinerated the body."

"But it's not Juanita? Please tell me the body isn't Juanita's."

He scowls before he replies. "We can't be absolutely certain, but probably not. The only witness . . ." he nods in the direction of a young woman with a fat toddler resting casually on her cocked hip ". . . says about an hour before the explosion she saw a pregnant woman get into the backseat of a car, which pulled out so fast it almost hit her kid's trike."

"Are you the officer in charge?" I ask.

"No, Detective Laurence caught the call. I'm here because of the possible connection to the Stanton homicide. Because of your information, really. I don't know what your interest in all this is, but I figure you don't deserve the shit Migill's rag suggested. You know, Migill did a hatchet job on my division last year. If you're Migill's enemy, you can't be all bad." He sighs. "Anyway, I've been here twice trying to confirm what you told me, but no luck finding Hadid or the cousin. If either of them were here, they didn't want to see me."

We cross the path in the chill morning air. People nod or tip their steaming cups as we pass. The whole scene has the feel of a family reunion or company retreat. Baca points toward two men conferring with a uniformed fire marshall. "The one on the left is Laurence. The other is Investigator Sanchez from the Attorney General's office. He was notified because of the counterfeits, the Indian jewelry. It seems you were right about that connection to Hadid. Let's go. Sanchez will want to talk to you."

"What happened here? Was it a bomb?" I ask Baca.

"No," he answers tersely. "The explosion was from an illegal butane hookup, easy enough to tinker with. The fire department declared it a possible arson a couple of hours ago."

"Agi? The cousin?" I guess.

"Could be. By the way, about the question you asked a few days ago, Ms. Donahue . . . uh . . . Matty, Sanchez does have some information about the cousin. His name, by the way, is the same as his cousin's, Hadid. He's Mohammed Agiberjan Hadid. Sanchez says he's here illegally on a Jordanian passport. Been traveling back and forth on it for years without drawing attention to himself. I don't know much more."

Sanchez nods when Baca introduces me. Laurence is silent. Sanchez picks up the story.

"We've been developing a case on what's beginning to look like an extended Arab family who've carved out a real lucrative niche for themselves in the counterfeit Indian jewelry market," he says. "In recent months the stuff has begun to show up locally, which is strange because the family and their operation have been almost invisible for a decade or more.

"But lately, one of the family members has been using the expensive 'old pawn' pieces to do everything but buy bread with. It's the break we've been waiting for."

"That makes sense," I say.

I repeat what Juanita told me about Rickie's family being so angry with him, taking away his walking-around money. "He must be the one who was using their jewelry inventory to buy what he needed. He tried to hire me with a concho belt. His cousin, Agi, was furious."

"Right." Sanchez nods. "It fits. Now, we just need to figure out if maybe one of these guys torched the other."

We step nearer the remains of the smoldering pile of twisted metal that had been Juanita's home.

"How are we going to find Juanita?" I am trying hard to swallow the guilt of leaving her in such danger. Surely I could have done something. Teddy had asked me to look after her. It's what Isadora would have wanted me to do.

"*We?*" asks Sanchez. "*We* don't know, at the moment, whether Juanita Jakes is a victim or a perpetrator or neither. And *we* don't know where their base of operation is. They almost certainly have a place where they assemble the pieces—polish the stones, carve the silver, get them ready for shipping. But we've had no luck finding it, and, from the looks of things . . ." he gestured glumly to the remains of the trailer, ". . . they may be closing down their operation for now. If we're going to find them, we probably have a narrow window of time."

Speaking of windows. "Do you mind?" I ask, trying to position myself parallel to where Juanita would have been sitting when she pointed out of her trailer window. "If I can just move a little closer . . . When I visited her here, Juanita told me . . ." I adjust my position until I have the direction clear in my mind.

". . . . Yes . . . see?" I point toward the semidesert which surrounds the south end of the city. "Over there. Juanita Jakes said, 'They make pretty things over there.'" Beyond the ragged, trailer-park-edge of Sante Fe nothing taller than a piñon bush is visible for miles. "If there's a place where they manufacture the pieces, it must be out there somewhere."

Baca drives, Sanchez rides beside him. From the back, I lean forward and rest my hands over the front seat. We travel dirt roads over shallow hills, which dip and rise like ocean swells. Traces of humanity materialize wherever a trough in the terrain provides a trickle of water. Here and there a shack or two hides in a nest of trees. Where there are people, Sanchez and Baca stop and chat briefly with the inhabitants.

After a fruitless hour or so, we circle back toward the city. We enter Sante Fe's laughably small industrial zone in a neighborhood generally invisible to tourists and residents. The city fathers like to zone this necessary, but ugly, muscle of the city out of the way and crammed into the smallest possible space.

This maze of narrow dirt streets seems likely, and Baca drives slowly past recyclers, auto junkyards, repair shops, storage units, and rows of transmissions and radiators organized behind chain-link. Most of these buildings have bars on the windows and stickers announcing the presence of alarms. There are no homes or lawns or children. A constant but erratic din fills the air.

"This is the kind of place they might choose, don't you think?" I'm excited, leaning far over the seat and more in their face than the cops welcome. But of course they have no search warrant and nothing about any one of maybe a hundred busy operations stands out as anything suspicious. "If a family of Arabs has been working here, the locals would know, wouldn't they? You can ask . . ."

"Maybe." Sanchez sounds dubious. "We know they had a couple of local Anglo goofs working for them in Gallup, doing dirty work and showing themselves when somebody had to be visible. It's likely they've got the same thing here. So even if they're here, they may not be very visible. In any event, we need some help. The work day will be over before we can get any men out here. I'll get on it first thing tomorrow. See what we can find."

Baca is sympathetic to my near hysteria about Juanita's welfare but, despite my protests, the two men drop me back at my car. The trailer park has nearly settled back to business as usual.

I watch evening fall through my windshield as I retrace each of the miles I took with the officers. When I reach the industrial zone again, it has changed. The bangs, thumps, and screeches of light manufacturing have given way to a near-profound silence. No vehicles move on the ugly streets. I park, drop the keys into my purse, stuff the purse under the seat, and begin to walk the streets of the instant ghost town. When, after twenty minutes, I hear a scrap of noise behind a building, I follow the sound to yet another corrugated metal Quonset building nearly swallowed by tall weeds at the far end of the lot. Two men are loading a van there. A gray Nova sits beside the van.

Through the weeds, lights are visible at the windows. I skirt to the far side, away from the activity, to get a look. I'm on my toes stretching to see inside.

TWENTY-SEVEN

———∽∾∾∽———

I DIDN'T FEEL THE BLOW. BUT THERE MUST HAVE BEEN ONE because pain stabs from the nape of my neck to the top of my skull. I can move my head only fractionally. I don't know how I got here. Wherever here is. I don't know if it is night or day. There is only darkness.

A tight sticky band about three inches wide runs across my eyes and temples. I must have been hit in the right eye or fallen on it because the gap between the eyeball and tape has been slowly filling with a liquid thicker than tears. I'm trying to stop worrying about my eye. I figure my eye may be the least of my troubles.

My hands are bound behind me, palms clasped as though in some kind of perverse backward prayer. My ankles are banded too, but my feet are free. My shoes have been removed and my toes touch cold metal. My arm lies on cold cement. The air smells slightly foul.

I begin to explore the space with my feet. My bare heel hits

something hard and cold. Porcelain. My toes tell me it is a toilet. I snake around until my head hits a wall and then I flop like
a fish until my head is in the other corner. A narrow thin mattress lies on the floor against this new wall. Exploration with
my feet reveals a zippered sleeping bag and pillow spilling off
the mattress. Two of the walls around me feel to my toes like
wallboard. The other two are corrugated steel; one is curved,
one straight. The whole space is about six by six. This must be
the back end of the metal Quonset building I'd seen from outside. And if it is, there is a door in the middle of the other cardboard wall.

I hunch painfully across the floor until I reach the door. I
lie still for minutes, my cheek on the cold sticky floor, my ear as
near the crack between the door and the floor as I can manage.

But there is nothing to hear, and consciousness begins
to fade.

When the high-pitched *skree* reaches me, it takes ages for me to
recognize that it isn't the screams from my dream but instead
the sound of a cellular phone on the other side of the door. I try
to hoist myself into a sitting position. I need to clear my head
and listen. It takes all my concentration to accomplish this, and
when I do bile rises without warning in my throat. The bile
keeps me from fainting.

"No," says the voice, talking to someone on the other end
of the phone line. Male, young. "We got the bitch tied up in
back. The lady lawyer. Nobody came with her. What do you
want us to do? . . . Yeah, yeah, the retard's still asleep. She's a
pain in the ass, too. 'Where's Rickie?' " his tone becomes high
and girlish and clearly mocking. " 'When is Rickie coming?'
That retard's driving me nuts. But Dell's kinky. He wants to do
her. Pregnant and all."

I'm consumed by pain but there is no choice. I must stay
alert, must listen, because I must understand what's going on.
My life depends on it. And, from what the man on the other
side of the door is saying, I'm guessing that Juanita's life depends on it, too.

"Dell's loading the heavy stuff now. . . . What? . . . Shit, man—we can't get all this equipment in the truck if we work all night. . . . How much extra . . . . ? Okay, okay, we'll do it. This place will be empty by morning and we'll be out of here. But what about the women?"

A long pause, then a vicious eruption. "How the shit should I know who she told? What do we care? We'll be outta here before . . . Okay . . . You got it," he says and snaps the cell phone closed.

Then he lets out a low whistle and a laugh that makes my blood run cold.

It is several minutes before there are voices again. Two this time. Dell—the heavy lifter, I guess. And the man who was on the phone. The latter explains to the new man: "The rag-head offered us a bonus to get everything out of this warehouse before morning. And another two hundred to find out who the lady lawyer told she was coming here if we can. Hadid wants to know what loose ends he's leaving. But we gotta get the information out of her before morning. Everything and everybody's gotta be outta here by morning."

"What about the women, Mike?" the new voice—Dell—asks.

"He don't give a shit what we do with the women. First we get this stuff on the truck, then we get the information. We get it, we get another two hundred; if we don't, we don't. Either way, when we're done here, we do the women."

"What you mean—do?"

The laugh again. "He left that up to us."

And slowly the other one begins to laugh too.

I let the tears come. I begin to rock my body on the hard floor, mucus flowing from my nose and the tears seeping into the tape. The tears mix with the blood and exert pressure on the tape, but more pressure on my eyeball. I want help.

"Please. Somebody," I pray aloud. "Please."

My blubbering goes on for many minutes. There is only endless blackness, until . . .

"Matty? Is that you?"

"What? Who?"

"Matty, what happened to you?"

Juanita's voice. She pulls the tape roughly from my mouth and begins to do the same with the tape around my eyes but my scream of pain shocks both of us. It also brings our captors on the run.

"What the fuck do you think you're doing?" Mike demands of Juanita. He seems to be in the process of moving her bodily out of my cell. Apparently, Juanita is resisting. I hear the shuffle and Juanita's protest. "She's hurt." More shuffling. "Matty's hurt." Suddenly Juanita's on the floor again, cradling me in her fleshy arms. "She's hurt," she insists, rocking me. Her skin feels slightly moist and she smells like new sweat and old cologne— lilac.

"Shit, we ain't got time for this crap," snarls Mike.

"Leave 'em be," advises Dell. "Look at the two of 'em. What the hell they gonna do? Let the retard clean her up for us."

Again the laugh as the men move out of ear shot.

For a long time Juanita works in the dark. On the floor of the cubicle, I lie docile while she unbinds my legs. She's been frightened by my scream of protest so she stays away from my eyes and tugs too gently on the other bindings. She's taking too much time. It's an eternity before she frees my hands and helps me up.

Juanita leads me into the outer room and sits me on something hard. The men are working somewhere in the large echoing room, lifting, grunting, moving things. They have left us to our own devices for the time being because we are so harmless. So little threat to anyone.

"Faster," I urge Juanita, and to my relief she obeys. Painfully she rips the tape from the back of my head, tearing hanks of hair out by the roots.

"Gentle, I have to do it gentle," she scolds herself. She tilts my head up and, more slowly, tugs the tape away from my left eye. "The blood." She is sucking in soft breaths with little wheezy sounds.

"The blood is coming from my other eye," I tell her. "I think this one may be okay."

And it is. My lashes stick together for a moment from the goo of the tape but when I flutter them open, I can see the fluorescent light near the ceiling and, despite the glare, I keep this eye open. I can see!

I've lived with the fear of blindness for only a short time, but that fear had reached every atom of every cell in my body. Now, I stare with my good left eye at the light, thanking a God I generally ignore and fervently promising Him that I won't ignore Him in the future, if He'll just grant me a future.

Each millimeter of tape she pulls from my right eye carries with it coagulating blood. Some of the pieces of tape bring up specks of flesh. Miraculously, Juanita's normally clumsy hands work on my eye with the delicacy of a surgeon.

While she works I talk to her. I ask questions. Not the hard ones. Not yet. Juanita tells me that she thinks one of the thugs, Mike, is not very nice but he's "okay" because he says he's Rickie's friend. Mike and Dell picked her up, she explains, because Rickie told them to bring her here to wait for him. She's been waiting for a long time and she keeps asking when Rickie will come but they don't say. It is clear that she doesn't even know that her trailer has disappeared in a wall of flames. No word can have reached her that a human being burned to death in that fire. I move my good eye down until I can see her innocent patient face.

And, in the background, I hear the laughing.

What do you mean, do? . . . He left that up to us. . . .

For the next hour there is more of the same. The sounds of the men emptying the warehouse in the background and, closer, the painstaking and painful cleaning of my wounded eye, bit by microscopic bit. Beneath the pain, however, my brain can still work. These two have to be the Hadid family's henchmen. One of the cousins has ordered the clearing of this warehouse. No doubt to get rid of all signs of their counterfeit jewelry operation.

He wants no evidence left.

Juanita is humming as she works now. The table in front of us is littered with wads of used duct tape amid jewelry-making paraphernalia. She is using these instruments—delicate tweezers and a metal probe like a crochet needle—to pick flecks from my eye.

"Juanita," my voice is low and I try to keep the terror out of it. "Pretty soon now those men over there—"

"Mike and Dell?"

"Mike and Dell. They're going to be finished loading the truck outside and when they do, Juanita, they're going to try to hurt us. We have to get out of here now. You have to help."

Juanita pats my shoulder. "No, Matty," she tells me firmly. "Rickie would not leave me with people who would hurt me. Mike says Rickie will be here tomorrow. We have to stay, Matty. Don't worry."

"Juanita!" This time I can hear my own panic. "Rickie isn't coming. Trust me, please. Those men are going to try to hurt us. We must get out of here. We need weapons, something to protect ourselves. Look for something; anything." I'm talking too fast. I know. My one good eye can't make out her expression but I can feel the sudden tension in her body. I can't begin to guess what she's feeling. Fear? Disbelief?

"Juanita, either Rickie did leave us here to be hurt, or else Rickie can't come to get you. I think Rickie may be dead."

Now it is her turn to scream. A loud banshee sound.

Her cry brings Mike and Dell back. They settle her down, promise her Rickie's on his way right now.

"Rickie'll be here before morning," Mike tells her. "Don't listen to the lawyer. Lawyers lie. Lawyers can't be trusted."

And it seems to work. Her sobs become sniffles and she begins to tidy up the table. Finally, she steadies her heavy body against my shoulder as she stands.

Before she leaves me she says, "Rickie's not dead, Matty. You should not say Rickie's dead."

Much later, the van is almost loaded. They have ordered me not to move and I've submitted. They've retaped my wrists in front of me but have otherwise left me alone. My undamaged eye is good enough to have located the only exit other than the one they're using to transport equipment and tools. I could make it there in two or three seconds. If the door is unlocked, I might even be able to get all the way to the street before they catch me.

When I entered this neighborhood a lifetime ago the

streets were already empty. It must be the middle of the night by now. There will be no one out there. I remember the alarm company stickers on every building along the streets. But, even if I could make it to the street, with my wrists bound, how would I set off the alarms? And I would have to leave Juanita behind. It is that thought which has so far stopped me.

The tables and shelves are almost bare. Everything is gone except for a small hot plate and skillets on a shelf where Juanita is preparing some kind of last meal. Juanita is humming to herself again, all trauma forgotten, all bad news untrue.

When Mike comes over to straddle the bench beside me he pulls from his back pocket a soldering iron the size and shape of a small gun with a tangle of wire wrapped around the handle. He plugs the iron into a socket in the floor. My mind is racing, but each plan I concoct fails as I follow it to its logical end.

He begins to lift my skirt an inch at a time with his finger while his dirty thumb caresses my thigh. Then he pulls a coil of solder from another pocket.

And now I know now how he plans to get information from me. How he plans to earn his extra two hundred dollars.

"We know you came here alone, sweetheart, but maybe you told somebody where you were going, huh?" While he speaks he turns a little switch on the soldering iron and draws a stick of solder to the end of it. He's left my skirt high up on my thigh.

"You're going to kill us anyway. There's no reason to tell you anything."

He watches the soft metal melt. One drop and then another falls onto the tabletop. Just in case I don't get the picture, he flips a third drop onto a scrap of paper. The paper flares and is consumed.

Do the women.

"There's a lotta of ways to die, lady."

He is sitting with his back toward Juanita. I can see her over his shoulder. She is shuffling a cast-iron skillet on the little hot plate.

"Rickie is dead, isn't he?" I say. "Rickie wouldn't leave Juanita here with rapists. Rickie loved Juanita." I'm trying to keep my voice loud for her.

Mike lifts my skirt another inch, then lays a coil of solder against the inside of one exposed thigh. He begins to laugh again low in his throat. Before I know it the other one is here too, kneeling by my knee—pulling to spread my legs.

"Grab her hands!" orders Mike.

The room explodes as the drop of burning metal hits my leg. All other pain is forgotten as the searing drop sinks deeper and deeper into my flesh. I am movement—thrashing—screaming—lunging. The bench tips over, but they are on top of me. Both of them grabbing and—

Then I hear the skillet as it cracks against his skull. She is trying for the other man but he grabs her wrist. Before he can wrestle the skillet from her, I grab the handle of the still-hot soldering iron with my bound hands and jab it at him with all the strength I have left. I feel it graze his cheek.

It isn't much, but it is enough for Dell to jump and cry "shit, hell," before Juanita whacks him with the skillet and he falls into my lap.

We are moving so fast that all is instinct. Run. Door. Gate. Street. I hear her panting beside me. This can't be good for a pregnant woman. Can't be good for a fetus. Run! Run! Run!

When we are outside into the darkness, I am abruptly and utterly blind again.

"Look for a brick, a rock—" panting, running.

"Rickie wouldn't . . . leave me . . . with a rapist."

"A rock!" I'm struggling to stay upright. Running blind. "A rock, Juanita. Set off the alarms!"

"What? . . . I don't under—"

"The alarms . . ." Out of breath. An engine starts behind us.

"Rock . . . through window . . . I can't see, Juanita . . . I can't get my hands free. It's up to you. Make the alarms sound. Throw a rock . . . through a window. NOW!"

TWENTY-EIGHT

———— ✦◈✦ ————

AND SHE DOES IT. WINDOW AFTER WINDOW. WITHIN SEC-onds alarms ring and dogs bark. Within minutes there are sirens and police cars. Mike and Dell are arrested as they drive the loaded van out of the gate. I'd imagined I was there to save Juanita Jakes's life, but in a striking reversal of roles, Juanita has saved mine.

SATURDAY, DECEMBER 21

And I tell her so. She's sitting in a wheelchair at the end of my hospital bed, wearing a maternity version of my crumpled smock and clapping her hands with what can only be described as glee. Her mind, thankfully, is unchallenged for now by the mystery of Rickie Hadid's whereabouts.

"Tell it again, Matty."

And I do. I tell it for her and, this time, too, for the benefit of the doctor and nurse who have come to examine my eye again. They've arranged a sort of pirate patch over the now smaller bandage and have momentarily removed both to have another look. When I finish my story for the second time by describing Juanita's skillet-whacking and rampage of brick-throwing, the doctor shines his penlight into the right eye. "It looks like your friend here has saved your eye, too."

Juanita claps again. "I saved you," she says and struggles out of her wheelchair and to the edge of my bed where she tries to hug me. But a series of straps is gartered around my leg to hold a small doughnut-shaped contraption in place. The doughnut, directly over a screw-sized hole in my flesh, prevents anything, even my hospital gown, from accidentally touching the wound. When the paraphernalia interferes, Juanita settles for resting her head on my abdomen and patting my hand.

My room has been crowded this morning, with men and women in white coats doing one job and men and women in uniforms with badges doing another. But the man who walks in the door isn't wearing either. He's wearing a sport jacket, a pink shirt, and knife-creased jeans.

"How are you doing, Matty?" he asks.

"Not as bad as I look. Juanita, this is Detective Daniel Baca."

Baca points to my purse to show me that he's retrieved it. He places it in the cabinet of my bedside table and pulls a chair up as the last nurse exits. The police have had most of the day to interview the thugs, he says. Mike and Dell have been falling all over themselves to cooperate. "They're afraid of murder charges stemming from the trailer fire, and they want to deal the other charges," Baca tells us. "They're talking, we're listening."

"Fire?" Juanita's voice is so small that Baca doesn't hear her.

"The one called Dell, real name Delbert Rakestraw, was the one in your office parking lot, Matty. He's also the one who tapped your home phone. Apparently they'd tried to get that job done before; Rakestraw says Agi Hadid, himself, scouted your place one night and only gave it up when the dog next door attacked him. Guess he was the prowler you saw from your window. According to Rakestraw, they only wanted to find out what Miss Stanton had told you about their operation."

"But why?"

"Apparently, Agi Hadid was trying to salvage the jewelry scam. Everybody knew that a group of Arabs had been dealing in counterfeit Indian pieces, but the Hadid family hadn't yet been identified. So their question was, had Isadora Stanton discovered the truth before she was killed? And had she shared her suspicions with anyone else? If not—and if Rickie could be reined in or deported—they could go back to business as usual as soon as the heat died down. Otherwise, they had to close up shop and they had to do it right now."

"But why me? Why did they bug me?"

Keeping his voice sympathetic, Baca turns to Juanita. "Apparently, Ms. Jakes here told her fiancé that you'd be the one that Miss Stanton might have talked to. And that's what Agi was trying to find out."

"Juanita?" I ask.

"Fire?" she answers.

Detective Baca explains patiently to Juanita that an hour after Mike and Dell had collected her, her trailer burned to the ground and that there was someone in the trailer at the time. "It's likely Rickie Hadid is either dead or . . . or else he was the one who gave Dell and Mike their orders."

The planes in Juanita's face sag as comprehension dawns. She'd managed to put what I told her in the warehouse out of her mind. But here is this policeman telling her that there are only two options.

"If Rickie was alive—he wouldn't—leave me with . . ." she protests haltingly, choking on tears. Her cries gradually become loud, bone-chilling wails. Eventually a nurse comes into the room and wheels her away, but I can still hear her far down the hallway after she has gone.

"Why did they take her?" I ask Baca.

He shrugs. "According to Mike and Dell, the family was— what do shrinks call it?—'deeply conflicted' . . . about what to do about her because of the baby. If the baby was going to be a boy—a boy of normal intelligence—they wanted it. If not . . ." Baca shrugs again. "Anyway, by the end there, whoever was giving the orders wanted nothing but out, and . . ."

I'm trying to give Baca my full attention but the ache in my thigh is like nothing I've felt before. It's deep down, near the bone, where the drop of searing metal sank. I've missed a couple of Baca's sentences. Through my fog I hear, ". . . may be a connection to the Stanton homicide after all."

To keep the pain under control, I've been given medication every four hours. But when the nurse comes in now with the pills, I ask her to leave them on the nightstand. She looks concerned, ushers Baca out, and tells me it's important to stay ahead of the pain curve. But the medication produces strange visions and muddled thought. I need my wits for a while longer so I merely smile, thank her, and murmur, "Soon. I'll take them soon."

I only want to hold off long enough to think through what has happened. Teddy's hearing is Monday morning. It should be easy now to implicate one or both of the Hadid cousins for Isadora's murder. I assume that Joleen will try to do that. There's only one problem. I don't believe either of them did it.

I try to sort through the complicated strings. I almost get them untangled for a second or two before the pain overwhelms me. Agi wanted to keep a lid on things. He only resorted to violence after every possibility of saving the business was lost. Would he have engineered a hideous murder which could only have served to bring more attention to their activities? As indeed it has done? If Teddy Bellasandro hadn't existed, a severed hand might well have been read as an Arab signature. I almost did that myself.

When the nurse returns and sees the pills still on the nightstand, she raises an eyebrow, picks them up, pours a fresh glass of water. "It's going to get much worse if you don't take the medication," she says kindly. This time I don't protest.

As I descend into drugged sleep, my mind conjures a Hieronymus Bosch vision, with groups of ragged guests groaning in agony as they drink cocktails and gobble hors d'oeuvres. I limp through the party-scape with injured hands—hands nailed to boards or nearly severed and dripping blood. I show my hands palms up, like a gypsy alms beggar, to the party sufferers. They laugh and, one after another, open cloaks or shirts to display their own bleeding cuts or suppurating sores. All of them wounded. No less than me.

The shake on my shoulder has been going on for several minutes before I know it is of this world, not that other.

"Matty," she whispers, "wake up."

"Juanita?"

She has wheeled her chair near my bed. "It's my fault, isn't it? They hurt you because of me."

"What? Of course not."

"And Teddy. That's because of me, too."

I hoist myself up on an elbow and stare at her. "What do you mean?"

"You remember when you came to my trailer?" she asks. "You remember you told me to tell the truth?"

"Yes." I hold my breath.

"Matty . . . I think I need to tell something."

TWENTY-NINE

———◦∞◦———

As I turn the key in my ignition Sunday morning in the dawn light, I give a little thanks to Daniel Baca, who managed to get my car moved to the hospital parking lot, and a little more thanks that the engine still turns over, and still more to the pills that are keeping pain at a distance. And, of course, to Juanita.

What Juanita had to say to me yesterday was repeated again two hours later to a court reporter and a video cameraman brought to her room by Joleen. The caption on the court reporter's file was not *State of New Mexico* v. *Anybody Hadid*. It was *State of New Mexico* v. *Theodore Bellesandro*. I'd placed only the one call to Joleen. After that things moved at breakneck speed.

Because Juanita's doctor felt that recent events might have endangered her pregnancy, he forbade her leaving the hospital to provide testimony. It was Joleen who'd made the difficult arrangements for the formal deposition to be taken in the hospital on a Saturday. A very disgruntled, very junior attorney represented the District Attorney's office. Rocks was there, pissed off because he was being given no role in the proceedings except to be solicitous of Juanita. Joleen, on the other hand, was so thrilled by the turn of events that she was actually courteous to one and all.

Thrilled because what Juanita had to say was pure gold for the defense of Teddy Bellasandro. And it had come just in time for tomorrow's hearing. Juanita was sheepish and relieved all at once. She had, indeed, heard Teddy "arguing and arguing" with Isadora the day she died. But it had been in the *morning*. Just as Teddy said. Before he left with Charlie Lee for Puye Cliffs. Just as Teddy said.

At the edge of the parking lot, I briefly consider my decision one last time. I could turn left toward Canyon Road, go home as I'd promised the doctor last night that I would. Lie down and put my feet up as Joleen pointedly encouraged me to do.

"You've been great," she'd apologized. "Get some rest. It's all over now," she'd said, pounding congratulations into my sore shoulder.

But I'd gone instead to the hospital gift shop to buy clean underwear and a blouse. They had only a packet of men's Fruit of the Loom T-shirt and briefs. I paid for them and for a comb and a toothbrush. This morning, I washed as well as I could in the small bathroom, careful to keep water away from my eye and my thigh. I pulled and pinned my too-short hair into an untidy ponytail to disguise its filthiness and stepped gingerly into the boy's briefs ignoring the odd extra flap of material between my legs. I threw my old stuff in the trash receptacle as I left the hospital minutes ago.

Joleen has a right to feel satisfied. Under oath and with a day to spare, the state's key witness has recanted her testimony. In her euphoria Joleen speculates that the D.A. might even join in her Motion to Dismiss the case against Teddy.

After a final pause to regret the sleep I'm not going to get, I turn right, toward the Interstate. If removing a piece of damning evidence against her client weren't enough to puff Joleen up, there was more: a rare (for Joleen) opportunity to point the finger of guilt at someone with little fear that it could come back to haunt her.

The Arabs, whether alive or dead, have engaged in a criminal conspiracy across state and national borders. Enough time has passed for one with a valid passport to be back in the Arab world. Even if one could be found alive and extradited, he would almost surely be the problem of the Federal Prosecutor and the Federal Courts. The Arabs are not, in short, Joleen's problem. And thus, it is finally perfectly apparent to her that one or all of the Arabs committed not only arson and abduction but the crime with which her client has been charged as well. The client who *is* her problem.

"Perfectly frigging obvious," she'd told the young A.D.A. late yesterday. As far as Joleen is concerned it's all wrapped up. The Arabs murdered Isadora Stanton. "Motive, means, opportunity," she argued passionately to the A.D.A., who didn't give her much one way or the other.

I left the room when she began to tick off the items of proof on her fingers. It had been a long day. My leg hurt. My eye hurt. I thought she was wrong.

I'd stopped at Juanita's room as I left the hospital. I was surprised to find Rocks in a chair watching her sleep.

"What are you doing here?" I whispered.

Rocks yawned and looked a little embarrassed. "Nobody was watching out for her and I just thought . . . I mean, we don't know *for sure* if she's out of danger yet . . ." He trails off, rests his eyes on Juanita as she sleeps. "Hell, Matty . . . I don't know. She's not able to figure things out for herself. She needs help, and I can't help thinking, you know, wondering . . . what's going to happen to them. Her and the baby. Now that it's all over."

He didn't mean it as a question and even if he did, I didn't know the answer. But, as I pull out onto the Interstate and turn south, I do know that it isn't all over.

THIRTY

━━◦◦◦◦◦━━

THE LANDSCAPE CHANGES ALMOST INSTANTLY AS I HIT THE highway headed south. Piñon and juniper and rolling hills give way to mesquite and tumbleweed along flat expanses cut by steep arroyos. The New Mexico south of Santa Fe is a different world from the New Mexico north of Santa Fe. And the difference is even more pronounced as you leave the ticky-tacky developments on the west side of Albuquerque in the direction of Canoncito. When I reach the top of Nine-Mile Hill, I can see before me a hundred bleak miles of tumbleweed and blond stubble grass.

I think I know who killed Isadora. Tito Sena's description of Isadora's trip gave me an important piece of the puzzle. But if I am to understand what the piece means I have to make the trip myself. And I have to go easy on the feel-good pills.

The village of Canoncito is uniformly impoverished and dreary. I've been directed to pass by the village itself. "Keep going until you can't go any farther," Sena had told me, and so I do.

The road dead-ends about a mile farther on, at a campus of cinder-block buildings dominated by a gymnasium. The tidy wooden sign at the edge of the dirt yard is carved with the words "Canoncito Schools" and below that, "Navajo Nation."

Except for two enormous leafless cottonwoods, the campus of the Canoncito Schools is as barren as the moon. A circle drive surrounds the campus and, equidistant along one side of the dusty circle, there are once-identical frame stucco houses in various stages of dilapidation. "Canoncito Teacherage" announces a second wooden sign.

"The fourth house from the end," Tito had directed. I pull the Toyota to a halt at what would be a curb if there were any elevation change between the dirt street and the dirt front yard of the fourth house from the end. The house is as unremarkable as the other brown stucco clones. I get out, rub some of the ache out of my thigh, and stick my eye patch in my pocket.

I wipe some spattered mud from the side of the metal mailbox but there is no name painted there. So, with a glance heavenward, I start across the bare dirt toward the front door.

Just to the side of the concrete slab-stoop is an upturned box upon which are two blue plastic bowls of mud, two plastic spoons, and three yellow birthday candles. Next to the box stands a little girl.

"Hi," I say.

She cocks her head to the side until her ear nearly touches her shoulder and she eyes me.

"My name's Matty. What's yours?"

"Lander."

"Lander?"

"Uh-huh."

"Lander's a nice name. Do you live here?"

"I do live here," she says softly.

"How old are you, Lander?"

"I are not three," she says as she hands one of the candles to me. Lander has dark brown hair and huge brown eyes.

"I see. Then you must be tw—"

"Yo . . . lan . . . daaa! I need some water. Bring me the water right n—"

The high-pitched order comes from a little girl a few years older than Lander. She rounds the corner and halts in midstride when she sees me. She is a sight to behold. Like the other, not quite Navajo, not quite Anglo. She is dressed in a pink skirt with black polka dots, and mud-spattered paisley tights wrinkled at the knee and torn down the length of one leg. A long, once-yellow, adult-sized apron with a dragging ruffle is tied around a thick fuchsia-and-red parka.

She raises a wooden spoon and a green bowl filled with thick mud in front of her like a sword and shield. Then, she steps quickly to guard the smaller child. The whole effect is something like that of a mad, midget, master-chef, champion defender.

"Hello," I say. "You must be Lander's sister."

"Yolanda," she says.

"Your name is Yolanda?"

With some disgust at my ignorance, she shakes her head. "No, *I'm* Lucy."

Lucy taps the younger child on the head a few times with the fat end of the spoon. "*She's* Yolanda."

"Oh, I see. But you call her Lander?"

"She named herself. She can't say her name yet."

Lucy remembers her role as protector. Her eyes narrow. "Who are you?"

I plop myself down on the stoop next to a bundle of advertizing flyers tied with string and tell the girls that my name is Matty and that I have a last name, too. "My last name is Donahue," I say. "What's yours?"

"Marlson," says Lucy.

"Marlson," echoes Lander.

I'm not surprised. I expected it. But, as another piece falls into place, a sense of satisfaction washes over me.

"And your daddy? Is your daddy's name Jeff? I'm looking for someone named Jeff Marlson."

"He's still at school." Lucy points with the spoon toward the campus across the street.

"On the weekend?"

"Uh-huh. Daddy's not teaching today. He's just messing around with papers and stuff. Mamma's inside."

"I are not three," Yolanda repeats her earlier assertion and tries to arrange her sticky fingers to illustrate her age.

"I see that. You have two yellow candles. And this must be the cake," I say pointing to the mud. "Did you make it?"

Yolanda nods. "I are two."

"You're two and a half," corrects Lucy sternly. One can see that Lucy has been teaching Yolanda to get it right for some time. "And *I* made your cake. *You* just helped."

"I helped," agrees Yolanda amiably.

The children keep chattering at me as I sit on the stoop looking out at the uninterrupted browns of the teacherage. A couple of tumbleweeds roll languidly across the schoolyard on the other side of the street and I watch one of them roll until it reaches the booted foot of the man striding toward us with a young Navajo boy of about four astride his shoulders.

The man looks very different from the smart-assed kid flipping the bird to the camera, but I recognize him immediately. By the time he reaches me, Lander is wiggling on my lap and I'm trying to protect my thigh and not to flinch. She clings like a chimp as I rise to shake her father's hand.

"Mr. Marlson? If you have a minute I'd like to talk to you about your grandmother."

"You're the second one in three months," he says with concern but a welcoming smile.

"Yeah, I thought I might be." I explain briefly that Isadora was murdered shortly after she was here. Jeff sobers instantly.

"Yes," he says as he lowers the little boy to the ground and opens the door. "We saw it on television. I tried to call the Santa Fe police but the line into the reservation was down. The next story I saw said they got the guy who did it so I just let it drop. I didn't think there was a connection. Was I wrong?"

"Yes, I think you probably were."

"Come in, come in," he says. "My wife's in the kitchen; come on back."

Jeff is obviously not the biological father of the third child, a full-blooded Navajo. A pretty young woman with slate black hair sits on a stool at the counter peering at the monitor of a small computer and sipping a Coke. More stacks of advertising flyers line the countertop around her. Jeff kisses her on the cheek and introduces her as Bernice. She smiles briefly but holds up a finger to signal him to wait until she saves what is on the screen.

In a few minutes, all six of us are seated around a red Formica table with Diet Coke cans in front of us. I'm explaining why I came and asking for the answers I need to fill in the missing pieces.

"Miss Stanton asked mostly about my drug use," Jeff explains. "When I had stopped using, and—"

"And especially if it had been before he turned thirty. Remember, Jeff? She asked if it was a whole year before your thirtieth birthday? That was the most important question to her, wasn't it?" prompts Bernice.

"Right. I didn't mind telling her. I'm one of the luckiest guys alive. I'm proud to tell people about turning my life around."

I look around at the decidedly humble, not to say bleak, surroundings. I look into the flat face of the Navajo boy with its distinctive telltale features and back at Jeff's contented face.

"Anyway, it seems they were girlhood friends, Miss Stanton and my grandmother. I'm sure I must have met her when I was young. Gran came out to this part of the country to be with her from time to time. The last period was a few years before Gran got real sick. She stayed with Miss Stanton for more than a year that time. That's how I ended up going to college here. I only visited my grandmother once after I flunked out. Course, I was in bad shape and, let's just say, the visit was short."

The boy has moved to Jeff's lap. He's having trouble sitting still. He spills his soda on the red Formica. Without skipping a beat, Jeff makes a dam with the edge of his hand to contain the spill while he goes on talking.

"When she visited us here, Miss Stanton brought an old letter from my grandmother. She told me Gran had sent it on to her just before she died. She'd been keeping it for me all these years."

Bernice tosses Jeff a towel and says to me, "The letter was wonderful. His grandmother must have loved Jeff very much. I would like to have known her."

Jeff uses the towel to sop up the spill. "It was a pretty emotional visit," he explains. "Miss Stanton began to cry. She just kept repeating 'I'm sorry, I'm sorry, it's my fault. It was my responsibility. I'll make it up to you. I'll fix it, I promise.'

"I didn't know what she was talking about," Jeff continues, "and she wouldn't explain. When I read the letter my grandmother wrote to me across the years, I just about broke down. I fucked up those years so bad. Hurt her so bad. I wish she could have seen this tribe." He sweeps his arm around the table.

"Are they all yours?"

The boy has wiggled down and moved to the end of the table where he's tentatively punching Lucy's back. I take in his small stature; I look into his small eyes.

"Yes, they are," Bernice says, following my gaze. "Richard joined us just recently. In fact, that's how Miss Stanton located us. It turned out she had a lot in common with us. She was as interested as we are in Fetal Alcohol Syndrome. She'd read a newspaper article about the need for adoptive parents. Next to it was a photograph of a bunch of us who'd taken the plunge, adopted F.A.S. kids. Miss Stanton said she looked at that picture for a week—with a magnifying glass—thinking maybe she recognized Jeff. Finally, she called the paper and came looking for him."

At Lucy's stern instruction, Richard is trying to sit still. He grins and curtails his wild rocking as Lucy ties her yellow apron around his back.

"It was your grandmother who got Isadora interested in alcoholism in the first place," I say. "Did you know that?"

Jeff laughs. "How not? Even though it took a decade or so, it was my grandmother who got *me* interested. My grandmother tried to get everyone she ever met interested in the problem of alcohol abuse and its victims. She was a champion, or a zealot, depending on your point of view. You see, she was raised by alcoholic parents. Yet all of their wealth came from making, bottling, and distributing alcohol. She'd been both a victim of alcohol and a beneficiary. Much of her life was about trying to make sense of that paradox. Gran's time in New Mexico got her focused on the alcohol problem among Native Americans. The rate of F.A.S. among Natives is six times the national average, you know."

"Nowadays," Bernice jumps in, "the effect of alcoholism on a growing fetus is clearer. It's natural that Miss Stanton's interest would focus on Fetal Alcohol Syndrome."

"When I got myself straight, I began to look for ways to help others who are dependent," Jeff adds. He gestures toward the stack of flyers on the counter. "That's how Bernice and I met."

"Did Isadora talk about your grandmother's estate?"

"Obliquely, yes. I knew that her estate was in the ten-million range. And I knew she'd cut me out of her will. You see, the one thing she wouldn't stand for from me was substance abuse. And that's the one thing I did. I don't know if it was in my genes; I do know, finally, it was my choice. As to the money, I always assumed she'd left it where she thought it would do some good."

Bernice, who has been scrubbing at Richard's face while Jeff spoke, shoos the children into the next room. "Miss Stanton spent almost an hour playing with the kids that day. She was so sweet with Richard. She said he reminded her of somebody, and she said that Yolanda looked like Skeeter. Skeeter was her name for Jeff's grandmother." Bernice chuckles. "The kids were scared of her at first. But by the time she left, Lucy was trying to twirl her cane like a baton."

We talk for a while longer about Fetal Alcohol Syndrome. Dealing with the root and stem of the problem has long been Bernice's passion.

"Somehow we've got to turn this curse around." Bernice hands me one of the flyers she's printed up. The text says that Native Americans are four times more likely to die of alcoholism than other groups in the United States. "We've got to find a way to keep our women from drinking while they're pregnant, and find a decent way to raise the kids of those we don't reach in time. We've got to get our people to see what we're doing to our future."

No one looking upon Bernice's face at this moment could doubt her intensity and depth of feeling about this blight upon the future of her people. Hers is an enormous aspiration. But doubt and defeat are hiding in the lines around her eyes. She has little reason to hope for much change.

As I pull back onto the Interstate from the Canoncito feeder road and head east toward Albuquerque, the sun is at my back and the desert is empty. All the pieces of the puzzle are in place now, but my mind is not at peace. The problem is that I can't prove any of it. Evidence does not exist.

Without much hope that the police will listen to me, I pull off the highway at Albuquerque and into the first parking lot near a telephone stall. To be heard over traffic, I yell into the receiver at Detective Baca. I tell him what I think and what I need.

"What?! Ms. Donahue, why in God's name are you even out of the hospital?" He's back to calling me "Ms. Donahue," I notice. "The last time you tried to help us do our job you nearly got yourself killed, remember? Go home! Leave it alone!"

I urge and goad and beseech, but he wants no part of any crazy scheme to smoke out a respected citizen.

"Look," Baca says with finality, "you come in to the station next week after you've had some time to rest and calm down. Until then, Matty, get a grip." "Matty" again.

I can't blame him. There's only my hunch that Isadora was killed to erase traces of a decade of criminal activity. Only my analysis of how it must have happened.

But the murderer can't know for sure that there's no evidence. The murderer might even believe that something was overlooked. It's a big chance to take without help, but I can't think of another way.

I watch the traffic for a while and then occupy myself reading the graffiti on the telephone backboard for divine inspiration. I'm looking for some slogan like, "Screw your courage to the sticking place and ye shall not fail."

The closest thing I can find is, "Screw yourself!"

Close enough.

To make it work, I need a few props. Albuquerque Printing is a lawyer's supply house that stocks everything including, luckily, antique legal-length blue paper stock. I buy a single sheet and a ream of long white bond. They are kind enough to loan me a typewriter, with which I make a fair replica of the first page of a document that should pass muster from across a room. In too great a hurry to fake the rest, I make a few copies of the first page and the copies become the subsequent pages.

It's getting late and I need to get this done before the end of the day. But I want authenticity. Unfortunately, my best quick shot at that is the cinder-block, grilled, and graffiti-adorned pawn shop on Central Avenue.

"Look who's back for whips and chains," Manson calls from his chair before my eyes adjust to the darkness. Buzz-cut politely gets down the metal courier case for me and I shell out sixty-five bucks plus another fifteen for two tape recorders. Buzz-cut throws in a couple of blank tapes he scoops from a bin.

Using the "shed" key, I let myself in the back door of the house on Acequia Madre and flip the switch, grateful that the electricity is still on. I get everything set up. I test my voice from a distance. The first recorder picks up my voice perfectly. I test the second, reverse the tape, and push play. Nothing happens. I try again. *Oh, shit, no!* The second cassette—my backup tape—is defective. It's too late to replace it: I've already made the phone call.

Calm down, I order myself. *What you have to do is calm down and think. Think and wait.*

THIRTY-ONE

⟿⟾

I SIT WAITING LIKE A TIBETAN MONK WITH A TROUBLED soul—motionless—except for my eyes, which irresistibly dart to the watch on my wrist. I ignore the throbbing in my thigh. My hands lie folded in my lap in a circle of mellow lamplight. Otherwise there is darkness in this room where Teddy once played Cajun rhythms to cheer a stubborn old lady and soothe her shredding mind.

It usually takes about half an hour to get from Bishop's Lodge Road to this old neighborhood on the east side. But tonight, according to my watch, only sixteen minutes pass since my phone call until the Lexus pulls onto the gravel of the walled yard. I move to the window, where I watch Joe begin to circle the house on foot.

His wariness is just below the surface of his charm as we greet at the front door. I guide him into the living room, toward the circle of light.

"Thanks for coming, Joe."

He hesitates. ". . . Of course, Matty . . . of course. I'm glad you feel you can still call on me." He flips on the overhead light. "I wish I'd had a chance to talk to you before Norman sent his letter. The letter was so . . . impersonal . . . cruel, really. But after what you'd done, I couldn't really have changed anything." Joe takes my hand, squeezes it.

"Now, what's this all about?" he asks. "You said you know something new about the Stanton murder. Something I have to hear tonight? Matthew, I hope this isn't more crap about Norman."

"In a way it is."

"Goddamn it, Matty! What's wrong with you? Do you need a building to fall on your head? This obsession with Norman has already cost you your job. Now, what is it you *think* you know?"

"I know what happened here that night, Joe. I know how it happened. And I know why it happened."

His expression doesn't change.

"Would you like to look around to . . . get a feel for how it was that night?"

He accepts my invitation, surveys the room, moves to the archway leading to the hall, lingers there, switches on the hall light. He inspects its length and begins to prowl the rooms. He does this swiftly but with real interest, pausing at each doorway, flipping the lights on and back off as he goes. His inspection tour ends at the door of Isadora's bedroom.

"This is where it happened," I tell him, turning on the final light myself. "Go on in."

He enters this room more slowly, touches surfaces, even checks behind the curtains. I casually sit on the edge of Isadora's bed and watch him as I reach into her nightstand for the handcuffs I bought in Albuquerque a week ago.

As though this were a play we were rehearsing, he does what I knew he would do. He pulls the chair from the dressing table to the center of the room and flips it with a practiced wrist so that he can straddle it backward. His arms hug the ladder back. He rests his chin on his stacked fists. I've seen him in this pose so often. I should have recognized the remnant of it in the unlikely position of the chair that first morning. He studies me over the chair back, notes the handcuffs, and an unsettling calm settles over him. "I repeat, Matty—what is it you think you've discovered?"

Discovery is a funny thing. Sometimes the most unlikely little thing can turn you around, point you in a new direction. The first time I wondered about Joe was when the story came out in *At Large*. He and Judge Sandoval were with Eamonn Migill at the Christmas party and the next thing I knew, my awful life story was all over the headlines. Sandoval knew part of it, of course. But only Joe knew it all.

I say: "You deliberately ratted on me with Migill, didn't you?"

I slip one of the cuffs onto my left wrist and snap it closed.

"So I asked myself, why would Joe Danforth want to spoil what little reputation I have?"

He doesn't answer.

"It was to make me tuck in my tail, wasn't it? To do what you knew I'd done before . . . run away from the problem . . . stop trusting myself."

"You were dragging my law firm through the mud, Matty. When you confronted Norman at the party, I knew you had to be stopped."

"Mmm, but, you know, if it hadn't been for that little betrayal I might never have begun to put all the other pieces together. I'd missed so many clues before. Like when I found out George had brought a packet of material from the D.A.'s office addressed only to Frederick and Danforth, it didn't even occur to me that either one of the senior partners could have opened it. Either one of you could've known enough to duplicate Teddy's crime."

"You're crazy! I never saw a D.A.'s report on Bellasandro."

"And," I continue, only slightly deterred, "when I saw Gil Rodriguez's old courier case, identical to Norman's right down to the F.D.R. initials . . ." I reach my free arm between table and bed and lug my own newly purchased metal case up onto the bed beside me ". . . I should have realized that meant all the senior partners in Frederick, Danforth and Rodriguez probably once had identical cases. So, the tall man with the silver box entering Isadora's house that night could have been you."

Joe is silent.

"But no!" I continue, "It couldn't be my friend Joe. Not Joe Danforth, the guy sticking his neck out for me."

I thread the still-open second cuff through the handle of the case. "Not the guy who'd agree to let me pursue the investigation . . . on the condition, of course, that I keep him informed about things. Things like, say, witnesses who might trip up the murderer. Witnesses who coincidentally disappeared or died after I told you about them.

"The Magill article was such an obscure little thing, but it made me understand *you* differently." I look from the case to Joe and straddle the moment.

"You know, Joe, you should never have brought Alice Marlson's trust document into this house. And you should never have let Isadora get her hands on your metal case. Because, when she had her wits about her, Isadora was too canny for you. And . . . she had this bad little habit of shackling herself to things, to even up odds that didn't suit her. But you wouldn't have known that, would you, Joe? You'd never laid eyes on Isadora Stanton before that afternoon."

He is so devoid of motion that he seems inert.

"Of course, that's really the part that kept me from seeing what you'd done to my friend. The fact that you didn't *know* her. You couldn't possibly have had a motive to kill someone you never met . . . right?" My heart is pounding as I snap the second cuff shut on the handle, securing my left arm to the steel case.

I'd banked on his being unnerved at seeing me shackled to the case just as he must have seen Isadora moments before her death. I need to loosen his rigid self-control. Unless I can provoke Joe enough to incriminate himself, the evidence that he killed and mutilated will never be found. He came here that night to remove Isadora's evidence of his embezzlement. And he succeeded. Without that, there is nothing to tie him to her murder. So now I must get him to provide enough detail to prove to the authorities that he was here. That his need to save his professional life was motive enough to kill the old woman who'd threatened to end it.

But so far, I'm the only one who seems unnerved.

"Ahh, but no," I say, dripping sarcasm. "It turns out that isn't right! It turns out you *did* know Isadora. At least you knew *about* her. And there came a time when she knew about you too."

"What are you talking about, Matty?" His voice is still under tight control.

"You may not have met Isadora all those years ago when Alice Marlson first set up the trust for her grandson, Jeff. Isadora probably directed her best friend to the firm because Norman was her lawyer. It was just providential that you ended up drafting the Marlson trust." With my free hand, I unhook the latches and open the case a couple of inches.

"Isadora Stanton was probably only a name to you then. The name dictated to you by Alice Marlson, the name of a cotrustee who was supposed to help you decide . . ." I hesitate—searching for admission in his eyes—searching for some sign that I'm right. This is my big gamble. I take another deep breath and push myself over the threshold. I reach my hand inside the case and draw out the long blue-backed legal document. I dangle it in the air between two fingers.

". . . Isadora Stanton was the name of the cotrustee named by Alice Marlson to help you decide if Jeffrey Marlson was drug-free by the time he turned thirty. If he was, then he was eligible to inherit under the terms of his trust, wasn't he? How much money was in the trust, Joe? It must—"

Joe rises from the chair. I replace the document and close the case.

"—have been a lot." I keep the tremor locked in my chest and out of my voice.

Joe approaches the bed fast, even as he must have that

night. I lock one of the latches. My fingers search anxiously for the other. His hands are on the case. I find the second latch. I snap it home.

He yanks wildly at the case, twisting it so savagely that pain shoots through my arm and I gasp.

"Hell of a thing, isn't it, Joe," I manage. "Reliving it like this? Must be like a nightmare you can never escape."

The cuff bites deeply into my wrist. I've borne too much pain in recent days, and an ancient part of my brain recoils from more. A long animal sound breaks the air. The sound is coming from me.

Startled back to his senses, Joe releases me abruptly. He gulps air deeply to gain composure. He doesn't bother to open the case. Even that night with Isadora, once she was locked to the case, the document ceased to matter. He could easily have opened the case and removed it, then killed the woman who knew its contents. No, by then it was the case itself—sturdy as a safe and etched with the initials "F.D.R."—that he couldn't leave behind.

Joe begins to pace. He open drawers, rifles contents. He's looking for something. He's begun to think about where this goes from here. The recorder with the only good cassette tape is attached beneath Isadora's dresser. I figure there's about a half hour of tape left. I reach deep into the right-hand pocket of my skirt, bring out the key to the handcuffs, and felt a shudder of relief as I free my wrist.

"If there'd been a key to her handcuffs that night, you wouldn't have mutilated her, would you?"

"I didn't mutilate anybody, Matty. And I didn't kill anybody, either." He bends. He runs his hands under the furniture. I know what he's looking for. He still hasn't incriminated himself. Both time and tape are running out.

"Okay, where is it?" he demands. "Are you wearing it? I know you wouldn't have set this up without protecting yourself . . . Where's the tape?"

"I don't need you on tape for protection, Joe. I have this." I pat the case lying beside me with complete conviction. I hold his stare. "I made more than this one copy of the trust agreement you drew up for Alice Marlson," I lie. "I left a second copy and a letter explaining everything with a reliable friend. Once the police compare the trust provisions with your financial records, it'll be all over. You'll be charged with embezzlement."

"I see." His voice has grown hoarse. His eyes bore holes in me. He gestures toward the case. "Where did you get that copy of the Marlson trust? I took her only copy."

His first admission. But I'm on extremely thin ice here. The bogus document contrived by me in fifteen minutes at Albuquerque Printing has passed the flash test, and I've apparently guessed correctly at the gist of the original. But I can't afford to invent more details. So, I change the subject.

"If you really didn't kill her, Joe, you could still pay the trust back, make restitution."

His body grows slack all at once. He laughs sourly, gets almost to the edge of a jag before he catches himself. "There's no money left to pay back, Matthew." His body shudders slightly. "Not enough to matter, anyway. The original principal was over ten million. At first I thought I could replace it all. I only took a million the first time. And I paid it back. No harm was done. The next time I took a bit more. I began to replace that, too, but then things went to hell. Investments failed. I borrowed again . . . and again."

"Liza needs a lot of money?" I venture.

"Everybody thinks she came from money. It's not true. Not for generations. Her family lived on pity and the charity of rich relatives. But she has such a hunger . . . By the time the Marlson kid was thirty, off drugs and eligible to inherit, the trust was already down by more than five million. The kid didn't need the money. What the hell did he need the money for? He's a teacher on some Indian reservation, for Christ's sake!"

Joe sees no similarity between Jeff's poverty and Liza's.

"So to keep Jeff's money for yourself, you notified Isadora Stanton that he was dead, didn't you? But when Isadora saw Jeff in the flesh, she knew what you'd done."

Joe's momentary recklessness is vanishing before my eyes.

"And she made the mistake of telling you she knew . . . didn't she?"

He tenses. He doesn't answer. He waits.

"That was the hardest part for me, Joe. You know, I wanted Norman to turn out to be the murderer. And that wanting blinded me. So I couldn't put it all together, until Tito Sena told me Isadora said she spat in the eye of the devil."

"What?"

"That's right. Her driver told me that at about five-thirty the evening before she was killed, Isadora came to our office. She confronted somebody inside and came back out satisfied. For a couple of minutes, I still I assumed it was Norman."

"But?" he asks cautiously, his eyes darting around the room.

"But at five-thirty on that particular evening Norman was giving the keynote address to a medical-legal conference in Los Alamos. Norman couldn't have been in the office when Isadora barged in loaded for bear. So, I asked myself, in whose eye did Isadora Stanton spit?"

He turns his head away from me, back to his search. He bends before the dresser and runs his arm along the bottom slowly. I see the sudden satisfaction in his face before he turns his full attention to ripping off the adhesive. He rises with my new tape recorder in his hand.

". . . Now, see, Matty, this wasn't smart at all. I take it your plan here was to get me to make a full confession while you recorded the whole sorry tale. Well . . ." He chuckles, pulling the magnetic tape loose from the cassette. ". . . I was careful here tonight. All you've got on this tape is what you already had, proof of the embezzlement. And, if it comes to it, I can plea-bargain that away in a heartbeat . . . three months of my life and all my remaining worldly goods into the bargain—"

"And," I interrupt recklessly, "your license . . . your reputation."

"Matthew, I'm not Norman. You know my creed, I do what I must. I move on. I'd survive losing my ticket . . . like I say . . . if it came to that." As he speaks, Joe is taking the saucer from under a candle on Isadora's desk, picking up the nearby packet of matches. "But perhaps it needn't come to that. There was a time when you were in professional trouble yourself, remember, Matty?"

He touches the flame to the tape, and the small evidence he has given me tonight begins to evaporate before my eyes. "You needed some help then, someone willing to overlook your professional transgressions and give you a second chance. Remember?"

"I remember."

"And, speaking of professional transgressions, of making restitution to clients," his voice is casual, almost nonchalant, "are you still making payments yourself? Must take—what? Half your salary?"

I nod and watch the flame consume the last of the tape. A whisper of ash is left in the saucer.

"So maybe now there's a way we can both walk away from our . . . difficulties . . . in better shape." He considers how thick a slice to cut me and decides to start low. He suggests that he could pay all my old debts and get me a new job—out of state, of course. "Good pay," he urges lightly, "a safe harbor."

"A safe harbor doesn't sound too bad to me right now, I'm ashamed to say. But I owe something to Isadora."

"You can't bring the old woman back, Matty, and you owe something to me, too."

"What happens to Jeff Marlson?" I ask. Joe thinks the question means he's passed the only real hurdle and now it's just a matter of haggling over price.

"Hell, if that's really a problem for you, I'll do what I should have done in the first place, what I told the Stanton woman I'd do. There's still a bit of money left in the trust. And I can sell a few things . . . even borrow some. Of course, it won't come to ten million, but . . . maybe, with luck . . . close to two million?" Hope and caution merge in his smile. "Maybe enough. What do you say?"

"You made this offer to Isadora? That you would replace Jeff's inheritance . . . some of it?"

"I did. And she accepted it."

To my dismayed expression, he answers, "Why wouldn't she? Like you say, she was a smart old curmudgeon. My offer was her last best hope of doing right by her old friend. If she turned me in, all of the Marlson kid's money would have gone to my lawyers."

"So help me get this straight, Joe." I falter through my vision of that night—Isadora confronting Joe—he, coming to her home to assess and mend the damage—she, trying to trap him with her handcuffs. Now that there is nothing to record Joe's words, he readily makes corrections, even contributes details. He admits everything. Everything except for knowing about Teddy's record and for the actual murder. Although I've shown him I'm willing to make a deal with the devil, he doesn't know for sure what I'll do if he admits to killing and mutilating my friend.

But he does know—*must* know—there's no credible account he can invent which has Isadora alive when he left her with her wrist shackled that night, but dead hours later with her hand severed from her wrist. He's considering his options. So I help him out.

"You don't need to pay my debts, Joe. And you don't need to find me a job. Lately, I'm finding the practice of law more trouble than it's worth. . . . Maybe, as you say, there *is* a way for us to help each other . . . but it'll have to be the whole two million."

"Agreed!"

"And it'll have to be within a month."

"Agreed, again."

"Okay, here's how it will work. One week after the money is turned over, you'll receive all copies of the Marlson trust . . . on two conditions. When you hear the second condition, you'll see why my only choice is to keep my word to you."

"I'm intrigued."

"First condition, you tell me the rest of the story."

"And the second?"

"Screw Jeffrey Marlson. The money will go to me. I'll give you the number of an offshore account as soon as I can arrange it."

A long moment passes before his smile breaks. A moment

more and he is laughing, gathering his things. "You're a girl after my own heart, Matty. I'm really going to miss you. And . . . you've got yourself a deal."

He supposes now that the story he spins doesn't even have to be a good one. He claims that once Isadora had agreed to his offer, he asked her for the key to the handcuffs but it was nowhere to be found. He says that he eventually found a toolbox and managed to remove the handle of his case with a screwdriver. "I left her right there in her bed like that, with her damn cuffs still on her wrists," he finishes.

I choose not to point out the coincidences one must swallow to buy his story. Instead, I stand up and put my hand out to him. The gesture says we are the same, he and I. He shakes my hand, congratulates me for my good sense, and finds his own way out. As the sound of the car leaving the courtyard dies, I stare at the ashes Joe's brief saucer-fire has left. Then I turn and lower myself to the floor. I get on my belly, careful once more not to damage my injured leg, and stretch again as far under the bed as I can reach. With the tips of my fingernails I peel the duct tape from the center bed slat and bring out the second tape recorder.

This evidence will clinch an embezzlement case. All by itself, it won't convict Joe of Isadora's murder. But, together with Juanita's statement, it'll go a long way to freeing Teddy. Sitting straight-legged on the floor, I feel fatigue and pain returning as adrenaline subsides. But, at the sight of the tape resting in my hand, it all seems worth it.

When I'd conceived this plan on the drive back from Canoncito, I knew Joe would probably find one of the recorders. I could only hope he wouldn't look for a second one. I had a bad moment getting things prepared before Joe came— when the second tape from the pawn shop proved to be a dud. But, sometimes, when it has to, your brain can tease out a little memory and present it to you.

The tape I'd been carrying around in my purse since Isadora's funeral was still in the never-used makeup pocket. As I rewind it now, I feel a pang. I'm sorry to have recorded over that little piece of Teddy and Isadora's world—Teddy singing "Amazing Grace" to Isadora like it might save her life. Who knew that it might save his own?

I play the backup tape twice to make sure it's all there before I call Detective Baca.

THIRTY-TWO

———⟡———

MONDAY, DECEMBER 23

OUTSIDE, EVERY STARK BRANCH OF THE APPLE TREE IS
topped with a thin band of new snow. Inside, I sink deep
into the quilts and prop the receiver up to my ear with the extra
pillow. It is Joleen again, calling to tell me more about this
morning's nondevelopments. I called her last night immediately after turning the tape over to Baca.

Fickle as ever, Joleen has spun a hundred degrees to take
advantage of the opportunity the tape presents. She's moved at
dizzying speed in the intervening hours. But, despite her huff
and her puff, the rest of the world is operating at a more
leisurely pace. Contrary to her demands, a criminal complaint
against Joe Danforth on embezzlement charges hasn't yet begun to be considered. And, despite the fact that the beleaguered
young A.D.A. from Saturday has now had the benefit of a dawn
meeting to hear the Danforth tape, the District Attorney's office
still hasn't made up its collective mind about joining the public
defender in today's Motion to Dismiss Theodore Bellasandro.

"We have two hours to go and there is no damned excuse for this fucking around," Joleen rages. "The little dick-head turned green when he listened to that tape. He knows Danforth killed Isadora Stanton but he's scared blue of a case against one of the state's most powerful lawyers."

"He's a pretty colorful guy—all green and blue." My lazy voice is in stark contrast to her aggravation. As far as I'm concerned this is all over but the shouting. With Juanita's deposition and the Danforth tape, I believe the court will dismiss the case against Teddy with or without the D.A.'s blessing. "Why not just let things take their natural course?" I ask.

"You haven't talked to Teddy lately, have you?"

"Joleen, do you even remember you're the one who specifically ordered me not to speak to Teddy?" I shoot back.

"Okay, okay. I'm sorry. Mea culpa. I was wrong. You were right. Now, let's get on with it. Teddy needs to put this behind him soon! Real soon."

"Sure, but we're only talking about a few—"

"Teddy may not have a few days . . . He's not . . . how shall I say this? Not . . . easy in his mind. One minute, he's all right. The next, he seems to be . . . collapsing somehow. I'm concerned about leaving everything unresolved for even a few more days. If he doesn't get out today, he's in over the holidays."

My good eye lingers on the slender mantle of snow at the base of my windows and I resist hearing her concern. I've worked hard in considerable pain. I've done enough. I'm tired. I want some sleep.

"This time it really is over," I say. "Relax."

When she hangs up, I burrow even further into the bed. But my eye begins to twitch, and I have a sudden jarring memory of the glass eyeball in Faye Stanton's socket. I haven't worn the patch since I took it off going into Canoncito. Now I'm suddenly very sober about testing my eye. I quickly focus back and forth on the near quilt pattern, then on the far branches, then back again. Happily, my eyes seem to work about as well as ever. I flex my thigh muscles. The pain is mild—quite bearable. While I wasn't watching, my body has been healing itself.

I'm feeling pretty good otherwise, too. More than just vindicated about Teddy. I'm slowly realizing it might not be possible to walk this earth without doing some harm. Grappling with the harm we do to each other is part of the human condition. Another part of it is moving on. And that thought leads to another.

I stretch, push the phone away, and reach for the fat envelope from Max that was in my mailbox when I finally got home last night. I open the mouth and let the cascade of photographs, mostly pictures of Sarah, slip into my lap. A few show Enid in the background, smiling, looking pensive and entirely too interesting. Sarah has her father's dark curls and open face. One of the photographs rivets me: Max and Sarah lie on the floor facing each other over a chess board, two pointy chins in cupped palms balanced on elbows. Two profiles intensely focused, concentrating fiercely on the game before them.

I put the pictures away and, with a wistful look at the cozy bed, rise and start to dress. Maybe there is a bit more to do after all. I consign the remaining pain pills to the toilet bowl and watch them swirl away with no regret. A phone call needs to be made. I've been thinking about it since Faye Stanton asked about finding someone to house-sit for her. I've been sure I'd eventually make the call since I read Isadora's second will in Fullerton's office in Albuquerque.

I call Faye and make a reasonable proposal, under the circumstances. I know full well that I should be going through Norman for this, but I opt not to. In due time, Juanita or Teddy or Jeffrey Marlson can formally protest Isadora's original will in probate court. But, right now, I just want a temporary solution for Juanita. Auspiciously and perhaps not surprisingly, Faye agrees to my suggestion.

I make arrangements and pick up Juanita from the hospital. I'd feared her distress, so I'm relieved when she seems content—even happy—to be back in the Acequia Madre house. At least she will have a place to live for a few months. I leave her puttering in the kitchen as though nothing had changed.

It's after noon by the time I get to the Public Defender's office. The conference room is cramped and junky. Lawyers and staffers are coming in and out. Mostly in. Joleen is sitting low in her chair, her head hunched into her shoulders. Both of her sturdy legs are on the conference table. Headphones still connected to the tape player on the table dangle from her neck. She has the Bellasandro file on her lap. Stone Allen slumps opposite. Neither of these two defenders of Teddy Bellasandro is nearly as happy as they ought to be right now.

Rocks has apparently been cranky since early morning, when Joleen took his shot at glory away by easing the file from him and going over to court without him to argue the *Motion to Dismiss the State of New Mexico* v. *Theodore Bellasandro* on the basis of newly discovered evidence.

Joleen is pointedly ignoring him, but she drags her nose out of the file from time to time to regale staff members—and me—with impersonations of her counterpart from the D.A.'s office at this morning's hearing. Unlike the Public Defender's office, which is miles from the courthouse, the office of the Santa Fe district attorney is located inside it, only a few cozy feet from the courtrooms and the judges' chambers.

"So there the little twerp is—pacing up and down in the hallway," Joleen says, her head craning on her neck like a fan's at a tennis match. "Back and forth, back and forth. He gets stopped every pass or two by other A.D.A.'s who put their two cents in. And the goddamn D.A. is hiding three feet away in his office while his minions run around like ants—touching heads to see what their shared brain is coming up with.

"They all know they can't bring a murder charge against Danforth while Bellasandro sits in jail on the same charge. And they know in their tiny hearts that eventually they've got to bring a murder charge against Danforth. No matter how much it scares the shit out of them to charge someone with muscle. Spreading their cheeks for hotshot private lawyers is S.O.P. for the D.A.'s office. Like what A.D.A. Martinez did, turning over Bellasandro's criminal record to Norman Frederick in the first fucking place. Which, incidently, they're denying now. The part of the tape that turned their bowels to jelly was that—not, 'Oh my God, we're prosecuting the wrong guy.' Uh-uh—who gives a shit about that? But, 'Hey, maybe our own office has some kind

of culpability.' Martinez himself gets buttonholed by his clones
to see how this part of the story might play out. Martinez stam-
mers around, claiming he never sent the record after all. Says he
ran it but then had second thoughts—says the only thing he
ever sent by courier to Frederick and Danforth was about selection committee business. All these guys are such scum bags. My
defendants are more honorable."

The Public Defender staff lawyers are mostly young, too.
They drink coffee from mugs stenciled with the motto, "A reasonable doubt for a reasonable price." The coffee is acrid but
the regulars don't flinch at the bitterness of the brew or of
Joleen's diatribe. They've tasted both before.

"Anyway, they dick around with shit like that until the last
possible second. Finally the D.A. himself comes out sucking his
lip like he's about to give up Al Capone on a technicality. He allows as how maybe it would be a good idea for Judge Peña to
hear the Danforth tape—take the onus off his bony hind-end.
Of course Judge Peña went ballistic when he heard what Danforth *admitted* to doing to Isadora. And with Juanita Jakes's re-
traction, it was a done deal. The A.D.A. takes Peña's rectal
temperature with his lips and graciously informs the court that
the charges against Teddy are being dropped."

"See, I could've handled that," contributes Rocks. "The
D.A.'s office was just going to roll over. I don't see why . . ." His
petulant tone trails off as a few more P.D. staffers drift into the
conference room. They are discussing the case—asking questions that Stone answers tentatively at first then, as no one corrects him, more boldly.

"See," he explains to one of the younger women as she
hoists herself up into the window well. "It was never about
Isadora Stanton's estate. It was all about Alice Marlson's estate.
Not about two million dollars—but about ten million dollars."

"I still don't get it," says the woman. "Why didn't Jeffrey
Marlson demand his inheritance? And wouldn't there have
been a second beneficiary?"

"Sure," I interject. "But the charity that was named as alternate beneficiary wouldn't have known unless the alternate provision naming it kicked in. And of course Jeff, himself, never

knew about the alternative provision. Only Joe and Isadora even knew there was a trust fund. When Isadora was notified of Jeff's death, she would have assumed the money had gone to the charity Alice Marlson had selected, just as intended."

"Jesus Hardball Christ!" Joleen explodes. She pushes off from the table, and punches at something in the file she's been reading with so much attention. "*This* is what they hadn't quite gotten around to telling me. The cops found Charlie Lee alive and well over a week ago and notified the D.A. They *talked* to the guy. My notification from these 'officers of the court' was put in the *mail*. Look at this shit! *Two frigging days ago!* And you can bet your booties that Lee was a terrific alibi witness for us. Otherwise, he'd a been shoved down my throat so fast I'd still be gagging on him!"

By now, several clerks and young lawyers stand against the walls and a couple more perch on the deep window shelf listening to the postmortem on one of the office's murder cases.

"See what I told you, Matty. This is what it's really like," Joleen instructs me solemnly, for their benefit. "It ain't no Sunday-school search for the truth. It's us against the jackboots. It's *this* crap." She rattles the Notification Of Witness Location at me.

The phone rings. Joleen stretches across the scarred conference table to grab it. She listens for a second. "We'll be here," she says and hangs up.

"He's out!" she calls. "They're bringing him over now."

There is near exhilaration in the room. No doubt they would rather have seen the defendant released as a result of good lawyering, but these particular lawyers have a vested interest in seeing any accused recognized as an innocent man. Things like that go a long way to justify their existence. Two of the lawyers exchange high fives, and a pretty young secretary pats Stone Allen's back.

While we wait for Teddy, Joleen stretches and cracks various joints in her body. She's still holding the notice concerning the location of Charlie Lee—still studying it. She turns and motions me to a relatively quiet corner of the room.

"What do you make of Charlie Lee being found unharmed?"

"What do you mean? What should I make of it?"

"I don't know. I thought it was part of your scenario that the killer had gotten rid of Lee because he was Teddy's alibi. Didn't you tell me that?"

"So I was wrong. I made a mistake. So?"

"Nothing, I guess."

I begin to turn away when she adds, "You made the same mistake about Hadid's death, huh? Assuming it was Rickie Hadid, he died as part of a family feud. So, that wasn't about getting rid of a witness either, was it?"

"What the hell are you trying to suggest?"

"I was just thinking. Danforth knew about both of them, didn't he? I mean . . . you told him. Told him what each of them knew or saw, right?"

"Right."

"So, he knew how dangerous they were to him, right?"

"Right."

"And according to us, he'd already committed one murder, right? . . . So, why didn't he?"

"Why didn't he what?"

"Why didn't he kill them?"

I open my mouth but nothing comes out.

"Hell." She slaps my back, and seeing that I have no answer adds, "Don't worry about it. I'm a defense lawyer. I'm hard-wired to look for the faults in a case. But *that* defendant ain't my problem. He's not yours either. Forget I mentioned it."

There's a stir in the hallway and both of us turn toward it. A woman clears a path into the room. In her wake Teddy follows. His eyes are bright and excited. They take in the room and come to rest on me.

"Son of a bitch if I don't owe you an apology, Matty. I try t' fire you, and you turn 'round and save my lousy hide. I can't tell you how sorry I am. I should'a trusted you." As Teddy reaches me, he pulls me to him in a bear hug that reminds me that my healing body has a ways to go.

Surprised at this lighthearted demeanor after what Joleen had warned about, I look questioningly at her. She seems as confused than I am, but shrugs broadly, shaking off her doubt.

Teddy's psychological recovery seems terrific to me, too. I squirm out of his embrace, smile at him, and ask, "You want to see Juanita? I told her I'd bring you over as soon as you were released."

"You bet," he says. "Let's blow this joint. No offense, Joleen. I want to thank you for your help."

Joleen laughs and says, "Oh, what the hell, I guess innocent is as good a way as any for beating a rap."

After that Teddy turns to Rocks and adds generously, "You too, Stone. Thanks."

Rocks moves solemnly forward and shakes Teddy's hand for a second too long.

"Glad I could be there for you," Rocks says to Teddy. I have to turn my head away.

THIRTY-THREE

———∞∞∞———

As he stares out the open window of my Toyota, sucking the cold sunny air deep into his lungs, Teddy lapses into silence. For a month and a half he's seen daylight only through slits of wired pebble glass.

"It's done," I finally say. "You're going to be all right."

He doesn't turn his head toward me when he says, almost to himself, "I don't think I'm going to be all right, Matty."

"It's too soon," I insist. "Too much has happened, but eventually . . ."

He rolls the window up, cutting off the outside world.

"Not ever." His voice is flat—final. "See . . . I remembered . . . things. You told me I should try to remember things. You said I had to." He turns to face me.

"But it turns out I didn't have to." His voice is accusatory and I see now there is something like hatred in his eyes. "I didn't have to remember."

"Teddy, I'm sorry, but—"

He interrupts, "I didn't have to remember nothing. Now I can't get things out of my head. Things ain't ever going to be all right."

"Sometimes we have to face things."

"What the fuck do you know?" he explodes. "You carry around your little piss-pot of guilt and you think it's heavy. You think me and you is alike. Well, we ain't alike! You can still find your way back from what happened to you. You don't know jack-shit-nothin' about *me*!"

As we pull into the courtyard and park next to the limo, Teddy runs the fingers of both hands through his hair, rests his forehead in his palms, and sits in silence. When he looks up, his composure is back and he's trying for a smile.

"God, Matty, I'm sorry. I been gettin' like this lately ... all ... all sideways-like. I know I gotta get hold of myself. I'm sorry."

"Forget it. Come on, let's go in."

As we enter, we hear Juanita in the kitchen singing. Something back there smells good. I guess Juanita has done whatever she had to do to make her peace with being back in Isadora's house. But Teddy is going to be another matter. As we move toward the warm kitchen I see him steal a glance toward Isadora's bedroom door and shudder.

But like someone has dialed a brightening knob, he lights up again as he enters the kitchen and sees Juanita. She appears to be preparing a meal primarily from canned goods. She has opened spinach, clam chowder, evaporated milk, and chili. She seems also to have found a sack of old potatoes from somewhere. These she's peeling and chopping on the bare counter. Teddy pops a slice of raw potato into his mouth, pats her enormous belly, and makes his eyes big in mock awe. She likes his teasing and bats his hand away as she looks for something. "I can't find the chopping block," she says.

Teddy's good mood evaporates as fast as it arrived. His shifts make him seem disconcertingly unpredictable. Joleen was right to be concerned about him.

"Hey," he says, "I'm feeling a little, I don't know . . . I think . . ." his eyes dart around as if trying to light on something safe. ". . . Hey, we can't have supper without wine, can we? How about if I take the limo and go buy us some wine to go with supper, huh?"

"Sure," I say doubtfully, "but . . . here, take my keys. Faye took the limo keys."

"Don't you worry about that, kiddo. I got ways to get in that car, and let's see if I can't work some Cajun magic on the ignition. You like your wine red or white?" he asks, turning on his heel, eager to be gone. He's out the door before I can answer.

I feel buffeted by Teddy's too-rapid changes, and when he's gone I stare dumbly at where he stood a moment before. Juanita repeats that she can't find the big wooden cutting board that was always on the counter.

"What?"

"The cutting board," she respeats patiently. "It was always here. Did the police take it?"

I'm considering that question. Perhaps if I hadn't been considering that particular question at that particular moment, the sudden engine roar from the courtyard wouldn't have penetrated. But the sound outside joins Juanita's question in my ear and they travel into my brain together.

And the thought they give rise to takes my breath away. I bolt for the front door and race across the portal. Teddy is on his back under the dash taping the wires he has just twisted together. I don't stop. I get in the Toyota, slam it into gear, and tear out of the driveway, almost skidding into the small open ditch.

Not wrong again! Please! I grip the wheel and drive fast, too fast for these narrow winding streets. I make reckless turns, skirting the center of town and turning north on the Old Taos Highway. I don't know if he'll still be there, but I'm not about to call ahead this time. I drive past Camel Rock and the Nambe Pueblo. A sign reads "Espanola, Low Rider Capital Of The World," and I think, Christ . . . one of Baca's kids—Chuey—he could have figured this out. It just took a different point of view, an unclouded view.

I think I've just about reached the limit of my guilt. I did what seemed right when I did it. If it turns out I was wrong— God forbid, wrong *again*—I will just have to live with that. No matter how many times you get it wrong, my choice has to be to forgive myself and go on. The other choice—is the choice to die.

I begin to slow at the southern edge of Espanola. The sign reads, "Los Alamos And Santa Clara Next Left." I make the turn.

I pull into the Santa Clara Pueblo, and the road floats downward at a drifty angle into the center of the village. It is quiet. Few people stir outside of their houses.

I park near a dirt plaza and walk toward a kiva entrance where an old man and a young man stand together in silence, watching my approach without sign of greeting or rejection. I know a white woman will not be welcome inside the kiva, the exclusive domain of the men of the tribe. When I reach the men, I keep my eyes away from their place of ancient ritual and speak to the air, glimpsing the elder in quick glances. He is about fifty with straight razor-cut iron hair and unblinking eyes. He is appraising me with those eyes.

"I'm trying to find a man, a Santa Clara man."

There is no answer.

"His name is Charlie Lee."

"Why are you looking for this man?"

I hesitate. ". . . An old woman was killed. Charlie Lee may know something about that—about the man who killed her. The old woman was a friend of mine."

"The old woman was . . . a white woman?"

"Yes."

"And the man, he is a white man?"

"Yes."

Another minute passes in a kind of eerie serenity while the man considers my request. My pulse has slowed somewhat by the time he nods to the younger man who motions for me to follow him.

We walk through the village single file along paths so narrow in some places that if I were to reach out both my arms at once I would touch an adobe dwelling on either side. We emerge on the eastern edge of the village. Here, the land falls gently under yellow fields and winter gray trees to the banks of the Rio Grande. Minutes later, we reach a fenced yard. Within it sits a skinny dog, a blue Ford pickup, and a yellow stucco house. My guide knocks at the door of the stucco house, enters, and seconds later emerges with another man.

This man is not happy to see me. I judge this mostly from the shape of his mouth since I can see little of his face. Charlie Lee's eyes are invisible behind the mirrored aviator glasses which he settled into place as he came out the door. What I can see of his hair under the baseball cap is black and thick and long enough to try to curl around the collar of his nylon ski jacket.

"Do you know who I am?" I ask.

"I can guess," he says quietly. "You're the Donahue woman."

I want information that Charlie Lee isn't going to want to give me. His posture says he didn't invite me here. As always, I feel a bit of the weight of everything from the purchase of Manhattan Island to Coronado's plunder resting on my shoulders, silently demanding repentance and atonement.

"Right. I'm sorry to bother you."

There is not a hint of invitation in his stance. I look at my own reflection in his glasses.

"The last time I talked to you," I press on, "you said you'd be willing to give a statement to the District Attorney about you and Teddy at Puye. But then you were gone."

"I made a statement when I got back."

"Yes, but that was a month too late. What happened, Charlie? Where were you? Would you tell me?"

"Me and a friend went out to California," he says flatly.

"But you said—"

"I said I'd make a statement if I had to. And if it went to court, I'd of come." He smiles at me like a teacher. "A lot of things just go away if you wait long enough. Like this case against Belly."

"How did you know? That it went away? That only happened this morning."

"Didn't. But I see how Anglo courts work. Lots of fuss. Lots of money. But you don't get any more done than we do." The smile again. He's enjoying this. "Do you?"

I cock my head, conceding the point to him. "Would you

mind talking to me just a little more about the day you picked
Teddy up? Would you tell me if he was angry when he left Santa
Fe? Was he mad at Miss Stanton?"

"No. He wasn't mad." After another moment, he adds, "But
he was worried. She wanted him to take her someplace. All the
way he kept saying she might need him. Maybe he should go
back. He kept it up. The more he drank, the more he worried."

I think there is no way to do this now but straight as a
string. I point to the blue pickup.

"That your truck? The one you drove that night?"

He nods.

"You said you had the keys the whole time . . ."

He nods and pulls them out of his back pocket as if that
would prove the point.

". . . but maybe he didn't need the keys. He could have hot-
wired your pickup, couldn't he?"

Lee looks dubious.

"I just saw him hot-wire a car," I go on. "It took him less
than two minutes."

Charlie Lee studies the pickup now and purses his lips. He
shrugs, then ambles over to the truck, opens the door, and
cranes his head inside to see beneath the dash. When he
straightens up, he give me another shrug.

"The wires've been taped," he says.

I feel like I've been punched in the stomach.

"Don't necessarily mean he did it," he says.

"Right," I say.

In a flash, the sort-and-batch part of my brain runs through
the options of getting tribal authorities or calling Baca. Won't
work. Be even worse this time than it was with Joe. The tribe may
even shut us all out.

"You said you camped at Third Pond?"

"Yeah. Caught fish every day. Teddy cooked them. He
chopped enough firewood and caught enough fish to feed the
village."

"Where exactly did you camp?"

I can't see the man's eyes, but I can see the wariness return
to his posture.

"You Belly's friend, or is this about something else?"

It's a simple question. I don't have a simple answer. "Could you tell me where exactly around Third Pond?" I repeat instead.

Charlie Lee shakes his head with finality, shutting me out. "You can't go up in there, if that's what you're thinking. The ponds are off limits to you."

I know we're done here, but I can't quite walk away. "I guess I don't know if he's my friend," I say, and I feel the melancholy of those words seep through me as I turn to leave.

When I am nearly out of earshot, I hear Charlie Lee say to my back, "He *is my* friend, you know."

THIRTY-FOUR

※◈◈※

T HE SUN IS LOW IN THE SKY AS I LEAVE THE PUEBLO.
Twelve miles to the south, at the roadside monument that
marks the Puye Cliff Dwellings, I turn abruptly west into the
setting sun to begin the long climb up and into the canyon.

The Santa Clara Canyon is one of many deep scars cut by
rushing creeks between high mesas of volcanic rock and sand-
stone. They point like splayed fingers down to the Rio Grande.
Shadows far off to my left creep across the Los Alamos ski runs.
High on the right, against the stark cliff faces, are the remnants
of a fourteenth-century Anasazi village. Other than the caves
themselves, what remains today are the long rows of carefully
aligned holes where poles extended over long-gone outer rooms
and porches.

Homes for nurturing ancient tribal families and homes
birthing nuclear weapons. Both hidden in the same high desert
mesas. Both built in the name of self-protection.

Ahead, the road splits. At the left fork, a sign on a gate

drawn across the road reads: "CLOSED TO ALL BUT TRIBAL MEMBERS." I edge around the barrier and continue driving.

The canyon narrows rapidly. The valley floor rises, but not as dramatically as the sheer cliff walls on either side. The curving road is rock-strewn and potholed, edged with huge ponderosa pines. I drive in and out of twilight and sunlight.

I still hope I'm wrong. But if I've learned anything these past weeks, it is that hoping doesn't make it so. I emerge from yet another canyon-night and, before my eyes can adjust, I've bounced past a ranger station and I see First Pond in a clearing off to my left.

By Second Pond there are frequent deep snow patches. I push this old car up the worsening road until I reach the wide clearing that surrounds the earthen dam which forms Third Pond. I turn onto twin ruts just below the dam and rattle across a narrow wooden bridge, looking for the site. At the crest of a ridge scattered with primitive remains of old campsites, I park the Toyota. I lean against the steering wheel to survey the scene.

If the evidence is here, how do I find it? How do I look for one particular old campsite? I get out of the car and stand very still for a long time. I'd dressed for celebration today and I'm still, foolishly now, in high heels and a suit. The dry air chills me to the bone but, if I am to find anything, it must be now. By tomorrow Charlie Lee will have alerted the Santa Clara rangers about my intent to trespass. Perhaps he already has. Given the intricacies of tribal jurisdiction and my shabby reputation with the Anglo authorities, it's unlikely anyone else will ever look here on my word alone.

I see an extra-large pile of cordwood stacked neatly between me and the pond. I trudge over to the fire pit nearest the pile and grab a stick to stir the ashes. Blackened but unburned pine knots, some crumpled aluminum foil, a beer can, and shards of a whiskey bottle surface. Nothing!

I squat and stir slowly through the ashes, inch by inch, then back again. And then I find the first little wood remnant. Maybe it means nothing, but it sure isn't mountain woodland firewood. This is no part of a tree cut in its natural state. It's a charred splinter of milled wood with squared edges. After several seconds of sifting, one more small piece of milled board surfaces. My heart sinks only a little. I can't say for sure these squares of wood came from a chopping block. There has to be more for me to believe what they suggest, to say nothing of any-one else believing it.

But where is the rest of it? Where is the stuff that would be hard to burn? The hatchet blade? The handcuffs? I look bleakly at the pond. It is covered with a skim of ice.

It's freezing now. I stand in the twilight, arms wrapped around myself to stop the shaking. And I will myself to be steady. I begin to survey the ground methodically. Back and forth, again, and again. I am as cold as the truth.

Finally, I spot a slight depression in the earth, about as big as a watermelon. In contrast to the surrounding ground, there is absolutely nothing growing in the dirt within the depression. A shallow path extends from the depression for a few feet then disappears. What happened to the boulder which must have lain recently in that depression? The sucker didn't just vaporize. Someone moved it. But, from the size of the depression in the earth, not very far!

When at last I see it, I don't know how I missed it. It's so incongruous, so absolutely out of its place. It is a white watermelon-sized boulder, wedged between two dirt-darkened outcroppings. The rock's pale midsection is topped by a cap of dark brown dirt so even and uniform that it could have been drawn on with a magic marker. There is no question. That rock was here at my feet in this shallow hole and now it is over there standing on its head. Someone moved it recently. Someone must have had a reason to do so.

I think I hear something on the road, the sound of an en-gine. Fuck! Lee must have alerted the rangers already. I listen. The sound stops. I cross to the outcrop, staggering slightly in my high heels. In exasperation I kick the damn shoes off, drop to my knees and start to tug. The rock won't budge. I dig around and beneath it. The dirt is cold and hard but I keep go-ing until my fingers are scraped and bleeding. But I don't feel any pain. I grab sticks and scrape and pry. My sweat freezes as it hits the air. I realize that I'm digging like a crazed person.

The sound again. I have to get whatever is hidden under here before the tribal ranger finds me. Before he stops me.

As the boulder teeters, then drops into the shallow crease I've dug under it, I can peer into the top of a steeply descending cavern behind it. With torn fingers, I keep scrabbling to get more clearance so I can—The vehicle is closer now, rattling as my car did, over the little bridge below the dam—get my arm into the hole. Only a minute or two left. The vehicle stops. The engine turns off. "Let me just finish," I whisper. "Please, let me finish."

I lay both arms over the rock and anchor my fingers into its pitted backside. I can feel the muscles in my stomach, the veins in my neck, my breath coming in short spurts as I strain to move it . . . I hear footsteps crunching up the slope. Then, without warning, the rock suddenly tumbles down and away and I plunge my arm deep into the void.

The tips of my fingers touch metal. I stretch as far as I can. Another inch. Smooth, flat, circular. A chain. And another connected bracelet. It slips, dings against the stone, then comes to rest on something . . . something soft . . . and makes no further sound. I can just feel some kind of heavy cloth. I pull gently. It is heavy, thick. I pull again, and it begins to unfold and, as it does, I hear with alarm a little clanking echo as the handcuffs topple deeper into the hole. Damn it! Damn it!

But there's no time to stop. Hand over hand now, I pull the heavy cloth out of the opening. And then I know what this is, too. A quilt. There is just enough light to see the pattern. Blue and yellow flowers.

Tired, satisfied, and very sad, I turn to see the ranger. But it is not the ranger. I recognize his shape before I can make out his features. I know he knows what I have found. And I know he knows what this means.

THIRTY-FIVE

———⟋⟍———

MY MUSCLES BECOME FEEBLE. MY ADRENALINE EVAPO-rates. I slowly let my back scrape down against the rock outcropping until I'm sitting against it. Isadora's flowered quilt—the one that wasn't on her bed the morning after her murder—rests in a mound across my lap.

He watches silently as I unfold the heavy tangle of cloth, uncovering the tools which were swaddled in its folds. An ice pick, a screwdriver, and finally a foot-long hatchet spill to the ground.

"Charlie called you?" I ask, knowing the answer.

Teddy nods, then squats before me and shakes his head sadly. "Why couldn't you just give it up, Matty? What harm was there? That high-class lawyer sure as hell ain't gonna burn for no murder. They'll be lucky to hold him on what he did do. You could'a let it be. Nobody would'a been hurt."

"Juanita," I say, hugging the quilt to me as the chill from the outcrop seeps into my body. "Juanita and her baby."

"I wouldn'ta hurt Juanita," he says. "I don't think it would'a ever happened again." He hesitates. "But I guess you gotta worry about somethin' like that, huh, Counselor?"

"You might have ended up sharing a house with them. And, if not them, maybe eventually it would have been somebody else."

"Oh, God!" Not a prayer nor a curse. More like consideration of a novel idea.

I hold the quilt up so that even in the dim light he can see the dark stains spattered across it.

"This is why there was so little blood around her bed, isn't it? You wrapped everything—the bloody cutting board, the hatchet, the cuffs—everything in this, didn't you?"

He lowers himself all the way to the ground and leans forward across his raised knees.

"You'll be in good hands with Joleen, Teddy," I continue. "She can mount a defense. You said you could live with a prison sentence."

"That was before . . . before I remembered." He falls silent and, in the quiet, I hear another vehicle in some distant part of the canyon.

"You want to tell me about it?" I ask. I want to understand this. I have to understand this.

"I loved the old geezer, Matty," he says quietly, stretching out his hand toward the hatchet. I'm too slow to stop him as his fingers close around the handle. "She was all I had." His voice is soft and full of pain. "I was all she had. She treated me like her son. Don't you see? I loved her." He hacks at the ground with the hatchet.

"I know you did, Teddy. Charlie said you were worried about her all the way up here. Is that why you went back that night? To see if Isadora was all right?"

"And she was anything but all right!" he answers. As he talks, he chops at the hard ground absently, rhythmically. "The Caddy'd been moved; the front door was unlocked; the lights were on way past her bedtime. Somethin' was wrong. Soon as I got near the door, I heard her yellin'. And, there she was all by herself, those cuffs locked to one wrist and her poking at the lock with a goddamned little ice pick. She'd stabbed it into her wrist a couple a' times and she was bleedin' all over the place.

"Right away she sees me, she starts yellin' at me. 'It's about time you showed up!' " He imitates Isadora. " 'Where's the key? I know you hid the damn key.'

"I couldn't say no different," Teddy says as his hatchet blade keeps time. "I took the key to her handcuffs a couple a' months ago. And I hid the damn thing. I was sick of her messin' me around with them fuckin' cuffs all the time. I should'a took the cuffs themselves, but she'da seen and raised hell. But that night, seein' her like that, bleedin' and out of control, an' I'm sick to my stomach. Whatever happened there must of been my fault.

"So I start right away lookin' for the key. I'm runnin' around lookin' everywhere like a chicken with his head cut off. But she's got me so rattled with her screamin' I can't think . . . I can't find it. She's got tools all over her bed. My big toolbox is on the floor. She's pointin' at it—shoutin' and cussin'—she wants the cuffs cut off her RIGHT NOW! It can't wait. I try to find out what happened to her but she won't shut up. 'You gotta help me. It's all your fault, you should'a been here,' she keeps yellin'.

"Course she was right. I shouldn't of took the key. I should of been there to help. I should of protected her. It was all my fault, Matty. All my life, it's been all my fault . . . know what I mean?"

Though he seems oblivious to his own steady chopping motions punctuating his words, I'm riveted by the foot-long hatchet in his hand. The evening has grown too dark to see clearly, but the wide hatchet blade catches and reflects an occasional glint of light.

"So anyway, I use the quilt to sop at her wrist. I wanted to call a doc, but she wouldn't have it. She's rantin' like a wild woman, worse than ever. She's wavin' her wrist and blood's runnin' down her arm and she's yellin' at me how I don't protect her and how useless I am; how, if I wasn't so useless, this—whatever the hell it was—wouldn't of happened. She kept saying, 'Help me! Help me get this damn thing off!' "

I am so still, trying to disappear, trying to eliminate myself from the picture Teddy must be seeing in his mind. He's talking faster now, in harsh bursts. The hatchet swings are faster too and his body rocks more fiercely with each chopping motion.

" 'Chop it off!' she kept screamin' and he was beatin' the crap outta her. An' I tried to help. I said . . . I said, 'Be still, Mamma, lie still!' But she wouldn't shut up and he wouldn't stop hittin' her."

Teddy is chopping faster and faster as he remembers.

"Who is beating the crap out of her? Teddy, what are you talking about?"

"She's screaming, I gotta help her and so I go to the kitchen for the chopping block to steady her hand, you know. And when I get back . . . now, all of a sudden she settles down. She's being good because I'm gonna do what she wants, like always. So she lays her hand on the chopping block all nice and I get the hatchet from the toolbox and I'm gonna hack the chain but it's so close to her wrist.

"I got the hatchet up in the air," he chokes. "Her hand's coming in an' out of focus. There's blood all over. The cuffs are slippery from the blood. I can't bring it down. She won't hold still any more.

"She starts in yellin' again, 'Cut the damned thing off! Cut if off! Cut if off!' She won't hold still no more. She says, 'Cut the damn thing off!' His cock, she means. You know, she wants me to cut off his prick. She yells 'He won't be struttin' his stuff no more. Won't be beatin up women no more.' She's screamin' 'Cut if! Cut it off, Teddy!' "

I begin to understand what he is seeing. It's not one memory anymore. It's two now, blending, blurring, bleeding together. "Teddy, do you mean Isadora? Or do you mean your mother?"

"I did it! I did what she wanted," Teddy explains with a childish whine. "I cut him with that goddamn ax. Then again! And again! I stopped him. He was dead but Mamma didn't even know it. She turned against me. She tried to protect *him*! Had her hands all over him like always, calling him 'Honey.'

" 'Wake up, honey,' she said. I told her to get the fuck out of the way, but she wouldn't let him go."

Snot is rolling down Teddy's face now. He's using his hand,

the one with the hatchet in it, to show me how he directed his mother away from Eldon Lamont's bloody body.

"Stupid goddamn woman! Always protected him! He'd hit her and hit her and she'd tell me to help her—to *protect* her. First she'd whine about I was useless, I was never there when she needed me. Then he'd come at her again and I'd try to help. But then she'd protect *him* from *me*! How could I help her when she did that?

"But, that time I *was* there for her, dammit!" He swings the hatchet hard, burying it in the dirt for a second before he yanks it free. "I did what she wanted! But like always, it ain't what she wanted after all. That asshole was dead, his cock was just hanging there by a thread, and she's singin' 'Wake up, baby. Look what Mamma's got for you.' And she started rubbing it. Rubbing his dick like she always did when she wanted to distract him."

Teddy stops chopping and mops snot from his face with the side of the hatchet handle. He peers at me in the darkness, seeking some response, asking me if I can believe the picture he is painting, asking me if I don't see, don't see that he had to do what he did.

"What do you mean, like she always did?" I ask instead, shrinking from the understanding even as it forms in my mind.

"She'd always calm him down that way. She'd tell me it was okay. If she got him horny he wouldn't hit us. It's how she could control him, you know; keep the son of a bitch from killin' us. When I got old enough, I used to have to leave the house when she started to rub him like that. 'Go to the movies, kid,' the bastard'd always say. He'd hand me a wad of money."

Teddy looks at his hatchet and seems to suddenly really see it. A change comes over him. He stops rocking and lays his hand down on the ground palm up. I feel in my gut what he intends before I see the dark profile of the hatchet against the night sky as he raises it high in the air.

There's no time to think. As the blade descends toward his wrist, I heave the quilt and my body toward him. It's an ungraceful upward lunge and it comes a second too late.

THIRTY-SIX

⟨⟩

I'M SPRAWLED ACROSS HIS BODY. ISADORA'S QUILT IS WRAPPED in a loony cocoon around and between us. I don't know if the blade has struck home.

"Are you all right, Teddy?"

"Oh, shit!" he howls. "Oh, fuck! Get the hell off me, Matty." He thrashes wildly, fighting the quilt and fighting me. When he gets loose, he's immediately on his knees patting the earth frantically, searching blindly for the hatchet. In another instant, I'm on my knees searching with him. I find it first, scoop it up, and raise my arm above my head to cast it away.

"No!" he shrieks, grabbing at my arm as I throw the damn thing into the darkness with all my strength.

"Goddamn it! Goddamn son of a bitch!" He sobs and pounds weakly at the ground until he collapses and lies spent. Little choking sounds eventually die of their own accord.

I pull myself slowly forward, reaching for his wrist, searching for a wound. My fingers find it and probe until he recoils.

Blood seeps from a long shallow cut. It won't kill him rapidly but it must be treated.

His recognition that he's bleeding seems to animate him a bit. He heaves himself into a sitting position, spitting words at me as he does: "I was all right before you made me remember. I could'a kept from . . . Shit! I didn't have to remember. I didn't have to," he wails.

Didn't he? I wonder. Wasn't not remembering what doomed him to repeat his worst nightmare? If he'd let this horror into his conscious mind a long time ago, could he have saved himself?

"Teddy, hold your arm still." I'm ripping at the quilt with my teeth, trying to tear off a long enough piece to make a tourniquet. "You could bleed to death."

He shoves me away roughly with his undamaged hand and pulls the other one near his chest to protect it from my assistance. "Leave me the hell alone," he snarls.

If he's to survive, I need to bind that wound. I stretch toward him again. This time he punches me quick and hard in the face and I fall back, nearly undone by the pain.

I close both eyes and ask myself to be calm. I listen hard for the engine sound in the distance but can detect nothing. I'm going to have to leave him to get help. I drag myself to my feet, find my shoes, and shove cold feet into cold leather.

"Sit down!" Teddy orders.

When I don't move, he screams, "SIT DOWN!"

I still don't move, and he says more gently, "Listen—please—sit down. The thing me and you gotta do here is—we gotta let it go."

I vacillate. My face burns. My leg trembles. I don't sit. But I don't leave either.

"I thought it was over, you know," he begins. "I forgot it—almost forgot it. I almost forgot it," he repeats, and falls silent. The next sound is an eerie kind of singsong humming under his breath.

Minutes pass before he speaks again. "I went nuts once. It was done and over. But . . . she . . ." He struggles to go on. He wants to say this. He wants somebody to know. "I guess it was in me. Tangled up . . . just, you know, in me," he finishes.

He starts humming again. This time there are bits of old songs mixed in. *"Jackamo fee na ney,"* he murmurs. The sounds are like those of a child who's been left alone to soothe himself too long. Tune fades to tuneless hum to nothing. When he speaks again, it's as though there'd been no interruption.

"When I saw the blood on Mamma's wrist and she kept screeching at me that I was a useless . . . a useless little boy . . . I laid her hand on her heart . . . on her bed jacket. It made a red spot on the pink. I cleaned up everything else. I had to use her quilt. But he was on the floor, too. His blood was on her hand . . . and I couldn't find the key and I didn't know how to help her. I watched her hand go up and down on that bastard and I wished . . ."

I know he should have been listened to a long time ago. So, however late it is, I listen now.

"You wished what?"

"Up and down. Him. Not me. Not ever on me. It was a sin to want her to do it to me. I know that. I know that. I know that."

"Teddy—"

"Izzy loved him. She didn't love me. I was just her little boy . . . her useless little boy," he sobs.

"You mean your mother, Teddy. Not Izzy. You've got them mixed up in your mind. It was your mother you wanted to love you." But he's beyond hearing me.

"I wanted her to rub *me* . . . that way. Since the first time I seen the two of 'um." He begins to cry without restraint now.

Teddy was right when he said I didn't know jack-shit about guilt. And he may be right now about leaving him alone here to die, too. But, when he is quiet, I take a step anyway. Then another.

"I've got to leave you for a while, Teddy . . . Teddy? Do you hear me?"

"Mama, what did you want with him, anyway? What should I have done . . . ?"

I leave him there like that, asking the only questions he's ever had.

Once in my car I drive down the rough mountain road. By

the time I get to the ranger station near First Pond, nearly fifteen minutes have passed. The ranger is nowhere to be seen. I honk my horn. I take paper from the car and slide a crude note between the door and door jamb of the station. I begin driving again—driving and honking the horn. I drive and honk for another fifteen minutes before the ranger finds me, just outside the park gate. We return together in his Bronco. When we get back to Third Pond, the limo is still as it was in the clearing. But Teddy has vanished. The ranger's floodlight shows clearly where Teddy has walked into the woods, but the Bronco can't travel the narrow path. I take his keys so that I can alert others while the ranger tries to track Teddy through the night on foot.

The next morning, near dawn, Teddy's body is found at the base of a steep ravine. He died in the night from massive loss of blood from his wrist. He died as the women in his life had died. He died at the hands of a madman. He died because of a crippled soul. He died because he'd killed his chance to recover.

EPILOGUE

Joe Danforth enters the New Mexico State Prison, five miles south of Santa Fe's city limits, on the same week that the first blossoms appear on my apple tree. Through his lawyer, Joe plea-bargained the embezzlement charge down by offering to pay back what he could of Jeff Marlson's inheritance. His offer was as generous as possible—five million dollars. It was less than he stole, but it was everything he owned. Jeff and Bernice will use much of the money to fund a foundation to support victims of Fetal Alcohol Syndrome and their families. Joe lost his licence to practice law, of course. But all, save eighteen months, of his five-year sentence was suspended. Surprisingly, Liza has stuck with him like a bright angel.

Perhaps not so surprisingly, Barbara Frederick has not been so loyal. She filed for divorce and pressed hard for a generous property settlement. As it happens, her lawyer has been forced to negotiate not so much with Norman's divorce lawyer as with Frederick & Danforth's malpractice carrier. The carrier announced it would deny coverage in the suit that Jeffrey Marlson has filed against the firm for recovery of the remainder of his inheritance. Its policy, the company asserts, covers only the intentional bad acts of the law partners.

Some academicians call the law a seamless web. But wildly vectoring human pathways and the laws that regulate them create not a web but a bizarre patchwork quilt. And the law frequently creates pairings of odd bedfellows to lie together beneath it. In one of the oddest of these, Norman Frederick and Jeffrey Marlson have joined to force the firm's insurance company to pay for Joe's malfeasance.

Norman is fortunate to have such an ally to protect the assets of what is now Frederick & Associates. Fortunate because Jeffrey Marlson's lawyer is a mad dog. Jeffrey Marlson's lawyer is me.

SUMMER

On the second of February, Richard Hadid, Jr., was born. Today, he is a happy, squirmy, demanding baby with Rickie's amazing eyes and a mop of black ringlets. Faye calls him Poodle and shakes his tiny hand when introduced. "Arab man-child meets the daughters of Sappho," she sings. From a chair in the shade of the portal, Juanita rocks her baby and explains innocently to Rocks and me that Faye will stop pretty soon. "She always does." This sets Faye off again. She laughs so hard that it's difficult not to laugh with her, and both Juanita and I nearly succumb. Rocks is not amused, however. On this hot August day, as on others before and, from the look of things, for some time to come, he looks stricken.

Due to the irregularities of Isadora's wills and the failure of the probate court to make a final determination in this millennium, Faye has temporarily been left to wrestle with her own conscience in the matter of Juanita's rights. So, for now, Juanita lives in Isadora's house as not-quite-housekeeper and not-quite-owner. Faye and her companion and Angel Bird come up on weekends as much to look in on Juanita as to look in on the house.

But Faye isn't the only one looking after Juanita these days. To my astonishment, Rocks came courting even before the baby was born. His life has given him a unique empathy with being a little less quick than some. And, less charitably, being with Juanita makes him feel like a genius. For her part, Juanita was never much bothered by being slow. It's simply a fact of her life. She likes that Stone is nice to her and she doesn't talk about Rickie much.

And Juanita never mentions Agi. After six months, Agi has not been located. There was no budget for a forensic anthropologist to definitively identify the charred remains found in the trailer park. The police assume that Agi is alive but has left the country. They have stopped looking. Counterfeit "old pawn" has disappeared from the market. At least for now.

On this day, Rocks glowers at Faye and smiles at Juanita and tries to position himself between hedonist and sweet innocence. Faye cackles like a crow at the attempt to eliminate her influence.

AUTUMN

I'm lazy this morning, back in bed with a coffee mug in hand and the Sunday paper spread out over my knees. The window above my head is ajar and, somewhere in the distance, someone is playing mariachi music. I stretch, turn, and open the window wider to hear better and to see and smell the fragrant world below.

Max is just turning off the street and into the compound. He's walking, by himself, slowly, head down. My heart jerks like its been touched with a cattle prod.

On the first of January, and for days afterward, I expected Max to come walking up my drive. But he didn't come then or for any of the months that followed. He sent a letter instead—a troubled, troubling letter. He hadn't worked out his professional dilemma, the letter said. He thought a little more time would help. The time would be as much for me as it was for him. I'd been working my way through hell without him and he didn't want to undermine my trust in myself. It said he loved me. It said it had been too soon after therapy to have begun to love me. It said he was afraid of screwing around now until it was too late, but he didn't have a choice. "Please try to understand," the letter said.

So after Teddy was buried, I was pretty much alone with my own thoughts. I've struggled with problems like free will and moral guilt and how to trust myself again. My guilt had paralyzed me for a few years. Teddy had buried his for almost a lifetime. My way was better. But it wasn't good. I've concluded that while both paralysis and denial are useful to keep emotional terror at bay for a time, they come at too great a cost. They cost a clouded brain and a damaged will.

Max slows even more as he gets closer, stopping before the cedar-pole gate. Before he steps into my yard, he rakes his fingers through his hair and straightens, as though bracing for an encounter he dreads.

Max wasn't here to talk to—to support me for these past months. So I talked to myself—supported myself. I realized that I hadn't really relied on Max since my therapy ended. Maybe that was what he wanted me to realize.

At the sound of his knock, I shove the newspaper aside, pull on a pair of slacks, and run downstairs. My hand is on the door. The man on the other side is here for a reason. He will tell me something or he will ask me for something. I realize I'm holding my breath as I turn the knob. He stands in the morning dapple of golden leaves and, when he sees me, it is he who catches his breath.

"I had to be sure I could handle it," he says with no introduction and no conclusion. "I had to take the chance that when I was sure, it wouldn't be too late."

After a frozen moment, I step back and hold the door open for him. I am a creature of ambivalence. Once, I was sure I wanted this moment. But it has taken him a long time to get here.

Much has happened since I last heard Max's voice. I've been taking on a few clients—those not too put off that I'm working out of my home. My infamy turned me into a celebrity for about a minute and a half and my resurrection has actually left me with a pleasant little aura of respectability. This small patch of the world invites me once more to drink from the well—even to take positions of trust. Trusting myself is still hard, but little by little I've been accepting the invitation. I really don't have any choice. To make a real life for myself I have to trust *me*. And I will make a life. I've been thinking I could make a life without Max Cortino.

He smiles and reaches out his hand to touch my cheek and I find myself covering his hand with my own. He draws me into his arms and it feels good. Very good. But very late. It may be a while before I know if it is too late.

ABOUT THE AUTHOR

Pat Frieder is a lawyer and former teacher who lives with her husband in Albuquerque, New Mexico. Like the protagonist, Matty Donahue, in *Signature Murder*, Pat grew up in Santa Fe. Also, like Donahue she has practiced law both in Santa Fe and Albuquerque. During part of this time she served as an Assistant Attorney General for Criminal Appeals for New Mexico.

She has been writing fiction for several years. *Signature Murder*, her first mystery novel, won the first place award in the mystery novel category in the prestigious Southwest Writer's Workshop Fiction Competition.

BANTAM MYSTERY COLLECTION

____ 57204-0 **KILLER PANCAKE** Davidson • • • • • • • • • • • • • • • $5.99

____ 56860-4 **THE GRASS WIDOW** Peitso • • • • • • • • • • • • • $5.50

____ 57235-0 **MURDER AT MONTICELLO** Brown • • • • • • • • • $6.50

____ 57300-4 **STUD RITES** Conant • • • • • • • • • • • • • • • • • $5.99

____ 29684-1 **FEMMES FATAL** Cannell • • • • • • • • • • • • • • $5.50

____ 56448-X **AND ONE TO DIE ON** Haddam • • • • • • • • • $5.99

____ 57192-3 **BREAKHEART HILL** Cook • • • • • • • • • • • • • • • $5.99

____ 56020-4 **THE LESSON OF HER DEATH** Deaver • • • • • • • • $5.99

____ 56239-8 **REST IN PIECES** Brown • • • • • • • • • • • • • • • • $5.99

____ 56976-7 **THESE BONES WERE MADE FOR DANCIN'** Meyers • • $5.50

____ 57456-6 **MONSTROUS REGIMENT OF WOMEN** King • • • • • $5.99

____ 57458-2 **WITH CHILD** King • • • • • • • • • • • • • • • • • • $5.99

____ 57251-2 **PLAYING FOR THE ASHES** George • • • • • • • • • $6.99

____ 57173-7 **UNDER THE BEETLE'S CELLAR** Walker • • • • • • • • $5.99

____ 56793-4 **THE LAST HOUSEWIFE** Katz • • • • • • • • • • • • • $5.99

____ 57205-9 **THE MUSIC OF WHAT HAPPENS** Straley • • • • • • $5.99

____ 57477-9 **DEATH AT SANDRINGHAM HOUSE** Benison • • • • • $5.50

____ 56969-4 **THE KILLING OF MONDAY BROWN** Prowell • • • • • • $5.99

____ 57191-5 **HANGING TIME** Glass • • • • • • • • • • • • • • • • • $5.99

____ 57590-2 **FATAL DIAGNOSIS** Kittredge • • • • • • • • • • • • • $5.50

- -

Ask for these books at your local bookstore or use this page to order.

Please send me the books I have checked above. I am enclosing $____ (add $2.50 to cover postage and handling). Send check or money order, no cash or C.O.D.'s, please.

Name _____

Address _____

City/State/Zip _____

Send order to: Bantam Books, Dept. MC, 2451 S. Wolf Rd., Des Plaines, IL 60018
Allow four to six weeks for delivery.
Prices and availability subject to change without notice.   MC 2/98

PENNY WARNER

DEAD BODY LANGUAGE

Deaf newspaper reporter Connor Westphal was the most
exciting thing to hit Flat Skunk, California—at least until
the first lady of this one-horse town, Lacy Penzance, was
found sprawled across her husband's grave at the Memory
Kingdom cemetery, cold as his headstone. Lacy had
secretly visited Connor the day before her death to place
an anonymous ad in the *Eureka!* supposedly looking for a
lost sister. Now Connor is determined to uncover Lacy's
secret and nail a killer—if she can avoid moving into a
Memory Kingdom plot of her own.

____57586-4 $5.50/$7.50

CURSO
DE FORMACION
TEOLÓGICA
EVANGÉLICA

La Iglesia,
Cuerpo de Cristo

CURSO
DE FORMACIÓN
TEOLÓGICA
EVANGÉLICA

La Iglesia,
Cuerpo de Cristo

F. Lacueva

editorial clie

EDITORIAL CLIE
M.C.E. Horeb, E.R. n.º 2.910-SE/A
C/ Ferrocarril, 8
08232 VILADECAVALLS (Barcelona) ESPAÑA
E-mail: libros@clie.es
Internet: http:// www.clie.es

LA IGLESIA, CUERPO DE CRISTO

Depósito legal: B-52997-2007
ISBN: 978-84-7228-091-5

Impreso en Publidisa

Printed in Spain

Clasifíquese:
460 ECLESIOLOGÍA:
Concepto de la Iglesia
CTC: 01-06-0460-01
Referencia: 22.02.40

INDICE DE MATERIAS

SEXTA PARTE:

LAS DIMENSIONES DE LA IGLESIA

SEPTIMA PARTE:

LAS ORDENANZAS DE LA IGLESIA

INTRODUCCION

Si el caballo de batalla de la lucha teológica, en el siglo XVI, entre la Reforma y Trento, fue el tema de la justificación por la fe sola, *que fue justamente señalado por los grandes Reformadores como el «articulus stantis et cadentis Ecclesiae», hoy el caballo de batalla es, sin duda, la naturaleza misma de la Iglesia, de modo que el concepto correcto, es decir, bíblico, de Iglesia y del ministerio en la misma viene a ser indispensable para entender adecuadamente el hecho y el alcance de nuestra membresía en el Cuerpo de Cristo y el punto álgido en el debate ecuménico.*

«Estamos en el siglo de la Iglesia» —ha dicho con razón O. Dibelius—.[1] En las cuatro décadas que van de 1925 a 1965, se ha hablado y escrito acerca de la Iglesia más que en los cuatro siglos que van desde la Reforma hasta 1925.

Este hecho implica que el tema de la Iglesia ha llegado a adquirir en nuestros días una suprema importancia en el plano ecuménico. Todas las grandes confesiones que se precian del nombre de «cristianas», se están poniendo rápidamente de acuerdo en materias tan importantes como la justificación por la fe,[2] la soberanía de la gracia de

---

1. Citado por A. Kuen, *Je bâtirai mon Eglise,* p. 13.
2. V. el libro, ya famoso, de H. Küng, *Rechtfertigung (Justificación),* que en la década del 60 causó un impacto formidable en los círculos teológicos, tanto católicos como protestantes. También P. Fannon, *La faz cambiante de la Teología,* pp. 53-56.

Dios, la autoridad suprema de las Sagradas Escrituras, el sacerdocio común de los fieles, etc., pero el concepto de «Iglesia» sigue constituyendo la gran barrera entre Roma y la Reforma. Ya en 1948 decía W. A. Wisser't Hooft, entonces Secretario General del Consejo Mundial de Iglesias: «Si existiera una eclesiología aceptable para todos, el problema ecuménico estaría resuelto.» [3] *En efecto, el día en que nos pongamos de acuerdo acerca del concepto de Iglesia y, sobre todo, acerca del concepto de* ministerio *en la Iglesia, y del* alcance y función del carisma correspondiente, la unidad de los cristianos será una realidad visible.*

No cabe duda de que, a la sobreestimación de la institución eclesial por parte de la Iglesia de Roma, sucedió la subestimación protestante de la iglesia visible y el énfasis puesto en la salvación individual. Es curioso constatar, sin embargo, como nos lo hacía notar V. Fábrega,[4] que, a pesar del absolutismo institucional que en la Contrarreforma provocó la relativización individualista de la Iglesia, llevada a cabo por la Reforma, con todo, Ignacio de Loyola enfatizó el aspecto individual de la salvación, aunque en las reglas de discernimiento de espíritus se muestra tan reaccionario y absolutista como Trento. Y P. Fannon [5] no duda en escribir: «Desde la Contra-Reforma se ha desarrollado entre nosotros una eclesiología burocrática, en oposición a las nociones de Iglesia del Nuevo Testamento y de los Padres, que eran más profundas y más realistas.»

El Concilio Vaticano II dio, en nuestra opinión, como suele decirse, «una de cal y otra de arena». Muchas de sus expresiones, como «pueblo santo de Dios»,[6] y una «Iglesia que encierra en su propio seno a pecadores, y siendo

---

3. Citado en la revista *Concilium*, abril de 1970, p. 15, nota 9.
4. En un cursillo sobre *Aspectos eclesiológicos en el Libro de Hechos*, dado en el otoño de 1970 en la Facultad de Teología «San Francisco de Borja» de San Cugat del Vallés (Barcelona).
5. *O. c.*, p. 57.
6. *Constitución Dogmática sobre la Iglesia, passim.*

al mismo tiempo santa y necesitada de purificación, avanza continuamente por la senda de la penitencia y de la renovación»,[7] podrían parecer salidas de la pluma de Calvino, pero el énfasis en la institución jerárquica y el carisma de la infalibilidad nos convencen de que el «clima» oficial no ha variado respecto al punto álgido del debate ecuménico. Digo «oficial» porque es preciso reconocer el mérito que suponen los esfuerzos hechos por muchas de las llamadas «comunidades de base» en tomar conciencia del papel y responsabilidad que competen a cada miembro de iglesia, así como del lugar y función de la iglesia local, como verdadera «comunidad de creyentes». Dice así Manuel Useros:

«El misterio escondido del pueblo de Dios en la tierra se manifiesta en la realidad concreta de la existencia personal, cuando surge y se desarrolla la comunidad de creyentes. Es ésta el espacio donde la verdad cristiana se hace opción transformadora, conversión, confesión de fe y compromiso, donde los sacramentos se hacen celebración, donde los imperativos evangélicos se hacen testimonio de vida, donde la comunión en Cristo se hace fraternidad y servicio; es la comunidad cristiana el espacio donde realmente la obra de salvación se hace historia.»[8]

Esto no quiere decir que los obstáculos para un mejor conocimiento de la íntima naturaleza de la Iglesia de Cristo hayan desaparecido en nuestros días. Hoy más que nunca se puede hablar de «crisis de la Iglesia», puesto que, junto a un grupo minoritario que se esfuerza en repensar y reformar la Iglesia de acuerdo con el Nuevo Testamento, tomado como infalible Palabra de Dios, el Modernismo bíblico y el Humanismo existencialista[9] están adulterando

---

7. *Id.*, punto 8.
8. *Cristianos en comunidad*, p. 13.
9. V. mi libro *Catolicismo Romano*, pp. 71-85, así como J. Grau, *Introducción a la Teología*, pp. 202-214.

el mensaje de Dios y el concepto escritural de Iglesia en círculos cada día más extensos de las grandes confesiones llamadas «cristianas», sin excluir a ninguna. El liberalismo en exégesis, el existencialismo en la cultura, y el excesivo «compromiso social» de casi todos los grupos progresistas de la «Nueva Catolicidad» nos obligan a mirar con recelo los anhelos, en los que no dudamos que el Espíritu de Dios tiene Su parte, de muchos individuos y grupos que, deseando vivamente una verdadera reforma de su Iglesia, no aciertan a comprender el fallo fundamental del sistema.

Con todo lo que llevamos escrito, no queremos insinuar que la suprema importancia del tema de la Iglesia radique en su actualidad como tema de estudio o de debate ecuménico. Su importancia deriva primordialmente de la propia voluntad del Señor, así como de nuestra misma condición de creyentes, salvos para la gloria de Dios.

Por el Nuevo Testamento, está claro que Jesucristo tuvo interés en fundar Su Iglesia (Mat. 16:18), que la amó y Se entregó a la muerte por ella (Ef. 5:25). El coste del precio que pagó para rescatarla nos da idea del valor que la Iglesia tenía a Sus ojos. Cristo murió para reunir en uno los dispersos hijos de Dios (Jn. 11:52). Este único Cuerpo de creyentes redimidos que es la Iglesia, ha sido elegido para ser en la tierra «columna y baluarte de la verdad» (1.ª Tim. 3:15), para proyectar esa verdad salvadora hacia el mundo entero (Mat. 28:19), e incluso para darla a conocer «a los principados y potestades en los lugares celestiales» (Ef. 3:10).

El lugar que la Iglesia ocupa en el Nuevo Testamento es muy importante: el Libro de Hechos es un recuento de fundaciones de iglesias tras el impresionante descenso del Espíritu en Pentecostés; a las iglesias son predominantemente dirigidas las Epístolas apostólicas (mención especial merece la 1.ª de Pablo a los corintios); la Epístola a los fieles de Efeso viene a ser como un resumen de «Teología de la Iglesia»; y es a las siete iglesias del

Asia Menor a las que el Espíritu dirige, en el Apocalipsis, la revelación de los planes de Dios para el futuro, junto con Sus promesas, alabanzas y reprensiones.

Por lo que toca a nosotros, los miembros de la Iglesia, recordemos que por la Iglesia nos ha sido transmitido el Evangelio;[10] *una vez nacidos de nuevo, por el mensaje de la Iglesia y el poder del Espíritu, la Iglesia nos ha nutrido, educado, corregido y hecho crecer (cf. Ef. 4:11a). Dentro de la Iglesia, hemos hallado las oportunidades de comportarnos cristianamente y de extender el radio de acción de nuestro ministerio y de nuestro testimonio.*

Si se ha dicho bien que «los hombres no son islas», con mayor razón hay que recalcar que un cristiano solitario no puede existir; incluso viene a ser una contradicción en sus propios términos. El Nuevo Testamento desconoce un cristianismo individualista. Tan pronto como alguien nace de nuevo y cree en el Señor, Dios lo añade a la Iglesia (Hech. 2:41, 47), es decir, a la «comunidad de los creyentes o cristianos».[11] *«Estar en Cristo» y «estar en la Iglesia» son fórmulas que se implican mutuamente, porque el ser miembro de Cristo comporta el ser co-miembro de los demás miembros del mismo Cuerpo.*

En cuanto al método para una correcta Eclesiología, una genuina investigación no puede comenzar por «considerar la Iglesia según existe ahora» y tratar luego de modificar, o mejorar, sus estructuras; ni siquiera es correcto el remontarse a los tiempos de la Reforma, lo cual equivaldría a depender de una tradición humana, sino que es preciso volver decididamente a un estudio sereno, profundo y sincero del Nuevo Testamento y estar todos dispuestos a empezar desde allí.[12]

---

10. Este es, en nuestra opinión, el verdadero sentido de la discutida frase de Agustín de Hipona: «Si no fuera por la Iglesia, yo no creería en el Evangelio.»

11. Dejamos para más adelante el papel del bautismo en este «añadir a la Iglesia».

12. V. M. Lloyd-Jones, *Qué es la Iglesia*, pp. 1-10, y A. Kuen, *o. c.*, pp. 11-17.

Para comodidad del lector estudioso, dividiremos este Tratado sobre la Iglesia en ocho partes: 1) Naturaleza de la Iglesia; 2) Fundación de la Iglesia; 3) Membresía; 4) La autoridad en la Iglesia; 5) El ministerio en la Iglesia; 6) Notas y dimensiones de la Iglesia; 7) Las Ordenanzas o Sacramentos de la Iglesia; 8) La Iglesia en el mundo. Añadiremos un breve apéndice sobre «La Iglesia hoy: su situación, causas y remedios».

Estamos abiertos al diálogo y a toda crítica constructiva. No hay obra humana perfecta; si la Iglesia, aun teniendo un fundamento divino, es imperfecta por lo que afecta a sus miembros, hombres siempre imperfectos, ¡cuál no será la imperfección de todo libro que se atreva a desvelar el «misterio» que es la Iglesia de Cristo! Sin embargo, estamos convencidos de que el empeño en estudiar con oración y sinceridad, desde las páginas del Texto Sagrado, todo lo que acerca de este «misterio» se nos ha revelado, obtendrá como fruto un enriquecimiento espiritual de nuestras almas y un paso más en el peregrinaje hacia la culminación de la unidad (cf. Ef. 4:13), que es la meta del «varón perfecto».

Mi gratitud a cuantos, con sus preguntas y sugerencias, me han ayudado en esta tarea (difícil, pero no ingrata), especialmente al escritor evangélico D. José Grau y a la «Misión Evangélica Bautista en España», bajo cuyos auspicios se publican los volúmenes de este CURSO DE FORMACION TEOLOGICA EVANGELICA.

Primera parte

Naturaleza de la Iglesia

LECCION 1.ª NOCION DE IGLESIA

1. Etimología de la palabra "iglesia".

Como advertía V. Fábrega en su cursillo sobre Eclesiología del otoño de 1970, cuando una persona pronuncia el vocablo «iglesia», el primer contenido que la Semántica tradicional ofrece al hombre de la calle es el de un edificio *cúltico* (ir a la iglesia); en segundo lugar, viene la acepción equivalente a *jerarquía* (¿quién manda en la iglesia?); la tercera acepción afecta al aspecto *confesional* (Iglesia Católica, Anglicana, Luterana, etc.); finalmente, topamos con el único sentido bíblico del término «iglesia»: *comunidad* de creyentes cristianos.

El término castellano «iglesia» (como sucede en catalán, vasco, gallego, portugués, italiano y francés) procede, a través del latín «ecclesia», del griego «ekklesía». Cuando se escribió el griego del Nuevo Testamento, este término servía, en lo profano, para designar una asamblea democráticamente convocada. De ahí que Hech. 15:4, 12, 22 nos ofrezcan un paralelo con las asambleas helénicas con su doble elemento: la «bulé», o grupo de dirigentes, y el «démos», o pueblo, que también toma parte en las deliberaciones. En el v. 12 aparece incluso la «multitud» o «pléthos», que habla, discute y comenta.

El vocablo «ekklesía» consta de dos partes: la preposición «ex» = de, que se convierte aquí en «ek» por aglutinación, y la forma nominal «klesía», derivada del verbo «kaló» = llamar; o sea, que significa «llamada de». El Nuevo Testamento usa más de cien veces este vocablo «ekklesía». Aunque en el griego del Nuevo Testamento dicho tér-

mino no implique necesariamente una «segregación» o separación, sin embargo el concepto cristiano de «iglesia»
la exige, como veremos más adelante.

2. El nuevo "qahal".

Es interesante ver el uso del Antiguo Testamento a este
respecto. El Señor, cuando fundó *Su* Iglesia, tenía, sin
duda, en Su mente el concepto del «qahal» judío. Ni Mateo
ni Lucas inventan el término ni introducen el concepto, sino
que ya se encontraba como término *técnico* en la comunidad cristiana, como reflejo del antiguo «qahal». Por eso
los LXX vierten el hebreo «qahal» por «ekklesía», ya que
dicho término hebreo designaba «la congregación del pueblo de Israel», y, tras el destierro a Babilonia, parece ser
que dicha palabra significaba tanto la comunidad del pueblo de Israel en sí misma, como la reunión en asamblea
de tal comunidad, aunque esto último era expresado con
mayor precisión con el término hebreo «edah», al que corresponde el griego «synagogué». El «qahal» englobaba la
asamblea de *hombres* de Israel, mientras que el «'am»
era el pueblo en general. La voz «qahal» se deriva de
«qol» = voz o grito (así se ve no sólo la semejanza semántica con el término griego «ekklesía», sino también la
similaridad fonética). Jer. 44:15 es la única excepción en
que asisten mujeres.

Así el «Qehal Yahveh» es el «Pueblo Escogido» de Dios.
Esto tiene una gran importancia para nosotros, puesto que
el Nuevo Testamento empalma con el judaísmo tardío o
«re-interpretado» después de la cautividad. El que hubiese
perdido su soberanía política da a este judaísmo unas características peculiares. Tenemos también el caso de los
esenios, según nos lo han descubierto los textos de Qunram,
los cuales forman su propio «edah», creyéndose el verdadero «qahal», como resto *fiel* que se retira al desierto y
ya no cree en el templo ni en el sacerdocio oficial, creán-
dose su propia jerarquía y su propio sacerdocio.

La diferencia más notable entre el «antes» y el «después» de la cautividad de Babilonia está en que *antes* el «qahal» o «ekklesía» estaba ligado a la *tierra* repartida a cada tribu, mientras que *después* la tierra deja de ser un bien salvífico, siendo sustituida por la Ley o «Torah». Si observamos la identificación que el Nuevo Testamento hace entre el *Logos* (el Verbo Encarnado, Jesucristo) y la *Torah*, no nos extrañará que el remanente espiritual judío comprendiese y aceptase la *nueva* etapa centrada en el Cristo muerto y resucitado y entendiese el nuevo «qahal» o «ekklesía» como el conjunto de comunidades o congregaciones locales caracterizadas como «discípulos» o «seguidores de Jesús».

No ha de extrañar, pues, que, siendo la Iglesia el nuevo «Israel de Dios», las promesas mesiánicas hechas a Israel se hagan extensivas a la Iglesia,[1] la cual viene así a ser «linaje escogido, real sacerdocio, nación santa, pueblo adquirido por Dios» (1.ª Ped. 2:9-10. *Cf.* Apoc. 1:6). Así, la Iglesia es la continuadora del «remanente» de la nación judía y, por tanto, acreedora al título de «pueblo de los santos del Altísimo» (Dan. 7:13-27. *Cf.* Rom. 9:8; 11:1-5; Gál. 3:29; 6:16).

3. Diferencias entre el "qahal" judío y la "ekklesia" cristiana.

Sin embargo, hay notables e importantes diferencias entre el «qahal» judío y la «Iglesia» de Cristo. Diferencias que los grandes Reformadores, especialmente Lutero y Calvino (siguiendo a Agustín), no tuvieron en cuenta. Dice A. Kuen: «El error fatal que más parece haber contribuido al establecimiento de ese sistema político-religioso al que se ha llamado la "Cristiandad" es, sin duda, la confusión entre la Antigua y la Nueva Alianza.»[2] Tres son las diferencias más notables:

---

1. No entramos aquí en la discusión dispensacionalista, habiendo quienes, como L. Sp. Chafer, opinan que Mat. caps. 5-7 y 24-25 se refieren exclusivamente a Israel en la futura dispensación.
2. *O. c.*, p. 55.

A) Mientras el «qahal» estaba circunscrito por los límites de la nación de Israel, la Iglesia no conoce fronteras, subsistiendo supranacionalmente en cada localidad. Por eso, al candelabro de los siete brazos (símbolo de un solo pueblo, sobre el que reposaba la promesa mesiánica de los siete espíritus —V. Is. 11:2-3—) suceden en la visión de Juan *siete* candelabros, entre los que pasea el Señor Jesús, para designar a *siete* iglesias, excluyendo así la alusión a límites geográficos o jurisdiccionales que encierren la Iglesia y poniendo como centro de unidad la autoridad de «un solo Señor» (Ef. 4:5), Jesucristo, el Soberano, Salvador y Juez único de todas las iglesias (*cf.* Apoc. 1:12 y siguientes).

B) La historia de la salvación recorre en el Nuevo Testamento un camino inverso al del Antiguo Testamento: Dios comienza la historia de la redención escogiéndose *una nación: una viña con muchas vides* (Is. 5:1-7). Pero, a medida que el Mesías se acerca, se realiza un proceso de concentración: las promesas serán para los hijos de Abraham «según la fe», no según la circuncisión. Esta concentración alcanza su punto límite en Jesucristo: *una sola vid con muchos pámpanos* (*cf.* Jn. 15:1 y ss.). Así que, ahora, ya todos los escogidos lo son «en Cristo».[3]

C) Mientras la apelación de la Ley y de los profetas al pueblo de Israel se hace siempre en tono colectivo: «Observaréis... Escucharéis...», el Nuevo Testamento recalca el carácter personal —distributivo— de la llamada de Dios a la fe y a la salvación: «Si crees..., sígueme...» El Nuevo Testamento contiene más de 700 expresiones de este carácter *personal* de la llamada de Dios, en frases como «Cualquiera que..., Todo el que..., Si alguno...», etcétera. Esto tiene una importancia capital para el estudio de la Eclesiología en general y para el tema del Bautismo en particular.

---

3. V. O. Cullmann, *Historia de la salvación*, pp. 179-182.

4. Acepciones novotestamentarias del término "iglesia".

El término «ekklesía» = iglesia, se usa en el Nuevo Testamento de tres maneras:

A) Para significar simplemente una «asamblea» (Hechos 19:32, 39, 41). Así se emplea en muy pocos casos y equivale entonces al término griego «synagogué» (compárese con Mat. 4:23; Hech. 13:43; Apoc. 2:9; 3:9).

B) Para designar el conjunto de los redimidos por Cristo (Ef. 5:25-27). La primera de las dos únicas veces que Jesús mencionó la palabra «iglesia» (Mat. 16:18) tomó este término en sentido universal, o sea, «el conjunto de los creyentes de todos los tiempos y lugares a partir de Pentecostés».[4] Otros ejemplos en el Nuevo Testamento son: Hech. 9:4, 31; 1.ª Cor. 15:9; Ef. 1:22; 5:23-33; Col. 1:18, 24; Heb. 12:23.

C) Para designar una comunidad local o congregación particular de los creyentes o «santos», y éste es el sentido más corriente. La segunda vez que Jesús mencionó el término «iglesia» (Mat. 18:17) lo hizo para referirse a una comunidad local. En esta acepción en que la «iglesia» (con minúscula) se contradistingue como comunidad concreta y visible a la «Iglesia» (con mayúscula), realidad trascendente y misteriosa (aspecto invisible, sólo conocido por Dios), es como la Iglesia toma cuerpo y queda circunscrita en el tiempo y en el espacio, tiene su inauguración, se la puede convocar, se puede uno dirigir a ella, tiene expresión, desarrollo, decadencia, desaparición, etc. De las 108 veces que este término ocurre en el Nuevo Testamento, 90 se refieren a la iglesia local (cf. Hech. 8:1; 13:1; 14:23; 15:41; Rom. 16:5; Col. 4:16; 1.ª Ped. 5:13, etc.). Tertuliano, de acuerdo con Mat. 18:20, asegura: «Dondequiera que hay dos o tres personas, aunque sean laicos (es decir, no dirigentes de la iglesia), allí hay una iglesia.»[5]

---

4. A. Kuen, o. c., p. 50.
5. De exhortatione castitatis, 7.

Por tanto, en la mayoría de los casos la palabra «iglesia» significa *la congregación local de los santos, organizada conforme al Nuevo Testamento,* ya sea grande o pequeña (incluso circunscrita a una *casa; cf.* 1.ª Cor. 16:19; Col. 4:15), y que se reúne periódicamente en un lugar (o en varios, según el número) de la localidad para propósitos religiosos. El Nuevo Testamento, como para evitar que la palabra «iglesia» pudiese ser tomada en el sentido de una organización mundial, nacional, etc., jamás dice, por ejemplo, «la *Iglesia* de Galacia», sino «las *iglesias* de Galacia» (en plural), o (en singular) «la *iglesia* de Dios que está *en* Corinto» (como para indicar la concreción visible de la Iglesia en una parcela determinada), o (también en singular) «la *iglesia de* los tesalonicenses» (como para indicar la pertenencia geográfica —local— de los fieles).

5. Noción bíblica de "Iglesia".

De todo lo dicho se desprende que los términos «iglesia de Dios» o «templo de Dios» se aplican en el Nuevo Testamento, tanto a la Iglesia Universal, en sentido de realidad trascendente, como a una iglesia local (*cf.* 1.ª Corintios 3:16; 15:9; 2.ª Cor. 6:16; 1.ª Tim. 3:5). Esto nos lleva a una observación de primerísima importancia: LAS IGLESIAS LOCALES NO SON PROPIAMENTE PARTES DE UN TODO SUPERIOR QUE LAS ENGLOBE, SINO CELULAS LOCALES COMPLETAS EN LAS QUE LA IGLESIA UNIVERSAL SE CONCRETA Y MANIFIESTA. Es decir, la Iglesia de Dios no está compuesta de comunidades subordinadas, sino de creyentes individuales. Como dice H. Küng, «la iglesia local no puede decirse meramente que *pertenece* a la Iglesia, sino que *es* la Iglesia...; no es una pequeña célula de un todo mayor, como si no representara al todo... Es ella la Iglesia real, a la que en su propia situación local se le ha dado y prometido cuanto necesita para la salvación de los hombres en su peculiar situación».[5 bis]

---

5 bis. En *The Church,* p. 85.

Por ser «iglesia de Dios» (1.ª Cor. 1:2; 2.ª Cor. 1:1; 1.ª Tim. 3:15), o «edificio de Dios» (1.ª Cor. 3:9), o «iglesia del Señor» (Hech. 20:28) o «de Cristo» (Rom. 16:16), y aun cuando, con referencia a los miembros, pueda adoptar formas como «iglesias de los gentiles» (Rom. 16:4), «iglesias de los santos» (1.ª Cor. 14:33), «congregación de los primogénitos» (Heb. 12:23), nunca encontramos en el Nuevo Testamento expresiones como «iglesia paulina» o «petrina», a pesar de que Pablo y Pedro fundasen iglesias; ni tampoco «congregacionalista» o «presbiteriana», por más que dichas formas de gobierno pudieron existir en la primitiva Iglesia. La incongruencia es aún mayor cuando una denominación se llama a sí misma «Iglesia luterana», contra la expresa voluntad de Lutero, quien dejó dicho: «Yo os ruego que dejéis mi nombre y toméis el de cristianos. ¿Quién es Lutero? Mi doctrina no es mía. Yo no he sido crucificado por nadie.»[6]

6. Iglesia y Reino de Dios.

El término «Reino de Dios» («Basíleia tû Theû») se encuentra unas 100 veces en el Nuevo Testamento. Si examinamos tal término a la luz del Antiguo Testamento, veremos que tal concepto implica la intervención decisiva y soberana de Dios en la Historia. De ahí que el «Reino de Dios» se *acerca* con Jesucristo (*cf.* Mat. 3:2; 4:17; 12:28; Marc. 1:15; Jn. 16:11), porque Jesús ha comenzado a vencer el pecado, la enfermedad y la muerte, íntimamente ligados entre sí y con la derrota original, que puso al género humano bajo la esclavitud de Satanás.[7]

Así se percibe la analogía que hay entre «entrar en el Reino de Dios» y «entrar en, o adquirir, la vida eterna» (*cf.* Mat. 18:3; 19:17; Marc. 9:43; 10:17; Luc. 18:17-18, 29-30). Ambos (el Reino y la vida eterna) se han *acercado,* están ya *entre nosotros,* al alcance de la mano (compárese

6. Citado por A. Kuen, *o. c.*, p. 53.
7. V. Feuillet, *Etudes joanniques,* pp. 181-182.

Luc. 17:21 con 1 Jn. 3:14), para ser introducidos silencio-
samente, por la fe, en nuestras almas, hasta prolongarse
y perfeccionarse definitivamente en la era escatológica
(comp. Mat. 25:34 con Marc. 10:30).

El Reino de Dios es «de arriba» y «para arriba». También la Iglesia, como don de Dios, es de arriba y para
arriba (Apoc. 21:1 y ss.). «Iglesia» y «Reino de Dios», sin
embargo, no son sinónimos: La Iglesia, como «segregada»
del mundo, surge de abajo, mientras que el Reino de Dios
irrumpe desde arriba, no precisamente como un territorio
donde Dios vaya a ejercer Su realeza, sino más bien como
un ámbito vital en que Dios va a ejercitar Su soberana,
poderosa, libre y graciosa iniciativa de salvación de los
pecadores, aunque ello comporta también una exigencia de
decisión radical por parte del hombre.

Podríamos decir que la Iglesia es el sector en que se
encuentran dos círculos tangenciales que mutuamente se
invaden: del círculo inferior, que es el mundo o *cosmos*
sujeto a condenación, puesto bajo el Maligno (1.° Jn. 5:19),
va emergiendo, por el don de la fe, el pueblo de Dios o
«Iglesia», en la misma medida en que, por la gracia de
Dios, irrumpe en el *cosmos* el círculo superior, o Reino
de Dios; cuando el número de los elegidos se haya completado, la Iglesia habrá llegado al «éschaton» o meta
final de la vida eterna.

CUESTIONARIO:

*1. ¿De dónde se deriva la palabra iglesia? — 2. ¿Qué
relación tiene la Iglesia de Cristo con el antiguo qahal
judío? — 3. ¿Qué acepciones tiene el término iglesia («ekklesía») en el Nuevo Testamento? — 4. ¿Cuál es la noción
bíblica de iglesia? — 5. ¿Qué analogía hay entre la Iglesia y el Reino de Dios?*

LECCION 2.ª CONCEPTO DE IGLESIA: (I) LO QUE NO ES LA IGLESIA

1. La Iglesia no es un templo material.

Como ya dijimos en el punto 1.º de la lección anterior, hay muchos que, al oír la palabra «iglesia», inmediatamente piensan en un edificio o templo material, como si lo más importante fuese el lugar de reunión. Es cierto que el lugar de reunión tiene su importancia, como la tienen la capacidad del local, sus condiciones acústicas, su decoración sobria, digna y atractiva, que inviten al respeto y a la comunión fraterna, y el disponer de las convenientes dependencias anejas, con destino a la Escuela Dominical, reuniones de jóvenes, etc.

Sin embargo, no debemos perder de vista que un lugar *sagrado* es todo aquel en que dos o tres creyentes se hallan reunidos en nombre de Jesucristo (Mat. 18:20); este lugar bien puede ser un piso o una casa corriente (*cf.* Romanos 16:5). Los primeros creyentes judeo-cristianos «partían el pan por las casas» (Hech. 2:46), aun cuando también se reunían a orar en el Templo.

En su discurso en el Areópago de Atenas, el apóstol Pablo destacó que «el Dios que hizo el mundo y todas las cosas que en él hay, siendo Señor del cielo y de la tierra, no habita en templos hechos por manos humanas» (Hechos 17:24); y el mismo Señor Jesús había dicho a la mujer samaritana que «la hora viene cuando ni en este monte ni en Jerusalén adoraréis al Padre...; los verdaderos adoradores adorarán al Padre en espíritu y en verdad» (Jn. 4:21, 23); es decir, desde el fondo de nuestro espíritu y guiados por el Espíritu de Dios hacia la realidad de un Dios que es Espíritu, superando así en la era mesiánica la antigua dispensación de símbolos y figuras. El templo vivo y verdadero del único Dios vivo y verdadero lo constituyen las personas de los mismos creyentes (cf. 1.ª Cor. 3:16; 6:19; 2.ª Cor. 6:16; Ef. 2:21).

Los peligros del «templo-centrismo» son bien notorios a lo largo de la historia. Los grandes templos macizos, con sus altares de sacrificio, tuvieron un origen judío-pagano. Después, el enorme fausto y riquezas materiales de los templos del Medievo, con sus costosos cálices, ostensorios, retablos, imágenes y paramentos, estaban basados en la idea de la transubstanciación, puesto que si el mismo Cristo habitaba físicamente en el templo, todo era poco para tan divino huésped. Sin embargo, Jesús mismo había dicho: «A los pobres siempre los tendréis con vosotros, mas a Mí no siempre Me tendréis» (Jn. 12:8). No es extraño que, ya en el siglo IV, Juan el Crisóstomo (santo doctor y padre de la Iglesia, según la Iglesia Romana) lanzase desde el púlpito sus invectivas, no sólo contra las rozagantes matronas que adornaban sus cuellos con joyas cuyo precio hubiese bastado para el sostenimiento de una familia, sino también contra la ya naciente ostentación en los ornamentos y decoración de los templos.

2. La Iglesia no es tampoco una "confesión de fe".

Al cumplir su comisión de predicar el Evangelio, los apóstoles solían resumir su mensaje en unos cuantos puntos vitales para la salvación o edificación de sus oyentes. Véase el sermón de Pedro en Hechos 2:22-36 y, más conciso aún, el esquema de Pablo en 1.ª Cor. 15:3-4. Pasado el tiempo de las grandes persecuciones, y en su lucha con las nacientes herejías, la Iglesia comenzó a sintetizar sus creencias básicas en confesiones de fe llamadas «credos», palabra latina que significa «creo», porque tales fórmulas comenzaban de esa manera.

La línea histórica de las «confesiones de fe» corre paralela a las desviaciones doctrinales que se sucedían a lo largo de los siglos. Después de la Reforma también surgieron diversas «confesiones de fe» que resumían la doctrina reformada con más o menos ajuste a la verdad revelada, pues sólo la Palabra de Dios goza de total infalibilidad. No se puede dudar del valor de los «credos» y confesiones de fe, en cuanto que resumen de una manera explícita y sistematizada las enseñanzas más importantes de la Escritura.

No hay que olvidar que la Biblia no es un acta de fe ni un texto de Teología, sino una historia de la salvación, en que las enseñanzas doctrinales quedan entramadas dentro de una problemática de actualidad, según la capacidad y las necesidades espirituales de los destinatarios. Por tanto, para hacer un texto de Teología, así como para redactar una confesión de fe, es preciso sistematizar en una serie de puntos las verdades que se hallan desparramadas o implícitas en la Palabra de Dios.[8] Tal es la utilidad de las «confesiones de fe».

Un hecho que ha obligado recientemente a tornar más y más necesarias las «confesiones de fe» o «profesiones de fe» es la progresiva ignorancia de los mismos miembros de iglesia con respecto a su Biblia, con el peligro consiguiente de que una congregación «indocta e inconstante» (cf. 2.ª Ped. 3:16) pervierta la Palabra de Dios y desvíe, por el voto de una mayoría (en la que el Espíritu no puede soplar aparte de la Palabra), la marcha misma de la iglesia.

Dicho esto, añadamos que los «credos» y «confesiones de fe» siempre albergan dos peligros:

A) Que, habiendo sido redactados en circunstancias peculiares y en un lenguaje que responde al tono cultural de una época, queden desfasados en su formulación; tanto más si ésta no corresponde al genuino sentido de la letra

---

8. V. J. Grau, *Introducción a la Teología*, pp. 27-29.

y del espíritu de la Biblia. Por otra parte, los que redactan los «credos», aun reunidos en gran asamblea, sólo pueden ser infalibles en la medida en que sus formulaciones se ajusten por completo a la Palabra de Dios.

B) Que los miembros de las iglesias que profesan tales «credos» pueden llegar a sentirse satisfechos con unas *ortodoxas* formulaciones escritas, sin vivir su contenido (*cf.* Apoc. 3:1), transformando así en *ortodoxia muerta* la más pura declaración de principios, y en hipocresía manifiesta la profesión de un «credo» religioso.

El sistema teológico de los primeros cristianos era, sin duda, muy somero y embrionario; quizá poco definido en algunos perfiles accesorios; pero les bastaba con vivir intensamente el misterio de su comunión (e *intercomunión*) con el Cristo muerto por sus pecados y resucitado para su justificación (*cf.* Rom. 4:25), guardando la unidad del Espíritu en el vínculo de la paz (Ef. 4:3). Seguramente desconocían muchas de las lucubraciones teológicas posteriores, pero poseían una característica de suprema importancia: ¡estaban espiritualmente vivos! [9]

3. La Iglesia no es una "denominación".

La división de los cristianos en «confesiones» o «denominaciones» es uno de los mayores obstáculos para nuestro testimonio y para la difusión del Evangelio. El mundo no ve la unidad del Espíritu existente en miembros de diversas confesiones (especialmente cuando el espíritu de «capillita» prevalece sobre la comunión de todos los verdaderos creyentes) y sólo se fija en las distintas «etiquetas». El argumento principal que suele esgrimirse contra los evangélicos es que «estamos divididos, mientras que los católicos son todos una misma cosa».[10] Este argumento esconde una falacia de la que, por falta de formación bíblica, son casi siempre inconscientes quienes lo esgrimen. Nues-

---

9. V. Lloyd-Jones, *Qué es la Iglesia*, pp. 7-11.
10. Dejamos para las lecciones 34.ª-36.ª la discusión sobre este tema de la unidad.

tra unidad es *en Cristo*, y la comunión eclesial que esto comporta no queda agrietada con los distintos puntos de vista sobre detalles más o menos accesorios. Naturalmente, cuando todo el énfasis se carga sobre la exterior unidad de unas instituciones jerárquicamente estructuradas, la diversidad denominacional y la independencia administrativa de las iglesias locales suena a cisma o herejía. Pero lo conclusivo es investigar, no el tipo de institución que vemos, sino si se ajusta al concepto bíblico de iglesia. Por otra parte, ¿no admite la Iglesia de Roma en su seno, conjuntamente, diversidad de opiniones en puntos tan importantes como la predestinación, la eficacia de la gracia, etc.? ¿Qué más da que se las llame «escuelas» (escuela tomista, molinista, escotista, agustiniana, etc.) que «denominaciones»? ¿Puede ser un monolito material la expresión de una unidad espiritual?

El nombre dado primitivamente a los cristianos fue el de «discípulos», o sea, seguidores del Maestro, y todos cuantos nos preciamos de tener a Cristo por nuestro único Señor y Salvador deberíamos contentarnos con el epíteto simple y llano de «cristianos».[11] Fue precisamente en Antioquía (Hech. 11:26) donde por vez primera se llamó así a los discípulos de Cristo. En Palestina no hubiera sido posible que se les hubiese llamado así, puesto que los judíos se oponían tenazmente a la idea de que Jesús fuese el «Cristo», o sea, el verdadero Mesías.

Es de notar que la palabra «católico» significa «universal», y en este sentido, aunque no sea un epíteto bíblico, lo adoptaron para sí las iglesias nacidas de la Reforma, como puede verse en la Confesión de Fe de Westminster y en el famoso Catecismo de Heidelberg, pero no estamos de acuerdo en que la Iglesia que se llama a sí misma «Católica» (a H. Küng le desagrada el apellido «Romana»)[12]

---

11. V. Lloyd-Jones, *o. c.*, pp. 1-8.
12. V. en *The Church*, p. 306. V., del lado evangélico, *Actualidad y Catolicidad de la Reforma* (Barcelona, EEE, 1967), especialmente P. Courthial, pp. 29-38.

conserve las características que corresponden al genuino, o sea, bíblico, concepto de iglesia de Cristo; por eso evitamos usar para nosotros el epíteto «católico», ya que podría engendrar confusión.

En realidad, las denominaciones son el resultado de uno de estos tres factores: 1) la *tradición* de siglos (en cuanto a doctrinas, estructuras, apelativos), acumulada en las enseñanzas e instituciones de la Iglesia oficial, y de la que muchos de los grandes Reformadores no acertaron a desprenderse del todo. A causa de esta remanente escoria de tradición, las iglesias específicamente llamadas «reformadas» retuvieron el bautismo de infantes y un concepto de iglesia como organización institucional reformada (mezcla de *Civitas Dei* agustiniana y del *qahal* judío), frente a la oficial institución romana. Los anglicanos retuvieron incluso gran parte de las estructuras romanas, aunque la doctrina quedó radicalmente reformada. Unicamente algunas denominaciones más recientes, como los «Hermanos», etc., y los Bautistas (que ya preexistían a la Reforma, empalmando, a través de muchas vicisitudes, con el Nuevo Testamento), se ven libres de esa espúrea cascarilla de tradición y están en las mejores condiciones para mantenerse en una actitud de continua y profunda Reforma. 2) El énfasis peculiar que cada grupo confesional pone en una *parte* del mensaje, que les parece que ha sido preterida o mal entendida por las demás denominaciones. Por ejemplo, los Bautistas recalcan la necesidad del bautismo de adultos por inmersión; los Pentecostales enfatizan el bautismo del Espíritu y la necesidad del uso constante de los carismas, en especial del don de lenguas desconocidas; los Calvinistas se atienen con fuerza a las consecuencias doctrinales que la soberanía de Dios y de Su gracia comportan; los Arminianos intentan salvar la posibilidad universal de salvación y la responsabilidad del libre albedrío en aceptar o rechazar el mensaje de salvación, etc. 3) La *traición* (es curioso que las palabras «tradición» y «traición» procedan del mismo término latino «tradere» = entregar) que algunas denominaciones o iglesias locales hacen a la Palabra de Dios, lo que obliga a los creyentes verdaderos a una dolorosa, pero necesaria, separación y a tomar un apelativo que los distinga del grupo o iglesia de donde hubieron de salir.

Sin embargo, la causa fundamental del denominacionalismo está en la peculiar condición de la Iglesia peregrinante: santa y pecadora a la vez; baluarte de la verdad, pero expuesta a equivocaciones. Equivocaciones que se deben, a su vez, a dos motivos: a) la imperfección mental y espiritual de los creyentes, quienes, aun después de estudiar y meditar mucho la Palabra de Dios, no aciertan a penetrar en el verdadero sentido que el Espíritu de Dios ha querido dar a ciertos pasajes; b) aunque cualquier creyente, por poco instruido que sea, puede captar claramente los puntos vitales del mensaje bíblico de salvación, hay, sin embargo, muchos detalles accesorios que están implícitos y aun velados, de tal manera que, aun después de mucho estudio y oración, los más competentes exegetas no se ponen de acuerdo sobre su interpretación. Sólo en la Escatología se cumplirá la perfección de la unidad de que se nos habla en Ef. 4:13.

Para concluir, digamos que la división denominacional, aunque obstaculiza la unidad visible de los cristianos y entorpece el poder de nuestro testimonio (cf. Jn. 17:21), es un defecto ineludible que, a la vez que muestra nuestras actuales limitaciones humanas, origina un sano pluralismo, propio de personas humanas que no se sienten coaccionadas por una minuciosa Dogmática o Casuística en el uso de sus facultades específicas; lo cual contrasta con la encorsetada uniformidad que las dictaduras religiosas imponen. Lo que hay que rehuir a toda costa es el fanatismo de «secta», lo cual sólo se consigue, como dice F. Schaeffer,[13] esforzándose en mantener con la misma firmeza, sin echarlos jamás en el olvido, todos y cada

---

13. En *Los caminos de la juventud hoy* (Barcelona, EEE, 1972), pp. 47-51.

uno de los aspectos o facetas que componen la verdad *total* del Evangelio.

CUESTIONARIO:

1. *¿Cuál es la importancia del templo, capilla o lugar de reunión? — 2. ¿Qué utilidad tienen y qué peligros albergan las «confesiones de fe»? — 3. ¿Qué factores han influido en la división denominacional? — 4. ¿Cuál es la causa fundamental del denominacionalismo?*

LECCION 3.ª CONCEPTO BIBLICO DE IGLESIA:
(II) LO QUE ES LA IGLESIA

1. La Iglesia es un grupo de PERSONAS.

Ya hemos visto que la Iglesia no es ni un edificio, ni una confesión de fe, ni una denominación; ¿qué es, pues? Sencillamente: una congregación de *personas*. «¿No es eso lo que encontramos en el libro de Hechos de los Apóstoles?», pregunta el Dr. Lloyd-Jones. Y continúa: «Una congregación de personas: 120 en el Aposento Alto; 3.000 añadidas a ellas; otras 2.000 añadidas a éstas; y así sucesivamente.» [14] Y más adelante: «Eso fue lo que atrajo a la multitud el día de Pentecostés. Allí había un cierto número de personas reunidas; tal era el fenómeno: personas. No declaraciones sobre un papel, sino personas.» [15]

Pero ¿qué tiene de peculiar ese grupo de personas que llamamos «iglesia»? En el mundo hay muchas sociedades, muchas asambleas, muchos grupos de personas, pero ¿qué es lo que distingue a esos grupos de personas y a esas asambleas que llamamos «iglesias», de los demás grupos, sociedades y asambleas? La respuesta es que aquí se trata de algo peculiar, diferente, único en el mundo: la iglesia es un grupo de personas que han sido *segregadas* del mundo (Hech. 2:40).

En efecto, el término «ekklesía», como ya advertimos en la 1.ª lección, comporta un llamamiento a *«salir de»*. El mismo Señor habló de llamar a Sus ovejas por Su nombre para que vengan a formar un solo rebaño bajo Su

14. *O. c.*, p. 8.
15. Pág. 11.

único pastorado (Jn. 10:16). Como sinónimo de *rebaño* tenemos en castellano la palabra *grey*. Así vemos que la formación de la iglesia comienza con un llamamiento de Dios (*cf.* Rom. 8:30; 2.ª Tes. 2:14). Dios, Cristo, el Espíritu, siguen llamando a las iglesias (*cf.* Apoc. caps. 2 y 3). Este llamamiento tiene como consecuencia una «segregación», término que significa «separación de ovejas» (V. Hech. 26:18; 2.ª Cor. 6:17; Gál. 1:4; 1.ª Ped. 2:9). Esto nos recuerda de dónde hemos salido (2.ª Ped. 1:4: «... de la corrupción que hay en el mundo»). Por eso, como el mismo apóstol intima, hemos de sentirnos en el mundo como «extranjeros y peregrinos» (1.ª Ped. 2:11); es decir, como «gente que pasa de largo junto a los poblados» («paroíkus» —de donde se deriva «parroquia»—) y «que no pertenece al país por donde pasa» («parepidémus»).

Pero este «salir de» tiene como término un «entrar en». Por eso, después de la *segregación* viene automáticamente la «con-gregación», es decir, la «reunión de ovejas», como el término indica (V. Jn. 11:52; Hech. 12:12; 1.ª Corintios 14:26; Ef. 1:10; Heb. 10:33). Al ser «extranjeros y peregrinos» en este mundo, hemos adquirido una nueva ciudadanía en los Cielos (Filip. 3:20).

Este profundo cambio se lleva a cabo por lo que el Nuevo Testamento presenta como un «nuevo nacimiento» o «nacimiento de arriba» por la acción regeneradora del Espíritu y la fuerza purificadora de la Palabra de Dios (Juan 3:3, 5; 15:3; Ef. 5:26; Sant. 1:18; 1.ª Ped. 1:23). Se nace de Dios por el Espíritu, participando así de la naturaleza divina (Jn. 1:12-13; 3:5-8; Rom. 8:14-21; Gál. 3:26; 4:5-7; Ef. 1:5; 5:1; Filip. 2:15; Heb. 12:6-7; 1.º Juan 3:1, 9; 4:7; 5:1, 4, 18). Este nacimiento es de nuestra parte como una «nueva creación», o sea, un «salir de la nada», pues nada hay en nosotros que pueda aportar fuerza, mérito ni disposición en este plano espiritual (Gál. 6:15; Ef. 2:10). Así somos trasladados de la muerte a la vida; de las tinieblas, a la luz; de la corrupción moral, a la santidad del hombre nuevo (Rom. 13:12; Ef. 2:1-6; 5:8; Col. 1:13; 1.ª Tes. 5:5; 1.ª Ped. 2:9-10; 2.ª Ped. 1:4-5; 1.º Juan 1:7; 3:2-3).

2. Estas personas son añadidas POR DIOS a la Iglesia.

Si la Iglesia es un grupo de personas que han sido llamadas por Dios y que han experimentado un «nuevo nacimiento» por obra del Espíritu, es obvio que dichas personas son hechas «cristianas» y añadidas a la Iglesia *por Dios* (Hech. 2:41, 47), no por su esfuerzo, mérito o decisión natural, ni por la mediación sacramental de una casta sacerdotal.

Como muy bien recalca el Dr. Lloyd-Jones,[16] el Libro de Hechos 2 nos aclara que la Iglesia no es un lugar para buscar la verdad, ni un foro de discusiones, ni un medio de diálogo para llegar a un acuerdo, sino que los creyentes son añadidos a la Iglesia precisamente cuando la discusión ha terminado y la experiencia espiritual ha tenido lugar, de la misma manera que las piedras con que se construyó el Templo fueron sacadas de la cantera y talladas a cincel antes de ser colocadas *en silencio* para formar el edificio.

¿Cómo se produce esa experiencia que da lugar a la formación de la iglesia? Leamos una vez más el cap. 2 de Hechos, que por sí solo vale por un texto de Eclesiología. Allí vemos lo siguiente: *a)* Unos testigos de Cristo (los apóstoles), llenos del poder del Espíritu (Hech. 1:8; 2:4), comienzan a predicar en lengua que todos entienden, por donde Pentecostés resulta el reverso de Babel; *b)* tomando la palabra en nombre de todos, Pedro pronuncia su primer sermón: escritural, incisivo, valiente, cristocéntrico, con peroración sobria y contundente (v. 36). Buen modelo de sermón evangelístico; *c)* la reacción provocada por el Espíritu, mediante la instrumentalidad de la predicación, en los corazones de «los que habían de ser salvos» (v. 47), origina el fenómeno espiritual que llamamos «conversión» —una vuelta de 180 grados—, siguiendo el itinerario marcado por Dios: 1) reciben la Palabra (vv. 37, 41); 2) son convictos de pecado y claman por su salvación (v. 37);

---

16. *O. c.*, pp. 16-17.

3) se arrepienten («metanoesate» —v. 38—, término que significa un «cambio de mentalidad» —cf. 1.ª Tes. 1:9: «os convertisteis a Dios de los ídolos»—); 4) se bautizan (versículos 38, 41), profesando así simbólicamente que han muerto con Cristo al hombre viejo y que han resucitado con Cristo a una nueva vida (Rom. 6:1-14).

3. Estas personas viven su nueva vida COMUNITARIA-MENTE.

Como pámpanos de una misma cepa, como piedras vivas de un mismo edificio, como miembros de un mismo cuerpo, los cristianos han de vivir *comunitariamente* su nueva vida, para poder formar realmente una *iglesia*. Ya Jesús había dicho: «Donde están dos o tres congregados en Mi nombre, allí estoy Yo en medio de ellos» (Mat. 18:20). Y Lucas nos refiere: «Todos los que habían creído estaban juntos» (Hech. 2:44); «comían juntos con alegría» (Hechos 2:46); «la multitud de los que habían creído era de un corazón y un alma» (Hech. 4:32). Esta *unidad viva* de todos los creyentes, por Cristo y en Cristo, es tema predilecto del apóstol Pablo (V. Rom. 12:5; 1.ª Cor. 1:10; 12: 12-27; Gál. 3:28; Ef. 4:3-16; Col. 2:2, 19). Jesús había rogado al Padre por esta unidad (Jn. 17:11, 21, 23). Es una unidad ya *realizada* en el momento de nuestra regeneración espiritual (1.ª Cor. 12:13), al haber recibido todos a un mismo Cristo, Señor y Salvador nuestro (Gál. 3:28), pero esta unidad debe ser *guardada* (Ef. 4:3), mutuamente *enriquecida* (Ef. 4:16) y *perfeccionada* (Ef. 4:12-13).[17]

4. Con un programa bien definido.

¿Y qué hacían juntos aquellos primeros cristianos? Hechos 2:42-47 nos ofrece escuetamente todo el rico programa de vida cristiana comunitaria de la primitiva Iglesia, el cual debe servirnos constantemente de modelo:

---

17. V. lección 35.ª.

a) «*Perseveraban*...» La primera característica es la *asiduidad* con que se reunían para participar en esta vida comunitaria, en culto y testimonio conjuntos y con mutua edificación (Hech. 2:42, 44, 46; 4:23-31; 5:12). Algunos años más tarde ya se daba el ahora tan frecuente y lastimoso caso de quienes tenían por costumbre dejar de asistir a las reuniones (Heb. 10:25).

b) «... *en la doctrina de los apóstoles*», es decir, en la asistencia a las instrucciones que los apóstoles impartían. Vemos aquí que la doctrina *va por delante de todo lo demás*. Y es que sólo cuando se coincide en una misma «fe» objetiva se puede tener auténtica comunión. Pretender una mutua comunión antes de ponerse de acuerdo en lo fundamental del Evangelio es un absurdo (Amós 3:3).

c) «... *en la comunión unos con otros*», o sea, en la intercomunicación de bienes, tanto espirituales como materiales (que a todo ello debe alcanzar la «koinonía» —cf. 1.º Jn. 3:17), como miembros de *un* cuerpo (V. Hechos 2:44; 4:32; Rom. 15:26; 2.ª Cor. 8:4; 9:13; Heb. 13:16).

d) «... *en el partimiento del pan*», comiendo juntos y celebrando la Cena del Señor (Hech. 2:46; 1.ª Cor. 11:20-34), como el mismo Jesús había hecho al instituirla («haced esto...») en la víspera de Su Pasión y Muerte. Esta Cena era un sello más de amistad fraterna y expresión comunitaria (V. 1.ª Cor. 10:17), a la vez que una proclamación de la muerte del Señor hasta que vuelva.

e) «... *y en las oraciones*». El carácter devocional, cultual, de estas asambleas exigía la práctica de la oración. La Iglesia primitiva era una iglesia *orante* y ello daba la medida de su potencia y de su testimonio (V. Hechos 4:31).

f) «... *con alegría y sencillez de corazón*» (v. 46). Como hace notar el Dr. Lloyd-Jones,[18] eran gente feliz y manifestaban un gozo radiante, del que nuestras iglesias carecen a menudo, dando ante el mundo la impresión de unos

---

18. *O. c.*, pp. 21-26.

tipos raros que se sienten miserables frente a la gente que pretende disfrutar de la vida al margen del Evangelio.

g) «... *alabando a Dios*» (v. 47). Ensalzando a Dios por Su santidad infinita, por su bondad inefable, por haberles entregado a Su Hijo Unigénito en propiciación por sus pecados (1.° Jn. 2:2), por haberles rescatado de la condenación, por haberles hecho hijos Suyos, por lo que eran y por lo que les quedaba por ser (1.° Jn. 3:2).

CUESTIONARIO:

1. ¿Qué distingue a la iglesia de otros grupos? — 2. ¿Quién añade a la iglesia a los que se salvan? — 3. ¿Qué pasos comprende, según Hechos 2, la conversión personal? — 4. ¿Qué es lo que hace de la vida cristiana una vida eclesial? — 5. Programa de Hech. 2:42.

LECCION 4.ª DEFINICION DE IGLESIA

1. Dificultad de una definición exacta.

Después de todo lo que llevamos dicho sobre el concepto de iglesia, parece obvio que podemos pasar ya a definir teológicamente lo que es la Iglesia. Sin embargo, es difícil dar una definición *exacta* de la Iglesia.[19] La razón de esta dificultad estriba en que una definición escueta puede resultar demasiado simplista, como la de K. Barth: «La Iglesia es la comunidad viva del viviente Señor Jesucristo.»[20] Por otro lado, una definición suficientemente descriptiva habrá de ser demasiado larga y, aun así, imprecisa, puesto que la Iglesia, a pesar de ser una noción sencilla de captar, es un *misterio* difícil de describir con exactitud; y si se deja de señalar algún aspecto importante de su concepto, hay peligro de formarse de la Iglesia una idea inadecuada.

2. Dos tipos de definición de Iglesia.

A falta de fórmulas más claras para una definición de Iglesia que sea aceptable (al menos dentro de nuestro marco confesional), creemos que son bastante acertadas las dos definiciones que Pendleton nos ofrece [21] y que, con ligeros retoques gramaticales, copiamos a continuación:

---

19. A. Kuen, *o. c.*, dedica cuatro páginas a la presentación de distintas definiciones.
20. En *Schrift und Kirche*, p. 37 (citado por A. Kuen, *o. c.*, p. 48, nota 22).
21. En *Compendio de Teología Cristiana*, p. 323.

A) **Definición esencial:** «Una iglesia es una congregación de discípulos de Cristo, bautizados,[22] unidos en la creencia de lo que El ha dicho y comprometidos a hacer lo que El ha mandado.»

B) **Definición descriptiva:** «Una iglesia es una congregación de discípulos de Cristo bautizados, que Le reconocen a El como su Cabeza, que confían en Su sacrificio expiatorio para la justificación delante de Dios, que dependen del Espíritu Santo para la santificación, que están unidos en la creencia del Evangelio y comprometidos a mantener Sus ordenanzas y a obedecer Sus preceptos, reuniéndose para el culto y cooperando para la extensión del reino de Cristo en el mundo.»

3. Definición católico-romana de Iglesia.

Para conocer el fondo del concepto católico-romano de iglesia y, por tanto, para saber a qué atenerse en un diálogo ocasional sobre este punto, estimamos conveniente presentar la que, durante cerca de cuatro siglos, ha sido la definición «oficial» dentro de la Iglesia de Roma: «La Iglesia es la congregación de todos los fieles que, habiendo sido bautizados, profesan la misma fe, participan de los mismos sacramentos y son gobernados por sus legítimos pastores, bajo una sola cabeza visible en la tierra.» Como puede verse, dicha definición recalca suficientemente la constitución jerárquica de la Iglesia Romana.

Una definición descriptiva de Iglesia, dada reciente y oficialmente por Roma, sólo se puede obtener leyendo atentamente los 16 primeros puntos de la *Constitución Dogmática sobre la Iglesia,* del Concilio Vaticano II.[23] Pero quizá sea lo bastante expresiva, dentro de su concisión, la que nos ofrece el párrafo 1.º de dicho documento, que

---

22. Téngase en cuenta que tratamos de la iglesia *local,* única realidad concreta de la Iglesia de Cristo como realidad trascendente.

23. V. mi libro *Catolicismo Romano,* pp. 20 y ss.

dice así: «La Iglesia es en Cristo como un sacramento, o sea, signo e instrumento de la unión íntima con Dios y de la unidad de todo el género humano.» Analicémosla brevemente, pues hay en ella cuatro aspectos dignos de observación:

A) «La Iglesia es *en Cristo* como un sacramento», o sea, así como la naturaleza humana de Cristo es vehículo de salvación, también lo es la Iglesia «por una notable analogía con el misterio del Verbo Encarnado».[24]

B) «La Iglesia es... un *sacramento*», es decir, un signo sensible que simboliza y confiere (según la doctrina de Roma) la gracia de la salvación. Como dice Semmelroth, la Iglesia es como una mano gigante con siete dedos (los siete sacramentos), con los que toma al hombre y lo pone en contacto con la salvación divina.

C) «... *instrumento* de la unión íntima con Dios»; sólo por medio de la Iglesia —no sólo como proclamadora del mensaje, sino como conducto sacramental— Dios toma al hombre con Su gracia, y el hombre se encuentra con el Dios Salvador.

D) «... y de la unidad de *todo el género humano*», lo cual implica que toda persona de buena voluntad (ateos incluidos) se halla en el camino que lleva a la salvación y pertenece, de algún modo, a la Iglesia.[25]

4. Diversos aspectos dentro del concepto de Iglesia:

A) IGLESIA INVISIBLE E IGLESIA VISIBLE. Al hablar de este modo no pretendemos insinuar que haya dos iglesias diferentes o que la iglesia conste de dos partes, sino sólo distinguir dos *aspectos* de una misma realidad, la cual es invisible en cuanto a su íntima esencia *espiritual,* ya que es invisible la regeneración que nos imparte la vida divina, como invisibles son también las operaciones del Espíritu en los creyentes y en la Iglesia, y la comunión de

24. V. el punto 8.º del citado documento.
25. V. el punto 16 de la misma *Constitución.*

los fieles con el Señor y entre sí. Pero esta realidad invisible toma forma concreta *visible* en los hombres que la componen, en el lugar de reunión, en los actos de culto y testimonio y en la organización y gobierno de las comunidades locales.

B) IGLESIA-ORGANISMO E IGLESIA-ORGANIZACIÓN. En una perspectiva similar, vemos que la iglesia como *organismo* es algo vivo espiritualmente, donde los diversos órganos y funciones esenciales vienen dados por el hecho de la unión vital con Cristo y de la participación en los dones del Espíritu, mientras que la iglesia como *organización* es como el andamiaje o caparazón por el que dicho organismo se manifiesta al exterior en determinadas formas de administración y de gobierno. Para distinguir bien entre ambos aspectos téngase en cuenta lo siguiente: *a)* como *organismo*, la iglesia es la comunidad de los creyentes, unidos a Cristo por el Espíritu; como *organización*, es una agencia divina para la conversión de los pecadores y la edificación de los fieles; *b)* como *organismo*, la iglesia está dotada de carismas o dones que posibilitan el ministerio común de cada miembro de iglesia; como *organización*, adquiere forma institucional y funciona a través de los oficios y demás medios convenientes para su buen funcionamiento;[26] *c)* como *organismo*, la iglesia tiene dentro de sí misma el objetivo de su constitución: hacer de los inconversos (aunque ya elegidos por Dios), por la Palabra y el Espíritu, cristianos que crezcan hasta la medida de un varón perfecto (Ef. 4:13); como *organización*, es un medio para el perfeccionamiento de los santos (Efesios 4:11-12).

El hecho de que la iglesia como *organismo* preceda lógicamente a la iglesia como *organización*[27] (puesto que la

---

26. La confusión de estos dos aspectos, haciendo de una institución jerárquica la garantía de ciertos carismas, ha sido, a nuestro juicio, el error básico de la Iglesia de Roma.

27. La organización debe ser una proyección del organismo, no viceversa (¿acaso corresponde el fruto al esfuerzo exterior de las organizaciones?).

experiencia del «nuevo nacimiento» es anterior a la *agregación* a la Iglesia —no somos salvos *por* pertenecer a la Iglesia, sino que pertenecemos a la Iglesia *por ser salvos*—; *cf.* Hech. 2:41), arroja suficiente luz para disipar muchas confusiones, notorias no sólo en el campo católico-romano, sino aun entre los llamados «protestantes». Ya dijimos anteriormente que la Iglesia no consta de iglesias, sino de creyentes. Pero hay otras dos principales fuentes de confusión: 1) mantener un concepto de «iglesia» como de una personalidad abstracta, un algo distinto de los miembros que la componen, siendo así que la iglesia no es sino *la comunidad de los creyentes* (como si dijéramos «la suma de los sumandos») ligados a la Cabeza-Cristo en la unidad del Espíritu (*cf.* Mat. 18:20; Ef. 4:3-6). 2) El identificar la iglesia con los que ejercen un oficio o un ministerio específico en la misma, y que se expresa (especialmente entre los católicos) en frases como «hay que obedecer a la Iglesia», «pregúnteselo a la Iglesia», «con la Iglesia hemos topado», etc., como si no fueran «iglesia» igualmente todos y cada uno de sus miembros. Esta confusión induce a muchos a sentirse súbditos de otros hombres en el terreno espiritual y a mirar a los ministros de Dios como «los profesionales de la religión», a quienes compete el conocimiento de la Biblia y la responsabilidad exclusiva en los asuntos de iglesia, y a quienes se acude de la misma manera que se va al abogado, al médico, etcétera, en materias de la respectiva competencia; como si la Palabra de Dios y los carismas del Espíritu estuviesen bajo la exclusiva de una casta, o como si el pastor de una iglesia hubiese de cargar con todas las responsabilidades de la congregación.

C) IGLESIA MILITANTE E IGLESIA TRIUNFANTE. La primera, a la que con mayor propiedad se aplica el nombre de *iglesia* (Cuerpo de Cristo en edificación), es la comunidad cristiana que peregrina por el desierto de esta vida hacia la nueva Tierra Prometida y a la que llamamos *militante*, no porque haya de adoptar un talante ofensivo, sino porque cada cristiano debe estar armado con la *panoplia* de Dios, para *estar firme* contra el demonio (*cf.* Ef. 6:12 y ss.).[28] La iglesia *triunfante* es el grupo incontable de creyentes trasplantados al Cielo, tras cambiar la espada corta («máchaira») por la palma; las lágrimas, por el cántico; la cruz, por la corona.[29]

CUESTIONARIO:

1. ¿Cómo podemos definir la Iglesia? — 2. ¿Cómo la define la doctrina tradicional de la Iglesia de Roma? — 3. Explíquese la definición contenida en el párrafo 1.º de la Constitución Dogmática sobre la Iglesia, del Vaticano II. — 4. ¿Qué entendemos por iglesia invisible? — 5. ¿En qué se distingue el organismo de la organización de la Iglesia? — 6. ¿Por qué llamamos «militante» a la Iglesia peregrina? — 7. ¿Existe una Iglesia llamada «purgante»?

---

28. Analizando este pasaje bíblico, descubrimos que se trata de una lucha: a) *constante* (v. 18), y b) *defensiva,* puesto que el creyente pisa *ya* terreno de victoria y, por eso, no se le exhorta a *marchar,* sino a «estar firme» y a «resistir» (vv. 11, 13, 14).

29. La Iglesia de Roma añade una tercera Iglesia «purgante», que expía en el Purgatorio la pena temporal de los pecados que quedó sin ser satisfecha en esta vida. Los evangélicos vemos en esto una abierta contradicción con pasajes como Rom. 8:1; 2.ª Corintios 5:21; Col. 2:14; Heb. 9:26-28; 10:12-18; 1.ª Jn. 1:7-9; Apocalipsis 1:5; 3:5; 14:13, entre otros.

Segunda parte

Fundación
de la Iglesia

LECCION 5.ª EL FUNDADOR DE LA IGLESIA

1. La Iglesia es una sociedad de fundación divina.

La gran mayoría de las organizaciones que existen en el mundo, incluyendo muchas sociedades religiosas, deben su origen a personas humanas, pero la Iglesia ha sido fundada por Dios mismo. La palabra «iglesia» indica ya un llamamiento por parte de Dios para salir de la perversidad del mundo. Esta fundación de la Iglesia se remonta, en los designios divinos, a la misma eternidad, ya que Ef. 1:4-5 nos asegura que Dios nos escogió «antes de la fundación del mundo»; y no precisamente como se escoge a individuos aislados, sino como «miembros de la familia de Dios» (Ef. 2:19).

La Iglesia, como ya dijimos en la lección 3.ª, implica una *segregación,* la cual se apunta ya en Génesis 3:15, donde Dios pone *enemistades* entre lo diabólico y lo divino, marcando así la frontera entre el mundo y la iglesia. Siglos después, cuando la corrupción humana ha difuminado esa frontera, Dios envía el Diluvio y se reserva un remanente en Noé y los suyos (Gén. caps. 6 y 7). Más tarde hace lo mismo con Abraham (Gén. 17). Después con Jacob (Gén. 28:10-22). Finalmente, la Trinidad toda interviene explícitamente en la fundación de la Iglesia de Cristo.

2. El Padre elige y llama.

Yahveh (Dios-Padre), para quien Israel era «Su Elegido» (Is. 45:4), elige, sella y envía a Su Hijo Jesucristo (Jn. 3:16; 6:27; 10:36) y, en El, elige, sella y llama a Sus escogidos (Ef. 1:3-6, 13; 1.ª Ped. 1:2) para formar la Iglesia. Esto lo hace *por amor*, «*según el puro afecto de Su voluntad*» (Ef. 1:5), a Sus predestinados, es decir, «a los que conforme a Su propósito son llamados...» (Rom. 8: 28-30). Por eso, la Iglesia es «linaje escogido..., pueblo adquirido por Dios» (1.ª Ped. 2:9).

3. El Hijo redime.

El Hijo de Dios, ya Encarnado, *redime*, es decir, compra la Iglesia, rescatándola de la esclavitud del pecado y del demonio, al precio de Su propia sangre (Jn. 10:11; Hech. 20:28; Rom. 5:8-10; Gál. 2:20; Col. 1:13-14).

Siendo el «único Mediador entre Dios y los hombres» (1.ª Tim. 2:5), Cristo es el puente tendido por Dios para nuestra salvación (Jn. 3:16). El hace de puente, o sea, es nuestro «Pontífice» o «Sumo Sacerdote» (Heb. 4:15), único capaz de tornar a Dios propicio para nosotros (Heb. 7:26-27; 9:11-15; 10:12-21; 1.º Jn. 2:2). Sólo por El se va al Padre (Jn. 14:6). El es «la puerta» (Jn. 10:7-9). Cristo es *siempre* la *única* puerta que permite a los pastores el acceso a Cristo y a las ovejas, y la única puerta que permite a las ovejas el acceso al Padre y a los bienes salvíficos.[1] Cristo es la puerta de cada persona salva y de la misma Iglesia, pues es por fe en El («recibieron la palabra» —Hechos 2:41—), y por la expresión simbólica de dicha fe por el Bautismo, como el Espíritu añade cada día a la Iglesia a los que son salvos. Triste cosa es que algunas iglesias lleguen a tal estado de postración (por negligencia o autosuficiencia —cf. Apoc. 3:14-19—) que el propio Señor de la Iglesia, que es también su Puerta, se quede fuera —«a la puerta» (Apoc. 3:20)—, ignorado, desdeñado o desobedecido. Sin embargo, por triste que sea tal condición, Cristo sigue llamando y ofreciendo su banquete nupcial; siempre hay motivo de esperanza, gracias a Aquél que no quebran-

---

1. V. W. Hendriksen, *The Gospel of John* (London, Banner of Truth, 1961), II, p. 109.

ta la caña rajada, ni extingue totalmente el pábilo que humea.[2]

Por tanto, la Iglesia *no es* la puerta. Si mantenemos el concepto bíblico de «iglesia» como congregación de los creyentes, es evidente que tal iglesia no puede ser la puerta del redil, por ser ella misma el rebaño de los *congregados*. Es un concepto introducido por la Iglesia de Roma el que una estructura jerárquica sea la puerta de la salvación, mediante el poder sacramental. Dice Möhler: «Primero es la iglesia visible; después la invisible; la primera engendra a la segunda»[3] (¿la organización *madre* del organismo?). Pero Hech. 2:47 nos dice que es el Señor, no la jerarquía de una iglesia, quien añade a esa misma Iglesia a los salvos.

4. El Espíritu regenera y abre la puerta.

El Espíritu Santo infunde la vida, el movimiento y la unidad en la Iglesia. El, por medio del «nuevo nacimiento», nos da la vida espiritual en Cristo (Jn. 3:3, 5-8; Ef. 2:1); con la vida, la atracción en Cristo al Padre (Jn. 6:44); con la atracción, la fe (Ef. 2:8; Filip. 1:29); con la fe, el conocimiento de las cosas espirituales (1.ª Cor. 2:10-14; 12:3). Fue el Espíritu quien con su operación sobre los reunidos en el Aposento Alto (Hech. 2:33), y sobre los corazones de quienes oían a los apóstoles (Hech. 2:38; 16:14), añadía a la Iglesia a los creyentes (Hech. 2:41, 47). El preserva la unidad de la Iglesia y reparte los varios dones (1.ª Corintios 12:4; Ef. 4:3-4, 7).

Estas realidades grandiosas nos deben llenar de asombro, de gratitud, de adoración, de afán de servicio y de celo misionero. ¿Cómo puede permanecer frío e inactivo

2. Es una equivocación el presentar Apoc. 3:20 como una intimación a los inconversos, según se hace en algunas campañas evangelísticas, con lo que se insinúa el error arminiano de que es el *hombre* quien abre la puerta a Jesucristo.
3. *Symbolism* (London, 1847), II, p. 108.

quien se percata de haber sido objeto de tan gran amor por parte de Dios Padre, de tan gran sacrificio por parte de Dios Hijo y de tan exquisito cuidado por parte de Dios Espíritu Santo? ¡Hemos de considerarnos siempre *como perdonados para perdonar y servir, como salvos para ser santos!* (*cf.* Ef. 1:4).

5. Diferencias entre la fundación de la Iglesia y la de otras sociedades.

La Iglesia no es la única sociedad fundada por Dios. Dios fundó también la familia (Gén. 2:18-24) y el Estado (Rom. 13:1). Pero hay notables diferencias entre estas dos últimas sociedades y la Iglesia:

A) Sólo al hablar de la fundación de la Iglesia usó Cristo el posesivo «mi» (Mat. 16:18). Y con razón, porque Cristo es el *Salvador,* y la Iglesia consta de *salvos,* lo cual no ocurre con la familia ni con el Estado. En otras palabras, la Iglesia pertenece a la esfera de lo *sobrenatural,* siendo la comunidad de los que han nacido *de arriba;* por tanto, los no regenerados no son *de* la Iglesia (1.° Jn. 2:19), mientras que la familia y el Estado pertenecen a la esfera de lo *natural* y, por ello, son sociedades abiertas a todos, aunque los cristianos son exhortados en el Nuevo Testamento a formar familias cristianas y a ser los mejores ciudadanos.

B) La familia y el Estado son sociedades a las que se pertenece por *necesidad.* Uno se hace miembro de una familia humana por nacimiento, hereditariamente. De la misma manera, uno nace en un territorio definido y se convierte en miembro de un Estado antes de quererlo libremente. Por el contrario, la pertenencia a la Iglesia es *voluntaria,* puesto que la membresía respecto de la iglesia es consecuencia de la regeneración espiritual, la cual no se opera por herencia ni por un certificado de nacimiento, sino por la recepción interior, consciente y voluntaria, de Cristo y de Su Evangelio, aunque dicha recepción sea efecto de la operación libre y eficaz del Espíritu Santo. El que la fe sea un don de Dios no es obstáculo para que sea también un acto consciente y voluntario del hombre.

C) Hay también razones internas esenciales para convencernos de que la Iglesia es una sociedad de fundación *específicamente* divina: *a)* la Iglesia, como congregación de cristianos, es una sociedad religiosa, es decir, un conjunto re-ligado a Dios. Ahora bien, sólo Dios puede tomar la iniciativa de vincular consigo al hombre en la esfera espiritual, de la que Dios tiene la exclusiva. *b)* La iglesia local es la concreción espacio-temporal del Cuerpo de Cristo; por tanto, todo su ser y todo su haber le vienen de su Cabeza que es Cristo. *c)* La Iglesia es llamada «Iglesia de Cristo», «Iglesia de Dios» (Mat. 16:18; 18:17-20; Hechos 20:28; Rom. 16:16; 1.ª Cor. 1:2; 10:32; 11:22; 2.ª Corintios 1:1; Gál. 1:13; 1.ª Tim. 3:5, 15), porque Dios es su Fundador, su Soberano, su Salvador y su Juez.[4]

CUESTIONARIO:

1. ¿Por qué decimos que la Iglesia es una sociedad de fundación divina? — 2. ¿Qué papel corresponde a cada una de las Personas de la Deidad en la fundación de la Iglesia? — 3. ¿Qué diferencias hay entre la fundación de la Iglesia y la de otras sociedades fundadas por Dios? — 4. ¿Quién es el que añade nuevos miembros a la Iglesia?

---

4. Para todo este tema véase R. B. Kuiper, *The Glorious Body of Christ*, pp. 36-40.

LECCION 6.ª EL FUNDAMENTO DE LA IGLESIA

1. Cristo es la piedra angular de la Iglesia.

Como muy bien ha dicho Griffith Thomas, «el Cristianismo es la única religión en el mundo que se apoya en la Persona de su Fundador».[5] «No hay otro nombre [es decir, otra persona] bajo el cielo, dado a los hombres, en que podamos ser salvos», afirma Pedro (Hech. 4:12). Y el apóstol Juan pone como test de la ortodoxia esta misma confesión: «Todo espíritu que confiesa que Jesucristo ha venido en carne, es de Dios» (1.º Jn. 4:2), lo cual adquiere su pleno sentido si se contrasta con 1.ª Tim. 3:16: «Dios fue manifestado en carne» (cf. Jn. 1:14). No es extraño que Jesús exigiera esta misma confesión para reconocer el verdadero discipulado: «Y vosotros, ¿quién decís que soy Yo?» (Mat. 16:15; cf. Marc. 8:29; Luc. 9:20; Jn. 6:69).

El apóstol Pablo dice que «nadie puede poner otro fundamento («themélion») que el que está puesto, el cual es Jesucristo» (1.ª Cor. 3:11); toda edificación doctrinal de la Iglesia ha de hacerse sobre este fundamento. El término «themélios» lo aplican Pablo (Ef. 2:20) y Juan (Apoc. 21:14) a los apóstoles, es decir, a los «Doce», como testigos insustituibles del Cristo muerto y resucitado (cf. Hech. 1: 21-22). Sobre este fundamento de los apóstoles, o sea, de su mensaje sobre Cristo, se levanta todo el edificio de «piedras vivas» que es la Iglesia (1.ª Ped. 2:5). Esta misma iglesia, como *comunidad* es llamada «columna *(stylos)* de

---

5. En *Christianity is Christ* (Grand Rapids, Eerdmans, 1955), p. 7.

la verdad», por su encargo de «mantener en alto» la verdad; pero también a cada creyente («al que venciere») se aplica este epíteto en Apoc. 3:12.

Sin embargo, sólo a Jesucristo aplica el griego del Nuevo Testamento el término «akrogoniaios» (piedra angular, o «piedra principal del ángulo» —Hech. 4:11; Ef. 2:20; 1.ª Ped. 2:6—). Los apóstoles tomaron este epíteto del hebreo «eben hapinnah» o «eben bojan pinnat» (*cf.* Isaías 28:16). En hebreo, el término significa «una piedra bien probada, costosa y segura como fundamento», pero el término griego con que fue vertido a los LXX y, a través de los LXX, al Nuevo Testamento, significa, como ha demostrado F. Rienecker,[6] «una piedra que, al mismo tiempo, sostiene el edificio, está en el ángulo, como para marcar la rectitud de la pared que se levanta, y le sirve de cima o cúpula» («ákros»).

Con esto ya tenemos desbrozado el camino para analizar el gran texto de controversia entre católico-romanos y evangélicos que es Mat. 16:18.

2. Interpretación católico-romana de Mateo 16:18.

La primera vez que la palabra «iglesia» aparece en el Nuevo Testamento es en Mat. 16:18: «sobre esta piedra edificaré MI IGLESIA». Advirtamos de antemano: 1) que Cristo habla en futuro: «edificaré»; 2) que habla de la Iglesia como algo «Suyo». ¿En qué estriba la relevante y peculiar importancia de este texto? En primer lugar, en el número y calidad de enseñanzas que de él se desprenden. Cinco cosas hay en él, según el obispo anglicano J. C. Ryle,[7] que merecen especial atención: en él se nos habla del edificio de la Iglesia, de su Constructor, de su Fundamento, de los peligros que la acechan y de la seguridad de su supervivencia. En segundo lugar, aunque no

---

6. *Der Brief an die Epheser* (Verlag, Wuppertal, 1968), p. 103.
7. V. Ryle, *Perlas Cristianas* (London, The Banner of Truth, 1963), pp. 349-363.

menos importante, en las consecuencias dogmáticas que
la Iglesia de Roma ha pretendido deducir de él; consecuencias que constituyen toda la clave dogmática del sistema católico-romano. Veamos cómo desarrolla la Teología
Romana su argumento a base de Mat. 16:18:

> «Cristo hizo a Pedro el fundamento de Su Igle-
> sia, esto es, el garante de su unidad y de su forta-
> leza inconmovible, y prometió a Su iglesia una
> duración perenne (Mat. 16:18). Ahora bien, la
> unidad y la solidez de la iglesia no son posibles
> sin la recta Fe. Por tanto, Pedro es también el
> supremo maestro de la Fe. Como tal, debe ser in-
> falible en la promulgación oficial de la Fe, tanto
> en su propia persona como en la de sus suceso-
> res, puesto que, por voluntad de Cristo, la Iglesia
> ha de continuar hasta el fin de los tiempos. Igual-
> mente, Cristo invistió a Pedro (y a sus sucesores)
> del supremo poder de atar y desatar. Así como en
> la expresión rabínica "atar y desatar" se com-
> prende también la declaración auténtica de la ley,
> así también se contiene aquí el poder de declarar
> auténticamente la ley del Nuevo Pacto, el Evan-
> gelio. Dios en el Cielo confirmará el juicio del
> Papa. Esto supone que, en su capacidad de supre-
> mo Doctor de la Fe, está preservado del error.» [8]

Por tanto, la Teología de Roma lee así este pasaje: «Tú
eres KEFA (piedra) y sobre este KEFA (que eres tú) edificaré Mi Iglesia.»

La referida interpretación de la Teología Romana tiene
carácter de «dogma» y, por tanto, es irreformable (por lo
que ha sido refrendada por el Vaticano II, con lo que no

---

8. L. Ott, *Fundamentals of Catholic Dogma* (Trad. de P. Lynch.
Cork, 1966), p. 287. V. también p. 280, acerca del Primado de Pedro.
V. también M. Fernández, *¿Tu camino de Damasco?* (Estella, Verbo
Divino, 1963), pp. 77-89, refutado por mí en la 2.ª edición de *Mi ca-
mino de Damasco* (Westcliff-on-Sea, The Power House, 1970), pp. 49-55.

cabe debate ecuménico sobre tal tema). Las consecuencias doctrinales son las siguientes:

A) El Papa es, como Cabeza y Fundamento visible de toda la Iglesia, el principio y raíz de la unidad de la Iglesia: el Vicario de Cristo en la Tierra.

B) El Papa tiene sobre la Iglesia un poder de jurisdicción (verdadera autoridad o *ius*) universal (sobre *toda* la Iglesia que se llame «cristiana»), supremo (inapelable) e inmediato (directo sobre cada uno de los pastores, fieles e iglesias). Como definió Bonifacio VIII:[9] «toda creatura humana está sometida al Romano Pontífice, como algo necesario para su salvación». Vemos, pues, que la definición de Bonifacio VIII es más inclusiva que la del Vaticano I. Las razones por las que se pretende que el Papa posee esta jurisdicción universal son las siguientes: *a)* los bautizados le están sometidos porque —según Roma— el Bautismo es la puerta de la Iglesia Universal (no se olvide que, para Roma, la única iglesia *verdadera* es la suya); *b)* los no bautizados le están sometidos en el ámbito religioso-moral, ya que se pretende que el Papa, como representante supremo de Dios en la Tierra, tiene el supremo y universal poder en la esfera ético-religiosa.

C) El Papa, ya solo, ya con el Colegio de obispos (pero no el Colegio de obispos sin él), es el único intérprete infalible de la Escritura y de la Tradición. Así que, cuando ejerce esta función *ex cáthedra*, o sea, en calidad de Maestro Universal de la Cristiandad, todo el mundo debe aceptar su interpretación, so pena de eterna condenación.

D) Hay, pues, en todo esto algo de suprema importancia que nosotros, guiados por la Palabra de Dios, estimamos como antibíblico: *los carismas de enseñanza y de gobierno quedan institucionalizados en una persona y jurídicamente garantizados por el mismo Dios (de derecho divino* —asistencia del Espíritu Santo—), a pesar de que esta persona puede carecer del Espíritu Santo, por no po-

---

9. En su bula *Unam Sanctam* (V. Denzinger-Schönm., n.º 875).

seer un corazón converso o regenerado (como los mismos católicos lo admiten de algunos papas), y carecer también de la capacidad para interpretar correctamente la Escritura (como lo muestra notoriamente la misma Bula de Bonifacio VIII, entre otros documentos).

3. Correcta interpretación de Mateo 16:18-19.

Resumiremos la interpretación que creemos más ajustada a la Palabra de Dios.[10]

Después de preguntar a sus discípulos qué opinaban las gentes de Él y escuchar los falsos rumores acerca de Su Persona, Jesús se encara con los apóstoles y les pregunta: «Y vosotros, ¿quién decís que soy YO?» (v. 15). Tomando la palabra en nombre de todos, responde Pedro: «Tú eres el Cristo, el Hijo del Dios viviente.» Esta confesión expresa el meollo de la fe cristiana; más aún, es el centro de la fe salvífica (cf. Jn. 20:31; Rom. 10:10). Pedro confiesa que Jesús, el hombre que está delante de él, es el «Cristo», el «Ungido» de Dios y enviado a este mundo, o sea, el verdadero «Mesías»; más aún, el Hijo Predilecto, Unigénito, de Dios vivo, en contraste con los dioses falsos, muertos —inertes— y vacíos de poder salvador. *Esta confesión de Pedro es la piedra fundamental del Cristianismo (cf. 1.* Tim. 3:16).

Jesús felicita a Pedro por esta confesión, que nadie, sino el Padre, por el Espíritu, ha podido revelar del Hijo, y añade: «Tú eres Pedro —una piedra— y sobre esta piedra edificaré Mi Iglesia.» Advirtamos que Cristo no dice: «y sobre ti edificaré Mi Iglesia» —no la edifica sobre la persona de Pedro *como tal*. Tampoco dice: «y sobre esta piedra —que soy Yo— edificaré Mi Iglesia», puesto que ni la expresión gramatical ni el sentido de la frase admi-

---

10. V., entre otros, J. A. Broadus, *Comentario sobre el Evangelio según S. Mateo* (Trad. de Sarah A. Hall, El Paso, Texas, sin fecha), pp. 446-463.

ten tal interpretación.[11] Jesús no funda Su Iglesia sobre la persona de Pedro, pero el sentido de *piedra (kefa)* no es ajeno a Pedro en cuanto *roca-confesante*. Estamos de acuerdo con A. H. Strong:

> «Los Protestantes se equivocan al negar en Mateo 16:18 la referencia a Pedro: Cristo reconoce la *personalidad* de Pedro en la fundación de Su Reino. Pero los de Roma yerran igualmente al ignorar que es la *confesión* de Pedro lo que le constituye "roca".»[12]

En otras palabras, la única Roca objetiva o Piedra Angular de la Iglesia es Jesucristo y *sólo El*. Pero Pedro es también un relevante «themélios» o cimiento —piedra fundamental— de la Iglesia; una de las tres grandes «colulumnas» (Gál. 2:9 —nótese el epíteto «Cefas», o «kefa», en labios de Pablo en dicho texto—), por cuanto con su testimonio apostólico —común a los Doce, pero de especial relevancia en él— echó los fundamentos de la fe cristiana, la cual se basa, hasta el fin de los siglos, en dicho testimonio apostólico.

¿Por qué se dirigió Jesús a Pedro en tal ocasión? Porque Pedro había respondido en representación de los Doce, e incluso en nombre de toda la Iglesia en ellos representada. Oigamos a Agustín de Hipona:

> «En esta confesión, Pedro representaba a toda la Iglesia... Por consiguiente —dice—, sobre esta piedra que has confesado, edificaré Mi Iglesia. Pues la piedra era Cristo, y el mismo Pedro fue edificado también sobre este fundamento.»[13]

---

11. Es una lástima que exegetas modernos, como Gander, sigan manteniendo esta ridícula interpretación, que O. Cullmann se ha encargado de triturar en su *Sant Pere* (Trad. al catalán de M. Balasch, Barcelona, 1967).
12. *Systematic Theology*, p. 909 (V. también A. Kuen, *o. c.*, páginas 103-115).
13. *Tractatus in Joannem 124, 5*. Para un análisis penetrante y práctico de la frase de Jesús: «Yo fundaré... mi Iglesia», véase L. Sp. Chafer, *Systematic Theology*, IV, p. 43.

De manera parecida se expresa la mayoría de los llamados «Santos Padres». Aunque dichos «Padres» no son infalibles, merecen cierto crédito en la medida de su antigüedad y conocimiento de la Palabra de Dios y, por eso, Lutero, Calvino y muchos teólogos evangélicos no han desdeñado su testimonio, sino que los citan a menudo.

Para mejor entender toda esta perícopa, analicemos brevemente el resto de ella:

A) «... *edificaré Mi Iglesia*». G. Gander [14] sostiene que la frase «edificaré Mi Iglesia» implica la construcción de la Iglesia como la «casa», edificio o templo de Cristo, [15] a la luz de Jn. 2:19-22. Metáfora que se entrelaza con la de «cuerpo» en Ef. 4:12, 16, y está explícita en Ef. 2:20; 1.ª Cor. 3:11; 1.ª Ped. 2:4-8; Apoc. 21:14. Dentro de esta interpretación se explica mejor todo el alcance de la frase siguiente.

B) «*Y las puertas del Hades no prevalecerán contra ella.*» Las, puertas del Hades (término griego que vierte el «sheol» de los judíos) no son los poderes del Infierno, ya que el Nuevo Testamento sitúa los poderes diabólicos en las regiones superiores de nuestra atmósfera terrestre o «primer cielo» (*cf.* Ef. 6:12), sino los poderes de la muerte; con la frase se indica, no que la Iglesia sea infalible ni indefectible, sino que —como edificio construido por Cristo— está a salvo de los embates del sepulcro, porque Cristo ha vencido a la muerte y esta victoria es extensiva a los Suyos, los cuales son la «piedras vivas» (comp. 1.ª Pedro 2:5 con Mat. 12:40; 16:21; Jn. 2:19-22; Rom. 6:9; 1.ª Cor. 15:55-58). Siendo la Iglesia el edificio construido por Cristo sobre la *Roca*, es claro que ninguna tempestad, vendaval o inundación podrán echarla por tierra (Mateo 7:24; Luc. 6:48). [16]

14. En la revista *Etudes Evangéliques*, Janv.-Sept., 1966, pp. 34-88.
15. V. también lección 8.ª, punto 2.
16. V. Gander, *o. c.*, pp. 89-102, y K. Barth, *Dogmatique* (edición francesa), III, vol. 2, 1961, p. 285.

C) «*Y a ti te daré las llaves del reino de los Cielos.*» En esta frase se pretende fundar el llamado «poder de las llaves» atribuido a las jerarquías eclesiásticas, en el sentido de que el sacerdocio ministerial, y especialmente los obispos y el Papa, tienen el poder de abrir y cerrar las puertas de la salvación, ya mediante la jurisdicción en el fuero externo, por la cual admiten dentro de la Iglesia por el Bautismo y excluyen de ella por la excomunión, ya mediante la jurisdicción en el fuero interno del confesionario, absolviendo o reteniendo los pecados de quienes se acercan al «tribunal de la Penitencia».

Para entender correctamente esta frase de Jesús es preciso tener en cuenta las siguientes observaciones: *a*) Como hace notar el propio H. Küng, Jesús no dijo: «A ti te daré las llaves de la Iglesia», sino «del reino de Dios».[17] Pedro empleó estas llaves para abrir las puertas del «Reino» a los judíos el día de Pentecostés (Hech. 2), y a los gentiles en casa de Cornelio (Hech. 10). *b*) Los judíos entendían bajo la metáfora de las llaves: 1) la función de declarar —abrir— las Escrituras (V. Luc. 24:32); ésta era la llave del *conocimiento;* 2) la función de admitir a, o excluir de, la comunidad eclesial (Mat. 18:18); ésta era la llave de la *disciplina.* En este aspecto, la facultad de Pedro era extensiva a todos los discípulos (y después a cada iglesia local, por medio de sus oficiales), aunque Pedro llevase, como suele decirse, «la voz cantante» en el período narrado en los doce primeros capítulos del Libro de Hechos.

G. Gander [18] hace notar que la entrega de las llaves a Su Iglesia era una metáfora consecuente con el empleo hecho por Jesús del verbo «edificar» en relación con el nuevo «Pueblo de Dios», ya que a partir de Pentecostés los discípulos de Cristo ejercitarían el ministerio evangélico, según los carismas a cada uno concedidos, para la salvación de las almas, lo que implicaba el abrirles las

---

17. V. *o. c.,* pp. 43 y ss.
18. *O. c.,* pp. 102-111.

puertas del Reino de los Cielos, cosa que los rabinos judíos no podían hacer. Es aquí donde Ef. 4:11 entronca con Mat. 13:52; 23:34, como realización de la promesa de enviar a Su Iglesia «escribas» dotados de carismas: apóstoles, profetas, evangelistas, pastores y maestros.

D) «Y *todo lo que atares en la tierra será atado en los Cielos; y todo lo que desatares en la tierra será desatado en los Cielos.*» Estas palabras se extienden a los demás discípulos en Mat. 18:18. «Atar y desatar», en el argot rabínico, indicaban la función del escriba judío de aplicar la Ley a los casos particulares (hoy diríamos: de sentar jurisprudencia), para permitir o prohibir ciertas acciones de acuerdo con una determinada interpretación de la Ley. Así se podía hablar de que lo que, por ejemplo, la escuela de Hillel «ataba», la escuela de Shammai lo «desataba», o viceversa. El fondo veterotestamentario de esta expresión la hace sinónima de «abrir y cerrar» cuando, como aquí, se halla dentro de una metáfora de edificio. Gander lo demuestra [19] haciendo referencia a lugares como Mateo 12:29; Marc. 5:3; 7:35; Luc. 8:29; 13:16; Hech. 20:22 (presentado también de otra forma en Jn. 20:23).

Dentro de este contexto se pueden interpretar mejor Mat. 16:19; 18:15-22 y el ya aludido —y tan falseado— texto de Jn. 20:23, especialmente a la luz que arrojan otros pasajes-clave como Luc. 24:47 y 2.ª Cor. 5:18-20 (donde el «ministerio de la reconciliación» se identifica con «la palabra de la reconciliación», es decir, con la predicación del mensaje de salvación).

Sobre el oficio de Pedro en la primitiva Iglesia, con la consiguiente discusión de los privilegios que se han atribuido tanto a él como a sus pretendidos sucesores, hablaremos más adelante.

---

19. *O. c.*, pp. 112-125.

CUESTIONARIO:

1. ¿Quién es el fundamento de la Iglesia? — 2. ¿En qué sentido son los Apóstoles fundamento de la Iglesia? — 3. ¿Cómo interpreta la doctrina tradicional de la Iglesia de Roma el texto de Mat. 16:18-19? — 4. ¿Cuál es la exégesis correcta de dicho pasaje?

LECCION 7.ª

¿CUANDO FUNDO CRISTO SU IGLESIA?

1. La pre-Iglesia.

En un sentido amplio, la Iglesia comenzó con el primer hombre, quien seguramente, ante la revelación del misterio de la futura Redención por la Simiente de la Mujer (Gén. 3:15), aceptó por fe al Que había de venir. No se puede perder de vista que cuantos fueron salvos antes de la 1.ª Venida del Señor *lo fueron por la fe,* no por el cumplimiento de la Ley. De ahí que, a lo largo del Nuevo Testamento, Abraham aparezca como el padre de los creyentes. Romanos 3 y 4; Gál. 3 y Heb. 11 bastan para convencernos de este hecho que tanta luz arroja sobre el tema del Bautismo. A esta pre-Iglesia o «congregación de los primogénitos que están inscritos en los Cielos», se nos dice en Heb. 12:22-23 que hemos sido acercados. Ellos son la «tan grande nube de testigos» que nos anima a correr «la carrera que tenemos delante» (Heb. 12:1).

Pero, estrictamente hablando, la Iglesia de Cristo comenzó a formarse cuando dos de los discípulos del Bautista dejaron a su maestro para seguir a Jesús (Jn. 1:37). La frase merece ser ponderada: «Le oyeron hablar (a *Juan*) y siguieron a *Jesús.*» ¡Qué bien está expresado aquí el correcto papel del ministerio cristiano, el cual, para ser bíblico, ha de formar siempre un triángulo, en uno de cuyos ápices se sitúa el ministro del Evangelio, apuntando con una mano al pecador que ante sí tiene, y con la otra al «Cordero de Dios que quita el pecado del mundo»! (Juan

1:29, 36). Sólo cuando el ministro *mengua*, puede Cristo *crecer* en la Iglesia (Jn. 3:30).

Aquel pequeño grupo, del que se nos habla en Jn. 1: 37-51, fue creciendo, siempre bajo la iniciativa divina («Ven y sígueme»); primero hasta Doce (Luc. 6:13-16), en representación de las doce tribus del pueblo escogido; después hasta otros 70 (Luc. 10:1 y ss.), en representación de los 70 ancianos que Moisés se escogió de entre la congregación de Israel. En el Aposento Alto encontramos ya 120 (12 × 10) discípulos. Quizás el número sea simbólico, pues Pablo nos dice que el Señor resucitado «apareció a más de quinientos hermanos a la vez» (1.ª Cor. 15:6).

2. Fundación de la Iglesia de Cristo.

Cuando Pedro, en representación de los Doce, confesó la divinidad de Cristo, el Señor, como ya hemos visto, anunció *en futuro* que edificaría Su Iglesia (Mat. 16:18), por lo que Sus palabras tienen un sentido profético que sólo después de Pascua había de convertirse en plena realidad. El contexto inmediato de la promesa (vv. 21-23) daba a entender bien a las claras que el nacimiento de la Iglesia seguiría al misterio del Cristo muerto y resucitado. Pero, como dice A. Kuen comentando el v. 18, «la primera piedra para el edificio que Jesús quería construir, estaba allí».[20]

Después de Su resurrección, Cristo, que había previsto Su Iglesia como «misterio» (escondido y pequeño grano de mostaza), la envió —«misión»— encargándole la grande y divina *comisión* de predicar el Evangelio (las «buenas noticias» de salvación) a todas las naciones, haciendo «discípulas» a todas las gentes («mathetéusate»), bautizándolas y enseñándoles cuanto Cristo había ordenado (Mateo 28:18-20; Marc. 16:14-16; Luc. 24:36-49; Jn. 20:21-23; Hechos 1:8). Además del Bautismo, como rito simbólico de la sepultura y resurrección espiritual con Cristo mediante

---

20. *O. c.*, p. 104.

la fe, Jesús instituyó, con el mismo carácter de perennidad («hasta que El venga» —1.ª Cor. 11:26), *Su Cena*, la cual constituye una proclamación («katanguéllete») del mensaje de la muerte del Señor, juntamente con el anuncio profético de Su 2.ª Venida.

3. Inauguración oficial de la Iglesia.

El nacimiento oficial de la Iglesia tuvo lugar el día de Pentecostés. «Pentecostés» significa «quincuagésimo», porque la fiesta judía de tal nombre daba fin a las siete semanas en que culminaba la recogida de la cosecha de cereales, que había empezado en la Pascua, como ofrecimiento de las «primicias» (*cf.* Sant. 1:18). Así también, si el misterio de Pascua de Resurrección significaba que la segur quedaba puesta a la raíz de la cosecha, el Día de Pentecostés manifestaba, con el Descenso del Espíritu Santo, la fabricación del gran Pan de la Iglesia (compárese Lev. 23:17-20 con 1.ª Cor. 10:16-17. Cf. también 1.ª Corintios 5:7), es decir, la culminación del proceso de gestación de la Iglesia, mediante la poderosa acción (la «dynamis») del Espíritu, rubricando así el acta de nacimiento de la comunidad cristiana.

La Venida del Espíritu Santo en Pentecostés había sido profetizada por Cristo (Marc. 1:8; Jn. 7:39; 14:16-17; 16:7-13; Hech. 1:4, 8). Más aún, Jesús había asegurado que convenía que El marchase para que el Espíritu descendiese (Jn. 16:7). El Espíritu había descendido ya sobre los santos del Antiguo Testamento *individualmente,* así como con carismas especiales sobre algunos individuos (profetas, sacerdotes, jueces), pero en Pentecostés descendió sobre la Iglesia *distributivamente* (a todos y a cada uno de los creyentes) y *corporativamente* (a la comunidad cristiana, como Cuerpo de Cristo),[21] produciendo la integración de los creyentes como comunidad viva de cristia-

---

21. Por eso vemos que, mientras Israel *tenía,* por ejemplo, un sacerdocio, la Iglesia *es* regio sacerdocio (1.ª Ped. 2:9).

nos, con poder de testimonio y de mutua edificación (Hechos 1:5; 11:15-16; 1.ª Cor. 12:13; Gál. 3:26-28). Como dice C. H. Dodd:[22] «Pentecostés marca la efusión definitiva del Espíritu Santo para la fundación de la Iglesia y la regeneración de los creyentes. El Espíritu Santo es la prueba de que los nuevos tiempos han comenzado.»

Los frutos no se hicieron esperar: aquellos tímidos e iletrados galileos se tornan valientes y sabios testigos y, a través de ellos, el Espíritu lleva a cabo en un solo día, con la añadidura de 3.000 personas a la Iglesia, lo que Jesús no había podido realizar durante más de tres años (cf. Jn. 14:12).

¿Por qué hubo de comenzar la Iglesia en Pentecostés? La respuesta es sencilla: Porque la Iglesia vive de la *obra acabada* de Cristo; sólo después de presentar al Padre el botín de la victoria pudo Cristo repartir la presa enviando al Dador de los dones para activar o «energizar» (permítaseme el neologismo) Su Iglesia (cf. Ef. 4:7-11).

CUESTIONARIO:

1. ¿Quiénes constituyen la «pre-Iglesia»? — 2. ¿Cómo se formó el primer grupo de discípulos? — 3. Promesa de fundación de la Iglesia. — 4. Entrega de comisión a la Iglesia. — 5. ¿Cuándo y cómo se inauguró oficialmente la Iglesia de Cristo?

---

22. Citado por A. Kuen, *o. c.*, p. 117.

LECCION 8.ª COMO FUNDO CRISTO SU IGLESIA (I)

La Iglesia de Cristo es una realidad tan rica, densa y misteriosa que la Palabra de Dios echa mano de una extensa gama de metáforas para presentarnos en diversas imágenes las distintas facetas de su contenido objetivo. Así, el Nuevo Testamento nos dice que Jesucristo fundó Su Iglesia:

1. Como una planta.

La planta que crece es una de las primeras metáforas que Jesús emplea para mostrar las leyes del crecimiento de Su Iglesia. Esta metáfora tiene tres variantes:

A) Jesús compara el Reino (es decir, la Iglesia como zona de irrupción del Reino de Dios) a un grano de mostaza que, una vez sembrado, germina y crece fuera de la proporción normal («atacado de gigantismo» —como dice A. Kuen—),[23] hasta convertirse en árbol, en cuyas ramas se posan «las aves del Cielo», expresión con que el Señor designa a los demonios (cf. Mat. 13:4, 19, 32). Con ello, Cristo profetizó probablemente el estado anormal de una futura Iglesia gigantesca, con muchedumbre de cristianos de nombre y con superestructuras antievangélicas. Posiblemente, la parábola de las tres medidas de levadura profetiza también la futura corrupción y desviación de la Iglesia (mediante la introducción de falsas doctrinas —cf. Col. 2:8, comp. con Mat. 16:6; Marc. 8:15; Luc. 12:1; 1.ª Cor. 5:6-8; Gál. 5:9), ya que la levadura siempre tiene

---

23. O. c., p. 82.

en la Biblia un sentido peyorativo, exigido también en el contexto de Mateo 13.[24]

B) Una metáfora semejante es la del trigo. En Marcos 4:26 se nos habla de un desarrollo lento, progresivo y silencioso, como toda obra del Espíritu en los individuos y en las iglesias. En Jn. 12:23-28 se nos ofrece en otra perspectiva: sólo el grano que «muere» sepultado en el surco, da cosecha. Esta ley de vida a través de la muerte se cumplió en Cristo y se cumple en cada cristiano y en cada iglesia (cf. Rom. 6:4-10; 8:13-16; 1.ª Cor. 15:31 y ss.; 2.ª Cor. 5:14; Col. 2:20; 3:3-5; 2.ª Tim. 2:11). En Mateo 13:24-30, 36-43 la cizaña crece junto al trigo, lo cual indica el peligro que siempre acecha a la Iglesia de parte del mundo en que está inmersa, a pesar de su segregación espiritual. La enseñanza de esta parábola no implica que hayamos de consentir que los no regenerados permanezcan en las iglesias (como equivocadamente la interpretó Agustín de Hipona), puesto que el mismo Jesús aclaró que «el campo es el mundo», no la Iglesia. Es en 1.ª Corintios 3:6-9 donde la Iglesia es el campo de Dios en otro contexto: el ministerio es comparado al sembrar y al regar, pero sólo Dios da el crecimiento.

C) Finalmente, una tercera variante aparece en Juan 15:1 y ss., donde la viña, imagen familiar del pueblo de Dios (cf. Sal. 80:9; Is. 3:14; 5:1-7; 27:2 y ss.; Jer. 2:21; 10:12; Ez. 15:2; Os. 10; Joel 1:7), queda reducida a una sola cepa, de cuya vitalidad todos los pámpanos han de participar en íntima comunión para poder dar fruto. La Iglesia es así un *misterio* de invisible unión con Cristo, pero también una irradiación de vida por la evangelización y el servicio: un campo de trabajo (Mat. 20:1-16; 21-28). En esta alegoría de la vid y los pámpanos dos verdades se ponen de relieve: a) hay un énfasis especial en la comunión vital y permanente de los cristianos con

---

24. V. L. Sp. Chafer, *Systematic Theology*, IV, p. 55, y *Holy Bible's Pilgrim Edition*, p. 1247, nota 3.

Cristo; [25] b) Jesús declara que, «aparte de El» (v. 5), no podemos dar fruto. El fruto que dan los pámpanos se debe a la unión con, y derivación de, la cepa. Pero también es verdad que la cepa sólo da fruto *en los pámpanos;* es decir, Jesús, por Su Espíritu, da Su fruto a través del *ministerio,* empleando la instrumentalidad humana.

2. Como un edificio.

El edificio construido para casa o templo de Dios es también imagen favorita del Nuevo Testamento para designar a la Iglesia. Jesús fue «el hijo del "tekton"» (Mateo 13:55); es decir, no de un simple «carpintero», sino de un trabajador en madera, que incluía el oficio de *constructor,* [26] a la usanza judía de aquel tiempo. Así se entiende mejor Mat. 16:18, en que Cristo habla de *edificar* Su Iglesia. En ella, El es la «piedra angular»; los apóstoles, los «cimientos»; los creyentes todos, «piedras vivas» (1.ª Corintios 3:9-11; Ef. 2:20; 1.ª Ped. 2:6-7; Apoc. 21:14), edificadas sobre el fundamento apostólico. La metáfora de edificio o templo para designar la Iglesia comporta las siguientes consecuencias doctrinales y prácticas:

A) Cada creyente es como una piedra sacada de la cantera del mundo y labrada con el cincel divino antes de ser colocada en el edificio, para que la edificación de la Iglesia, como ya dijimos, se haga en silencio, al igual que el templo de Salomón. [27]

B) Cada creyente, como piedra viva de un conjunto orgánico que avanza hacia su meta de crecimiento, es un *edificador* del Cuerpo (Ef. 4:16), mediante el uso de los dones que capacitan a cada miembro para un determinado

---

25. Nótese que hablamos de *comunión vital,* no de *unión posicional* en Cristo; el creyente puede fallar en la comunión, pero no puede ser *separado* de la unión con su Señor (*cf.* Jn. 10:28-29).

26. Por eso, el vocablo «arquitecto» significa «jefe de constructores» (*cf.* 1.ª Cor. 3:10).

27. V. Lloyd-Jones, *o. c.,* pp. 16-17.

servicio. No se puede encontrar perfección en los materiales humanos, pero sí en el *amor* que el Espíritu de Dios infunde en el Cuerpo de la Iglesia (*cf*. Mat. 5:48; Rom. 5:5; 1.ª Cor. 13:7-13; Ef. 4:15-16; Filip. 3:15; 1.º Jn. 4:12, 18).

C) Cada creyente, como piedra *personal* del edificio de la Iglesia, tiene su configuración peculiar: su carácter, temperamento, dones, cualidades y defectos propios (sus «entrantes y salientes»), mediante los cuales se ajusta precisamente a las peculiaridades de las demás piedras, gracias al uso que de tales diferencias hace el divino Arquitecto.

D) La Iglesia local es a la vez: a) *edificio* que cobija, como el redil en que las ovejas entran y salen y encuentran pastos (Jn. 10:9), sintiéndose al abrigo de Cristo en medio de una generación perversa; b) *templo* en que se rinde culto a Dios: se adora, se alaba y se intercede (*cf*. 1.ª Cor. 3:16-17; 2.ª Cor. 6:16; Ef. 2:21; 1.ª Tim. 3:15, comp. con Marc. 11:17 y Jn. 2:16).

CUESTIONARIO:

1. ¿Qué variantes tiene la metáfora de plantación aplicada a la Iglesia? — 2. ¿Qué peligros comporta un crecimiento anormal? — 3. ¿Quiénes constituyen la «cizaña» de Mat. 13:24-30, 36-43? — 4. ¿Qué lecciones deducimos de Jn. 15:1 y ss.? — 5. ¿Qué implica, para cada uno de los creyentes, el ser «piedras vivas» del edificio de la Iglesia?

3. Como un cuerpo.

A) SIGNIFICADO DE LA METÁFORA. Esta es la metáfora predominante en las Epístolas paulinas. Hay quienes han pretendido ver en la metáfora del cuerpo un elemento helenizante, o sea, de origen griego y ajeno a la mentalidad judía, lo cual es inexacto, como veremos en la lección 13.ª. Pero también es cierto que es Pablo el único escritor del Nuevo Testamento que usa esta metáfora, no porque él la invente, pues se encuentra ya al fin del siglo v antes de Cristo en la literatura griega, pero él la engarza en un concepto nuevo.

Como dice G. Millon,[28] esta imagen de la Iglesia como cuerpo

> «tiene muchas ventajas sobre las demás: subraya el hecho de que la Iglesia es una realidad espiritual viva y formada de miembros vivos; pone de relieve la diversidad de los miembros y sus relaciones mutuas; la cohesión viva del conjunto; la relación del Cuerpo con la Cabeza ("kephalé" = = "jefe") que es Cristo; las nociones de vida individual y de vida colectiva; de crecimiento hacia una meta precisa —la estatura perfecta de Cristo; crecimiento que interesa a cada miembro y a todo el Cuerpo; la relación fundamental entre el Cuerpo y el Espíritu; y la importancia del bautismo en un solo Espíritu».

28. En *L'Eglise*, p. 6.

Pablo usa esta metáfora para decirnos: «*a*) que los cristianos son bautizados en un solo Cuerpo (1.ª Cor. 12:13); *b*) que forman un solo Cuerpo (1.ª Cor. 10:17); *c*) que son un solo Cuerpo en Cristo (Rom. 12:5); *d*) que son el Cuerpo de Cristo (1.ª Cor. 12:27); *e*) que son los miembros del Cuerpo de Cristo (1.ª Cor. 6:15; Ef. 5:30); *f*) que son miembros los unos de los otros (Rom. 12:5; Ef. 4:25); *g*) que son llamados a formar un solo Cuerpo (Col. 3:15); *h*) que son miembros de un mismo Cuerpo con los judíos (Efesios 2:16; 3:6); *i*) que la Iglesia es el Cuerpo de Cristo (1.ª Cor. 12:4-27; Ef. 4:1-16; Col. 1:24); *j*) que Cristo es la Cabeza del Cuerpo (Ef. 1:22-23; 4:15-16; 5:22-23; Colosenses 1:18; 2:19).» [29]

B) CONCLUSIONES QUE SE DEDUCEN DE ESTA METÁFORA. Comoquiera que toda la Tercera parte de este volumen está dedicada al tema de la membresía en el Cuerpo de Cristo, nos limitaremos aquí a resumir en epígrafes las conclusiones prácticas de esta enseñanza. La metáfora del Cuerpo implica: 1) que la Iglesia es una unidad viva e indivisible, por lo que tanto el bienestar como el malestar de sus miembros *afectan al todo*. 2) La Iglesia, como el cuerpo humano, es una unidad completa en sí misma; es cierto que la intercomunión de las iglesias locales enriquece, fortalece y renueva el vigor de cada una de ellas, pero cada iglesia se basta a sí misma para subsistir y crecer. 3) La Iglesia, como el cuerpo, es una unidad organizada y en crecimiento. Ningún miembro puede vivir para sí, si no vive para el conjunto; tampoco puede funcionar normalmente si no obedece al cerebro. Lo mismo pasa con la Iglesia: sólo cuando cada creyente cumple debidamente con su función, en íntima comunión con Cristo, es cuando una iglesia crece conjunta, simétrica y normalmente. 4) La Iglesia, como el cuerpo, es una unidad en la diversidad: sólo así puede darse un *organismo;* «si todo el cuerpo fuese ojo, ¿dónde estaría el oído?», pregunta Pablo (1.ª Corintios 12:17). Por eso, el *pluralismo* es en la Iglesia tan

---

29. A. Kuen, *o. c.*, pp. 90-91.

necesario como la *unidad*. 5) La Iglesia, como el cuerpo, está sometida a su Cabeza, que es Cristo. El cuerpo recibe de la cabeza la unidad, la vida y el movimiento. La misma dependencia tiene la Iglesia respecto a Cristo. Pero hay algo en la Iglesia, respecto a su Cabeza, donde se quiebra la analogía con el cuerpo humano. La diferencia consiste en que, en el cuerpo humano, la cabeza posee la misma identidad individual física con él y, por tanto, participa de su debilidad tanto como de su fortaleza; mientras que Cristo, sin dejar de ser verdadera Cabeza de la Iglesia, transciende soberana e infinitamente la condición espiritual de Su Iglesia, propinándole vida y fuerza sin participar de su debilidad o languidez. Esta observación es de importancia extraordinaria, pues por haber llevado demasiado lejos la analogía con el cuerpo humano, ha podido entrar en la Iglesia de Roma la línea llamada «encarnacional», que hace de la Iglesia la continuación de la Encarnación del Señor.[30]

4. Como una novia o esposa.

Ya en el Antiguo Testamento, Yahveh aparece como el Marido de Su Pueblo, Israel (Is. 54:4-5; 62:5; Jer. 3:1, 14, 20; Ez. 16:8; Os. 2:18-21). Todo el *Cantar de los Cantares* describe poéticamente el conflicto de la Sulamita entre el amor de un pobre pastorcillo y la seducción del poderoso y rico monarca. De manera parecida, la comunidad de Dios se halla siempre en conflicto entre el amor de Dios y la seducción del mundo. En esta imagen del matrimonio de Dios con Su pueblo se apoyan las expresiones que aluden a la infidelidad y al adulterio de Israel, de las que parece hacerse eco, en su Epístola, Santiago 4:4).

En el Nuevo Testamento, Cristo aparece como el Esposo de Su Iglesia. Después de comparar a Sus seguidores con

---

30. V. V. Subilia, *Il Problema del Cattolicesimó* (Torino, Libreria Editrice Claudiana, 1962). V. también mi libro *Catolicismo Romano*, pp. 20 y ss.

un cortejo de boda (Mat. 9:15), Cristo gusta de presentar el Reino de Dios en su etapa escatológica como un banquete de bodas. Juan el Bautista designa también a Cristo como el «Esposo», mientras él se denomina a sí mismo como «el amigo del Esposo» (Jn. 3:29); es decir, como el «paraninfo» (o sea, asistente del novio) o «ninfagogo» (conductor del novio a la cámara nupcial) del Mesías-Esposo del nuevo Israel. Allí terminó Juan su oficio: introdujo a Cristo en presencia de la Esposa, al apuntar hacia el Cordero en presencia de sus discípulos, y... desapareció, «menguó», gozoso de que las gentes se fuesen tras Jesús, mientras él se quedaba a las puertas del tálamo nupcial escuchando el grito del Esposo ante la comprobación de que se le había entregado una Esposa *virgen*, es decir, purificada por el mensaje y bautismo de Juan y libre de violación por parte de aquel modelo de ministros del Señor que fue Juan, quien supo limitarse a ser un *eco* de la *Palabra*, sin arrebatar para sí la gloria del Salvador.[31]

El apóstol Pablo recoge esta metáfora (2.ª Cor. 11:2; Ef. 5:25-26, 32), presentando a la Iglesia, incluso a una iglesia local, como la Esposa de Cristo. Juan nos habla de la Esposa y de las nupcias del Cordero (Apoc. 19:7-8; 21:2, 9; 22:17). Los místicos han aplicado frecuentemente esta metáfora a la relación íntima del alma con Cristo, pero la Palabra de Dios da a entender claramente que la Esposa de Cristo es *la iglesia toda*, no un miembro particular. Nótese el singular «virgen pura» de 2.ª Cor. 11:2 al hablar de una iglesia local como esposa de Cristo.[32]

L. Sp. Chafer advierte [33] que, al ser la Iglesia esposa o *consorte* de Cristo, participa de su regio sacerdocio

---

31. V. C. Spicq, *Agapè dans le Nouveau Testament*, III, páginas 238-239.

32. El epíteto «Esposa de Cristo» aplicado a religiosas conventuales, con todos los ritos simbólicos que acompañan a estos «desposorios», insinúa una especie de «exclusiva» en la consagración al Señor cuando ésta es común a todos los creyentes.

33. *O. c.*, IV., p. 135.

(1.ª Ped. 2:9; Apoc. 20:4-6). Sin embargo, aunque la Iglesia participe de la gloria de su Esposo (Jn. 14:3; 17:24;
Rom. 8:17; Ef. 1:20-21; Col. 3:4 —por tanto, no se trata
de un matrimonio «morganático»—), no deja por eso de
estar sometida a Su señorío (cf. Apoc. caps. 2 y 3). Ninguno
de los miembros de la iglesia ni la congregación entera
puede suplantar la autoridad y soberanía de Jesucristo; lo
cual no le impide ser una iglesia (escatológicamente) «gloriosa» (Ef. 5:27), porque *servir a Dios es reinar* (cf. Apocalipsis 22:3, 5).

El amor sacrificado de Cristo a Su Esposa queda patente en Ef. 5:25.

5. Como un rebaño.

En el Antiguo Testamento, Yahveh se presenta como
Pastor de Su pueblo escogido (Sal. 23; 74:1; 79:13; 80:1;
95:7; 100:3; Is. 40:11; Jer. 23:1; Ez. 34:11-16; Zac. 11:7-9;
13:7). Era una imagen llena de sentido especial para un
pueblo de estirpe nómada y pastoril, y que había pasado
40 años en el desierto bajo la guía de su Dios.

Jesús usa la metáfora del rebaño para aludir a los
Suyos. En Mat. 26:31 habla de la dispersión de Sus ovejas
cuando hayan herido al Pastor. En Luc. 12:32 se dirige a
ellos como «manada pequeña». Pero es en Juan 10 donde
la imagen del pastor y del rebaño cobra todo su sentido y
profundidad. Jesús es el Pastor Hermoso («kalós»), que
«llama por su nombre a las ovejas y las saca» (v. 3 —hecho
implicado en el mismo vocablo «iglesia» = llamada de, así
como en «congregación» = reunión de ovejas, que han sido
«segregadas» del mundo para pertenecer a Cristo). Jesús
va delante de Sus ovejas, a la usanza oriental (v. 4),[34] da
Su vida por ellas (vv. 11, 15), las *conoce* (con toda la carga
afectiva que este término comporta en la Biblia) y profetiza el día en que otras ovejas que no pertenecen al *redil*
judío vendrán (derribando el muro de separación —Efe-

---

34. Esto es también corriente en Cataluña.

sios 2:14—) para formar «un solo rebaño» tras un solo Pastor (v. 16).

La Vulgata Latina, al usar dos veces la misma palabra («ovile» = redil) en el v. 16, cuando el original distingue bien entre «aulé» = redil, y «poímne» = rebaño, introdujo una confusión (en la que cayó también la versión oficial inglesa), favoreciendo la idea de un solo redil para todos los cristianos, bajo un pastor visible. Esta interpretación queda refutada por Heb. 13:20 y por el mismo san Pedro (1.ª Ped. 2:25; 5:4). Lo cual no excluye el ministerio de pastores humanos (Hech. 20:28; Ef. 4:11; 1.ª Ped. 5:2-3), quienes en cada iglesia han de prestar el servicio (no el dominio) del pasto espiritual, siendo responsables de su cometido ante el Supremo Pastor (v. 4).

Como observa A. Kuen,[35] el peligro de esta metáfora está en que los creyentes se sientan tentados a tomar una actitud pasiva (*gregaria*) en la iglesia, dejándose llevar como corderos sin iniciativa propia, lo cual es ajeno a la Palabra de Dios y al sentido que sugieren las demás metáforas con que se expresa el misterio de la Iglesia.

CUESTIONARIO:

1. ¿Qué sentido tiene la metáfora de cuerpo aplicada a la Iglesia? — 2. ¿Qué se desprende de la organización, funcionamiento y pluralidad que esta metáfora, sin merma de la unidad, comporta? — 3. ¿En qué sentido es la Iglesia «esposa» de Cristo? — 4. ¿Qué enseñanzas deducimos de Juan 10:1-16?

---

35. *O. c.*, p. 82.

LECCION 10.ª COMO SE RECONOCE A LA VERDADERA IGLESIA DE JESUCRISTO

1. Las verdaderas NOTAS de la Iglesia.

El problema que el epígrafe de esta lección plantea, equivale a investigar las «notas» de la Iglesia, es decir, las señales por las que pueden ser fácilmente descubiertas las características *notorias* de la verdadera Iglesia de Cristo. Los Manuales de Teología Católico-Romana trataban de la unidad, santidad, catolicidad y apostolicidad como de las «notas» de la verdadera Iglesia. H. Küng las denomina acertadamente «dimensiones», y en este sentido trataremos de ellas en su debido lugar.

El Nuevo Testamento señala claramente dos «supernotas» de la verdadera iglesia: la *fidelidad* al mensaje del único Evangelio, y el *amor fraterno* (cf. Jn. 13:35; 17:21; 1.ª Cor. 15:1-4; Gál. 1:6-9; Ef. 4:15; 1.º Jn. 3:14-19; 4:1-6; 2.º Jn., vv. 9-10). Todas las demás «notas» o se reducen a éstas o no muestran *notoriamente* la genuina Iglesia de Cristo.

En un contexto que afecta más de cerca a cada iglesia local, podríamos decir que las *notas,* o caracteres distintivos, de una verdadera comunidad cristiana son tres: 1) la *ortodoxia* en la profesión y predicación de la Palabra de Dios; 2) la recta *observancia de las ordenanzas* del Señor; 3) la *correcta práctica de la disciplina.*

2. Método para reconocer a la verdadera Iglesia.

Como ya adelantamos en la Introducción, el Dr. Lloyd-Jones indica certeramente cuál es el único método correcto para tratar el problema de la Iglesia, realizar su reforma y practicar el único Ecumenismo que la Biblia garantiza.[36] Este método no consiste en considerar la Iglesia cual existe ahora y cavilar sobre la manera de reformarla en algún punto que otro, y mirar dónde se puede introducir una renovación en las estructuras. Esta es la falacia del Movimiento Ecuménico y el, a nuestro juicio, fallido intento del Vaticano II de llegar a la base del problema.

Ni siquiera es suficiente el retrotraerse al tiempo de la Reforma para seguir las huellas de Lutero, Calvino, etcétera, ni aun de volver al comienzo del movimiento no conformista o de una particular denominación. Por muy grandes que fuesen los pioneros de la Reforma o de cualquier otro movimiento de renovación y reavivamiento, eran hombres falibles, hijos de su época e influidos por la circunstancia. Seguirlos incondicionalmente equivaldría a defender una *tradición,* cosa que ellos mismos habrían sido los primeros en condenar.

El único método correcto de estudiar la naturaleza de la Iglesia y de encontrar el modo de reformarla continuamente es *volver a las fuentes del Nuevo Testamento.* Es, también, el único modo de reconocer dónde se halla una verdadera iglesia cristiana. Esto no significa que hayamos de echar por la borda cuanto nuestros antepasados en la fe hicieron para una mejor comprensión del mensaje bíblico. Por el contrario, los escritos de los Reformadores, y aun mucho de lo que escribieron Agustín, Crisóstomo, Jerónimo, etc., e incluso nuestros grandes místicos de los siglos xvi y xvii, forman parte del acervo común de nuestra cultura cristiana.[37] Sin embargo, aun habida cuenta de lo mucho bueno que nos han legado, la última e inapelable norma de fe y costumbres, a cuya luz todos ellos han de ser discernidos, es para nosotros la Biblia, es decir, la Palabra de Dios.

---

36. *O. c.,* pp. 7-8.
37. Nos referiremos a esto más adelante, al citar un discurso de A. H. Strong.

Afortunadamente, este método de *volver a las fuentes* se está imponiendo entre los más competentes teólogos y exegetas modernos de la Iglesia de Roma. Basta ojear el magnífico libro de H. Küng, *La Iglesia*, aunque los argumentos empleados por él para mantener su actual membresía nos parecen indignos de un teólogo de su talla.[38]

El retorno a las fuentes significa lisa y llanamente que hemos de encararnos con el *invariable mensaje apostólico*, fundamento de nuestra fe cristiana, con el que toda doctrina posterior debe contrastarse. Como dice O. Cullmann:[39] «la fijación del canon significa que la Iglesia misma ha trazado una clara y neta línea de demarcación entre el tiempo de los apóstoles y el tiempo de la Iglesia». Y el artículo 6.° de la Iglesia Anglicana está en lo seguro al afirmar: «La Sagrada Escritura contiene todo lo que es necesario para la salvación, de tal manera que lo que no se lee en ella ni se puede probar por ella, a nadie se le puede exigir que lo crea como artículo de fe o que lo juzgue como requisito indispensable para la salvación.»

La Iglesia de Roma ha mantenido oficialmente un criterio opuesto en esta materia: las formulaciones de la fe que la Escritura y la Tradición apostólica nos presentan deben contrastarse con las nuevas decisiones del Magisterio Eclesiástico (es decir, con las definiciones «infalibles» de la Jerarquía), no viceversa.[40]

3. Las desviaciones.

Como hemos visto en la lección 8.ª, el mismo Señor comparó Su Iglesia a un grano de mostaza que crece desmesuradamente hasta convertirse en un gran arbusto, don-

---

38. Los he refutado en mi libro *Catolicismo Romano*, p. 30, nota 18.
39. *La Tradition*, p. 43. Un buen resumen de este importante libro puede verse en *Christianity Divided* (edited by D. J. Callahan, etcétera, London, Sheed & Ward, 1962), pp. 7-29.
40. *Cf.* mi libro *Catolicismo Romano*, pp. 66-69.

de el diablo mismo encuentra cobijo (Mat. 13:4, 19, 32).
Echemos una rápida ojeada a la Historia de la Iglesia:

A) El canon de los Libros Sagrados quedó fijado a
mediados del siglo II,[41] una vez que se rechazaron como
no inspirados y carentes de origen apostólico algunos libros
que circulaban con dudosa filiación en las comunidades
cristianas.[42] La falta de un canon preciso en el lapso de
tiempo que media entre la muerte del apóstol Juan (a. 106?)
y la fijación del correcto canon (hacia el a. 160), hace que
los primeros escritores eclesiásticos no tamizasen bien sus
citas de la Palabra de Dios. Por ejemplo, la *Didaché*, que
es tenido como el primer documento no inspirado de la
Iglesia (comienzos del siglo II?), ya tuerce el precepto que
Jesús expresó en forma positiva (V. Mat. 7:12; Luc. 6:31),
presentándolo (al estilo de Confucio) en forma negativa:
«*no* hagas a otro lo que *no* quieras que te hagan a ti»
(*Rouet*, 1).

B) A la era de los llamados «Padres Apostólicos» (por
haber recibido su información directa de los Apóstoles o
de inmediatos discípulos de éstos) sucede la de los así
llamados «Padres Apologistas», porque se dedicaron especialmente a la *defensa* de la fe cristiana. Desgraciada-
mente, algunos de ellos introdujeron en la Iglesia las corrientes filosóficas griegas (platónicas y estoicas), merced
a las cuales la filosofía pagana comenzó a mezclarse con
el mensaje revelado, se inició la excesiva identificación de
Cristo con la Iglesia (e incluso con toda la Humanidad) y
se consideró a la mente y a la voluntad humanas como
poseedoras de una capacidad y de un poder en el orden
de la salvación que contrastan con la «locura de la cruz»
y la incapacidad del inconverso para las cosas espirituales (*cf.* 1.ª Cor. 1:18; 2:14).

C) Entre fines del siglo II (Ireneo) y mediados del III
(Cipriano) y, sobre todo, con la entrada *masiva* de los gen-

---

41. *Cf. Rouet de Journel (Enchir. Patristicum)*, n.° 190.
42. Remitimos al lector a los libros de J. Grau *El fundamento
apostólico* e *Introducción a la Teología* (vol. I de esta serie teológica).

tiles en la Iglesia, al ser proclamado el Cristianismo «religión oficial del Imperio», comienzan a introducirse en la Iglesia tanto doctrinas como costumbres y ritos de origen pagano-judaico; especialmente, surge el «sacerdotalismo» (casta separada del pueblo —reminiscencia del judaísmo e infiltración del paganismo) y el «sacramentalismo» (con su énfasis en la eficacia del *rito*, como resabio de la magia de los ritos paganos). Como ha puesto de relieve G. Millon, la noción de «sacerdote individual» (el «cohen» hebreo y el «hiereús» griego) es totalmente ajena a la Nueva Alianza, en la que Cristo es el único «hiereús» y «archiereús» (Sumo Sacerdote),[43] mientras que todo el pueblo (sin castas) es *colectivamente* llamado «sacerdocio regio» (1.ª Pedro 2:9; Apoc. 1:6; 5:10). «El "hiereús" de los paganos —añade Millon— no era sólo un mediador; poseía poderes mágicos y practicaba también la adivinación.» [44]

D) Paralelamente a este proceso de evolución de la casta sacerdotal, se organiza paulatinamente la superestructura jerárquica de la Iglesia. Una ambigua noción de «obispo», como representante de Dios y principio de unidad, lanzada por Ignacio de Antioquía,[45] aunque teñida de contenido espiritual y en denuncia del peligro de cisma, dio origen al llamado «episcopado monárquico» (el obispo resulta la única autoridad responsable de la iglesia local o de un grupo de iglesias); esta noción alcanza su apogeo con Cipriano de Cartago.[46]

E) Quedaba el último estadio por alcanzar: el poder papal. Este tiene su origen más remoto en el obispo de Roma, León I († 461), que alcanzó gran prestigio por haber preservado la capital de Occidente de la invasión de Atila. Gregorio I († 604) sumó nuevo prestigio para la Sede romana, aunque rehusó el título de Obispo Universal o Papa,

---

43. *Cf.* Heb. 2:17; 3:1; 4:14; 5:6, 10; 6:20; 7:17, 21, 24, 26; 8:1; 9:11; 10:21.
44. *Cf.* G. Millon, *L'Eglise*, pp. 43-44, y *L'Eglise de Jésus-Christ*, pp. 11-12.
45. *Rouet de Journel*, núms. 44 y 48.
46. *Cf. Id.*, núms. 555-557.

siendo uno de sus inmediatos sucesores quien, al amparo del emperador bizantino Focas, se alzó con el título. Gregorio VII († 1085) reforzó la autoridad papal en sus luchas con Enrique IV de Alemania. Inocencio III, de gran carácter e indudable talento político, llevó a su culminación el absolutismo del poder papal con su célebre frase: «Dios me ha dado la mitra como signo del poder espiritual, y la tiara como signo del poder temporal.» Bonifacio VIII († 1303) elevó a *dogma* el señorío papal sobre «toda creatura humana».[47] Este proceso tuvo éxito con ayuda de un cuerpo de «decretales» espúreas, falsamente atribuido a la pluma de Isidoro de Sevilla, como los mismos historiadores católicos confiesan. Finalmente, Pío IX vio definidos solemnemente en el Vaticano I (1870) los «dogmas» del primado universal y de la infalibilidad del Papa.

F) Entre otras desviaciones doctrinales, los evangélicos consideramos (a la luz de la Escritura) las siguientes: *a)* el Purgatorio, en el siglo III, por un falso comentario de Tertuliano a Mat. 5:26; *b)* el culto a las imágenes, refrendado en el Niceno II (a. 787); *c)* la transubstanciación (a. 1202); *d)* el sacrificio de la Misa y la obligación de la confesión auricular al sacerdote (1215); *e)* las indulgencias (aludidas en 1215 y solemnemente confirmadas en 1563); *f)* la Inmaculada Concepción de María (1854), y *g)* su Asunción corporal a los Cielos (1950).[48]

4. Puntos vitales y detalles secundarios.

Los Reformadores del siglo XVI resumieron el núcleo del mensaje cristiano en su famoso tríptico: «SOLA GRATIA, SOLA FIDE, SOLA SCRIPTURA», que podemos parafrasear así: Somos salvos de pura gracia, mediante la sola fe, y tenemos la Escritura por única norma de fe y conducta. Este tríptico fue completado así: Sólo Jesucristo es el Salvador necesario y suficiente (Señor y Juez

---

47. *Cf.* Denzinger-Schönm., n.º 875.
48. Para detalles, véase mi libro *Catolicismo Romano.*

de la Iglesia) y sólo el Espíritu Santo es el regenerador espiritual y constante santificador de la Iglesia.[49]

Este quíntuple aspecto del mensaje cristiano, o núcleo de verdades bíblicas *vitales* para la salvación, constituye el «test» de la ortodoxia de la Iglesia y es la única base para un sano Ecumenismo. Aparte de este núcleo, hay puntos o detalles discutibles que no deberían empañar la fraternidad cristiana ni la intercomunión eclesial. Si la misma Iglesia de Roma, a pesar de su organización monolítica, admite diferentes escuelas teológicas y diversas liturgias, y tiende hoy hacia una mayor descentralización en la administración y gobierno, poniendo un énfasis creciente en el valor de las comunidades locales, no vamos a ser nosotros, los «evangélicos», quienes, a causa de nuestras diferencias, nos neguemos «la diestra de compañerismo» (Gál. 2:9) y rehusemos recibir a los hermanos, como el autoritario y cismático [50] Diótrefes (2.° Jn., v. 10; 3.° Jn., v. 10). En las lecciones 34.ª y siguientes trataremos en detalle de esta importante materia. Juan 17:23 y Ef. 4:13 tienen una decisiva relevancia para entender la dinámica de la unidad cristiana, la imperfección de nuestro conocimiento de la fe cristiana, y la existencia de denominaciones.

Ello no significa que, con tener una correcta base doctrinal, tengamos suficiente para llevar una vida genuinamente cristiana. Más aún, el supremo énfasis en los «credos», como si ellos constituyesen el núcleo *vital* de la Iglesia, «ha sido —dice Lloyd-Jones— [51] un camino real para una ortodoxia muerta». No puede olvidarse que el «Amor» es tan «supernota» de la Iglesia como la «Verdad» (Efesios 4:15). No negamos que la doctrina va lógicamente

---

49. En realidad, el Espíritu Santo es el único «Vicario de Cristo» en la Tierra, el *otro Consolador... para siempre»* de Juan 14:16.

50. Como advierte L. Berkhof, «cismático» no es sólo el que *se separa* de la Iglesia, sino también el que *separa* indebidamente a los hermanos.

51. *O. c.*, pp. 8-11.

delante de la comunión (*cf.* Hech. 2:42), pero sí hemos de advertir seriamente que, a menos que *vivamos* nuestra fe en el servicio mutuo y en el crecimiento espiritual, la ortodoxia sola no nos va a salvar (2.ª Tim. 3:5).[52]

Concluiremos diciendo que los «credos», etc., son siempre indispensables para saber cuáles son las bases doctrinales en que se asienta nuestra posición eclesial, sobre todo en épocas de confusión y medias tintas, como es la nuestra. Es preciso que haya *claridad* tanto en la exposición de la doctrina como en el testimonio de la conducta. Es menester que nadie se llame a engaño respecto al lugar que tomamos en relación al Movimiento Ecuménico, etc., pero no perdamos de vista que la Iglesia es, antes que nada, *un grupo de personas espiritualmente vivas:* de creyentes, que *han nacido del Espíritu* y siguen las huellas de Jesucristo (1.ª Ped. 2:21).

CUESTIONARIO:

1. ¿Cuáles son las verdaderas notas de la Iglesia? — *2. ¿Cómo se reconoce a la Iglesia verdadera?* — *3. ¿Cuál es, en resumen, el proceso de las desviaciones en la Iglesia?* — *4. ¿Qué puntos son vitales en la ortodoxia de la Iglesia?* — *5. ¿Es suficiente la mera ortodoxia doctrinal?*

---

52. Citado por Lloyd-Jones, *o. c.*, p. 19, quien añade: «El único medio para salvaguardarnos de una ortodoxia muerta es poner la vida por delante incluso de la ortodoxia. Se trata de una *vida.*»

LECCION 11.ª   OBJETIVOS DE LA IGLESIA

1. La gran comisión.

A partir de Pentecostés la Iglesia comenzó a desempeñar la comisión que el Señor le había encargado, incluso antes de que las primeras iglesias importantes (Jerusalén, Antioquía, Corinto) se hubiesen tornado fuertes y maduras. Esta tarea durará hasta el fin de los tiempos (Mateo 28:20, comp. con Is. 11:9).

Ni siquiera en el Antiguo Testamento faltó este espíritu de expansión del mensaje salvador. Dios prometió a Abraham que todas las familias de la tierra serían benditas en él (Gén. 12:3). El salmo 86:9 canta la gloria y el culto que todas las naciones ofrecerán un día al Señor. Y todo el Libro de Jonás es un ejemplo relevante y conmovedor de que la predicación de la Buena Nueva a los gentiles no era ajena al Antiguo Testamento.[53]

Pero es después de la resurrección de Jesucristo cuando la Iglesia, con el poder del Espíritu descendido en Pentecostés, se entrega de lleno a cumplir su objetivo primordial de fomentar la expansión del Reino de Dios. La comisión para esta tarea se encuentra, con algunas variantes, en los cuatro evangelios (Mat. 28:18-20 —hacerse discípulas a todas las gentes, bautizándolas y adoctrinándolas—; Marc. 16:15-16 —predicar el Evangelio a todos para salvación; quien rechace el mensaje, se condenará—; Lucas 24:46-49 —predicar el arrepentimiento y el perdón [comp. con Hech. 1:7-8; 2:38; 2.ª Cor. 5:17-20]—; pasajes

53. *Cf.* R. B. Kuiper, *o. c.*, pp. 160-161.

necesarios para entender mejor Jn. 20:21-23, donde, junto a la división que produce la predicación del mensaje —comp. con Jn. 9:39-41—, se incluye también el ejercicio de la disciplina eclesial —comp. con Mat. 16:19; 18:18).

Esta comisión dada por el Señor mismo a la Iglesia hace que todas y cada una de las iglesias locales sean *esencialmente* MISION.[54] Decimos *esencialmente* porque el darse a sí misma para transmitir el mensaje de salvación es esencial para la misma vida de la Iglesia. R. B. Kuiper[55] pone como símbolo los dos grandes lagos de Palestina: el Mar de Galilea, al norte, recibe sus aguas del Hermón y del Líbano y las trasvasa al Jordán, y tiene abundancia de peces en sus aguas frescas y vivas, mientras que el Mar Muerto, al sur, se cierra en sí mismo, recibiendo sin dar; sus aguas salobres y bituminosas no pueden albergar pez vivo alguno. Así también, una iglesia que piensa recibir edificación sin darse en misión, enfermará hasta morir, mientras que una iglesia bíblicamente misionera tiene en esta actividad el mejor termómetro de su vitalidad interior.

2. La Iglesia, colaboradora de Dios.

Hablar de los objetivos de la Iglesia equivale a hablar del fin que Cristo se propuso al fundarla, o sea, de la *utilidad* de la Iglesia en los planes de Dios. Al dirigirse a los fieles de Corinto (1.ª Cor. 3:9), dice Pablo que la edificación de la Iglesia es una colaboración con Dios en obra de labranza, en la que los ministros plantan y riegan (operan desde fuera) y Dios da el crecimiento (opera desde dentro). Aunque Dios es soberano y siempre tiene la iniciativa en la obra de la salvación, sin embargo ha querido admitir colaboradores en esta obra, como había dispuesto la colaboración de nuestros primeros padres en la tarea de prolongar la obra de la creación y, sobre todo, de pro-

---

54. V. las lecciones 41-44 de este volumen.
55. *O. c.*, p. 161.

pagar la especie humana, multiplicando la vida. De la misma manera, Cristo ha encomendado a Su Iglesia la continuación, por el Espíritu, de la obra cuya consumación se llevó a cabo en el Calvario, pero que ha de ser *aplicada* en la Iglesia y por la Iglesia, mediante el ministerio de la palabra, el ejercicio de la disciplina y la práctica del testimonio.

Para evitar confusiones, recuérdese lo ya dicho en otro lugar: Aun cuando la Iglesia es esposa de Cristo y continúa Su obra, tiene que dar testimonio de Cristo apuntando siempre hacia El, *no hacia sí misma,* y reconociendo constantemente la dependencia en que se encuentra respecto al que es su Juez, tanto como su Salvador. Esta es la doctrina bíblica sobre el genuino objetivo de la Iglesia como continuadora de la obra de Cristo, y muy diferente de la línea «encarnacional» del Vaticano II, preconizada ya por Agustín de Hipona y audazmente expuesta por J. A. Möhler, hace más de un siglo, de la forma siguiente:

> «La Iglesia visible es el mismo Hijo de Dios, que se manifiesta perennemente a Sí mismo entre los hombres en forma humana, que se renueva y se rejuvenece perpetuamente —la permanente Encarnación del mismo, así como también en la S. Escritura los creyentes son llamados el cuerpo de Cristo.» [56]

3. Primer objetivo de la Iglesia: mantener una antorcha.

Dirigiéndose a su discípulo Timoteo, dice Pablo que la Iglesia de Dios es *«columna y baluarte de la verdad»* (1.ª Tim. 3:15). Estas palabras significan que, de la misma manera que los pilares de un edificio mantienen el techo, y el baluarte fundamental sostiene toda la superestructura, así también la Iglesia ha de mantener en alto, sin

---

56. *Symbolism*, II, pp. 5 y 35 (citado por Bannerman, *Church of Christ*, I, p. 85).

desmayo y sin descanso, incólume e incorrupta, la verdad del Evangelio.[57] No se olvide que la Iglesia es:

A) Producto de la Verdad. Si somos «renacidos... por la Palabra de Dios» (1.ª Ped. 1:23); si «la fe es por el oír, y el oír, por la Palabra de Dios» (Rom. 10:17); y si los que reciben la Palabra son añadidos a la Iglesia (Hechos 2:41), resulta obvio que la Iglesia es producto de la Palabra de verdad, siendo cada iglesia una comunidad de creyentes, justificados por la fe (Rom. 3:28; 5:1), hijos espirituales de Abraham, «padre de todos los creyentes» (Romanos 4:11).

B) Guardián y Heraldo de la Verdad. En la Antigua Alianza, Dios se escogió quienes proclamasen Su mensaje ante el pueblo con la consigna: «Así dice el Señor.» De ahí que el término «profeta» significa primordialmente «el que habla en lugar de otro», siendo portavoz de otra persona. Igualmente, Cristo eligió doce *enviados* (eso quiere decir el término «Apóstol») que le fuesen testigos especiales, constituyéndolos así en cimientos de la Iglesia (Ef. 2:20), e hizo de la Iglesia misma un pueblo de profetas que publicasen las maravillas de Dios en la salvación de los Suyos (1.ª Ped. 2:9). Esta proclamación tiene en el griego del Nuevo Testamento un término específico: «kerysso», que implicaba el oficio de un heraldo o alguacil respecto a un bando u orden de la autoridad. De este «bando» o «decreto real» no se puede quitar nada (Mateo 28:20: «... todas las cosas»; Jn. 14:16; 16:15; Hechos 28:20; «todo el consejo de Dios»). Sólo una iglesia en la que se predique *todo* el mensaje, explicándolo y aplicándolo a todos los problemas y a todos los individuos, puede gloriarse de ser «columna y baluarte de la verdad».

C) Intérprete de la Verdad. De ello hablaremos más adelante, pero podemos hacer notar, ya desde ahora, que todo creyente que, estudioso y orante, se deje conducir por el Espíritu, irá penetrando progresivamente en los te-

---

57. *Cf.* W. Hendriksen, *Timothy and Titus* (London, The Banner of Truth, 1964), pp. 136-137.

soros de la Palabra. Con todo, la interpretación más segura de la Escritura es fruto de una tarea comunitaria, es decir, *eclesial*. No queremos decir con ello que se requiera una persona o casta aparte, con un carisma institucionalizado de interpretación «infalible», pero es igualmente peligroso el irse al otro extremo de conceder a cualquier miembro un carisma de interpretación correcta. Los dones se dan para bien del Cuerpo de Cristo, y es dentro de ese Cuerpo, sobre todo, donde tienen cierta garantía de eficiencia, aunque nunca de infalibilidad. Cualquier miembro de iglesia puede y debe ejercitar su don profético, enseñando la Palabra de Dios a quienes no la conocen, especialmente a los inconversos, como Felipe al eunuco etíope (Hech. 8:35), pero ello ha de hacerse en nombre y como por comisión de la respectiva comunidad eclesial, siendo un ministerio que requiere dones y competencia que no siempre son comunes a todos los miembros de la iglesia.

Por todo ello, la Iglesia tiene la responsabilidad, al proclamar el Evangelio, de ofrecer las «Buenas Noticias» de la Verdad, pues esa Verdad nos libera (Jn. 8:32), trayéndonos la Luz que es la Vida eterna (Jn. 1:4); luz para el Camino que es Cristo (Jn. 14:6). Por eso, el Evangelio no sólo es *doctrina* de vida, sino que es *vida*, y vida para la *eternidad* (Jn. 4:14).

Ya en el Antiguo Testamento los judíos veían en la Ley («Torah»), no sólo la verdad de Dios, lámpara segura para los pies del caminante (Sal. 119:105), sino también la fuente de vida para el pueblo (Jn. 5:39). Por eso, la Ley era un «depósito» (Rom. 3:3, comp. con 1.ª Tim. 6:20), que debía pasar de padres a hijos (Deut. 17:18-20) y permear todas las instituciones, prácticas y costumbres de la vida judía. Los levitas estaban encargados de guardar la Ley en el Arca de la Alianza, mientras que los «cohanim» o sacerdotes estaban encargados de explicarla al pueblo.

El desvío de la Ley de Dios y la acumulación de tradiciones al margen de la Ley marcó el final del judaísmo como religión verdadera. La Iglesia que emergió de Pentecostés, «el nuevo Israel de Dios», ha recogido la antorcha, y su primera tarea ha de ser mantenerla en alto y presentarla sin aumento, pérdida ni alteración (Apoc. 22: 18-19, comp. con Is. 8:20).

Se ha acusado a las iglesias nacidas de la Reforma de haber descuidado la misión de llevar el Evangelio a todas las gentes, lo cual no es cierto. Los Reformadores tenían muy presente que toda la Europa del siglo xvi era un enorme campo de misión. No se puede olvidar que toda misión auténtica ha de realizarse en círculos concéntricos (Hechos 1:8). Pero tampoco entonces faltaron las misiones a países lejanos: en 1555 se formó la Misión Reformada francesa en Brasil; en 1602 la Compañía holandesa de la India del Este ejerce gran labor misionera, y en 1622 se fundó en la Universidad de Leyden un Seminario para la formación de misioneros. Es cierto que en los siglos xvii y xviii bajó mucho el nivel misionero en muchas denominaciones, pero el siglo xix conoció un nuevo despertar del afán misional en las iglesias evangélicas.

4. Segundo objetivo de la Iglesia: alimentar una vida.

La tarea de la Iglesia no se limita a difundir el mensaje de la verdad, sino que ha de ocuparse también de la edificación progresiva de los nuevos miembros. Por este ministerio (tanto común —de todos los miembros— como específico o pastoral) el Señor prosigue y acaba Su obra (Filip. 1:6; 1.ª Tes. 5:23-24). El ha puesto en Su Iglesia diversidad de ministerios, de acuerdo con los diferentes dones del Espíritu, a fin de que «la ley de crecimiento» se verifique y se consume en la Iglesia (Ef. 4:11-16; Colosenses 1:9-11; 2:19; 2.ª Ped. 3:18 y ss.). La *calidad* de una iglesia tiene su piedra de toque en la atención que dedica a esta tarea de *edificación*. Como dice Millon,[58] cuando en una iglesia no se sabe discernir un cristiano de un mundano, un niño espiritual de un hombre maduro

---

58. *L'Eglise*, pp. 57-58.

en la fe, tenemos asambleas de niños conducidas por niños, lo que es contrario a la Palabra de Dios (V. Is. 3:19).

Al convertirse una persona, pasa por una experiencia que se realiza de una vez por todas: es salvo y justificado para siempre; ha pasado de muerte a vida, y su *posición* en Cristo es total, como total es la *posesión* que Cristo ha tomado de él (Filip. 3:12). Pero es una vida recién estrenada, y toda vida tiende a desarrollarse, a crecer; un cuerpo que no crece es un cuerpo raquítico, si no es que está muerto. Y para crecer hay que alimentarse (*cf.* 1.ª Pedro 2:2). Es cierto que cada cristiano tiene el derecho y la obligación de buscar por sí mismo ese alimento mediante el estudio y la plegaria, pero en muchísimos casos tal estudio es insuficiente por falta de tiempo o de competencia; de ahí que sea necesaria la debida instrucción, clara y metódica, por parte de los pastores de la grey de Dios. De ahí la seriedad de la exhortación, primero del Señor a Pedro (Jn. 21:15-17), y después de Pablo y del mismo Pedro (Hech. 20:28; 1.ª Tim. 4:13-16; 2.ª Tim. 2:15; 4:1-4; Tito 2:1, 15; 3:8; 1.ª Ped. 5:2).

5. Tercer objetivo de la Iglesia: la multiplicación de la vida.

Como observa Millon,[59] la imagen de los siete candelabros, de que nos habla Apoc. en sus caps. 1, 2 y 3, implica directamente la expansión de la luz en torno a ellos y, de este modo, la expansión de la vida. Esta expansión, por ser espiritual, se realiza por el Espíritu. Las lámparas, como las estrellas, se unen por medio de su luz, no por medio de sus masas. O, como ha dicho C. S. Lewis, la geografía de los espíritus se distingue de la geografía de los países en que, mientras éstos se unen por sus fronteras, aquéllos se unen por sus centros. Esos centros de energía vital y expansiva de las iglesias (su evangelización, su servicio y su testimonio) son los que favorecen la verdadera multiplicación de la vida en medio del mundo.

---

59. *O. c.,* p. 58.

Es cierto que al mundo le cabe una tremenda responsabilidad por no recibir a Cristo (Jn. 1:10; 3:19; 16:9); pero también es cierto que las iglesias presentan un gran «escándalo», o sea, un gran tropiezo al mundo, cuando dejan de ser luces sobre el candelero; es decir, cuando no son lo que deberían ser, ni dan el testimonio que deberían dar. Falla entonces su tarea profética (*cf.* 1.ª Ped. 2:9). Con todo, la actividad iluminadora y vivificante, de la que la Iglesia tiene el ministerio, no ha de confundirse con el activismo ni el burocratismo. Puede haber mucho apostolado de «fichero», sin que por eso haya vida en las estructuras. Es de notar que, aunque la imprenta (lo mismo digamos de la radio, televisión, etc.) es un vehículo colosal para el Evangelio (como lo es para confusión y corrupción también), el Señor oró al Padre por aquellos que habían de creer por la *palabra* de los apóstoles (Jn. 17: 19-20) sin esperar —como observa Millon [60]— a la invención de la *imprenta.* Y aun ahora nada puede sustituir a la *viva voz* del Evangelio, acompañada de una vida santa.

El Espíritu puede convertir al mundo sin necesidad de repartir tratados, ni aun de Sociedades Bíblicas (sin desdeñar el importante servicio de unos y otras), mientras que toda actividad que no vaya impulsada y vivificada por el Espíritu, por muy bien que se organice y por mucho dinero que maneje, no será otra cosa que «metal que resuena o címbalo que retiñe» (1.ª Cor. 13:1). El caso de la pesca milagrosa en Juan 21:1 y ss., en que todos los esfuerzos nocturnos resultan estériles hasta que, con el amanecer del Resucitado, el mismo Señor da la orden de echar las redes, así como la espera expectante de la Iglesia hasta la Venida del Espíritu en Pentecostés (Hech. 1:7; 2:1 y siguientes), son muestras palmarias de que la expansión del Reino de Dios en el mundo es obra del poder *divino,* no del esfuerzo *humano.* El hombre queda reducido al papel de *ministro,* esto es, de *mano* que sirve a un cerebro superior; y la mano se mueve tan sólo cuando el ce-

---

60. *Id., ibid.*

rebro lo ordena; no antes, ni tampoco después. Tan antibíblica resulta la actitud de una iglesia cuando pretende
empujar al Espíritu, o tirar de El a destiempo, como cuando no se deja empujar por el Espíritu ni llevar la dirección que Este le marca.[61]

CUESTIONARIO:

*1. ¿Qué es lo que hace de cada iglesia una «misión»? —
2. ¿En qué sentido es la Iglesia colaboradora de Dios?
— 3. ¿Cómo ha de cumplir la Iglesia su papel de «columna y baluarte de la verdad»? — 4. ¿Olvidó la Reforma el
carácter misionero de la Iglesia? — 5. ¿Por qué es necesario en la Iglesia el ministerio de edificación? — 6. ¿Qué
papel corresponde a la Iglesia como reflectora de luz y de
vida? — 7. ¿Qué clase de poder es el que convierte al
mundo y multiplica la vida?*

61. Un denso pero magnífico resumen de cuanto constituyen los
objetivos de la Iglesia puede verse en el folleto *The Christian
Church - A Biblical Study* (Port Talbot, Evangelical Movement of
Wales, 1966).

La membresía en la Iglesia

LECCION 12.ª CONCEPTO DE MEMBRESIA

Dos conceptos de «iglesia» divergentes imponen dos conceptos de membresía también diferentes: 1) según la Teología católico-romana tradicional, la Iglesia viene a ser «la sociedad de los bautizados, cuya cabeza visible es el Papa»; 2) según el Nuevo Testamento, la iglesia es «la congregación de los creyentes, cuya única Cabeza es Jesucristo».

1. Concepto católico-romano de membresía.

El cardenal R. Belarmino hizo famosa la distinción entre *cuerpo* y *alma* de la Iglesia, distinción que ha estado vigente hasta el 2.º tercio del presente siglo. Según él, sólo los creyentes que poseen la gracia «santificante» (libres de pecado mortal) pertenecen al *alma* de la Iglesia, aunque puedan encontrarse involuntariamente (por ignorancia invencible) fuera de la estructura visible de la Iglesia Romana. Al *cuerpo*, o estructura social visible, sólo pertenecen los que han sido válidamente bautizados, profesan íntegramente (al menos, de forma implícita) la fe católico-romana y están sometidos a la cabeza visible de la Iglesia, que es el Papa, y a los obispos y sacerdotes que están en comunión con el Papa. Esta membresía no se pierde por el pecado «mortal», ni siquiera por la herejía o la incredulidad interior; únicamente la excomunión, o la herejía, apostasía o cisma notorios separan del cuerpo social de la Iglesia.

El famoso exegeta Cornelio a Lápide inventó una distinción más sutil.[1] Comentando Ef. 4:16, distingue en la Iglesia *dos almas:* una la de la *fe* (como profesión externa de unas mismas creencias), que es como la forma exterior del cuerpo de la Iglesia en cuanto sociedad visible, y establece la membresía de todos los que profesan la misma fe católica, aunque interiormente sean herejes; otra, la del *amor,* o caridad, que es un alma mucho más perfecta y hace a los fieles participantes de la vida de Cristo; sólo los *santos* (es decir, los que poseen la gracia santificante y, con ella, la caridad) poseen esta alma; «de ahí – dice él— que ellos solos son llamados por Pablo el «cuerpo», o sea, la Iglesia».

Estas explicaciones no tenían en cuenta que *un* alma sólo puede animar un cuerpo, y que *un* cuerpo no puede vivir *sin* alma o con *dos* almas. De ahí que por los años 30 de este siglo comenzó a hablarse en términos de pertenencia *visible* e *invisible* al mismo cuerpo y alma de la Iglesia. Esta distinción pareció ser favorecida por la Encíclica *Mystici Corporis* de Pío XII, en 1943;[2] pero tampoco tuvo éxito durable, pues no se entendía cómo una Iglesia que es esencialmente una estructura *visible* puede albergar miembros que sólo *invisiblemente* pertenezcan a ella. Por tanto, la distinción que finalmente se impuso en el Vaticanc II, en 1964, es entre membresía *imperfecta* y membresía *plena.*

En efecto, la *Constitución Dogmática sobre la Iglesia,* párrafo 14, dice que

> «a esta sociedad de la Iglesia (entiéndase: de Roma, *cf.* párrafo 8) están incorporados *plenamente*[3] quienes, poseyendo el Espíritu de Cristo, aceptan la totalidad de su organización y todos los medios de salvación establecidos en ella, y en

---

1. *Cf. Comment. in omnes Divi Pauli Epistolas* (Antuerpiae, 1665), pp. 512-513.
2. V. Denzinger, núms. 3.800 y ss.
3. El subrayado es nuestro.

su cuerpo visible están unidos con Cristo, el cual la rige mediante el Sumo Pontífice y los obispos, por los vínculos de la profesión de fe, de los sacramentos, del gobierno y comunión eclesiástica. No se salva, sin embargo, aunque esté incorporado a la Iglesia, quien, no perseverando en la caridad, permanece en el seno de la Iglesia "en cuerpo", pero no "en corazón".»

Por otra parte, el mismo Concilio asegura que todos aquellos que «se esfuerzan en llevar una vida recta», aun cuando no conozcan a Dios (es decir, incluso los ateos de «buena voluntad»), disponen de «los auxilios necesarios para la salvación» (párrafo 16). En otras palabras, la «buena voluntad» es la condición para que todo el mundo pueda pertenecer de algún modo a la Iglesia de Roma, en mayor o menor grado, según la mayor o menor aproximación a las creencias y estructuras de la Iglesia de Roma. Para remachar mejor esta enseñanza, el párrafo 8 de dicha *Constitución* aclara que

«la única Iglesia de Cristo... que nuestro Salvador, después de su resurrección, encomendó a Pedro para que la apacentara... subsiste en la Iglesia católica, gobernada por el sucesor de Pedro y por los obispos en comunión con él, si bien fuera de su estructura se encuentren muchos elementos de santidad y de verdad que, como bienes propios de la Iglesia de Cristo, impelen hacia la unidad católica».

En este párrafo está condensado el concepto de membresía que la actual Iglesia Romana defiende, así como su modo de entender el ecumenismo. De ahí que a los evangélicos ya no se nos llame «herejes», o sea, «gente que profesa una religión falsa, guiados por razones humanas» (frases del Vaticano I),[4] sino «hermanos separa-

---

4. V. Denzinger, n.º 3.014.

dos», ya que estamos en posesión de «muchos elementos de santidad y de verdad», aunque estos elementos, como bienes propios de la Iglesia Romana, nos habrían de llevar, en la medida en que nos dejemos conducir por el Espíritu de Cristo, a la unión con Roma, para quedar así incorporados *plenamente* —según el Vaticano II— a «la única Iglesia de Cristo».

En este concepto de membresía se implican dos principios que los evangélicos no podemos admitir:

1.°, la identificación que la Iglesia de Roma hace de sí misma como «única Iglesia de Cristo». No sólo no admitimos que sea la única Iglesia verdadera, sino que no la tenemos por *verdadera* Iglesia de Cristo mientras no se atenga fielmente, en su doctrina y en su estructura, a la Palabra de Dios.

2.°, que baste la «buena voluntad» para pertenecer, de alguna manera, al Cuerpo de Cristo. De sus hermanos de raza dice, en Rom. 10:2, el apóstol Pablo: «yo les doy testimonio de que tienen celo de Dios (es decir, *buena voluntad*), pero no conforme a ciencia (o sea, según el conocimiento correcto de la verdad)». Comentando este versículo dice J. Murray: «El celo es una cualidad neutra y puede ser el mayor de los vicios, pues lo que determina su carácter ético es el objetivo al que se dirige.»[5]

2.   Concepto bíblico de membresía.

Puesto que cada iglesia local no es más que la concreción espacio-temporal de esa realidad trascendente que llamamos, con mayúscula, «la Iglesia», una *verdadera* membresía en la iglesia local implica la unión vital con Cristo-Cabeza, mediante el *nuevo nacimiento* y conversión.[6] Por tanto, es contra la misma esencia de la Iglesia

5. *On Romans* (London, 1967), II, p. 48.
6. Los bautistas y Hermanos tenemos el bautismo de inmersión como expresión visible, simbólica, de la regeneración y, por ello, lo requerimos para admitir en la membresía de la iglesia local.

(congregación de los creyentes) el que figuren en el registro eclesial miembros no regenerados. Sin embargo, como el interior de los corazones es conocido solamente por Dios (2.ª Tim. 2:19), puede darse el caso de que algún inconverso se encuentre, como adherencia postiza, en la estructura visible de una iglesia local (incluso en lugar prominente de la estructura exterior —cf. Ef. 4:14; 1.ª Tim. 4:1 y ss.; 1.º Jn. 2:18-19—). 1.º Jn. 2:19 es un pasaje sumamente luminoso a este respecto. Dice así: «*Salieron de nosotros, pero no eran de nosotros; porque si hubiesen sido de nosotros, habrían permanecido con nosotros; pero salieron para que se manifestase que no todos son de nosotros.*»

La importancia de este pasaje es extraordinaria. En él se nos dan dos enseñanzas fundamentales:

A) «*Si hubiesen sido de nosotros, habrían permanecido con nosotros*»; es decir, el verdadero creyente *permanece* hasta el fin, no como mérito para alcanzar la salvación final, sino como indicio de la salvación adquirida. Los que permanecen con nosotros muestran ser de los nuestros, mientras que, como dice Calvino, «los que se marchan, nunca han sido completamente imbuidos del conocimiento salvador de Cristo, sino que sólo han tenido una ligera y pasajera degustación de él» [7] (*cf.* Heb. 6:4-8). O sea, aquí se nos enseña la perseverancia final de los santos.

B) «*Salieron de nosotros, pero no eran de nosotros.*» Esto significa que puede darse el caso de que alguien esté *con* nosotros (que se halle aparentemente *en* la iglesia), sin que sea *de* la iglesia, por falta de unión vital con Cristo-Cabeza. Como dice J. R. W. Stott:[8] «estos tales participan de nuestra compañía terrenal, pero no de nuestro nacimiento celestial». Su defección final muestra su verdadero color: «para que se manifestase que no todos son de

---

7. Citado por J. Stott, *Epistles of John* (London, The Tyndale Press, 1966), pp. 105-106.
8. *Ibidem*, p. 106.

los nuestros», es decir, con el designio providencial de que los elementos espúreos salgan a la luz y dejen de seducir a los escogidos (Mat. 24:24). En último término, el Gran Día del Señor descubrirá la escoria entre el oro, y la cizaña entre el trigo. Esto no significa que la iglesia haya de tolerar en su seno a los falsos cristianos. Ya hablamos de la falsa interpretación dada por Agustín a la parábola de la cizaña en Mat. 13:38. Como dice A. H. Strong,[9] «la parábola da razón, no del porqué no hemos de echar de la iglesia a los malvados, sino del porqué Dios no los saca inmediatamente de este mundo». Como dice el mismo autor, citando a H. C. Vedder: «La Iglesia es un cuerpo espiritual que consta únicamente de los regenerados por el Espíritu de Dios.»

Por tanto, cada uno debe examinarse a sí mismo para ver si posee los caracteres de un verdadero cristiano [10] y así evitar que el Señor pueda decirnos un día: «¡No os conozco!» (Mat. 25:12). ¡Terrible cosa es ser un desconocido para Dios!

CUESTIONARIO:

1. ¿Cuál es el concepto católico-romano tradicional de membresía de la Iglesia? — 2. ¿Cómo lo describe el Vaticano II? — 3. ¿Qué principios, inadmisibles para nosotros, implica la declaración del Vaticano II? — 4. ¿Cuál es el concepto bíblico de membresía? — 5. ¿Qué luz arroja sobre este tema el pasaje de 1.° Jn. 2:19?

---

9. *Systematic Theology,* p. 888.
10. Recomendamos a este respecto la lectura del librito *Los Rasgos distintivos del verdadero cristiano,* de Gardiner Spring (Trad. de F. Lacueva, Barcelona, EEE, 1971).

LECCION 13.ª EL HECHO DE LA MEMBRESIA (1)

1. Antecedentes corporativos.

Decíamos en la lección 9.ª que la metáfora de cuerpo no es totalmente ajena al Antiguo Testamento, porque el pueblo de Israel es considerado siempre como un todo *corporativo*. El mismo nombre «Israel» ya implica una especie de personificación corporativa, pues Israel es el nombre puesto por Dios a Jacob después de su lucha con el ángel en Peniel (Gén. 32:28). De ahí que Dios solía castigar a todo el pueblo por el pecado de un individuo (p. ej.: Jos. 7:11 y ss.; 2.º Sam. 24:12 y ss.). De igual modo, por la oración de Moisés, Dios se arrepiente del mal que había pensado hacer a todo el pueblo (Ex. 32:14). Era Israel, *como pueblo*, a quien Dios había desposado con El mismo (Is. 54:5). Por eso, a diferencia del Nuevo Testamento, donde tanto abunda el singular en las condiciones de la salvación y en las exhortaciones a la conversión y a la santificación, el Antiguo nos ofrece casi siempre en plural la imposición de mandatos y las exhortaciones de los profetas.

Sin embargo, no es en la perspectiva de Jacob, ni siquiera de Abraham, como el Nuevo Testamento empalma la metáfora de cuerpo. Es más bien en función de *Postrer Adán* como Cristo toma a la Humanidad para hacerse un pueblo, no sólo de los judíos, sino de todas las gentes y razas. Basta estudiar el pasaje de Rom. 5:12 y ss. para percatarse de que la salvación en Cristo es la contrapartida del contagio corruptor con que nuestra naturaleza fue infectada en Adán, por quien entró la prevaricación; en

él perdimos todos la rectitud original, y a él imitamos
todos en nuestros personales desvíos (cf. Rom. 5:12; Ecle-
siastés 7:29; Is. 53:6; Rom. 3:10-12, 19-23).

2. "Somos un cuerpo en Cristo" (Romanos 12:5).

La Iglesia es el cuerpo de Cristo. No es una parte de
Su cuerpo físico, lo que implicaría una identificación absoluta con Cristo, sino Su cuerpo místico (escondido) o *espiritual*. Es decir, cada cristiano vive su vida espiritual
dependiendo de la acción del Espíritu de Cristo, quien vi-
vifica, impulsa y une a la Iglesia toda y a cada miembro
con Cristo, así como a los mismos miembros entre sí.

Por ser la Iglesia un cuerpo *espiritual*, es preciso que
sus miembros hayan nacido de nuevo por el Espíritu. Sólo
así pueden ser «piedras vivas», edificadas sobre la Piedra
vivificante que es Cristo (1.ª Ped. 2:5 y ss.). Sólo estas
piedras vivas poseen la elasticidad funcional necesaria
para adaptarse al lugar que cada una ocupa en el edificio.
Sólo las piedras vivas son garantía de que el edificio entero vivirá y crecerá (Ef. 4:16), sin deteriorarse ni des-
componerse. Por eso, dice Pablo a los fieles de Corinto:
«¿no sabéis que un poco de levadura leuda —corrompe—
toda la masa?» El fracaso de las iglesias de *multitudes* se
ha debido, sobre todo, al hecho de que se haya tenido por
cristianos verdaderos a quienes fueron admitidos por el
bautismo en su primera infancia, sin garantías de que
después hubiesen de conducirse como creyentes; así como
a quienes asisten a los servicios o hacen profesión externa
de unas creencias cristianas, sin haber experimentado una
verdadera conversión y, por tanto, *sin haber nacido de
nuevo*.

La doctrina y la práctica del Nuevo Testamento sobre
este punto está bien clara. Las corrupciones posteriores
(filosofía, entrada masiva en la religión oficial, sacramentalismo, organización de la «Cristiandad» medieval, estructurada jerárquicamente sobre *masas*) alteraron totalmente el concepto de verdadera membresía. La misma

Reforma no acertó a modificar seriamente las posiciones oficiales respecto a este punto, e incluso persiguió violentamente a quienes proponían una reforma más radical, con una vuelta total a la enseñanza y práctica de la Iglesia apostólica. El caso de Conrado Grebel perseguido por Zuinglio, el de los anabaptistas (aun los exentos de iluminismo o de afán revolucionario) por Lutero y Calvino, y el del bautista John Bunyan (el autor de *El viaje del Peregrino*) por parte de la iglesia oficial de Inglaterra, son claras muestras de lo que venimos diciendo. De ahí que las comunidades llamadas «no conformistas» (disidentes de las iglesias «oficiales»), especialmente las de tipo congregacional, sean las herederas legítimas de una verdadera *Reforma*.

3. Co-miembros.

La noción de miembro de iglesia comporta la idea de que el creyente es *parte* del organismo eclesial y, por tanto, vive y funciona de acuerdo con este concepto. Por eso, guarda una íntima relación con la Cabeza-Cristo y con los demás miembros; relación que el apóstol expresa por medio de vocablos acuñados por él mismo, en los que entra como prefijo la partícula *con*, que indica una participación conjunta. Así dice que somos *co*-sepultados, *co*-plantados, *co*-crucificados, *co*-resucitados (Rom. 6:4-7), *co*-vivificados y *co*-sentados en los Cielos con Cristo (Ef. 2:5-6).

Aquí tiene, por otra parte, todo su sentido el término griego «koinonía» = comunión («communio» en latín indica un «munus» = «cargo y regalo *común*» y, de ahí, una creencia común, una vida común, una participación en común de los bienes) con que el Nuevo Testamento expresa la relación íntima de los miembros con la Cabeza y entre sí, de tal manera que ningún cristiano vive de sí, para sí, por sí, en sí solo; sino que podemos afirmar que todos los miembros de la iglesia *con*-creen, *con*-viven, *com*-parten y *con*-sufren. Esta *comunión* es tan esencial para la iglesia y para cada miembro, que Juan la pone como

test de una verdadera conversión (1.° Jn. 3:14-18). Ya Jesús
había hecho de ella la «super-nota» de Su Iglesia (Jn. 13:35;
17:21; *cf.* 1.ª Cor. 13:1-13).

4. Relación de los miembros con la Cabeza.

Efesios 1:22; 4:15; 5:23; Col. 1:18; 2:19 son los lugares
donde encontramos *explícita* la afirmación de que Cristo
es la Cabeza de la Iglesia. Examinemos dichos textos:
Efesios 1:22; 5:23; Col. 1:18 contienen la misma frase
con ligeras variantes: «... lo dio (a Cristo) por cabeza
sobre todas las cosas a la iglesia, que es su cuerpo» (Efesios 1:22). Efesios 4:15; Col. 2:19 enseñan lo mismo con
diferente fraseología: «crezcamos en todo en aquel que
es la cabeza, esto es, Cristo, de quien todo el cuerpo...»
(Ef. 4:15-16); «y no asiéndose de la Cabeza, en virtud de
quien todo el cuerpo... crece con el crecimiento que da
Dios» (Col. 2:19).[11] Las enseñanzas que de estos textos,
así como de los citados al pie de página, se deducen, son
las siguientes:

A) A la vista de Col. 2:10 (*cf.* 1:16-17), donde Cristo
aparece como Cabeza *cósmica* (especialmente sobre todos
los ángeles, para que nadie piense que éstos pueden me-
diar o interferirse entre Dios y nosotros), la idea de *Cabeza* implica primero que Cristo es el Jefe *Soberano* y
Señor *Propietario* de la Iglesia. Ha de tenerse en cuenta
que Pablo nunca dice que formamos «un cuerpo *con* Cristo», sino que «somos un cuerpo *en* Cristo» (Rom. 12:5), y
que la Iglesia es el cuerpo *de* Cristo, o sea, del que Cristo
es Cabeza-Jefe; pero Cristo no es *parte* de ese Cuerpo.
En esto hay una notable diferencia con una cabeza física. Por tanto, *toda* la Iglesia Le está sometida como a
Jefe-Cabeza.

B) De la Cabeza-Cristo, toda la Iglesia recibe el suministro de energía espiritual por medio de los diversos

11. *Cf.* también Rom. 12:4-5; 1.ª Cor. 10:17; 12:12-27; Ef. 2:16;
4:4 12; Col. 1:24.

dones que el Espíritu reparte a cada uno. Este reparto es tan abundante que Pablo puede decir que la Iglesia es la *plenitud* («pléroma») de Cristo (Ef. 1:23), no en el sentido de que la Iglesia complete intrínsecamente o añada algo a Cristo, sino porque «es designio divino que la Iglesia sea expresión *plena* de Cristo, siendo *llenada* por Aquél Cuyo destino es *llenarlo* todo».[12] Del mismo modo que no hay verdadero Rey sin reino, ni Redentor sin redimidos, así tampoco el Señor, Jefe-Cabeza, halla su pleno sentido sin la comunidad —Cuerpo— de los Suyos, unidos íntimamente con Él para siempre.

C) Con el suministro, por el Espíritu Santo, desde la Cabeza al cuerpo, Cristo da a este cuerpo espiritual, no sólo *vida* («zoé» —la vida eterna suya—, Jn. 1:4), sino también *unidad;* «bien *concertado y unido...*» (Ef. 4:16 —el primer término significa en griego «cuidadosamente conjuntado»; el segundo, «engarzado hacia arriba»—); es decir, el Espíritu de Cristo armoniza conjuntamente las distintas partes —miembros— de la Iglesia y engarza hacia Cristo —en la comunión espiritual que de Él emana— esas distintas partes unidas entre sí. Como toda cabeza, Cristo da también *movimiento* a Su Cuerpo, puesto que la vida cristiana es algo dinámico: *crecimiento, edificación, marcha codo con codo* (Ef. 4:13, 15-16; Col. 2:19).

5. Relación de los miembros entre sí.

A base de los textos citados en el punto anterior, podemos decir lo siguiente:

A') La ayuda mutua entre los miembros, de la que habla Ef. 4:16, y que es esencial a la noción de co-miembro, se ejerce por medio de las «junturas», es decir, por el mutuo contacto y enlace de unos miembros con otros. Los miembros de la Iglesia se enlazan por medio de sus

---

12. Así resume felizmente F. Foulkes, *Ephesians* (London, Tyndale Press, 1968), p. 67, la interpretación más probable de este difícil versículo.

ministerios peculiares, los cuales han de ejercitarse de acuerdo con los dones que cada uno ha recibido.

B') Cada miembro tiene el derecho y la obligación de ejercitar y mantener *vivo* (activo) el don recibido, no permitiendo que pierda su calor bajo el rescoldo, sino reavivándolo a golpe de fuelle (éste es el sentido del vocablo «anazopyreîn» de 2.ª Tim. 1:6). (Véanse también el «úsese» de Rom. 12:6 y el «se preocupen» de 1.ª Cor. 12:25.)

C') El derecho a ejercitar los dones proporciona a cada miembro una parte *activa* en la edificación de la Iglesia, mediante la diversidad de dones, especialmente mediante el *más excelente* camino del amor fraternal (1.ª Cor. 12:31; 13:1 y ss.), del que *todos* (sin jerarquías ni clases) pueden y deben usar. En la Iglesia no puede haber *inútiles* (pues todos tienen algún don), ni *parados* (pues nunca se acaba el trabajo), ni *mutilados de guerra* (porque cualquier debilidad, congénita o adquirida —no siendo orgánica, sino funcional—, queda superada por el *poder* («dynamis») del Espíritu que se imparte a cuantos son de Cristo.[13] Todo ministerio debe ser respetado dentro de su competencia peculiar, pero nadie debe *imponerse* a los demás: los miembros no *sirven* al pastor, ni a los diáconos, etc., sino al Espíritu, cuyo don es ejercitado por el pastor, etc.; de la misma manera, el pastor ha de escuchar la voz del Espíritu en el don y ministerio de cada miembro vivo de la iglesia.

D') La obligación de usar los dones al tope de nuestras fuerzas está basada en dos consideraciones de suprema importancia: *a)* por el bien del miembro mismo, quien adquiere la plenitud de su *personalidad* espiritual (se realiza a sí mismo en plenitud), en la medida en que ejercita *su* don; *b)* por el bien del *cuerpo,* ya que, por negligencia en el uso del don, se impide el normal desarrollo de todo el cuerpo (queda enclenque o deforme), ya que su crecimiento depende de la acción concertada de todos los miem-

---

13. *Cf.* 2.ª Cor. 12:9-10; 13:4; *Ef.* 3:20; 6:10; Filip. 4:13; Col. 1:11; 2.ª Tim. 4:17.

bros que lo componen, de la misma manera que el cuerpo humano se desarrolla por la acción concertada de todos sus órganos y sistemas.

CUESTIONARIO:

1. ¿Es la metáfora de «cuerpo» totalmente ajena al Antiguo Testamento? — 2. ¿Qué significa «ser un cuerpo en Cristo»? — 3. ¿Qué implicaciones se deducen del hecho de que Cristo sea la Cabeza de la Iglesia? — 4. ¿Por qué llama Pablo a la Iglesia «plenitud» de Cristo? — 5. ¿Qué comporta el concepto de co-miembro? — 6. ¿Tiene algún miembro excusa para permanecer inactivo?

LECCION 14.ª EL HECHO DE LA MEMBRESIA (II)

6. ¿Qué constituye a la iglesia en "cuerpo de Cristo"?

¿Cuál es el elemento *esencial* que constituye intrínsecamente (la *causa formal*, como dirían los Escolásticos)
como *iglesia*, o cuerpo de Cristo, a una congregación de
creyentes? A esta pregunta, de peculiar importancia para
comprender lo que es una iglesia cristiana, respondemos
así:

A'') El cuerpo eclesial no es un club de personas que
se reúnen por motivos *intelectuales* (para aprender religión o, incluso, estudiar la Biblia), o *afectivos* (para disfrutar de la compañía de otros que tienen las mismas
creencias o anhelos), o *sociales* (emprender campañas de
beneficencia, compromisos políticos o sociales, etc.). Todo
ello puede ser legítimo, y aun necesario, pero eso no constituye *la iglesia*. Más aún, es sumamente peligroso identificar las opiniones culturales y las ideas políticas y sociales con la condición de *miembro de iglesia* (factor de
UNIDAD), en la que *todos* los nacidos de nuevo que hayan
obtenido debidamente su membresía pueden encontrar su
lugar adecuado no obstante sus diferencias de cultura,
clase social y opiniones políticas y sociales.[14]

B'') Lo que constituye en *iglesia* a un grupo de creyentes es *su unión en la fe de un mismo Jesucristo* (Dios
y Hombre) *muerto y resucitado, por cuya gracia son salvos como efecto del amor selectivo del Padre, y por cuyo
Espíritu son inhabitados, capacitados y movidos a recibir*

---

14. *Cf.* M. Useros, *Cristianos en comunidad*, pp. 59-70.

*conjuntamente el mensaje revelado, a ponerlo por obra
en sus vidas, a ejercitar sus dones comunitariamente, a
rendir culto al Señor y a encenderse en afán misionero.*[15]

C'') Por tanto, podemos concluir: *El Cristo del Evangelio* (ortodoxamente entendido y comunitariamente vivido) es el *elemento esencial interno* (o causa formal) que constituye en *iglesia* a la congregación o comunidad de los creyentes. Así pues, volviendo del revés la incorrecta expresión (frecuente durante siglos en la Iglesia de Roma): «Donde está la Iglesia, allí está Cristo»,[15 bis] debemos decir: «*Donde está Cristo, allí está la Iglesia.*» En un memorable sermón, el actual pastor de la Strict Baptist Church en Crowborough (Inglaterra), Mr. Delves, decía en enero de 1964: «Aunque haya un círculo más íntimo de "hermanos" en los de mi propia denominación, todo aquél para quien Cristo es preciso, es mi hermano.» En el mismo sentido decía J. Bunyan: «Hay una base común de comunión que ninguna diferencia en los ritos externos puede borrar.» Y A. H. Strong observa que «en los momentos más sublimes de inspiración, el católico Tomás de Kempis, el puritano Milton, el anglicano Keble, se elevaron por encima de sus credos peculiares y de los límites que dividen a las denominaciones, a regiones más elevadas de un común Cristianismo».[16] Por eso, Lutero y Calvino no dudaron en hacer suyas muchas de las enseñanzas de Agustín y otros antiguos escritores eclesiásticos; y los evangélicos españoles no dudamos en aceptar mucho de lo que Juan de la Cruz, Juan de Avila, Teresa de Jesús y otros místicos de todos los tiempos dijeron y escribieron, como parte del acervo común de la Cristiandad.

Aunque en las lecciones 34.ª-36.ª hemos de extendernos en detalle sobre el tema de la unidad de la Iglesia, per-

---

15. *Cf.* Efesios 4:4-6 para darse cuenta de cuáles son los siete vínculos de la unidad eclesial. *Cf.* también A. H. Strong, *o. c.*, páginas 887-889.

15 bis. Puede tomarse en el sentido de Mat. 18:18, pero aquí nos referimos no al *lugar*, sino al *test* de una verdadera iglesia.

16. *O. c.*, p. 888.

mítasenos copiar, a este respecto, una bella página de
A. H.Strong:

«La cooperación con Cristo implica la unidad
espiritual no sólo de todos los bautistas entre sí,
sino también de todos los bautistas con toda la
compañía de cristianos verdaderos de cualquier
denominación. Es cierto que no podemos ser fieles
a nuestras convicciones sin organizarnos en corporación con los que están de acuerdo con nosotros en la interpretación de la Escritura. Nuestras
divisiones denominacionales son al presente una
necesidad natural, pero deploramos estas divisiones y, conforme vamos creciendo en gracia y en
el conocimiento de la verdad, nos esforzamos, al
menos en espíritu, en remontarnos por encima
de ellas. En Norteamérica, nuestras haciendas
están separadas por vallas, y en la primavera,
cuando el trigo y la cebada están todavía brotan-
do de la tierra, estas vallas se notan demasiado
y dan al paisaje un aspecto poco agradable; pero
al llegar el verano, cuando el cereal ha crecido y
se acerca el tiempo de la recolección, las espigas
son tan altas que las vallas quedan completamente
ocultas, y en muchos kilómetros a la redonda aparecen a los ojos del viandante como una sola
hacienda. Así pues, es nuestro deber ineludible
confesar siempre y en todo lugar que somos, en
primer lugar, cristianos, y sólo después bautistas.
El vínculo que nos une a todos con Cristo es más
importante (y así debe aparecer a nuestros ojos)
que el que nos une con quienes son de nuestra
propia denominación. Nos anima la esperanza de
que el Espíritu de Cristo tendrá a bien impartirnos
a nosotros, como a todas las demás denominaciones genuinamente cristianas, un crecimiento tal
en nuestras mentes y en nuestros corazones que
el sentimiento de nuestra unidad no sólo llegue a

remontar y ocultar las barreras que nos separan, sino que al final dará al traste con las mismas barreras de una vez.» [17]

D") Estas consideraciones tienen importantes aplicaciones prácticas en una doble dirección:

a) *ecuménica*. No somos enemigos de todo Ecumenismo, sino del Ecumenismo que, a nuestro juicio, no está fundado en una base bíblica, como sucede con el Consejo Mundial de Iglesias, que minimiza lo doctrinal en aras de un pretendido frente común en el amor y en el servicio. Admitimos el Ecumenismo en el sentido de Efesios 4:1-16.[18]

b) *social*. El cristiano está llamado a ser «luz del mundo» y «sal de la tierra». La misión de la Iglesia es la expansión del Reino de Dios, cumpliendo los objetivos que estudiábamos en la lección 11.ª. Si por «Reino de Dios» en Cristo entendemos el reinado visible de Cristo, esto sólo será posible cuando el Rey vuelva visiblemente a llevarse a Su Iglesia. Si se entiende en un sentido espiritual, ese reino se extiende a medida que van siendo más y mejores los corazones que se entregan a Jesucristo con fe amorosa. Como *ciudadano del mundo*, el creyente debe inspirarse en los principios del Evangelio, procurando así ejercer su profesión secular de la manera más recta y competente posible. Debe igualmente cooperar decididamente en todo lo que signifique mejoramiento moral, cultural y social de la Humanidad (dentro de la pluralidad de soluciones no contrarias al Evangelio), comenzando por los «domésticos de la fe», o sea, por sus co-miembros de iglesia. Romanos 8:16-25 define la situación y la postura del cristiano en un Universo que gime por la esperanza de su total redención. Pero este pasaje no implica que el mundo camine por sí solo hacia un mejoramiento progresivo *en el orden espiritual*, como soñara P. Teilhard de Chardin. No hay otra forma de renovarse espiritualmente que el

---

17. *O. c.*, p. 914.
18. V. la lección 35.ª.

nuevo nacimiento, el cual acaece siempre a contra corriente del hombre natural y al margen del progreso técnico.

E'') El hecho de la membresía en el cuerpo de Cristo tiene en las Cartas del Apóstol Pablo una constante resonancia, como advierte el Dr. Lloyd-Jones.[19] En efecto, con un ligero vistazo, por ejemplo, a la 1.ª Epístola a los Corintios, nos damos cuenta de que Pablo tenía siempre en su mente la idea del cuerpo. Ya en 1:11 condena con energía las contiendas en torno a las personas, y pregunta: «¿Acaso está dividido Cristo?» Todo el capítulo 3 vuelve sobre lo mismo, a la vez que establece el verdadero concepto de ministerio en los vv. 6-11. También en 5:6, tocante al problema del incestuoso, dice: «¿No sabéis que un poco de levadura corrompe toda la masa?» Lo mismo hace en 6:5, cuando les reprocha que ventilen sus litigios ante tribunales profanos; después, en los vv. 12-20, sobre el respeto al propio cuerpo; en el cap. 7, sobre el matrimonio y los hijos; y en el cap. 8, sobre «el hermano más débil». La idea de co-miembros alcanza su clímax en los capítulos 10 («un solo pan, ¡un solo cuerpo!»), 11 (sobre la Cena del Señor), todo el 12 en especial y en directo, el 13 sobre el «más excelente» carisma del amor, el 14 (el orden en los cultos y servicios) y el 15 (la glorificación conjunta —en espiga granada— con el Cristo resucitado).

CUESTIONARIO:

1. ¿Qué es lo que constituye como iglesia a un grupo de creyentes? — 2. ¿En qué sentido es correcta la expresión: «Donde está la Iglesia, allí está Cristo»? — 3. ¿A qué compara A. H. Strong la división denominacional? — 4. ¿Es la perfección en la unidad un producto de la evolución cósmica? — 5. ¿Qué relevancia tiene en las Epístolas paulinas el hecho de la membresía común de los cristianos?

---

19. *O. c.,* pp. 4-6.

LECCION 15.ª NOMBRES DE LOS MIEMBROS

Vamos a estudiar ahora los nombres que el Nuevo Testamento da a los miembros de iglesia. Estos nombres no sirven para *definir*, sino para *designar*, al creyente, de forma que por esos nombres pueden ser reconocidos por los de fuera. Formando una síntesis con todos ellos, podríamos llegar a un conocimiento bastante adecuado de lo que constituye la naturaleza misma del creyente.[20]

1. Discípulos de Jesucristo.

Como vemos por Mat. 22:16, el discipulado era bien conocido de los judíos. Por Jn. 1:35 comenzamos a enterarnos de que Juan el Bautista tenía sus discípulos. En Jn. 2:2 se comienza a hablar de los discípulos de Jesús. Ser *discípulo* de Jesús comportaba mucho más que ser alguien de entre las masas que le seguían para oír Sus enseñanzas y presenciar Sus maravillas. Era «seguirle», lo que implicaba dejarlo todo y estar con El cada día (V. Hechos 1:21-22). A partir de Pentecostés este título cobra más amplitud, pues designa a todos los que han sido ganados para Cristo por la predicación del mensaje y el poder del Espíritu (Mat. 28:19-20). Hechos 6:1 nos dice que había crecido mucho el número de los discípulos, o sea, de los convertidos y bautizados.

El nombre de *discípulo* añade algo al de *creyente* —como observa Millon [21]—, puesto que a la *fe* se añade la actitud *dócil* de la persona que está deseosa de apren-

---

20. *Cf.* G. Millon, *L'Eglise*, pp. 19-23.
21. *O. c.*, p. 20.

der de su Maestro. Y si algunos creyentes arrastran una vida espiritual enclenque, es porque se olvidan de esta condición de discípulos, lo que les expone al peligro de escuchar a falsos maestros. Así nos encontramos en Hechos 19:1 a ciertos discípulos ignorantes del Espíritu Santo y del bautismo cristiano. La verdadera actitud cristiana comienza con la pregunta de Hech. 2:36; 9:6. El nombre «discípulos» sólo se encuentra en los Evangelios y en el Libro de Hechos.

2. Cristianos.

Hechos 11:26 nos dice que fue en Antioquía donde por primera vez se llamó *cristianos* a los seguidores de Cristo. Había de ser precisamente en una ciudad de la gentilidad donde este nombre iba a comenzar a usarse. El nombre tuvo rápida aceptación, pues vemos en Hech. 26:28 que el rey Agripa dijo a Pablo: «Por poco me persuades a ser cristiano.» La tercera y última vez que el Nuevo Testamento lo usa es en 1.ª Ped. 4:16, donde se estimula al creyente a no avergonzarse si padece «como cristiano», sino que ha de glorificar a Dios por ello.

3. Hermanos.

El primer uso de esta palabra en Hechos es para designar, con mentalidad hebrea, a los copartícipes de las promesas de Yahveh, prescindiendo de su aceptación personal de la fe cristiana (*cf.* Hech. 1:16; 2:29, 37; 7:2; 13:15, 26, 38; 15:7, 13; 23:1, 6; 28:17).

A partir de Hech. 9:30 (como un eco de Jn. 20:17 —compárese con Heb. 2:17, etc.—) la palabra «hermano» adquiere otra cadencia. En Hech. 9:30 se refiere todavía a los fieles de Jerusalén. En 10:23 se aplica ya a los fieles de Jope. Después designa con suma frecuencia a todos los cristianos de cualquier raza (*cf.* Hech. 11:1, 29; 15:23; 16:40; 17:10, 14; 18:27; 21:7, 17; 28:14, 15; Rom. 14:10, 15; 1.ª Cor. 5:11; 6:5; 8:11, 13; 16:20, etc.).

Este nombre comporta la idea de una común paternidad de Dios, ya que mediante el *nuevo nacimiento* el creyente ha sido engendrado a una nueva vida (2.ª Ped. 1:4; 1 Jn. 3:1-2), adoptado por hijo y heredero e ingresado en la familia de Dios. Más aún, todo creyente ha sido predestinado a ser conforme a la imagen del Primogénito, para que Cristo sea el primero entre muchos hermanos (Rom. 8:14-17, 29).

Cuando un cristiano da a otro el nombre de «hermano», este epíteto tiene una resonancia particular que no puede aplicarse a nadie que esté fuera de la iglesia de Cristo, puesto que espiritualmente *hermanos* son sólo los que han nacido de nuevo del mismo Espíritu y tienen a Dios por Padre, ya que sólo los que creen en Cristo y le han recibido en sus vidas «tienen la potestad de ser hijos de Dios» (Jn. 1:12). 1.ª Cor. 5:9-13 es un pasaje sumamente iluminador a este respecto.

4. Santos.

Este título, usado frecuentemente por Pablo como saludo en sus cartas (Rom. 1:7; 1.ª Cor. 1:7; 2.ª Cor. 1:1; Ef. 1:1; Filip. 1:1; Col. 1:2, etc.), implica primordialmente que el cristiano ha sido *puesto aparte, separado* del mundo, como *posesión* exclusiva de Dios, a Quien ha *consagrado* toda su vida, y así debe vivir para El. Rom. 6 nos explica que dicha posesión tiene como principal título jurídico la redención, o sea, el rescate mediante compra (*cf.* 1.ª Ped. 1:18; Apoc. 5:9, etc.).

Esta nueva relación que nos vincula al Dios *Santo* supone una *elección* (2.ª Tes. 2:13; 1.ª Ped. 1:2); se inaugura en la *justificación,* con el perdón de los pecados y la imputación de la justicia de Cristo, y progresa en la *santificación,* la cual implica autopurificación (1.º Jn. 3:3) y docilidad al Espíritu (Rom. 8:14).

En 1.ª Cor. 7:14 se habla de *santidad* en otro sentido más amplio, al que no puede aplicarse lo anteriormente dicho, ya que ni el esposo *infiel* (pagano) puede llamarse «cristiano», ni (según el mismo contexto) el *niño* personalmente inconverso.

5. Hijos de Dios.

El apóstol Juan (1.° Jn. 3:1) prorrumpe en un grito de admiración alborozada: «Mirad cuál (literalmente: «de qué región») amor nos ha dado el Padre, para que seamos llamados hijos de Dios, *y lo seamos*» (esta última frase aparece en la mayoría de los MSS). La palabra griega usada aquí para hijos no es «hyioí», que indica más bien nuestra posición legal, sino «tékna», de «tikto» = engendrar, con lo que se resalta que el creyente es engendrado de Dios (Jn. 1:13; 3:3 y ss.).

Por eso, somos *nuevas creaturas* (2.ª Cor 5:17; Gálatas 6:15; Ef. 2:10), no nacidos de carne y sangre, ni por el esfuerzo humano. Por tanto, hemos sido llamados a participar de la naturaleza divina (2.ª Cor. 3:18; 2.ª Ped. 1:4). Todos los creyentes podemos apuntar hacia atrás al recordar ese «ahora» de 1.° Jn. 3:2, como línea divisoria entre un pasado de perdición y un gozoso presente de salvación adquirida, llenos de una bendita esperanza hacia la eternidad (Rom. 5:5; 12:12; Gál. 5:5; Heb. 11:1, etc.).

Esta *regeneración* por la que somos hijos de Dios es simbolizada en el bautismo; no porque las aguas del bautismo tengan virtud mágica para regenerarnos (*cf.* 1.ª Pedro 3:21), sino porque expresan en un símbolo apto nuestra sepultura y resurrección con Cristo mediante la fe (Romanos 6:1-11; Tito 3:5). Por ser hijos de Dios, los cristianos somos «miembros de la familia de Dios» (Ef. 2:19). La palabra griega «oikeioí» indica que somos a la vez *hijos* y *servidores* de Dios: puestos bajo la autoridad del amo de la casa, que por otra parte es el Padre (nuestro Padre) de familia.

6.   Creyentes o fieles.

«Creyente —dice Millon— es el que cree; fiel es aquél en quien se puede confiar sin ser engañado. La misma palabra griega «pistós» tiene esta doble significación.» [22] Aunque en su lugar respectivo hablaremos de la naturaleza de la fe cristiana, diremos ya que la auténtica fe es la que surge de la angustia de sentirse perdido, se vuelve hacia la Cruz de Cristo con esa angustia en esperanza de salvación (Jn. 3:14-15), se arraiga totalmente en Cristo (Jn. 1:12; 3:16; Rom. 3:24-28; Col. 2:6-7), se hace operante por el amor (Gál. 5:6), dando frutos de buenas obras (Ef. 2:10; Sant. 2:17-19), y se mantiene en obediencia al Evangelio (Rom. 1:5; 16:26).

En esto se distingue el creyente de los de la circuncisión (Hech. 11:2), de los incrédulos (1.ª Cor. 14:22; 2.ª Corintios 6:15), de los que no han sido puestos aparte para Dios (Ef. 1:1), de una mera pasividad «mística» (1.ª Timoteo 5:10), de un sentimiento subjetivo, no fundado en el hecho del Cristo Resucitado (1.ª Cor. 15:2-4). Toda otra fe es *vana* (1.ª Cor. 15:14) y termina en miedo y temblor (Sant. 2:19).

7.   Otros nombres y cualificaciones menos usuales:

A)   SERVIDORES DE DIOS. La expresión «siervos de Dios» (1.ª Ped. 2:16 —comp. con Apoc. 22:3) nos recuerda dos cosas: 1) que la libertad de *hijos* de Dios es compatible con el servicio a Dios. La obligación que nos impone la Ley de Cristo (1.ª Cor. 9:21) es más bien una norma sabia que orienta al amor, un carril o canal por el que la *vida* se protege a sí misma (el orden al servicio del amor) mediante el discernimiento de los verdaderos espíritus, de acuerdo con el Evangelio auténticamente interpretado por el Espíritu Santo; 2) que, aunque la «diakonía» haya pasado a ser la expresión técnica de un ministerio especí-

---

22. *O. c.*, p. 21.

fico, todo miembro de iglesia es un «diákonos» o servidor mediante el uso del don o carisma peculiar que ha recibido del Espíritu.

B) «CONCIUDADANOS DE LOS SANTOS» (Ef. 2:19). Esta expresión se refiere aquí a los gentiles convertidos, quienes no habiendo pertenecido antes al pueblo de Dios (Ef. 1:12), hemos sido hechos (por la fe y mediante la sangre reconciliadora de Cristo) ciudadanos del Israel de Dios juntamente con los judíos creyentes, una vez derribado por Cristo el muro de separación. En Filip. 3:20, Pablo dice que «nuestra ciudadanía está en los Cielos», como queriendo exhortarnos a considerarnos cual peregrinos en este mundo, formando una especie de «colonia del Cielo», que es nuestra ciudad nativa (por el nuevo nacimiento) y, por tanto, donde se guarda el registro en que figuramos como vecinos residentes.[23]

C) «LOS SALVOS» (Hech. 2:47). El vocablo está expresado en un participio de presente, tiempo que en griego posee un carácter incoativo-progresivo, o sea, que equivale a decir «los que iban siendo salvos» (no en futuro, como aparece en nuestra Reina-Valera). El sentido de «salvo» aquí, a la luz del v. 40, significa el acto inicial de la salvación, por el que somos arrancados del mundo perdido y puestos a salvo en Cristo e introducidos por el Espíritu en el cuerpo de Cristo (1.ª Cor. 12:13), que es la Iglesia. Es una 1.ª fase, que comportará las siguientes etapas de salvación.

D) «NEÓFITOS» (1.ª Tim. 3:6). Este término es, a veces, traducido por «recién convertido». Aunque el fenómeno espiritual que llamamos «conversión» está atestiguado suficientemente en ambos Testamentos, el Nuevo Testamento nunca designa al creyente con el término «convertido». «Neófito» significa «nueva planta» y alude al hecho de que el cristiano es *arraigado* (Col. 2:7) y *plantado con* («sym-

23. *Cf.* R. P. Martin, *Philippians* (London, Tyndale Press, 1960), pp. 160-161.

phytoi» —Rom. 6:5; *cf.* Jn. 15:1 y ss.—) Jesucristo, mediante la fe, cuyo símbolo es la inmersión bautismal.

CUESTIONARIO:

1. ¿Qué sentido especial comporta el apelativo «discípulo» de Cristo? — 2. ¿Dónde y por qué se comenzó a llamar «cristianos» a los creyentes? — 3. ¿Qué implica el epíteto «hermano» aplicado a los creyentes? — 4. ¿Cuál es el sentido primordial del vocablo «santo»? — 5. ¿Es un mero título de adopción o una realidad interna lo que hace que se nos pueda llamar «hijos de Dios»? — 6. ¿Qué sentido puede tener el término «conciudadano» de los santos? — 7. ¿Tiene esta expresión el mismo sentido en Ef. 2:19 que en Filip. 3:20?

LECCION 16.ª CUALIDADES DE LOS MIEMBROS (I)

Al hablar de cualidades de los miembros de iglesia nos referimos a lo que un miembro debería ser, pues en la práctica nos encontramos con que sólo un cierto porcentaje de dichos miembros están activa y espiritualmente dedicados al servicio de la iglesia. Romanos 12:1-2 nos muestra el carácter del miembro ideal.

1. Regenerado.

Aunque parezca superfluo, hemos de insistir en que la 1.ª cualidad de un miembro de iglesia es, naturalmente, que haya «nacido de nuevo», o sea, regenerado por el Espíritu, redimido por la sangre de Cristo, salvo de gracia mediante la fe. En una palabra, que haya recibido a Cristo en su vida y se haya entregado a El por completo.

Es lastimoso que pueda haber quienes figuran en el registro de la iglesia local y no hayan pasado por esta experiencia fundamental. Quizás hicieron sólo un acto de «profesión», sin comprender que ser salvo es un asunto de «posesión» (1.° Jn. 5:12). Muchos están tranquilos por haber sido bautizados, sin percatarse de que la inmersión en el agua es tan sólo un símbolo exterior de su inmersión en Cristo por la fe, y esta inmersión espiritual debe preceder a la inmersión material. En su lugar, hablaremos de la importancia del bautismo de agua.

2. Asiduo a los cultos.

Un miembro fiel asiste con regularidad a los cultos. dando así una muestra más de su condición de co-miembro

(Heb. 10:25). Es cierto que los quehaceres, cuidados y prisas de la vida moderna hacen a veces difícil esta asistencia asidua, pero no nos eximen de nuestro deber. Hemos de examinarnos bien, por si la causa más profunda fuese nuestro afán de contemporizar con las diversiones mundanas, o el poco atractivo que para nosotros supongan la comunión fraterna, el culto al Señor y las enseñanzas que recibimos. Debemos percatarnos de que el asistir al culto supone: A) Ir al encuentro del Señor y de nuestros hermanos (Sal. 84:2, 4; 133:1, 3); B) recibir al Señor, que viene a impartirnos Su bendición y una vida más abundante (Sal. 133:3; Mat. 18:20; Jn. 10:10); C) imitar el ejemplo de los primeros cristianos, que «*perseveraban unánimes cada día en el templo...*» (Hech. 2:46; *cf.* también Hech. 2:42; 4:32).

3. Activo.

Esto significa que cada miembro de iglesia debe ser consciente de los dones que ha recibido y usarlos en el servicio de Dios en comunión con sus hermanos. Predicar, enseñar, exhortar, consolar, socorrer, administrar fondos o cantar, son otros tantos servicios para distintas oportunidades de ejercitar nuestros dones. La iglesia local necesita las habilidades de todos sus miembros, y la moción del Espíritu, *discernida por la iglesia,* nos dirá en cada momento cuál es el don que debemos ejercitar del modo más conveniente para el provecho común.

Esta actividad no debe confundirse con el mero *activismo* (hacer por hacer). Más aún, todo miembro ha de estar siempre dispuesto también a *recibir:* a recibir formación y educación mediante el estudio y lectura de buenos libros y revistas; a recibir corrección y a ejercitarse en el examen interior de sí mismo, para descubrir los defectos ocultos (egoísmo, soberbia, celos, autoritarismo, etc.) que el demonio procura que entren en juego para inutilizar nuestro testimonio o entorpecer la comunión fraterna; a recibir consejo, enseñanza y dirección de nuestros pastores y maestros.

4. Consecuente.

Una persona es *consecuente* cuando practica lo que profesa, siempre y en todas partes. Uno de los mayores males con que se enfrenta la iglesia es la inconsecuencia de muchos de sus miembros. Y si este problema se resolviese, nuestro testimonio en el mundo sería eficaz (Juan 17:21). Seguir a Cristo *de lejos* suele llevar a sentarse junto a sus enemigos y, ya debilitados, a negarle como Pedro. Ser consecuente es llevar el ideal cristiano a todos los aspectos de la vida, tanto en privado como en público. A poco que pensemos en ello, nos daremos cuenta de que nuestra falta de poder frente al mal, así como la tibieza o timidez en presentar un testimonio vibrante de nuestra fe, se deben a que no *somos* de veras lo que *profesamos* ser y, con nuestra inconsecuencia, desacreditamos el mismo Evangelio que pretendemos proclamar.

Insistimos de nuevo en que nadie tendrá excusa si rechaza a Cristo a causa de la debilidad de nuestro testimonio; pero, con todo, es un hecho real que muchos no serán ganados para Cristo, porque nunca les convenció la clase de vida que llevan tantos de los que se dicen *cristianos*. ¡Seamos conscientes de nuestra responsabilidad como «luz del mundo» y «sal de la tierra!» ¿Cómo alumbraremos a los que están en tinieblas, si nosotros mismos llevamos una vida *oscura*? ¿Y cómo presentaremos al mundo el buen sabor y olor de Cristo, si nos volvemos *insípidos* y, quizás, hasta mal olientes?

5. Estudioso de la Biblia.

Hubo un tiempo en que el pueblo cristiano era conocido como *el pueblo del Libro* por excelencia, que es la Biblia. La Reforma se centró, ante todo, en el «SOLA SCRIPTURA», o sea, «sólo la Biblia». En realidad, de ella se derivan los otros dos lados del gran tríptico: «todo de gracia» y «por la fe sola». La Historia ha demostrado que tanto los individuos como las naciones que se apoyaron en la Biblia y vivieron de acuerdo con sus enseñanzas fueron bendecidos y prosperados por Dios. La Biblia ha sido y es *el pan de los fuertes*, y sólo los que se nutren de ella en abundancia son capaces de crecer en gracia y de hacer frente a tentaciones y pruebas de todo género.

Por eso, todo miembro de iglesia debe leer, estudiar y meditar su Biblia asiduamente. Textos como Deut. 6:6-7; Jos. 1:7-8; Sal. 1:3; todo el Sal. 119; Marc. 12:24; Jn. 5:39; Hech. 17:11 y 2.ª Tim. 3:16-17, son suficientes para estimularnos a estudiar y atesorar en la mente, en el corazón y en la conducta la Palabra de Dios. ¿Cuánto tiempo dedicamos a la lectura y estudio de la Biblia? Si creemos que, según nuestra profesión de fe, la Biblia es nuestra única «regla» de fe y práctica, no tenemos excusa para no conocer más a fondo lo que constituye la única norma de nuestra vida espiritual. La inconstancia y la falta de celo en esta preciosa y sagrada tarea son muestras de que una persona dista mucho de poseer las cualidades de un miembro ideal, mientras que el miembro fiel es como el «escriba docto» de Mat. 13:52, el «obrero aprobado» de 2.ª Tim. 2:15, y el creyente «siempre preparado para presentar defensa», de 1.ª Ped. 3:15.

6. Orante.

Agustín de Hipona decía que la oración es «la fuerza del hombre y la debilidad de Dios» (*cf.* Ex. 32:14), aunque esta «debilidad de Dios» procede de Su amor, *lo más fuerte* de Dios, pues nada hay tan fuerte como la rama que se inclina por el peso de un fruto abundante. Teresa de Avila dice que la oración es como «la respiración del alma». Otros la llaman: «la gran fuente de energía», «el poder que mueve todo». Algo muy necesario y muy fuerte ha de ser la oración, cuando Jesús mismo dijo: «Es necesario orar siempre y no desmayar» (Luc. 18:1), y así lo hacía El constantemente. Pablo también exhorta: «Orad sin cesar» (1.ª Tes. 5:17). Y Santiago asegura: «La oración eficaz del justo puede mucho» (5:16). En realidad, toda oración adquiere su eficacia de la constante intercesión de Cristo en los Cielos. Por eso, el Apoc. 8:3-4 nos presenta a un ángel con un incensario de oro, al que se le da desde el altar celeste «mucho incienso (símbolo de la oración —cf. 5:8—) para añadirlo a las oraciones de todos los santos».

Sin embargo, no todo ruego o petición es verdadera oración, pues ésta consiste, ante todo, en identificar nuestros afanes con los intereses de Dios, o sea, nuestra voluntad con la Suya. Por tanto, la oración implica esencialmente una actitud de dependencia respecto a Dios, de comunión con Dios, de absoluta confianza en Dios. De ahí que la mejor oración es la de adoración, alabanza y acción de gracias.

Nos impresiona el extraordinario avivamiento que supuso Pentecostés, pero a veces olvidamos que, como disposición para aquella maravillosa experiencia, Hech. 1:14 nos dice que los discípulos «perseveraban unánimes en oración y ruego». Algo similar ocurriría también ahora si nuestras iglesias adoptasen la misma actitud. La Iglesia primitiva tenía tanto poder (cf. Hech. 4:31) porque era una Iglesia orante.

¿Por qué no tienen respuesta muchas de nuestras oraciones? Agustín de Hipona decía que «o porque somos malos (faltos de comunión), o porque pedimos malamente (sin plena fe o confianza —cf. Sant. 1:5-6—), o porque pedimos cosas malas (o sea, cosas que no convienen para nuestra salvación)». Como el mismo Agustín añade: «No pide en nombre del Salvador —cf. Jn. 14:13— quien no pide cosas conducentes a la salvación.» Podemos añadir que Dios siempre escucha la súplica de un hijo suyo, pero, a veces, en Su infinita presciencia da una respuesta dife-

rente (más conveniente) [24] en cuanto a lo que nos da, cuándo lo da y cómo lo da. Dios es eterno y, por eso, *siempre llega a tiempo*.

CUESTIONARIO:

1. *¿Basta con ser asiduo al culto, o con bautizarse, para ser miembro de iglesia?* — 2. *¿Puede excusarse un miembro de tomar parte activa en la iglesia?* — 3. *¿Qué quiere decir ser* consecuente *con nuestra profesión cristiana?* — 4. *¿Qué importancia tiene para un creyente el estudio de la Biblia?* — 5. *¿Qué nos enseñan Ex. 32:14; Hech. 1:14; 4:31; Sant. 1:5-6 y Apoc. 8:3-4 acerca de la eficacia de la oración?* — 6. *¿Por qué no escucha Dios, a veces, nuestras oraciones conforme a nuestros deseos?*

---

24. Un ejemplo elocuente de esta respuesta *diferente* de Dios a una súplica *eficaz* lo tenemos en Heb. 5:7-9: La satisfacción de contemplar el fruto de Su muerte (Is. 53:11; Heb. 12:2) fue para Cristo una respuesta *diferente* (pero mejor) que el que Dios le librara de los tormentos de la Pasión.

LECCION 17.ª CUALIDADES DE LOS MIEMBROS (II)

7. Dador generoso.

En Hech. 3:43 44; 4:32 vemos que la primera comunidad cristiana practicaba una *voluntaria* comunidad de bienes. 1.º Jn. 3:16-17 contiene una fuerte intimación a este respecto. El creyente, pues, ha de estar dispuesto a compartir con los hermanos, no sólo el servicio de sus dones espirituales, sino también el disfrute de sus bienes materiales. Además de esto, el creyente es responsable de la «obra» de evangelización del mundo (la gran *comisión* de la Iglesia), lo cual requiere también grandes dispendios. Como alguien ha dicho: «el agua viva del Evangelio hemos de darla gratis, pero las vasijas en que la transportamos cuestan dinero». La membresía en la iglesia postula también la sustentación de «pastores y maestros», el socorro a los necesitados, literatura e instrumental pedagógico para los niños, etc.

Tan sólo el genuino creyente sabe dar con generosidad para esta «obra del Señor» por la que la Iglesia ha de laborar. La espiritualidad y la comunión de cada miembro muestran su grado y sus quilates en la medida de esa generosidad. Dios no aprecia el valor material de lo que se da, sino el amor y entrega propia que el don comporta, como Cristo expresó en el caso de la viuda, que «de su pobreza echó todo el sustento que tenía» (Luc. 21:4), y en el de María de Betania, que rompió el gollete del frasco de perfume (Marc. 14:3), derramándolo *todo* sobre Jesús, sin reservarse nada para sí.[25] El Antiguo Testamento nos ofrece también, entre otros, dos casos de suma generosidad: En 2.º Sam. 19:30, Mefiboset renuncia a toda su hacienda, satisfecho con que el rey David haya vuelto sano y salvo. En 24:22 es Arauna quien se dispone a ofrecer al rey todo cuanto necesite para el sacrificio en favor del pueblo, aunque David no lo aceptó gratis: «No ofreceré a Yahveh mi Dios holocaustos que no me cuesten nada» (v. 24).

En 2.ª Cor. 8:9 vemos que *dar* es una «gracia». ¿Qué gracia es ésta? Leyendo el contexto, vemos que Cristo nos *dio* su riqueza y tomó a cambio nuestra *pobreza,* de modo que nosotros fuésemos *ricos.* ¿Qué le movió a ello? Pablo dice: «... por *amor* a vosotros se hizo pobre». Y, escribiendo a los efesios, dice: «... así como Cristo amó a la Iglesia y se entregó a Sí mismo por ella» (5:25). Vemos que el *entregó* va después del *amó,* para indicarnos que no hay verdadera *entrega* donde no existe *amor (cf.* Juan 3:16; 15:13; Rom. 5:5).

Tan sólo cuando comprendemos que hemos sido comprados a gran precio (1.º Ped. 1:18-19) y que ya no somos nuestros, sino de Quien nos compró (1.ª Cor. 6:20), estamos en condiciones de ejercer una correcta mayordomía de nuestros bienes. ¿No es una grave inconsecuencia de nuestra parte que Le llamemos «Señor» nuestro y Le regateemos lo que Le pertenece? *(cf.* Mal. 3:8-10). ¿No será la falta de *consagración* lo que merma el módulo de nuestra

---

25. D. W. Brealey (en *La Iglesia,* compil. de J. B. Watson, páginas 184-186) dice que los tres principios de generosidad, según 2.ª Cor. caps. 8 y 9, son: a) *mano abierta* (8:1-2; 9:6, 11, 13); b) *mente dispuesta* (8:3, 12; 9:7), y c) *corazón alegre* (9:7; *cf.* Hechos 20:35). 1.ª Cor. 16:1-3 introduce tres modos: a') *con regularidad;* b') *sistemáticamente,* y c') *proporcionalmente.* Todo ello ha de hacerse, además, *honestamente* (2.ª Cor. 8:20-21). No es honesto lo que vemos en Marc. 7:11-13 (dar a Dios, privando a la familia de lo necesario); Rom. 13:8 (hasta caer en deudas); 2.ª Cor. 12:14 (hasta ser gravoso a otros) y 1.ª Tim. 5:8 (dejando de proveer para los suyos).

generosidad? «Darse a sí mismo primeramente» es la condición necesaria para «abundar en riquezas de generosidad» (2.ª Cor. 8:2, 5). El «probadme en esto» de Mal. 3:10 es la garantía divina de que, si cumplimos nuestro deber de dar, Dios no se dejará vencer en generosidad.

8. Ferviente.

Un miembro ideal de iglesia *vive por fe,* arraigado en Cristo (Col. 2:7) y guiado siempre por el Espíritu Santo (Rom. 8:14), avivando constantemente, por medio del amor, la llama de su fe (Gál. 5:6) para que nunca languidezca. Pablo atestigua que la vida que él vive, en contraste con la que llevaba antes de su conversión, es «en la fe del Hijo de Dios» (Gál. 2:20). Y Juan asegura: «Esta es la victoria que vence al mundo, nuestra fe» (1.° Jn. 5:4). Por tanto, lo que todo cristiano ha de inquirir es cuán grande es su fe: su fe en los designios de Dios, en el poder de Dios, en la acción de Dios. Como dijo a Sus discípulos (Luc. 8:25), Jesús podría repetirnos a veces: «¿Dónde está vuestra fe?» ¿Cuál es la causa de este fallo? Podemos decir que son dos: 1.ª, una falta de *seguridad* en el poder de Dios, que suele realizar sus maravillas contando con débiles efectivos humanos, a condición de que obedezcamos con humildad; 2.ª, una falta de *confianza* en los dones que hemos recibido; lo que, en cada caso, hemos de preguntarnos no es: «¿seré capaz de realizar eso?», sino «¿estoy dispuesto a que Dios me use para eso?». Romanos 4:20 dice que Abraham, a pesar de todas las circunstancias aparentemente adversas, «tampoco dudó, por incredulidad, de la promesa de Dios, sino que *se fortaleció en fe,* dando gloria a Dios».[26]

---

26. Alguien quiso burlarse de una anciana, fervorosa creyente, preguntándole: —¿También obedecería usted a Dios si le mandase meter la cabeza por una pared?— A lo que contestó ella: —¡Claro que sí! Mi obligación sería meter la cabeza, y la obligación de Dios sería hacer el agujero.

Un cristiano fervoroso es el que, según Romanos 12:1-3:

A) Ofrece su «*cuerpo*», es decir, su actividad exterior y concreta, en perfecta consagración («sacrificio») a Dios, haciendo de toda su vida un «culto» religioso *racional;* es decir, no un rito mecánico, sino una adoración *consciente,* en espíritu y en verdad (v. 1. *Cf.* Jn. 4:24).

B) Comprueba cuidadosamente (con las antenas alerta al soplo del Espíritu) en cada caso «cuál sea la buena voluntad de Dios, agradable y perfecta» (v. 2); o sea, escogiendo siempre, entre varias opciones, lo más perfecto, de acuerdo con el beneplácito divino: *hacer el mayor bien posible de la mejor manera posible.*

C) Piensa y obra «conforme a la medida de fe que Dios repartió a cada uno» (v. 3), o sea, utiliza con fe firme y dedicación absoluta el don que Dios le ha impartido; con humildad, pero sin complejos; con esperanza, pero sin impaciencia; sin especular acerca del éxito o resultado exterior de su obrar, pues sólo Dios ve el fin desde el principio y nunca llega demasiado pronto ni demasiado tarde, sino siempre *a punto,* como quien obra desde la eternidad que es una perenne *actualidad.* Jesús solía decir: «Hágase conforme a tu fe» (*cf.* Mat. 9:29). Sea nuestro lema el de Guillermo Carey: «Esperemos grandes cosas de Dios y emprendamos grandes cosas para Dios».

9. Ganador de almas.

Una señal segura de verdadera conversión y de fiel membresía en la iglesia es el celo por ganar almas para el Señor. No todos pueden subir a un púlpito o a una tribuna, pero todos pueden, en privado y por medio de contactos personales, hacer conocer a otros lo que Dios ha hecho en sus vidas y lo que el mensaje evangélico ofrece a todos, mediante el poder del Espíritu, para salvación: «Ven y ve» (Jn. 1:46).

La comisión de Cristo a Su Iglesia para testificar de El en todo el mundo no fue dada sólo a unos pocos, sino a *todos* los discípulos que veían ascender a su Señor y habían de vivir en tensa expectación de Su 2.ª Venida (Hech. 1:7-11). Este mandato tiene un carácter tan permanente como la existencia de la Humanidad sobre la Tierra y, por tanto, posee hoy el mismo poder y la misma vigencia que entonces. Cada creyente debería ser, pues, un *ganador de almas*. El testimonio fiel e instruido de cada cristiano (1.º Ped. 3:15) es el más seguro y eficaz medio para ganar para Cristo a los perdidos. Por otra parte, ninguna otra obra en esta vida tendrá mayor galardón en el Cielo: «Los entendidos resplandecerán como el resplandor del firmamento; y los que enseñan a la multitud, como las estrellas a perpetua eternidad» (Dan. 12:3).[27]

En el mundo hay miles de millones de personas que no conocen a Cristo o que le conocen mal. Es entre ellos donde debemos ser «testigos». ¿Nos ha salvado Cristo? ¿Hemos experimentado el *fruto* del Espíritu, «amor, gozo y paz»? (Gál. 5:22). ¿No nos ha dado Dios un nuevo designio, brillante y triunfal, para nuestras vidas? Entonces, vayamos sin demora, con mansedumbre, pero también con decisión, a comunicar la Buena Noticia. Todo lo bueno que no disminuye con la participación, debe compartirse; así nosotros debemos compartir la victoria y el gozo que hemos hallado en Jesucristo.

Nuestra actitud debe ser semejante a la de los cuatro leprosos de 2.º Rey. 7:8-9. Luego que comieron y bebieron, y tomaron del grandioso e inesperado botín que Yahveh había provisto para Su pueblo, «se dijeron el uno al otro: No estamos haciendo bien. Hoy es día de buena nueva, y nosotros callamos; y si esperamos hasta el amanecer, nos alcanzará nuestra maldad. Vamos, pues, ahora; entremos y demos la nueva en la casa del rey». También nosotros, si somos salvos del imperio de Satán y hechos partícipes del abundante botín de Cristo (Ef. 4:7-10), salgamos *ahora*

---

27. Aquí no puede menos de venir a las mientes aquello de 1.ª Cor. 15:41-42: «... pues una estrella es diferente de otra en gloria. Así también es la resurrección de los muertos».

a dar la *Buena Noticia* («Evangelio», en griego), antes que amanezca el Día del Señor (2.ª Ped. 1:19).

CUESTIONARIO:

1. ¿Qué nos enseñan Hechos 2:43-44; 4:32 y 1.º Juan 3:16-18? — 2. Ponga algunos ejemplos de suma generosidad, tanto en el Antiguo Testamento como en el Nuevo. — 3. ¿En qué pone Pablo su énfasis acerca de la generosidad de los corintios, en 2.ª Cor. 8:5? — 4. ¿Cuál es el reto que Dios lanza a los Suyos en Malaquías 3:10? — 5. ¿Por qué es tan mezquina nuestra fe? — 6. ¿Qué nos enseña Romanos 12:1-3? — 7. ¿Por qué debe ser cada creyente un ganador de almas?

LECCION 18.ª

COMO SE OBTIENE LA MEMBRESIA (I)

1. Dos clases de membresía.

Hablar de la membresía de la Iglesia implica el hablar de la entrada en la Iglesia. Así pues, la pregunta ¿cómo se obtiene la membresía en la Iglesia? es equivalente a esta otra: ¿cómo se entra en la Iglesia? La respuesta no puede darse en un solo sentido, puesto que hay que distinguir entre la *Iglesia* en su realidad trascendente y misteriosa (el grupo de todos los salvos en Cristo, sin fronteras de tiempo ni de espacio), y la *iglesia local,* o concreción espacio-temporal de esa realidad trascendente y universal que, para distinguirla, escribimos con mayúscula.

Antes de presentar la doble respuesta que corresponde a estos dos aspectos, bueno será tener en cuenta que la Iglesia de Cristo es una realidad divino-humana: El aspecto divino se muestra *verticalmente* (desde arriba): en Dios Padre, que hace la *convocación,* o llamamiento de la «ekklesía»; en Dios-Hijo, que hace la *redención,* o rescate de los llamados, constituido único Jefe y Cabeza de la «ekklesía»; en Dios Espíritu Santo, que realiza la *aplicación* de la obra consumada de Cristo a los ya elegidos, constituido alma de la Iglesia (Ef. 4:4) y Vicario de Cristo durante la era presente (Jn. 14:16), mediante la distribución de dones y carismas (todo desde arriba) y mediante la Escritura, por El inspirada para que sea norma inapelable de fe y conducta en la Iglesia. Todo esto es puramente divino y sin fallo posible. El aspecto humano es el plano *horizontal* en que la Iglesia toma concreción visible y se muestra en los miembros que la componen. Este aspecto humano de la Iglesia puede fallar por dos conceptos: 1.°, porque el «nuevo nacimiento», que determina la unión espiritual de cada miembro con la Cabeza-Cristo, es un fenómeno invisible en sí y, por tanto, pueden introducirse subrepticiamente en la iglesia local personas que no han nacido de nuevo; 2.°, porque los mismos miembros de iglesia, regenerados ya espiritualmente y bautizados bíblicamente, están todavía expuestos a tentaciones del enemigo y a fallos internos que son producto de nuestra naturaleza pecaminosa, cuyo poder sólo progresivamente va siendo contrarrestado (nunca destruido en esta vida) [28] por el poder del Espíritu Santo en el proceso de la santificación.

2. Entrada en la Iglesia trascendente.

La entrada en la Iglesia como realidad espiritual trascendente es absolutamente necesaria para la salvación (por ser salvos, pertenecemos a ella —entiéndase bien—) y se realiza por el *nuevo nacimiento*, como ya dijimos en la lección 5.ª. De esta Iglesia fue miembro el ladrón que en su cruz llegó a ser salvo y discípulo de Cristo, sin tener tiempo de entrar en una iglesia local. El nuevo nacimiento nos capacita para ser añadidos a la Iglesia por Dios (Hechos 2:41, 47), puesto que nuestra entrada en el Reino de Dios es obra del Padre (Col. 1:13), del que recibimos la adopción de hijos por la fe (Jn. 1:12-13), siendo co-resucitados con Cristo (Ef. 2:4-6; Col. 2:13).

En esta entrada en la Iglesia trascendente juega un papel de primera importancia la fe, medio subjetivo de la justificación, no como obra que consigue dar alcance a la gracia, sino como mano desnuda que la recibe como

---

28. Traducir el «katargethê» de Rom. 6:6 por «destruido», como suelen hacer las versiones, tanto de Roma como de la Reforma, es inexacto gramaticalmente y falso bíblicamente, pues el poder del pecado nunca queda destruido en esta vida, sino solamente contrarrestado. Dicho verbo significa «hacer ineficaz» o «resistir la acción».

un regalo total e inmerecido (Hech. 16:31; Ef. 2:8). No es suficiente con creer en un Dios remunerador (Heb. 11:6); es preciso profesar también una creencia con base objetiva determinada en la S. Escritura: la exaltación del Jesús crucificado (Hech. 2:36; 1.ª Cor. 15:3-4) y el descenso del Espíritu Santo (Hech. 19:1-7).[29] Dicha fe ha de ser *viva* para ser salvífica. Como decían los Reformadores: «Sólo la fe justifica, pero no justifica la fe que está sola.»[30] O como escribe G. Millon: «Es evidente que no hay arrepentimiento verdadero, ni fe real, si el pecador no se hace seriamente la pregunta: «Señor, ¿qué quieres que yo haga?» (Hech. 9:6) ni hace lo que el Señor le diga. Ni el discípulo puede ser un discutidor, ni el arrepentido puede ser un desobediente.»[31]

Esta Iglesia trascendente forma una sola unidad (universal) en todo el mundo. Escribiendo a los corintios, dice Pablo: «Porque por un solo Espíritu fuimos todos bautizados en un cuerpo» (1.ª Cor. 12:13). Este texto nos ofrece, entre otras, las siguientes enseñanzas:

A) Pablo y Sóstenes, que escriben la carta, y los destinatarios que la reciben (los fieles de Corinto), han conocido un momento que divide sus vidas en *antes* y *después* (1.ª Cor. 6:9-10; Ef. 2:12-13; 1.º Jn. 3:1): el momento en que, tras el llamamiento de Dios, han sido santificados y pueden invocar a Cristo como Señor (1:2), salvados (1:18), nacidos de nuevo (4:15), lavados y santificados (6:11) y rescatados (7:23). El pronombre «todos» se refiere a los que han pasado por la experiencia de la espiritual regeneración.

B) Todos éstos han sido bautizados «por el Espíritu», es decir, han sido sumergidos en Cristo por el Espíritu (lo

---

29. En cuanto a la salvación de quienes no tuvieron la oportunidad de ejercitar una fe explícita en Jesucristo, cf. J. Grau, *Introducción a la Teología*, pp. 149-155.

30. Para más detalles sobre la justificación por la fe véase mi libro *Doctrinas de la Gracia* (vol. V de esta serie teológica —en preparación—).

31. En *L'Eglise*, p. 24.

cual es simbolizado en el bautismo de agua, aun cuando éste no coincida cronológicamente con el bautismo espiritual). *Todo regenerado recibe el bautismo del Espíritu.* De donde se sigue: *a)* que los no regenerados no pueden formar *un cuerpo* con los regenerados; *b)* que no existe un cuerpo de *bautizados en el Espíritu,* distinto de los *simplemente regenerados.*[32]

C) «Todos hemos sido bautizados *en un cuerpo*»; literalmente: en orden a formar un solo cuerpo. Todo el contexto del capítulo 12 de esta Epístola habla del *único cuerpo* que los regenerados forman en Cristo. El Nuevo Testamento no conoce creyentes-islas, como células vivas que vivan una vida independiente. Hoy, como en el primer siglo de la Iglesia, todos los que nacen de nuevo son llamados a formar un solo cuerpo con sus hermanos y hermanas. Todo el que tiene por Cabeza a Cristo, forma un solo cuerpo con todos los demás que tienen también a Cristo por Señor y Cabeza.

3. Entrada en la iglesia local.

Las disensiones entre nuestras denominaciones comienzan al tratar de la entrada en la iglesia local. La cosa era sencilla en la Iglesia primitiva, pero las tradiciones humanas la han complicado. Volvamos al Nuevo Testamento y sólo a él.

A) IMPORTANCIA DE OBTENER LA MEMBRESÍA EN UNA IGLESIA LOCAL. Hay creyentes sinceros que sienten cierta repugnancia a formar parte de una iglesia local determinada. Hay incluso quienes pretenden apoyar en la Escritura su equivocada actitud. Sin embargo, se trata de algo muy importante. El contexto entero del Nuevo Testamento, al hablar de iglesias locales, nos está indicando que todos los creyentes de una localidad determinada formaban parte de la «familia de la fe» (Gál. 6:10), a no ser que se les marginase como medida disciplinar correctiva.

---

32. V. A. Kuen, *o. c.,* pp. 75-77.

El ser miembro de una iglesia implica tanto privilegios como responsabilidades, que deben extenderse a toda la familia eclesial. Los creyentes no pueden descuidar el servicio que deben prestar a su iglesia, ni ser negligentes en el testimonio que compromete a la comunidad. Rom. 12, 1.ª Cor. 12, Ef. 4, etc., nos enseñan que somos miembros los unos de los otros, con la consiguiente vida de relación en verdad y amor, y no es lícito eludir la responsabilidad y el privilegio que ello implica.

La relación familiar que la iglesia local comporta, se muestra congregándose en un determinado lugar de culto, comunión, servicio, plegaria, observancia de las ordenanzas del Señor, donación generosa y afán misionero y evangelizador *colectivos* (1.ª Cor. 16:2; 2.ª Cor. caps. 8 y 9). La iglesia local es el lugar a donde han de ser encaminadas las personas ganadas para Cristo, y donde, mediante el ministerio de la Palabra, son después formadas y edificadas en la fe y en el reconocimiento de Cristo (Ef. 4:11-14; 2.ª Ped. 3:18; Judas 20). ¿Dónde mejor que en la iglesia local vamos a hallar el lugar apropiado para educar a nuestros hijos en la disciplina y en la amonestación del Señor? (Ef. 6:4). Hebreos 10:25 exhorta a asistir con asiduidad a los servicios de nuestra iglesia. Romanos 12:13; Gál. 6:6; Heb. 13:16 nos recomiendan el sostener la obra de la iglesia y a sus ministros. Todo regenerado (y sólo él) debe hacerse miembro de una iglesia local. Si alguien, repensando su situación eclesial, descubre que no es realmente salvo, una de dos: o acepta entonces al Señor, quedando así cualificado para una genuina membresía, o debe marcharse en paz de la congregación.[33]

B) Cómo se obtiene la membresía en la iglesia local. La práctica de la Iglesia primitiva nos dice que la entrada en la iglesia local es por medio del bautismo, lo cual implica (para nosotros) la inmersión en agua. Quienes han creído de corazón en Cristo y han recibido el Espíritu

---

[33]. *Cf. Baptist Distinctives* (Ed. Dr. M. R. Hull, Des Plaines —Illinois—, Regular Baptist Press, 1965), pp. 41-42.

deben ser sumergidos (Hech. 2:38-41; 8:35-38; 10:47-48; 16:31-33), y quienes han sido solamente sumergidos, deben creer y recibir al Espíritu Santo (Hech. 8:14-18; 19:1-7).

Uno no debe bautizarse a sí mismo; es la iglesia local la que bautiza mediante el ministerio de un miembro suyo. Así la iglesia está presente en el bautismo cuando un nuevo miembro es incorporado a ella por el Señor: la iglesia recibe a aquél que es *añadido* por Dios; no es ella la que añade, aunque es ella la que ha recibido la orden de sumergir; no es ella la que da el Espíritu, aunque sea ella la que ruega e impone las manos como símbolo de la extensión de las promesas y dones del Espíritu al nuevo miembro que confiesa su fe pasando por las aguas del bautismo. En la Iglesia apostólica *todos* eran bautizados en agua y en Espíritu, incorporados a Cristo y a la iglesia local (Hech. 2:41, 47; Rom. 6:3 y ss.; 1.ª Cor. 12:13; Gálatas 3:27). La enseñanza clara del Nuevo Testamento es que cuantos creen y son salvos, se bauticen y entren así a formar parte del cuerpo de creyentes de la comunidad local. A través del Libro de Hechos vemos que, siempre que el bautismo tuvo lugar, los bautizados se agregaron en seguida a la iglesia local. Aunque nada se diga del etíope de Hech. 8, es seguro que su testimonio y su mensaje serían ministerio de salvación y, por ende, de formación de iglesias locales.

Si alguien, en flagrante desobediencia al mandato del Señor (Mat. 28:18-20), rehúsa someterse a la comisión dada a la Iglesia a este respecto, no debe ser admitido a formar parte de la comunidad local. Un estudio atento de Gál. 3:27 refuerza nuestro argumento: «Porque todos los que habéis sido bautizados en Cristo, *de Cristo estáis revestidos.*» El término usado en el original para expresar la frase que hemos subrayado, está tomado del argot militar, para indicar el acto por el cual un soldado se viste su uniforme. Un soldado queda obligado al servicio desde el momento en que presta juramento, pero no queda públicamente identificado con las Fuerzas Armadas hasta que se pone el uniforme militar. De modo similar, nosotros somos salvos y quedamos unidos a Cristo desde el momento en que creemos, pero el bautismo constituye como el acto solemne en que nos revestimos (simbólicamente) del uniforme que nos muestra al exterior como identificados con Jesucristo. Ahora bien, es imposible la pretensión de estar uniformado exteriormente como soldado de Cristo, sin la voluntad de manifestarse identificado con todos aquellos que, en virtud del mismo bautismo, se han puesto el mismo uniforme.[34]

La iglesia local tiene igualmente la obligación de proclamar el evangelio, exhortar a la fe (a los inconversos) y a la confesión y arrepentimiento [35] (a los creyentes) y discernir los frutos del nuevo nacimiento antes de bautizar en el nombre del Padre y del Hijo y del Espíritu Santo, «para no tomar el nombre de Dios en vano», como dice G. Millon.[36] Juan el Bautista no se avino a bautizar a la «raza de víboras», por más que intentasen escapar de la cólera venidera. Es Cristo el que «agrega»; quien no congrega con Cristo, dispersa (Mat. 12:30); es decir, hace la obra del demonio. Esto llena de responsabilidad a las iglesias en la admisión de nuevos miembros.

CUESTIONARIO:

1. ¿Por dónde puede fallar la Iglesia? — 2. ¿Cuál es el requisito indispensable para pertenecer a la Iglesia (con mayúscula) de Cristo? — 3. ¿Qué comporta una genuina fe salvífica, según Millon? — 4. ¿Qué entiende usted por «bautismo del Espíritu»? — 5. ¿Es importante el hacerse miembro de una iglesia local? — 6. ¿Cómo se obtiene la membresía en la iglesia local?

---

34. *Id.*, pp. 46-47.
35. Como demuestra L. Sp. Chafer (*Systematic Theology*, III, páginas 372-378), como comentario a Marc. 1:15 y pasajes similares, el arrepentimiento *como acto distinto de la fe* se requiere sólo a quienes están ya *dentro del pacto* con Dios.
36. *O. c.*, pp. 24-25.

LECCION 19.ª

COMO SE OBTIENE LA MEMBRESIA (II)

4. Inclusividad y exclusividad de la Iglesia.

Como corolario de la lección anterior, y para clarificar nuestras ideas sobre este tema, vamos a tratar de averiguar en el presente apartado los límites exactos de una correcta membresía, o sea, quiénes son *todos* (inclusividad) y *solos* (exclusividad) los que pueden ser miembros de iglesia. Vayamos por partes:

A) INCLUSIVIDAD. Todos los verdaderos creyentes (que profesan una correcta creencia en el Señor y están dispuestos al testimonio, al servicio y a la obediencia) están cualificados para la membresía en una iglesia local. Por tanto, en ella caben:

a) *Todas las razas.* El color de la piel y la peculiaridad de la raza no pueden ser obstáculo para una membresía común con gentes de otra raza y de otro color. Es cierto que cada raza comporta tradiciones y mentalidades distintas, pero Col. 3:11 y Apoc. 5:9 nos enseñan que la sangre de Cristo ha superado las diferencias entre las razas y condiciones sociales. Una iglesia que hace distinción entre sus miembros por el color de la piel o se niega a admitir en membresía a personas de otra raza no es verdadera iglesia cristiana.

b) *Todas las clases sociales.* Cualesquiera que sean las condiciones sociales o políticas de un país, la iglesia ha de considerar y tratar por igual a todos los miembros, sin establecer diferencias por su condición social. ya que todos los que participamos de un mismo pan somos un solo cuerpo (1.ª Cor. 10:17). En 1.ª Cor. 11:20-22 se trata de esta discriminación como de algo grave contra el cuerpo de Cristo; no debe haber más diferencia que la que establece la diversidad de dones. Col. 3:24 y 4:1 y, sobre todo, Sant. 1:9-10; 2:1-4 son pasajes que exigen seria atención a este respecto. No se puede reservar una butaca afelpada para el millonario, mientras el menesteroso se sienta en un banco sin respaldo o en el suelo.

c) *Todos los caracteres.* Basta una rápida ojeada a los Evangelios para darnos cuenta de las notables diferencias caracteriales de los Doce que seguían al Maestro constantemente. ¿Qué mayor diversidad que la que existía entre un Pedro activo, impetuoso, irreflexivo, o un Juan apasionado, pero contemplativo, y un Tomás escéptico y pesimista? No obstante, los tres fueron *apóstoles,* es decir, testigos cualificados (excepcionalmente) del Señor. Una diferencia similar encontramos entre las hermanas Marta y María de Betania, dos de las más fieles discípulas de Cristo. Es precisamente esta diferencia de temperamentos la que ofrece campo a la diversidad de miembros de un mismo cuerpo, como dice Pablo en 1.ª Cor. 12:17-22.[37]

B) EXCLUSIVIDAD. Hemos dicho anteriormente que *sólo* los verdaderos creyentes pueden ser miembros auténticos de una iglesia cristiana. La conducta correcta de una iglesia consiste en huir de dos extremos igualmente antibíblicos: el de aquellos que niegan la membresía a quienes no manifiesten una experiencia iluminista o una conducta totalmente intachable, arrogándose así una especie de participación en la infalibilidad divina o albergando un concepto perfeccionista de iglesia,[38] y el de aquellos que se dan por satisfechos con que una persona *diga* ser creyente, sin dar pruebas claras de haber nacido de nuevo. Los

---

37. V. mi libro *Cómo beneficiarse del complejo de inferioridad* (Barcelona, Bruguera, 1968), pp. 179-180.
38. En otro lugar referimos la respuesta de Spurgeon a uno que iba en busca de la «iglesia perfecta».

tests para admitir correctamente a una persona en la membresía de una iglesia son tres:

a') ¿Tiene el candidato un conocimiento ortodoxo, vivo, experimental —aun sin detalles de una Teología técnicamente elaborada—, de su Salvador, precedido y también acompañado de verdadera convicción de pecado y sed de salvación, y sin confiar en sus propias obras o méritos para salvarse?

b') ¿Consiste su fe en una entrega total a Cristo, Dios manifestado en carne, como a su único Salvador, y en una firme creencia en lo que la Palabra de Dios nos dice de Su persona, de Su doctrina y de Su obra?

c') ¿Muestra en su conducta los frutos de un regenerado (Mat. 7:20; Gál. 5:22), es decir, un progreso en la santificación (que sigue a la gracia de la justificación), sin caer en el perfeccionismo ni en el antinomianismo? Hechos 5:11-14 nos ofrece el asombroso contraste de un grupo purificado que sigue siendo *atrayente*.

Quien no ofrezca una prudencial evidencia (siempre falible) de responder con la debida satisfacción a estos tres *tests* no debe ser admitido en membresía (Romanos 10:10).[39]

La actual situación de las iglesias hace de la correcta membresía un problema nada fácil. Los Reformadores vieron clara la situación cuando hubieron de salir de la Iglesia oficial, no por impulso de una rebeldía cismática, sino en actitud de sumisa obediencia a la Palabra de Dios (Apoc. 18:4). Ahora, en cambio, la Reforma está en decadencia, deteriorada por dos escándalos: el escándalo de la *división* (a veces, ineludible, pero no siempre fundamentada) y el escándalo —mucho peor— de la *debilidad,* por haberse apartado de la creencia ortodoxa y de la correcta sumisión a la Palabra de Dios. ¿A dónde encaminar, a veces, a un neófito espiritual, sin la discreción suficiente para poder resistir a todo viento de doctrina? (Ef. 4:14).

---

39. Para todo este tema, *cf.* R. B. Kuiper, *o. c.*, pp. 281-296.

Quizá la única iglesia «protestante» de su localidad es una iglesia modernista, o se encuentra allí con una docena de iglesias entre las que resulta difícil escoger. Si se deja conducir por el Espíritu pedirá membresía en la que vea una mejor ortodoxia en la predicación del Evangelio y una mayor observancia de las ordenanzas y de la disciplina, pero habrá de estar dispuesto, a medida que vaya creciendo espiritualmente, a decidirse tal vez un día por la elección legítima de una comunidad que se acomode mejor al espíritu del Evangelio de Jesucristo.[40]

5.   Transferencia de membresía.

La membresía en una iglesia local comporta, según dijimos ya, privilegios y responsabilidades que no pueden tomarse a la ligera. Cada miembro debe dedicarse, según sus dones y en la medida en que sus ocupaciones profesionales se lo permitan, al servicio y edificación de la iglesia. Hay personas que, pensando hacer así más labor, disipan sus energías en muchas direcciones, perteneciendo a la vez a muchas organizaciones, a veces de manera antibíblica (*cf.* 2.ª Cor. 6:14-18). Nuestra primordial dedicación ha de ser para la iglesia de la que formamos parte. Aunque sólo podamos ofrecer al Señor la décima parte de nuestros ingresos, y la séptima parte de nuestro tiempo para Su obra, podemos, sin embargo, y debemos entregar *por entero* nuestro propio ser (*cf.* Rom. 12:1) y nuestras energías.[41]

En caso de trasladar nuestra residencia habitual a otro lugar, deberíamos en seguida buscar allí otra iglesia cristiana donde establecer membresía. Siendo *una* sola la Iglesia de Cristo, la cual subsiste visiblemente en cualquiera de las comunidades cristianas locales, el cambio de residencia no requiere una especie de nuevo empadronamiento o «nacionalización» y, por tanto, no debería presentar

---

40.   Del tema de la separación hablaremos en la lección 36.ª.
41.   V. *Baptist Distinctives*, p. 24.

ningún problema. No se hace uno miembro de Cristo mediante la pertenencia a una iglesia local, sino viceversa, puesto que la Iglesia total no consta de *iglesias*, sino de *creyentes*, siendo la localidad o nacionalidad «un mero accidente» geográfico.[42]

Hay iglesias (y, sobre todo, pastores) que miran la marcha de un miembro a otra iglesia local como una pérdida, y hasta se muestran reacias a permitir la transferencia, cuando la nueva membresía debería ser algo casi automático como consecuencia del nuevo domicilio, siendo la baja y alta un mero expediente administrativo en favor del orden y comportando así la transferencia como una especie de *carta comendaticia* de una iglesia del Señor a otra iglesia hermana.

Terminemos toda esta Tercera parte del presente volumen con la acertada frase del pastor de una de nuestras iglesias hermanas: «SOLAMENTE CON LA VESTIDURA DE LA HUMILDAD HAREMOS EFECTIVA NUESTRA PARTE EN LA IGLESIA.»

CUESTIONARIO:

1. ¿Son obstáculos para la membresía en una iglesia las diferencias de raza, clase o temperamento? — 2. ¿Cuáles son los tests correctos para admitir a un candidato? — 3. ¿Qué debe hacer un neófito para asegurarse una correcta membresía? — 4. ¿Por qué causa y de qué modo ha de realizarse una transferencia de membresía?

---

42. V. W. H. Griffith Thomas, *The Principles of Theology*, p. 268.

Cuarta parte

Las autoridades
de la Iglesia

LECCION 20.ª

LA UNICA NORMA DE LA IGLESIA (I)

1. Noción de autoridad.

«Autor», según su etimología latina, significa «el que añade». Por eso, se llama autor a toda persona que añade algo, mediante su actividad creadora, al acervo de la cultura, del arte, de la técnica, etc. En esta acepción, la cualidad de autor se llama «autoría», no «autoridad». Sin embargo, el vocablo «autoridad» tiene el mismo origen, aunque haya adquirido distinto sesgo en la historia del lenguaje. Fue ya entre los latinos aplicado a los generales que, mediante sus conquistas militares, *añadían* nuevas provincias al Imperio. Esto los constituía en árbitros del botín adquirido; les daba *autoridad*. Y así, de todo aquel que, con su investigación especializada sobre un asunto, ha obtenido en ello una peculiar competencia, se dice que es una *autoridad* en la materia.

La *autoridad* comporta, pues, cierta primacía o dominio, ya sea por derecho de creación, ya sea por derecho de conquista. Pero hay también otra clase de *autoridad* delegada, que consiste en la habilitación provista por una autoridad superior para el desempeño de un cometido que se ajuste a la norma de quien ejerce el verdadero dominio. Así tenemos, tanto en griego como en latín, dos clases de *autoridad*: en griego, el «krátos», propio del «kyrios» o *señor,* y la «exusía» o facultad para ostentar una dignidad o desempeñar un cometido; en latín está el «ius», propio del magistrado que ejerce justicia y sienta jurisprudencia, y la «auctoritas» de quien en virtud del «ius» tiene facultad para hacer cumplir la ley. Por eso, en tiempos de la República Romana, al pasar el «ius» o «krátos» al pueblo («demo-cracia» es un vocablo griego que significa «el poder en manos del pueblo»), el Senado se quedó con la «auctoritas», que implicaba una mera representatividad, como la de todo Parlamento en una verdadera democracia.

Todo lo que antecede, va dicho, no por vía de mera erudición, sino por la enorme importancia que estas distinciones tienen para comprender el concepto de *autoridad* en la Iglesia. De acuerdo con lo dicho, y de acuerdo con la Palabra de Dios (compárese la «exusía» de Jn. 1:12 con la advertencia de Pedro a los ancianos a que no se comporten como «teniendo señorío» —«katakyrieúontes»— de la grey que se les ha encomendado), tenemos que afirmar que la verdadera *autoridad* («krátos» o «ius») en la Iglesia no la puede tener *ningún hombre*, sino sólo Dios; más concretamente: sólo *hay tres autoridades en la Iglesia: la Palabra de Dios, como única norma inapelable; el Hijo de Dios, Jesucristo, como único Señor y Gobernador; y el Espíritu de Dios, como único principio vital y «Vicario de Cristo» en la tierra.*[1] Todo «pre-fecto» o «prelado» (que significan «puesto delante») dentro de la Iglesia ha de ser, por consiguiente, no un «jerarca» o *príncipe sagrado*, sino un «ministro» o «servidor», como veremos en la siguiente sección (Quinta parte) de este volumen.

2. La Palabra de Dios y la Iglesia.

Siguiendo el orden indicado en el punto anterior, comenzamos por la Palabra de Dios, o sea, la Biblia o *Sagradas Escrituras* (no porque tenga la primacía en el dominio, sino por su prioridad *lógica*, ya que es en *Su Palabra* donde Dios muestra la autoridad de Jesucristo y la del Espíritu Santo).

En su *Institución de la Religión Cristiana*, libro IV, cap. I, puntos 8 y ss., hace observar Calvino que la pri-

---

1. V. M. Lloyd-Jones, *La autoridad.*

mera y más importante *nota* de la Iglesia verdadera es su *fidelidad* a la Palabra de Dios. De ahí que la relación entre la Iglesia y la Santa Biblia, donde se encuentra la verdad revelada por Dios, ha de ser íntima y estrecha. ¿Cuál es esta relación? Al dar respuesta a esta relevante pregunta, percatémonos de que aquí se establece la principal línea divisoria entre la Reforma y la Iglesia de Roma. Mientras la Reforma devolvió a la Biblia su verdadero lugar en la Iglesia, al proclamar que la Iglesia —toda la Iglesia y todas las iglesias— han de someterse a la Palabra como UNICO TRIBUNAL INAPELABLE EN MATERIAS DE FE Y CONDUCTA, la Iglesia de Roma mantuvo su doctrina de un jerarca humano, investido de un carisma institucional de infalibilidad (definido como «dogma» en 1870), no como *superior* a la Biblia, pero sí como *único intérprete inapelable* de la Biblia. Así se constituyó a la Iglesia —como dice J. Grau— en garantía del Evangelio, en vez de constituir al Evangelio en garantía de la Iglesia, según el orden que dicta la razón y la misma Biblia.

Como quiera que este problema de la relación entre la Iglesia y la Biblia ha sido ya tratado en detalle en otros volúmenes de esta serie teológica, ya publicados,[2] a ellos remitimos al lector estudioso, resumiendo, sin embargo, dos puntos que, en el contexto del presente volumen, revisten un peculiar interés, pues nos explican qué significa para la Iglesia la Palabra de Dios como *autoridad:* la Biblia es el mensaje de salvación que: *a)* determina la ortodoxia de la Iglesia, y *b)* constituye la totalidad de la Revelación Especial de Dios a los hombres. De estos dos puntos se derivan dos consecuencias de suma importancia: 1.ª, en la Biblia encuentra la Iglesia todo lo que está obligada a creer, predicar y practicar en relación con Dios; 2.ª, la Iglesia no puede añadir, quitar o alterar la menor partícula de dicho mensaje.

---

2. *Cf.* J. Grau, *Introducción a la Teología,* espec. las lecciones 51.ª-52.ª, y mi *Catolicismo Romano,* espec. las lecciones 7.ª y 8.ª.

3. La Santa Biblia, mensaje de salvación.

Se ha dicho muy bien que la Biblia es como la Carta Magna de la salvación, descendida del Cielo para los hombres perdidos, así como del Padre Celestial para Su Pueblo. Su mensaje es, pues, un mensaje de salvación ofrecida por pura, gratuita y misericordiosa iniciativa divina.

Pero este mensaje ha sido transmitido, desde el principio, envuelto en las vicisitudes de la Historia de un pueblo. Por un proceso de progresiva selección (Seth, Noé, Abraham, Isaac, Jacob), Dios se formó un pueblo que fuese vehículo de su mensaje salvífico, así como objeto de Su presencia y acción salvíficas. Este proceso tiene diversas etapas, siendo la era cristiana con la Nueva Alianza, al menos en lo que afecta a la Iglesia,[3] la última de ellas. Con la Encarnación del Verbo, con Su predicación y Su obra redentora, Dios da cumplimiento a la fase decisiva de las profecías mesiánicas, poniendo en clara luz el espíritu de la Ley (como «nuestro ayo, para llevarnos a Cristo» —Gál. 3:24), que las tradiciones fariseas habían oscurecido.

Esta renovación y «plenitud» que Cristo vino a traer a la Antigua Alianza, dio ocasión al hecho tremendo del rechazo, por parte de la gran masa del pueblo judío, del mensaje salvador ofrecido por Dios en su Mesías al pueblo elegido, como una nueva etapa de la Historia de la salvación,[4] que empalmaba convenientemente, dentro de los planes divinos, con la etapa anterior. Este rechazo

---

3. No queremos entrar aquí en la discusión dispensacionalista respecto al futuro de Israel (V. el vol. VII —en preparación— de esta serie teológica).

4. Por eso, como hace notar L. Sp. Chafer (o. c., III, pp. 372-378), la exhortación a la «metánoia» o *cambio de mentalidad*, así como a creer, al mismo tiempo, en el *Evangelio* (la «Buena Noticia» del cumplimiento de los tiempos), que forman el esquema del primer sermón de Juan el Bautista y del mismo Jesucristo (Mat. 3:2; 4:17; Marc. 1:15), van dirigidas, ante todo, *a los judíos.*

hizo que los apóstoles se volvieran *entonces* a los gentiles (Hech. 13:46).

Nosotros, pues, gentiles (es decir, no pertenecientes a la nación judía) debemos a ese rechazo el haber obtenido más de prisa las Buenas Nuevas de la salvación (Romanos 11:11), hechos ahora hijos espirituales de Abraham por la fe; ya que, de lo contrario, la Iglesia de Cristo (= Iglesia de Dios) sería probablemente una comunidad universal (el gran *qahal* del nuevo eón) de base israelita con prosélitos gentiles. El hecho de que el mismo Pablo —el apóstol de la incircuncisión (Gál. 2:7)— fuese *primero* a predicar en la sinagoga, dondequiera que existía una comunidad judía, parece avalarlo.

De aquí se desprende que toda la historia de la salvación, según la registra la S. Biblia, está enhebrada en un hilo único, que es Jesucristo. El Mesías profetizado en el Antiguo Testamento, y encarnado, muerto y resucitado para inaugurar la Nueva Alianza, presta la solución clara al crucigrama que el mensaje de la Biblia hebrea parecía presentar. Agustín de Hipona lo expresó magníficamente en una de sus frases lapidarias: «El N. Testamento está *latente* en el Viejo, y el Viejo Testamento está *patente* en el Nuevo.»

Recalquemos de nuevo que la Biblia es una *Historia de salvación que comporta un mensaje de salvación.*[5] Lo cual implica dos consecuencias muy importantes, que conviene tener en cuenta para evitar dos extremos igualmente peligrosos: el literalismo y el modernismo; *a)* la Biblia es un libro de *religión,* no de astronomía, física, biología, etcétera; *b)* la Biblia está escrita en el lenguaje de la época, dentro de una cosmovisión típica del Oriente y con un estilo semita, que varía según la formación humana y cultural de los redactores humanos o «hagiógrafos» y el designio de la vocación divina para cada uno de ellos, que la inspiración se encargaba de llevar a cabo a través de

---

5. Para más detalles, *cf.* J. Grau, *Introducción a la Teología,* lecciones 45.ª-51.ª.

ellos. Junto a estas características, hemos de señalar que la revelación del mensaje salvador ha sido *progresiva,* como una planta que se desarrolla a partir de una semilla, o como un cono de luz, cuyo vértice inicial o minúsculo haz es Gén. 3:15, y cuya base amplia, final y definitiva, es la Revelación completada en y por Jesucristo (Hebreos 1:1-2).

CUESTIONARIO:

1. ¿Qué sentido y acepciones comporta el vocablo «autoridad»? — 2. ¿Cuáles son las verdaderas autoridades de la Iglesia? — 3. ¿Cuál es la correcta actitud de la Iglesia frente a la Palabra de Dios? — 4. ¿Es la Biblia un libro de Astronomía o de Geología? — 5. ¿En qué estilo literario está redactada la Sagrada Escritura?

LECCION 21.ª

LA UNICA NORMA DE LA IGLESIA (II)

4. "La fe dada una vez a los santos".

Terminábamos la lección anterior diciendo que la Revelación Divina (Especial) ha quedado completada en y por Jesucristo, y, por ello, fijada para siempre (Jud. 3). Así pues, no queda ya para la Iglesia *progreso en la revelación divina*, sino *en la comprensión del mensaje revelado*. Por eso, al hablar Jesucristo en la víspera de Su muerte acerca de la futura labor del Espíritu en la Iglesia, no dijo que el Espíritu *revelaría* nuevas cosas, sino que *enseñaría y recordaría todo lo que El había dicho*.[6]

¿Significa esto que la vida del cristiano y de la Iglesia misma es algo estático, inmóvil? ¡No! La vida cristiana, por ser *vida* («zoé» = el más alto —divino— nivel de vida), es algo *dinámico* (por la «dynamis» del Espíritu),[7] en progreso constante hacia una meta (*cf.* Filip. 3:10 y ss.), hacia un «superior reconocimiento —epígnosis— del Hijo de Dios» (Ef. 4:13); pero no es la fe objetiva la que va creciendo, sino la penetración del creyente en dicha verdad y la vivencia espiritual progresiva de dicha viva verdad en Aquél que, siendo el Camino, es también la Verdad y la Vida (Jn. 14:6).

Ello no significa que nuestra fe personal y eclesial se funde en algo subjetivo e inmanente, como enseña el Mo-

---

6. *Juan 14:26. Cf.* Jn. 15:26; 16:14 (V. R. B. Kuiper, *o. c.,* pp. 79-85).
7. René Monod ha escrito un librito titulado *La Dynamite de Dieu* (Strasbourg, La Voix de l'Evangile, 1971).

dernismo, sino que es una «praxis» basada, no en opiniones meramente humanas o en experiencias subjetivas, sino
en algo esencialmente *objetivo* y estable: sencillamente,
nuestra fe se funda en *hechos*. Es curioso notar que el
Libro de Hechos se llame en griego «Práxeis Apostolôn».[8]
También es notable que sea Lucas el único evangelista
que hace una plena reflexión sobre la primitiva comunidad
cristiana, quien centre su relato en la «práxis» de los apóstoles y de la Iglesia, así como que sea él quien llame
«obra» (Hech. 5:38; 13:2; 14:26) a la tarea salvífica de la
Iglesia mediante la predicación de la Palabra, y «Camino»
(Hech. 9:2; 18:26; 19:9, 23; 22:4; 24:14, 22) a la Iglesia
misma, como realización práctica del definitivo plan salvífico de Dios.

Igualmente, cuando Pablo quiere dar un resumen de
su Evangelio, dice: «Porque primeramente os he enseñado
lo que asimismo recibí: Que Cristo murió por nuestros
pecados, conforme a las Escrituras; y que fue sepultado,
y que resucitó al tercer día, conforme a las Escrituras; y
que apareció a Cefas, y después a los Doce...» (1.ª Corintios 15:3-5). He aquí *hechos*: los grandes hechos de la salvación, garantizados por la Palabra de Dios y proclama-
dos por los *testigos* escogidos para tal menester. Pablo
teme que pueda en alguna iglesia (aquí, Corinto) formarse
una especie de «cofradía» basada en un esoterismo hele-
nístico alrededor de un Dios, pero sin admitir la resurrección —vv. 14 y ss.—, con lo que todo lo más fundamental
de la salvación quedaría en crisis. Por eso, cuando Pablo,
al enfatizar que el nuevo «Israel de Dios» (Gál. 6:7) inaugura una nueva etapa de salvación, universal y sin fronteras, habla de este nuevo Israel como «nacido según el
Espíritu», en oposición al «nacido según la carne» (Gálatas 4:29), no porque el primero sea menos concreto que el

---

8. El vocablo «praxis», del que se deriva «práctica», se aplica
a la realización concreta, palpable, sujeta a experiencia (*cf.* Hebreos 11:1, donde se llama «prágmata» a «las cosas que esperamos»),
en oposición a la «teoría» o mera «contemplación» de un espectador.

segundo, ya que este Israel «katà pneúma» es el que se hace visible en cada una de las comunidades locales, sino porque la nueva etapa inaugura también una nueva «práxis». Ya la *Torah*, en cuanto Ley, o código ético, da paso a un Evangelio de salvación por la *fe*. Pablo alza su protesta contra el legalismo (2.ª Cor. 3:17; Gál. 5:1, 13-14, 18), como contra todo Código que pretenda encerrar y cuadricular la vida en el minucioso entramado de la casuística, mientras realza la suprema norma del amor al hermano como poder avasallador mediante el que la fe cumple y rebasa las exigencias de la Ley entera (Gál. 5:5-6, 13-14).

5. El mensaje diferencial del Cristianismo.

Dijimos ya en la lección 15.ª que el primero y más significativo epíteto aplicado en el Nuevo Testamento a los creyentes fue el de *discípulo*, en el sentido de «seguidor del Maestro». Aquí cobra nuevo énfasis el término «Camino», al que hemos aludido en el punto anterior, puesto que los cristianos *andamos* (sinónimo de conducta) arraigados en *un Camino que anda* (comp. Col. 2:6-7 con Juan 14:2, 6). Por eso, late constantemente en los escritos del Nuevo Testamento la idea de «éxodo» y «peregrinación», porque la salida de los hebreos de Egipto, a través del Mar Rojo, por el desierto hacia la tierra prometida, era para los judeo-cristianos el gran símbolo de la vida cristiana, cuya esencia se resume en salir del pecado (el Egipto mundanal), ser salvos mediante la roja sangre de Cristo, peregrinar por el desierto de esta vida y arribar finalmente a la verdadera Tierra Prometida (comp. Jn. 1:14, en que se nos dice que el Verbo hecho carne «habitó» —literalmente «plantó su tienda de campaña»— entre nosotros, con 1.ª Ped. 2:11; Heb. 11:13-16). Ello tiene también su importancia para mejor entender el simbolismo del bautismo cristiano, pues el «pasar a través de las aguas» representa la *transmersión* de la muerte a la vida, mediante la fe (cf. 1.ª Ped. 1:21-23; 3:21), con el Cristo muerto, sepultado y resucitado a la perenne vida de la gloria (Romanos 6:3-10). Paradójicamente, con la desconcertante sabiduría de las divinas paradojas, el Cristo en que nos sumergimos por la fe es también el único puente de acceso al Padre (Jn. 14:6; 1.ª Tim. 2:5), o sea, es nuestro único «Pontífice», para lo que necesitó poseer la naturaleza divina y la naturaleza humana indisolublemente casadas en la unidad de la única Persona del Hijo de Dios. ¡He aquí la quintaesencia diferencial del Cristianismo! (Mt. 16:16, 18; Marc. 8:29; Luc. 9:20; Jn. 6:68-69).

Por atentar contra este núcleo del mensaje cristiano, toda enseñanza que *disuelva* a Cristo, o sea, que niegue o la perfecta divinidad, o la perfecta humanidad, o la unidad de persona, de Cristo, es esencial y especialmente *anticristiana* (*cf.* 1.ª Tim. 3:16; 1.º Jn. 2:22-23; 4:2; 2.º Juan 9-10). No es extraño, pues, que la fe dada a los santos de una vez para siempre (Jud. 3) coincida con la medula misma del Cristianismo: Jesús, verdadero Dios y verdadero hombre (el «Hijo de Dios» y el «Hijo del Hombre»), único Salvador necesario y suficiente, muerto y resucitado, y recibido por fe, sin las obras de la Ley (Rom. 3:28). Esta fe objetiva constituye el *único Evangelio posible*, atreviéndose Pablo a decir que si alguien, aunque sea un ángel del Cielo, predicare un Evangelio *diferente* («par'hó» = sobreañadido), sea *anatema* (Gálatas 1:6-9).

Por tanto, toda enseñanza eclesial ha de contrastarse con este Evangelio, al que nada se puede ya añadir o quitar, del que nada se puede cambiar o alterar, contra el que se puede pecar lo mismo por parte de *menos* que por parte de *más* (*cf.* Is. 8:20; Apoc. 22:18-19). El apóstol Pedro, uno de los Doce cualificados testigos de vista de las humillaciones, así como de la más gloriosa manifestación de Jesucristo en el Tabor, asegura que, por encima de su propio testimonio de primera mano, está «la palabra profética más segura», inspirada e inapelable (2.ª Pedro

1:16-21; 2:1-3), o sea, las Sagradas Escrituras, a las que todos harán bien en «estar atentos», para no ser seducidos por «falsos maestros, que introducirán encubiertamente herejías destructoras».

Ya hemos aludido (y aludiremos de nuevo más adelante) a las consecuencias de suma importancia que de todo esto se desprenden en orden al Ecumenismo y a la separación: no podemos *transigir* con fórmulas que minimicen el objeto nuclear de nuestra fe, pero tampoco hemos de ser intolerantes, hasta oscurecer y negar la fraternidad que nos une en Cristo con personas y grupos que coinciden con nosotros en lo fundamental, aunque difieran en detalles secundarios de doctrina, disciplina, gobierno o administración. Como decía Agustín de Hipona, todos debemos esforzarnos en mantener «la unidad en lo necesario, la libertad en lo discutible, la caridad en todo».

Cerramos esta lección con una advertencia acerca del valor de la «Tradición». El uso que el Nuevo Testamento hace del término «parádosis» nos indica que su sentido es el de *una enseñanza de origen divino que, primero Jesús y después los apóstoles, entregaron a la Iglesia*, en contraposición a las tradiciones fariseicas y a toda tradición humana (*cf.* Mat. 5:22-44; 6:25; 15:3, 6, 9; Marc. 7:6-9; Luc. 1:2; Rom. 6:17; 1.ª Cor. 11:2, 23; 15:3; Gál. 1:6-16; Ef. 4:20-21; Col. 2:8; 2.ª Tes. 2:15; 3:6-7; 1.ª Tim. 5:18; 6:20; 2.ª Ped. 1:16-19; 3:16; Judas 3). *Esta tradición apostólica luego cristalizó en los escritos del Nuevo Testamento.* Por tanto, fuera de estos *escritos,* no podemos admitir ninguna otra tradición *constitutiva* (o sea, que tenga autoridad y garantía para ser creída y observada en parangón con la Escritura). Sólo admitimos una tradición *interpretativa* (una cierta línea de interpretación de la Biblia), sólo válida en la medida en que esté de acuerdo con el genuino sentido de la Palabra de Dios, sirviéndonos muchas veces de guía e ilustración, pero nunca como norma infalible de fe y conducta; de modo que *toda interpreta-*

ción (por autorizada que nos pueda parecer) ha de ser contrastada con la Biblia, y no viceversa.[9]

CUESTIONARIO:

1. ¿Puede darse progreso en la fe cristiana? — 2. ¿Cuál es el núcleo diferencial de nuestra fe? — 3. ¿Cómo puede formarse un Evangelio «diferente»? — 4. ¿Cómo resumió Agustín de Hipona el verdadero ecumenismo? — 5. ¿Podemos admitir alguna «tradición» como norma de fe y conducta?

---

9. Para más detalles, *cf.* J. Grau, *El fundamento apostólico* e *Introducción a la Teología,* así como *The New Bible Dictionary* (London, IVF, 1962), pp. 1290-1291.

LECCION 22.ª

JESUCRISTO, SEÑOR DE LA IGLESIA (I)

1. Jesucristo, único Señor y Rey de la Iglesia.

En Apocalipsis 1:13-15, Juan relata cómo vio al Señor en medio de siete candelabros de oro, que son figura de siete iglesias del Asia Menor, y nos lo describe con varios símbolos que expresan los atributos que más resaltan Su sacerdocio, Su divinidad y, especialmente, Su *soberanía* sobre las iglesias.

Ya antes de nacer, Jesús es llamado «mi Señor» por Isabel (Luc. 1:43). De no tratarse de citas del Antiguo Testamento, el Nuevo Testamento reserva a Cristo el término «Señor», que corresponde al hebreo «Adonai» con que los judíos nombran aun hoy a Dios, para no pronunciar el sagrado e inefable nombre de «Yahveh», que Dios se puso a Sí mismo en Ex. 3:14. El griego «Kyrios», que vierte el hebreo «Adonai», implica *posesión* y *soberanía*. Cristo es el único Señor y Señor total de cada uno de nosotros y de todas y cada una de las iglesias. De ahí que Su señorío sea para Pablo el primer fundamento de la unidad de la Iglesia (Ef. 4:5). Otros textos importantes son: Hechos 2:36; 4:12; 1.ª Cor. 8:5-6; Filip. 2:9-11; Col. 1:15-18; 2:6-9; 1.ª Tim. 2:5; Heb. 1:1-13.

La primera acepción del término «Cabeza», aplicado a Cristo respecto de Su Iglesia, indica que Jesucristo es su *Jefe* [10] y *Señor*, tanto como su *Salvador* y su *Juez* (V. los

---

10. Nótese que la palabra «jefe» se deriva del griego «kefalé» = = cabeza.

tres primeros caps. del Apoc.). El es Cabeza de todos los redimidos, como Adán lo fue de todos los perdidos (*cf.* Romanos 5:12 y ss.). Cristo nos recuperó con creces todo lo que Adán nos perdió, pues Su perfectísima obediencia al Padre contrarrestó y superó la desobediencia de Adán y de todos sus descendientes. «Quizás es por esto —concluye R. B. Kuiper—[11] por lo que la Escritura habla del Salvador como del *postrer* Adán, más bien que del *segundo*.»[12]

Jesucristo es el Dueño y Señor soberano de la Iglesia: A) por derecho de creación y fundación (Mat. 16:18; Juan 1:3; Col. 1:16); B) por derecho de redención o rescate (1.ª Cor. 6:20; 1.ª Ped. 1:19); C) por derecho de matrimonio (Ef. 5:23-27, 32). Así pues, comprados y adquiridos *totalmente,* somos *totalmente* Suyos; por eso, hemos de glorificarle con *todo* nuestro ser; y Le hemos de servir y glorificar siempre y en todo lugar, como individuos y como *iglesia.* Pablo dice en Ef. 4:5: «UN SOLO SEÑOR.» El común señorío de Cristo une a todos Sus vasallos entre sí más que a los de otros amos, pues, Su señorío y derecho de propiedad alcanzan a todo nuestro ser, y Su soberanía es absoluta y sin competencia. De aquí se deriva que los cristianos han de estar acordes en la sumisión a su Señor, no teniendo muchos amos, ni usurpando el dominio unos sobre otros. ¡NO PODEMOS SERVIR A DOS SEÑORES! Este señorío se ejerce sobre una Iglesia visible que El fundó, para la que instituyó Sus medios de gracia, y en la que estableció los correspondientes oficios, servicios y ministerios (Ef. 4:7-11).

J. M. Stowell advierte[13] que la Biblia usa generalmente el término «Señor» para aplicárselo a Cristo en relación con la *Iglesia,* mientras que el vocablo «Rey» connota más bien la relación de Cristo con *Israel.* Y añade: «Hablando con propiedad, podemos decir que Cristo es nuestro Señor presente y nuestro Rey venidero.»

---

11. *O. c.,* p. 92.
12. En efecto, 1.ª Cor. 15:45 dice «*éschatos*», no «*deúteros*».
13. En *Baptist Distinctives,* p. 32.

Dios Padre es quien, al resucitar por el Espíritu a Su Hijo Jesucristo, Le ha manifestado pública y definitivamente como el *Ungido* y el *Señor* (Hech. 2:32-36). Mientras la Iglesia va peregrinando por este mundo, el reinado de Cristo puede ser menospreciado, negado y combatido, pero tiene asegurada la victoria ya desde el principio (Génesis 3:15). Siendo Cristo el Príncipe de la Paz (Is. 9:6), posee un reinado de lucha y de conquista, mas cuando el último enemigo haya sido sometido, Cristo pondrá Su Reino a los pies del Padre (1.ª Cor. 15:24). El poeta francés J. C. Renard, en su poema «Señor, he aquí al hombre», lo expresa gráficamente diciendo que Cristo exprimirá entonces todas las uvas de Su cepa (Jn. 15:1) en los labios del Padre.

R. B. Kuiper [14] dice que la Iglesia tiene el derecho y el deber (podríamos añadir: y el privilegio) de predicar la realeza de Jesucristo, su Señor y Cabeza. En cuanto Dios, Cristo es Rey de toda la creación por Su *esencia* o esencialmente. Como Hombre, es Rey Universal por *mediación,* o sea, en calidad de Mediador o Medianero. Este reinado de Cristo, aunque no sea de momento reconocido y aceptado por todos los hombres, no es exclusivamente *escatológico* (para el final de los tiempos), contra la opinión de K. Barth y Emil Brunner (*cf.* Mat. 28:18; 1.ª Cor. 15:25; Ef. 1:20-22; Apoc. 1:5). Es cierto que Satanás no ha sido aún lanzado definitivamente al lago de fuego y azufre, pero ha quedado desprovisto del poder de hacer daño a quien no se encuentre en la atmósfera mundana (*cf.* 1.º Juan 5:18), donde todavía conserva un dominio relativo y provisional (*cf.* 1.ª Cor. 5:5). A pesar de todos los ataques del enemigo (y aun *por medio* de ellos —*cf.* Sal. 76:10—), la Iglesia tiene un Rey invencible, destinado a reinar siempre y universalmente (Apoc. 11:15), y de este reinado hará partícipe a Su Iglesia (*cf.* Luc. 12:32; Apoc. 33:5).

---

14. *O. c.,* pp. 195-200.

CUESTIONARIO:

1. ¿Qué implica el término «Señor» aplicado a Jesucristo? — 2. ¿Por qué se llama a Cristo «el Postrer Adán»? — 3. ¿Qué se deduce de la frase «Un solo Señor» de Ef. 4:5? — 4. Si Cristo era el Señor desde Su encarnación, ¿cómo se explica lo que dice Pedro en Hech. 2:36? — 5. ¿Está ya presente el reinado de Cristo o reinará solamente al final de los tiempos?

LECCION 23.ª

JESUCRISTO, SEÑOR DE LA IGLESIA (II)

2. Jesucristo, único Gobernador de la Iglesia.

En la lección 20.ª, párrafo 1.º, nos hemos referido al hecho de que, en contraste con la Iglesia de Roma, todos los evangélicos mantenemos que Cristo (así como Su Palabra y Su Espíritu) es el único que tiene el *poder* o *dominio* («krátos» o «ius») en la Iglesia y, por tanto, la verdadera *jurisdicción* sobre las iglesias, mientras que el ministerio específico *pastoral* dispone de una *facultad* («exusía» o «auctoritas») de regir a la congregación en el sentido de «apacentarla» (Hech. 20:28 dice «poimaínein», equívocamente vertido a la Vulgata Latina por el verbo «regere», en lugar de «pascere» que sería lo correcto). Esta *facultad* ministerial del pastor humano, aunque de algún modo pueda llamarse *autoridad*, en el sentido de quedar señalado y equipado por Dios para tal ministerio, no comporta ningún poder sobre la congregación, sino una grave *responsabilidad* ante Dios y un *servicio* específico a la comunidad, admitiendo que dicho servicio exige honor, respeto y obediencia (Heb. 13:17).[15]

¿Cómo ejercita Cristo Su gobierno en la Iglesia? No lo hace física y visiblemente, como los gobernantes humanos, sino por medio de dos agencias suyas: 1) *subjetivamente* (en el interior del sujeto), por medio de Su Espíritu,

---

15. En la Quinta parte trataremos sobre el ministerio en la Iglesia y sobre la diferencia radical entre Roma y la Reforma, respecto a este punto.

quien da el *poder* (la «dynamis» de Hech. 1:8, etc.) y comunica así la *operación* (*cf.* Ef. 4:16) o «enérgeia» que viene del Padre (1.ª Cor. 12:6), para la edificación y crecimiento de la Iglesia; 2) *objetivamente* (desde fuera), por medio de la Palabra de Dios, a la que *todos* han de estar sometidos, como a los mandatos del Rey, ya que la Biblia es la múltiple expresión del *Verbo,* o sea, de la única Palabra personal del Padre (Jn. 1:1, 18; Heb. 1:1-2). Sólo esta Palabra de Dios es «ley en sentido absoluto» —como dice L. Berkhof.[16]

Por Jesucristo y en Jesucristo, la Iglesia es una congregación de reyes, sacerdotes y profetas (1.ª Ped. 2:9-10), de tal manera que ninguna otra persona en la Iglesia puede llamarse con propiedad «Pontífice», «sacerdote», «clero», etc., en sentido singular o como una casta aparte.[17]

3.   Jesucristo, único Salvador y Juez de la Iglesia.

Jesús es el único «Nombre», es decir (conforme al estilo semita), la única Persona por quien podemos ser salvos: «Porque no hay otro nombre bajo el cielo, dado a los hombres, en que podamos ser salvos» (Hech. 4:12). A Cristo ha sido dado «*el* nombre [el original griego lleva artículo] que está sobre todo nombre» (Filip. 2:9). El *nombre es,* evidentemente, *Jesús,* que en hebreo significa «Yahveh salva» o «Dios Salvador», «para que en el nombre de Jesús se doble toda rodilla» (vers. 10 —acto de latría que sólo a Dios puede tributarse; *cf.* Deut. 6:13; 10:20; Mat. 4:10; Luc. 4:8). Buscar la salvación en cualquier otra persona es hacer un blasfemo agravio al Señor y desviarse del único camino de salvación. Sigue vigente la Palabra de Dios que dice: «Así ha dicho Yahveh: Maldito el varón que confía en el hombre, y pone carne por su brazo [es decir: pone en un hombre mortal la esperanza y el poder de salvarle], y su corazón se aparta de Yahveh» (Jer. 17:5).

---

16.   En su *Systematic Theology,* p. 583.
17.   Sobre esto hablaremos en detalle en la lección 27.ª.

Siendo el nombre de Jesús el único que salva, resulta obvio que Cristo sea el único Mediador entre Dios y los hombres (1.ª Tim. 2:5. *Cf.* Heb. 4:15-16; 10:11-22). Por Él, con Él y en Él, nuestros sacrificios de alabanza, generosidad y dedicación personal (Rom. 12:1; Heb. 13:15-16) son aceptables a Dios. De Su Trono Celestial sale el *incienso*, o sea, la intercesión constante y eficaz, que da valor y urgencia a nuestras oraciones (Apoc. 8:3). *Nadie* —ni individuos, ni iglesias— va al Padre sino por Él, porque Él es el único «Camino, Verdad y Vida» (Jn. 14:6): La única fuente de *Vida* —por Su Espíritu— de la Iglesia; el único Maestro infalible de la *Verdad* (para un judío, la verdad es una *seguridad*) y la única norma de conducta —*Camino*— de la Iglesia. Los tres epítetos llevan artículo en el original, para recalcar que Cristo no es un camino entre otros, sino *el Camino* único y suficiente. Como ya dijimos en otra lección, resulta curioso que el Libro de Hechos presente repetidamente el Cristianismo y la Iglesia con el nombre de «Camino», como una *Vía sacra* identificada con Cristo (*cf.* Hech. 9:2, 4; etc.), que anda *en* Cristo (Colosenses 2:6-7) y *por* la que Cristo anda (Apoc. 1:13).

Así el papel de Cristo en la Iglesia es de una relevancia sin igual. Por ello, Él es la piedra angular de la Iglesia, o sea, el «líthos akrogoniaîos» = «piedra principal del ángulo» —como dice el apóstol Pedro (1.ª Ped. 2:6)—.[18] Así, este «líthos akrogoniaîos», esta piedra principal del ángulo, escogida y preciosa, que es Jesucristo, hace superfluo y nulo todo otro fundamento y toda otra clase de bóveda humana que se pretenda imponer a la Iglesia como centro, raíz y principio de la unidad cristiana.[19] Hemos de distinguir cuidadosamente entre el «líthos akrogoniaîos» que es Cristo, y el «themélios» de los apóstoles (comp. Mat. 16:18 con 1.ª Cor. 3:11; Ef. 2:20; 1.ª Ped. 2:4-6 y Apoc. 21:14).

Pero Jesucristo no es sólo el Jefe y Salvador de Su Iglesia. Es también el *Juez* supremo e inapelable de la Iglesia:

---

18. Véase la lección 6.ª, punto 1.º.
19. V. lo dicho en la lección 6.ª sobre el fundamento de la Iglesia.

de *toda* la Iglesia y de cada una de las iglesias o comunidades locales. Los caps. 1 al 3 del Apocalipsis nos presentan a Jesucristo salvando, consolando, exhortando, reprendiendo y amenazando a las siete iglesias del Asia Menor (incluyendo a los pastores, lo mismo que a los creyentes en general). 1.ª Cor. 3:13 nos presenta el juicio que se hará a los edificadores de la Iglesia, especialmente a los predicadores (pastores y maestros). Cristo aparece además como Rey y Juez de las naciones en Mat. 25:31-46; Jn. 5:26 y ss.; Apoc. 20:4 y ss.; 22:10 y ss.

CUESTIONARIO:

1. ¿Quién tiene verdadera jurisdicción *sobre la Iglesia? — 2. ¿Cómo ejercita Cristo Su gobierno en la Iglesia? — 3. ¿Qué sentido tiene «el Nombre» en Filip. 2:9-10? — 4. ¿Por qué asegura El mismo ser «el Camino, y la Verdad y la Vida»? — 5. ¿Qué significa la expresión «principal piedra del ángulo», aplicada a Jesucristo en 1.ª Pedro 2:6? — 6. ¿Dónde se muestra mejor el papel de Juez que Cristo ejercita con respecto a la Iglesia?*

LECCION 24.ª

EL ESPIRITU SANTO Y LA IGLESIA (I)

1. La Persona del Espíritu Santo.

Vamos a presentar un brevísimo resumen de la doctrina bíblica sobre la Persona del Espíritu Santo, remitiendo al lector a nuestro volumen II para un estudio más detallado.

El Espíritu Santo es la 3.ª Persona de la Trina Deidad. El nombrarlo en tercer lugar (cf. Mat. 28:19) no indica inferioridad alguna, pues las tres Personas poseen la misma individual esencia divina, sino sólo un *orden* lógico fundado en el origen íntimo, puesto que el Espíritu Santo —«Aliento Santo y santificador» (Amor Personal de Dios)— procede del Padre y del Hijo (Jn. 15:26; 16:7, 15). Su carácter *personal* —no es una mera fuerza divina, sino una Persona— y *divino* se muestra en textos como Mat. 28:19 (el griego denota una alianza y consagración, que sólo tienen sentido cuando se refieren a una persona divina); Jn. 14:26; 15:26; 16:7, donde se le llama «Parácletos» = = Consolador, Confortador (literalmente: una persona a quien se llama para que venga al lado de uno para ayudarle); 1.ª Cor. 12:4, 8-11, donde se dice que reparte dones «como El quiere»; Ef. 4:30, donde se dice que puede ser «contristado»; Hech. 5:3-4, donde mentir al Espíritu Santo equivale a «mentir a Dios»; 1.ª Cor. 3:16; 6:19, donde «templo de Dios» y «templo del Espíritu Santo» son sinónimos; etc.

2. El Espíritu Santo y la vida espiritual de la Iglesia.

En 1.ª Cor. 12:13 dice Pablo: «Porque por un solo Espíritu fuimos todos bautizados en un cuerpo»; es decir, por la recepción de un mismo Espíritu hemos sido hechos todos los creyentes miembros de un solo Cuerpo de Cristo. Y en Ef. 4:4, al enumerar los siete vínculos de unidad de la Iglesia, dice el mismo apóstol: «... un cuerpo y un Espíritu...» .Comentando este versículo, dice el gran teólogo Charles Hodge:

> «Así como el cuerpo humano es uno porque está informado por una sola alma, así el Cuerpo de Cristo es uno porque está penetrado por un mismo Espíritu, quien, al habitar en todos, es un principio común de vida. Por tanto, todos los pecados contra la unidad son pecados contra el Espíritu Santo, puesto que tienden a separar lo que el Espíritu une.» [20]

Vemos, pues, la analogía que hay entre las funciones de Cristo como Cabeza y las funciones del Espíritu Santo como Alma de la Iglesia, pues tanto Cristo como el Espíritu son en la Iglesia principio de *unidad, vida y movimiento.* En realidad, Cristo es Cabeza vivificante de la Iglesia *por Su Espíritu* (1.ª Cor. 15:45), hasta tal punto que el Espíritu Santo es el verdadero «Vicario de Cristo» en la Tierra (*cf.* Jn. 14:16). Más aún, si Cristo —en cuanto Hombre— puede dar vida y crecimiento espiritual a Su Cuerpo, la Iglesia (Ef. 4:15-16), es porque Él mismo recibió el Espíritu *sin medida* (cf. Jn. 3:34), mientras que nosotros recibimos los dones *según la medida* (Ef. 4:7-11).[21]

---

20. *The Epistle to the Ephesians* (Grand Rapids, sin fecha), p. 204.

21. Por eso se dice en Jn. 1:14 y ss. que todos recibimos *gracia sobre gracia* de la *plenitud* que hay en Jesucristo, así como el blanco del espectro solar contiene virtualmente en sí todos los colores del iris, los cuales manifiestan toda su rica gama al refractarse a través de un prisma translúcido.

Dejando para el vol. V el estudio de las funciones vivificadoras que el Espíritu realiza en el creyente individual, consideramos aquí su acción en la Iglesia. El Espíritu Santo descendió visiblemente en Pentecostés como lenguas de fuego, precedidas de un viento huracanado (Hech. 2: 2-3). La violencia del viento, cuyo sonido fue perceptible a todos, simbolizaba la potente, majestuosa y divina acción del Espíritu (recuérdese que *pneuma* significa también viento —cf. Jn. 3:5-8). Las «*lenguas...* como de *fuego,* asentándose *sobre* cada uno de ellos» (los discípulos), simbolizaban el poder transformador y vivificante (desde el interior) del Espíritu, que todo lo iba a penetrar, transformar y purificar —como el fuego—, y la eficacia de una *predicación* con poder, no en un estado de loca exaltación propio de la embriaguez física (v. 15), sino con la *sobria ebriedad* en que la pasión mística produce el éxtasis (versículo 17), antes de la proclamación del mensaje de alabanza en *lenguas,* haciéndose entender de todos (cosa muy diferente del hablar en lenguas *desconocidas*) y convirtiendo el Día de Pentecostés en el reverso del Día de Babel. Todo ello, hecho de una manera *consciente,* como lo indica el que las lenguas aparecieran *sobre* las cabezas, no *en* las mismas bocas. Que el fuego indicaba una renovación interior, una vitalidad espiritual, se muestra por la contraposición que Juan el Bautista hizo entre su bautismo de «agua», y el bautismo «en Espíritu y en fuego» que el Mesías venía a inaugurar (Mat. 3:11).

Ordinariamente se considera el Día de Pentecostés como el día del nacimiento de la Iglesia;[22] con todo, la comunidad de creyentes cristianos existía ya antes de ese Día (*cf.* Hech. 1:15). Juan 20:22 asocia la recepción del Espíritu con el Misterio Pascual.[23] Más rotundamente aún, Pablo hace de la Resurrección, o Misterio Pascual, el

---

22. V. la lección 7.ª.

23. Según algunos intérpretes, Jn. 19:30 asocia también la *transmisión* («parédoke») del Espíritu con la *expiración* de Jesús en la Cruz.

punto-clave por el que Cristo se constituye en «espíritu vivificante» (1.ª Cor. 15:45). Sin embargo, Pentecostés representa como la partida de nacimiento de la Iglesia, pues al descender visiblemente sobre ella, el Espíritu hace que la Iglesia realice una profunda «toma de conciencia» de sí misma y comience a testificar con poderes carismáticos; o sea, la Iglesia nace ese Día *en cuanto comunidad plenamente investida del poder de cumplir su misión en el mundo;* pero, así como la vida precede al *dar a luz,* el feto al niño, y la gestación al parto, así también el grupo del Aposento Alto poseía el Espíritu Santo en su seno: como individuos, desde su conversión; como grupo netamente cristiano, desde la Resurrección; como grupo consciente de su misión, desde Pentecostés.

Como el Espíritu sigue vivificando a la Iglesia después de Pentecostés, cada nuevo creyente es incorporado al Cuerpo de Cristo mediante «el bautismo del Espíritu». Por eso, el hecho de Pentecostés es irrepetible, ya que cierra una etapa previa. De ahí que, antes de ese Día, se completa el círculo cerrado de los Doce con la elección de Matías; pero ya no se sustituye a Santiago, martirizado después de Pentecostés.

El Espíritu también *libera* a la Iglesia, puesto que al darle vida *divina,* la saca de la esclavitud del mundo (1.ª Cor. 2:12 y ss.) y le confiere la verdadera libertad (2.ª Cor. 3:17), puesto que al hacerla un Cuerpo con Cristo y, con él, unirla a Dios, hasta ser «un espíritu con Él» (1.ª Cor. 6:17), es libre con la libertad de Dios que nos independiza de toda otra servidumbre.[24]

---

24. *Cf.* también Jn. 8:32, 36; Rom. 6:14-18; 7:4-6; 8:2-12; Gálatas 5:1, 13. Como decía nuestra Teresa de Avila: «Quien a Dios tiene, nada le falta; sólo Dios basta.» Y H. Küng añade (*The Church,* p. 152): «La libertad es un don, un don de Dios. La base y el origen de la libertad del hombre no está en el hombre mismo, sino en la libertad de Dios, en la libertad de Su gracia, que nos libera en Cristo.»

CUESTIONARIO:

1. ¿Por qué nombramos al Espíritu Santo en tercer lugar? — 2. ¿Cómo sabemos que se trata de una Persona divina, no de una fuerza? — 3. ¿Por qué decimos que el Espíritu Santo es como el alma de la Iglesia? — 4. ¿Qué símbolos encierra Hech. 2:2-3? — 5. ¿Qué representa Pentecostés para la Iglesia? — 6. ¿Cómo libera el Espíritu a la Iglesia?

LECCION 25.ª

EL ESPIRITU SANTO Y LA IGLESIA (II)

3. El Espíritu Santo y la actividad de la Iglesia.

A) EL ESPÍRITU GOBIERNA A LA IGLESIA. Y lo hace de una manera libre y soberana. Como advierte H. Küng,[25] el Espíritu *no* es la Iglesia, ni es el Espíritu *de la Iglesia*, sino de Dios. Por eso, el Espíritu obra donde, cuando y como quiere. No es la Iglesia la que *posee* el Espíritu, sino el Espíritu quien posee la Iglesia. El es enteramente *divino;* la Iglesia es en sí *humana*, aunque convocada y santificada por Dios. Por eso, es juntamente santa y pecadora: *comunión de los santos* y, al mismo tiempo, *comunidad de pecadores*. De ahí que nadie en la Iglesia puede arrogarse *autoridad* sobre el Espíritu ni sobre los nacidos del Espíritu. Por eso, el Nuevo Testamento nunca usa para indicar el ministerio específico los clásicos términos griegos *arkhé* (principado) o *timé* (dignidad), sino el más modesto de *diakonía* (servicio).[26]

B) EL ESPÍRITU DIRIGE LA ACCIÓN DE LA IGLESIA. Esto se manifiesta especialmente en el Libro de Hechos, con razón apellidado «Hechos del Espíritu Santo». En 1:4 y ss. es prometida la Venida ostentosa y poderosa del Espíritu, la cual tiene lugar para los judíos en el cap. 2 y para los gentiles en el cap. 10. Es cierto que en Mat. 28:18-20 el Señor había dado ya a la Iglesia el encargo de extender

---

25. *O. c.*, p. 173.
26. Para el tema de esta lección y de la anterior véase la magnífica exposición de H. Küng, *o. c.*, pp. 162-179.

el Evangelio, pero Su último mandato antes de la Ascensión fue no que «marcharan», sino que «no se fueran de Jerusalén» hasta que recibiesen *poder* mediante la Venida del Espíritu (Hech. 1:4, 8).

En todo momento, los apóstoles desempeñan su misión por el poder del Espíritu, y la aceptación del mensaje que predican va también acompañada, precedida o seguida de manifestación visible y carismática del Espíritu. El Espíritu dirige y controla la extensión del Evangelio. Como dice P. Tucker,[27] «al leer Hechos de los Apóstoles del principio al fin, he notado que no se encuentra allí ninguna decisión hecha por alguien situado en posición prominente para la extensión de la obra, sin una clara dirección y guía del Espíritu Santo». Esto nos muestra que el Espíritu Santo es el agente indispensable, insustituible, de todo verdadero evangelismo. Si nuestras campañas de evangelización no tienen en nuestros días el éxito apetecido, ello se debe a que no se concede al Espíritu el lugar que le compete en la extensión del Evangelio.

El Espíritu guía igualmente los movimientos de los predicadores (8:29, 39; 10:19 y ss.; 16:6 y ss.). El dirige a la iglesia de Antioquía en la separación de Pablo y Bernabé para la tarea misionera que se les encomienda (13:2 y ss.); ocupa el puesto de honor en las decisiones del concilio de Jerusalén (15:28); habla por medio de los profetas (11:28; 20:23; 21:4, 11); es el principal *testigo* de la verdad del Evangelio (5:32) y constituye a los pastores en su ministerio (20:28).[28]

C) EL ESPÍRITU SANTO HABITA EN LA IGLESIA COMO EN SU TEMPLO. La iglesia de Corinto, comunidad local que distaba mucho de ser perfecta, es llamada por Pablo «el templo de Dios en el cual habita el Espíritu de Dios» (1.ª Cor. 3:16). A pesar de todas sus debilidades, la Iglesia es la mansión peculiar del Dios tres veces Santo (1.ª Cor. 3:17; Ef. 2:17-22; 1.ª Ped. 2:5 y ss.). Uniendo

---

27. En *The Gospel Magazine,* sept. 1970, p. 416.
28. *Cf. The New Bible Dictionary,* p. 11.

dos metáforas, dice Pablo que la Iglesia es «un cuerpo que se edifica» (Ef. 4:16), ya que el mismo Espíritu que, como alma de la Iglesia, hace de ella un «cuerpo espiritual», la convierte, como divino huésped de ella, en un «templo espiritual», para que los creyentes, como «piedras vivas» y prescindiendo de cualquier lugar «santo», puedan adorar al Padre en espíritu y en verdad (Jn. 4:24).

D) EL ESPÍRITU DIRIGE EL CULTO DE LA IGLESIA. Por ser la Iglesia templo de Dios, el Espíritu Santo dirige también el culto, puesto que ese culto que se ofrece a Dios «en espíritu y en verdad» no es fruto de la actividad humana, sino de la acción del Espíritu. Por eso:

a) En Filip. 3:3 dice el original: «los que con el Espíritu de Dios adoramos». El apóstol rebate aquí a quienes querían rendir culto a Dios apoyados en ciertas observancias culturales judías, oponiéndose así a Juan 4:24.

b) Heb. 9:14 enseña igualmente que es el Espíritu Eterno quien purifica nuestras conciencias por la sangre de Cristo, para que podamos servir y dar a Dios el culto correcto («latréuein»).

c) Ef. 2:18 nos muestra cómo nuestro culto y el confiado acceso al trono de la gracia (cf. Heb. 4:16) tiene una dimensión trinitaria, puesto que nos acercamos al Padre a través del Hijo por el Espíritu.[29]

d) Finalmente, el Espíritu nos ayuda y enseña a orar. Efesios 6:18 muestra que la oración eficaz ha de ser hecha «en el Espíritu». Romanos 8:26-27 nos dice que el Espíritu nos ayuda para que oremos como conviene —sintonizando con la voluntad del Omnipotente—. 1.ª Corintios 12:3 asegura que ni siquiera se puede nombrar debidamente a Jesús como Señor «sino por el Espíritu Santo».

---

29. Podríamos decir que, en nuestro culto oracional, entendido como una audiencia que Dios nos concede, el Padre es quien *recibe* en audiencia, el Hijo —Jesús— es la *puerta*, y el Espíritu es como el *ujier* o encargado de introducirnos en la cámara divina (V. Paul Tucker, en *The Gospel Magazine*, n. c., p. 415).

4.   El Espíritu Santo y la comunión eclesial.

El Espíritu que habita en cada creyente es el mismo que habita en la Iglesia, haciendo de ella una comunidad de creyentes cristianos y, por ello, el creyente es *miembro* de la Iglesia. De ahí que —conviene repetirlo— el Nuevo Testamento no conoce un Cristianismo individualista, sino *esencialmente* comunitario. Esto se muestra en el uso que Hechos y las Epístolas hacen del vocablo *koinonia* = comunión. La etimología de esta palabra parece sugerir participación en un mismo «munus»;[30] así, el sentido del vocablo, tanto en latín como en castellano, etc., se ha extendido a todo aquello que es *común* a varios, que se aplica a varios o en lo que varios intervienen. La palabra *comunión* (y su derivada *comunicación*) ha venido a ser sinónima de *participación;* sin embargo, la etimología de ambas ofrece una variedad digna de ser tenida en cuenta. En efecto, *participar* indica que cada uno toma una *parte* de un objeto, el cual se divide al repartirse; en cambio, *comunicar* es hacer extensivo a otros algo que, al impartirse, no se divide, sino que permanece íntegro en todos aquellos que lo reciben. Así, el amor del Padre, la gracia de Jesucristo, el poder del Espíritu, la salvación adquirida, y todas las demás bendiciones celestiales, son bienes divinos de los que todos los creyentes disfrutamos *en común*, sin que se fraccionen al recibirlos y sin que mengüen al aumentar el número de beneficiarios. Este disfrute en común de los mismos bienes divinos es el elemento aglutinante de la unidad de la Iglesia. En efecto:

A)   EL ESPÍRITU SANTO ESTABLECE LA COMUNIÓN ECLESIAL. Esta *comunión* es atribuida al Espíritu en la bendición final de 2.ª Cor. 13:14. En 1.ª Cor. 12:13 se dice que todos los creyentes «hemos bebido de un mismo Espíritu». Efesios 4:3 habla de «guardar la unidad del Espíritu en el vínculo de la paz», o sea, en el lazo que es la paz. Esa

---

30.   «Comunión» viene, según F. Díez Mateo, de «com-munus» = = participación en un mismo *don* o *cargo*.

paz es consecuencia del amor, humildad, mansedumbre y mutuo soportarnos los unos a los otros (v. 2), y es esencial a la comunión eclesial, como fruto y manifestación de la presencia del Espíritu (*cf.* Gál. 5:22).[31] Por ser el Espíritu Santo como el lazo o vínculo de amor personal entre el Padre y el Hijo, la comunión que se establece entre el creyente y las personas divinas implica necesariamente la acción amorosa y unitiva del Espíritu; de tal manera que, aun en aquellos pasajes que no mencionan explícitamente al Espíritu, es obvia la referencia implícita a Su persona (*cf.* Jn. 17:21; 1.º Jn. 1:3 —en ambos lugares el vínculo de *comunión* es el Espíritu—).

Por otra parte, el Espíritu actúa especialmente a través de la *comunidad: a)* lanzando a la Iglesia al cumplimiento de la gran comisión que ha recibido (Hech. 1:8; 13:2); *b)* enseñando en común a *toda* la Iglesia, no sólo a una «jerarquía» (Hech. 15:23, 28), puesto que la acción del Espíritu se ejerce sobre los «congregados en *uno*» (v. 25); *c)* dando un poder extraordinario a la oración comunitaria (*cf.* Hech. 2:1 y ss.; 4:31).

B) EL ESPÍRITU SANTO PRODUCE LA UNIDAD DE LA IGLESIA. Recordemos que la Iglesia es algo *más* que un grupo de creyentes que se reúnen en un lugar por tener los mismos gustos, ideas, intereses, etc. Los creyentes forman *iglesia, una* iglesia, por la recíproca comunión que los vincula al Señor Jesucristo mediante la acción del Espíritu Santo (2.ª Cor. 13:14; Filip. 2:1). Tanto la comunión eclesial como la *unidad* que ella implica, son producto del Espíritu Santo, no del esfuerzo humano. Hoy se habla mucho de Ecumenismo y de esfuerzo por la reunión de los cristianos, pero se olvidan a menudo dos conceptos bíblicos de suma importancia: 1.º, que la unidad sólo puede ser producida por el Espíritu de Dios; 2.º, que esta unidad se realiza automáticamente por la comunicación de todos los creyentes verdaderos en unos mismos vínculos de unidad, garantizados en el «nuevo nacimiento» de una persona;

---

31. V. Ch. Hodge, *Ephesians*, pp. 201-202.

por eso, el apóstol no exhorta a *realizarla*, sino a *guardarla* y a *perfeccionarla* (Ef. 4:3, 13). Aparte de esto, lo único que el hombre suele hacer es ponerla en peligro con sus fallos y pecados y quebrarla visiblemente con divisiones y cismas, aunque la íntima esencia de esta unidad es irrompible.

CUESTIONARIO:

1. ¿Puede la Iglesia, o alguien en ella, acaparar *el Espíritu?* — 2. *¿Cómo dirige el Espíritu la acción de la Iglesia?* — 3. *¿Cómo habita el Espíritu en la Iglesia?* — 4. *¿Quién y cómo dirige el culto de la Iglesia?* — 5. *¿Qué significa el vocablo* comunión *aplicado a la Iglesia?* — 6. *¿Cómo se establece la comunión eclesial?* — 7. *¿Quién* hace *la unidad de la Iglesia?*

LECCION 26.ª

EL ESPIRITU SANTO Y LA IGLESIA (III)

5. El Espíritu Santo y los dones en la Iglesia:

A) EL ESPÍRITU SANTO, SUPREMO DON. El Espíritu Santo es llamado en el Nuevo Testamento el *don* (o dádiva) de Dios por excelencia (Jn. 4:10; 7:37-39; Hech. 2:30; 8:20; 10:45; 11:16-17) y el *Dador* de los dones (Rom. 5:5; 1.ª Corintios 12:4). Siendo el Espíritu Santo el Amor personal de Dios, podemos decir que Dios nos da Su Amor o Su «Corazón» antes de darnos cualquier otro don; así se entiende por qué el «*amó Dios*» va delante del «*entregó a Su Hijo Unigénito*» en Jn. 3:16. Como escribe Tomás de Aquino, todo buen dador da por delante su amor; tanto que, si se sospecha en la dádiva un motivo egoísta por parte del dador, en seguida despreciamos el regalo mismo y al que nos lo ofrece. Pero Dios está infinitamente lejos de tan bastardo motivo, ya que en Dios resulta absolutamente imposible el egoísmo, por ser infinitamente rico y no poder acrecentar, por tanto, su haber con lo que otros puedan darle. Más aún, el amor que Dios nos tiene, parte siempre de nuestro *cero;* mejor dicho, de nuestro gran *déficit* (Rom. 5:8). Este pensamiento nos hará apreciar mejor el don de Dios.

B) EL ESPÍRITU SANTO Y LOS DONES. El Espíritu Santo es el distribuidor de los dones en la Iglesia (1.ª Cor. 12:4, 7-13). Aunque estos dones son dados a *personas,* con todo se dan en un contexto eclesial y para el servicio, edificación y promoción misional de la Iglesia; de manera que tales personas no marchan solas con sus dones a cuestas, sino que ejercitan estos dones *dentro* de la iglesia, como *miembros* de la misma. Es el Espíritu quien da *dones* a los hombres, mientras que Cristo da *hombres* (ministros) a Su Iglesia.[32] La *kharis = gracia,* que en el contexto del Nuevo Testamento suele significar *favor* (*cf.* Ef. 2:8) o *poder* (*cf.* 2.ª Cor. 2:19) divinos en beneficio propio del creyente, puede también significar un *don* —poder— al servicio de la comunidad (Ef. 4:7, 11). Cuando este don comporta la visible y extraordinaria manifestación de un *khárisma,* no es, por sí solo, garantía de una mayor espiritualidad por parte del individuo o la comunidad que lo reciben, como puede verse por la primitiva comunidad local de Corinto, en la que, a pesar de sus muchos fallos, no faltaba ninguno de los *carismas.* El hecho mismo de que estos dones o carismas se impartan, no para directa exaltación del individuo mismo que los recibe, sino para servicio y edificación de la iglesia, elimina la ocasión de celos o envidia.

Hay que distinguir entre los *dones* y el *fruto* del Espíritu Santo. En Gál. 5:22-23 encontramos nueve aspectos de ese *fruto,* que afectan a la personalidad entera del cristiano y, por tanto, deben reflejarse en la conducta de cada creyente, mientras que 1.ª Cor. 12:8-10 presenta nueve dones que no modifican nuestra personalidad interna, sino que nos equipan para determinados servicios y ministerios en bien de la iglesia local, en la cual unos tienen un don y otros tienen otro. Estas dos series de gracias distintas corresponden a la división que, con terminología no muy feliz, estableció la Teología Romana del Medievo, entre «gracia que hace grato» y «gracia dada gratis», puesto que toda gracia es, por definición, *gratis* o gratuita.[33]

C) CARISMAS ORDINARIOS Y EXTRAORDINARIOS. El griego *khárisma* suele expresar, indistintamente, los dones al servicio de la comunidad, los cuales comportan tanto los mi-

32. Según la frase feliz de W. Nee en *La Iglesia normal,* p. 25.
33. V. mi libro *Catolicismo Romano,* p. 140.

nisterios ordinarios de predicar, enseñar, etc., como los extraordinarios de profetizar, hablar en lenguas, curar sobrenaturalmente, etc. (1.ª Cor. 12:28-31). Es evidente por Hech. 2:4 y ss. que los primeros discípulos, *en general*, fueron investidos por el Espíritu Santo de dones extraordinarios. ¿Eran estos carismas dones peculiares de los primeros cristianos, en orden a la rápida plantación e irrigación de la primitiva Iglesia, como manifestación notoria de la gran irrupción del Espíritu, como muchos piensan? Marcos 16:17-18 parece indicar lo contrario. No negamos que el nacimiento de la Iglesia comportase una mayor abundancia de tales carismas, pero habría que preguntarse si el hecho de que tales maravillas no sean hoy frecuentes no se deberá a que nuestra *fe* no es lo suficientemente fuerte como para trasladar montañas (1.ª Corintios 13:2, como un eco de Mat. 17:20; Marc. 11:23; Lucas 11:1; 17:6; Jn. 14:13-14). La fe que obra maravillas requiere, ante todo, *una perfecta sintonía con el poder de Dios*. Santiago 1:5-7 nos enseña cuál ha de ser nuestra fe; en 4:3-10, la pureza que ha de acompañar a la fe; y en 5:15-18, la eficacia milagrosa de tal fe. Si no hacemos maravillas, es porque nuestra fe es falsa o débil. Los grandes santos, como Pablo en el siglo I y Jorge Muller en el XIX, cuya fe en la oración era pura, perfecta y confiada, obtenían resultados que a nosotros se nos antojan imposibles. Quizás hemos perdido la fórmula: fe firme, dedicación absoluta, profunda humildad y exquisita pureza.

D) EL DON DE LENGUAS. Entre los dones de 1.ª Cor. 12 y 14 destaca, por la frecuencia de las referencias y el énfasis que en él ponen los Pentecostales, el *don de lenguas*. Hay que distinguir dos especies de tal don, según el contexto: *a*) lenguas *extranjeras*, inteligibles para los nativos de los países respectivos. Este es el caso de Hechos 2:4-8, 11. Luego viene el discurso de Pedro (versículos 14 y ss.) en arameo o, según piensan otros, en el griego común o *koiné*.[34] Este fenómeno, que marca la nueva era

---

34. V. P. Tucker, *The Gospel Magazine*, Novemb. 1970, p. 521.

de la predicación del mensaje a los judíos, se repite en la predicación a los primeros gentiles (Hech. 10:45-46, comp. con 11:17) y en el perfeccionamiento de los efesios de Hech. 19:6; b) lenguas *desconocidas*, que requieren interpretación profética (1.ª Cor. 14:19, 23) y que, más que en un lenguaje sistematizado, consistían en expresiones extáticas y enigmáticas, sólo inteligibles para el Espíritu Santo. Hech. 8:12-17 y 1.ª Cor. 12:29-30 implican que este don de lenguas no lo tenían todos, a pesar de su parigual membresía. Más aún, Pablo tiene por niñería el sobreestimar tal don (1.ª Cor. 14:20) e impone condiciones que controlen su uso (vv. 27-34). Lloyd-Jones ve en ello una muestra de exuberancia que hay que controlar para que no se desborde:

«el gran problema era el problema del control y de la disciplina. Y, con todo, ésta es la gloria de la vida en el Espíritu: que puedan coexistir la vitalidad y el control al mismo tiempo. No hay en ello tumulto, no hay exceso, sino este divino orden —la vida que se protege a sí misma para la gloria de Dios».[35]

E) EL CARISMA DE INTERPRETACIÓN DE LA ESCRITURA. La agencia que el Espíritu usa para edificar e incrementar la Iglesia es la Palabra de Dios. «Toda la Escritura es *expirada por Dios*» (*theópneustos*) —dice Pablo en 2.ª Timoteo 3:16—. Y el apóstol Pedro, refiriéndose a los redactores humanos de la Escritura, dice que «hablaron siendo inspirados por el Espíritu Santo» (2.ª Ped. 1:21). Y el mismo Espíritu que inspiró la Biblia es el único intérprete autorizado de la misma.[36] En Jn. 14:26; 16:13, Cristo prometió a Sus discípulos que el Espíritu les enseñaría y recordaría todas las cosas que el mismo Señor había dicho, a fin de que, tras la visible Descensión del Espíritu en

---

35. En *Qué es la Iglesia*, p. 27.
36. Para todo este punto ver J. Grau, *Introducción a la Teología*, lecciones 33.ª y ss.

Pentecostés, pudiesen predicar fielmente el mensaje del Evangelio y, después, ponerlo por escrito inspirados por el mismo Espíritu, de modo que nos fuese transmitido sin pérdida ni adulteración.

¿Quién posee el carisma del Espíritu para interpretar auténticamente la Escritura? Este es un punto en que la Reforma hubo de situarse claramente frente a la Iglesia oficial, defendiendo el derecho y el deber de cada creyente a inquirir, mediante el estudio, la meditación y la plegaria, el recto sentido que el Espíritu Santo ha inspirado, para nuestra edificación, en la S. Biblia. Que la jerarquía de Roma no ha abandonado la pretensión de ser la única intérprete válida de la Biblia lo muestran las siguientes afirmaciones formuladas por Pablo VI en su mensaje con ocasión del 5.º aniversario de la clausura del Vaticano II (documento firmado el 8-12-1970 y hecho público el 6-1-1971):

> «Por necesaria que sea la función de los teólogos, no es a los sabios a quienes Dios ha confiado la misión de interpretar auténticamente la fe de la Iglesia: esta fe descansa en la vida de un pueblo, cuyos responsables ante Dios son los obispos. A ellos corresponde decir a ese pueblo lo que Dios le exige creer... Porque es a nosotros, obispos, a quienes se dirige la exhortación de Pablo a Timoteo: "Te conjuro delante de Dios, etc." (2.ª Timoteo 4:1-4).» [37]

Dejando para más adelante el problema que presenta el magisterio en la Iglesia, así como la aclaración de la antinomia: «Iglesia institucional - Iglesia carismática», podemos adelantar lo siguiente:

a) Juan afirma (1.º Jn. 2:20, 27), dirigiéndose a los fieles en común, que ellos poseen «la unción del Santo»,

---

37. V. también cómo interpreta el C. Vaticano II Luc. 10:16 en su *Constitución Dogmática sobre la Iglesia*, al final del punto 20.

o sea, el Espíritu de Cristo, y conocen «todas las cosas», de modo que no tienen necesidad de que nadie les enseñe, tratándoles como «no iniciados» a quienes fácilmente se puede engañar. En verdad, todos los fieles poseen este carisma profético (1.ª Ped. 2:9), por el cual Timoteo había sido hecho *sabio* mediante el estudio constante de las Escrituras (2.ª Tim. 3:14-15), en las que había sido instruido desde su niñez, no por una «jerarquía», sino por su madre y por su abuela.[38]

b) El «libre examen» significa que el creyente puede encontrar por sí mismo, mediante el Espíritu que en él mora, el recto sentido de la Escritura y, por tanto, de la *fe* cristiana. Ello no significa que cada fiel disponga de una especie de «hilo directo» con el Espíritu, de modo que, con la simple lectura de un pasaje, sea iluminado sobrenaturalmente para conocer el recto sentido literal del texto, pues esto haría infalibles a los creyentes (y a las iglesias), lo cual negamos en redondo, sino que, con la luz del Espíritu, el estudio constante, humilde y orante de la Biblia (especialmente cuando se hace en común, o sea, *eclesialmente*) sirve «para hacernos sabios para la salvación..., enteramente equipados para toda obra buena» (2.ª Tim. 3:15-17). Ello no hace superfluo el ministerio pastoral, don del Espíritu «para perfeccionamiento de los santos» (Ef. 4:11-12); de lo contrario, la misma Epístola de Juan sería superflua; pero la diferencia radical entre Roma y la Reforma está en que, mientras las definiciones dogmáticas de la jerarquía de Roma no admiten apelación alguna a la Palabra de Dios, en cualquier iglesia realmente reformada, un simple fiel conocedor de la Palabra, y guiado por el Espíritu, puede llamar la atención a su propio pastor, si éste se desvía notoriamente de la ortodoxia, aunque tal pastor se llame «Arzobispo de Canterbury».[39]

---

38. En cuanto a la recta interpretación de 2.ª Ped. 1:20, que podría objetársenos, *cf.* J. Grau, *Introducción a la Teología*, lección 34.ª.

39. V. el Artículo XX de Religión de la Iglesia Anglicana.

c) Permítansenos dos breves apostillas al párrafo citado del discurso de Pablo VI: 1.ª, si por «teólogo» entendemos un *exégeta* competente, diremos que sólo un pastor *sabio* (el de 2.ª Tim. 3:15, no el de 1.ª Cor. 1:26) puede alimentar y guiar espiritualmente a su congregación; por eso, Ef. 4:11 habla de «pastores y maestros» como de dos servicios de *un* mismo ministerio. 2.ª, la función del pastor no es imponer a la congregación «lo que ha de creer», sino edificarla mediante la predicación de la Palabra, sabiendo que no es él quien da autoridad (por poseer un carisma *institucional*) a una cierta interpretación de la Palabra, sino quien recibe de la Palabra (por carisma *ministerial*) el encargo de exponerla *fielmente,* aunque nunca *infaliblemente.* NO HAY MAS AUTORIDAD INFALIBLE QUE LA MISMA PALABRA DE DIOS.[40]

CUESTIONARIO:

1. ¿Cuál es el Don de Dios por antonomasia? — 2. ¿Quién da los dones a la Iglesia? — 3. ¿Cuántas clases de dones distingue el Nuevo Testamento? — 4. ¿En qué se distinguen los dones del fruto del Espíritu? — 5. ¿Se acabó ya el tiempo de los carismas extraordinarios? — 6. ¿Qué distinciones y observaciones son precisas al hablar del don de lenguas? — 7. ¿Quién tiene el carisma de interpretación de la Escritura?

---

40. V. el libro del obispo católico F. Simons, *Infalibilidad y Evidencia* (Edic. Ariel, Esplugues de Llobregat, Barcelona, 1970).

Quinta parte

El ministerio
en la Iglesia

LECCION 27.ª CONCEPTO DE MINISTERIO

Llegamos ahora a la parte más delicada y discutida de este volumen. Si lo que ahora vamos a tratar es bien estudiado y entendido, se habrá dado un gran paso hacia la comprensión del *misterio* de la Iglesia, así como hacia una clara toma de posición frente a las diferencias denominacionales y al diálogo ecuménico.

1. Noción de ministerio.

La palabra «ministerio» indica la función del «ministro». Este vocablo se deriva del latín *minister*, que los antiguos romanos oponían a *magister*,[1] pues mientras el término *magister* era aplicado a los encargados de administrar justicia (los *magistrados*) y se les atribuía un *magis* = más que los demás (en competencia y honestidad),[2] el término *minister* suponía un *minus* = menos que las «autoridades» (al servicio de ellas), como lo demuestra el término «menestral» con que fue en seguida vertido al romance.[3] En este sentido, *ministro* equivale a criado o persona al servicio de otra u otras.

---

1. V. J. Ortega y Gasset, *Una interpretación de la Historia Universal* (Madrid, Revista de Occidente, 1966), p. 100.

2. En el pueblo judío esta función noble pertenecía a los jueces, a quienes la Biblia llama *dioses* por participar de la función —estrictamente divina— de juzgar a los demás (comp. Mat. 7:1 y ss. con Sal. 82:6; Jn. 10:34-35).

3. En oposición al «magister» —magistrado y maestro—, al que se le reconocía un «magis» = más, el «minister» era el «servidor o criado», o sea que, en realidad, al *ministro* se le adjudica un «minus» = menos (V. *Oxford Dictionary*), puesto que, en una democracia (o en una teo-democracia), el ministro es un servidor del pueblo, representado en sus «magistrados».

2. Uso bíblico del término "ministro".

El término *ministro* tiene ya en el Antiguo Testamento una cadencia similar a la del uso latino, lo cual ha de ser tenido en cuenta al hablar de ministerio en la Iglesia. El término hebreo «*mesharét*» expresa normalmente el servicio en el templo y, por eso, la versión de los LXX lo vertió por «*leiturgós*» (de donde viene *liturgia*), que significa alguien que está al cargo de un servicio público. Los elementos mismos son llamados «ministros» de Dios en el Sal. 104:4 (Heb. 1:7 lo acomoda a los ángeles). En un sentido más general, son llamados *mesharét* los inmediatos servidores de un prominente personaje bíblico (*cf.* Exodo 24:13; Jos. 1:1), con lo que empalmamos con el sentido etimológico, arriba apuntado, del vocablo *ministro*.

El Nuevo Testamento usa preferentemente el término *diákonos* = servidor, que se emplea primero en sentido general (*cf.* Filip. 1:1) y luego en sentido técnico, o sea, específico para designar un oficio determinado dentro de la iglesia (diácono). El uso del término *diákonos* (Mateo 20:26; Marc. 10:43; Luc. 22:27 —*ho diakonôn*, aplicado a Cristo, así como en Rom. 15:8) para indicar que aun el más alto de los ministerios eclesiales debe ser un acto de servicio a la comunidad, ilumina esplendorosamente el verdadero papel del ministerio cristiano (*cf.* 1.ª Cor. 3:5; 2.ª Cor. 3:6; 6:4; 11:23; Ef. 3:7; 6:21; Col. 1:7, 23, 25; 4:7; 1.ª Tes. 3:2; 1.ª Tim. 4:6). La humildad aneja a este servicio cobra aún mayor énfasis con la sinonimia del vocablo «*dúlos*» = esclavo, que Pablo aplica a Cristo («tomando la forma de un esclavo» —Filip. 2:7—) y luego a los apóstoles y a sus cooperadores (Rom. 1:1; Gál. 1:10; Col. 4:12; Tito 1:1. *Cf.* Sant. 1:1 y 2.ª Ped. 1:1).

Otro vocablo griego sinónimo es «*hyperétes*», que indica el oficio de un remero de galeras subordinado al comandante de la nave (comp. con Hech. 13:5) y que corresponde al hebreo *hazzán*, que designaba al guardián de los rollos de la Ley en la sinagoga (Luc. 4:20). Lucas 1:2 lo usa para el ministerio de la Palabra, y el apóstol Pablo se lo apropia a sí mismo en Hech. 26:16; 1.ª Cor. 4:1.

Finalmente, el Nuevo Testamento usa también el término «leiturgós» para expresar el carácter *sacral* del ministerio, no sólo como servicio a la Iglesia, sino como culto al Señor (Hech. 13:2; Rom. 13:6; 15:16, 27; Filip. 2:25; Heb. 1:14; 8:2).

Dentro de un contexto típicamente trinitario, Pablo dice que el *Espíritu* imparte los dones o *carismas,* mediante los cuales podemos ejercitar los ministerios o *diaconías* del *Señor* (Jesucristo), siendo *Dios* (Padre) quien, como fuente primera de la vida y de la acción («enérgeia» o «energémata» = operaciones concretas), «obra todo en todos» (1.ª Cor. 12:4-6). Por este texto vemos que todo ministerio eclesial puede definirse como *un servicio para provecho de la Iglesia* (v. 7), *que se ejercita en virtud del don que el sujeto recibe conforme a la medida que el Espíritu distribuye a cada uno de los miembros de iglesia* (V. todo el contexto post. y Rom. 12; Ef. 4:7 y ss.).

3. Ministerios y oficios.

Es preciso distinguir cuidadosamente entre *ministerio* y *oficio.* El primero se ejercita en virtud del don que sólo el Espíritu concede (aunque la iglesia ha de discernirlo y reconocerlo), mientras que el oficio se desempeña en virtud de un nombramiento o designación. El ministerio es un servicio para crecimiento y edificación del *organismo* o Cuerpo de Cristo; el oficio está para el buen orden de la *organización* eclesial. El ministerio tiende al bien *universal* de la Iglesia, aunque sea susceptible de localización en muchos aspectos; el oficio emerge del mismo concepto de iglesia *local,* aunque puede trascender los límites de una localidad (salva la independencia de las iglesias locales).

Ambos (ministerio y oficio) pueden darse, según *diversos* aspectos, en una misma persona. Así, v. gr., Felipe era *diácono* (por oficio) de la iglesia de Jerusalén (Hechos 6:5) y *evangelista* (por ministerio) más allá de Jerusalén (Hech. 8:5, 26; 21:8);[4] Pedro era, por ministerio, *apóstol* (Hech. 1:22; 1.ª Ped. 1:1; 2.ª Ped. 1:1), pero era también, por oficio, *anciano* («presbyteros» —1.ª Ped. 5:1—) y así daba su informe y parecer a la iglesia de Jerusalén (Hech. 11:2 y ss.; 15:7 y ss.); Pablo era igualmente apóstol por designación *ministerial* de Dios (Gál. 1:1, 11), pero ejercía también el oficio de *maestro* en la iglesia de Antioquía (Hech. 13:1), de la que era enviado y a la que regresaba con el informe de sus viajes misioneros (Hechos 13:2-3; 14:26-27). Juan era asimismo, por ministerio, uno de los *Doce* y, por oficio, *anciano* de Efeso cuando escribía sus Epístolas 2.ª y 3.ª.

4. Ministerio común y ministerio específico.

El ministerio en la Iglesia se divide en *común y específico*. *Común* es el que cada miembro de iglesia ejercita de acuerdo con el don o dones que ha recibido del Espíritu y que han sido discernidos y reconocidos por la iglesia. *Específico* (por así designarlo, ya que cada distinto ministerio es «específico») es el que se ejercita en la predicación y enseñanza de la Palabra, por lo que se llama también «ministerio de la Palabra». De alguien que estudia en un Colegio o Seminario bíblico-teológico decimos que se prepara para el «ministerio». En la lección siguiente veremos la interrelación entre el ministerio específico y el común.

5. Concepto de ministerio en la Iglesia de Roma.

El ministerio específico es tenido en la Iglesia de Roma como una casta aparte, jerárquicamente institucionalizada y provista de cierto poder mediador con su carisma corres-

---

4. Aunque nunca desvinculado de su iglesia o incontrolado (¡Hechos 8:14 y ss.!).
5. Véase también mi libro *Catolicismo Romano*, lecciones 4 y 5.

pondiente, que garantiza su normal funcionamiento. Este poder es triple: *a)* de gobernar a los súbditos y dar leyes, pudiendo excomulgar a los contumaces; *b)* de enseñar (*infaliblemente,* en las condiciones determinadas por el Vaticano I), exigiendo fe o asentimiento respetuoso, según los casos, en todo lo tocante a la fe y costumbres; *c)* de regenerar espiritualmente y santificar mediante los sacramentos. Los jerarcas representan (vicariedad) a Jesucristo ante los fieles. Por eso, el Vaticano II cita [6] Lucas 10:16 en su favor, como si tal pasaje estuviese dirigido *sólo* a los *Doce* (de los que los obispos pretenden ser sucesores) y connotase un carisma de infalibilidad en la transmisión del mensaje. La diferencia *esencial,* y no sólo de grado, que la Iglesia de Roma sostiene, aun después del Vaticano II,[7] entre el sacerdocio común de los fieles y el sacerdocio ministerial o jerárquico, establece una separación de castas en los tres planos del ministerio: 1) en lo *profético,* distinguiendo entre la *ecclesia docens* o iglesia que enseña, y *ecclesia discens* o iglesia que aprende; 2) en lo *cultual,* distinguiendo entre *clérigos* y *laicos,* según el distinto nivel específico de *consagración* y aplicando el término técnico *hiereús* = sacerdote, a un grupo aparte dentro de la comunidad, aplicando además el término «pontífice» a los obispos (equivalente al «archiereús» de Hebreos —aplicado allí a Cristo—) y el de «sumo pontífice» al Papa u obispo de Roma; 3) en lo *regio* o gubernativo, estableciendo la llamada «jerarquía de jurisdicción», por la que el Papa es el Jefe supremo de la Iglesia, y los obispos son los jefes diocesanos, subordinados al Papa, siendo simples *súbditos* todos los demás fieles (incluyendo los simples sacerdotes o de 2.º orden).

En cambio, entre los evangélicos, el ministerio específico está considerado como un servicio peculiar, reconocido por la comunidad, para el que se ha recibido el don

6. *Constitución Dogmática sobre la Iglesia,* p. 20, al final, y 21, al final.

7. *Ibid.,* p. 10.

y el llamamiento correspondientes. Este servicio consiste en confrontar directamente (sin mediación) con Jesucristo al individuo no regenerado, o al miembro de iglesia, y diciéndole como el Bautista: «He ahí el Cordero de Dios, que quita el pecado del mundo» (Jn. 1:29). Así el ministro de Dios no se interfiere en el camino de la salvación ni ejerce una mediación que estimamos antibíblica, sino que, en vez de convertirse en centro de atracción (culto a la personalidad),[8] desaparece y mengua para que sólo Cristo crezca (Jn. 3:30): «Le oyeron (a Juan) y siguieron a Jesús» (Jn. 1:33). Así es como, por Jesucristo y en El, la iglesia entera es una comunidad de reyes, sacerdotes y profetas (1.ª Ped. 2:9-10), sin que ningún individuo dentro de tal Cuerpo pueda llamarse «pontífice», «sacerdote», «clérigo», etcétera, en sentido de casta aparte. Efectivamente, el Nuevo Testamento reserva exclusivamente a Cristo los vocablos técnicos *archiereús* = sumo sacerdote, y *hiereús* = = sacerdote, mientras que los oficios de la iglesia reciben nombres como *episkopos* = supervisor, *presbyteros* = anciano, *poimén* = pastor, *diákonos* = servidor, y *proestôn* = = presidente, que no se refieren en modo alguno al ejercicio de una jurisdicción o a la celebración de un sacrificio. También es curioso notar que el Nuevo Testamento no sólo desconoce la división en *clérigos* y *laicos* como dos castas distintas, sino que a *todo el pueblo de Dios* (el *«laós* Theû» —de donde viene *laico*— de 1.ª Ped. 2:9-10) le llama *«klerôn»* (heredades del Señor» —1.ª Ped. 5:3—), o sea, lotes de la grey *de Dios* (v. 2), no de los pastores, como si éstos pudieran enseñorearse («katakyrieúontes») de ella. Por tanto, tales pastores o presbíteros no son una casta o *clero*

---

8. Se suele replicar que dicha personalidad es sólo *representativa*, pero lo cierto es que fácilmente se margina la representatividad en aras de la propia estimación, y así tenemos el «culto a la personalidad». Recordamos la anécdota de cierto abad de un monasterio que solía repetir: «vuestro abad que indignamente os preside». Todo fue bien hasta que un inocente novicio, al aludirle, dijo: «y nuestro abad, que indignamente nos preside...». Ello bastó para que la aparente humildad se tornase orgullosa cólera.

peculiar, distinto y distante de las ovejas, sino que son precisamente las ovejas las que —según el apóstol Pedro— forman el *clero*, y no los pastores (aunque, naturalmente, también ellos —si han *nacido de nuevo*— forman parte de la heredad).

En efecto, la organización de la Iglesia de Cristo no es en forma *piramidal*, con alguien en la cúspide encargado de enseñar infaliblemente, de mandar inapelablemente y de oficiar cultualmente por sí solo en lo más sustancial del oficio sacerdotal, mientras los demás se limitan a escuchar, obedecer, rezar calladamente y pagar religiosamente.[9] Si la Iglesia es el Cuerpo de Cristo, *todos* los miembros tienen en ella su función específica, sus dones que ejercitar, sus servicios que realizar. En otras palabras, la iglesia en sí es una construcción *horizontal*, donde las distintas posiciones indican *diferencia* de ministerios y funciones, pero no *jerarquía* de unos *sobre* otros; es decir, Cristo distribuye, por Su Espíritu, los dones que descienden a la comunidad, *de la que emergen los ministerios específicos con sus dones anejos.* ES CIERTO QUE UN CREYENTE NO ES INVESTIDO DEL DON NI LLAMADO AL MINISTERIO POR LA COMUNIDAD, SINO POR EL ESPIRITU; PERO SU DON Y SU LLAMAMIENTO HAN DE SER DISCERNIDOS, RECONOCIDOS Y ACEPTADOS POR LA COMUNIDAD. También es menester tener presente que los *dones* que capacitan para un ministerio específico no tienen por qué ser, de suyo, *vitalicios.*[10]

---

9. Así definió, en la primera sesión del C. Vaticano II, el obispo de Metz la función tradicional de los seglares en la Iglesia de Roma.

10. El escalafón burocrático que tradicionalmente ha comportado el concepto de ministerio en la Iglesia de Roma, ha servido para distorsionar su funcionalidad, con perjuicio de un verdadero servicio a la comunidad, *estatificando* las estructuras y *fijando*, de por vida, los oficios. Resulta refrescante leer lo que dice R. Laurentin en la revista *Concilium* (n.º 80, p. 452): «La lección primera y capital es que los ministerios del Nuevo Testamento son funcionales; su fin

6. Ministerios ordinarios y extraordinarios.

Siendo el ministerio el ejercicio de un don o carisma, se sigue que un ministerio será ordinario o extraordinario según que el carisma sea lo uno o lo otro. Sin entrar en discusiones sobre el condicionamiento (Rom. 12:3) y la perduración de los dones extraordinarios, diremos que se pueden tener por *ordinarios* los ministerios que se hallan fácilmente en la Iglesia de todos los tiempos, porque no desbordan el cauce ordinario por el que el Señor provee a las necesidades de Su Iglesia, como son los presentados en 1.ª Cor. 12:8-9 (discutible el último), mientras que pueden llamarse *extraordinarios* los presentados en el versículo siguiente: don de milagros, de lenguas, de interpretación, etc., que resultaban ordinarios en el tiempo fundacional de la Iglesia y, en cambio, son excepcionales en nuestros tiempos, quizás —como ya dijimos en otra lección— porque nos falta la fe de un Jorge Muller, por ejemplo.

También pueden llamarse extraordinarios los ministerios que sirvieron para echar los fundamentos de la Iglesia, como son los de los *apóstoles* y *profetas* (no simplemente como ejercicio ocasional del don de profecía, sino como ministerio profético específico), los cuales eran irrepetibles y no admitían *sucesión* (Ef. 2:20; Apoc. 21:14).

---

es el servicio de la comunidad, y no han de determinarse por los imperativos internos de una máquina burocrática. Según el ejemplo del Nuevo Testamento, las finalidades prevalecen sobre las reglas *a priori*, los impulsos del Espíritu sobre las conveniencias administrativas, si bien es verdad que esos impulsos del Espíritu en materia de ministerios exigen una regulación, como lo demuestra Pablo al intervenir en Corinto (1.ª Cor. 11-14). No se trata, por consiguiente, de eliminar la autoridad ni de impedir que sea ejercida en nombre de Cristo, sino de situarla, ante todo, en función de la fe que estructura las comunidades desde dentro, a imagen de la vida orgánica.» V. también en el mismo número de la misma revista el artículo de M. Houdijk (pp. 573-583, espec. p. 581, párrafo 2, líns. 10-20).

7. Ministerios localizados y ministerios no localizados.

G. Millon [11] llama ministerios *localizados* a los de los supervisores, pastores, ancianos, diáconos y diaconisas; y *no localizados* a los de apóstoles, profetas, evangelistas y doctores.[12] Efectivamente, estos últimos, incluyendo bajo el epíteto de evangelistas a los *misioneros,* de los que hablaremos en la lección 41.ª, tienen ministerios que desbordan los límites de las iglesias locales, aunque los misioneros y actuales evangelistas hayan de ser también miembros, como los doctores, de iglesias locales, por las que son *enviados* a expandir el Evangelio, mientras que pastores, ancianos y diáconos ejercen un ministerio de suyo ligado a la iglesia local. Estos ejercen oficio en virtud de la propia organización *interna* de la iglesia (por eso, el Nuevo Testamento nos detalla sus cualificaciones y tareas), mientras que hay otros oficios, como secretario, tesorero, etc., que, siendo también desempeñados dentro del ministerio *común* en virtud de un peculiar don, pertenecen más bien a la administración burocrática de la organización externa de la comunidad.

---

11. *L'Eglise,* pp. 28 y ss.

12. Esta división nos parece harto discutible a la luz de lo que hemos dicho en el punto 3 de la presente lección, ya que Millon enumera, entre los ministerios *localizados,* algunos que figurarían mejor como *oficios.* También podríamos añadir a lo dicho allí, que los *ministerios,* por ser de esencia del *organismo,* pertenecen al *esse* de la Iglesia, mientras que los *oficios,* por pertenecer a la *organización,* sirven para el *bene esse* de la Iglesia.

CUESTIONARIO:

1. ¿Cuál es el sentido profano del vocablo ministro? —
*2. ¿Qué términos usa la S. Biblia para darnos el concepto
de ministro del Señor? — 3. ¿En qué se diferencian los
ministerios de los oficios en la Iglesia? — 4. ¿Qué entendemos por ministerio común y específico? — 5. ¿Cuál es
el concepto de ministerio específico en la Iglesia de Roma?
— 6. ¿Qué se entiende por ministerios ordinarios y extraordinarios? — 7. ¿Cómo distingue G. Millon los ministerios
por razón de su diferente inserción en la iglesia local?*

LECCION 28.ª EL MINISTERIO PROFETICO

1. El ministerio profético en la Iglesia.

Abundando en alguno de los conceptos vertidos ya en las lecciones 10.ª y 11.ª, insistiremos en que, frente al derecho que la jerarquía de la Iglesia de Roma se arroga de ser la única intérprete auténtica e infalible de la Palabra de Dios, la Reforma sostiene el libre y directo acceso de cada creyente a la Biblia, de acuerdo con el ministerio profético común a todo el pueblo de Dios (1.ª Ped. 2:9; 1.ª Jn. 2:20, 27).

En un libro realmente revolucionario contra la infalibilidad de la Iglesia, el obispo católico F. Simons dice así:

«¿Cómo podemos conocer el contenido de la revelación? Ha de existir un camino que nos lleve a un conocimiento cierto de ella. Para las Iglesias de la Reforma, el único camino es la Biblia. Para la Iglesia católica, el principal, incluso el único digno de confianza en última instancia, es el magisterio vivo instituido por Cristo y conservado hasta nuestros días en la Iglesia de Roma. Contra el juicio falible de los hombres acerca del significado de las palabras de la Biblia, la Iglesia católica apela al juicio infalible del magisterio vivo. En esta diferencia estriba la más importante de las disensiones fundamentales que separan a Roma de la Reforma.» [13]

---

13. *Infalibilidad y evidencia*, p. 27.

Efectivamente, el Vaticano II, remachando la definición de la infalibilidad papal, proclamada por el Vaticano I (*cf.* «Denzinger-Schönmetzer», n.° 3.074), afirma:

«Esta infalibilidad compete al Romano Pontífice, cabeza del colegio episcopal, en razón de su oficio cuando proclama como definitiva la doctrina de fe o de conducta en su calidad de supremo pastor y maestro de todos los fieles, a quienes ha de confirmar en la fe (*cf.* Luc. 22:32). Por lo cual, con razón se dice que sus definiciones por sí y no por el consentimiento de la Iglesia son irreformables, puesto que han sido proclamadas bajo la asistencia del Espíritu Santo prometida a él en san Pedro y así no necesitan de ninguna aprobación de otros ni admiten tampoco la apelación a ningún otro tribunal.»[14]

Por el contrario, la Reforma enseñó, de acuerdo con la Biblia, que *toda* la Iglesia debe someterse a la Palabra de Dios. De ahí que incluso la Iglesia Anglicana, hoy tan cercana a la Iglesia de Roma, después de establecer en su Artículo XIX de Religión la falibilidad de las iglesias, y en el XX la incompetencia de la Iglesia para decretar algo que esté en contra de la Biblia o para exigir el creer, como necesario para salvarse, algo que no esté contenido en la misma, dice en el XXI que incluso los decretos emanados de los Concilios Generales no tienen, en orden a la salvación, ninguna fuerza o autoridad, a no ser que pueda demostrarse que han sido tomados de la Sagrada Escritura.

En el vol. VIII de esta serie teológica[15] examinamos los textos bíblicos en que la Teología católica tradicional pretende apoyar el «dogma» de la infalibilidad del Papa. El propio obispo Simons[16] se encarga de desmantelar cum-

---

14. *Constitución Dogmática sobre la Iglesia*, p. 25.
15. *Catolicismo Romano*, lección 4.ª, especialmente p. 36, nota 23.
16. *O. c.*, pp. 144-145.

plidamente el argumento montado sobre Luc. 22:31-32. Ya hemos aludido en otra ocasión a Luc. 10:16, donde Roma pretende ver cierto carisma de infalibilidad para la jerarquía eclesiástica. Lo mismo hacen los Manuales de Teología católica con Marc. 16:15-16, conectando la propia salvación con una presunta infalibilidad por parte del Magisterio de la Iglesia, cuando este texto ha de interpretarse a la luz de sus paralelos: Mat. 28:18-20; Luc. 24:47; Hech. 1:7-8 y, especialmente, 2.ª Cor. 5:18-20, donde el *ministerio de la reconciliación* es llamado *«la palabra de la reconciliación»*, que consiste en predicar el mensaje de salvación como «embajadores en nombre de Cristo», cometido que los apóstoles realizaron en función especial e irrepetible, pero que perdura hasta la consumación de los siglos en el *ministerio específico de la Palabra*.

2. El ministerio específico de la Palabra.

En el Antiguo Testamento (Núm. 11:24-29; comp. con Marc. 9:38-40; Luc. 9:49-50) está el episodio de dos individuos que profetizaban lejos del Tabernáculo, sin ser por ello desechados por Moisés. En Joel 2:28-29 se profetiza el derramamiento del Espíritu sobre toda carne; profecía que se cumplió en plenitud en Pentecostés (Hech. 2:1-4). La rasgadura del velo del Templo (Mat. 27:51) simbolizaba el acceso de todo el Pueblo al Santísimo (Heb. 4:16; 10:19-22) por poseer ya un sacerdocio común (1.ª Ped. 2:9), para ofrecer, por Cristo y en Cristo, sacrificios vivos de alabanza, acción de gracias, dedicación al Señor y a los hermanos (Rom. 12:1-2; Heb. 13:15-16); sin intermediarios humanos entre el creyente y Dios (1.ª Tim. 2:5; 1.ª Jn. 1:9), ni entre el creyente y la Biblia (2.ª Tim. 3:14-16; 1.ª Pedro 2:2; 2.ª Ped. 1:14-19; 1.ª Jn. 2:20, 27), ni entre los creyentes entre sí (Mat. 18:15, 18). Todos los fieles hacen bien cuando, como los judíos de Berea, se afanan en escudriñar cada día las Escrituras, para ver *si son así* las cosas que se les predican (Hech. 17:11).

Pero este ministerio común de los fieles no es óbice a la existencia de un ministerio específico de la Palabra (Ef. 4:11): servicio especial de edificación (1.ª Cor. 3:5-15); pastoreo que demanda de todos honor, respeto y aun obediencia (Hech. 20:28; 1.ª Tim. 4:11-14; 2.ª Tim. 1:6-8; Hebreos 13:7, 17); ejercicio de un don *que no se da a todos* (Rom. 12:6-8; 1.ª Cor. 12:29; Ef. 4:11). Mención especial merece este último texto, sobre el que queremos hacer tres breves observaciones, antes de pasar a su estudio en el punto siguiente: A) Que se trata de ministerios destinados *para toda la Iglesia* (no localizados, excepto el *pastoreo*); B) Que *todos ellos* van orientados a la predicación de la Palabra; C) Que se dan para el equipamiento de los *santos*, en orden a la obra del ministerio común y, así, a la edificación y al crecimiento de todo el Cuerpo de la Iglesia.

3. El ministerio de edificación.

En un contexto de gran riqueza y densidad, importantísimo para conocer la verdadera unidad de la Iglesia, el apóstol Pablo introduce, como dones del Señor a Su Iglesia, los ministros de la Palabra, cuyo servicio especial está destinado a «perfeccionar a los santos para la obra del ministerio», a fin de que, mediante el progreso en la unidad y en el reconocimiento del Hijo de Dios, el Cuerpo de Cristo se edifique, crezca y se desarrolle armónicamente, hasta llegar a la madurez de un varón perfecto, gracias al suministro constante de energía espiritual que desciende de la Cabeza (Ef. 4:1-16). La traducción exacta de los versículos 11 y 12 es como sigue:

> «*Y él* (Cristo ascendido) *dio unos, los Apóstoles; otros, los Profetas; otros, los Evangelistas; y otros, los Pastores y Maestros; a fin de perfeccionar a los santos para una obra de servicio, para edificación del Cuerpo de Cristo.*»

Examinemos de cerca cada uno de estos ministerios:

A) APÓSTOLES. Por este nombre se designa primordialmente a los *Doce*, testigos de excepción de la resurrección de Cristo, de entre los discípulos que habían convivido con el Señor desde el bautismo de Juan (Hech. 1:21-22). Estuvieron dotados de carismas especiales, mediante los cuales echaron los cimientos de la Iglesia (Ef. 2:20; Apocalipsis 21:14, comp. con Mat. 16:18). Este ministerio fue irrepetible y, por tanto, no ha podido tener sucesores. De ahí que a Judas le sustituye Matías *antes de Pentecostés;* pero a Jacobo, muerto antes de que se escribiera ningún libro del Nuevo Testamento, ya no se le sustituye (Hechos 12:2). J. R. Rollo, citando a Hort, dice: «La autoridad de los apóstoles era moral más bien que formal; una invitación a la deferencia más bien que el derecho a ser obedecido.» [17]

Las condiciones para este ministerio peculiar e irrepetible, según Hech. 1:21-22, son tres: *a)* que fuesen *varones* («andrôn»). La mujer judía estaba excluida de tribunales, cargos de juez y de testigo, etc. Así se explica que, habiendo sido precisamente *mujeres* los primeros testigos de la resurrección de Cristo, no se les diese crédito hasta que Pedro y Juan fueron al sepulcro (*cf.* Luc. 24:22-24), y que cuando Pablo enumera muy detalladamente, en 1.ª Corintios 15:5-8, las personas a las que Cristo resucitado se apareció, comience por Cefas (Pedro) y no mencione ni una sola mujer; *b)* que hubiesen acompañado a Jesús, desde el bautismo de Juan hasta el día de la Ascensión, durante toda Su vida pública («entraba y salía» es una expresión judía para resumir la totalidad de la conducta); *c)* que fuesen *testigos* de la Resurrección; todo esto los

---

17. En *La Iglesia* (compil. de J. B. Watson), p. 55. Así parece indicarlo Hech. 15:31. Este es también el parecer de V. Fábrega en el cursillo *Aspectos eclesiológicos del Libro de Hechos,* ya aludido. El nos demostraba cómo Mat. 19:28 y paralelos predicen un *poder judicial en la Escatología final,* no en la era presente. Para más detalles, *cf.* mi tesis doctoral *La unidad de la Iglesia en Efesios.*

cualificaba especialmente para la proclamación del mensaje («kérygma») centrado en la persona y la obra de Cristo.

Pablo pasa a ocupar un lugar similar, incluso superior en muchos aspectos (1.ª Cor. 9:1 y ss.; 2.ª Cor. 11:22 y ss.), a los Doce (Gál. 2:7 y ss.), pero no idéntico a ellos. Así en Hech. 13:31 él mismo se excluye del grupo de testigos cualificados. Aunque su apostolado no era «de hombres ni por hombre... sino por revelación de Jesucristo» (Gál. 1:1, 11), él vio una luz y oyó una voz, pero no vio en realidad a Jesucristo resucitado (cf. Hech. 9:3-5); además su don ministerial tuvo que ser reconocido eclesialmente (Hechos 9:10-19; Gál. 2:9). En 1.ª Cor. 9:6 equipara a Bernabé y a sí mismo a «los otros apóstoles» (v. 5).

Finalmente, la palabra *apóstol* («apóstolos» en griego) significa *enviado, mensajero*, y, en este sentido amplio, se aplica a todo misionero.[18]

B) PROFETAS. Este vocablo (del griego «profétes») no significa primordialmente «anunciador del futuro», sino «portavoz de otro»; en este caso, de Dios mediante una peculiar inspiración. La diferencia entre los apóstoles y los profetas del Nuevo Testamento está en que la inspiración de éstos era ocasional y, por ello, su autoridad como maestros estaba subordinada a la de los apóstoles. Este ministerio profético, distinto del don extraordinario de profecía, estaba destinado en especial a la interpretación de las Escrituras y era un servicio de principal relevancia dentro de las iglesias locales (cf. Hech. 13:1). En Ef. 2:20 aparecen alineados junto a los apóstoles como fundamentos —cimientos— de la Iglesia.

C) EVANGELISTAS. Esta palabra significa «anunciador de Buenas Noticias». Son, pues, los proclamadores del mensaje de salvación, o «*kerygma*» en su sentido más preciso. Ahora bien, todo apóstol es evangelista, pero no viceversa. En tiempo de la Reforma prevaleció la opinión de que se

---

18. V. lección 41.ª.

trataba de una especie de «vicarios apostólicos», comisionados por los apóstoles para ciertos encargos y con ciertos poderes. Pero un estudio más profundo del Nuevo Testamento nos hace ver que se trata de misioneros o predicadores itinerantes, enviados como pioneros. Es el caso de los 70 discípulos de Lucas 10, y de Felipe en Hech. 8:26 y siguientes. Cuando Timoteo es exhortado a hacer «obra de evangelista» (2.ª Tim. 4:5), se trata de predicar el Evangelio. Por tanto, el *evangelista*, como proclamador del mensaje a los inconversos, se distingue del *profeta*, que es un anunciador de revelaciones o inspiraciones divinas, y del *maestro*, que enseña para edificación de los creyentes.

D) PASTORES Y MAESTROS. Calvino interpretó equivocadamente este versículo al pensar que se trataba de ministerios que habían de ser ejercidos por distintas personas. Sin embargo, ya en el siglo IV, decía Jerónimo: «Nadie debe arrogarse el título de pastor si no puede enseñar a los que apacienta.» Ch. Hodge advierte [19] que no hay lugar en la Escritura donde aparezcan ministros de la Palabra no autorizados tanto a exhortar como a pastorear; además, la ausencia del artículo griego delante del término *didaskálus*, tras una enumeración jalonada con artículos, es un fuerte indicio de que se trata de dos funciones ejercitadas por una misma persona. Con todo, los recientes comentarios de Foulkes, Rienecker, etc., hacen notar que, aunque ambos ministerios están bajo un solo artículo, no se sigue necesariamente que vayan a coincidir siempre en una misma persona dentro de una comunidad local (*cf.* Romanos 12:7; Hech. 13:1; 1.ª Cor. 12:28, etc.). Por otra parte, puede asegurarse que el término *pastor* designa primariamente al supervisor o *epískopos*, mientras que el de *maestro* designa al *instructor*.

1.ª Tim. 3:2 y Tito 1:9 dicen que el pastor o *epískopos* ha de ser «apto para enseñar y para exhortar». Podemos concluir diciendo que todo pastor es maestro, pero no todo

---

19. *Ephesians*, pp. 226-227.

maestro puede ser tenido por *pastor*. En realidad, cualquier ministro de la Palabra que, con su estudio y experiencia, ha adquirido una especial competencia para la docencia o *didaché*, es decir, una formación bíblica y teológica para edificar a la comunidad, puede ser reconocido y usado con gran provecho como investido del *don de enseñanza*, mientras que el pastoreo específico requiere, ante todo, *dones prácticos de gobierno, de guía espiritual y de orientación personal*, los cuales, como es obvio, estarán carentes de poder y provecho sin la debida formación bíblica y sin la debida temperatura espiritual.

Digamos, para terminar esta lección, que los ministerios de Efesios 4:11 no eximen a la congregación de procurarse la debida formación bíblica doctrinal y espiritual. Más aún, el ministerio específico es dado a la iglesia para equipar a todos los demás miembros para el desempeño más cabal de sus respectivos servicios, como miembros activos del mismo Cuerpo (*cf.* Ef. 4:12-16).

CUESTIONARIO:

1. ¿Cuál es la diferencia radical entre Roma y la Reforma respecto al ministerio específico de la Palabra? — *2. ¿Qué importancia tiene Efesios 4:11 dentro de su contexto?* — *3. ¿Qué ministerios específicos comportan los epítetos apóstol, profeta, evangelista, pastor y maestro?*

LECCION 29.ª   EL MINISTERIO CULTUAL

El Cristianismo comporta, junto a un ministerio profético, un ministerio cultual y un ministerio regio (*cf*. 1.ª Pedro 2:9; Apoc. 1:6; 5:10; 22:3, 5). En la lección anterior hemos tratado del primero; en la siguiente trataremos del tercero, y en la presente vamos a tratar del segundo.

1. El culto cristiano.

El culto cristiano implica fundamentalmente un *servicio* a Dios. Tanto el término hebreo *'abodâ* del Antiguo Testamento, como el griego *latreía* significan originalmente el servicio de un siervo contratado para trabajar por y para su señor. Para ofrecer este servicio *cultual* de la manera más expresiva los siervos de Dios se prosternan (hebreo: *hishtahavâ*; griego: *proskineîn*), mostrando así su temor reverencial y su pavor asombrado ante la majestad divina.

Así podemos decir que la adoración constituye la medula misma del culto. En torno a este núcleo, la alabanza, la acción de gracias y la petición, expresadas comunitariamente, tanto en tono hablado como por medio de cánticos, forman parte del servicio cultual que la congregación tributa a Dios. De arriba abajo, como voces de Dios, están la exhortación, la corrección mutua y el perdón, así como la predicación de la Palabra y la celebración de las ordenanzas, o sea, del Bautismo y de la Cena del Señor. El Nuevo Testamento no nos presenta un esquema estereotipado de servicio cultual. Podemos vislumbrar que el modo de celebrar los cultos revestía una notable variedad, conforme a la libertad espiritual de los hijos de Dios.

El primer esquema completo de un servicio dominical aparece a mediados del siglo II, en Justino,[20] con el siguiente orden: lectura de la Palabra, sermón, oración de pie en la que todos pueden participar, la Cena del Señor tras las plegarias y acción de gracias del presidente, y, finalmente, la colecta que se entrega al pastor o presidente, para ayuda de huérfanos, viudas, enfermos, encarcelados y demás necesitados.

2. El orden en el culto.

El Nuevo Pacto de Dios con Su Pueblo lleva consigo, como ya estaba anunciado, una enseñanza directa, sin intermediarios, de Dios a Sus hijos (Is. 54:13; Jer. 31:31-34; Jn. 6:45; Heb. 8:10-11; 1.ª Jn. 2:20, 27). Por otra parte, cuanto mejor se deja llevar el creyente por el Espíritu de Dios (Rom. 8:14) y mejor dispuesto está a cumplir la voluntad de Dios, tanto mejor puede discernir la doctrina (Jn. 7:17). De ahí que todo creyente puede usar los dones del Espíritu para hablar, exhortar, orar, etc. ¡Ojalá todas las iglesias estuviesen tan llenas de carismas y de vida como la iglesia de Corinto! (*cf.* 1.ª Cor. 14). Pero hay en este mismo cap. 14 de 1.ª Corintios algo que es preciso considerar atentamente. El apóstol deja bien claro que todo ha de hacerse para *edificación* (vv. 3, 5, 12, 17, 26), decentemente y *con orden* (vv. 33, 40), o, como dice Ch. Hodge:[21] «como un ejército bien disciplinado, donde cada uno ocupa su lugar y actúa en el momento oportuno y de manera adecuada». ¿Cómo ha de ponerse orden en una congregación donde abundan los carismas de exhortación, plegaria, lenguas, profecía? Responde Pablo: «los espíritus de los profetas están sujetos (o «estén sujetos» —según Hodge—, aunque el original sugiere el indicativo) a los profetas»;

---

20. *Apologia*, I, 67.
21. Ch. Hodge, *1.ª Corintios* (Trad. de Miguel Blanch, London, The Banner of Truth, 1969), p. 283.

es decir, el espíritu de profecía que el Espíritu Santo imparte no obra irresistiblemente forzando a hablar, sino que ha de ejercitarse con el debido control por parte del sujeto (para no extralimitarse en la forma, tiempo, etcétera) y por parte del ministro que dirige el culto.

No se puede olvidar que la vitalidad ha de coexistir con el orden, y que hay creyentes que pueden tomar como impulso del Espíritu lo que es impulso del propio espíritu de vanidad o de ignorancia. Aquí reside la tensión entre lo *carismático* y lo *edificante*, rondando a veces el borde de lo extravagante. Es cierto que *todos* los creyentes tienen el derecho y el deber de ejercitar sus dones peculiares respectivos, pero también es cierto que entre esos dones está el de discernimiento de espíritus, y este don *suele* (no es regla fija) abundar más en los «maestros y profetas» de la congregación (*cf.* Hech. 13:1-2). Por otra parte, el v. 34 no significa —según la opinión más probable— que las mujeres hayan de abstenerse de orar o dar testimonio en los servicios; este versículo ha de interpretarse a la luz de otro más claro, que es 1.ª Tim. 2:11-12. Lo que Pablo parece prohibir a la mujer es *la enseñanza autorizada* en un servicio cultual.[22] Por eso, apoyados en esta Palabra, nos resulta muy problemática la promoción de la mujer al ministerio específico; sobre todo, al pastorado.

3. ¿Sacrificio cultual?

La Epístola a los hebreos deja bien claro (caps. 9 y 10) que Cristo ofreció en la Cruz, *de una vez para siempre,* el

---

22. Sin embargo, no puede pasarse por alto el contexto judío (farisaico = puro) en que Pablo está expresándose. Ya hemos visto, en la lección anterior, su intencionada omisión de las mujeres como *testigos* de la Resurrección. Hacer válido para siempre un contexto típicamente espacio-temporal (estamos exponiendo nuestra opinión personal, a falta de otra prueba mayor) nos obligaría a perpetuar el lavamiento de los pies de Jn. 13:14 (entonces no se usaban zapatos), así como la unción de Sant. 5:14-15 (donde la oración con fe —curativa— iba asociada al aceite, tenido como medicamento popular).

único sacrificio propiciatorio y expiatorio de la Nueva Alianza. Así, en Heb. 10:12, el «sentarse» simboliza que Cristo ha terminado su tarea sacrificial, la cual, por ser definitiva (vv. 14, 18), no puede repetirse, ni por Sus propias manos ni «por manos de los sacerdotes».[23] Jesús ejerce ahora Su eterno sacerdocio intercediendo por quienes se acercan, por El, a Dios (Heb. 7:24-25), pero no en actitud de *orante* (de pie), sino *regia* (sentado). Apocalipsis 5:6 lo presenta de pie, en contexto diferente, para indicar que está vivo —resucitado—, a pesar de haber sido inmolado. Todo creyente tiene ahora acceso al «Santísimo», sin necesidad de intermediarios (*cf.* Heb. 4:16; 10:19; 1.ª Jn. 2:1-2). Nuestro sacerdocio común queda magníficamente expresado en Rom. 12:1-2; Heb. 13:15-16.[24]

CUESTIONARIO:

1. ¿En qué consiste la quintaesencia del culto cristiano? — 2. ¿Qué elementos pueden y cuáles no pueden faltar en un culto? — 3. ¿Es necesario poner orden al ejercicio de los dones? — 4. ¿Cuál es el verdadero sentido de 1.ª Corintios 14:34? — 5. ¿Cómo replicaría usted al «dogma católico-romano» sobre el sacrificio de la Misa?

---

23. Como definió el C. de Trento, sesión XXII, cap. 2 (*cf. Denzinger-Schönm.*, n.º 1.743).
24. Para más detalles, véase mi libro *Catolicismo Romano*, lección 36.ª, así como el vol. IV de esta serie teológica (en preparación).

LECCION 30.ª EL MINISTERIO REGIO O REAL

1. El oficio de gobernar.

En su 1.ª a Timoteo 5:17 dice el apóstol: «Los ancianos que gobiernan bien, sean tenidos por dignos de doble honor.» El original dice «hoi proestôtes», término que se aplicaba a los prefectos y presidentes o jefes de partido o de grupo en la antigua Grecia. El hecho de que el único Jefe o Gobernador de la Iglesia, con autoridad propia y dominio sobre las comunidades locales, sea Jesucristo, no es obstáculo para que en las iglesias haya oficios con el cometido de regir, presidir y ejercer funciones de gobierno; a ellos hay que «obedecer y sujetarse» (Heb. 13:17) voluntariamente, alegremente, en el Señor.

En efecto, como ya adelantamos en la lección 27.ª, párrafo 3.º, los oficios emanan de la *organización* de la iglesia, mientras que los ministerios están insertos en el *organismo*. En otras palabras, cada *don* del Espíritu a los miembros de iglesia comporta un ministerio, y así todos los miembros tienen un servicio y una *función* que ejercer; entre ellas están el exhortar, el predicar, enseñar, aconsejar, etc. Son funciones espirituales que comportan, no un oficio *superior*, sino un ministerio *peculiar* más específico y restringido. Estos ministerios específicos pueden ejercitarse sin estar investidos de un *oficio,* sino sólo en cumplimiento de una *función* para la que se ha recibido del Espíritu el don necesario. En cambio, una persona no debe ejercer el cometido de gobernar y presidir, etc., a no ser que haya sido investido para ello de una autoridad *oficial,* ya se ejerza ésta temporal y provisionalmente, ya se ejerza de por vida. Este oficio no emana de la constitución intrínseca de la iglesia *como organismo* (de lo contrario, sería uniforme e invariable), sino de la *organización* que la iglesia, como toda sociedad bien ordenada, debe tener. De ahí que admitamos cierto pluralismo en el modo de gobernar las iglesias.

2.   Origen y autoridad de los oficios.

Cristo es el Rey y Señor de Su Iglesia, y El mismo, con Su sangre, nos ha hecho profetas, sacerdotes y reyes («real sacerdocio» —dice 1.ª Ped. 2:9). Así como el ministerio profético, común a todos los miembros, asume una forma específica en los «maestros y profetas» (Hech. 13:1), o *ancianos que enseñan,* así también el ministerio regio, común a todos los miembros, asume una forma especial en los *ancianos que gobiernan.* Así pues, podemos concluir con R. B. Kuiper,[25] que «los oficios específicos tienen su raíz en el oficio universal». Por ello, corresponde a la iglesia misma el elegir los oficios: o sea, de abajo arriba, no de arriba abajo (impuestos por una autoridad superior), como aún viene haciéndose en la Iglesia de Roma.

Si el *organizarse* mediante el nombramiento de oficios corresponde a la iglesia local misma, se sigue necesariamente que los oficios gobiernan la iglesia con el consentimiento expreso de sus miembros, de tal manera que la imposición de un pastor u otro oficial de iglesia sin el consentimiento de los miembros es una negación del oficio universal de éstos, y aun del mismo concepto de iglesia como cuerpo de Cristo-Cabeza. Este mismo concepto de *cuerpo* exige que los oficios emerjan de la propia congregación; o sea, una iglesia ha de elegir sus oficiales de entre su membresía. Como quiera que el pastorado no es un mero oficio, sino un ministerio localizado que requiere ciertos dones específicos y un llamamiento de parte del Señor, la iglesia puede reconocer y aceptar como

---

25.   *O. c.,* p. 134.

pastor a una persona debidamente dotada, aunque proceda de otro lugar y aun de otra denominación, con tal que dicha persona acepte previamente la constitución y orden de la iglesia referida y quede así afiliada dentro de la posición doctrinal y disciplinar de la membresía correspondiente.

La forma correcta de gobierno de cualquier iglesia local siempre será una «teo-democracia», donde la única verdadera autoridad es *divina* (de Cristo) y en la que el Espíritu de Cristo distribuye los dones y constituye los ministerios, llamando a desempeñar los servicios. En este sentido, la iglesia se gobierna en forma de *teocracia.*[26] Pero es la iglesia *toda* (no un «superior») la que discierne los dones y reconoce los ministerios, nombrando y aceptando los oficios; en este sentido, es una *democracia.* Entender este doble aspecto es de suma importancia. Por no hacerlo así, se cometen graves equivocaciones en el gobierno de muchas iglesias. Téngase en cuenta que el pastor ha de obrar con el consentimiento de la congregación, pero su última responsabilidad no es ante la congregación, sino ante el verdadero Señor de la Iglesia, Jesucristo.

Una ortodoxa comprensión de la membresía, cual la hemos enseñado en la Tercera parte de este volumen, implica que todos los miembros han de tener voz y voto en los asuntos de la iglesia, pero hay dos obstáculos que dificultan el buen funcionamiento del sistema: A) la falta de la debida formación, así como de la necesaria dedicación y responsabilización de cada miembro, lo que puede hacer de un voto mayoritario una resolución imprudente y peligrosa; B) la pasividad que va aneja a un concepto «gregario» de membresía, favoreciendo la anómala situación de una iglesia en que el pastor ordena todos los pro-

---

26. También aquí la desviación de la práctica apostólica fue rápida, buscándose la Iglesia oficial un «Rey» visible. Como dice J. B. Watson (*La Iglesia,* p. 11): «El estilo de gobierno —pura teocracia— dado al Israel de antaño no les satisfizo por mucho tiempo. Desearon, como las otras naciones, tener una cabeza visible antes que retener a Dios como su invisible rey.»

gramas, expone todas las iniciativas y toma todas las resoluciones; lo cual resulta más peligroso cuando tal pastor posee características temperamentales que le predisponen a asumir actitudes dictatoriales o paternalistas.

3. Variedad de gobierno en la época apostólica.

En el Nuevo Testamento encontramos, al menos, tres tipos de organización:

A) Jerusalén, la primera iglesia local y, en cierto sentido, la «madre y maestra» de todas las demás, aparece en Hechos 15 con una organización típica del judaísmo: junto al presidente, los ancianos, los servidores y la congregación. Allí tenían un puesto específico los *Doce,* por su misión peculiar e irrepetible de *testigos cualificados del Resucitado,* pero con un carácter esencialmente itinerante (sin dejar, por eso, de quedar integrados, con especial autoridad, en la iglesia local). Por eso, había también un presidente o *pastor* fijo, Jacobo, «el hermano del Señor», quien, con Pedro y Juan, es llamado «columna» de la iglesia en Gál. 2:9. Junto al pastor, Jacobo, y los apóstoles, aparecen allí los ancianos y toda la iglesia —los «hermanos»— (*cf.* Hech. 15:22-23).

B) Antioquía, a mitad de camino entre Jerusalén y Corinto, aparece en Hech. 13 gobernada por un grupo de «profetas y maestros» que «ministran» y a quienes compete, en nombre de la congregación, el envío de misioneros. Son ancianos con oficio de enseñar los que aquí parecen formar el presbiterio.

C) Corinto, ya en el corazón de Grecia, tenía desde el principio una membresía numerosa (Hech. 18:8), con organización claramente congregacional, pues ni en Hechos ni en 1.ª y 2.ª Corintios se mencionan ancianos o pastores, sino un grupo exuberante de carismas, con banderías en torno a «nombres» humanos (*cf.* 1.ª Cor. 1:12; 3:4), con algún desorden en el ejercicio de los dones (1.ª Cor. 14) y descuido en el terreno de la disciplina (1.ª Cor. 5).

4. Variedad de gobierno en la época actual.

Dejando para el vol. VIII el estudio de la organización de la Iglesia de Roma, mencionaremos aquí el gobierno de las iglesias salidas de (o afines a) la Reforma:

A) GOBIERNO EPISCOPALIANO. Mantiene una estructura similar a la de Roma (sin Papa): cada parroquia (distribución territorial) tiene su rector (el «vicar» inglés), con o sin coadjutores; las parroquias se agrupan por diócesis, al frente de la cual hay un obispo, con autoridad de tipo prácticamente administrativo o burocrático, más bien que espiritual. Los obispos de una provincia eclesiástica están presididos por un arzobispo. La comunión anglicana tiene además como «Primado» al arzobispo de Canterbury, aunque la Iglesia de Inglaterra tiene por Cabeza oficial visible al Jefe del Estado; sin embargo, como dice E. Kevan:[27] «El Episcopalianismo no tiene una conexión necesaria con la idea de una iglesia estatal; es un mero accidente histórico el que tal relación con el Estado haya llegado a surgir.»

B') GOBIERNO PRESBITERIANO. Así como en el Episcopalianismo hay una «jerarquía» oficial, impuesta a las iglesias desde fuera adentro y de arriba abajo, en el Presbiterianismo hay igualdad en el plano ministerial; pero, junto a él, se alza también, aunque de abajo arriba, una especie de pirámide jerárquica, con poderes legislativos, judiciales y ejecutivos, al estilo de un Estado constitucional de base democrática: cada congregación nombra un cuerpo de ancianos (presbíteros), asociados al pastor (que es un anciano separado para el oficio de enseñar), con el que forman la *sesión*. Los ministros y ancianos representativos de cada sesión hacen un *presbiterio*. Los presbiterios se agrupan en *sínodos*. Sobre los sínodos está la

27. *Dogmatic Theology* (Curso por Correspondencia), vol. VI, lección IV, p. 4, a.

Asamblea General. Los Metodistas se rigen por un gobierno similar.[27 bis]

C') GOBIERNO CONGREGACIONAL. Muchas de las iglesias llamadas «libres» (es decir, independientes), así como las iglesias *congregacionalistas* y *bautistas* se rigen por el sistema «teo-democrático» que hemos expuesto anteriormente. Dentro de este sistema de gobierno, Cristo es la única autoridad gubernativa de las iglesias y Su autoridad jamás es delegada a los hombres, sino que es comunicada a la iglesia (congregación) por el Espíritu de Cristo, de tal manera que puede decirse que no se trata de un gobierno del pueblo *por* el pueblo, sino por el Espíritu Santo *a través* del pueblo. Así, la iglesia no intenta meramente descubrir la opinión de la mayoría, sino la mente de Cristo expresada por el Espíritu a través de la oración y de la comunión eclesial. En esta organización hay lugar para un ministerio específico: pastorado escogido y llamado por el Señor, y reconocido y aceptado por la iglesia, así como ancianos y diáconos.

D') ASAMBLEA DE HERMANOS. En ellas, el *ministerio* pastoral está diluido en la congregación, no admitiendo el pastorado único y específico, mientras que la función supervisora y gubernativa está en manos de un grupo de «ancianos». Hay, sin embargo, lugar para ancianos encargados especialmente del ministerio de la Palabra, que pueden incluso dedicarse exclusivamente a esta obra. La administración está en manos de los ancianos, los cuales no son elegidos por el voto de la congregación, sino reconocidos por los hermanos como equipados por el Señor para tal ministerio.

---

27 bis. En el régimen presbiteriano actual, al menos en algunas iglesias, hay una proporción casi igual —o igual— de laicos y de ancianos.

CUESTIONARIO:

1. ¿De dónde emerge en la iglesia el oficio de gobernar? — 2. ¿Qué parte tiene la membresía en el nombramiento y aceptación de pastores? — 3. ¿Cuál es la correcta forma de gobierno de una iglesia local? — 4. ¿Qué diferencias de gobierno advertimos en Jerusalén, Antioquía y Corinto? — 5. ¿Qué variedades de gobierno se dan en las iglesias reformadas o afines a la Reforma? — 6. ¿Es el régimen de nuestras iglesias una «democracia»?

LECCION 31.ª LOS PODERES DE LA IGLESIA

1. Qué poderes competen a la Iglesia.

Vamos a examinar ahora brevemente cuáles son los poderes de la Iglesia, desarrollados en virtud del ministerio regio o real que le compete.

Frente al concepto católico-romano y episcopaliano de jurisdicción eclesiástica (*ius ecclesiasticum* = derecho eclesiástico), según el cual una clase aparte (presbíteros, obispos, papa) tiene verdaderos poderes sobre el resto de la iglesia, sostenemos que *toda* la iglesia (ministros, oficiales y miembros comunes) está sometida al poder de Jesucristo, ejercitado mediante el Espíritu que reside en cada uno de los miembros de la congregación. Por eso, el primer nombre dado a los cristianos fue el de *discípulos*, con lo que se manifestaba, no sólo la condición de seguidor de Cristo que el discipulado cristiano comporta, sino también la radical actitud de iglesia *discente* que correspondía a toda la comunidad cristiana, no sólo a los *«simples»* fieles. Por eso, Griffith Thomas [28] hace notar que en Apocalipsis, caps. 2 y 3, no se dice: «oiga lo que la Iglesia dice a sus hijos», sino «oiga lo que el Espíritu dice a las iglesias».

Por otra parte, siendo cada iglesia local autónoma, o sea, independiente en cuanto a su administración y gobierno, dentro de una intercomunión eclesial en la fe y en el amor, ningún comité u órgano superior puede imponer sus leyes a las iglesias locales. Todo Comité o Consejo dedicado a coordinar los esfuerzos misionales, evangelís-

---

28. *O. c.*, p. 289.

ticos, sociales, etc., de las iglesias, debe ser un mero servidor de las iglesias y de la obra, sin que sus decisiones tengan más valor que el que las iglesias mismas les den mediante el voto de sus delegados y la aceptación de las respectivas comunidades.

2. Naturaleza, división y límites del poder eclesial.

Al hablar del *poder eclesial* ha de tenerse en cuenta que:

A) Es un poder: a) *espiritual,* porque se recibe del Espíritu, se ejercita en nombre de Cristo, por el poder de Su Espíritu, que pertenece a los nacidos del Espíritu y se ejerce de manera espiritual, aunque se proyecta visiblemente y alcanza al ser humano entero, no sólo al alma; b) *ministerial,* porque no es soberano, sino relativo, subordinado y dependiente de la Palabra, de Cristo y del Espíritu (que son las tres *autoridades* soberanas de la Iglesia); o sea, es una *diakonía* y una *leiturgía:* un *servicio* y un *ministerio.*

B) Es un poder: a') *dogmático* o *didáctico,* o sea, una autoridad espiritual para dar testimonio del Evangelio y para interpretar fielmente (no infaliblemente) y en forma proclamatoria (no definitoria) la verdad de la Palabra de Dios; b') *diatáctico,* o facultad para administrar las ordenanzas del Señor y gobernarse teodemocráticamente según las normas de la Escritura; no cabe lugar alguno para el ejercicio de un poder físico, mediador de salvación, mediante la acción sacramental *ex opere operato* (en virtud del rito mismo), ni imposición coercitiva sobre las conciencias; c') *diacrítico,* o facultad para ejercer la disciplina, así como para admitir en, o excluir de, la comunión eclesial. Lo cual no se puede hacer por medios coactivos, sino por la amonestación, corrección, instrucción y amorosa intimación o censura. Berkhof añade: d') el poder de la *misericordia,* que se ejercita mediante los carismas de curación y el ejercicio de la benevolencia con los necesitados.

C) Por su carácter espiritual, relativo, subordinado y dependiente, el poder de la iglesia tiene sus límites; está limitado: a'') por su naturaleza espiritual, no pudiendo ejercerse en la esfera temporal (política, civil o penal); b'') por su subordinación a las ya mencionadas tres autoridades (la Palabra, Cristo y el Espíritu), por lo cual nunca puede ser un poder absoluto, despótico o tiránico. Los oficiales son servidores, no dominadores de la grey (Mateo 23; 1.ª Ped. 5), y el ejercicio de su autoridad está enteramente sometido a la Palabra, de modo que no puede imponer nada que no se halle en la Escritura. c'') por la condición de los miembros mismos de la iglesia, que son hijos de Dios, libres con la libertad del Espíritu, y en cuyas conciencias sólo Dios puede entrar, habiéndose de tener por intruso a quien pretenda forzar las puertas de tal santuario.

3. ¿Puede admitirse en la iglesia un primado universal?

La Iglesia de Roma sostiene como «dogma» el Primado Universal, supremo, directo e inmediato del Papa sobre todas y cada una de las iglesias y sobre todos y cada uno de los pastores. El obispo de Roma Siricio, a fines del siglo IV, interpretó en favor de su universal superintendencia la frase paulina «mi preocupación por todas las iglesias» (2.ª Cor. 11:28). Dejamos para el volumen VIII el examen de este tema. Por ahora, baste con decir que el apóstol expresaba con tal frase: 1.º, que su misión *apostólica* rebasaba *de suyo* las fronteras de las iglesias locales; 2.º, como se ve por el contexto, que en lo profundo de su corazón simpatizaba con todos los problemas, penas y alegrías de todas las comunidades. Una función autoritativa, con jurisdicción sobre varias iglesias, es totalmente ajena a la Palabra de Dios. Sin embargo, podemos admitir con E. Kevan [29] que «hay dentro de la Iglesia actualmente hombres de Dios, cuyos eminentes dones y gene-

---

29. *O. c.*, vol. VI, lecc. IV, p. 2.

ral aceptación de muchas iglesias les cualifican para una preocupación general por las iglesias». Citemos como un ejemplo contemporáneo al Dr. Lloyd-Jones, reconocido líder de los evangélicos ingleses por su gran competencia, experiencia y espiritualidad.

CUESTIONARIO:

1. ¿En qué sentido caben en la Iglesia autoridades humanas? — 2. ¿De qué naturaleza es el poder eclesial? — 3. ¿Cuáles son los aspectos de tal poder? — 4. ¿Cuáles son sus límites? — 5. ¿Puede alguien hoy cargar con la paulina preocupación expresada en 2.ª Cor. 11:28?

LECCION 32.ª LOS OFICIALES DE LA IGLESIA

Como observa Pendleton,[30] «no puede decirse que los oficiales son esenciales para la existencia de una iglesia, porque la iglesia debe existir antes de que pueda nombrar sus oficiales». Así como los *ministerios o funciones* son esenciales para el desarrollo del *organismo* eclesial, los *oficios* pertenecen a la *organización* de la iglesia local y, por tanto, no son necesarios para la *vida* misma de la iglesia, sino para el *buen funcionamiento* de sus estructuras.[31] Los oficios que comportan un ministerio específico se reducen a dos: ancianos y diáconos.

1. Supervisores, ancianos, pastores o conductores.

Todos estos nombres designan distintas funciones de una misma persona:

A) SUPERVISOR (griego: «epískopos») —que muchas versiones traducen por «obispo»— es un término que expresa los deberes y responsabilidades de un pastor. Que es sinónimo de «anciano» (griego: «presbyteros») queda patente por Hech. 20:17, 28, donde a los «presbíteros» de Efeso se les llama «obispos», así como por Tito 1:5, 7, donde los «ancianos» nombrados para cada localidad son llamados «obispos». En 1.ª Ped. 5:1-2 se exhorta a los «ancianos» a «pastorear», «teniendo cuidado («episkopúntes» —esta palabra falta en unos pocos MSS) de la grey». Filipenses 1:1 alinea a los «obispos» junto a los diáconos. Finalmente,

---

30. *Compendio de Teología Cristiana*, p. 324.
31. V. lección 27.ª.

en un pasaje paralelo al de Tito, 1.ª Tim. 3:1 y ss. nos presenta las cualificaciones *pastorales* de un «obispo». Todavía Jerónimo, entrado ya el siglo v, dice: «El apóstol enseña claramente que los presbíteros son los mismos que los obispos».[32]

B) ANCIANO. Es un término extraído de la tradición judía, mientras *supervisor* es de tradición griega. La institución de los ancianos pertenecía ya a la misma estructura de las tribus de Israel e indicaba una edad madura, junto con una experiencia demostrada. El Nuevo Testamento no insiste en la edad, pero sí en las cualificaciones y en la experiencia, en la cual se exige cierta *veteranía.* Por eso, en 1.ª Tim. 3:6 se intima que no se nombre «obispo» a «un neófito [o sea, a un recién convertido], no sea que envaneciéndose caiga en la condenación del diablo». En 1.ª Tim. 5:17 se habla de «ancianos que gobiernan» (griego: «proestôtes» —que presiden, dirigen o gobiernan), «especialmente los que trabajan en la Palabra y en la enseñanza». Hebreos 13:7 llama «egumónon» (conductores o líderes) a estos mismos ancianos que enseñan. Este mismo término se repite en los vv. 17 y 24 del mismo capítulo, así como en Hech. 15:22, 32, donde Judas y Silas son llamados «líderes» (sin duda, ancianos) y «profetas» de la iglesia de Jerusalén, que es la que los envía.[33]

C) PASTOR. Efesios 4:11 alinea a los *pastores* («poiménas») con los *maestros* con un solo artículo, lo que indica que se trata de la misma persona.[34] Este término aparece en Hech. 20:28 y 1.ª Ped. 5:2 en forma de verbo («poimaínein» = pastorear). Que se trata del *pasto* de la Palabra

---

32. *Epist. 146 (cf. Rouet de Journel*, n. 1.357).

33. Respecto a las cualidades humanas de los *ancianos*, observa W. R. Lewis (en *La Iglesia*, compil. de J. B. Watson, pp. 117-118): «Alguien dijo en una ocasión que el anciano necesita "la sabiduría de un padre, el afecto de una madre y la piel de un rinoceronte".» V. Fábrega, en el cursillo citado, nos hacía notar que los «presbyteroi» judíos no eran los sacerdotes, sino los nobles de sangre o en posesiones.

34. V. lección 28.ª.

de Dios, es evidente por el contexto de todos los pasajes citados. «Pastor y Obispo» son dos términos que se atribuyen conjuntamente a Cristo en 1.ª Ped. 2:25. El salmo 23 y Juan 10 son hitos relevantes en la trayectoria bíblica del pastorado aplicado a Yahveh y a Jesucristo. Si ya Homero pudo decir que los reyes eran «pastores de pueblos», a nadie mejor que a Cristo puede aplicarse el vocablo, ya que El fue proclamado, según el título de la Cruz, «Rey» que dio Su propia vida en pasto abundante para Sus ovejas (Jn. 10:10). No es extraño que Pedro apele al «Príncipe de los pastores», Cristo, cuando intima a los *ancianos* su responsabilidad como pastores de la grey de Dios (1.ª Pedro 5:4). Siendo el *pastorado* un ministerio específico que, bajo tal nombre, engloba todas las funciones que venimos enumerando en este apartado, bueno será resumir aquí algunos aspectos dignos de consideración:

a) *Deberes y cualificaciones del pastor:* 1) El pastor debe ser un maestro espiritual, forjado en la experiencia, el estudio y la oración; celoso de ganar almas y edificar las ya ganadas; ejemplo de su casa y de la grey. 2) Aunque no posee ningún *carácter* sacerdotal, siendo su principal ministerio predicar el evangelio más bien que presidir el culto, a él corresponde administrar las ordenanzas, aunque cualquier otro miembro designado por la iglesia puede administrarlas con igual legitimidad en una emergencia. 3) El es el superintendente nato de la disciplina, así como el presidente de las reuniones. Sólo Jesucristo posee el poder legislativo en la Iglesia, pero el pastor representa el poder ejecutivo de la congregación; y esto nunca en *forma* coactiva, sino por la enseñanza y la persuasión. Mateo 18:17 y 1.ª Cor. 5:2-5 muestran que el ejercitar la disciplina compete a toda la comunidad. 4) Así merece ser honrado y sostenido económicamente por la iglesia (*cf.* 1.ª Cor. 9:7-14; 1.ª Tim. 5:17-18).

b) *Elección de pastor.* En 2.ª Cor. 8:19 (como en la *Didaché*, 15, 1),[35] el verbo «cheirotonéo» retiene quizá su

---

35. V. *Rouet de Journel*, n.º 9.

sentido clásico de «levantar la mano para votar» y, con el precedente de Hech. 1:15-23, donde el plural «éstesan» muestra que todos intervinieron en la elección, ya que Pedro (sujeto en singular del v. 15) se dirige a todos en el v. 16, vemos que la elección corresponde a toda la congregación. En Tito 1:5, Pablo le manda nombrar o instituir («katastéses») ancianos en Creta. Hechos 14:23 nos presenta a Pablo y Bernabé «imponiendo las manos»[36] para designar ancianos en las iglesias de Listra, Iconio y Antioquía de Pisidia. El nominativo del participio y el dativo «autoís» hacen aquí imposible el sentido de votación general.[37]

2. Diáconos.

Los pastores no pueden atender a todas las necesidades espirituales y materiales de una congregación; sobre todo, si ésta es numerosa y dispersa. Ya en Hech. 6 vemos cómo los apóstoles, necesitando todo su tiempo para dedicarlo a la oración y a la predicación de la Palabra, buscaron ayuda mediante el nombramiento de siete varones de buen testimonio y llenos del Espíritu Santo, elegidos por la congregación e instituidos por los apóstoles mediante la oración y la imposición de las manos («epéthekan autoís tas cheirás» —v. 6—), para que sirvieran a las mesas. Tres observaciones son convenientes a propósito de este pasaje: A) Los siete tienen nombre griego, debido sin duda a que eran precisamente las viudas de origen griego las que se quejaban de quedar desatendidas. B) Aunque es una peculiar «diakonía» o servicio lo que se les encomienda, el texto no les da el título específico de «diáconos». C) De los siete mencionados en el v. 5, sólo dos vuelven a aparecer, y no precisamente como administradores de la comunidad, sino como *testigos* del mensaje (Esteban —el primer «mártir», testigo hasta el ofrecimien-

---

36. Véase el punto 4 de la presente lección.
37. V. E. Trenchard, *Comentario a Hechos*, p. 308.

to de su vida, tras dar testimonio con poder, elocuencia y milagros—; incluso, un crítico severo de la religión y del culto judíos; y Felipe —capítulo 8, etc.— haciendo labor de *evangelista*).

El actual oficio de *diácono* comporta el ayudar a los pastores, tanto en lo espiritual como en lo material. Sus deberes y cualificaciones están detallados en 1.ª Tim. 3: 8-13, y pueden resumirse de la manera siguiente: *a*) Relevar al pastor en funciones externas, informándole de las condiciones y necesidades de la iglesia y sirviendo de lazo de unión entre el pastor y la congregación; *b*) ayudar a la propia congregación, encargándose del alivio de enfermos y necesitados en lo material así como en lo espiritual, y también de todo lo relacionado con los cultos en su parte material, como es la distribución de los elementos en la Cena del Señor; *c*) el v. 9 muestra que el diácono ha de desempeñar su oficio «concienzudamente», «guardando el misterio de la fe», o sea, en atención, y por amor, al Señor encarnado, crucificado y ascendido (v. 16); *d*) a semejanza de Esteban y Felipe, ha de tener celo por cooperar en primera línea a la obra evangelizadora y edificadora de la iglesia, siendo como una extensión de la obra pastoral en los servicios no culturales.

INSTITUCIÓN DE LOS DIÁCONOS. 1.ª Tim. 3:10 manda que los diáconos sean sometidos a un tiempo de prueba, hasta ser hallados irreprensibles. Hechos 6 requería una solución rápida, de emergencia, pero en 1.ª Tim. 5:22 ya encarga el apóstol a Timoteo que «no imponga las manos con ligereza a ninguno, para no participar en los pecados ajenos», o sea, para no hacerse responsable de los fallos en que, por su incapacidad o su falta de espíritu, vaya a incurrir la persona a quien Timoteo se disponga a imponer las manos. Por otra parte, los siete varones de Hechos 6 eran recomendados por todos por su conducta intachable y estaban reconocidos como «llenos del Espíritu Santo». Como es obvio, los diáconos han de ser reconocidos y aceptados por la congregación y especialmente por los dirigentes de la comunidad, sobre quienes pesa una peculiar responsabilidad en los asuntos de la iglesia.

3. Diaconisas y viudas.

En Rom. 16:1-2, Pablo menciona a Febe, a la que se da el apelativo de «diákonos» en la iglesia de Cencrea, suburbio de Corinto. En 1.ª Tim. 3:11, en un inciso dentro de las cualificaciones de los diáconos, se habla de «mujeres» (sin artículo). Los más competentes teólogos y exégetas [38] piensan que no se trata aquí de las esposas de los diáconos, sino de mujeres que les ayudaban en las funciones externas de la iglesia. Es curioso notar cómo las cuatro cualificaciones del v. 11 corresponden a las del v. 8; mientras en el v. 8 se requiere a los diáconos que sean «sin doblez», o sea, que no digan una cosa al pastor o a los ancianos, y otra a la congregación, en el v. 11 se intima a las mujeres (¿diaconisas?) que no sean «diablos», es decir, chismosas o calumniadoras, pues esto es lo que significa la palabra griega empleada allí («diabolus»). Tanto en los Evangelios como en las Epístolas, puede encontrarse una lista respetable de mujeres que, con todo amor y dedicación, ofrecían su tiempo, su dinero y su trabajo en favor del Señor o de Su Iglesia. Estas cristianas, fieles y generosas, nunca han faltado en nuestras iglesias. Exceptuando quizás el ministerio de enseñanza con autoridad (1.ª Tim. 2:12), son muchos los servicios que las buenas creyentes pueden prestar. 1.ª Tim. 5:3-16 habla de las *viudas*. No se trata aquí de mujeres que hayan de prestar servicios a la iglesia, sino viceversa (*cf.* Hech. 6:1 y ss.).

4. La imposición de manos.

Hechos 6:6; 13:3; 1.ª Tim. 4:14; 5:22 nos hablan de «imponer las manos» («epitíthemi tas cheirás») o de «im-

---

38. *Cf.* A. H. Strong, *o. c.*, p. 918; W. Hendriksen, *Thimothy and Titus*, pp. 132-134; G. Millon, *L'Eglise*, p. 41.

posición de manos» («epíthesis ton cheirón»). La Iglesia de Roma ve en este simbolismo un rito sacramental de ordenación. Sin embargo, este símbolo tiene, dentro de la tradición judía, un claro sentido: *identificación* con aquél a quien se imponen las manos, como para extender a él, en prolongación sucesoria o proyección comunicativa, las promesas o las bendiciones divinas (Gén. 48:8-20), o el propio espíritu y autoridad (Núm. 27:18-23), o una común comisión (Núm. 8:10; Hech. 13:3), o incluso, para cargar sobre él los propios pecados en sustitución expiatoria (*cf.* Lev. 16:20-22). La transmisión de poderes *sacerdotales* es incompatible con el simbolismo de tal rito.[39]

CUESTIONARIO:

1. ¿Para qué son necesarios los oficios en las iglesias? — 2. ¿Cómo demostraría usted que «obispo» y «presbítero» designan una misma persona? — 3. ¿Cuáles son los deberes y derechos del pastor? — 4. ¿Cuáles son los cometidos de los diáconos? — 5. ¿Qué simbolismo comporta la «imposición de las manos»?

---

39. En efecto, los sacerdotes del Antiguo Testamento eran consagrados con óleo, pero no se les imponían las manos. En el Nuevo Testamento sólo hay un «*Christós* = Ungido», por excelencia, con el Espíritu, porque Él es también el único «*hiereús* = sacerdote de la Nueva Alianza, con quien todo el nuevo «Pueblo de Dios» es un «hieráteuma» = sacerdocio (1.ª Ped. 2:9), que recibe en común el «crisma» o «unción del Santo» (1.ª Jn. 2:20). Por eso, la *epíthesis tôn cheirôn* o imposición de manos transmite un *oficio* o *comisión*, pero no un poder sacerdotal.

LECCION 33.ª LA DISCIPLINA EN LA IGLESIA

1. Necesidad de la disciplina.

Entendemos por *disciplina* la acción que la iglesia local se ve obligada a tomar con alguno de sus miembros, cuando éste rehúsa apartarse de un grave error doctrinal o de un pecado notorio y escandaloso. La disciplina es algo necesario para preservar el testimonio y la pureza de una iglesia. Tiene aquí aplicación el llamado «poder de las llaves», que Lutero condensó en la frase: *«predicar y aplicar* el Evangelio».[40] Esta es *la llave de la disciplina* (ya mencionada en la lección 6.ª), a la que ya se alude en Mat. 16:19; 18:18, y cuya aplicación está detallada en 1.ª Cor. 5:1-13.

2. Clases de disciplina.

A) PRIVADA. Es la mencionada en Mat. 5:23-24; 18:15-18. Dado que las palabras «contra ti» de Mat. 18:15 faltan en la mayoría de los MSS, podemos decir que, más bien que de dos clases de ofensas (personales y públicas), se trata de dos modos distintos de ejercitar la disciplina, siendo *privada* cuando el miembro ofensor es corregido por otro hermano en secreto y con amor (Ef. 4:32). La frase de Mat. 18:15 «has ganado a tu hermano» demuestra que el pecado de cualquier hermano no es sólo una pérdida para Dios y para él mismo (vv. 11-14), sino también para los demás miembros de la iglesia, puesto que todo fallo en el Cuerpo de Cristo hace descender el nivel espiritual de la

---

40. *Cf. The New Bible Dictionary*, pp. 1017-1018.

comunidad. Nunca se debe llevar una queja contra un hermano a la iglesia o al pastor, sin haber antes intentado corregirle en secreto.

B) Pública. Cuando la ofensa es grave y pública, o el ofensor rehúsa corregirse tras la corrección privada, debe aplicarse la disciplina *eclesial* de acuerdo con 1.ª Corintios 5:1-13; 2.ª Tes. 3:6. Por el primer pasaje se puede ver que Pablo no concede moratorias para despedir al incestuoso. Allá el pecador con Dios y con su conciencia, donde ha de buscar el sincero arrepentimiento y el decidido propósito de la enmienda, pero la iglesia no puede ni debe esperar cuando su reputación y su necesidad de continua autopurificación están comprometidas. La iglesia no es una Sociedad de Socorros Mutuos, sino una comunidad de creyentes *segregados* del mundo.

3. "Excomunión" y reconciliación.

Aparte de los crímenes que eran castigados con la muerte, los judíos practicaban tres clases de excomunión: *a)* la separación durante un mes, llamada en hebreo «niddu» y en griego «aphorismós»; *b)* la exclusión de las asambleas, o «jerem» (en griego «anáthema»); *c)* la permanente separación de la comunidad, o «shammattah». En el Nuevo Testamento no aparecen distinciones en el tiempo o en el grado de separación, sino que sólo se menciona la necesidad de apartarse decidida y totalmente de cuantos manchan el nombre cristiano. Así han de entenderse lugares como 1.ª Cor. 5:1-13; 2.ª Cor. 2:6-8; 2.ª Tes. 3:6; 2.º Jn. vv. 9-11. Especial atención merecen los vv. 9-11 de 1.ª Cor. 5, donde vemos que la *separación* ha de mantenerse dentro de los ya *segregados* del mundo, puesto que es esta mezcolanza *dentro* de la iglesia la que contamina el Cuerpo y embota el testimonio, mientras que el contacto con el mundo depravado, del que no se puede esperar otra cosa y al que hemos de presentar nuestro testimonio, es ineludible.[41]

En el terreno cultual, la excomunión comporta esencialmente la exclusión de la *comunión* eclesial y, por tanto, de la participación de la *Cena del Señor,* que la simboliza (*cf.* 1.ª Cor. 10:16-17). No se excluyen las oraciones por los ofensores.[42] Tampoco se les prohíbe que asistan a la predicación de la Palabra, siendo éste el medio primordial para que recapaciten, se arrepientan y vuelvan al buen camino.

1.ª Cor. 5:5 no implica una *pena de muerte,* sino el ser arrojado al mundo, donde Satanás, «el príncipe de este mundo» ejerce su dominio, lo cual lleva al creyente indigno a nuevas pruebas espirituales y también a penalidades de tipo corporal (la enfermedad y la muerte están en la órbita del pecado —comp. con 1.ª Cor. 11:30-32, en un contexto de la Cena del Señor, y Heb. 12:6 y ss.—). Cuando una iglesia, obediente a la Palabra de Dios, ejercita la disciplina, como en 2.ª Cor. 2:6-11, los frutos de la corrección amorosa, tanto privada como eclesial, no se harán esperar.[43]

4. ¿Quién tiene que aplicar la disciplina.

La disciplina ha de ser ejercitada *por la iglesia misma, en el nombre de Cristo, en obediencia a la Palabra de Dios*

41. Acerca de la correcta interpretación de la parábola de la cizaña, hablamos ya en la lección 8.ª.

42. Sobre el problema que plantea 1.ª Jn. 5:16 trataremos en el vol. V, aunque podemos adelantar como probable la solución que ofrece L. Sp. Chafer, *o. c.,* vol. III, p. 310, de que se trata de alguien que ha cometido pecado que suele ser castigado por el Señor con la muerte (como el «muchos duermen» de 1.ª Cor. 11:30) y por cuya sanación física Juan *no manda* —tampoco lo prohíbe— que se ruegue. Que no se trata de apostasía ni pecado contra el Espíritu Santo, ni de muerte eterna, como suele interpretarse, lo muestra el hecho de que Juan habla de un «hermano», vocablo que sólo se aplica a creyentes.

43. Como alguien ha dicho: «Cuando uno de los nuestros cae, es que los demás no le hemos ayudado bastante.»

y en el poder del Espíritu Santo. Sin embargo, el pastor, los ancianos y los diáconos tienen en ello un doble papel: 1.º, de *supervisión,* procurando informarse fiel e imparcialmente sobre las ofensas y sus circunstancias y presionando para que se den los pasos que señala la Palabra de Dios; 2.º, de *ejecución,* en la que el pastor no ejerce ninguna autoridad propia, sino que es el órgano ejecutor de la iglesia y el superintendente especialmente responsable de la purificación de la comunidad, para el buen nombre del Señor y para el bien espiritual de la misma persona ofensora, pues éstas deben ser las metas u objetivos de toda comunidad verdaderamente cristiana al usar la llave de la disciplina.[44]

5. Razones de una buena disciplina.

Wayne Mack [45] resume así las razones para la disciplina eclesial:

> «Las razones para la disciplina de la iglesia son tres: Una es por la gloria del Señor. "Viendo que la iglesia es el cuerpo de Cristo, no puede ser mancillada... sin acarrear cierta deshonra a su Cabeza" —dice Calvino en sus *Instituciones,* II, p. 454—. Es Cristo quien nos ha ordenado el ejercitar la disciplina eclesial, y no podemos honrarle si desobedecemos Su mandato... Una segunda razón para la disciplina es procurar que otros no se desmanden a causa de un mal ejemplo: "Un poco de levadura leuda [es decir, corrompe] toda la masa" (1.ª Cor. 5:6); "A los que persisten en pecar, repréndelos delante de todos, para que los

---

44. *Cf. Baptist Distinctives,* pp. 51-52; R. B. Kuiper, *o. c.,* páginas 297-312; W. H. Griffith Thomas, *Principles of Theology,* pp. 434-438; *The New Bible Dictionary,* p. 402 («Excommunication») y páginas 1017-1018 («The power of the keys»); A. H. Strong, *o. c.,* páginas 924-926; E. Trenchard. *La Iglesia, las iglesias y la obra misionera,* pp. 34-42.
45. En la revista *Reformation Today* (Winter, 1971), p. 20.

demás también teman» (1.ª Tim. 5:20). Una tercera razón para la disciplina es que el pecador puede ser así convencido de pecado e incitado al arrepentimiento. El designio de la disciplina no es primariamente punitivo, sino reformativo, protectivo, correctivo y restaurativo (2.ª Tes. 3:14; 1.ª Corintios 5:5; Mat. 18:15; 2.ª Cor. 2:6-8; Gál. 6:1).»

Y, citando a G. I. Williamson, añade que la disciplina eclesial es «un acto de amor y preocupación, propio del buen pastor que va en busca de la oveja perdida». Finalmente, como el mismo W. Mack hace notar, «una forma —podríamos decir: la primordial— de ejercer la disciplina es el ministerio público de la Palabra. Cada vez que la Palabra es predicada, reprende, corrige e instruye».

CUESTIONARIO:

1. ¿Cuál es el deber de la iglesia en cuanto a la disciplina? — 2. Clases de disciplina y cómo se ejerce cada una. — 3. Contexto judío de «excomunión» y su uso en el Nuevo Testamento. — 4. ¿Qué comporta la excomunión en el plano cultual? — 5. ¿Cuál es el significado de 1.ª Cor. 5:5? — 6. ¿A quién compete aplicar la disciplina? — 7. ¿Cuál es la meta última de toda disciplina bien aplicada? — 8. ¿Por qué razones ha de ejercitarse la disciplina eclesial?

Las dimensiones
de la Iglesia

LECCION 34.ª CONCEPTO DE UNIDAD

1. Introducción.

Comenzamos con esta lección el estudio de lo que la Iglesia de Roma ha venido llamando «notas de la Iglesia» y que H. Küng, con mejor acuerdo, llama «dimensiones».[1] Estas dimensiones son: unidad, santidad, catolicidad y apostolicidad. La doctrina tradicional de la Iglesia de Roma es que estas cuatro «dimensiones» son las «notas» (o sea, *características* notorias) de la verdadera Iglesia de Cristo, y que estas *notas* se encuentran *solamente* (o, al menos, de un modo más perfecto) en la Iglesia Católica Romana. De ahí que se niegue a cualquier otra comunidad cristiana el título de «verdadera iglesia de Cristo».

2. Noción de unidad.

La unidad es la característica trascendental por la que todo ser es algo *integrado en sí* y diferenciado de cualquier otro. La materia inorgánica tiene una unidad *visible* que le presta su aparente continuidad en objetos no fraccionados. Lo orgánico debe su unidad a un principio interior de vida, organización y movimiento. Tanto la materia inorgánica como la orgánica albergan interiormente otras *unidades* a nivel subatómico, atómico y molecular, etc.

Los seres racionales pueden unirse entre sí mediante sus coincidencias en las mismas ideas y en los mismos gustos e intereses. Así se forman los distintos grupos, par-

---

1. *O. c.*, pp. 263-269. En cuanto a lo que nosotros llamamos «notas» de la Iglesia, véase la lección 10.ª.

tidos, clubs, etc. La comunidad de sangre, raza, cultura, etcétera, es también un multiforme factor de unidad. Finalmente, el «nuevo nacimiento» a la vida *espiritual*, con la consiguiente participación de la naturaleza divina (2.ª Pedro 1:4), nos da una nueva y más fuerte *unidad*, como hijos de un mismo Padre y como miembros de un mismo Cuerpo de Cristo, que es la Iglesia (*cf.* Rom. 8:14; 12:4 y siguientes; 1.ª Cor. 12; Ef. 4, etc.).

3. Historia de la unidad.

La unidad del *qahal* de Israel estaba basada en los pactos de Yahveh-Dios con Su Pueblo escogido: el pueblo de las promesas y de las bendiciones divinas. Ahora bien, ¿qué es lo que establece la continuidad del *Israel de Dios* a través de ambos Testamentos? No es la nacionalidad judía, expresada en la circuncisión, sino la *fe*, por la cual todos los creyentes somos hijos espirituales de Abraham (Gál. 3:7-9, 14-16, 26-29), lo que *unifica* a la Iglesia de todos los tiempos. La cuidadosa distinción entre los términos griegos «aulé» y «poímne» de Jn. 10:16, muestra que la Iglesia no está ya circunscrita a una nación o territorio («redil»), sino que es «un solo *rebaño*», liberado de vallas territoriales, porque Cristo ha derribado el muro de separación mediante el derramamiento de Su sangre en la Cruz (Ef. 2:11-22), lo cual constituye para Pablo el «misterio» por antonomasia (Ef. 3:3-6). Romanos 11:13-36 nos presenta la misma verdad bajo distinta metáfora: el injerto de ramas ajenas en el «buen olivo». Hechos 7:38 viene a darnos incluso la coincidencia entre los términos *qahal* (hebreo) y *ekklesía* (griego) de la Iglesia de Dios a través de los tiempos.

El concepto de «Iglesia» es expresado en el Nuevo Testamento bajo las metáforas de planta, cuerpo, edificio, rebaño, esposa, etc.,[2] de naturaleza *espiritual*. La unidad de la Iglesia es, pues, unidad del Espíritu y de caracte-

---

2. V. las lecciones 8.ª y 9.ª.

rísticas *espirituales*, aunque debe proyectarse también *visiblemente*, como veremos en la siguiente lección. Una unidad así entendida admite sana libertad y pluralismo de formas dentro de su núcleo irrompible. Los pecados contra la ortodoxia y el amor (herejía y cisma) son los que de verdad la dañan.

La *oficialidad* de la Iglesia y el concepto de la misma como *Ciudad de Dios* oscurecieron lamentablemente el concepto de *unidad*, haciéndola depender durante más de un milenio (desde el siglo IV hasta la Reforma) de la sumisión a unos poderes jerárquicos y a unas estructuras monolíticamente centralizadas; sobre todo, cuando comenzó a considerarse al Bautismo como instrumento de *regeneración* espiritual, al mismo tiempo que como *puerta* de la Iglesia Universal. En esta perspectiva hay que examinar las rupturas de unidad visible ocurridas en la Iglesia a lo largo de los siglos.[3]

CUESTIONARIO:

1. ¿A qué podemos llamar «dimensiones de la Iglesia»? — 2. ¿Cómo influye el «nuevo nacimiento» en la unidad de la Iglesia? — 3. ¿Qué es lo que unifica a la Iglesia de Dios en ambos Testamentos? — 4. ¿Qué clase de unidad expresan las metáforas de cuerpo, rebaño, planta, etc.? — 5. ¿De dónde arrancó la desviación en el concepto de unidad?

---

3. Repásese la lección 12.ª para mejor entender el concepto de unidad.

LECCION 35.ª

CARACTERISTICAS DE LA UNIDAD ECLESIAL

1. Profundidad de la unidad de la Iglesia.

Entramos en una materia de suma importancia, no sólo por lo que la unidad de la Iglesia significa en sí, sino por el concepto de iglesia que esta unidad comporta y por las consecuencias que tiene en el terreno del Ecumenismo. Es sabido que el «slogan» del Consejo Mundial de Iglesias, supuesto portavoz y órgano del Movimiento Ecuménico Mundial, es: «*Que todos sean uno*» (Jn. 17:21). Estudiemos, pues, este pasaje dentro de su contexto.

Como preliminar digamos que hay autores que sostienen (y dan sus razones) que Jesús elevó al Padre esta grandiosa oración teniendo en Su mente y ante Su vista *sólo* a los Doce, siendo el v. 20 un paréntesis. Si se admite esta interpretación, Jesús habría orado para que el Espíritu consagrase en la verdad y mantuviese en unidad compacta de mensaje y testimonio, a los Doce fundamentos de la Iglesia, para que el mundo recibiese, mediante la unidad de vida y testimonio de ellos, la prueba de que el Padre había enviado a Su Hijo como Mesías-Salvador.

Pero concedamos que el v. 21 se refiere tanto a los apóstoles como a cuantos habían de creer por la palabra de ellos. ¿Qué dice el versículo?

A) «*Para que todos sean uno.*» Más que de la unidad inicial, invisible, pero inquebrantable, que todos los creyentes tienen con el Señor y entre sí desde el momento en que fueron salvos, *naciendo de nuevo*, se trata de una unidad que hay que guardar, fomentar y manifestar.[4]

B) «*Como tú, oh Padre, en mí, y yo en ti, que también ellos sean uno en nosotros.*» Aquí aparece como modelo y raíz de la unión entre los creyentes la unidad e inmanencia mutua que existe entre las personas divinas. ¿Y cómo son *uno* dichas personas divinas? Por la perfectísima comunión en la Esencia, la Verdad, el Amor, etc., divinos. El Padre está en el Hijo *expresando toda Su Verdad;* el Hijo está en el Padre como *Verbo* revelador de dicha Verdad. El Padre y el Hijo están en el Espíritu *imprimiendo todo Su Amor;* el Espíritu Santo está en el Padre y en el Hijo como la impresión personal del Amor de ambos (Romanos 5:5).

C) Por tanto, la dinámica de la unidad de la Iglesia (v. 23 —lit. «para que sean perfectos *hacia* la unidad») tiene dos ejes notorios: la *Verdad* total, o sea, la ortodoxia del Evangelio, y el *Amor* en la *koinonía* del Espíritu. No pueden excluirse mutuamente la *doctrina* y el *servicio*. Han de marchar siempre unidos la Verdad y el Amor, la Ortodoxia y el Entusiasmo. La Verdad sin Amor es fría, pero el Amor sin Verdad está vacío. Por eso, no pueden arrumbarse, sin más, las diferencias doctrinales en aras de un servicio y cooperación mutuos. Como dice W. Hendriksen,[5] «los creyentes deberían siempre suspirar por la paz, *pero nunca a expensas de la verdad,* porque la «unidad» ganada al precio de tal sacrificio no es digna de tal nombre» (el subrayado es suyo).

2. Unidad VISIBLE de la Iglesia.

Juan 17:21 termina así: «*para que el mundo crea que tú me enviaste*». Esto implica que la unidad de los creyentes es necesaria para testimonio ante el mundo, lo cual es imposible si tal unidad no puede ser vista desde el exte-

---

4. V. el punto 3 de esta misma lección.
5. *The Gospel of John*, II, p. 365.

rior. Es, pues, necesario que, a través de nuestras diferencias de toda índole, el mundo pueda ver la *unidad* de los creyentes a triple nivel:

a) A nivel *personal:* unión espiritual de cada creyente con Cristo-Cabeza, de tal manera que nuestra posición doctrinal y nuestra conducta diaria puedan traslucir e irradiar los rasgos de Cristo (Rom. 8:29; 1.ª Cor. 11:1; 2.ª Corintios 3:18; Ef. 5:1; Col. 3:1; 1.ª Tes. 1:6; etc.).

b) A nivel de *iglesia local:* testimonio propio de una comunidad cristiana *viva,* en unión espiritual de todo el Cuerpo con su Cabeza-Cristo, y en comunión de criterios, sentimientos, afanes, problemas y bienes con los demás co-miembros. Notemos que la *koinonia* o «comunión de los santos» indica, sobre todo, «comunión de las cosas santas» (*cf.* 1.ª Cor. 1:10; Filip. 2:2-4; Tito 3:10; 1.ª Jn. 3:16-18; etcétera).

c) A nivel de *Iglesia Universal,* puesto que cada comunidad local no es sino la concreción espacio-temporal de la única Iglesia (con mayúscula) de Jesucristo. Todas las iglesias genuinamente *cristianas,* a pesar de sus legítimas peculiaridades, deberían manifestar *visiblemente* su unidad mediante un «credo» bíblico común y una pronta disposición a darse mutuamente *las manos diestras de compañerismo* (Gál. 2:9) en las comunes tareas de evangelización, testimonio y beneficencia.[6] En este punto vemos dos extremos igualmente equivocados: 1) el de la Iglesia Romana, que acentúa el aspecto *externo* de la unidad, identificando a la Iglesia Universal con una determinada estructura, mundialmente organizada, con detrimento del núcleo espiritual de la unidad *en Cristo;* 2) el de los que niegan o evitan todo nexo de las comunidades cristianas entre sí, quizá por miedo a caer en el peligro de las estructuras organizadas a escala nacional o mundial. Por eso, cuando empleemos el adjetivo «independiente» aplicado a una igle-

---

6. Es lamentable que algunas denominaciones, grupos y «Misiones» parezcan buscar (al menos, subconscientemente) su propia gloria más bien que la del común Señor.

sia, hemos de explicar su sentido: independencia de toda estructura oficial organizada de fuera adentro (o de arriba abajo), pero no como opuesto a la intercomunión eclesial.

3. Amplitud y riqueza de la unidad de la Iglesia.

Efesios 4:1-16 es, sin duda, el pasaje que mejor condensa las características de la unidad de la Iglesia. Allí aprendemos que:

1. La unidad eclesial está ya *hecha*, puesto que el apóstol no exhorta a *hacer*, sino a *guardar*, la unidad (versículo 3). La unidad de la Iglesia es obra del Espíritu, quien regenera, convence de pecado, da poder al mensaje, imparte el don de la fe y, así, *añade* a la Iglesia única de Cristo.

2. La unidad eclesial requiere *abnegación* para su fiel custodia, pues la mutua solicitud por la unidad se sostiene sobre cuatro pilares: humildad, mansedumbre, paciencia y amor (v. 2).

3. Es *esencialmente espiritual* y está trabada por siete lazos espirituales: formamos un solo Cuerpo, con una sola Alma, creciendo y marchando a una misma meta (v. 4); tenemos un solo Señor a quien seguir; una sola fe que profesar y un solo Bautismo que recibir (v. 5); todo lo hace en nosotros un solo Dios y Padre de todos los creyentes (v. 6).

4. Es una unidad en la *variedad*, pues siendo todos miembros del mismo Cuerpo, tenemos diversos dones (v. 7), distintos ministerios específicos (v. 11) y se nos han encomendado diferentes servicios, «según la actividad propia de cada miembro» (vv. 12, 16).

5. Es una unidad obtenida *al precio de la sangre de Cristo* y ganada en batalla con el demonio (vv. 8-10), pues sólo tras su humillación y exaltación pudo el Señor repartir el botín de los dones que consagran y potencian la unidad.

6. Es una unidad que debe *crecer* y perfeccionarse, hasta llegar a la medida de madurez de un varón perfecto, como corresponde a un Cuerpo que ha crecido simétrica y armónicamente con su Cabeza. Este crecimiento se realiza por medio de una progresiva profundización en la fe (de ahí la importancia de la formación bíblica para el fomento de la unidad) y una mayor intimidad en el conocimiento experimental de Jesucristo (de ahí la necesidad de una honda espiritualidad para todo sano ecumenismo —versículos 12-13—).

7. Es una unidad que exige conjuntamente *adhesión práctica a la Verdad en el Amor,* para escapar así tanto de una ortodoxia muerta como de un entusiasmo huero. Una formación madura, tanto doctrinal como espiritual, nos prevendrá contra los falsos maestros y los cantos de sirena de toda índole, que engañan a los indoctos *pueril- mente fluctuantes y versátiles* (vv. 14-15; comp. con 2.ª Pedro 3:16).

8. Tres observaciones finales, de suma importancia práctica, nos ofrece este pasaje: A) Es importante constatar que entre los siete vínculos de la unidad eclesial (vv. 4-6) no figura una cabeza humana visible, pretendido «principio y raíz de la unidad»; B) Los pecados que directamente afectan a la unidad eclesial son: *a)* la *herejía,* que toma partido por un aspecto de la verdad revelada, suprimiendo u oscureciendo el contexto total del mensaje; *b)* el *cisma,* o escisión injustificada en el Cuerpo de la Iglesia, lo cual se debe frecuentemente al afán de hallar la *iglesia perfecta.*[7] C) El verdadero método para guardar y fomentar la unidad de la Iglesia consiste en una continua *«metánoia»,* que comportan los requisitos de los versículos 2-3. Cuando los creyentes y las iglesias reconozcan sus defectos; cuando estemos todos dispuestos a sufrir

---

7. Cuentan que Ch. H. Spurgeon dijo a uno de estos «perfeccionistas»: «Si usted no se tiene por perfecto, deje ya de buscar la iglesia perfecta, porque ésta dejará de serlo en el momento en que usted se haga miembro de ella.»

y a esperar, a sobrellevar con amor y paciencia los fallos ajenos y a confesar los propios, a dejar nuestras opiniones y vanas tradiciones y ceñirnos a la Palabra, irá madurando la verdadera unidad.

CUESTIONARIO:

1. ¿Por qué es tan importante el tema de la unidad? — 2. ¿De qué unidad se trata en Jn. 17:21? — 3. ¿A qué niveles ha de ser visible la unidad de la Iglesia? — 4. ¿Qué extremos han de evitarse en esta materia? — 5. ¿Qué características de la unidad nos presenta Ef. 4:1-16? — 6. ¿Qué pecados afectan directamente a la unidad de la Iglesia? — 7. ¿Qué debemos hacer (creyentes e iglesias) para fomentar la unidad?

LECCION 36.ª   UNION Y SEPARACION

1. La división denominacional.

Repetidas veces, dentro de contextos diferentes, hemos aludido al problema de la división denominacional, así como a la necesidad de separarse de una iglesia falsa. Insistiremos en estos aspectos desde el punto de vista de la *unidad*.

Una vez estudiados el concepto y las características de la unidad de la Iglesia, nos percatamos de que el aparato exterior de una estructura monolíticamente organizada no es señal de mayor unidad eclesial, y de que, siendo la Iglesia un *organismo*, más bien que una *institución*, las distintas denominaciones no laceran realmente la unidad del Cuerpo.

Pero ¿se puede decir que la división denominacional es una virtud? ¡No! El apóstol Pablo, que no toleró banderías en torno a personas, no hubiese tolerado tampoco la división en denominaciones. Sin embargo, hay una diferencia radical entre la era apostólica y la nuestra. La Iglesia primitiva, aunque imperfecta, era mantenida en la fidelidad a la Palabra de Dios por la autoridad apostólica, siendo expulsados de la comunidad quienes fallaban gravemente en la doctrina o en la conducta. En cambio, las iglesias que se llaman cristianas a partir de la Reforma, o se quedaron a medio camino en su intento de adaptarse al Nuevo Testamento, o se han desviado oficialmente de la Palabra de Dios. Con estas posiciones semirreformadas o desviadas, la única opción de todo verdadero creyente ha sido salir de ellas y adoptar nombres *diferen-*

ciales que expresasen de algún modo su posición bíblica frente a la posición oficial de las comunidades que, habiendo perdido el contenido, seguían arrogándose (a veces, en exclusiva) los títulos de «Iglesia católica», «Iglesia de Cristo», y hasta de «Iglesia evangélica».

2. El Movimiento Ecuménico.

Con todo, subsiste el hecho de que la división denominacional entre comunidades eclesiales ortodoxas que coinciden en lo fundamental, presenta caracteres de *anomalía* antibíblica, así como de notorio *contratestimonio* frente al mundo que sólo ve el aspecto exterior de una división desconcertante. No es, pues, extraño que, ante una renovada toma de conciencia de la realidad eclesial, en su doble aspecto de *misterio* (un Cuerpo) y *misión* (una tarea común en el mundo), todo creyente que esté de veras alerta a la voz del Espíritu, sienta en su corazón la urgencia de una tarea ecuménica que favorezca la manifestación *visible* de la unidad de la Iglesia.

Pero siempre que se habla de «ecumenismo» nos exponemos a tergiversar las nociones. Como dice G. Millon,[8] «jamás se ha hablado tanto de unidad como hoy, pero jamás ha sido tan ilusoria, por no decir mentirosa, la búsqueda de la unidad». Podemos decir que hay tres clases de «ecumenismo»: A) El de la Iglesia de Roma, según el cual la única verdadera Iglesia de Cristo es la Romana y, por tanto, todo afán de unidad ha de estar encaminado, en fin de cuentas, a la reintegración de todas las comunidades separadas en la única «Santa Madre Iglesia Católica Apostólica Romana». Entretanto, los católicos deben renovarse espiritualmente, adoptar un tono caritativo y comprensivo, procurar conocer mejor la doctrina y vida de los «hermanos separados» y exponer a éstos claramente toda la doctrina católica, estando dispuestos a colaborar en la promoción de la paz, de la justicia social y de

8. *L'Eglise*, p. 52.

la beneficencia.[9] B) El del Consejo Mundial de Iglesias que, sobre una base aparentemente bíblica, se esfuerza en realizar la unión y la cooperación entre todas las iglesias que se denominen cristianas, enfatizando el amor, el servicio y la colaboración, sin exigir una posición doctrinal claramente ortodoxa y esperando que la Iglesia de Roma acepte este programa para darle la más cordial bienvenida. Como ha escrito Forsyth,[10] *el término favorito es "ancho" y el resultado general "delgado"*. C) El ecumenismo evangélico, fundado en la Palabra de Dios, que implora el auxilio divino para que, mediante el poder del Espíritu, el Señor reavive a Su Iglesia, le inspire un profundo afán de continua Reforma, de profundización en Su Palabra, de testimonio por el anhelo misionero y la conducta santa y por el agrupamiento, *en un frente visible,* de todas las iglesias evangélicas fieles a la autoridad infalible de la Escritura, a la única jefatura de Jesucristo y al único impulso verdaderamente unificador: el poder y la gracia del Espíritu Santo.[11]

3. Las relaciones intereclesiales.

Como ha puesto de relieve Griffith Thomas,[12] la unidad entre las iglesias de la era apostólica y subapostólica se expresaba de modo muy simple: mediante la mutua hos-

---

9. V. el *Decreto sobre Ecumenismo* del C. Vaticano II, puntos 9-12.

10. *The Church and the Sacraments*, p. 28.

11. Un gran líder de este ecumenismo bíblico es, en los actuales tiempos de peligrosa confusión, el Dr. M. Lloyd-Jones, quien, además de numerosos sermones y conferencias dedicados a este tema, ha escrito, entre otros, dos importantes opúsculos: *The Basis of Christian Unity* y *Qué es la Iglesia*. Más bibliografía sobre este asunto: J. Grau, *El Ecumenismo y la Biblia* (Barcelona, 1969); G. W. Bromiley, *The Unity and Disunity of the Church* (Grand Rapids, 1969); O. Cullmann, *Verdadero y falso Ecumenismo* (Trad. de E. Requena, Ediciones Studium, 1972). De parte católica romana, J. Sánchez Vaquero, *Ecumenismo. Manual de Formación Ecuménica* (Salamanca, 1971).

12. *O. c.*, p. 276.

pitalidad, recibiendo cordial y fraternalmente la visita de
profetas y misioneros y mediante cartas. Darse la diestra
en señal de compañerismo era un modo de expresar la
coincidencia en lo fundamental del Evangelio (Gál. 2:9), y
recibir a los hermanos con amor y hospitalidad se reco-
mienda como conducta auténticamente eclesial (3.ª Juan
vv. 5-10).

Todas las iglesias verdaderamente evangélicas pueden
y deben coordinar sus esfuerzos en orden a la predicación
del Evangelio y a un testimonio conjunto dondequiera que
la verdad y la justicia lo demanden. Sin perder jamás su
independencia comunitaria y su autonomía administrativa,
las iglesias que sostienen unos mismos puntos de vista en
lo referente a lo doctrinal, la disciplina y el gobierno
harán bien (de acuerdo con el Nuevo Testamento) en aso-
ciarse, con el fin de cultivar su intercomunión, de estimu-
larse a una común obra misionera, de ayudarse en la tarea
de formación de ministros y obreros y de suplicar al Espíritu por un auténtico reavivamiento.

Como advierte J. M. Stowell,[13] «surge siempre en las
organizaciones democráticas una tendencia a centralizarse
por mor de la eficacia. Debemos estar alerta para que
esta tendencia no nos lleve a los bautistas a una jerarquía que pretenda imponerse a la iglesia local». Es, por
tanto, de suma importancia el que los comités o consejos
de dichas asociaciones, así como los representantes de las
iglesias en ellos, no se sientan como una corporación de
delegados que imponga unas normas o usurpe la tarea
de las iglesias, sino como *enviados* de las mismas iglesias
para intercambiar iniciativas y experiencias, sirviendo de
organismo coordinador y orientador, no de tribunal de apelación, puesto que las iglesias no pueden abdicar de su
autoridad y autonomía y son ellas las que, en último término, han de refrendar o rechazar los acuerdos de los
plenos y comités.

---

13. *Baptist Distinctives*, p. 27.

A nivel individual, la intercomunión se hace visible de una manera precisa y bíblicamente simbólica mediante la admisión a la Cena del Señor (símbolo de la unidad de la Iglesia —cf. 1.ª Cor. 10:17) a todo fiel de creencia ortodoxa, de buena conducta, y miembro normal de una iglesia local. Si se trata de una persona desconocida, debería presentar carta comendaticia de su propia iglesia. Tan abusiva es la comunión «cerrada» como la comunión indiscriminada.[14]

4. El problema de la separación.

Llegamos a un punto muy claro en teoría, pero a veces difícil en la práctica: ¿Cuándo puede y debe un creyente separarse de su iglesia? ¿No es un cisma toda separación de la estructura visible de la única Iglesia? ¿Por qué no quedarse en la iglesia para reformarla desde dentro, en vez de romper con ella en un afán de perfeccionismo? Contestaremos brevemente a tan frecuentes preguntas:

A) Notemos que el Nuevo Testamento exhorta frecuentemente a los cristianos a separarse de los no creyentes o de los falsos creyentes (cf. 1.ª Cor. 5:11-13; 15:33; 2.ª Corintios 6:14-18; Ef. 5:5-7; Apoc. 18:4). La misma obligación hay de separarse de una iglesia falsa, es decir, una iglesia que enseña un «evangelio diferente» (Gál. 1:6, 8-9) o mantiene prácticas contrarias a la Palabra de Dios, o que rehúsa someterse a la clara voz de la Escritura y escuchar

---

14. No es unánime la opinión entre los evangélicos sobre si se puede admitir a la Mesa del Señor a hermanos que sean genuinos creyentes, pero que no han sido bautizados, o lo han hecho en su infancia por aspersión o infusión. Personalmente creemos que sólo los bautizados deben participar de la Cena del Señor, pudiéndose admitir a la misma a quienes no lo hayan hecho por inmersión, con tal que no sea de continuo, pues esto implicaría una membresía anómala. Sin embargo, no subestimamos las razones de otros hermanos, quienes, viendo en la Cena del Señor un símbolo de unidad de *todos los salvos* por la muerte de Jesucristo y que esperan con gozo Su 2.ª Venida, piensan que no debe negarse la comunión a creyentes que no han sido aún bautizados.

nuestra protesta en nombre del Evangelio. Hay detalles doctrinales accesorios que no justifican un cisma, pero cuando se niega o se pervierte la enseñanza sobre un Dios en tres personas, o la verdadera divinidad y humanidad de Cristo en la única persona del Verbo, Su expiación suficiente en el Calvario, Su resurrección corporal, la salvación de pura gracia, la justificación mediante la sola fe, la autoridad infalible de las Escrituras, etc., se trata de una iglesia *herética*. Si, a pesar de nuestra protesta (no de nuestro silencio), la tal iglesia, *en su capacidad oficial* (sesión, presbiterio o voto mayoritario), *enseña el error, obliga a sus miembros a creer o hacer lo que es contrario a la Palabra de Dios, o rehúsa ejercitar la necesaria disciplina con los herejes notorios y con los cristianos indignos de tal nombre*, a pesar de estar bien probados los cargos contra ellos, nuestro derecho y nuestro deber es separarnos de tal iglesia y buscar otra que se conduzca de acuerdo con la Palabra de Dios.

B) Tal decisión no es un cisma, sino la preservación de la unidad y santidad de la única verdadera Iglesia de Cristo. Cuando los Reformadores rompieron con Roma, no pretendieron negar la unidad visible de la Iglesia verdadera, sino llevársela consigo, al ser rechazadas sus protestas por una estructura oficial que rehusaba someterse a la Escritura; por eso tuvieron a la Iglesia oficial de entonces por herética y cismática.

C) La Palabra de Dios y la experiencia enseñan que el empeño en reformar *desde dentro* una iglesia oficialmente desviada es una utopía que empaña nuestro testimonio y engendra confusión. La verdad y la obediencia están por encima del sacrificio, de la falsa caridad y de las buenas intenciones. En frase de Spurgeon, «el deber de uno es hacer lo recto; de las consecuencias se encarga Dios». Hay quien cita Mat. 13:24-30 sin percatarse de que allí no se trata de la *iglesia*, sino del *mundo* («el campo es el mundo»). Los más apelan al argumento de que a una madre (*cf.* Gál. 4:26) no se la deja, por fea o mala que sea; pero éstos no se dan cuenta de que la iglesia no es una abstracción superior, cuya naturaleza permanece a salvo, a pesar de la falsedad o apostasía de sus miembros, o de los defectos en las estructuras, sino *la congregación espiritual de los verdaderos creyentes,* cuyo «ser o no ser» dependen enteramente de la ortodoxia y de la «ortopodia» (Gál. 2:14), o sea, de la recta conducta de sus miembros.[15]

CUESTIONARIO:

1. *¿Dónde radica la verdadera unidad de la Iglesia?* — 2. *¿Qué piensa de la división denominacional?* — 3. *¿Existe un verdadero Ecumenismo bíblico?* — 4. *¿Cómo debe expresarse la intercomunión eclesial?* — 5. *¿Qué peligros han de evitarse en las asociaciones de iglesias?* — 6. *¿Cuándo existe el derecho y el deber de separarse de una iglesia?*

---

15. Conviene aquí recordar que la *iglesia* no es algo aparte o encima de los miembros —una organización, madre del organismo—, sino, como ya dijimos en otro lugar, algo así como «la suma de los sumandos» = la congregación de los creyentes en torno a su Señor.

LA SANTIDAD DE LA IGLESIA

1. Lo "santo" y lo "profano".

Toda religión implica una distinción entre lo *santo* y lo *profano*. Lo «santo» es lo que *se separa* para *consagrarlo* a la divinidad; lo «profano» («pro-fanum») es lo que queda alejado del santuario, sin traspasar los linderos de lo sagrado; por eso, resulta un *sacrilegio* tanto la profanación de lo sagrado como la sacralización de lo profano. Los términos bíblicos que corresponden al vocablo «santo» son *qadosh* en hebreo y *hagios* en griego. Cuando la idea de santidad implica una relación de amor por parte de Dios, con correspondencia piadosa por parte del hombre, suele usarse *hasid* en hebreo y *hosios* en griego (Hechos 2:27; Tito 1:8).

El término «santo» se usa por primera vez en la Biblia para referirse al día del sábado (Gén. 2:3). Después son designados «santos» determinados lugares, tiempos, cosas y personas, en virtud de su conexión con el culto divino.

2. El Pueblo santo de Dios.

Basta con tomar una buena Concordancia para darse cuenta de que el primer sentido del término «santo» aplicado a la Iglesia encierra la idea de separación ya implicada en el vocablo «ekklesía»: separación de lo profano, es decir, de lo mundano, para ser dedicados totalmente a Dios. Así Deut. 7:6 empalma con 1 Ped. 2:9. Pero existe una gran diferencia entre el Israel de la circuncisión y la

Iglesia de la fe: Israel era un pueblo santo como nación escogida para Yahveh, con una Ley santa y un ceremonial santo; pero dentro de esta *nación santa* había individuos abominables, incluyendo muchos de sus más altos jefes en lo sacerdotal y en lo político. En cambio, la Iglesia es, por definición, la congregación de los verdaderos creyentes, realmente *santos* en virtud de su llamamiento eficaz, de su regeneración y justificación; por eso, los inconversos o no regenerados no son miembros de la Iglesia, aunque aparezcan visiblemente insertos en su caparazón exterior.

Esto no quiere decir que todos los creyentes sean ya moralmente santos desde su justificación. La santificación interior es un proceso que se realiza paso a paso por medio de la docilidad al Espíritu Santo, siendo fruto de la salvación y teniendo por meta la vida eterna, es decir, el estadio final o escatológico en que la Iglesia entera será sin mancha ni arruga. Pero, ya desde el comienzo, es un principio de santidad (espiritual) el que gobierna (Romanos 8:14) y orienta *habitualmente* al cristiano (el llamado «estado de gracia»), haciendo del pecado habitual algo incompatible con la nueva naturaleza que hemos recibido (1.ª Jn. 3:9), pues ésta tiende a dar fruto de santidad (Romanos 6:19, 22; Gál. 5:22; Ef. 2:10; 1.ª Tes. 4:3, 7; 2.ª Tesalonicenses 2:13 —cf. también Ef. 1:1, 4; 5:27; Apoc. 21:2), aunque *todos* estamos expuestos a continuas caídas *actuales,* aun después de regenerados (cf. Sant. 3:2; 5:16; 1.ª Jn. 1:8-10; 2:1).

La santidad de la Iglesia se proyecta sobre todo en dos sentidos: el profético y el sacerdotal. La Iglesia es una agencia *santa* de salvación, mediante la comisión que ha recibido para extender el Reino de Dios por el mensaje y el testimonio de una conducta santa (Mat. 5:13-16; 28:19-20; 1.ª Ped. 2:9). Es también un sacerdocio *santo,* no por un ceremonial externo y con víctimas ajenas, sino con, en y por Jesucristo, mediante la alabanza, la beneficencia y el sacrificio vivo y total de nuestras personas en el seguimiento de Cristo (Mat. 16:24; Rom. 12:1; Heb. 13:13-16).

3. La Iglesia santa y pecadora.

En contraste con la doctrina tradicional de la Iglesia de Roma,[16] los modernos teólogos católico-romanos (especialmente H. Küng) y el mismo Vaticano II han reconocido que la Iglesia necesita una continua purificación y renovación espiritual. Por otra parte, admiten que fuera de su estructura visible hay muchos elementos de santificación y de verdad.[17]

La Reforma enseñó siempre que la Iglesia de Cristo, en su condición de Iglesia peregrina, o sea, hasta la segunda Venida del Señor, es *santa y pecadora*: santa, por su llamamiento, regeneración, justificación y progresiva santificación; pecadora, por el poder del pecado (remanente de la vieja naturaleza) que todavía le acecha y le hace caer en cada uno de sus miembros. Si la Iglesia es la congregación de los creyentes, y cada uno de ellos es imperfecto, defectuoso, falible y pecador, es lógico que la Iglesia entera sea, al mismo tiempo, la *congregación de los santos* y la *comunidad de los pecadores* salvos de pura gracia.

Es cierto que la Iglesia entera no puede fallar en el sentido de que vaya a desaparecer de este mundo la «columna y baluarte de la verdad», puesto que esa Iglesia (con mayúscula) es inmortal (Mat. 16:18). Pero cada una de las iglesias locales (únicas concreciones de la Iglesia trascendente) es falible, defectible y mortal, o sea, no inmune contra la desaparición. Por otra parte, es preciso distinguir bien entre iglesia *defectuosa* e iglesia *falsa*. La primera es aquella en que se enseña correctamente la Palabra de Dios, se observan debidamente las ordenanzas y se practica puntualmente la disciplina, aun cuando sus miembros sean más o menos defectuosos, fríos o pecadores; la segunda es aquella que en su mayoría o en sus órganos representativos se ha vuelto infiel a la Palabra

---

16. V. mi libro *Catolicismo Romano*, pp. 46-47.
17. C. Vaticano II, *Constitución Dogmática sobre la Iglesia*, p. 8.

de Dios o tolera en su seno a herejes o indignos. En la primera se *debe permanecer*, cooperando a su reavivamiento; de la segunda *se debe salir*, según las normas de la lección anterior.[18]

4. "Ecclesia semper reformanda".

Cuando se habla de la «Reforma» o de «Iglesia reformada», no debemos pensar que la renovación de la Iglesia es un hecho escueto del pasado, desde el que se alza sólido y airoso un edificio que, durante siglos, permanecerá incólume desafiando la erosión del tiempo. ¡No! La Iglesia es un organismo vivo, con su asimilación y desasimilación, con sus altibajos de salud y enfermedad, en perpetua construcción y en constante reparación. Toda suerte de excrecencias y desviaciones le acechan en su tarea de recibir y presentar el mensaje; toda clase de connivencias y complicidades atentan contra la pureza de su testimonio. Unas veces es la ortodoxia la que se desnivela, otras es la disciplina la que se relaja. En otras palabras, una «iglesia reformada» es siempre una «iglesia en necesidad de perpetua reforma». ¿De dónde le viene a la Iglesia de Cristo esa continua erosión que postula una reforma también continua? Citemos las causas más generales:

A) De la propia condición de sus miembros, pecadores salvos o santos pecadores, que es lo mismo. El cristiano, mientras peregrina por este mundo (1.ª Ped. 2:11), es un ser extraño con dos centros de gravitación: el cuerpo de pecado, que le atrae hacia la tierra, y el espíritu vivificante que le atrae hacia el Cielo; tiene la Cabeza en el Cielo (Ef. 2:1 y ss.; Col. 3:1-3) y los pies en el suelo, que se ensucian cada día con el polvo del camino (Juan 13:10; 1.ª Jn. 1:8-10). Es una persona con dos naturalezas: divina (2.ª Ped. 1:4) y pecadora (Rom. 7:25). Siendo la iglesia el conjunto de estos *santos pecadores*, la santidad

---

18. Es lamentable que esta distinción no esté clara en el libro de H. Küng, *The Church*, pp. 319-344, a pesar de lo mucho bueno que hay en dichas páginas, pues la confusión de conceptos influye decisivamente en la posición eclesial del mismo Küng.

de la Iglesia se ve empañada con los pecados de todos sus miembros; tanto más cuanto que el pecado del cristiano es un pecado *eclesial,* es decir, contra el Cuerpo del que es miembro (1.ª Cor. 5:6; Gál. 5:9), del mismo modo que el ejercicio de sus dones es una virtud *eclesial* (Ef. 4:16).

B) Del ambiente mundano que, como una atmósfera, rodea a la Iglesia y penetra en el mismo santuario. La Iglesia no está inmune del contagio de las malas corrientes mundanas de todo orden. Todo cristiano y toda iglesia se ve obligada a luchar contra la epidemia general, a nadar contra la corriente del mundo y de la carne y, en última instancia, a batallar contra el demonio (Ef. 6:11 y ss.). Los siete mensajes que el Espíritu dirige a las iglesias del Asia Menor en los caps. 2 y 3 del Apocalipsis son siete magníficas lecciones sobre este tema: de la decadencia de Efeso a la tibieza de Laodicea, de la connivencia de Pérgamo a la transigencia de Tiatira, de la correctísima ortodoxia muerta de Sardis a la debilidad de Filadelfia, sólo Esmirna se salva de todo reproche, y eso... gracias al flagelo de la tribulación. En el momento en que la Iglesia triunfalista cambió la púrpura de la sangre por la de las clámides romanas, comenzó a decaer.

C) De la fosilización que el hábito y la rutina, los ritos y las estructuras burocráticamente organizadas producen siempre en los seres vivientes y, con más razón, en una sociedad espiritual como la Iglesia, que, para ser auténtico Cuerpo de Cristo, necesita vivir cada día su propia crucifixión, muerte y resurrección.

CUESTIONARIO:

1. ¿Cuál es el sentido primordial de la santidad de la Iglesia? — 2. ¿Qué lugar ocupa la santidad moral en tal contexto? — 3. Concepto católico-romano y concepto reformado de santidad eclesial. — 4. ¿En qué se distingue una iglesia defectuosa de una iglesia falsa? — 5. ¿Cuáles son las razones para una perpetua reforma de la Iglesia?

LECCION 38.ª

LA CATOLICIDAD DE LA IGLESIA

1. La "Católica".

El vocablo «católico» proviene del griego «kath'ólu» y significa: referente o dirigido hacia el total; equivale al vocablo «universal» (del latín «uni-versum» = un todo que tiende hacia la unidad). El Nuevo Testamento no usa este término, y la única vez que sale en la Biblia (en forma adverbial —Hech. 4:18—) significa «enteramente», con la connotación negativa de «en ninguna manera».

El primero en usar la expresión «Iglesia Católica» fue Ignacio de Antioquía en su Carta a los fieles de Esmirna 8, 2.[19] Allí, como en el *Martirio de S. Policarpo,*[20] designa a la Iglesia total o universal, representada en cada una de las iglesias locales.

2. Catolicidad externa e interna.

Aunque la catolicidad de la Iglesia se entendió desde un principio como algo característico de la única Iglesia de Cristo extendida por todas partes, en cumplimiento de la gran comisión (Mat. 28:18-20) —catolicidad *extensiva* o *externa*—, pronto surgió la noción de catolicidad *interna* o *intensiva*, o sea, de *ortodoxia comúnmente admitida en todo tiempo y lugar.*[21] En este sentido escribía Tertuliano

---

19. *Cf. Rouet de Journel,* n.º 65.
20. *Ibidem,* n.º 77.
21. *Ibidem,* n.º 2.168.

de la *contesseratio hospitalis* entre las iglesias,[22] por la que el mismo credo o «símbolo de fe» era como la *tessera* o piedrecita blanca con que los amigos se reconocían mutuamente (*cf.* Apoc. 2:17).

Así podemos decir que el adjetivo *católico* significa, ya la Iglesia Universal, a la que pertenecen todos los redimidos en todo el mundo, ya la doctrina *total* del mensaje cristiano; contra la primera acepción de catolicidad está el cisma, que significa *escisión;* contra la segunda, la herejía, que significa *partido* o toma de posición en favor de una verdad fragmentaria, absolutizándola y cortándola del contexto total del mensaje. Un concepto afín es el de secta, que significa *cortada.* A. Alonso distingue perfectamente entre secta y comunidad eclesial, al decir: «La secta es un individualismo colectivo; la comunidad es una personalización socializada.»[23] Así, mientras la comunidad mantiene abierta su catolicidad a todo hombre salvo de gracia mediante la fe, la secta se cierra en un exclusivismo fanático que enfatiza, en vez del núcleo del Evangelio, detalles fragmentarios, junto con la negación de verdades fundamentales de la Biblia.

Es necesario poseer ideas claras acerca de estos términos para no incurrir en confusiones de las que no están exentos los grandes teólogos. Así, nada menos que el ya famoso moralista católico-romano B. Häring, en un artículo publicado en 15-2-1971 en la revista *La Familia Cristiana*, p. 11, decía: «Los Testigos de Jehová es una de esas sectas protestantes que todavía no se han abierto al Movimiento Ecuménico.»[23 bis]

---

22. *De praescriptione haereticorum*, pp. 20-36.
23. *Comunidades eclesiales de base*, p. 122.
23 bis. Es innecesario decir que los protestantes protestamos (y aquí cuadra bien el adjetivo) enérgica y rotundamente contra esta errónea opinión de Häring. Los mismos «Testigos de Jehová» lo harían también. Ellos no quieren ser considerados como secta protestante, ya que llaman, a todas las iglesias cristianas, organizaciones de Satanás. Por nuestra parte hallamos en los «Testigos de Jehová»

3. Evolución del concepto de catolicidad.

Como observa H. Küng,[24] «es obvio que unidad y catolicidad son conceptos correlativos». De ahí que un concepto católico-romano tradicional que enfatiza la estructura institucional, jerárquica, piramidal, como principio y raíz de la unidad de la Iglesia, forzosamente ha de definir la catolicidad en función de la misma estructura visible, jerárquicamente organizada; de tal modo que cuantos están fuera de dicha estructura quedan automáticamente excluidos de la «nota» de *catolicidad*. Queda así distorsionado el concepto de membresía de la Iglesia.

La concepción agustiniana de *La Ciudad de Dios* favoreció el nacimiento de este concepto de catolicidad, cobrando así un nuevo sentido la expresión de Cipriano: «Fuera de la Iglesia no hay salvación.» Todos los que, por diversas causas, disentían en lo más mínimo de la Iglesia oficial, pasaban *ipso facto* a ser unos «apóstatas», «herejes» o «cismáticos», separados de la *católica* y, por ende, de la única «Arca de salvación». Esta concepción ha perdurado hasta el siglo actual. El Vaticano I daba por perdidos («seducidos por opiniones humanas, seguidores de falsas religiones»)[25] a quienes se mantenían fuera de la Iglesia Romana sin ser atraídos hacia «el conocimiento de la verdad» (1.ª Tim. 2:4). El reciente cambio de perspectiva en este punto por parte de la Iglesia de Roma se ha debido a la introducción de dos nuevos conceptos de suma importancia, que han tenido una decisiva influencia en la actitud hacia las demás religiones, y que han hecho cambiar los epítetos de «herejes» e «infieles» por los de «hermanos separados» o «hermanos en vías de unión». Estos dos conceptos han sido: A) la «buena voluntad» o «buena fe» como factor básico en la salvación personal (supuesta la gracia

---

doctrinas demasiado separadas del común acervo de la fe cristiana para poder considerarles como una denominación u organismo eclesial evangélico. — *(Nota editorial.)*

24. *O. c.*, p. 299.
25. *Cf. Denzinger-Schönmetzer*, n.º 3.014.

de Dios, que a nadie se niega); B) el *votum Ecclesiae*, o deseo de pertenecer a la única Iglesia Católica, el cual se supone, al menos implícitamente, en todos los que, deseando llevar una vida moralmente honesta, manifiestan así su deseo de una salvación de la que quizá nunca oyeron hablar, y que sólo en la «Católica» tiene su «sacramento primordial».

En el otro extremo están los ecumenistas a ultranza, quienes piensan que todo grupo que se llame a sí mismo «iglesia» es parte integral de la Iglesia Universal. Quedan así incluidas muchas *sectas* y también muchos grupos religiosos que niegan verdades tan fundamentales como la Trinidad, la divinidad de Jesucristo, Su expiación sustitutoria en el Calvario, la infalibilidad de la Biblia, etc. Esta parece ser la mentalidad del Consejo Mundial de Iglesias, el cual, aceptando de algún modo el concepto romano de visibilidad y encarnacionalismo de la Iglesia, se va al otro extremo únicamente por su amplísimo concepto de catolicidad interna, mientras que el concepto romano de tal catolicidad abarca sólo a los que mantienen *toda* y *sola* la fe católica y obedecen al Papa como Jefe infalible de la Iglesia.

4.   Concepto Reformado de catolicidad.

Mientras la Iglesia de Roma atribuye en exclusiva la «nota» de catolicidad a su propia estructura visible eclesial, que tiene por suprema cabeza visible al obispo de Roma, reclamando así el derecho de ser considerada como la única iglesia *católica*, tanto por la *extensión* universal de su organización, como por atribuirse la posesión de la *totalidad* del mensaje y de los medios de gracia (teniendo a las demás confesiones religiosas por ramas desgajadas y dispersas, que arrastran partículas de verdad), el concepto evangélico de catolicidad es radicalmente diferente. Para nosotros, la catolicidad de la Iglesia no se expresa en forma de grandes cifras ni de estructuras jerárquicamente organizadas a escala mundial. Las parábolas de

Mat. 13 —insistimos— aluden proféticamente a un fenómeno de gigantismo, anormal en la verdadera iglesia (comp. Mat. 13:33 con Col. 2:8), la cual no debe escandalizarse de ser *pequeña* (cf. Luc. 12:32), sino de hacerse *mundana*. Creemos que la verdadera Iglesia Católica o Universal es la invisible compañía de los verdaderos creyentes de todo tiempo y lugar, cuyo mensaje salvador va dirigido a *todos* los hombres y debe permear la vida *toda* del hombre converso. La catolicidad es también atributo o dimensión de la iglesia visible, en cuanto que la Iglesia Universal se concreta y *realiza* existencial y temporalmente en todas y cada una de las comunidades locales bíblicamente constituidas y mutuamente enlazadas por los siete vínculos de unidad expresados en Efesios 4:4-6. En suma, sólo una iglesia ortodoxa y obediente a su Jefe y Cabeza Jesucristo merece el apelativo de «católica», por ser una concreción local totalmente representativa del conjunto *universal* de los creyentes.

5. ¿Es la catolicidad un concepto totalmente novotestamentario?

Aunque el Pacto Antiguo, con las promesas de salvación que comportaba y la Ley que le servía de estatuto, fue hecho exclusivamente con Israel (Sal. 147:19-20), esto no elimina, sin embargo, la posibilidad de que las bendiciones salvíficas se extendiesen a otros pueblos. Ya desde el llamamiento de Abraham para formar un pueblo que fuese el peculio de Dios, Yahveh le dice: «serán benditas en ti todas las familias de la tierra» (Gén. 12:3). Como dice R. B. Kuiper,[26] «el nacionalismo nunca fue una meta en sí mismo, sino que desde el comienzo fue un medio para la meta del universalismo». Otros lugares significativos son: el salmo 72, que profetiza el reinado universal del Mesías; el cap. 60 de Isaías (comp. con Apoc. 21:22-26; y también Is. 45:22 con Jn. 3:14-15), con su profecía sobre

---

26. *O. c.*, p. 62.

la futura gloria de Sión, y todo el libro de Jonás, con su emocionante final sobre la entrañable misericordia de Yahveh hacia la ciudad de Nínive, que se hallaba lejos del recinto del Pueblo escogido.

Con todo, la catolicidad llegó a su verdadera expresión con la muerte de Cristo, quien derribó el muro de separación entre judíos y gentiles (Ef. 2:14-22) y, levantado en la Cruz, atrajo hacia Sí a todos (Jn. 12:32), uniendo así a los dispersos hijos de Dios (Jn. 11:52). Consecuencia necesaria de esta salvación, procurada para gentes de todo linaje, lengua, pueblo y nación (Apoc. 5:9), fue la comisión encargada a la naciente Iglesia de ir y predicar a todas las gentes (Mat. 28:19), comenzando por Jerusalén y, en círculos concéntricos, hasta llegar a los últimos confines de la tierra (Hech. 1:8). Por eso, el Día de Pentecostés se hallaban en Jerusalén, para oír el primer sermón de la Iglesia, «judíos, varones piadosos, de todas las naciones bajo el cielo» (Hech. 2:5), y, por otra parte, fue desde Jerusalén y en manos de Pablo como el Evangelio, cual una antorcha olímpica, emprendió su marcha triunfal hacia Roma; desde la capital del judaísmo hasta la capital del Imperio.

6. Ontogénesis de la catolicidad.

Así pues, la catolicidad de la Iglesia se produce de dentro afuera. Con un símil tomado de la biología, podemos decir que la Iglesia crece y se multiplica en extensión universal, por un proceso de reproducción «cariocinética», es decir, semejante al de la célula viva, que, al llegar a su plena madurez, se escinde en dos, y así sucesivamente; de una manera parecida, toda iglesia que ha llegado a la madurez se convierte en *misión:* tiende a extenderse, a llevar el mensaje al exterior y, mediante la siembra fructífera de la Palabra, a plantar nuevas iglesias locales, las cuales reflejarán la misma constitución orgánica de la iglesia enviante, no por escisión celular, sino por comunicación —sin fraccionamiento— de la misma luz y de la misma llama de fe y amor con que el Espíritu Santo, mediante el ministerio de la Palabra, enciende nuevos *candeleros de oro* (Apoc. 1:12-13), por medio de los cuales anda el mismo y único Señor, principio y raíz de la *unidad* y, por tanto, de la *catolicidad* de todas las verdaderas iglesias.

CUESTIONARIO:

1. ¿Qué significa el término «católico»? — 2. Catolicidad extensiva e intensiva. — 3. ¿En qué se distingue una secta de una comunidad eclesial? — 4. ¿Cómo ha evolucionado en la Iglesia oficial el concepto de catolicidad? — 5. ¿Cuál es el concepto evangélico de catolicidad? — 6. ¿Dónde se halla, en realidad, la base de la universalidad de la Iglesia? — 7. ¿Cómo se produce internamente el proceso de la catolicidad?

LECCION 39.ª CONSECUENCIAS PRACTICAS DE LA CATOLICIDAD DE LA IGLESIA

1. La Iglesia Universal es supranacional.

Del concepto bíblico de universalidad o catolicidad de la Iglesia se desprende que la teoría de una iglesia *nacional* o *internacional* es un absurdo. La Iglesia, por su naturaleza espiritual y su íntima unidad en Jesucristo, sólo puede ser *supranacional*. Como demuestra A. H. Strong,[27] el concepto de iglesia nacional es antibíblico y tiende a construir una organización jerárquicamente estructurada.

En efecto, aunque en Hech. 9:31 el singular *ekklesía* se vea refrendado por los mejores MSS, fácilmente se echa de ver que no indica allí una organización regional o nacional de iglesias, sino que es una mera generalización sustitutiva de la pluralidad de iglesias locales. Algo similar se observa en 1.ª Cor. 12:28; Filip. 3:6; 1.ª Timoteo 3:15. El uso constante del Nuevo Testamento es el empleo del plural para designar varias iglesias de una región o nación, y el empleo del singular para referirse a una iglesia local. Por otra parte, la lectura atenta del Nuevo Testamento nos ofrece una intercomunión eclesial fundada en la independencia administrativa y autonomía de gobierno de las iglesias. Sirva de ejemplo el llamado «Concilio de Jerusalén» de Hechos 15. Un cuidadoso e imparcial análisis del texto nos lleva a la conclusión de que no se trata allí de una imposición jurisdiccional, sino de una respuesta (desde la iglesia «madre») a una consulta sobre un tema doctrinal de importancia vital.

---

27. *O. c.*, pp. 912-914.

Tampoco cabe duda de que la teoría de la iglesia nacional produce normalmente una estructuración jerarquizada, puesto que inmediatamente se siente la necesidad de una autoridad superior que centre las iniciativas y difumine las diferencias, con lo cual el camino hacia una iglesia *mundial* queda allanado. Más aún, Rainey [28] observa agudamente que tal unidad como la que la Iglesia nacional (Anglicana o Episcopaliana) representa, favorece la división entre las iglesias nacidas de la Reforma, mientras aspira a una organización similar a la de la Iglesia de Roma, llegando a darse el caso de que «no reconocen a iglesias (evangélicas) que los reconocen a ellos, y reconocen a iglesias (la de Roma y las Orientales separadas) que no los reconocen a ellos».

Finalmente, hemos de percatarnos de que Pentecostés marcó el fin de una iglesia-nación e inauguró la era de la separación entre la Iglesia y el Estado, como consecuencia de la verdadera universalidad y supranacionalidad de la Iglesia.

2. La Iglesia es independiente en su misión.

La implicación más directa y positiva de la catolicidad de la Iglesia está en el derecho inalienable y en el solemne e ineludible deber que tienen las iglesias de proclamar el Evangelio a todas las gentes, con la libertad que tal comisión demanda, de modo que puedan predicar, exhortar, amonestar y argüir a todos con la Palabra de Dios, sin interferencias ni obstáculos por parte del poder público, o de una clase dominante, o de un grupo cualquiera de los llamados «de presión».

3. La Iglesia ha de evitar el espíritu de secta.

Otra consecuencia de la catolicidad de la Iglesia es la necesaria oposición al espíritu sectario. Ya hemos exami-

---

28. Citado por A. H. Strong, *o. c.*, p. 912.

nado el concepto de *secta*. Añadamos que tal espíritu comporta, junto al indebido énfasis en un detalle del mensaje, con detrimento de todo el contexto, la condenación indiscriminada de todos cuantos no piensan del mismo modo y, por ende, un cierto *fanatismo*, el cual, como dice Santayana, consiste en suplir con la violencia del gesto la debilidad de la propia convicción.

Aquí aparece igualmente el peligro de sectarismo latente en el intento de confundir la Iglesia de Cristo con la propia denominación o grupo, con la estrechez de juicio y los prejuicios que esto lleva consigo. R. B. Kuiper alude,[29] a este respecto, a los extremos doctrinales sostenidos, por ejemplo, lo mismo por el Arminianismo que por el Ultracalvinismo, al tratar de la soberanía de Dios y de la responsabilidad del hombre. Lo mismo hemos de decir de un extremo puritanismo que imponga como grave obligación el abstenerse de cosas que ni Dios ha prohibido, ni causan daño al sujeto, ni escándalo al «hermano más débil».[30]

Pero esta acusación de sectarismo puede también emplearse injustificadamente contra quienes, con una correcta exégesis del Texto Sagrado (dentro de *todo* el contexto) se ven obligados a tomar una posición denominacional, como hacemos los bautistas y Hermanos, etc., en favor del bautismo de creyentes. El hecho de que teólogos de la talla de K. Barth (luterano) y H. Küng (católico-romano) se hayan rendido a la evidencia que el Nuevo Testamento presenta a este respecto, debiera hacer meditar a quienes, siguiendo a personas o tradiciones humanas, nos acusan de sectarios.

---

29. *O. c.*, p. 65.
30. De todo ello hablaremos en el vol. X (*Etica Cristiana*) de esta colección.

4. La Iglesia ha de mantener en Jesucristo su unidad esencial.

R. B. Kuiper cuenta [31] que, en el invierno de 1909, Sir A. Balfour dio en Edimburgo una conferencia sobre *Los Valores Morales que unen a las Naciones*, mencionando el mutuo conocimiento, los intereses comerciales comunes, la diplomacia y los lazos de la amistad. Cuando cesaron los aplausos, resonó una voz desde la galería: «Señor Balfour, ¿no hay nada que decir de Jesucristo?» Un estudiante japonés había así abochornado al líder del, a la sazón, mayor imperio cristiano del mundo.

Terminemos este tema de la *catolicidad* uniéndolo —como hicimos al comienzo— con el de la *unidad* en Cristo, Verdad salvadora y unitiva de todos los Suyos. A la secular objeción contra la Reforma: «eres diversa; luego no eres la verdad», debemos responder: «el supuesto y la consecuencia son falsos; nuestro pluralismo denominacional no obstaculiza nuestra íntima unidad en Cristo». El correcto raciocinio habría de ser: «eres heterodoxa; luego no eres la verdad»; puesto que a la *verdad* no se opone la diversidad, sino la falsedad.

CUESTIONARIO:

1. ¿Qué opinión le merece la idea de una iglesia nacional? — 2. ¿Por qué necesita la Iglesia su independencia espiritual? — 3. ¿Cuándo es justa la acusación de sectarismo? — 4. ¿Cómo respondería usted a la objeción: «sois distintos; luego no estáis en la verdad»?

---

31. *O. c.*, pp. 65-66.

LECCION 40.ª LA APOSTOLICIDAD DE LA IGLESIA

1. Concepto de apostolicidad.

Cuando hablamos de apostolicidad de la Iglesia, queremos decir que la Iglesia de Cristo está fundada sobre los apóstoles, no en el sentido de que sus *personas* fuesen los fundamentos sobre los que la Iglesia había de edificarse, pues este papel es exclusivo de Jesucristo, «principal piedra del ángulo», sino en el sentido de que los apóstoles, mediante la predicación del Evangelio, echaron los cimientos de la Iglesia sobre Cristo y de una vez para siempre (cf. Mat. 16:18; 1.ª Cor. 3:11; Ef. 2:20-21; 1.ª Pedro 2:5 y ss.; Apoc. 21:14).

El vocablo «apostólica», aplicado a la Iglesia de Cristo, no aparece en el Nuevo Testamento, siendo empleado por primera vez (lo mismo que el de «católica») por Ignacio de Antioquía (en la inscripción de su Epístola a los tralianos) y después en el *Martirio de S. Policarpo*, 16, 2.

La apostolicidad es, por decirlo así, la dimensión que da cuerpo real a las otras tres, o, como dice H. Küng,[32] es el criterio crucial para hallar la genuina unidad, santidad y catolicidad de la Iglesia, pues sólo cuando están fundadas sobre el mensaje apostólico son auténticas dimensiones de la Iglesia de Cristo.

2. La sucesión apostólica.

Ya dijimos en otro lugar[33] que los apóstoles no pudieron tener sucesores en lo que constituía su ministerio es-

---

32. *O. c.*, p. 344.
33. V. la lección 28.ª.

pecífico, porque éste era peculiar e irrepetible. ¿Puede, no obstante, hablarse de una «sucesión apostólica» en el sentido de que los obispos de las actuales diócesis procedan, directa o indirectamente, como una cadena ininterrumpida, de un primer anillo que podría ser un apóstol o un obispo ordenado por un apóstol? Si el ministerio apostólico —como vimos— no coincide de suyo con el oficio de «epískopos» o supervisor, no se puede hablar de un apóstol como primer obispo de una diócesis. Incluso Ireneo, en su lista de obispos de Roma (lista que H. Küng considera como no digna de crédito), no cita a Pedro como primer obispo de Roma, sino que dice: «Los bienaventurados apóstoles (Pedro y Pablo) fundaron y constituyeron la iglesia (de Roma) y encomendaron a Lino el oficio ("episcopatum") de administrarla».[34]

¿Puede entonces hablarse de una sucesión personal ininterrumpida, a partir de un primer obispo que fuese instituido por algún apóstol? Esta es la tesis que sostienen las iglesias episcopalianas, las orientales separadas y la Iglesia de Roma, pero con estas diferencias: la Iglesia Anglicana (y la Episcopaliana) asegura que los tres grupos poseen dicha sucesión apostólica; la llamada Ortodoxa parece negarla a los otros dos grupos; y la Iglesia de Roma se la concede a la Ortodoxia, pero no al Anglicanismo.

Sin embargo, tal sucesión apostólica *personal* es una mera suposición legendaria, como el propio H. Küng reconoce. No hay una sola iglesia entre todas las que se atribuyen el título de «cristianas» que pueda demostrar en modo alguno tal sucesión. Y, aun en el caso de que pudiera garantizarse en todas las iglesias una correcta sucesión apostólica *personal*, ello no podría constituir *nota* distintiva de verdadera iglesia de Cristo,[35] porque dicha

---

34. *Cf. Rouet de Journel*, n.º 211.
35. No olvidemos que Jesucristo fue condenado a muerte por el Sumo Sacerdote Caifás, cuya correcta «sucesión aarónica» nadie ponía en duda.

sucesión no es, por sí misma, garantía alguna de que dicha iglesia conserve incorrupto el *mensaje apostólico*, en el que se basa la verdadera apostolicidad de la Iglesia de Cristo.

3. La apostolicidad del mensaje.

Por tanto, la única «sucesión apostólica» correcta es la *sucesión del mensaje apostólico* a través de esta era de la Iglesia, intermedia entre la Ascensión y la 2.ª Venida del Señor. Nadie lo ha expuesto con más franqueza y claridad que H. Küng.[36] Por provenir de una fuente católico-romana, aunque de vanguardia, su testimonio adquiere una fuerza especial.

Después de afirmar que, en su tarea de testigos y mensajeros peculiares del Cristo Resucitado, los apóstoles no tienen sucesores, advierte Küng que lo que resta es una tarea y una comisión que continuar. Esta comisión apostólica «está basada —dice— en la obediencia al original testimonio de los apóstoles como mensajeros del Señor». Y es la Iglesia entera, no unos cuantos individuos, la comprometida en esta sucesión apostólica de obediencia, puesto que toda la Iglesia es el pueblo de Dios. Por esto mismo, no existe una original tradición «apostólica» exterior al Nuevo Testamento. Las tradiciones eclesiásticas consisten sólo en interpretaciones, explanaciones y aplicaciones de la única tradición apostólica cristalizada en los escritos novotestamentarios. Küng concluye así su argumentación:

«Por tanto, la sucesión apostólica comporta una continua y viva confrontación de la Iglesia con el testimonio original y fundamental de la Escritura; la sucesión apostólica sólo se lleva a feliz término si este testimonio bíblico es seguido fielmente en la predicación, en las creencias y en la conducta, si la Biblia no permanece como un libro cerrado,

---

36. *O. c.*, pp. 354-359.

ni siquiera incluso como un libro, en el sentido de un manual de leyes o de historia, sino como una viva voz de testimonio, para ser oída y creída aquí y ahora como un mensaje de gozo, de liberación, de buenas nuevas. En este sentido, la sucesión apostólica significa seguir la fe y la confesión de los apóstoles.» [37]

CUESTIONARIO:

1. Concepto de apostolicidad e importancia de esta dimensión de la Iglesia. — 2. ¿Tuvieron sucesores los Doce Apóstoles? — 3. ¿Qué piensa de la sucesión apostólica personal? — 4. ¿En qué consiste la verdadera sucesión apostólica? — 5. ¿Quién hereda esa sucesión apostólica del mensaje?

37. *O. c.*, p. 357. Lo de «viva voz» necesitaría matizarse; creemos que Küng es aquí, por desgracia, un «eco» de K. Barth. V. también R. B. Kuiper, *o. c.*, pp. 67-72; J. Bannerman, *Church of Christ*, I, pp. 436-451, y II, pp. 217-228; A. Kuen, *o. c.*, pp. 29-30; F. Lacueva, *Catolicismo Romano*, pp. 48-49.

LECCION 41.ª

EL APOSTOLADO Y LA MISION DE LA IGLESIA

1. La tarea apostólica.

En la lección anterior hemos hablado de la apostolicidad como dimensión de la Iglesia, y en este sentido hemos dicho que la verdadera Iglesia de Cristo es apostólica, porque tiene su fundación en el mensaje apostólico. Pero la palabra «apostólico» significa también lo propio de un «apóstol». El término griego «apóstolos», al que corresponde el latín «missus», significa «enviado». De aquí que todo *enviado* de Dios es un *apóstol* o *misionero*. Esta tarea apostólica o misionera corresponde a toda la Iglesia de Cristo, en virtud de la *comisión* recibida por los primeros discípulos de parte del Señor antes de la Ascensión. Desde este punto de vista, toda la Iglesia no sólo *tiene* una misión, sino que *es* Misión: extender por todo el mundo el mensaje de las Buenas Nuevas de salvación, o sea, del Reino de Dios y, con el poder del Espíritu, aplicar ese mismo mensaje de salvación a los corazones de los escogidos en Cristo. Tarea urgente e ineludible, en la que no caben evasivas teológicas. Como decía Spurgeon, «la cuestión no es si el mundo será salvo sin el Evangelio, sino si nosotros lo seremos si no le predicamos el Evangelio». Es cierto que Dios puede salvar al mundo *sin nosotros*, pero el candelero que no brille será removido (*cf.* Apocalipsis 2:5).

2. El "Enviado" de Dios.

De la misma manera que, en el orden natural, Dios se sirve de las causas «segundas» (la energía creada, tanto consciente como inconsciente) para llevar adelante la construcción del mundo y la historia de la Humanidad, así también se sirve de Sus *enviados* como instrumentos ministeriales en la obra de la salvación. Dios Padre opera u *obra* por medio de Sus servidores, ministros del Señor Jesucristo (primer gran Enviado), capacitados con los dones del Espíritu (segundo gran Enviado). Véase 1.ª Corintios 12:4-6.

De aquí que Jesús es el primer «Apóstol» o «misionero», porque es el primer gran Enviado de Dios para consumar la revelación de Dios, la redención del hombre y la fundación de la Iglesia (*cf.* Luc. 9:48; Jn. 5:30; 6:38, 57; 13:20; 17:8, 18; 20:21; Rom. 8:3; Gál. 4:4; 1.ª Jn. 4:9, 14). Por eso, Cristo es llamado en Heb. 3:1 «el Apóstol». En realidad, es en su calidad de «Cristo» como es enviado, pues mientras el término «Hijo» designa Su personalidad en relación al Padre, el término «Señor» designa su función regia y soberana, el término «Jesús» designa su función sacerdotal —Dios salvador mediante el sacrificio del Calvario—, y el término «Cristo» designa su función *profética,* es decir, de enviado de Dios para comunicar el mensaje de salvación del Padre (Jn. 7:16-18).

3. ¿Quiénes son apóstoles?

En principio, podemos decir que «apóstol» es todo obrero de Dios, hecho ministro de Cristo y enviado por el Espíritu Santo a efectuar, con peculiar dedicación y responsabilidad, la obra a que ha sido llamado. Sin embargo, el término «apóstol» se aplica, de diferente manera, a distintos grupos de personas:

A) En primer lugar, están *los Doce apóstoles,* que representaban, como patriarcas del Nuevo Israel, las doce tribus y que fueron escogidos por el Señor como testigos excepcionales de Su vida, muerte y resurrección, para echar, con su mensaje de primera fuente, los cimientos de la Iglesia (Jn. 6:70; Mat. 16:18; Hech. 1:26; Ef. 2:20; Apoc. 21:14). (V. también lección 28.ª, párrafo 3.º.) Estos Doce forman el primer grupo misionero completamente especial, pero sin más atribuciones jerárquicas que las que Cristo les promete simbólicamente en el plano escatológico final (*cf*. Luc. 22:30).

B) En segundo lugar, pero también formando un apartado especial, está Pablo (Gál. 1:1-12). Aunque Pablo queda al margen del círculo cerrado de los Doce, su misión no es menos importante: se le encomienda el apostolado de los gentiles, como a Pedro se le había encomendado —de manera especial— el de los judíos (Gál. 2:7-8). Más aún, cuando leemos, sin más, «el Apóstol», entendemos que se habla de Pablo, porque él trabajó por el Evangelio más que todos los demás juntos (2.ª Cor. 11:23 y ss.). Sus escritos ocupan más de la mitad del Nuevo Testamento.

C) En tercer lugar, el Nuevo Testamento aplica el nombre de «apóstoles» a muchos otros obreros que, juntamente con los Doce y con Pablo, contribuían a la propagación del Evangelio (*cf*. Rom. 16:7 —según interpretación probable—; 1.ª Cor. 15:5-7; 1.ª Tes. 1:1; 2:6; Apoc. 2:2 —cuando Juan escribía esto, era el único superviviente de los Doce). Esto nos enseña que cabe la posibilidad de designar como «apóstoles» a personas que trabajan, después de la época «apostólica» propiamente dicha, en la difusión del Evangelio.

4. Concepto de misionero.

Partiendo del punto anterior, podemos decir que todo creyente, como miembro de una iglesia que ha recibido una comisión misional, tiene el privilegio y el deber de dar testimonio de su fe cristiana en todo tiempo y en toda circunstancia (V. Hech. 4:31 y 1.ª Tes. 1:8).

Sin embargo, en un sentido específico y particular, el término *misionero* se aplica a una persona elegida y separada por Dios para la comunicación de un mensaje (*cf*. Is. 6:9; Jer. 1:5; Jn. 15:16; Hech. 9:15). El misionero cristiano puede definirse así: «Es un hombre llamado por Dios, dotado por el Señor de las cualidades y condiciones necesarias y enviado al mundo para predicar el mensaje y fundar iglesias, de modo que éstas, a su vez, funden otras iglesias.»

Lo ideal es que el misionero específico dedique todo su tiempo a la tarea también específica de difundir el Evangelio, como obrero llamado aparte para tal función (V. Hech. 6:3-4). Sin embargo (sobre todo, cuando necesite ganarse el sustento), puede alternar su ministerio con una profesión secular, como fue el caso del apóstol Pablo, trabajador en lonas para tiendas de campaña.

Junto al misionero propiamente dicho, que *predica* el mensaje y funda iglesias, pueden existir misioneros *auxiliares,* que pueden realizar una labor evangelística mediante la literatura, radio, escuelas, hospitales, etc.

5. Cualidades del misionero.

A) HOMBRE DE ORACIÓN. La oración ha sido llamada «la primera palanca del apóstol» (pastor o misionero). En efecto, toda *competencia* apostólica viene de la unión con Dios (2.ª Cor. 3:4-5) y se conserva mediante la oración, mientras que un activismo disipado puede llevar a la herejía de considerarse suficiente por sí mismo o indispensable. La oración es siempre la expresión más tajante de la propia insuficiencia y de la subordinación ministerial al Dador de la gracia y del poder de salvación (V. Mat. 7:7-11; Jn. 15:7, 16; 16:23-24; Hech. 1:14, 24; 4:24-31; 6:6; 8:15; Rom. 8:26-27; 15:30-32; Ef. 6:11-13; Filip. 1:9-11; Col. 4:12; Sant. 1:5-6; 5:13-18; 1.ª Jn. 5:13-16.) La unión con Cristo, para la expansión del Reino, comporta igualmente el sacrificio del propio *yo* (Mat. 23:34; Luc. 9:23; Jn. 12:24-25; 15:18-20; Rom. 6:3-4; 1.ª Cor. 15:31; Gál. 2:20; 6:14; Filipenses 1:29-30; Col. 1:24).

B) AMOR A CRISTO Y A LOS HOMBRES. Si, para todo cristiano, el amor es la *perfección* (Mat. 5:45-48; 22:39; 25:31 y ss.; Rom. 13:8-10; Gál. 5:6, 14; 1.ª Jn. 3:16 y ss.; 4:11-20),

de tal manera que el amor a los hermanos es la gran
«supernota» del Cristianismo (Jn. 13:34-35), cuánto más
para el *hombre de Dios*, enviado especialmente por Dios,
pues a él, más que a otros, el amor de Cristo le apremia
a misionar, teniendo siempre en las mientes la obra de
la Cruz (2.ª Cor. 5:14-21). Hay cuatro versículos en el Evangelio según S. Juan (6:57; 15:9; 17:18; 20:21) que subrayan
la relación íntima entre la *misión* y el *amor:* Por fe y
amor se «come» al Enviado del Padre; y, por otra parte,
el gran Enviado del Padre envía a sus apóstoles como al
Padre le envió a El, y les ama como el Padre le amó
a El. Por eso, el sufrir misionero es señal de predilección
divina, a semejanza de Cristo (Jn. 15:18-21), que exige
una correspondencia similar. Para ser genuino, el amor
a las almas ha de proceder del amor a Cristo y a Su obra.
Este amor se manifiesta en hechos prácticos: en la comunicación de bienes (Heb. 13:16), en el remedio de necesidades perentorias (Rom. 12:13), en hacerse «todo a todos»
(1.ª Cor. 9:18-23), en la delicadeza en el trato (Hech. 28:15).
Pablo se conducía de acuerdo con su extraordinario pasaje
sobre el amor (1.ª Cor. 13).

C) OBJETO DE UN LLAMAMIENTO ESPECIAL. Todos los creyentes son *llamados* del mundo a trabajar en la viña del
Señor, según su don peculiar (Ef. 4:7), conforme al llamamiento para un servicio peculiar («vocación» = llamamiento). En los que son *enviados* a la tarea misionera este
llamamiento es más específico, pues supone una especial
elección por parte de Dios (Jn. 15:16), y una transmisión
del mismo Espíritu que fue dado a Cristo sin medida, para
la gran obra de la redención del mundo (*cf.* Jn. 20:21-22).
Así Cristo escogió, llamó y envió: 1.º, al círculo cerrado
de los Doce (Luc. 6:13; 9:1-2); 2.º, al círculo mayor de
otros setenta (Luc. 10:1, 16); 3.º, a los 120 que componían
la comunidad cristiana del Aposento Alto (Hech. 1:15; 2:1),
a quienes se dio el Espíritu Santo «con poder», en orden a
testificar de Cristo hasta los últimos confines de la tierra
(Hech. 1:7-8). Sin este llamamiento peculiar del Señor para
trabajar en Su obra, que a la iglesia local incumbe dis-

cernir y reconocer, la tarea misionera se convierte en una farsa que no puede esperar bendición de Dios, sino castigo al usurpador. (Léase detenidamente Jer. 14:14 y todo el cap. 23 del mismo libro.)

D) COMPETENCIA. Todo portador de un mensaje debe estar bien enterado del mensaje que lleva. El misionero debe conocer bien la Palabra de Dios, el modo de exponerla y los hombres a quienes la dirige. Si todo creyente debe estar preparado para dar razón de su esperanza (1.ª Ped. 3:15), cuánto más quien ha recibido el llamamiento a la tarea específica de difundir el mensaje de salvación. 2.ª Tim. 1:5; 2:2; 3:14-17 dicen mucho a favor de una formación bíblica temprana, sólida y perfecta por parte del que ha de ejercitar este ministerio. De ahí la necesidad del estudio bíblico, sistemático y profundo, en las iglesias. Todo aspirante a pastor o misionero debe, tras un período de estudio y experimentación bajo la guía de un «maestro», comprobar su vocación mediante una intensa vida espiritual y el gradual ejercicio de sus dones, de modo que tanto él como la propia iglesia puedan discernir, sin ilusiones ni engaños, la verdadera calidad de su llamamiento. A ser posible, debe formarse en una Escuela Bíblica o Colegio Teológico (he ahí una gran necesidad de nuestras iglesias), que sean recomendables *por la pureza de su doctrina, por su ambiente espiritual y por la modernidad y eficacia de sus métodos de enseñanza.* Al menos, necesitará un buen Curso por correspondencia y continuar ávido de una más completa instrucción. Una vocación sin brío, un estudio sin capacidad y un lanzamiento sin experiencia son los tres grandes enemigos de la Obra, aun contando con la «buena voluntad».

CUESTIONARIO:

1. ¿Qué significa, en realidad, la palabra «apóstol»? — 2. ¿Quién fue el gran Enviado? — 3. ¿A cuántos grupos de personas puede aplicarse el término «apóstol»? — 4. ¿A quién se aplica específicamente el título de misionero? — 5. Cualidades que debe poseer todo misionero.

LECCION 42.ª   PRINCIPIOS MISIONEROS

1. Toda la Iglesia está comprometida en la obra misionera.

En la Iglesia primitiva no existían Asociaciones, Convenciones ni Comités de Misión que se propusieran llevar a cabo la obra misionera. Por el contrario, en nuestros días, asistimos a la organización y proliferación de Sociedades misioneras que se esfuerzan por atraerse el interés de las iglesias, y de los creyentes en general, en favor de *sus* Misiones, como si las iglesias mismas pudieran ser sustituidas en este menester o pudieran delegar en otros lo que constituye su primordial comisión, de acuerdo con el mandato del Señor (Mat. 28:18-19; Hech. 1:8).

No queremos decir que las iglesias no puedan y deban agruparse, para hacer conjuntamente una obra que no podrían hacer por sí solas (ya sea por lo menguado de su membresía, ya por su penuria económica), pero sí que dichas iglesias deben hacerse directamente responsables de la tarea misionera, sin delegar en otras organizaciones, del tipo que sean, las atribuciones y responsabilidades que a cada una en particular corresponden.

2. La razón de ser de las Asociaciones Misioneras.

No queremos insinuar, con lo dicho anteriormente, que hayan de desaparecer todas las Juntas o Comités que, de parte y en nombre de las iglesias mismas, se ocupen de programar obras y métodos misioneros, sirviendo de guía y dirección a las iglesias locales. Pero sí se ha de evitar a toda costa el caer en una organización burocrática o super-iglesia, que disponga del dinero de las iglesias y lo administre como a ella le parezca, montando una Sociedad que retenga para sus propios usos una buena parte de las aportaciones pecuniarias, que deberían ser enviadas íntegramente a los distintos campos misioneros.

Por otra parte, las iglesias deben conocer a sus propios misioneros, conocer sus cualidades, los lugares a que son enviados y la obra que desarrollan. Para ello, necesitan mantenerse en contacto directo y frecuente con ellos y recibir de los mismos los correspondientes informes relativos a su vida de familia y a las actividades que ejercitan. Del mismo modo, la iglesia, conjuntamente y a través de sus oficiales, debe interesarse por los misioneros y por la obra que realizan; es decir, debe ser en miniatura una Sociedad Misional. Sus dádivas deben ir totalmente a las manos de los misioneros, como ella misma lo ha designado y sin que se retenga cantidad alguna para usos que no han sido propuestos por la misma iglesia.

Por tanto, desde un punto de vista bíblicamente correcto, todas las Juntas o Comités que, por comodidad y mayor eficacia, lleguen a crearse, deben estar al servicio de las iglesias, pues no son sino el canal a través del cual ellas mismas organizan su tarea misionera y envían sus aportaciones al campo de misión.

3. El espíritu misionero es inherente al "nuevo nacimiento".

Sólo quienes han pasado por la experiencia de la conversión o regeneración espiritual están capacitados y obligados a «ir y decir cuán grandes cosas el Señor ha hecho con nosotros». No perdamos de vista que el Señor nos ha elegido para que «vayamos y demos fruto» (Jn. 15:16). El mandamiento misionero o Gran Comisión fue dado para predicar el Evangelio, en círculos concéntricos, primero en Jerusalén (la ciudad o pueblo donde nos encontremos), después en Judea (toda la región), llegando hasta Samaria (las comarcas limítrofes) y proseguir hasta los extremos de la tierra. Podemos, pues, decir como Wesley: «el mundo es mi parroquia». O sea, nuestro mensaje es un mensaje para todos los hombres. Pablo habla del «Evangelio, el cual vosotros habéis oído, y el que ha sido anunciado a toda creatura bajo el Cielo» (Col. 1:23).

4. Necesidad de "ir".

A pesar de la orden imperativa de *ir* y anunciar el Evangelio a todos, la primera iglesia (la de Jerusalén) ya centró en sí misma y para sí misma todas sus actividades evangelísticas, y hubieron de pasar seis largos años antes de dar un solo paso por cumplir el mandamiento de Cristo de predicar el Evangelio a todo el mundo. En la providencia de Dios, fue menester que el fervor persecutorio de un joven fariseo, Saulo de Tarso, cambiase las cosas, dispersando a los miembros de la iglesia de Jerusalén, como por la explosión de una bomba, enviándoles así por todas partes a anunciar las «Buenas Nuevas» del Evangelio. Y su anuncio llegó hasta las partes más lejanas (Rom. 10:18), hasta la misma Antioquía, entre los gentiles, muy lejos de la capital de Judea. Bueno será comparar esta persecución con la experiencia de Jonás y aprender la lección que nos enseñan.

5. El ejemplo de Antioquía.

Fue Antioquía la que mereció ser honrada con el nombre de «iglesia misionera» y fue esta ciudad el centro más importante de misión hasta entonces conocido. Antioquía tomó a su cargo el glorioso deber que le fue confiado y, fieles todos a este deber, pusieron manos a la obra, cada uno conforme a su capacidad y de acuerdo con los dones recibidos, de modo que el Evangelio se extendiese hasta regiones muy lejanas. La iglesia en Antioquía y, después, otras iglesias que siguieron su ejemplo, trabajaron en cooperación y fueron las agencias por medio de las cuales los que fueron llamados a este trabajo llevaron el Evangelio por todas partes, organizando otras iglesias, como nos lo demuestra el ministerio de Pablo y de sus colaboradores.

CUESTIONARIO:

1. ¿A quiénes compete la tarea misionera en la iglesia? — 2. ¿Cuál es la razón de ser de las Sociedades Misioneras? — 3. ¿Para qué elige el Señor a Sus obreros? — 4. ¿Cómo cumplieron las iglesias de Jerusalén y Antioquía la orden del Señor de ir?

LECCION 43.ª METODOS MISIONEROS

Si tomamos como ejemplo a la Iglesia primitiva, veremos que sus métodos misioneros eran muy sencillos y, sin embargo, fueron muy efectivos y tuvieron resultados excelentes. Examinemos algunos de estos métodos:

1. La unidad oficial y responsable era la iglesia local.

De esto tenemos una prueba palmaria en la iglesia de Antioquía, la cual envió los primeros misioneros fuera de su propia región.

Las iglesias del Nuevo Testamento no poseían ninguna organización especializada a la manera de las que existen actualmente y, al principio, aun cuando no había otra iglesia fuera de Jerusalén más que la de Antioquía, ésta tenía tal fuerza y demostró tanto entusiasmo y celo en la empresa misionera, que tomó bajo su responsabilidad y cuidado, de acuerdo con el mandamiento recibido de Cristo, el llevar el Evangelio a otras regiones y hasta «los extremos de la tierra». Es de suponer que, con el tiempo, esta iglesia cuidaría de organizarse mejor y mejor, equipándose constantemente conforme a las necesidades que requerían un mayor incremento en su labor misionera.

2. Los misioneros, en cuanto sabemos, estaban bajo el control de la iglesia.

Es muy posible que dichos misioneros no estuviesen sostenidos por medio de sueldos fijos, aunque tampoco podamos asegurarlo con certeza. Sin embargo, es de su-

poner que la iglesia que los enviaba se hacía cargo de
su responsabilidad moral respecto a ellos y hacía todo lo
posible para que sus enviados tuvieran siempre lo indispensable para llevar a cabo su misión del modo más provechoso posible. Es muy probable que, al principio, Pablo
y Bernabé fueran sostenidos por la iglesia de Antioquía y
que, más tarde, por lo menos en lo que a Pablo se refiere,
éste se sostuviera por sus propios medios y con la ayuda
de otras iglesias. Sabemos, por ejemplo, que la de Filipos
le había ayudado en varias ocasiones (Filip. 4:16). De todos
modos, él deja bien sentado el principio de que, quien
consagra su vida al Evangelio, viva también del Evangelio
(1.ª Cor. 9:13-14). Una cosa es, pues, sin duda alguna,
cierta y es que la obra misionera en el primer siglo de
la era cristiana fue llevada a cabo por medio del sacrificio y abnegación de los enviados y de los que enviaban,
y siempre en directa relación y trato entre las iglesias y
los misioneros.

**3. Había también quienes trabajaban en la obra misionera
sin salario.**

Esto es lo que podríamos llamar *voluntarios;* entre
ellos, Aquila y Priscila son un ejemplo relevante. Ambos
fueron íntimos colaboradores, en la obra misionera, del
gran apóstol de los gentiles, y en el libro de Hechos tenemos varios testimonios de cómo evangelizaban a la vez
que se ocupaban de su negocio secular. Como ellos había,
a no dudarlo, un gran número de hombres que, mientras
viajaban por razón de su trabajo, iban también dando
testimonio y propagando el Evangelio. «Ellos fueron por
todas partes anunciando el Evangelio», y éste fue, en alto
grado, el secreto del gran éxito que tuvo el Cristianismo
en el primer siglo de su existencia.

4. ¿Qué método se seguía para fundar y sostener las iglesias en su labor misionera?

En el Nuevo Testamento no tenemos ninguna indicación de que alguna iglesia, fundada por misioneros extranjeros, fuera sostenida luego por alguna iglesia (o iglesias) que existiera en otras tierras. Aunque este principio no excluye la mutua ayuda y cooperación que debe existir entre las iglesias, el hecho cierto es que, al principio, todas las iglesias se sostenían a sí mismas en todos los aspectos y, en este sentido, eran verdaderamente independientes las unas de las otras. En cambio, vemos cómo las iglesias indígenas ayudaron, en muchas ocasiones, a la propagación del Evangelio y a la misma iglesia madre, como fue el caso de la gran colecta reunida entre las iglesias del campo misionero y destinada a la iglesia de Jerusalén.

5. Métodos de captación.

Todos estamos de acuerdo en que, supuesto el poder del Espíritu en la aplicación de la Palabra a los corazones de los hombres, el misionero o evangelista, etc., necesitan conocer lo más y mejor posible el contenido de su mensaje, los destinatarios del mensaje y el método (*méthodos* = camino o procedimiento) para llevar el mensaje a su destino de la manera más eficaz. Hay quienes se aferran a los viejos métodos, confundiendo modernidad con mixtificación, y alegan que lo único que se necesita es conocer a fondo el mensaje de la Biblia y tener un corazón encendido en el celo por la salvación de la humanidad perdida. Dos reflexiones habrían de bastar para sacarnos de semejante engaño: *a)* Todo mensaje necesita ser *comunicado;* ahora bien, no puede haber *comunicación* si no hay un Diccionario *común* para el que habla y para el que escucha. Por tanto, es del todo necesario estar *al día* (y *al lugar*) con la corriente cultural del ambiente en que nuestro mensaje va a ser proclamado. *b)* Es cierto que el Evangelio no es una «filosofía» religiosa, pero el evangelista hará bien en conocer el contexto filosófico, etc., en que se desenvuelve la cultura actual. ¿Hubiera podido Pablo pronunciar su maravilloso discurso de Hech. 17 sin conocer el ambiente cultural de los sabios del Areópago ateniense? ¿Se figura uno a Pedro o Juan hablando en un estilo *apto* ante tal Asamblea? [37 bis]

CUESTIONARIO:

1. ¿Quién se hacía responsable, en la Iglesia primitiva, de la tarea misionera? — 2. ¿Quién tomaba a su cargo el sostenimiento de los misioneros? — 3. Tenemos ejemplos de misioneros voluntarios, es decir, sin salario? — 4. ¿Cómo se sostenían las primeras iglesias en su labor misionera? — 5. ¿Qué métodos de captación exigen las circunstancias de cada época?

[37 bis]. Comprender estas realidades y tratar de inculcarlas ha sido el gran mérito del Dr. F. Schaeffer.

LECCION 44.ª MISION E IGLESIA LOCAL

1. El misionero y la iglesia local.

De todo lo dicho se desprende que el hombre apartado por Dios para la tarea de llevar el Evangelio a otras gentes no es enteramente independiente, en el sentido de que pueda lanzarse a la obra sin conexión con la iglesia local. Por el contrario, tanto su persona como su obra se han de desenvolver en completa conexión con la iglesia de la que es miembro. Hech. 13:1-3 es sumamente aleccionador a este respecto: Se trata de la iglesia de Antioquía, la segunda en fundación y la primera entre las iglesias de los gentiles; punto neurálgico y normal encrucijada en los caminos de Palestina, Siria, Grecia y Roma. En esta iglesia había «profetas y maestros»; se designan aquí dos ministerios que, sin duda, implicaban también oficio, como se ve por el «leiturgúnton» del v. 2, ya que, como estudiamos en la lección 27.ª, «leiturgós» es vocablo que el Nuevo Testamento aplica al ministerio local. A los ministros locales, pues, o «ancianos» dice el Espíritu que le separen a Bernabé y Saulo para una tarea misional. Ellos, en representación de la iglesia, les imponen las manos y los envían («apélysan» = los soltaron o dejaron marchar —el v. 4 nos aclara que el verdadero enviante era el Espíritu Santo—).

Por tanto, el primer requisito de un misionero es que sea miembro de una iglesia local; el segundo es que haya sentido el llamamiento del Señor; el tercero es que este llamamiento haya sido reconocido por la iglesia; el cuarto, que, siendo enviado por el Espíritu, sea la iglesia —por manos de sus dirigentes— la que «lo deje marchar». Gálatas 1:15-16 y 1.ª Cor. 9:16 nos ponen en la perspectiva necesaria para calibrar la correcta posición del misionero cristiano: es un llamado por Dios, íntimamente unido a Cristo, que siente en su corazón la urgencia de predicar el mensaje (cf. Jer. 20:7-9); por tanto, debe ser un *hombre de Dios* (1.ª Tim. 6:11), nunca un *profesional* de la predicación. Otra característica esencial del obrero misionero es su carácter itinerante. Está llamado a *extender* la Palabra; si se detiene a formar una iglesia, es para establecerla y nutrirla convenientemente, hasta que ésta haya madurado lo suficiente como para valerse por sus propios medios y elegir oficiales competentes. Una vez que la iglesia alcanza la madurez necesaria para ejercitar sus ministerios específicos y su autonomía administrativa, el misionero no tiene otra alternativa que, o marcharse a otra parte, o constituirse automáticamente en pastor de la misma iglesia, dejando así de ser «misionero».[38]

2. Papel básico de la iglesia local en la tarea misionera.

Se deduce de lo anterior que el papel básico en la tarea misionera corresponde a las iglesias locales. Las iglesias locales tienen gravísima responsabilidad en los siguientes puntos:

A) En conservarse espiritualmente *vivas,* no por una mera ortodoxia o por un exacto cumplimiento de sus estatutos, sino, sobre todo, por un constante espíritu de humildad, arrepentimiento y reforma, siempre de cara a la Palabra de Dios. Para ello se requieren tanto la predicación fiel, sistemática y profundamente *expositiva* de «todo el consejo de Dios» (Hech. 20:27), como también un conocimiento *experimental* de Jesucristo por parte de todos,

---

38. A los lectores que conocen el inglés es de recomendar la lectura del libro que lleva por título *Back to the Bible in Christian Missions,* del conocido escritor español D. Samuel Vila, quien condensa, en un centenar de páginas que no tienen desperdicio, su larga experiencia de más de medio siglo acerca de las misiones y misioneros, con sus virtudes y defectos.

tanto dirigentes como simples miembros. No se puede olvidar que Cristo es la Cabeza de las iglesias.

B) En avizorar y discernir los dones que Dios imparte a Su pueblo (Rom. 12:6-8), entre los cuales ocupa un lugar destacado la llamada a la función misionera específica. La iglesia no debe adoptar la actitud pasiva de esperar a que surjan los dones, sino que debe orar y observar su aparición para alentarlos (cf. Hech. 6:1-5; Tito 1:5). Asimismo debe considerar las cualidades y condiciones del presunto misionero, para discernir si se trata de un verdadero llamamiento de Dios o de un capricho emocional y aventurero.

C) En observar la forma correcta que el Nuevo Testamento enseña respecto al envío de obreros y plantación de nuevas iglesias. Aparte de casos extraordinarios como el de Pablo en Hech. 9 y el de Felipe en Hech. 8, la forma ordinaria en que Dios obra en la extensión de Su Reino es mediante el ministerio instrumental de las iglesias locales, y esto por ambos extremos: el de la iglesia *enviante*, que lanza a los obreros, y el de las iglesias *recipientes*, ya que los misioneros deben orientar a los recién convertidos hacia las respectivas iglesias locales, si las hay bíblicamente establecidas en el lugar, para que en ellas ejerzan sus servicios o sean por ellas enviados, a su vez, como misioneros.

D) En cuidar que el misionero se mantenga bajo la disciplina y el control de la iglesia que envía. Por «iglesia que envía» se entiende el cumplimiento de la gran comisión que dicha iglesia, sola o asociada con otras, debe llevar a cabo conforme a las órdenes de quien es Señor y Cabeza de la misma. Al mismo tiempo, y para que se mantenga un vínculo cordial, permanente y activo entre la iglesia enviante y las recipientes, es menester que éstas últimas acojan favorablemente al misionero y que éste sea capaz de adaptarse completamente a la mentalidad, idiosincrasia y demás circunstancias del país y aun de la región donde ha de ejercer su tarea. De ahí la ventaja de utilizar obreros nativos, aunque sean dirigidos doctrinalmente y ayudados económicamente desde fuera, hasta que las iglesias puedan valerse por sí mismas en ambos terrenos, proceso que es necesario acelerar en lo posible. Así como una iglesia enviante muestra su vitalidad íntima en el termómetro de su afán misionero, así también una iglesia recipiente la muestra en el afán por sostenerse a sí misma primero, y lanzarse después, a su vez, a la expansión del Evangelio.

3. Evangelismo e iglesia local.

Al hablar de *evangelismo,* en seguida nos viene a las mientes o lo que se ha venido en llamar *campañas evangelísticas* o el culto llamado de *evangelización.* Respecto de ambos aspectos evangelísticos haremos unas breves observaciones dentro de los límites de espacio que requiere el presente volumen.

A') No vamos a hablar de los métodos usados para congregar grandes multitudes y para recabar «decisiones» por Jesucristo.[38 bis] En cambio, hemos de enfatizar: *a)* que todo miembro de iglesia habría de sentirse *ganador de almas para Cristo,* no desaprovechando ocasión alguna, en casa, en la oficina, en la fábrica, en la calle, de ser luz y sal; *b)* que miembros e iglesias habrían de preocuparse en encontrar los métodos más aptos para presentar el mensaje. Como dice M. Goodman:[39] «Un hombre que descubre que el público no entra a su tienda sería un necio si culpara a la gente porque le evitó. Poco ganaría diciendo: "Bueno, después de todo, mi mercancía está a la disposición si ellos quieren comprar; son ellos los que pierden si no la toman." Esto puede que sea cierto, *pero la falla es de él.*» Si estamos convencidos de la importancia de descuidar «una salvación tan grande» (Heb. 2:3), segura-

---

38 bis. De ello hablaremos en el vol. V (*Doctrinas de la Gracia*).
39. En *La Iglesia* (compil. de Watson, cap. XI: «Evangelistas y evangelismo», de M. Goodman, pp. 189-206), p. 195.

mente pondremos todos los recursos de nuestra mente y de nuestro corazón al servicio del Evangelio.

B') El evangelismo no puede reducirse a un culto de iglesia que se celebra a una hora determinada de la tarde del domingo. Ello no sería «ir a todo el mundo». En un artículo importante, David Kingdon ha dado en la diana al decir:

«Mientras no recobremos la doctrina apostólica sobre la iglesia, no recobraremos la práctica apostólica del evangelismo. Con todo, el evangelismo apostólico no era templo-céntrico. Un estudio de los "métodos" de Pablo (si cabe la expresión) lo demuestra. Tan pronto predica al aire libre, como en el mercado y a la orilla del río en Filipos, o en la colina de Marte en Atenas. Se metía en las sinagogas cuando podía y predicaba allí un sábado tras otro mientras se lo permitían. En Corinto llegó a instalarse en el edificio próximo a la sinagoga, después que en ella le rechazaron. Por tanto, el evangelismo de Pablo, aunque estaba centrado en la iglesia, no estaba centrado en el edificio, como ocurre con gran parte de nuestro evangelismo de hoy. Más aún, podemos afirmar que era muy poco el evangelismo que se practicaba cuando la congregación se reunía. La iglesia se reunía para el culto y la instrucción más bien que para un servicio evangelístico. Lo demuestra la referencia puramente incidental al hecho de que un inconverso entre en el lugar de culto» (1.ª Cor. 14:24 y ss.).[40]

---

40. Traducido de la revista *Reformation Today*, n.º 8 (Winter, 1971), p. 10.

CUESTIONARIO:

1. ¿Qué conexiones debe guardar todo misionero o evangelista? — 2. ¿Qué nos enseña Hech. 13:1-4? — 3. ¿Cuáles son los requisitos de un auténtico misionero? — 4. ¿Cuál es la característica preponderante del misionero? — 5. ¿Qué puntos pueden señalarse como de grave responsabilidad de las iglesias locales respecto a la tarea misionera? — 6. ¿Cuál es el concepto genuino de «evangelismo»?

Séptima parte

Las ordenanzas de la Iglesia

LECCION 45.ª CONCEPTO DE ORDENANZA

1. Los medios de gracia.

Aparte de la *oración*, cuya eficacia en orden a la recepción de la gracia depende enteramente de la libre iniciativa divina,[1] los autores suelen señalar como *medios de gracia* la Palabra y los Sacramentos u ordenanzas. La Palabra de Dios obra, por el poder del Espíritu, mediante la lectura de la Santa Biblia y, especialmente, mediante la viva predicación del mensaje contenido en las Escrituras. Las ordenanzas o sacramentos operan como símbolos que activan la fe, expresan nuestra profesión y sellan nuestra obediencia y dedicación al Señor. En este sentido, podemos decir que *son especiales medios de gracia*, aunque *no son medios de gracias especiales*. Tanto la predicación de la Palabra como la administración de los sacramentos han sido encomendadas a la Iglesia, y de ahí la razón por la que los incluimos en el presente volumen.

2. ¿Sacramento u ordenanza?

La palabra «sacramento» (equívoca versión latina del griego «mystérion») significaba en su origen el juramento que los soldados romanos proferían de obedecer a sus je-

---

1. Aunque es cierto que, en Su misericordia paternal, se ha obligado con *promesa*, supuesta nuestra unión con la voluntad divina, a concedernos múltiples bendiciones celestiales (*cf.* Mat. 6:5-15; 7:7-11; Luc. 11:1-13; Jn. 15:7; Hech. 4:31; Rom. 8:26-27; 15:30; Efesios 6:18; 2.ª Tes. 1:11; 1.ª Tim. 2:1-8; Heb. 13:18-19; Sant. 5:14-17; 1.ª Jn. 5:14-16) como respuesta a nuestras oraciones (*cf.* lo que sobre la oración hemos dicho en la lección 16.ª, punto 6).

fes militares hasta la muerte, y en este sentido podemos decir que el Bautismo y la Cena son sacramentos, en cuanto que nos ligan con sumisión y fidelidad a nuestro Señor y Jefe Jesucristo. Todos los grandes Reformadores del siglo XVI y las iglesias más directamente vinculadas a ellos usaron y usan el término «sacramento». Sin embargo, nosotros preferimos el término «ordenanza», tanto porque dichos ritos simbólicos fueron *ordenados* e instituidos por el mismo Jesucristo, como por el sentido equívoco que el término «sacramento» ha adquirido con el correr de los siglos. A. H. Strong da la siguiente definición de ordenanza: «Son ritos externos que Cristo ha establecido para que sean administrados en Su Iglesia como signos visibles de la verdad salvadora del Evangelio.» [2] Como signos, expresan vivamente dicha verdad y la confirman en el creyente excitando la fe.

3. Símbolo, rito y ordenanza.

Aunque las ordenanzas son ritos simbólicos, no todo rito simbólico es ordenanza. *Símbolo* (del griego «symbolos» = contraseña) es todo signo exterior, o representación visible, de una verdad invisible o de una idea espiritual. *Rito* es toda fórmula verbal acompañada de una ceremonia simbólica, que se emplea con alguna regularidad y con sagrada intención, como es la imposición de manos, acompañada de oración, con que se deja partir a un misionero. *Ordenanza* es un rito simbólico, *ordenado por Cristo para ser observado siempre y en todo lugar,* como expresión figurativa de las verdades centrales de nuestra fe cristiana. En virtud de esta precisión diferencial, sólo los ritos simbólicos del Bautismo y de la Cena del Señor pueden recibir el nombre de ordenanzas.

---

2. *Systematic Theology,* p. 930.

4. Número de las ordenanzas.

Solamente del Bautismo y de la Cena del Señor nos consta que fueron instituidos por Jesucristo como ritos simbólicos perpetuamente obligatorios en toda la Iglesia. Por tanto, sostenemos con todas las iglesias fieles a la Reforma que las ordenanzas son *dos* y nada más que dos. Por el contrario, tanto la Iglesia de Roma como la llamada «Ortodoxia» y el sector anglo-católico de la Iglesia Anglicana sostienen que hay *siete* sacramentos, pues admiten como tales, además del Bautismo y la «Eucaristía», la Confirmación, la Penitencia, la Unción de los enfermos, la Ordenación y el Matrimonio. Los pasajes bíblicos invocados para fundamentar tal aserto son: para la Confirmación, Hech. 8:14-17; para la Penitencia, Jn. 20:22-23; para la Unción, Sant. 5:14-15; para el Orden, 1.ª Timoteo 4:14; 2.ª Tim. 1:6; y para el Matrimonio, Ef. 5:31-32.[3]

5. Eficacia de los sacramentos u ordenanzas.

Hay tres modos de explicar la eficacia de las ordenanzas o sacramentos.

A) *Roma,* la *«Ortodoxia»* y los *anglo-católicos* sostienen que los sacramentos confieren la gracia *en virtud del mismo rito* (*«ex ópere operato»*), de manera similar a como la virtud de curar se encuentra en una medicina. Por eso, los llaman «signos eficaces de la gracia» y «causas instrumentales de la gracia».

B) *Los seguidores de Calvino* sostienen que los sacramentos confieren gracia, no porque la contengan en sí mismos, sino por la operación concurrente de la Palabra y del Espíritu Santo. Por eso, el presbiteriano L. Berkhof da la siguiente definición: «Un sacramento es una sagrada ordenanza instituida por Cristo, en la cual, *por medio de signos sensibles,* la gracia de Dios en Cristo y los benefi-

---

3. Para más detalles véase mi libro *Catolicismo Romano,* lecciones 28.ª-39.ª.

cios del pacto de gracia son representados, sellados y aplicados a los creyentes, y éstos, a su vez, dan expresión a su fe y a su lealtad a Dios.» [4]

C) *Los Bautistas* (y grupos afines) afirmamos con Zuinglio que las ordenanzas no tienen otra eficacia objetiva que la de actuar como emblemas significativos de las grandes verdades del Evangelio, excitando así de modo especial la fe subjetiva.

CUESTIONARIO:

1. ¿A qué llamamos medios de gracia? — 2. ¿Por qué llamamos «ordenanzas» a lo que otros llaman «sacramentos»? — 3. ¿En qué se diferencian el mero símbolo, el simple rito y la ordenanza? — 4. Número y eficacia de las ordenanzas.

---

4. *Systematic Theology,* p. 617. (El subrayado es nuestro; en el original, toda la definición está en cursiva.)

LECCION 46.ª NATURALEZA Y SUJETO DEL BAUTISMO CRISTIANO

1. Noción.

Si prescindimos de detalles controvertidos, podemos definir así el Bautismo: Es un rito ordenado por Jesucristo a Su Iglesia, mediante el cual se expresa simbólicamente nuestra regeneración espiritual que nos une, por fe, al Señor.[5]

Desde nuestro punto de vista confesional lo definiremos como «la inmersión de un creyente en agua, en señal de su previa comunión, mediante la fe, en la muerte y resurrección del Señor».

2. Institución.

El bautismo cristiano tenía un precedente en el bautismo que los judíos administraban a los prosélitos antes de

___

5. En realidad, la palabra *bautismo* (o *bautizar*) tiene en el Nuevo Testamento un doble sentido: injertarse o *sumergirse*, por la fe, en Cristo, o revestirse de Cristo, llamado también bautismo *real* «en Espíritu Santo y fuego» (Mat. 3:11); y sumergirse «en agua», llamado también bautismo *ritual*. Un pasaje iluminador, a este respecto, es Jn. 1:29-34. Juan el Bautista opone, junto a dos bautismos, dos personas: la suya, que bautiza en agua, excitando al arrepentimiento, para preparar «el camino del Señor» (por eso, Jesús recibió de Juan el bautismo, pero no recibió «el bautismo de Juan»), mientras que Jesús bautiza como «Cordero de Dios, que quita el pecado del mundo». Al decir que Jesús es «*el que bautiza con el Espíritu Santo*», Juan daba a entender que Cristo era el gran dador del don mesiánico por excelencia (Is. 11:2; Ez. 36:26-27; 37:1-14; Joel 2:28 y ss.; Jn. 4:10; 7:37-39).

que pudiesen participar de la Pascua, y en el bautismo de Juan, «bautismo de agua para arrepentimiento de los pecados», el cual Cristo mismo dio a entender que era de origen celestial.[6] Jesucristo quiso que este rito fuese de obligación universal y perpetua para la Iglesia (cf. Mateo 28:19; Marc. 16:16). Así lo entendieron los apóstoles (cf. Hech. 2:38; 10:48; 22:16), y así lo observaron los creyentes de la era apostólica (cf. Hech. 2:41; 8:12, 36, 38; 9:18; 16:15, 33; 18:8; 19:5), y así lo han observado posteriormente todas las iglesias cristianas. Las únicas excepciones son el llamado «Ejército de Salvación», para el que las ordenanzas no tienen una obligación más permanente que el lavamiento de los pies de Jn. 13, y la «Sociedad de Amigos» (Cuáqueros), que entienden por bautismo sólo la renovación interior hecha por el Espíritu Santo.

3. Fórmula de administración.

La fórmula del bautismo, según palabras del mismo Señor, es «en el nombre del Padre y del Hijo y del Espíritu Santo». La preposición griega eís, seguida de acusativo, del texto original, indica que la expresión «en el nombre» no significa «bajo la autoridad de», sino «con relación a». ¿Qué relación es ésta? Lugares como Hech. 8:16; 19:15; 1.ª Cor. 1:13; 10:2, así como Rom. 6:3; Gál. 3:27, arrojan bastante luz a este respecto. La interpretación más obvia es: «dedicándolos o consagrándolos al Padre, etc.», e introduciéndolos así en la familia divina (el bautismo de agua es símbolo de la regeneración espiritual, por la que pasamos a ser hijos de Dios y participantes de la naturaleza divina —cf. Jn. 1:12; 2.ª Ped. 1:4; 1.ª Jn. 3:1-2—). La fórmula «en el nombre del Señor Jesús» (Hech. 19:5 —o «de Jesús» en Hech. 8:16—), aun cuando adopta la misma construcción gramatical, no implica una variación en la fórmula bautismal, sino que tiene el sentido de «sepulta-

---

6. Cf. Mat. 3:6, 11 —con el comentario de Broadus a estos lugares—; Mat. 21:25; Jn. 1:25-28.

dos en Cristo, para ser introducidos con Él en la familia divina». Como puede verse por Hech. 19:4, esta fórmula venía a poner en claro que el bautismo de Juan, ya recibido, adquiría así su pleno sentido *cristiano*.[7]

4. Simbolismo.

El bautismo tiene una riqueza simbólica extraordinaria, pues expresa:

A) *La inserción y unión íntima del creyente con Jesucristo.* Todavía podemos contemplar los baptisterios instalados en el centro de iglesias prerrománicas y románicas,[8] en los que los creyentes entraban en el agua por la escalerilla de un lado, como expresando que allí sepultaban al «hombre viejo», y salían por el lado opuesto,[9] indicando que resurgían con Jesucristo, del que habían sido revestidos, a la vida del «nuevo hombre», muerto y resucitado con el Señor (*cf.* Rom. 6:3-11; Gál. 2:19-20; 3:27; Col. 2:12; 3:3).

B) *La unión de todos los creyentes en Cristo,* pues el bautismo es uno de los 7 vínculos de la unidad cristiana (Ef. 4:5). 1.ª Cor. 12:13 expresa la misma idea —aunque la alusión al agua es aquí quizá más indirecta— (comp. con Ef. 4:4-5).[10]

C) *La salvación.* En 1.ª Ped. 3:21 vemos que «el bautismo que corresponde a esto [a la salvación del Diluvio

---

7. En Hech. 2:38 la fórmula lleva la preposición *epí* con dativo, lo que sugiere allí el sentido de «bajo la autoridad de».

8. Existen notables ejemplares en Tarrasa (Barcelona).

9. Por eso, sería más correcto hablar de «*transmersión*» (como el paso del «Mar Rojo», para salvación —liberación de Egipto—, y del Jordán, para purificación —antes de la definitiva entrada en la Tierra Prometida—) que de «*inmersión*». En nuestras iglesias bautistas de Inglaterra se dice «to pass through the waters of Baptism» = pasar *a través de* las aguas del Bautismo.

10. Como ocurre con otros muchos términos novotestamentarios, el sentido *espiritual* y *ritual* del bautismo se imbrican íntimamente en todos los pasajes, basculando alternativamente hacia uno de ellos más que hacia el otro.

por medio del arca, de lo cual el bautismo era *antítypos* =
= realidad figurada] ahora nos salva (no quitando las in-
mundicias de la carne, sino como la aspiración de una
buena conciencia hacia Dios) por la resurrección de Jesucristo». El paréntesis que el mismo Pedro introduce es una
advertencia para poner en claro que el bautismo de agua
no tiene en sí otra *eficacia* que la que comporta la *fe* en
el Cristo *resucitado,* siendo dicho bautismo el símbolo que
despierta la fe y la expresa exteriormente.[11] Por la figura
retórica llamada «metonimia», Pedro atribuye la salvación
al bautismo, tomando el *signo* por la *cosa significada.*[12]

D) Finalmente, el bautismo es *la puerta de entrada
en la iglesia local.* Hech. 2:41, 47 nos aclara que sólo después de creer, arrepentirse y *ser bautizados* hubo añadidura al núcleo inicial de la iglesia de Jerusalén.

5. Sujeto del bautismo.

Pocos temas han influido tanto en la división denominacional como el de la práctica del bautismo cristiano,
en lo que se refiere al *sujeto* a quien ha de administrarse
y al *modo* con que debe administrarse. El primer aspecto
tiene más importancia que el segundo y por eso lo tratamos en primer lugar.

Como advierte E. Kevan,[13] el punto de arranque de la
controversia está en el *significado* primordial del bautismo: quienes, ante todo, ven en él un *signo del pacto* de
Dios con el nuevo Israel, abogan por la admisión de los
bebés al bautismo de agua, ya que por él se hacen oficialmente partícipes de las promesas y bendiciones de la
Nueva Alianza y son añadidos al Pueblo del pacto; en

11. V. A. Stibbs, *The First Epistle General of Peter* (London,
Tyndale Press, 1959), p. 144.
12. *Cf.* también Hech. 2:38, en que se empalma el «perdón de·
los pecados» con el «arrepentimiento» (comp. con Mat. 3:6, 11 y
Marc. 16:16a).
13. *O. c.,* vol. VI, lecc. VIII, pp. 2-3.

cambio, quienes ven en él una profesión exterior de la salvífica fe personal —conectada con el «nuevo nacimiento»— (Jn. 3:3), abogan por la admisión de solos los adultos que den garantía suficiente de haber pasado por dicha experiencia *personal*.

¿Favorece la Biblia la posición bautista? Creemos que sí. En efecto: A) Mat. 28:19; Hech. 2:37-41; 8:12, 36-38; 10:47; 16:32, 34; 18:8 nos muestran que la instrucción y la fe personal preceden siempre al bautismo. B) El mismo concepto de iglesia como *congregación de creyentes*, en la que no se puede entrar sin la experiencia personal del *nuevo nacimiento*, implica que el bautismo de agua, signo de entrada en la iglesia local, ha de negarse a quienes son incapaces de un acto consciente de fe personal. C) Los lugares en que se habla de «bautizar a alguien con toda su casa» (*cf.* Hech. 16:32, 34) explican que la «casa» —familiares y criados— que fue bautizada es la que había recibido la palabra y había creído. D) El «y para vuestros hijos» de Hech. 2:39 no implica el bautismo de bebés, ya que el término griego no es *pais* = niño, sino *téknon* = hijo, en calidad de descendiente a quien se extienden las promesas de generación en generación. E) 1.ª Cor. 7:14 no puede ser aducido en contra, ya que Pablo no habla del marido bautizado, sino del marido inconverso.

Tampoco la Historia favorece el bautismo de bebés, ya que la primera mención que de él se hace es en el año 180 (Tertuliano), y no para aprobarlo, sino para condenar la naciente práctica. En realidad, la práctica del bautismo infantil no cobró auge hasta el siglo v, cuando ya se habían introducido los conceptos de *regeneración bautismal* y de institucionalización de la Iglesia como *Ciudad de Dios*. Así triunfó en la Reforma la idea de «pacto», de tradición agustiniana. Pero al invocar tal concepción, como si el bautismo fuese el sustituto actual de la circuncisión, los partidarios del bautismo infantil olvidan dos cosas: *a*) que la circuncisión era el signo de la pertenencia a la *nación* de Israel, no de la salvación personal (*por la fe* —*cf*. Heb. 11—); de ahí que los judíos estableciesen la costumbre de bautizar a los prosélitos *ya circuncidados,* antes de admitirlos a participar de la Pascua (hoy diríamos de la Mesa del Señor); *b)* que Pablo hizo circuncidar a Timoteo después de estar éste bautizado, lo que Pablo no habría permitido (*cf*. Gál. 2:18) si el bautismo sustituyera a la circuncisión.

Finalmente, la práctica del bautismo infantil ha ocasionado los siguientes males: 1) Introducir la persuasión de que una persona es *cristiana* por haber recibido el bautismo en la infancia,[14] dando así al bautismo de agua un valor y una eficacia que no posee. 2) Oscurecer el sentido del «nuevo nacimiento» y de la conversión personal, como línea de demarcación entre el mundo y la Iglesia, con lo que se introdujo funestamente un cristianismo *nominal.* 3) El sustituir así una iglesia de *profesantes* por una iglesia de *multitudes,* con la ambigüedad confesional —y el peligro de mundanización— que dicha situación comporta. De ahí que la parte más evangélica de las denominaciones que todavía practican dicho bautismo lo admitan como mero rito de presentación o dedicación —lejos de la idea de regeneración bautismal— y exijan seriamente a los padres la promesa de instruir cristianamente a sus hijos a fin de que en el futuro puedan ser dignos del apelativo «cristiano» que se les impuso.[15]

---

14. Decimos *infancia,* mejor que *niñez,* puesto que un niño que haya llegado al uso de razón suficiente como para sentir, por el poder del Espíritu, la convicción de pecado y la necesidad de la salvación, es capaz de un acto *personal* de fe y, por tanto, apto para recibir el bautismo. Comentando Gál. 3:27, alude H. Lacey (en *La Iglesia,* compil. de Watson, p. 83) a la *toga virilis* que todo romano asumía al llegar a la madurez viril. Podríamos añadir que el «revestirse de Cristo» por el bautismo viene a ser como «la puesta de largo» del hijo de Dios, para ser presentado en la sociedad eclesial.

15. Esta evolución es notoria en la Iglesia de Roma (sin negar todavía el «dogma» de la regeneración bautismal, definido en Trento). Para bibliografía sobre este tema del sujeto del bautismo, *cf*. Strong,

CUESTIONARIO:

1. Definición del bautismo cristiano. — 2. ¿Presenta Hechos 19:5 una fórmula distinta de la de Mat. 28:19? — 3. ¿Qué simboliza el bautismo de agua? — 4. ¿Cuál es la raíz de la polémica sobre el sujeto del bautismo? — 5. ¿Qué nos enseñan la Biblia y la Historia sobre este asunto? — 6. ¿Cuáles son las principales consecuencias funestas del bautismo infantil?

---

o. c., pp. 945-959; A. Kuen, *o. c.*, pp. 163 y ss.; J. M. Pendleton, *Compendio de Teología Cristiana*, pp. 343-348; *La Iglesia* (compil. de Watson), pp. 65-87, y, sobre todo, T. E. Watson, *Baptism not for Infants* (London and Southampton, Henry E. Walter Ltd., 1970).

LECCION 47.ª
MODO Y NECESIDAD DEL BAUTISMO

1. El modo de bautizar.

Tanto católicos como protestantes están de acuerdo en que la Iglesia primitiva practicó el bautismo, durante muchos siglos, por *inmersión*. Todavía hoy, en la Iglesia Anglicana, antes de proceder al bautismo por *infusión*, se pregunta al sujeto o al padrino si se desea el bautismo por inmersión.[16]

¿Qué nos dice el Nuevo Testamento? Al usar el verbo *baptizo* y los sustantivos *báptisma* y *baptismós*, la Biblia nos indica que el modo normal de administrar esta ordenanza es por inmersión, ya que dicho verbo sólo puede significar «sumergir» o «teñir», que equivale a lo mismo, ya que las telas se teñían *por inmersión*. Si el Nuevo Testamento hubiese tenido en cuenta la infusión o aspersión, hubiese usado el verbo *rantizo*, que significa *rociar*. Oigamos lo que dice H. Lacey sobre este punto:

> «La versión de los Setenta tiene dos veces *baptizo*: "El (Naaman)... se zambulló... en el Jordán" (2.º Rey. 5:14); y "el horror me ha intimidado" (Is. 21:4). En la primera porción se traduce a *tabhal*, que significa "sumergir" (zambullir —como en Lev. 4:6, 17; 9:9; 1.º Sam. 14:27; Job 9:31, etc.), y en la segunda se traduce a *ba'ath*, que da la idea de estar dominado por el temor, aterrorizado.

16. Ya hemos mencionado el testimonio que, en favor del bautismo *por inmersión*, ofrecen las iglesias prerrománicas y románicas.

Las iniquidades de Belsasar volvieron para intimidarle en terror y juicio. Es evidente que los traductores de la versión de los Setenta entendieron la palabra *baptizo* como sumergir, zambullir o abrumar.» [17]

Como puede verse en Pendleton,[18] los más distinguidos partidarios del bautismo por infusión confiesan que el significado propio de *baptizo* es *sumergir,* siendo también la significación simbólica del bautismo un argumento decisivo en favor de la inmersión, ya que sólo la inmersión expresa cumplidamente nuestra sepultura y resurrección con Cristo (*cf.* Rom. 6:3-5; Col. 2:12).

Es cierto que este tema del *modo* del bautismo no es tan importante como el del *sujeto.* Los documentos más antiguos de la Iglesia no ofrecen excepción alguna en favor del bautismo de bebés; en cambio, ofrecen alguna excepción, en caso de necesidad, al bautismo por inmersión, como puede verse en la *Didaché:*

«En cuanto al bautismo, bautizad así... en agua viva [es decir, en agua corriente], pero si no tienes agua viva, bautiza en otra agua [estancada]; pero si no tienes ninguna de las dos, derrama tres veces agua sobre la cabeza...» [19]

Fue, sin duda, la comodidad la que introdujo paulatinamente el bautismo por infusión. Y ello favorecido por dos circunstancias dignas de notarse: *a)* la introducción del bautismo llamado «clínico» —por ser recibido en el lecho de muerte (griego «klíne»)—, ya que muchos recién convertidos (?), asustados por el rigor de las penas disciplinarias que se imponían a los reincidentes, preferían

17. *O. c.,* p. 67.
18. *O. c.,* pp. 337-338.
19. V. *Rouet de Journel,* n.° 4. Se discute sobre la fecha de este documento. Aunque muchos no dudan en fecharlo a primeros del siglo II, otros autores dudan en asignarle una fecha tan temprana.

demorar el bautismo hasta el lecho de muerte, para escapar así a la disciplina eclesial de los primeros siglos; b) la práctica del bautismo de los bebés, a los que, por temor a dañar su salud, se fue sustituyendo la infusión en vez de la inmersión.

La purificación interior, que la justificación mediante la fe realiza, queda también expresada mucho mejor por la *inmersión* bautismal (*cf*. 1.ª Ped. 3:21).

2. Necesidad del bautismo.

La Iglesia de Roma, de acuerdo con su noción de *regeneración bautismal*, afirma que el bautismo de agua es un *medio* absolutamente necesario para salvarse, si bien, en caso de necesidad, el *deseo* del bautismo y el *martirio* suplen, en este aspecto, al bautismo de agua. Sin embargo, el Nuevo Testamento nos dice que los que habían creído y se habían arrepentido, eran los que recibían el bautismo (Hech. 2:37-41); lo cual indica claramente que no nos bautizamos *para salvarnos*, sino *para confesar que somos salvos*. Por tanto, para nosotros, el bautismo no es necesario con necesidad de *medio*, sino de *precepto*, o sea, porque así está mandado por el Señor (*cf*. Mat. 28:19).

Ningún grupo o denominación cristiana, excepto los Cuáqueros y el Ejército de Salvación, niega la necesidad de observar esta ordenanza, aunque disientan sobre el sujeto que debe recibirla y el modo de administrarla. Antes de bautizar a un converso, es preciso que éste dé muestras suficientes de haber *nacido de nuevo* y de conocer el mensaje fundamental de la salvación. Bautizar sin discreción es abrir la puerta de la iglesia local a gente no regenerada, pero hacer esperar con un catecumenado demasiado prolijo equivale a olvidar que el «enseñar todas las cosas que el Señor ordenó» va en Mat. 28:19 después del mandato de *bautizar*.

3. Suficiencia del bautismo de agua.

Juan el Bautista se refirió a Jesucristo como al que había de bautizar «en Espíritu y fuego» (Mat. 3:11; Lucas 3:16; Jn. 1:33; Hech. 1:5; 11:16), no porque Jesús hubiese de emplear un rito más perfecto de bautizar, sino porque el bautismo de agua es el *símbolo* de una vida renovada y purificada, la cual es *realmente* producida por el Espíritu Santo mediante la regeneración y santificación interna.

De ahí que las manifestaciones exteriores del Espíritu Santo, entre las que está el don de lenguas, a veces *siguen* (Hech. 8:17), a veces *preceden* (Hech. 10:44-48), al bautismo de agua. Exigir, pues, un nuevo rito (imposición de manos) para el llamado «bautismo del Espíritu», a fin de que el cristiano alcance su *necesaria* perfección,[20] es algo que no tiene ningún fundamento en la Escritura.

CUESTIONARIO:

1. ¿Cuál fue el modo de bautizar usado en la Iglesia primitiva? — 2. ¿Qué pruebas añaden el nombre mismo y el simbolismo del bautismo? — 3. ¿Cómo se introdujo la práctica de la infusión o rociamiento? — 4. ¿Es necesario el bautismo de agua para salvarse? — 5. ¿Qué se requiere por parte del sujeto? — 6. ¿Qué opina usted sobre la necesidad de un segundo bautismo «en el Espíritu Santo»?

---

20. Como sostienen los Pentecostales. En otro contexto sucede lo mismo con el llamado «Sacramento de la Confirmación».

LECCION 48.ª

INSTITUCION DE LA CENA DEL SEÑOR

1. Institución de esta ordenanza.

Mateo 26:26-28; Marc. 14:22-26; Luc. 22:19-20; 1.ª Corintios 11:23-25 son pasajes que nos dan abundante evidencia de que la «Cena del Señor» es una ordenanza cristiana, o sea, un rito simbólico instituido por Jesucristo para ser celebrado a perpetuidad por Su Iglesia. Lucas 22:19 y 1.ª Cor. 11:24, 25 nos dicen expresamente que Jesús dijo: «Haced esto en memoria de Mí.» 1.ª Cor. 11:26 nos enseña que esta ordenanza debe observarse hasta la 2.ª Venida del Señor.

2. Su observancia en la Iglesia primitiva.

Hechos 2:42, 46; 20:7; 1.ª Cor. 10:16 y ss.; 11:17 y siguientes nos muestran que la Cena del Señor era observada con regularidad en la primitiva Iglesia. Más aún, la frase de Hech. 20:7: «El primer día de la semana...», da a entender que la Cena del Señor era observada todos los domingos. 1.ª Cor. 16:2 nos dice que en este día se hacía la colecta. El testimonio de Justino Mártir [21] nos confirma que los primeros cristianos celebraban la Cena del Señor cada domingo, y en el mismo culto hacían la colecta para los pobres y para las necesidades de la iglesia.

---

21. *Apología*, I, 67.

3. Nombres dados a esta ordenanza:

A) CENA DEL SEÑOR. Pablo usa este nombre como epíteto primordial en 1.ª Cor. 11:20. La «Cena (*deípnos* = comida principal, banquete) del Señor» significa la Cena instituida por el Señor (anticipación del banquete escatológico —Apoc. 3:20), distinguiéndose del «Agape» fraternal, al que cada uno aportaba lo que tenía, y que servía de introducción o epílogo a la Cena del Señor. Por los desórdenes a que esto daba lugar, dichos ágapes fueron reprendidos por Pablo (1.ª Cor. 11:21-22) y prohibidos definitivamente en un Concilio de Cartago.[22] La palabra «cena» procede, según F. Díez Mateo,[23] del griego «thoine» = banquete. Una variante de este nombre es «*Mesa del Señor*», que encontramos en 1.ª Cor. 10:21.

B) PARTIMIENTO DEL PAN. Con este nombre se refiere Hech. 2:42 a la Cena del Señor. Quizás el v. 46 alude a esto mismo. Las palabras de la institución aluden a este partimiento que el Señor hizo del pan antes de darlo a sus discípulos, en señal de la futura rotura de Su cuerpo por nosotros (*cf.* 1.ª Cor. 11:24).

C) COMUNIÓN. En 1.ª Cor. 10:16 dice Pablo: «La copa de bendición que bendecimos, ¿no es la comunión de la sangre de Cristo? El pan que partimos, ¿no es la comunión del cuerpo de Cristo?» La palabra «koinonía» expresa el sentido en que debe tomarse el término «comunión»: no se trata de comer *físicamente* el cuerpo de Cristo, sino de una *participación*, por fe, del Espíritu, carácter, sufrimientos, gloria y salvación de Cristo; es tener comunión

---

22. *Cf.* Ch. Hodge, *1.ª Corintios, in loc.*
23. En su *Diccionario Español Escolar Etimológico.* (Lamentamos que el famoso J. Corominas, en su *Diccionario Crítico-Etimológico de la Lengua Castellana* —4 volúmenes de gran tamaño—, en este término, como en otros muchos, no vaya más allá de la raíz latina.) Ahora bien, la transcripción al latín «coena» nos hace dudar con vehemencia que pueda proceder de «thoine». Personalmente opinamos que procede del griego «koiné» = común, por ser una comida que siempre se tomaba en grupo (familiar o social).

con Cristo, en oposición a la comunión *con* los demonios (vv. 20-21).

4. Nombres introducidos posteriormente.

A') EUCARISTÍA. Este nombre, usado hoy en círculos «protestantes» y con el que se alude modernamente, en tono ecuménico-pastoral, a la Misa en los libros y textos litúrgicos de la Iglesia de Roma, no es aplicado por el Nuevo Testamento a la Cena del Señor, pero tiene su origen en la «acción de gracias» (en griego «eucharistía») que el Señor realizó antes del partimiento del pan.[24]

B') MISA. Este término está tomado de la despedida que, en la Iglesia de Roma, anuncia el final de la celebración eucarística, con la frase *«Ite, missa est»*, copia de la antigua fórmula romana con que el juez despedía al pueblo, después de pronunciar la sentencia en una causa, como señal de que la decisión había sido trasladada a la autoridad superior para su cumplimiento: «marchad, la causa ha sido enviada». Estas palabras aluden claramente al sentido *sacrificial* que dicho acto cultual tiene en la Iglesia de Roma. Examinaremos este contenido sacrificial en la lección siguiente.

5. ¿Quiénes deben ser admitidos a la Cena del Señor?

Podemos contestar brevemente diciendo: todos los miembros de una iglesia local que no estén excluidos en cumplimiento de una justa medida disciplinaria. Siendo una ordenanza *que expresa la unidad de la Iglesia* (1.ª Corintios 10:17), debe celebrarse *comunitariamente*. De ahí que sea un abuso la costumbre posteriormente introducida de llevarla a las casas, etc., para ser recibida por personas *particulares*. Muy distinto es el caso de celebrarla comunitariamente en una casa.

---

24. El título es muy antiguo, pues la *Didaché* ya llama «Eucharistía» a la Cena del Señor (*cf. Rouet de Journel*, n.º 6).

Como nadie puede ser miembro de una iglesia local sin estar bautizado, se sigue que sólo los legítimamente bautizados pueden ser admitidos a la Mesa del Señor. ¿Qué hacer con los bautizados en la infancia que hayan experimentado el «nuevo nacimiento» y pertenezcan a una iglesia local evangélica? Como ya dijimos en otra lección, nuestra costumbre, fundada en la Palabra de Dios, es que pueden ser admitidos ocasionalmente a la Cena del Señor en nuestras iglesias, pero no como concesión regular y continua, ya que ello implicaría una membresía que no puede existir sin la participación en los mismos principios doctrinales acerca de las ordenanzas del Señor.[25]

CUESTIONARIO:

1. ¿Qué es la Cena del Señor y cómo se prueba que la instituyó Jesucristo? — 2. ¿Cuándo y cómo fue observada por la Iglesia primitiva? — 3. ¿Qué otros nombres le da el Nuevo Testamento? — 4. ¿Cuáles son los nombres que han sido introducidos después y qué significan? — 5. ¿Quiénes pueden ser admitidos a la Cena del Señor?

---

25. A título personal, opino que, en localidades donde no haya iglesias verdaderamente evangélicas (de nuestra denominación o de otras), no se debería negar la Mesa del Señor y, por ende, la membresía (*comunión*) a quienes disientan de nosotros en puntos no nucleares del Evangelio. Más aún, habríamos de esforzarnos para que, como ocurría en la primitiva Iglesia, la única *división* fuese la *geográfica* o territorial (*cf.* W. Nee, *La Iglesia normal, passim*, y mi tesis doctoral *La unidad de la Iglesia en Efesios* —en preparación—).

LECCION 49.ª

CONTENIDO DE LA CENA DEL SEÑOR

1. Punto de vista católico-romano.

Puesto que en el volumen VIII de esta serie teológica examinamos en detalle la doctrina de Roma sobre la Cena del Señor,[26] nos limitaremos aquí a un resumen muy breve. Dos puntos de extrema importancia hay en tal doctrina por los que se distingue radicalmente de las doctrinas de la Reforma. Según Roma:

A) En la Misa, y al conjuro de las palabras de la consagración («Esto es mi cuerpo», «Esto es mi sangre»), correctamente pronunciadas por un sacerdote válidamente ordenado,[27] toda la sustancia del pan se convierte en el cuerpo de Cristo y toda la sustancia del vino en Su sangre, quedando sólo los *accidentes* (o propiedades físicoquímicas observables) del pan y del vino.

B) La Misa es un verdadero sacrificio *propiciatorio* por el que los frutos redentores del sacrificio del Calvario se aplican, en todo tiempo y lugar, a cuantos de ellos pueden beneficiarse de algún modo. De ahí que la «Eucaristía» es, para la Iglesia de Roma, el centro del dogma, del culto y de la piedad.

2. El punto de vista luterano.

Lutero defendió también la presencia *real* de Jesucristo en los elementos del pan y del vino, aunque no admitió la

---

26. Véanse allí las lecciones 34-37.
27. Aunque personalmente sea hereje, apóstata o excomulgado.

transustanciación. Según él, Jesucristo está *en, con* y *bajo* el pan, etc. El fundamento de esta doctrina es la equivocada interpretación que Lutero dio a la frase: «se ha sentado a la diestra de Dios» (Heb. 10:12), arguyendo que, puesto que la diestra de Dios está en todas partes, el cuerpo de Cristo está también en todas partes y, por tanto, en el pan y en el vino. Esto implica una cierta forma de monofisismo, atribuyendo a la naturaleza humana de Cristo una propiedad que es exclusiva de Su naturaleza divina.

Sin embargo, Lutero afirmaba que el efecto *sacramental* de esta unión de Cristo con el pan y el vino sólo se produce en el momento de la comunión, sin que las palabras de la consagración ejerzan ningún poder sobrenatural a los efectos de la presencia del Señor en la Eucaristía, y todo el fruto del sacramento depende de la *fe* del sujeto que lo recibe.

Por otra parte, Lutero, como todos los demás grandes Reformadores, negaba en redondo que la Misa sea un sacrificio propiciatorio. Por esta razón, la doctrina de la Reforma en este punto fue condenada por el Concilio de Trento, en el cual se reiteró solemnemente la definición dogmática de la transustanciación, ya proclamada por Inocencio III en el IV Concilio de Letrán *(año 1215)*.

3. La doctrina de Calvino.

El punto de vista de Calvino, seguido especialmente por las iglesias anglicanas y presbiterianas, es el siguiente: Jesucristo no está *físicamente* en los elementos del pan y del vino, pero en la comunión nos alimentamos espiritualmente del verdadero cuerpo y sangre de Cristo que están en los Cielos, mediante el poder infinito del Espíritu Santo, que conecta directamente el alma del creyentes que comulga, con la energía espiritual que fluye del cuerpo glorioso del Cristo resucitado y ascendido. El medio indispensable y único de participar así del cuerpo y sangre de Jesucristo es la *fe*.

Por tanto, la diferencia radical entre los puntos de vista luterano y calvinista es la siguiente: Según Lutero, al comulgar *con fe,* tomamos *corporalmente* el cuerpo y la sangre de Jesucristo *realmente* presentes en los elementos del pan y del vino, y nos beneficiamos espiritualmente de tal comunión. Según Calvino, al comulgar *por fe,* participamos *espiritualmente* del verdadero cuerpo y sangre de Cristo (que se halla solamente en los Cielos), por obra del Espíritu de Cristo que habita en El así como en nosotros.

4. El punto de vista de Zuinglio.

Zuinglio es, para nosotros, en esta materia de la Cena del Señor, el correcto intérprete del Nuevo Testamento. Según él, los elementos del pan y del vino son meros *símbolos* sagrados de la obra que Cristo, una vez por todas, realizó en la Cruz. «Comer el cuerpo» de Cristo y «beber Su sangre» equivale a *creer en la obra de la Redención llevada a cabo en el Calvario,* de modo que los elementos de la Cena del Señor son signos que excitan nuestra fe en el Crucificado, induciéndonos a proclamar, cuando los tomamos en obediencia a El, Su muerte hasta que vuelva. Así, la Cena del Señor es un medio de gracia como símbolo que suscita espiritualmente el recuerdo («anámnesis» —1.ª Cor. 11:24, 25—) de la muerte de Cristo, sin conexión física ni espiritual con la *realidad* misma del Cuerpo y de la Sangre de Jesucristo.

Por consiguiente, la diferencia radical entre Calvino y Zuinglio, en este punto, es la siguiente: Según Calvino, la Cena del Señor es una *comunicación* de Cristo, ya que, si comemos y bebemos con fe los elementos, el Espíritu Santo nos conecta con el Cuerpo y Sangre de Jesucristo. Según Zuinglio, la Cena del Señor es una *conmemoración* de Cristo, ya que la recepción de los elementos sirve para reavivar nuestra fe y aumentar en nosotros, por el poder del Espíritu, el amor a Cristo y a Su Iglesia.

CUESTIONARIO:

1. ¿Qué punto de vista sostiene la Iglesia de Roma acerca de la Cena del Señor? — 2. Punto de vista luterano. — 3. Punto de vista de Calvino y en qué se diferencia del de Lutero. — 4. ¿Qué doctrina mantenemos los bautistas (y Hermanos) acerca de la Cena del Señor, y en qué se diferencia nuestra posición de la de Calvino y sus adeptos?

LECCION 50.ª

SIGNIFICADO DE LA CENA DEL SEÑOR

1. ¿Recuerdo o memorial?

En las palabras de la institución de la Cena, según nos las han transmitido Lucas y Pablo (Luc. 22:19; 1.ª Corintios 11:24, 25), Jesús dijo: «Haced esto en *memoria* [es decir, en *recuerdo*] de mí.» Nótese que el término usado en el original es «anámnesis» = recuerdo, en cuanto vivencia *subjetiva* del creyente, no «mnemósynon» = memorial, como signo *objetivo* que sirve de recordatorio. La adopción del término «memorial» en vez de «remembrance» en la reciente reforma del texto litúrgico de la Cena del Señor, llevada a cabo en la Iglesia Anglicana, denota un peligroso acercamiento hacia el concepto sacrificial del rito,[28] lo cual es totalmente ajeno al Texto Sagrado.

¿Qué es lo que nos *recuerda,* no los elementos mismos de la Cena, sino el rito simbólico que con ellos se practica? Que, así como se parte el pan y se nos da para comerlo, así fue quebrantado el cuerpo del Señor y ofrecido al Padre para nuestra salvación. Y que así como se derrama el vino en las fauces del creyente, así fue derramada la sangre de Jesús por la salvación del mundo. Por eso, el practicar la Cena del Señor es «anunciar, proclamar» («katangéllete» —1.ª Cor. 11:26—) la muerte de Jesucristo «hasta que venga». Esta proclamación implica el autoexamen, la confesión del pecado y el *valorar* debidamente lo que se

---

28. Recientes declaraciones y documentos confirman este peligro, pues ya se habla, sin rebozos, de *sacrificio.*

simboliza, para no practicar *indignamente* el rito que con-
memora la muerte del Señor. El requisito para «comulgar»
no es la ausencia de pecado, sino el reconocerlo y confe-
sarlo ante el Señor y ante los hermanos a quienes hayamos
ofendido.

2. El sello de un pacto.

Mateo 26:28 nos muestra cómo el rito de la Cena simboliza el nuevo pacto de Yahveh con Su pueblo, no mediante
la sangre de animales, sino con la sangre de Su propio
Hijo.[29] Heb. 8:6-8 nos aclara suficientemente cómo se llevó
a cabo la firma del nuevo pacto mediante la sangre del
único Mediador entre Dios y los hombres. Por tanto, la
Cena del Señor es también, para los fieles, el símbolo de
la garantía que tenemos en la sangre de Cristo de que
Dios ha perdonado nuestros pecados y nos ha hecho acep-
tos en el Amado (Ef. 1:6).

3. Un banquete festivo.

El Señor comparó el Reino de los Cielos a una gran
cena (comp. Luc. 14:16 con Apoc. 19:17). Mat. 26:29 y Lucas 22:18 se refieren también a la cena escatológica, dentro de la institución misma de la Cena del Señor.

Comparando Luc. 22:15 con 1.ª Cor. 5:7, se advierte
claramente la relación de la Cena del Señor con la celebración de la Pascua. Así como el banquete pascual re-
memoraba la liberación del pueblo de Dios, comiendo de
prisa el cordero y asperjando con sangre los dinteles
santos, para que el ángel exterminador no tocase a los
fieles, así la Cena del Señor rememora nuestra liberación
pactada con la sangre del «Cordero que quita el pecado
del mundo» (comp. Ex. 12-21-30 con Heb. 11:28).

---

29. V. Jer. 31:31-34, donde el nuevo pacto se anuncia con el perdón de los pecados y el envío del Espíritu para enseñar directamente a los fieles, y comp. con Is. 54:13; Ez. 36:22-27; Jn. 6:45.

La idea de *pacto* no debe inducirnos a pensar que nosotros contribuimos en algo al banquete pascual en que
Cristo sella Su testamento, entregándonos Su cuerpo y Su
sangre en los símbolos del pan partido y de la sangre
distribuida. E. Kevan hace notar [30] dos cosas importantes: *a*) que, al decir el Señor: «Esta copa es el nuevo pacto
en mi sangre», dio a entender claramente el sentido me-
tafórico de sus palabras al hablar de comer Su cuerpo y
beber Su sangre; *b*) que el pacto fue contratado entre
el Padre y el Hijo, no entre Jesús y nosotros, pues somos
meros beneficiarios, no co-autores del pacto. Por eso, el
Espíritu Santo no inspiró al redactor humano el prefijo
«syn», que quiere decir «con», sino «diá», que significa
«por medio de» (por eso, el término que el Nuevo Testamento usa no es «synthéke», sino «diathéke»). En otras
palabras, el pacto no se hizo *con* la sangre, sino *mediante*
la sangre, de Jesucristo.

Este aspecto de banquete pascual, en que Cristo sella
con Su sangre la amistad con los Suyos, y Su generoso
amor que le induce a *darse* por Sus amigos, es lo que hace
tan abominables los abusos que puedan cometerse con
ocasión de la Cena del Señor (*cf.* 1.ª Cor. 11:17 y ss.).

4. Comunión fraternal.

1.ª Cor. 10:16-17 introduce un nuevo aspecto en el rito
de la Cena del Señor al hablar de «koinonía» = comunión
o comunicación. La palabra «koinonía» —ya lo hemos dicho
en otra ocasión— comporta siempre, en el Nuevo Testamento, un participar con otros, conjuntamente, de los bienes salvíficos, en virtud de la efusión del Espíritu de Dios
sobre Su Iglesia (comp. Jn. 17:21 con 1.ª Cor. 10:16-17;
2.ª Cor. 13:14; 1.ª Jn. 1:3), lo que supone un conocimiento
fiel y cordial (comp. Jn. 6:69 con 1.ª Jn. 4:16) del Señor
y nos induce a compartir incluso los bienes materiales
(comp. Hech. 4:32 con 1.ª Jn. 3:16-18).

---

30. *The Lord's Supper*, pp. 32-42.

Esta *comunión,* o mutua comunicación de los bienes espirituales y materiales, sigue, en Hech. 2:42, a la ortodoxia y precede al partimiento del pan, para dar a entender que no hay verdadero amor cristiano sin la ortodoxa doctrina apostólica, y que es una hipocresía el acercarse a la «comunión» del Señor cuando no se ama de verdad a los hermanos. Como dice Agustín de Hipona, «es como si alguien intentara besar a Jesús en la frente y propinarle, a la vez, un pisotón». No estima el Cuerpo de Cristo quien desprecia a los miembros de Cristo. También nos enseña que, en la conjunta comunión con Cristo (Mat. 18:20), cada creyente es como un carbón encendido que mantiene su calor en la medida en que forma un solo «fuego» con los demás carbones.[31]

CUESTIONARIO:

1. ¿Qué nos recuerda la Cena del Señor? — 2. ¿Es un recuerdo o un recordatorio? — 3. ¿Con qué y entre quiénes fue sellado el pacto nuevo de Mat. 26:28? — 4. ¿Qué relación tiene la Cena del Señor con la Pascua? — 5. ¿Qué cadencia expresa la «koinonia» de Hech. 2:42 dentro del contexto de dicho versículo?

---

31. Bibliografía evangélica para todo este tema de la Cena del Señor, entre otros: E. Kevan, *The Lord's Supper* (London, 1966) y *Correspondence Course (Dogmatic Theology),* VI, less. IX; L. Berkhof, *Systematic Theology,* pp. 644-657; A. H. Strong, *Systematic Theology,* pp. 959-980; Ch. Hodge, *Systematic Theology,* III, pp. 611 y ss.; J. Bannerman, *Church of Christ,* II, pp. 133 y ss.; Pendleton, *Compendio de Teología Cristiana,* pp. 349-358; W. Griffith Thomas, *Principles of Theology,* pp. 388 y ss.

Octava parte

La Iglesia
en el mundo

LECCION 51.ª LA SEGREGACION DE LA IGLESIA

1. Segregados.

Desde la primera lección de este volumen hemos insistido en que «iglesia» significa «un grupo de llamados por Dios a salir del mundo y formar una santa congregación», es decir, un rebaño de ovejas pertenecientes al Divino Pastor como Pueblo Suyo. Agraciados con las promesas divinas, hemos sido hechos partícipes de la naturaleza divina (santidad y pureza de Dios), «habiendo huido de la corrupción que hay en el mundo» (2.ª Ped. 1:4) y debiendo comportarnos como «extranjeros y peregrinos», obligados a abstenernos de los deseos mundanos (1.ª Pedro 2:11), ya que somos el templo de Dios en el Espíritu (Ef. 2:22) y, por eso, llamados a ser santos y sin mancha (1.ª Cor. 1:2; Ef. 1:4). Hech. 5:1-11 nos muestran la seriedad con que los Apóstoles tomaron esta necesaria cualidad de la Iglesia como «santa comunidad de Dios».

2. Concepto de "mundo".

Al hablar de *segregación*, o apartamiento del mundo (en sentido moral, no en el físico —*cf.* Jn. 17:15; 1.ª Corintios 5:7-10—), necesitamos examinar el concepto de «mundo», ya que este término se emplea en la Escritura en distintas acepciones. El hebreo usa la palabra *'olam* para designar, tanto el *mundo* (griego «kósmos» = orden, Universo en orden) como el *siglo* o era temporal (el «aión» griego). Ciñéndonos a la palabra *cosmos* o mundo, veremos que el Nuevo Testamento la usa para significar:

A) El Universo con todo lo que contiene (Mat. 16:26; Jn. 1:10b; Hech. 17:24).

B) Este planeta que habitamos, al que Jesús vino (Jn. 1:9, 10a; 3:16; 11:27; 16:21).

C) La humanidad en general, objeto del amor de Dios para salvación mediante la fe (Jn. 3:16, 17).

D) Lo *mundano;* es decir, este mundo o *cosmos* en cuanto corrompido por el pecado, subyugado por el Maligno, que tiene al demonio como príncipe y dios,[1] que rechazó a Cristo y por el que Cristo no oró al Padre (Jn. 1:10c; 14:30; 17:9, 14, 16, 25; 2.ª Cor. 4:4; 1.ª Jn. 2:15; 5:19, entre otros muchos lugares). Este *mundo* en sentido peyorativo, más que un lugar, es una «atmósfera» de pecado, contagiosa, que todos respiramos y que penetra en el mismo santuario. Aunque el demonio lo gobierna, sigue, sin embargo, perteneciendo *de derecho* a Dios. Rom. 8: 19-22 muestra cómo la creación entera, corrompida por el pecado del hombre, gime a una para ser libertada «de la esclavitud de la corrupción». Cuando se intima a la Iglesia a salir de este mundo en sentido moral, o sea, a huir de «la corrupción del mundo», este término se entiende en esta cuarta acepción.

3. Mundanidad y purificación.

La Iglesia debe, pues, huir de la mundanidad y conservarse santa y pura para su Esposo Jesús. A lo largo de la Historia de la Iglesia siempre se ha mantenido la tensión entre la mundanidad y la pureza. Frente a las desviaciones y a las corrupciones de la Iglesia oficial surgieron en la Edad Antigua movimientos como el Montanismo, el

---

1. Por eso, cuando Satanás ofreció a Cristo los reinos de este *mundo* (Mat. 4:8-9), con la condición de que le adorase —servir el plan del diablo, en vez del que el Padre le había programado (Jn. 4:34)—, Jesús no le acusó de mentiroso, sino que tácitamente confesó que este mundo «yacía en el Maligno» (1.ª Jn. 5:19), y únicamente se opuso a la pretensión de Satanás de que le adorase y sirviese.

Donatismo y el Novacianismo. En la Edad Media, los Cátaros, los Valdenses y los Lolardos o seguidores de J. Wiclif. En la Edad Moderna, todos cuantos suelen designarse bajo el común denominador de «puritanos». La Reforma fue también un gran movimiento en favor de la purificación de la Iglesia. Poco antes de la Reforma, y del lado católico-romano, merece destacarse la actuación y predicación del dominico florentino Jerónimo Savonarola, cuya es la famosa frase: «En la Iglesia primitiva, los cálices eran de madera y los prelados de oro; en nuestros días, la Iglesia tiene cálices de oro y prelados de madera.»[2]

El Nuevo Testamento describe la vida de la Iglesia como una repetición espiritual del *Exodo*: salidos del Egipto de nuestra esclavitud anterior y salvos a través del Mar Rojo de la sangre de Cristo, caminamos por el desierto de esta vida, peregrinando hacia la Tierra Prometida, que es el Canaán Celestial (*cf.* Heb. caps. 3, 4, 11, 12, 13). Hay muchas clases de *mundanidad* de las que la Iglesia tiene que huir, entre las que destacamos: *a*) la mundanidad de los signos *externos* como la riqueza en templos y paramentos, el florecimiento numérico, la prosperidad económica,[3] la actividad burocrática, las atracciones mundanas; *b*) la indiferencia en materias doctrinales, el descuido de la debida disciplina, las discusiones bizantinas y agrias sobre problemas oscuros de Escatología, haciendo olvidar las graves y urgentes responsabilidades del presente en

---

2. Citado por R. B. Kuiper, *o. c.*, p. 15. El que consulte sin prejuicios los libros de escritores imparciales (¿los hay?) y artículos de Enciclopedias (comp. lo que se dice en la *Larousse* con lo que se dice en la *Enciclopedia Británica*) sobre este interesante personaje (un verdadero profeta con el espíritu —y los defectos— de Elías) verá *cómo se escribe la Historia* («todo es según el color del cristal con que se mira»).

3. No queremos insinuar que un negocio o trabajo próspero sea algo perverso —ya que la Biblia lo tiene por bendición de Dios a sus fieles—, sino los criterios regidos por la égida de Mammón, en que el dinero se convierte en el tirano del hombre, en vez de ser su servidor.

aras de un morboso énfasis en aspectos proféticos del futuro, etc.

Es cierto que el puritanismo tiene también sus excesos; se ha hecho constar, no sin razón, el carácter sombrío del clásico puritano, en contraste con el gozo y la alegría que caracterizaban a los primeros cristianos (cf. Hech. 2:46). Hay quienes sacan de quicio la frase de Pablo en 1.ª Timoteo 4:8 «el ejercicio corporal para poco es provechoso», para desacreditar la «gimnasia somática» —como dice el original—, cuando Pablo sólo pretende comparar el ejercicio corporal (que para algo es provechoso) con la «piedad que para todo aprovecha», puesto que da fruto que perdura para la eternidad.[4] Pero también es verdad que un verdadero seguidor de Jesucristo habría de abstenerse de todo lo mundano y de todo lo inútil (cf. Rom. 12:2; 13:12; Gálatas 5:19 y ss.; Ef. 4:29; 5:4; Filip. 4:8 —el vers. de las ideas positivas—). Uno no se imagina a Pablo acudiendo a ciertos espectáculos o perdiendo el tiempo en ciertas lecturas, visitas, diversiones, etc., sino teniendo siempre a la vista «la carrera» que tenía delante (cf. 1.ª Corintios 9:26-27; Filip. 3:12-14; 2.ª Tim. 4:7). Lo que ocurre con la mayoría de los creyentes es que, como decía Th. Brooks del cristiano imperfecto, «son demasiado buenos para ser felices con el mundo, y demasiado imperfectos para ser felices sin el mundo».

El cristiano ha de saber «controlarse» en todo. La «enkráteia» o control de sí mismo es fruto del Espíritu Santo y virtud cristiana de suma importancia (cf. Gál. 5:23; 2.ª Ped. 1:6), pues ayuda al creyente a mantener la legítima libertad de los hijos de Dios (Jn. 8:32; Rom. 6:22; 8:15; 2.ª Cor. 3:17; Gál. 5:18).[5]

---

4. V. el magnífico comentario de W. Hendriksen a este lugar (*Timothy and Titus*, p. 151).

5. Debo principalmente a mi esposa inglesa y a mis padres políticos el haber corregido mis criterios demasiado «españoles» a este respecto (por ejemplo, en cuanto a diversiones y modos de profanar el Día del Señor). Sobre la disciplina purificadora que la iglesia local ha de ejercer con sus miembros indignos hemos hablado ya en la lección 33.ª.

CUESTIONARIO:

1. ¿Qué nos sugiere la palabra «iglesia» respecto a la necesaria segregación del mundo? — 2. ¿Cuántas acepciones puede tener el vocablo «mundo»? — 3. ¿En qué sentido lo tomamos aquí? — 4. Mundanidad y purificación en la Historia de la Iglesia. — 5. El sentido de peregrinaje del cristiano y las formas de mundanidad. — 6. Anverso y reverso del puritanismo. — 7. ¿Cuál es la virtud que rige el «justo medio» en la vida del cristiano?

LECCION 52.ª INDEPENDENCIA DE LA IGLESIA

1. La doble ciudadanía.

El cristiano —insistimos— es una persona con doble ciudadanía: como *nacido de arriba*, su ciudadanía está en los Cielos (Ef. 2:19; Filip. 3:20; Col. 3:1); como *habitantes de este mundo* (aunque en calidad de «peregrinos»), los creyentes, «por causa del Señor» —es decir, en conciencia y como acto de obediencia al Señor y de testimonio de la propia fe cristiana), han de cumplir del modo más perfecto posible sus deberes de ciudadanos, sometiéndose, en todo lo que no contravenga a la Ley de Dios o a los postulados de la verdad y de la justicia, a las humanas autoridades que, en último término, están establecidas por el mismo Dios (*cf.* Rom. 13:1 y ss.; 1.ª Ped. 2:13 y ss.).[6]

2. Una mezcla funesta.

La Iglesia naciente hubo de soportar en seguida la persecución, tanto por parte de los poderes judíos (político-religiosos) como por parte de los emperadores romanos. Sin embargo, fue aquella Iglesia perseguida, imbuida de la «teología de la Cruz», la que se esparció vigorosa por todo el mundo. Como dice E. de Pressensé:

> «Los hombres que juzgan las cosas desde el punto de vista exterior, admiraban en Jerusalén la sinagoga mientras despreciaban el Aposento Alto. De un lado estaba una tradición gloriosa, una

---

6. Reservamos para el vol. X (*Etica Cristiana*) el entrar en detalles de conducta.

organización importante, el sacerdocio, la autoridad y las multitudes; del otro, el pequeño número, la debilidad, la ausencia de crédito, y el entusiasmo, siempre ridículo para la humana sabiduría. Sin embargo, de aquel templo no iba a quedar piedra sobre piedra, mientras que del Aposento Alto partirían los vencedores del mundo.» [7]

La llegada de Constantino al poder, su «conversión» y la entrada masiva de los gentiles en la Iglesia hicieron del Cristianismo la religión oficial del Estado. Con el Sacro Imperio, el poder civil adquirió privilegios espirituales, mientras el Papado llegó a tener en sus manos las riendas del poder temporal, sobre la pretendida «base bíblica» de *las dos espadas* (*cf.* Luc. 22:38), la espiritual y la temporal, en manos del Papa. Inocencio III y Bonifacio VIII llevaron a su clímax esta imposición del poder eclesiástico en los asuntos temporales.

Por su parte, los Estados totalitarios, tanto de un signo como de otro, han pretendido siempre controlar las actividades de la Iglesia. Justo es añadir que las iglesias que más daño han sufrido por ese lado han sido las que más implicaciones temporales se habían forjado o estaban estructuradas como instituciones jerárquicamente centralizadas.

En la Iglesia de Roma se nota hoy una clara evolución a este respecto, puesto que, mientras hasta hace poco se defendía la soberanía indirecta de la Iglesia sobre el Estado y se condenaba el laicismo de éste, ahora se tiende a una mera cooperación e incluso a una separación total de la Iglesia y del Estado.

3. Independencia de la Iglesia.

J. M. Stowell hace notar [8] que Dios ha fundado tres instituciones: la familia humana, el gobierno estatal y la

---

7. Citado por A. Kuen, *o. c.*, p. 285.
8. En *Baptist Distinctives*, pp. 53-56.

iglesia local (Gén. 2:18; 9:6; Mat. 16:18), y que cada una de estas tres instituciones son factores estabilizadores de la sociedad y están destinadas a funcionar dentro de sus propias esferas, con independencia de las demás: la familia tiene unos derechos inalienables y un área privada donde ninguna de las otras dos instituciones tiene derecho a inmiscuirse; el Estado está destinado a promover el bien común temporal mediante la ley y el mantenimiento del orden público, terrenos en que la Iglesia no tiene por qué entremeterse; y la Iglesia tiene la comisión de predicar el Evangelio a todas las gentes y de dar culto a Dios en la forma que El ha ordenado, lo cual puede y debe hacer independientemente de todo control temporal y de toda injerencia por parte del Estado.

Cuando la Iglesia se ha apoyado sobre el brazo secular, obteniendo privilegios de orden temporal, o ha tomado partido en las luchas políticas y sociales, sólo desastres se han obtenido de tal amalgama. Como dice el antes citado E. de Pressensé:

> «Dondequiera que encontréis una religión estatal, encontraréis una iglesia que ha renegado de su principio fundamental y que retorna de la Nueva Alianza a la Antigua.» [9]

Y Emil Brunner añade:

> «Vista desde la perspectiva de las iglesias libres, la herencia constantiniano-teodosiana de las iglesias de la Reforma en Europa es, hay que reconocerlo, una verdadera maldición.» [10]

4. La libertad religiosa.

Pío IX condenó la libertad de conciencia como una de «las libertades de perdición». Esta condena indiscrimina-

---

9. Citado por A. Kuen, *o. c.*, p. 286.
10. Citado por *id.*, *ibid.*

da se basaba, en parte, en un equívoco que es preciso deshacer. Cuando defendemos la libertad de conciencia y la libertad religiosa, no negamos que todo hombre tenga la obligación de obedecer la Ley divina y de creer en el mensaje del Evangelio, sino que afirmamos que todo ser humano debe estar libre de toda coacción externa en el ejercicio de sus deberes religiosos. La voluntariedad y responsabilidad necesarias del acto de fe son la base primordial de tal libertad, a lo que se añaden los derechos de la persona humana.[11]

CUESTIONARIO:

1. ¿Es el cristiano ciudadano del Estado? — 2. ¿Cuál es sumariamente la historia de las relaciones entre la Iglesia y el Estado? — 3. ¿Cómo ha querido Dios que funcionen las tres sociedades instituidas por El? — 4. ¿Qué daños se siguen de una Iglesia estatal? — 5. ¿En qué se funda la libertad religiosa?

---

11. Para más detalles sobre este tema véase nuestro capítulo sobre la libertad religiosa en el libro *30.000 españoles y Dios* (Barcelona, Nova Terra, 1972), pp. 239-277.

LECCION 53.ª EL COMPROMISO DEL CRISTIANO

1. El cristiano y la verdad.

La Iglesia como tal —todas las iglesias— y cada cristiano en particular están comprometidos con la *verdad*: tienen la obligación de proclamar la verdad, de comunicar el mensaje, de anunciar el juicio de Dios, por incómodo que ello pueda resultar, tanto al mensajero como al destinatario. Así lo hizo Samuel con Saúl, cuando éste se entremetió a ofrecer sacrificio (1.º Sam. 13:9-14); así Natán con David tras el doble crimen de éste (2.º Sam. 12:1-14); así Elías al rey Acab de Israel tras el asesinato de Nabot (1.º Rey. 21:17-29); así Jeremías durante todo el tiempo de su ministerio profético; así Pedro, ante el Sanedrín que les prohibía enseñar en el nombre de Jesús, replicó: «Es necesario obedecer a Dios antes que a los hombres» (Hech. 5:29); así, también, Lutero hubo de protestar ante la Dieta de Worms: «Esta es mi posición; no puedo obrar de otro modo; que Dios me ayude. Amén.»

Los cristianos han de ser «sal de la tierra», presentando, con el testimonio de su conducta, un reflejo del poder del Evangelio, a fin de que el mundo tenga un atisbo del sabor de Jesucristo, única explicación a los problemas de la vida, y sea, en algún grado, preservado de la corrupción que devoraría al mundo con más rapidez si desapareciese de él el testimonio cristiano, que es un freno a la creciente perversión y al desatamiento de la ira de Dios sobre la tierra. Han de ser también «luz del mundo». Como dice R. B. Kuiper:

«El gran honor de la Iglesia de Cristo está en que sus miembros son los hijos de la luz, que hacen brillar su luz mediante la predicación de Jesucristo como Salvador y Señor de individuos y naciones, presentándolo así como el único que es capaz de trasladar a los pecadores desde las tinieblas a la luz y de dispersar las negras nubes que envuelven a los pueblos de la tierra como una mortaja.» [12]

Con su palabra y con su conducta la Iglesia muestra a la Humanidad perdida y desorientada el único camino de la salvación y de la felicidad (*cf.* Jer. 2:13; Mat. 5:1 y ss.). La antítesis que la luz presenta a las tinieblas (antítesis de la que el propio creyente puede dar testimonio personal —*cf.* Ef. 5:8—) hace que los hijos de las tinieblas persigan a los de la luz,[13] pero la palabra, la conducta y la oración pueden ser usados por el Señor para derribar a muchos perseguidores, como lo hizo el testimonio de Esteban con el perseguidor Saulo.

2. El cristiano y la justicia.

El creyente, como cristiano y como ciudadano, tiene el derecho y la obligación de salir por los fueros de la justicia, contra la opresión, la explotación, la violencia (¡por difícil que esto sea, a veces!), el hambre, la miseria y !a ignorancia. Como cristiano y como ciudadano, tiene también la obligación de cooperar al justo orden y cumplir fielmente las leyes justas, comportándose en todo tiempo y lugar según el consejo del apóstol Pablo en Romanos 13 y 1.ª Tim. 2:1-3, así como el de Pedro en 1.ª Pedro 2:13-17. A este propósito dice E. Kevan:

---

12. *O. c.,* p. 265.
13. Es de notar que el mundo no odia a los cristianos por ser *buenos,* sino por ser *diferentes* (1.ª.Ped. 4:4: «... *cosa extraña...»*).

«Pertenece al departamento de la Etica Cristiana el discutir si la Iglesia tiene el derecho de "rebelión"; pero no cabe duda de que, habiendo la Iglesia de orar por los que están en autoridad y someterse al gobierno legítimo, ella debe ser enemiga de la anarquía y sostenedora del gobierno constitucional.» [14]

3. El compromiso temporal.

Puesto que la iglesia local es la única concreción espacio-temporal de la Iglesia Universal, es obvio que la realidad eclesial exige una *encarnación* en lo temporal, o sea, un comprometerse con las realidades temporales en las que está inmersa la vida cristiana. El cristiano, no lo olvidemos, posee dos ciudadanías y esto comporta sus problemas. Vamos a aventurarnos a proponer dos principios generales de conducta que nos parecen los más conformes a la letra y al espíritu del Evangelio:

A) El profeta Sofonías, de parte de Yahveh, hace el siguiente augurio para el remanente de Israel, que será el núcleo de la entonces futura Iglesia de Cristo: «Y dejaré en medio de ti un pueblo humilde y pobre, el cual confiará en el nombre de Yahveh» (Sof. 3:12). Así, los «'anavim» de Yahveh son, al mismo tiempo, los «pobres en espíritu» y los «mansos» de Mat. 5:3, 5; es decir: *todos los que en su corazón, piadosamente, se sienten insuficientes, destituidos, necesitados* (los desatendidos por el mundo, pero favorecidos de Dios); *pobres* [15] *y mansos,* que

---

14. *Dogmatic Theology (Correspondence Course)*, vol. VI, less. X, pp. 5-6.

15. Los «pobres *en el espíritu*», o sea, los que tienen corazón de pobre, de Mat. 5:3, no son precisamente los que viven en la miseria, sin un céntimo en el bolsillo, sino los que tienen su corazón desapegado del dinero, lo cual puede darse en un honesto jefe de una empresa próspera, mientras que un menesteroso puede estar dominado por la codicia y albergar un «corazón de rico», anhelando dinero, posición social y autosuficiencia o autoseguridad.

sólo en la gracia o favor de Dios encuentran un asidero para su salvación y para su felicidad, *no en sus riquezas, ni en su posición social, ni en sus méritos.* Desde Is. 61:1-3 hasta Sant. 2:1-13, pasando por Mat. 5:1-12; Luc. 4:16-21; 6:20-26; 7:22, etc., la Biblia nos muestra que el Evangelio (la «Buena Noticia» de parte de Dios) es para estos *pobres,* que la Iglesia ha de ser pobre,[16] como su Cabeza-Cristo; ésta es «la teología de la Cruz». La Iglesia, pues, ha de estar en favor de los pobres y oprimidos; no puede aburguesarse ni favorecer a los burgueses. Pero, *como tal Iglesia,* su arma contra la opresión es la predicación del Evangelio, no las armas mortíferas, ya que el Evangelio es el único *manifiesto* que procura la verdadera redención del proletariado al producir un *hombre nuevo,* liberado por la verdad (Jn. 8:32) y guiado por el Espíritu (Romanos 8:14) para afrontar todos los problemas temporales en amor, paz y justicia (*cf.* Tito 2:11-12), o sea, en una perspectiva *divina.*

B) El cristiano, como *ciudadano del mundo,* tiene el derecho y el deber de cualificarse para desempeñar puestos de responsabilidad en la administración pública, así como de dar su nombre y su voto a partidos sociales y políticos que, según su conciencia —guiada por la Palabra de Dios—, mejor respondan a los postulados de la justicia y del bien común. Pero *no debe implicar su condición de creyente,* ni comprometer a su iglesia, en la lucha política (*sí* en las justas reivindicaciones sociales), ya que la fe es un factor de *separación de lo mundano y de unidad en Cristo,* pero no de *separación,* por motivos políticos, *entre los creyentes.* De ahí la conveniencia (y aun necesidad) de que los que ostentan representación oficial en las iglesias se abstengan de *visibles intervenciones políticas* (aunque sí en favor de la justicia, de la cultura y del legítimo progreso).

---

16. Más bien que una «iglesia pobre», ha de ser una «pobre iglesia», como dice J. M. de Llanos; es decir, destituida de auxilio humano, despreciada y perseguida.

CUESTIONARIO:

1. Deberes de la Iglesia respecto a la proclamación de la verdad. — 2. ¿Qué implica para el creyente ser «luz del mundo» y «sal de la tierra»? — 3. Deberes del cristiano respecto de la justicia. — 4. ¿Cuál es la raíz del compromiso cristiano? — 5. ¿Cuál ha de ser la actitud de los creyentes y de las iglesias en lo político y en lo social?

APENDICE

LA IGLESIA HOY: SITUACION, CAUSAS Y REMEDIOS

1. Situación actual de la Iglesia.

La Iglesia de Cristo atraviesa hoy una de las peores crisis de su Historia. Es una crisis de indiferencia, de enfriamiento, de inadaptación y de compromiso.

A) La Iglesia sufre, como de rebote, el fenómeno moderno al que se ha llamado «descristianización de Europa». Esta descristianización se debe principalmente a dos causas:

a) El creciente dominio que el hombre ha conseguido, en los dos últimos siglos, de la materia, de la técnica y del confort, ha estimulado en él un desordenado interés en los aspectos materiales de la vida, con desprecio de lo espiritual. La cultura se ha orientado, sobre todo, hacia un mejor disfrute de lo material. Resulta, por otra parte, sintomático el que, mientras Dios y la religión van retrocediendo, en la consideración de nuestros contemporáneos, a zonas cada vez más lejanas (ya que la intervención divina en la vida y en la Historia les parece innecesaria con la «mayoría de edad» de esta generación, que ha hecho caer uno tras otro los mitos en que estaba envuelta la antigua concepción del Universo), grandes masas se vuelven de nuevo a la magia, a la astrología, al ocultismo, fundiendo la técnica occidental con la mística oriental de los yoguis. Es *el retorno de los brujos*.[1] Volvemos, pues, no a la *falta de religión,* como podía esperarse de una generación materialista, sino al *exceso de religión (cf.* Hechos 17:22: «... observo que sois muy religiosos»), o sea, a la *superstición* —a la que el ser humano retorna ineludiblemente cuando da la espalda al verdadero Cristianismo—. Con esta mentalidad triunfante en el mundo, la Iglesia ofrece muy poco interés para este siglo, a no ser que se mundanice ella misma, lo cual está ocurriendo en muchas iglesias de todas las denominaciones.

b) Después de muchos siglos en que las iglesias oficiales se han preocupado de aspectos administrativos y seculares, más bien que del Reino de Dios y de Su justicia (resultando así, más que una agencia espiritual, un poder social, político o cultural), las masas han perdido su confianza en la iglesia, vista especialmente a través de sus representantes oficiales. La situación está descrita gráficamente en la parábola de Kierkegaard acerca del payaso y el circo en llamas, que ha recogido Harvey Cox en su libro *La Ciudad Secular*.[2] Habiéndose declarado un incendio en un circo próximo a una aldea, uno de los payasos, en traje de faena, va a pedir socorro al pueblo cercano, pero los habitantes creen que está «haciendo el número» para conseguir concurrencia y se ríen de sus palabras y de sus lágrimas, hasta que el incendio, tras devorar el circo, devora también el pueblo. El profesional de la religión ha venido también apareciendo ante las masas como el payaso de circo que hace su número para conquistar «parroquianos» y, cómo no, dinero para la «parroquia». Como dice E. Brunner:

> «No se puede desconocer que existe hoy, sobre todo en Europa, una desconfianza considerable respecto a todo lo que se denomina "iglesia", in-

---

1. Véase Louis Pauwels y Jacques Bergier, *El retorno de los brujos* (Barcelona, Plaza y Janés, 1970).
2. Citado por J. Ratzinger, *Introducción al Cristianismo* (Salamanca, Sígueme, 1969), pp. 21 y ss.

cluso entre gentes perfectamente abiertas al Evangelio de Jesucristo. No debemos olvidar que la noción de iglesia alberga un pasado pesadamente cargado con una vieja historia de diecinueve siglos y que las iglesias han acumulado entre Jesucristo y el hombre individual obstáculos a menudo insuperables.» [3]

B) El enfriamiento ha sido consecuencia de esta indiferencia que se ha filtrado en las filas de los mismos creyentes. Las estadísticas ecológicas y sociológicas van dando periódicamente detalles del creciente porcentaje de «cristianos» de nombre, especialmente en las iglesias de multitudes, cuya membresía se adquiere en la primera infancia mediante el bautismo de bebés. Pero incluso en nuestras iglesias de profesantes cunde quizás el ejemplo de Sardis (Apoc. 3:1-2), en que la ortodoxia se mantiene incólume y todo parece marchar «evangélicamente», pero sin espíritu ni vida. Del extremo opuesto surgen movimientos aislacionistas, antieclesiales, grupitos cerrados, capillitas de «perfectos» y movimientos seudoespiritualistas de toda laya.

C) Un peligro que acecha también a nuestras iglesias es la falta de adaptación a las circunstancias, empeñándose en continuar con viejos métodos de predicación y de evangelización; en suma, de atracción hacia Cristo. El Espíritu y el mensaje son siempre los mismos, es cierto, pero la metodología tiene que adaptarse al hombre actual, al lenguaje y a la mentalidad de nuestra época. En el extremo opuesto tenemos la primacía de la «diversión», del entretenimiento, tratando de superar el aburrimiento de los insatisfechos, pero posponiendo sin fecha la salvación de los inconversos.

D) Finalmente, tenemos siempre la amenaza del compromiso: *a)* compromiso con lo mundano, participando de los criterios, intereses y aficiones de los mundanos y

---

3. Citado por A. Kuen, *o. c.*, p. 291, nota 3.

tratando de *no ofenderles; b)* compromiso con la cultura
y el ambiente, hasta hacer del Evangelio un libro más de
filosofía u ocultismo, o un manifiesto revolucionario, etcétera; *c)* compromiso con las demás religiones, tratando
de olvidar o subestimar las diferencias doctrinales, en
aras de un ecumenismo tan ancho como sea posible.

2. Las causas.

Hay quienes echan la culpa de todo lo que pasa en la
Iglesia a las corrientes filosóficas modernas, al materia-
lismo ambiente, al creciente ateísmo, al avance del marxismo, etc., y, con calarse un fácil y seudoheroico «anti»,
se creen los auténticos portaestandartes del Evangelio y
los únicos verdaderos «testigos» de Jesucristo en esta hora.
No quieren comprender que los avances del ateísmo y
del marxismo se deben, como ha señalado certeramente
A. Kuen, a que

> «el Cristianismo, que ocupaba el terreno y tenía
> la ventaja, se ha marchitado y desnaturalizado
> hasta el punto de no tener respuestas válidas que
> dar a los problemas de los hombres, ni metas de-
> seables que ofrecer a sus aspiraciones, porque la
> Iglesia que debía traer el mundo a Cristo ha cava-
> do ella misma, a menudo, el foso de separación
> entre ambos».[4]

Las verdaderas causas son otras más profundas, en-
quistadas dentro de la misma Iglesia y que, en aras de la
brevedad, vamos a resumir casi telegráficamente:

A') *Intelectualización de la fe,* sustituyendo el mensaje puro y sencillo de la Biblia, que mantiene siempre
su «garra» para salvar (*cf.* Rom. 1:16), por una filosofía
religiosa.

---

4. *O. c.,* p. 306.

B') *El comportamiento pelagiano,* acusado implícitamente en el constante recurso al empleo de los medios humanos, con evidente olvido y desprecio de la *oración* y del *poder* del Espíritu de Dios.

C') *La supervivencia del espíritu constantiniano,* por el que se pretende continuar favoreciendo el mantenimiento de las iglesias de multitudes y solicitando el apoyo de los poderes temporales.

3. Los remedios.

Resumiremos aquí la magnífica exposición que sobre este tema hace A. Kuen en su tantas veces citado libro *Je bâtirai mon Eglise.*[5]

A'') REAVIVAMIENTO POR EL PODER DEL ESPÍRITU. Cuando hablamos de «reavivamiento» no entendemos por ello una más grandiosa campaña evangelística (sin negar su valor inicial), ni un mayor compromiso social (que puede hacernos falta), ni un esfuerzo extraordinario para congregar multitudes interdenominacionalmente, como para demostrar la «vitalidad» del Protestantismo, ni una profunda renovación litúrgica, al estilo de Taizé (aunque deberíamos revisar la monotonía de muchos servicios de culto), ni una reunión urgente de todas las iglesias cristianas, en aras del Ecumenismo de moda (aunque muchas congregaciones han perdido la «conciencia», o sentido, de Iglesia —con mayúscula—). El único «reavivamiento» de base bíblica consiste en implorar una nueva venida del Espíritu de Dios y prepararnos a ella por medio de una verdadera «metánoia» o conversión colectiva. Como ha escrito K. Barth:

> «El camino hacia la unidad de la Iglesia, parta de aquí o de allí, no puede ser otro que el de su renovación. Pero renovación significa arrepentimiento. Arrepentimiento significa conversión: no

5. Páginas 319-358.

la de los demás, sino la nuestra *propia*. El Problema que el Concilio de Roma (el Vaticano II) presenta al Consejo Mundial de Iglesias ¿no es el de la conversión y, por tanto, de la renovación de *nuestras* iglesias?» [6]

B) NECESIDAD DE UNA CONTINUA REFORMA. Ya hemos dicho repetidamente en este volumen que los grandes Reformadores del siglo XVI fueron esclavos de una época y de una peculiar visión de la Iglesia, queriendo presentar, frente a la Iglesia oficial, que ante ellos aparecía como claramente desviada del núcleo central del Evangelio, otra Iglesia de multitudes «Reformada». Es cierto que consiguieron rescatar ese núcleo del Evangelio (la justificación mediante la fe sola) y colocar la Palabra de Dios en el centro de la Iglesia; pero, en cuanto al concepto mismo de «iglesia», no cabe duda de que se quedaron a mitad de camino. Y todos ellos persiguieron con saña a las iglesias independientes, que mantenían el principio del bautismo de creyentes y la separación entre la Iglesia y el Estado.

A esto se ha añadido que la mayoría de los seguidores de Lutero, Calvino, etc., han hecho de ellos y de otros muchos pioneros de la Reforma una especie de «papas protestantes», semi-infalibles, cuyas doctrinas se observan, hasta en los detalles desfasados o equivocados, como coincidentes en todo con la Palabra de Dios. El Dr. M. Lloyd-Jones habla de este método de remontarse al siglo XVI como de un camino equivocado para encontrar el auténtico concepto de iglesia y proceder a una reforma eficaz en nuestro tiempo.[7] Y, ya en 1620, en su despedida a los «Padres Peregrinos», que marchaban de Inglaterra a los Estados Unidos de Norteamérica (entonces Nueva Inglaterra), J. Robinson les decía:

«Os requiero de parte de Dios a que no me sigáis sino en la medida en que me habéis visto

---

6. Citado por A. Kuen, *o. c.*, p. 324.
7. En *Qué es la Iglesia*, pp. 7-8.

seguir a Jesucristo. Si Dios os revela algo por medio de otro servidor Suyo, estad tan prontos a obedecerle como si hubieseis recibido el mensaje por medio de mi ministerio... Por mi parte, no puedo deplorar bastante la condición de aquellas iglesias reformadas que han adquirido un determinado grado de religión, pero no quieren ir más allá de su primera Reforma. Los luteranos no pueden ver sino lo que vio Lutero, y preferirían morir antes que aceptar algún aspecto de la verdad revelada a Calvino. En cuanto a los calvinistas, se aferran sin discriminación a la herencia legada por aquel gran hombre de Dios, el cual, sin embargo, no lo sabía todo. Esto significa una lamentable pobreza, porque, si es cierto que tales hombres fueron en su tiempo lámparas que ardieron y brillaron en las tinieblas, también es cierto que no habían penetrado todavía en todo el consejo de Dios.» [8]

La iglesia que renuncia a reformarse constantemente, deja poco a poco de ser una auténtica iglesia *reformada*.

C) RESTABLECIMIENTO DE LA AUTORIDAD DE LA BIBLIA. Recorriendo los testimonios que, tanto de parte protestante como católica, de fundamentalistas como de liberales, de ecumenistas como de antiecumenistas o de ecumenistas «con reparos», presenta A. Kuen,[9] todos ellos coincidentes en que toda nueva reforma de la Iglesia supone una sumisión total a la Palabra de Dios por parte de todos, llega uno a pensar si no estaremos manteniendo nuestras diferencias a base de discusiones bizantinas o pormenores de detalle, pero el propio Kuen nos avisa que

«habría que preguntarse si todos los que hablan de someter todas las instituciones y prácticas de la Iglesia a la norma bíblica se dan cuenta del

---

8. Citado por A. Kuen, *o. c.*, p. 326.
9. *O. c.*, pp. 333-339.

reto que les lanza esa misma Palabra cuya autoridad querrían restablecer. ¿Es que las iglesias actuales están prestas a llevar a cabo la revolución que la puesta en práctica de sus propuestas iba a desencadenar?».[10]

También, y antes que nada, habría que preguntarse qué opinión tienen sobre la Biblia como Palabra infalible de Dios muchos de los que hablan de «someter todas las instituciones y prácticas de la Iglesia a la norma bíblica».

D) RESTAURACIÓN DE LA IGLESIA DE ACUERDO CON LA BIBLIA. Todo el problema de la situación actual de la Iglesia está en su apartamiento total o parcial del mensaje de la Biblia *en cuanto ésta contiene todo el consejo de Dios.* El hereje es *el que escoge,* entre las doctrinas de la Biblia, las que convienen a sus prejuicios o a su tradición denominacional, subestimando o ignorando las demás. Un estudio serio, profundo, completo, de la Palabra de Dios —*tenida toda como infalible*—, invocando la ayuda del Espíritu Santo que la inspiró, es un paso absolutamente necesario para la revitalización de la Iglesia. Ello comporta para cada uno de nosotros: la certeza experimental del nuevo nacimiento, la membresía en una ortodoxa y viva iglesia de *profesantes,* el seguimiento de toda la verdad en amor y el dejar que sea Jesucristo, no nosotros, quien continúe en todo momento reformando, es decir, *reedificando Su Iglesia* (Mat. 16:18).

BIBLIOGRAFIA

A. Alonso, *Comunidades eclesiales de base* (Salamanca, Sígueme, 1970).

J. Bannerman, *Church of Christ*, dos volúmenes (Edinburgh, 1868).

L. Berkhof, *Systematic Theology* (London, Banner of Truth, 1963). Hay edición castellana.

B. Besret, *Claus per a una nova església* (traducció de Pacià Garriga, Abadia de Montserrat, 1972).

Concilio Vaticano II. Especialmente, *Constitución Dogmática sobre la Iglesia* y *Constitución Pastoral sobre la Iglesia en el mundo actual* (Madrid, BAC, 1967).

O. Cullmann, *Del evangelio a la formación de la teologia cristiana* (Salamanca, Sígueme, 1972).

O. Cullmann, *Verdadero y falso Ecumenismo* (Trad. de E. Requena, Madrid, Studium, 1972).

O. Cullmann, *La Historia de la salvación* (Trad. de V. Bazterrica, Barcelona, Edicions 62, 1967).

L. Sp. Chafer, *Systematic Theology*, vol. IV (Dallas, Dallas Seminary Press, 1948).

P. Fannon, *La faz cambiante de la Teología* (Santander, Sal Terrae, 1970).

J. Gonzaga, *Concilios*, dos vols. (Grand Rapids, 1965).

J. Grau, *El fundamento apostólico* (Barcelona, Ediciones Evangélicas Europeas, 1966).

J. Grau, *Introducción a la Teología* (Tarrasa, CLIE, 1973).

W. H. Griffith Thomas, *The Principles of Theology* (London, Church Book Room Press, 1956).

A. Hortelano, *La Iglesia del futuro* (Salamanca, Sígueme, 1970).

E. F. Kevan, *The Lord's Supper* (London, Evangelical Press, 1966).

A. Kuen, *Je bâtirai mon Eglise* (Saint-Légier sur Vevey, Editions Emmaüs, 1967). Con amplia bibliografía en las pp. 361-368.

R. B. Kuiper, *The Glorious Body of Christ* (London, The Banner of Truth, 1967).

H. Küng, *The Church* (Translated by R. & R. Ockenden, London, Burns & Oates, 1968). Hay edición castellana. Lo mejor de este gran teólogo católico progresista.

H. Küng, *The Council and Reunion* (Transl. by C. Hastings, London, Sheed & Ward, 1961). Hay edición castellana.

H. Küng, *The Living Church* (Transl. by C. Hastings & N. D. Smith, London, Sheed & Ward, 1963). Hay edición castellana: *Estructuras de la Iglesia*.

H. Küng, K. Barth, O. Cullmann and others, *Christianity Divided* (London, Sheed & Ward, 1961).

F. Lacueva, *La unidad de la Iglesia en Efesios* (Tesis doctoral en preparación).

M. Lloyd-Jones, *La autoridad* (Trad. de D. E. Hall, Córdoba —Argentina—, Ed. Certeza, 1959).

M. Lloyd-Jones, *Qué es la Iglesia* (Trad. de F. Lacueva, London, Banner of Truth, 1970).

M. Lloyd-Jones, *The Basis of Christian Unity* (London, IVF, 1962).

J. M.ª Martínez - J. Grau, *Iglesia, sociedad y ética cristiana* (Barcelona, EEE, 1971).

G. Millon, *L'Eglise* (mimeografiado).

G. Millon, *L'Eglise de Jésuchrist* (Gaillard, France, Editions du Lien Fraternel, sin fecha).

W. Nee, *La Iglesia normal* (Trad. de A. Deras, Cuerna-
vaca —México—, Tipográfica Indígena, 1964).

J. M. Pendleton, *Compendio de Teología Cristiana* (Trad.
de A. Treviño, El Paso —Texas—, Casa Bautista de
Publicaciones, 1960).

F. Simons, *Infalibilidad y Evidencia* (Trad. de J. C. Bru-
guer, Barcelona, Ediciones Ariel, 1970).

J. R. W. Stott, Lloyd-Jones, J. Grau, *La evangelización y
la Biblia* (Barcelona, Ediciones Evangélicas Europeas,
1969).

A. H. Strong, *Systematic Theology* (London, Pickering &
Inglis, 1958).

E. Trenchard, *La Iglesia, las iglesias y la obra misionera*
(Kingsway, Lit. Bib., sin fecha).

M. Useros, *Cristianos en comunidad* (Salamanca, Sígueme,
1970).

J. A. Vela, *Las comunidades de base y una Iglesia nueva*
(Buenos Aires, Editorial Guadalupe, 1969).

J. B. Watson, etc., *La Iglesia,* compilación por J. B. Watson (Trad. y adapt. de J. A. Lockward P. y J. R. Co-
chrane, Buenos Aires, 1971).

T. E. Watson, *Baptism not for Infants* (London, H. E. Walter Ltd., 1970).